THE NEVER KING

THE
NEVER
KING

JAMES ABBOTT

PAN BOOKS

First published 2017 by Pan Books
an imprint of Pan Macmillan
20 New Wharf Road, London N1 9RR
Associated companies throughout the world
www.panmacmillan.com

ISBN 978-1-5098-0311-8

1 3 5 7 9 8 6 4 2

A CIP catalogue record for this book is available from the British Library.

Typeset by Palimpsest Book Production Ltd, Falkirk, Stirlingshire
Printed and bound by CPI Group (UK) Ltd, Croydon, CR0 4YY

For Tobias

ACKNOWLEDGEMENTS

Bringing a book into the world is always a team effort, and this one is no different. But in particular, I would like to thank Julie Crisp for her never-ending belief over the years, and for making the industry more fun; and John Jarrold for his guidance over the past decade of my writing career. It's safe to say that without them both I would not have inflicted so many words upon the reading public. And also, as ever, my wife, who has put up with me spending more evenings behind a laptop than I care to remember.

PROLOGUE

The Ninth Age, Year 126

Dress like an animal. Act like an animal. *By the thunder of the Goddess*, Jorund thought, *even* talk *like an animal.* Barbarism to combat barbarism.

Those had been the orders from one of King Cedius's messengers. Act like barbarians before the King's Legion arrived to bring the discipline of the king to the borderlands. Jorund had been posted to the town for just three months and had much to prove, and he was too wise a watchman to ignore a direct order from Cedius the Wise, despite not seeing the wisdom of such tactics himself.

Jorund daubed woad to his face within the cramped confines of his watchman's house and considered the grim situation ahead. Those too young and too old to participate in the coming battle were escorted into the nearby caves – Jorund's young, pregnant wife, Carmissa, among them. All who remained were willing fighters determined to protect their homes.

Clan markings were being ripped down in the town, and in their places crude animal totems were thrown up. And the reason for such deceptions? There was a dark flood of barbarian tribes from the north making forays into the Plains of Mica, their armies streaming forth into the northern reaches of Stravimon. That was a cause for concern to the king. If the tribes came together in their thousands it would be a bloody mess for the towns and cities far beyond Baradium Falls.

So it was that the most northerly settlements had been given the strange instructions to disguise themselves as tribal towns in the hope that the invading armies would consider the places their own territory and pass them by, looking for richer pickings. To Jorund this seemed wishful thinking, even if it had worked once before, two decades ago. Still, Jorund lived in hope that it might work or at least buy the townsfolk time until their rescuers arrived. Ahead of Cedius's First Legion were advancing the finest warriors in the kingdom – the Solar Cohort. Legends would be riding into his town. Jorund's heart thumped at the very thought of the great names: Xavir, Dimarius, Felyos and Gatrok among them.

Jorund hauled on his furs, grabbed his axe and strode outside into the thick cool air. At the top of the steps he surveyed the wide street. Above the braying townsfolk he could hear the roar of Baradium Falls itself, and smell its pungent aroma above the woad that caked his face. Well over a thousand savage-looking warriors looked towards him expectantly.

A grin came to Jorund's lips. *This will do.* 'Well, make a noise, you ugly bastards. You're meant to be savages!'

And with that the people of Baradium Falls roared like creatures of the woods.

Hundreds of townsfolk, pretending to be something they were not, waded into the line of trees beyond Baradium Falls. The next settlement, two miles to the east, Belgrosia, had reportedly put twice their number out. A long night lay ahead of them all. With luck, the ruse would work . . .

A blue mist settled, glowing ethereally in the gibbous moon.

The people looked like ghosts within the gloom. Men and women from young to old, each one covered in mud and woad and furs – he could barely recognize any of them.

He'd sent out scouts in an attempt to see where the northern barbarians were expected to strike first, and they were to report back at the first sign of trouble. The warriors' march slipped into a trudge. Jorund grew ever more tense. His breath coiled pale before him. Something did not feel right. His scouts had not returned yet and that unnerved him. In the distance, a wolf howled.

Wolves don't stray this far west, he thought. Then the woodland began to thunder around him, the ground shaking perceptibly. The people of Baradium Falls hastily arranged themselves, and began slamming the flat of their blades against their armour just as their barbarian enemies would. Should they encounter them the hope was that the barbarians would think them some of their own warriors – it was a slim chance. Jorund scanned the tree trunks around him breathlessly, searching for signs of incursion into the woodland. Screams drifted across the top of the forest from some distance away. His heart thumped.

'Riders!' someone shouted, from the darkness.

'The king's men!'

'Solar Cohort!'

Thank the Goddess. Jorund thought. If they were attacked now, help was at hand.

Something wailed like a banshee's scream and a torchbearer's light in the distance was extinguished.

It must be their foe. Jorund yelled for his people to charge. His longsword held aloft, he stepped over bracken, between the towers of oak. Moonlight penetrated a clearing, illuminating the ground ahead, but when he arrived he saw only corpses cleaved open on the earth. Corpses that he recognized from Baradium Falls.

Where are their attackers? Barbarians don't ambush – they don't have the finesse for it. There was something wrong about the wounds as well: too clean, too professional . . .

'Watchman!' someone screamed. 'Beyond the clearing—'

'Make haste,' Jorund shouted.

He saw the shapes dismount from their horses, and was confused again by the incongruity. *Since when did barbarians ride horses?* He could make little sense of who or what these warriors were. Six figures in black began to carve into the people of Baradium Falls like daemons from another world. The screams were intense. Jorund threw himself towards the front of the townspeople, then stopped in horror. Upon the black jerkins of the warriors were symbols of crenellated towers and the rising sun. The Solar Cohort.

It's not possible.

'Stop!' he shouted. 'We're Stravir! We're on the same side!'

But in the madness of slaughter his voce was lost to a melee of screams.

Blades blurred and wailed as they separated limbs and heads from their bodies. Within a brief moment, hundreds of people had been butchered. By just six warriors, legends indeed. Jorund fell to his knees as the warriors loomed. His sword slipped from his hand. He hurriedly stripped off his furs, removed the bone chains and tribal totems from his body and showed them the single leather breastplate bearing a watchtower he wore underneath.

'I am Stravir!' he sobbed, looking around him in anguish at the innocent villagers who had met such a grisly end. 'We are all Stravir . . .'

One man sheathed his two enormous curved swords over his

broad shoulders with a flourish and stepped across the corpses towards him. His face was lean and glistened with blood in the moonlight.

'Speak, man!'

'We are Stravir, all of us. We're not the northlanders. We're not barbarians.' He waved his hands towards the dead. 'They were from Baradium Falls.'

The tall man glanced to the others. 'Dimarius?'

A blond-haired figure approached, his face full of confusion. 'Why were you dressed like barbarians?'

'The king's orders,' Jorund muttered.

Dimarius shook his head at the tall warrior who was staring in horror and grief at the corpses surrounding them.

He looked back and Jorund flinched at the expression of intense anger and shame that crossed the soldier's features. 'What have we done?' he asked bitterly.

No one was able to answer him. The watchman stared through his tears. Nearby someone screamed in mourning.

The Ninth Age
Year 131

The Gates of Hell

'You'll die here if you're lucky.'

A gust of wind whipped across the wide courtyard, scattering flecks of snow from the mountain directly into Landril's face. It was as if the weather conspired with everything else to make him even more miserable than he already was.

As if the freezing conditions and his situation weren't hard enough, every few steps across the grime-caked grey slabs, the bastard guards heckled the prisoners, spat at them, or worse. Landril wondered what perverse enjoyment they got from their entertainment. Even their pathetic attempts would make anyone feel much more terrible than they already did for coming to a place like this.

'Get a move on, *mongrels*,' one snapped, jabbing for emphasis with his spear at those not moving quickly enough for his taste. 'Your mothers must have bedded yaks to spawn half-breeds like you.'

The old, balding man in front of Landril winced in pain and spat defiantly at the foot of his tormentor.

Fool. It's precisely what they want.

A response. An excuse. An opportunity to turn a simple game into a bloodsport.

The guards moved in quickly, knocking the man to the floor

while Landril quashed any instinct to help. The rest of the prisoners watched impassively, seemingly indifferent. It was every man for himself here. The guards beat the old man, dragged him, unshackled, across the stone and out into the blinding white. They seemed in no hurry to finish things off – making a show of their violence. A warning, perhaps, to those watching.

Landril kept his head down, so only caught glimpses as the four guards kicked the cowering prisoner over and over again. With a final, violent kick across the man's face, his neck snapped back. Blood sprayed and teeth rattled across the stone. He collapsed in the snow while the guards laughed and clapped each other on the back. They left him where he lay. Landril wasn't sure if he was dead or not. For a moment he couldn't take his eyes off the beaten corpse – would that be his own fate? He scanned his surroundings: huge slab-sided walls made from granite, a series of gateways interspersed by courtyards, designed to block the progress of rioting prisoners. *Have I done the right thing?* he wondered.

'Welcome to Hell's Keep,' one guard sneered at the prisoners before motioning them forwards.

Head down. Do not make eye contact.

Hell's Keep. An apt moniker. More so than its official designation, Citadel Thirty-Six. The grey, high, fortress-like walls were built into the third highest peak of the Silkspire Mountains, two thousand feet up from one of the long-abandoned merchant routes out of the eastern kingdoms. Well away from the home comforts of Stravimon. This was a place to send only the most hardened and dangerous criminals. Those too deadly to imprison in any normal gaol – but too important or useful to have killed. No one had ever escaped.

It was the location rather than the quality of the security that made it so invulnerable. Freezing temperatures at altitude, and visibility obscured by snow. Winding, rocky, treacherous paths that cut through coarse undergrowth. Witches at the foot of the mountain.

Landril looked appraisingly at the fifteen Stravir soldiers in crimson uniforms and bronze helms accompanying them. There were another four dozen within the gaol itself, probably huddled around coal fires and cursing their luck for being stationed at the arse-end of the world. They were as trapped as their own prisoners.

As his group were marched into the innermost part of the gaol, the stench of shit and unwashed bodies massed together attacked his senses. More attuned to incense, perfumed rooms and the luxury of city life – Landril almost gagged at the cloying odours.

A horn's braying echoed around the walls, and the mammoth iron doors ahead of them screeched demonically as they opened. Landril took one lingering look at freedom before being pushed with the others through the gateway of hell.

Mercy of the Goddess. That bastard had better damn well be alive, or I'm buggered . . .

Through whispers and glances and gestures in the shadows, information came quickly to a man of Landril's learning. Within just a few hours of incarceration, he had found a shifty-looking man of some fifty summers who was grateful for a packet of Landril's smuggled herbs.

His name was Krund, a wiry fellow with damp grey shoulder-length hair and a scruffy beard. He was one of the three cellmates Landril was forced to share with. Each of the men here wore the same clothing, a thick grey tunic that itched all over like a dockyard rash.

'I don't get it,' Landril said, playing the part of a novice.

'Get what?' Krund sighed.

'Why not just kill us and be done with it?'

'Well, a different breed of men get brought here,' Krund muttered. 'A thief would get his hand severed at the wrist. A common murderer beheaded. Us? We were of value to someone on the outside and so we were spared immediate death.'

'Any famous people here, then? Well-known figures from the court?'

Krund cast him a sly glance. 'How should I know? Everyone's a no one in here.'

Landril fought back the disappointment. He would have to scrutinize the face of every inmate just to be sure. He'd have to look into cold, hard eyes to find the man he sought, the hero of Twelve Valleys, the Plains of Anguish and just about every campaign of old Cedius's rule.

'What'd you do to end up here?' Krund asked with barely concealed indifference. 'You have no accent. You don't look much like a man who knows his way around a blade.'

Information was power; Landril knew that better than any.

Landril smiled enigmatically. 'My offences were mostly, shall we say, *political*.'

Krund chuckled, his features softening, but he still appeared more interested in the package of herbs Landril had given him.

'And you? How did you come to be here, Krund?'

'I was a lawyer working on behalf of a Stravir duke. Suffice to say I became engrossed in things I ought not to have become engrossed in. But life can be cruel – no point in being angry about it, is there? I have accepted my lot in life. And I'm still alive, aren't I? But I'm tired, stranger. I could do with a rest and some time alone with your gifts.'

Landril left him to his corner, knowing that, when the time

came, Krund would make for a useful informant. He watched as the door to his cell was locked with a sudden finality. Moments later he could hear thud after echoing thud as other inmates were sealed into their tomb-like quarters. The sliver of light through the stone showed very little of the room. Stone beds with dirtied blankets for warmth. Someone had said that the blankets were donations from the nearby monastery; he just hoped they weren't already infested with fleas. There was nothing else but wet, graffitied walls, a bucket to relieve himself in, and the company of miserable, hopeless men.

This is it, then. Landril Devallios, spymaster, dies here next to a bucket of piss.

He focused on the task ahead. Tomorrow he would start the search for the one man who could get him out of here. He would deliver his message. A few days after that, if what people said of his target was true, they would both be free. If not, then he'd have to spend the rest of his days locked up in this miserable rat hole. Landril considered death to be a better option.

Even for a man like Landril, who liked to play the long game, the conditions of Hell's Keep made him feel tense and impatient. The conditions were beyond anything he'd ever encountered previously. And there was still no sign of his quarry. One day bled into another.

His life became measured by small miseries: his back aching from the stone slabs, the constant cold, the inedible food he gagged down at each meal. His searching became more desperate. The inmates were allowed to mix only once a day, which gave Landril just a small sliver of time in which to find his target. But the grim-faced prisoners all looked the same: unshaven, unkempt. Perhaps body shape would be the first indicator. Some men were scrawny, with little meat to their bones, but others had somehow maintained good musculature despite being here. Would the man he'd come to find have remained as strong as before? He'd been gone for years now, but he wouldn't shrink in height at least. Landril flitted from prisoner to prisoner each day, careful not to make his searching too obvious. Too much curiosity would only get you killed in here. He questioned Krund subtly about the prisoners but his cell-mate knew next to nothing about individuals. No one spoke of their past.

He eavesdropped on conversations, built up a network of inmates who reported to him. Ironically, he felt that the prison structure wasn't that different from the machinations of court life. The drugs he had smuggled bought him eyes in darkened corners of the gaol, just as they had done over a year ago whilst he was investigating the murders outside Stravimon's Court of Sighs. But the reports told him nothing more than he could see for himself: grim men, standing bored and constantly on the edge of violence. The usual prison politics.

As with anywhere, a hierarchy existed. There were gangs here, as if somehow these hardened men could not get by without some form of structure to offer stability and security. His informants told him of the Hell's King, the Bloodsports and the Chained Dead. The gangs divided the prison between themselves, looking out for their own men in different ways, ensuring a ready supply of illicit trade and backhanded favours. Landril figured that, if he wanted to discover anything at all about the man he'd come to find, joining one of these gangs might be the only way to do it.

He assessed that the most powerful faction was that run by a figure known as Hell's King: a brooding, serious man, apparently, who dealt both mercy and punishment equally, swiftly and, often, violently. His reputation was fearful, more so, Landril suspected, because he was rarely seen. None of Landril's hastily constructed network of informants could give him a description of the man or point him out in the yard. It seemed the King of Hell was not a man to be found easily. Unfortunately, Landril *was*.

Hell's King

For two days the tall prisoner had watched the shifty little newcomer with all the keenness of a hungry eagle at dawn. Initially he had thought him merely yet another assassin who had been issued his true name and taken it upon himself to end his days. Like those other failed attempts, this one would no doubt end sadly for the would-be assassin.

But then he'd recognized him from days gone past. And he wondered how he'd ended up here. It was a far cry from the sumptuous lifestyle either of them had enjoyed previously and a long way from the city. A long way from anywhere. After all this time here, he could barely remember when he'd first arrived. Monotony had made the days blur together, and he no longer trusted his own memories. He did not even *like* the memories he could trust.

When he had first arrived he had given no name and spoken to no one. He was uninterested in the power plays he saw being run between the gangs, had no wish to get involved with any aspect of it. But he wasn't given a choice. Vallos had been a gang leader for years — an ex-soldier of some seniority, judging by his neck tattoos — and he had attempted to prove his dominance. Both he and the prisoner were of similar, muscular proportions underneath their loose grey tunics, bodies honed to perfection by years of campaigns, and both were scarred enough to show they knew their way around a fight. So when the bearded gang leader pulled a sharpened piece of flint and attempted to slam it into the newcomer's shoulder, he saw the blow coming, saw the nod to the guards to allow it to happen and saw the others move to one side to give Vallos space in that narrow, stone corridor. In a movement that might have been missed with a blink, he seized Vallos's wrist, smashed it against the stone so the flint clattered to the ground, headbutted the attacker, then shoved his face into the wall. Vallos slumped downwards and the newcomer gripped the man's throat with one hand.

He could have ended Vallos's life there and then. Both of them, and the gathered, braying crowd, realized it. But he chose otherwise. He had seen too much blood in his life by that point. He had pushed Vallos away. Everyone was in awe, for no one had bested Vallos in a fight before. This newcomer had done it within seconds. From then on he gained a new name: Hell's King. That was the beginning of his dominion in Hell's Keep.

Eventually Hell's King decided he'd better talk to the spy before someone else got hold of him. He ordered his men to cause a distraction on the far side of the open courtyard and while the guards' attention was on them, he approached the spymaster.

'Landril,' muttered Hell's King. 'You're a long way from home. And if you're not careful your curiosity will end with a knife in a dark corner.' He nodded towards where a group of the Bloodsports were watching them.

Landril stared at him with surprise, then with unconcealed relief, which he quickly tried to hide. 'Xavir Argentum. Thank the Goddess. You're actually *alive.*'

'You have a knack for stating the obvious, spy.' Their voices were low. Xavir was conscious of being watched and overheard. Not even his own men knew of his past and he wanted to keep it that way. 'In here my name here is Hell's King,' he continued. 'You'd do well to use no other.'

Landril smiled. 'I came here to find you.'

'Well, now you have,' Xavir replied. 'Why?'

'I *must* speak with you about an urgent matter.'

'I have no business with the outside world.'

'Well, it bloody well has business with *you*.'

Xavir glared at Landril. 'The man I was, he died out there. Years ago. My swords were taken. I have innocent blood on my hands. They sent me here because of it and they were right to. There is no forgiveness for what we did.'

'You're wrong.' Landril's words were fierce, but his tone was fearful. 'You were in the Solar Cohort. And now you dwell with animals.'

'They're ordinary men, spy, just like you. Some were good men once.'

'They're prison dogs,' Landril sneered. 'Lowest of the low.'

'You don't believe that. Many in here come from good breeding. A man of your calibre would know that from their accents. And you're in here as well, are you not?'

'Ah, yes,' Landril replied. 'But *I* committed no crime.'

Xavir smiled coldly, straightened his back. 'Ask any of them in here and they would give you a similar answer.'

'But it's different.'

'Of course. Look, spy, whatever you were out *there* –' Xavir gestured with finger to the west – 'does not apply in *here*.'

'Technically it's . . . spy*master*. Anyway. You need to know what I have to say. It's over five years since you came here, Xavir. Things have changed a lot in that time.'

'That the world changes is its only constant. You came here to tell me poor man's philosophy?'

Landril had begun to wring his hands, cracking a knuckle. 'Just let me finish, dammit. It's been five years since *he* put you in here. Mardonius and his cronies.'

Xavir gave no response to this bold claim.

'He became king the year after, you know,' Landril continued. 'Once Cedius rotted away.'

'So he is definitely dead, then,' Xavir replied. 'I heard, but I didn't like to believe it.'

'Sadly so,' Landril said. 'The old man was never the same without you and the Legion of Six. Then Mardonius began his warmongering. He's expanded the clan territories and the duchies grow ever larger. People were happy. Metal merchants were happy. Those towns and villages on the borders were absorbed and Stravimon stands larger than even when you led the way.'

'Nations expand and retract like lungs, spymaster. Nothing new here, especially where the clans are concerned. We're people bred to fight. You didn't come here to tell me that all was prosperous with the world.'

'No I did not,' Landril said. 'Mardonius has begun a campaign to clear our nation of those who worship the Goddess and other gods.'

'I am not a religious man.'

Landril shook his head. 'You don't understand. He is committing genocide – thousands of our own people have been killed. Good Stravir are no more.'

'How so?'

'As you'd expect. First he demanded higher taxes from the clans affiliated to her, and then gods like Balax, Jarinus, Kalladorium and the Great Eye. Suddenly local stations of the King's Legion started to make life difficult for worshippers of all faiths. Those who worship the Goddess felt the brunt – they were treated like scum. A few families hid their faiths, but the majority – tens and tens of thousands – did not. When they refused to move from their homes, there was an increase in troops stationed nearby, and then many families just "disappeared". The clans have been whittled down from thirty to half that – nearly all of them remain on his side.'

Xavir considered the spymaster's words. 'How long ago was this?'

'The most brutal of the cleansing started last summer, when there were harvest festivals and offerings for the Goddess, but the seeds had been planted long before.'

'An ancient technique, that – to kill followers on their sacred holy days.'

'This is only *half* my news, Xavir. Your family's castles on the eastern border of the duchies have been ransacked. Only the fortress at Gol Parrak still stands, but no one stands with it.'

'Why not?' Xavir balled his fists.

Landril took a slow step back. 'Because the clans around Gol Parrak have been bribed over five years. The various families now fight for *him*.'

'Do any of my family still survive at least?' Xavir had not thought of his father and sister in years, assuming they felt shame for his being here.

Landril's face darkened. 'Your father passed away defending Gol Parrak with several kin. Your sister escaped with her children.'

Landril turned to three guards who marched by, none of them making eye contact with Xavir.

'You came all the way here to tell me this,' Xavir said softly. 'You risked your own life. Did they brand you too?'

A gentle nod. Landril lifted his sleeve to show the exposed 'X' upon his upper arm. The permanent mark of a prisoner.

'You have guts, spymaster, I'll give you that.'

'Admittedly, I took an elixir before they pressed the iron to my skin,' Landril said, with half a smile. 'I felt nothing, dammit, but I could smell my own flesh cooking.'

Xavir shook his head. 'Why did you do this? Why come here?'

'Has what I said not been enough?' Landril asked, a little exasperated.

'Why did you, spy, come to find *me*? You only work on others' behalf, so who sent you?' Xavir demanded.

A gust of wind howled by the side of the fortress, and Landril shivered.

'Lupara. The wolf queen.'

Forging Peace

In the darkened cells, Davlor, an irritating man of twenty summers with straggling brown hair, rat-like features and small eyes, shuffled towards Xavir, who was lying on his bare stone slab of a bed. Despite today's donation of blankets from the monastery, Xavir always ensured that he was the last to receive such comforts. The truth was that he had woken moments before, after experiencing a nightmare. A flashback. The harsher the stone under his back, the quicker he returned to reality from sleep. That was if he could sleep properly at all these days.

Davlor stood beside him with a bloodied nose, and waited.

'What happened?' Xavir asked.

'Someone claimed they had smuggled in a witchstone and I wanted to get it.'

'And what good,' Xavir said, 'would a witchstone be among men?'

Davlor shrugged. 'Thought it might be useful, boss.'

The statement felt even more petty and ridiculous given Landril's earlier news about the crimes going on in the wider world.

Xavir sighed. 'And who's responsible for the stone and for your nose?'

'Gallus from the Chained Dead,' Davlor replied sullenly.

'Valderon's men. As ever. I'll meet with him about it.'

'No revenge?' Davlor said, surprised.

'No, lad,' Xavir grunted. 'No revenge. They're still bitter about Jedral gouging Fellir's eyes ten days past.'

'But . . . my nose—' Davlor muttered.

'Looks a lot better than it did,' Xavir interrupted calmly. 'Don't be looking for battles over things as trivial as this.'

'I still wanna see Gallus's nose kicked in.'

'Save your enthusiasm for the real fights, Davlor. You've only been here a few months and it's not only your nose that will get disfigured, so get used to it or learn to keep your wits about you. Be vigilant at all times and keep your mouth shut unless it's necessary. When in a cell with others you don't trust, concentrate. Listen. Sense movements. But keep your damned mouth shut. Control your anger. Deploy it tactically. If you still have time to waste then listen to Tylos's poems.'

Someone nearby laughed. It might even have been Tylos.

'You always talk like a warrior, not like a prisoner.' Davlor eyed Xavir with an almost childlike enthusiasm for the supposed glory of military life.

Xavir waved him away.

There were five men in their shared cell, but it was still spacious. Xavir had come to an agreement with one of the guards in exchange for this particular place.

He could hear Davlor still muttering curses about Gallus. As a relatively new inmate, Davlor could not know of the sheer effort to keep some form of peace among the gangs, otherwise there would be blood every day.

Politicking.

Ironic that even in here there were hierarchies, negotiations and understandings reached. *Would things have been any different in the outside world?* Xavir wondered. This was *his* kingdom now. But, once, he might have had another. *It would have still been politicking, still the same, just in finer clothes.*

The conversation with Landril had stirred the burning embers within Xavir. This was a red heat he had suppressed, until suppression had become habit, and habit had become his character. He had never thought of leaving Hell's Keep after the first year. He had found a way of coping and his satisfaction came from stopping other ruined men from being worse than they were. His gang had become a substitute for his clan, and that sat well with him.

But . . . things were different now that Landril had given him a vision. The outside world – the duchies and Stravimon – was in crisis. People were dying. Lupara, of all people, was involved with Landril's scheme. That suggested ill times indeed. In a way, being in Hell's Keep was no longer a punishment, but a shelter from the storm.

Xavir laughed to himself at the very notion.

'What's so funny, boss?' Davlor called out from the darkness.

'The world is caving in,' Xavir muttered. 'And we're in the safest place we could be.'

'You know, I think he's finally lost it,' Tylos said with a smile. The black man's elegant ways made the statement seem charming rather than an insult. Tylos was in gaol for being a thief with expensive tastes. Xavir often enjoyed his company and his southern philosophy.

'The fucker was always mad,' said Jedral. 'Happens to us all eventually.' The wild-looking bald man often joked about having killed his own parents to claim an inheritance, but he was an inveterate liar and the reasons for his incarceration got wilder and wilder with each telling. But Jedral had watched Xavir's back in here more than once and that was enough for Hell's King.

The others chuckled darkly, a sound that was replaced by the wind groaning through the old stone corridors.

'Then you'll definitely think I'm insane for what I'm about to suggest,' Xavir announced.

Jarratox

Birds arced in a wide circle towards the sun, flocking tightly to form the shape of a hooded head in the orange-blue sky. The strange head, like that of an old crone, moved from left to right before scattering on the wind. From her bedroom window, with the breeze brushing against her face, Elysia watched the spectacle with a frown on her face, wondering if it signified anything meaningful.

At times she felt as if she was questioning the purpose of everything.

She peered out between the old stone spires towards the tip of the void that marked the limits of the island. Two hundred feet the other side of the drop was firm land, which could be accessed by one of three stone bridges — or levitation if one knew the right methods. She didn't. The sisters did not teach those skills until near the end of a young witch's education.

Across the way she could see where the cliff face was alight with the glimmer of gemstones in the soft afternoon light. Witchstones, the source of the witches' power, the various colours used for different spells and ready to be mined by the younger girls, who would abseil safely under the protection of numerous wards.

Today the blue sky was broken up only by wisps of cloud.

Green hills shimmered in the gentle heat, and here and there were copses of oaks, and stone dwellings. To the west were forested mountains where, at night, she had noticed the occasional crackle of magic, but by daybreak there were no signs of what might have caused it.

A floorboard creaked outside her room and a moment later there was a knock at her door.

'It is time for your lesson,' a voice called. It was the tutor, Yvindris.

Elysia's heart sank; she had hoped Birgitta might instruct her today. She at least enjoyed the lessons with her.

Sighing, she pulled on her simple brown tunic, the colour worn by all novice sisters, and paused by the mirror to check her black hair was tied back neatly and to the right, in the official manner. She jumped down from the stone windowsill and tiptoed between the piles of books and parchments to, no doubt, endure yet another pointless lecture.

The young novice and the old, blue-robed teacher walked in silence along the passageway. Yvindris had a slight limp because of a persistent pain in her left leg which she waxed lyrical about to the bored Elysia. This was typical conversation among the older tutors, seemingly more concerned about news of their health than about magic – and even talking about magic could be dull enough at times. It made Elysia more determined than ever to spend time practising the more physical arts, lest she turn into someone like Yvindris.

As their feet whispered along the ancient stone, there came the chatter of women's voices from hidden alcoves, utterances of prayer or readings of arcane texts. Lore was being passed on from generation to generation of sisters. The book learning was what she liked the least – Elysia preferred to be out in the forests with Birgitta. That, inevitably, meant many of the other sisters accused her of being stupid.

The two of them entered a wide courtyard, which contained a beautiful garden with a fountain in the centre. Privets no taller than her knee grew in intricate spirals, dividing up patches of different coloured flowers. Statues of former matriarchs lined the avenue ahead of her, and around the fringes of the courtyard were columns of stone half-strangled by ivy. A handful of crows loitered on the walls above. It was a bright day now and the faded stone glowed with the sun's warmth. Three other young women sat on a stone seat in quiet contemplation, reading from scrolls; two looked up and gave her a disdainful glance. Elysia didn't make friends easily – even among those brown-garbed novices of her own age.

One of the plants twisted its black-petalled flowerhead towards Elysia as she walked by. The thing was watching her; or rather the old women were using it to watch her from elsewhere. She rarely wandered through the garden, knowing that some-one, somewhere, would be following her every move.

Yvindris paused in the centre by the fountain. The old woman stood a little shorter than Elysia, who even at seventeen summers was now taller than most of the sisters. It was another reason she felt different from everyone else – not merely men-tally, but physically. Yvindris's pale, wrinkled face was shaded by the hood of her flowing rich, blue shawl, her eyes concealed in the darkness. One of her eyes had been replaced by a red witch-stone, and Elysia never knew what properties it had given her.

From her sleeve Yvindris produced a pale-blue witchstone and handed it to Elysia, before gesturing with a crooked finger towards the fountain. 'With this water elemental, I want you to stop the flow today. Do not do anything with it. Merely stop it. See if you remembered the lines of text from yesterday.'

Elysia sighed, stepped towards the ornate stone rim and peered into the rippling pool of water. About two yards away, in the centre of the pool, a stone fish rose up and from out of its mouth came a stream of clear water. Aside from their voices and the occasional shrill bird cry, the bubbling fountain was the only sound here.

She clutched the stone in her right hand, surprised by its weight and density, and calmed her heartbeat.

Yvindris peered over her shoulder. 'I hope you remember the formal words,' she hissed. There was more than a hint of glee in her voice. 'You have failed twice before. Your reputation as a failure will see you go to a poor clan and the time for allocation is almost upon you. A poor clan is no life for a sister, I can tell you.'

Because you'll end up back here as a one-eyed hag? Elysia wanted to say. It was an unspoken rule that many of the less fortunate sisters ended up back here as tutors.

Elysia squeezed the stone and muttered the chant in an ancient, Fourth Era tongue, trying her best to remember the forms of words that were no longer spoken beyond the bridges of Jarratox. She searched her mind to recall the right words, all the while feeling the breath of the old sister on the back of her neck. A heat began to spread through her body, a tightness in her chest . . .

'Two words are incorrect,' Yvindris snapped. 'Round the vowels and pronounce the endings more clearly.'

The water in the pool began to bubble, not become still, and steam started rising from the surface. The stone fish started shaking erratically.

Yvindris placed a hand upon Elysia's shoulder for her to stop talking, and her words ceased.

Elysia was breathless, her legs felt weak.

'You are too angry,' Yvindris scoffed.

Is it any wonder, with you looming over me?

Elysia merely shrugged her shoulders, handed over the blue stone and turned back into the bright courtyard, blinking as if she had just woken up from a deep sleep.

Nearby, the other girls barely concealed their laughter at her failure.

'Why can you not do what is a simple task for a sister of your advanced learning?' Yvindris's words were neither soft nor harsh, just the same emotionless monotone that most of the old matrons used with her. Only Birgitta was any different.

'Perhaps I'm just not going to be very good,' Elysia muttered, 'and I will fail the sisterhood.'

'That is not for you to foresee,' Yvindris replied. 'The matriarch has always been wary of you. It is not any lack of power that stops you, oh no. You're quite potent. Rather it is your attitude. You do not see the point in what we do. You do not *care* enough about getting things right.'

Elysia sighed. 'Should we not question what we are shown? *Is the world not an illusion?* That's what we're taught all the time. Those are the words above the archways as you enter the Forgotten Quadrangle.'

'The ways of the sisterhood *can* be trusted,' Yvindris continued. 'We are of the earth. We are part of the fabric of the world. Illusions do not apply to us.'

Elysia peered down to the smooth flagstones beneath her feet. If she questioned things, the answers would come in the form of another lecture. It had always been the same, and by now she had worked out that the best method was to ask nothing and find her own answers later.

A noise caught her attention and she looked up. On the far side of the garden a door opened violently, striking against the stone wall. A dozen figures, all wearing sun-yellow robes, strode from one part of the enclave across to the other. There was silence as they went. The older sisters seldom moved in large groups on the settlement, and certainly never with such a sense of urgency.

'You look worried,' Elysia said, watching Yvindris carefully.

'I am, child.'

Child?! At seventeen summers, is it any wonder I get so angry when you keep calling me a child?

'What's concerning you?' she replied.

'Our future. The world's future.'

'The future can never happen,' Elysia quoted the Eighth Era mystic Faraclyes.

'I see you have learned something then,' Yvindris muttered.

A bell began to ring, a sound that Elysia had never heard in her entire life here.

'I must go,' Yvindris snapped. 'Return to your quarters.'

The old woman pulled up her robes and scurried from the courtyard. Elysia looked across to the other novices and saw that they had stopped laughing. The strange, watching flowers had their heads bowed and moved no longer.

A Dark Court

Men whispered in dark corners. Messages were exchanged. Before long a meeting was arranged.

Two days later, in a remote part of the keep, Valderon, leader of the Chained Dead, stood before Xavir. No one else was even near these quarters. The two guards who permitted the meeting in exchange for Landril's smuggled herbs were probably too sensible to enter the cell to keep an eye on them. Perhaps they hoped the two gang leaders would kill each other.

'What do you want with me, gangman?' Valderon grunted. He refused to use Xavir's title Hell's King – *king* had connotations for Valderon that he openly despised.

'Gallus struck a blow to Davlor's face,' Xavir told him. 'Tylos witnessed it.'

'The black man is reliable enough.' Valderon sighed, his dark eyes glimmering with tension. He was a big man, as tall as Xavir. His shoulders were still huge despite eating prison gruel. There were no grey hairs in his dark mane yet. 'Petty squabbles among boys,' Valderon grumbled. 'This is why you summoned me?'

'No.' Xavir watched Valderon's every move. The last time they had met they had been surrounded by their own men in the courtyard, and nearly every guard stood on standby, spear or arrow pointed their way.

'Then what do you want?' Valderon asked, rubbing his dark, dishevelled beard.

'An end to it all,' Xavir said. 'To put an end to these pointless protection and retaliation scraps once and for all. To stop fighting over *nothing*, and begin fighting over *something*.'

Valderon rose and cracked his knuckles.

'Calm down.' Xavir waved him back, careful for the gestures to not be perceived as dismissive. 'I have not come to fight *you*.'

'Then how do we *end* things, as you say? Speak.'

'Are you at peace here?' Xavir asked.

'And what is *that* supposed to mean?' Valderon spat.

'Is this it? I don't know what rank you held before, but I suspect that you were military. I don't know what you did to end up here, but is this all you want to do for the rest of your life, to die in some gaol on the far end of the continent?'

Valderon looked at him appraisingly. 'This isn't so bad. You should know, being a fighting man yourself. You must have been on campaign. We've got it easy compared to that. Regular food. No worries over where to sleep. No pressures of men's lives being in your hands — at least to no great extent. A man can be at peace here.'

'A man can go insane, too,' Xavir said, contemplating his own night terrors.

'With any luck,' Valderon replied with a grim smile.

The leader of the Chained Dead stepped into the partial light of a barred window, revealing the faint scar along his cheek, above his thick black beard. This wound had come from long before Hell's Keep. It was whispered that Valderon had once been in the First Legion, one of Cedius's finest regulars.

'I need to leave Hell's Keep,' Xavir announced.

Valderon gave a coarse, guttural laugh. 'Of course. Well, just stroll out the front gate.'

'I'm serious,' Xavir replied. 'I must go.'

Valderon frowned at him. 'Why do you want to get out now?'

'There are things happening and my help is needed.' Xavir would say no more on the matter.

'As you say,' Valderon replied. 'Do you have any idea how many guards stand between you and freedom?'

'Two hundred and four,' Xavir replied, 'at my last estimation, and all of them armed. Not to mention fourteen locked, barred gates and the witches at the bottom of the slope. I'm sure the cook has a blunt knife somewhere in his armoury.'

Valderon gave another slight smile at that, and the tension eased slightly. 'So how exactly do you *propose* to leave?' he asked.

'With your help.' Xavir could tell he now held the man's interest. 'We're going. Both of us. Together. And we're taking as many of our men with us as possible.'

A moment of silence. Valderon laughed loudly then quietened as he saw the seriousness on Xavir's face. 'Speak, man of hell. Let's hear you out.'

It had not been easy to convince Valderon of the plan. That it relied mostly upon Landril, who didn't look the most capable of beings, did not exactly help their cause. But when Xavir explained the spymaster had managed to sneak *into* Hell's Keep purely to deliver news and smuggle Xavir out, Valderon was impressed.

'I dislike spies, Goddess curse their sneaking ways, but this one seems to have balls,' Valderon admitted.

'Hell's Keep,' Xavir told him, 'depends upon routines. Routines can be exploited and that is what our plan does so well.'

'If it is so easy, then why not just go on your own?' Valderon asked.

'I never said it would be easy,' Xavir muttered.

Valderon nodded. 'It will not be difficult to create a diversion, at least.'

'Like any war this depends on the *flow* of men. Where they are and at what hour of the battle. Numbers are a secondary factor. The guards outnumber us certainly, two to one at least, and they are armed and we are not. But they cannot be everywhere at once and we can easily take their weapons off them when they are dead. I have seen those who have come to serve here recently and their calibre is not as it was many years ago. The good soldiers are needed elsewhere.'

'You're a warrior,' Valderon said with a piercing stare. 'I knew as much.'

Xavir gave no reply.

'When does this begin?'

'With your agreement, in three days' time, in the courtyard. Landril has calculated the formula the guards use for deciding which prisoners go into the courtyard. We are seldom in there together, for obvious reasons, but in three days myself and Landril will be there, as well as a good number of your men. We just need your consent and for you to direct them.'

'How can I know you'll not let me rot in the cells?'

It was a fair question, and one Xavir had anticipated. 'Trust means very little around here, of course. But you know I cannot get out of here without a man of your calibre. We need you armed, swiftly, and to lead your men as if you were a warrior once again. As I say, either both of us leave together – or we'll both die in here.'

'What of the Bloodsports?'

Xavir shrugged. 'They are ten men, where our gangs total forty-two. Together we form the majority faction. I would be glad of their help, but for now it is best that they know nothing. There was an escape attempt two years ago, and I think it might have been successful if the Bloodsports had not let the guards know. You'll understand if I do not wish them to be a part of this plan.'

Valderon said nothing.

'We'll quickly become hunted men,' Valderon said, contemplatively.

'At least by being hunted we will feel *alive.*'

Once again there was an upward curve to Valderon's lips. Xavir extended his arm towards Valderon, and the gang leader shook it, clasping firmly at the wrist. It was a casual gesture, one shared by so many warriors who served in the armies of Cedius the Wise. In that unspoken moment there was an acknowledgement that they shared more than others realized.

Elysia

Birgitta burst into Elysia's room and spoke breathlessly. 'They're up to something.'

'Who?' Elysia asked, rising from her bed where she had been sprawled, trying to commit a scroll to memory, to perfect what she had failed at earlier.

'The sisters,' Birgitta said. 'By the source! That's what the recent bell was for – did you hear it earlier? Many of the older sisters have already been recalled from their clans. They came last night or this morning.'

'Why aren't you there?'

'Because *I*, as a mere tutor, have not been invited.' Birgitta folded her arms in mock offence. She was wearing a long, blue robe and a darker blue tunic underneath. There was beautiful but subtle detailing all across the chest and around the neck of the tunic, a minor rebellion, given that such adornments were frowned upon. Birgitta was between forty and fifty summers – young for one of the tutoring sisters – and she had bright, messy blonde hair which had a silver sheen to it that suggested she was much older. Her features were small, her eyes, nose and mouth, all of them delicate so that in the right light she looked vaguely like a doll. Hidden by her robe was a wiry, youthful physique. One of the reasons Elysia liked Birgitta so much was that she refused to grow feeble and frail like many of the sisters around here, who deemed that exercise was beneath them.

'What's everyone up to?' Elysia asked. 'What's going on?'

'We're going to watch.' Birgitta held out her hand. 'Come on.'

'Watch what?'

'I don't know yet, little sister. But we can find out.'

The two sisters headed out into the corridors, Birgitta leading the way down the stairs, and into the main thorough-fare. There was no one else around, which was unusual for the late morning; a time where early lessons were completed and the sisters were permitted leisure time before the quiet study of the afternoon.

Birgitta paused suddenly and turned to face an old limestone wall. Elysia, who did well not to step on her heel, was about to ask why, when the woman drew a black witchstone from her pocket and placed it into a hole that Elysia could barely see.

A doorway, stuttered into existence.

'Quick, in you go,' Birgitta said.

Elysia stepped cautiously into the void while Birgitta retrieved the stone. A moment later they were in total darkness surrounded by a musty, damp smell. Birgitta muttered, and a line of stones began to glow one by one, a ripple of white light spreading up ahead, illuminating a long, narrow corridor.

'Where are we?' Elysia asked. 'Are we even allowed to be in here?'

'You're too cautious! By the source, have I taught you noth-ing? If you risk nothing, then you will end up just like the others. You should be thrilled about a secret passageway.'

'Well I am, in a way . . . But where is this?'

'Within the walls. The sisters can quickly walk from one part of Jarratox to the other without being seen by means of these tunnels.'

'Why do they need to be secret about it?'

'The sisters don't like terms like *secret*. They pride themselves on being open and honest – or at least that is what they tell others. What I'm about to show you will prove that it is a lie.'

'Should you be showing me this?'

'You're old enough to decide for yourself,' Birgitta said. 'Now, come on.'

They continued following the glowing stones for a short while.

Elysia could hear the muffled sounds of chattering.

'Is this passage underneath some of the sisters' rooms?' she asked.

'This part is,' Birgitta said, pausing to perceive their location. Elysia could tell they were standing at some kind of crossroads, but the lights in front of them began to fade, their power seeping away slowly.

Birgitta gestured to the right and another line of stones began to glow.

'How did you do that?' Elysia asked.

'The stone,' Birgitta replied, showing her the same black stone she had placed into the wall earlier. 'The stone knows where I want to go.'

'I don't believe you.'

'Good,' said Birgitta mysteriously, and added, 'Now keep your voice to a whisper from here on.'

Elysia nodded and followed the older sister. The sound of voices became slightly fainter, then, after they'd climbed up a spiral stairwell, it became much louder once again.

Eventually the two of them stepped out into a low-roofed corridor. It featured a small, decorative iron grille to the stone-work on the outside, allowing in a slit of natural light to capture dust motes and cobwebs. There was a similar grille a little further on, on the left, only this time it faced down into a dimly lit auditorium.

'This is a conclave of sisters,' Birgitta whispered, her footsteps light on the boards. 'They have not held one for ten years or more.'

She directed Elysia towards the grille. The two of them sat down on the floor and pressed their faces against the ironwork.

Down below were about three dozen old women. Some wore yellow robes, indicating they were senior sisters close to the matriarch. Others wore grey robes with red sashes or hoods – the colours of those attached to a clan. All were seated on wooden benches looking towards where the matriarch, a white-haired lady wearing a shimmering white robe and cloak, stood before them on a raised platform. A handful of cressets had been lit, casting an eerie glow upon the sisters' faces, and wafts of incense drifted upwards.

'I still don't understand why you're not there with them?' Elysia whispered.

'Only the highest-ranking of the sisters are there – those with proper influence in the clans and in the wider world.' Birgitta tugged her blue robe to indicate her exclusion. 'Besides, they do not trust tutors like me.'

'Why not?'

Birgitta paused for a moment. 'They never do. I am not one of them. They frown upon my ways. To them, magic is all, the stones are all, the source is all, and to talk about training in other arts is a blasphemy of sorts.'

'They let you teach, though. They let you teach me.'

'They do, little sister, they do.' Birgitta sighed. 'In my darker moments, when I see them like this, I cannot help but think they view tutors merely as a means of looking after novices until the novices can be used in their games of power.'

'What games? This looks serious to me.'

'Can games not be serious too?' Birgitta asked. 'It is a game of strategy, whatever they play. The yellow-robed seniors play the game within these walls – they all compete for the matriarch's favour, or manoeuvre to replace her at some stage. As for what game the matriarch herself plays? That, I do not know.'

There was the sound of heavy footsteps down below. A figure in armour appeared – silver chainmail, black robes and a silver helmet that covered the face, with two horns protruding to evoke the image of a bull. As soon as the warrior came forwards to approach the matriarch, the other sisters fell into silence.

'Who's that?' Elysia asked.

'One of King Mardonius's soldiers.'

'It's a man?'

'It likely is.'

'I thought men weren't allowed on Jarratox?'

'It is rare,' Birgitta said quietly. 'But not unknown. Let us listen and find out why he's here.'

For a moment Elysia thought she saw another figure far behind in the shadows. It looked like a man, but now and then its armour – if it wore armour at all – burned like the embers of a fire. Whoever it was stood at the back, away from the attention here.

'Did you see that?'

'I think so. Oh . . .' Birgitta said.

'Do you know who it is?'

Birgitta never got to answer. Down in the dimly lit chamber, the matriarch began to speak. Elysia had rarely heard the great woman talk, had only really seen her passing with her yellow-robed entourage. Her image of the grand head of the sisterhood had been formed largely by the awed whispers of the other sisters – of a noble, stern woman who put the sisterhood before all else.

'Grave times befall us, my dear sisters,' she began, her voice carrying loudly across the auditorium. Her tone was bold and rich, and commanded respect.

'*Challenging* times,' the matriarch continued, 'times that have seen a great deal of unease in the world. Times that have also seen almost twenty of our own sisterhood vanish without a trace.'

The soldier made no response, aside from facing the other sisters. The figure in the shadows burned slowly.

'And in such times, we must make difficult decisions. It has always been the way for our sisterhood. As the ebb and flow of the outside world changes, we must change too. Today is no different.'

The rest of the sisters remained silent, but there was a tension that even Elysia could feel from her hidden position.

'We hold more sway outside than many of you know,' the matriarch continued. 'Our relationships with the clans are based on them adhering to the king's codes. Those sisters among you who have been recalled have been so because your clan has rejected the codes. They have therefore forfeited their sister and lost their connection to the source.'

'And what code would they have gone against, *precisely*?' one woman demanded.

A hush fell across the other sisters. Birgitta leaned into Elysia and whispered, 'That's Galleya, a strong woman. I like her. At one time she was believed to be part of a faction to usurp the matriarch, though I do not believe it myself. Hence she was *invited* to spend time beyond the bridge.'

'They have gone against King Mardonius's wishes,' the

matriarch announced, 'and it is he who binds together not merely Stravimon, but all the weaker nations who border it.'

'But how have *they* gone against his wishes?' Galleya repeated. It was clear from a few shakes of heads that some of the other sisters hoped she would remain silent. There was a strange inevitability about proceedings, and Galleya seemed to be just getting in the way.

'There are ancient laws that exist to keep all nations in peace,' the matriarch replied. 'Laws where magics are to be committed for the greater good. There have been refusals to enact such laws, among other things, and direct challenges to the king's authority. And so we are faced with a difficult decision. I cannot dither any longer. We have debated about the merits a dozen times, but parchment must be signed. Quite simply, we must commit to a formal allegiance to King Mardonius, not merely the seat of Stravimon. And by doing so, we will secure a more powerful and enduring future for the sisterhood. That is my purpose as your matriarch, and that is what I have done.'

Several sisters rose to speak at once, whilst the others whispered their disapproval to whoever was sitting next to them. The room was divided. After a few moments, once the matriarch had raised both her hands, the room fell into a relative calm.

'This is not a decision we can make lightly. King Mardonius wishes to make our union more formal. Deeper, you might say.'

'What do we get that secures our future?' someone asked.

The matriarch hesitated until a deep quiet settled on the chamber. 'Our ways of creating new novices are archaic and unreliable. Our stock of seed progenitors is as weak as ever. The traits we seek – or those traits we wish to remove from our stock – are often beyond our control. Mardonius has access to incredible techniques he has in turn gained from an alliance with that race that comes from beyond our shores. These techniques will permit us much more control over the newer novices. There will be no weak sisters in the future.'

During the resulting commotion at the declaration, Elysia turned sharply to Birgitta with a hundred questions she wanted to ask. She had heard rumours about how the novices were the results of unions between selected stock of men from the outside world and specific sisters. Novice weren't just born – they were bred.

'In addition,' the matriarch declared, 'in return for this formal arrangement, he has discovered large deposits of witchstones in several location across the nation, and he is willing to cede us these lands and offers the industry with which to mine these stones and deliver them to us. All the colours you can imagine have been found within the deposits.'

'He wants to buy our support,' someone said.

'Bribery!' shouted another.

'It is an *offer*,' the matriarch snapped, 'like any other. This is how the world beyond our bridges operates.'

'And ours too, by the sounds of it,' a sister said.

'This is a partnership, no more, no less,' the matriarch said, glancing to the soldier. 'He has promised our safety in these uncertain times.'

The warrior made no movement. The figure behind him burned again. Elysia thought she could see two red eyes.

'In return, all he asks is that if he needs our help then we will send some of our sisters to his aid. Our black-robed sisters have already journeyed to him and he gives us thanks for that.'

'He wants us to help kill innocents,' Galleya shouted, 'to butcher good people.'

The soldier to the left of the matriarch shifted threateningly. For a moment no one said anything. They were too shocked at the gesture. The burning figure in the shadows was no longer to be seen.

Eventually, the matriarch gave an awkward laugh. 'You insult our guests,' she began. 'They are no butchers. They bring stability. They are defenders of the freedoms of innocent people. Besides, these are all concerns of the world beyond the bridges.'

'Are we not a part of that same world?'

'What do you ask of us?' another asked. 'It sounds as if a decision has been made.'

'No, it has not been made. That is what you are all here for. We stand today at a crossroads. We can turn towards Mardonius. In exchange for this, we will stabilize how we breed new novices in a manner never before known, and be given an unlimited resource of witchstones, which would allow our skills to reach new heights. This is an incredible opportunity that we cannot ignore. All that is required of us is that those of you who are now unaffiliated with a clan help Mardonius's own territories out when needed, and that we withdraw any support from those clans who stand against him.'

'What is the other option?' came a voice from the back, almost directly underneath Elysia. 'What if we decline?'

'We can of course decline the deeper union with the king. Bear in mind that we are already aligned due to pacts that were formed at the beginning of this Ninth Era. To decline would put a centuries-old relationship in jeopardy. It would mean weakening our resources, letting our stock of novices become weaker and it would cause instability elsewhere – for those of you who remain concerned with the *outside* world.'

A murmur of discontent spread across the group and the matriarch held up her hand once again.

'For two days and two nights, Mardonius's messengers will wait here. We have no urgency to decide. I realize this is a difficult decision for some of you, but we are a *democratic* sister-hood and protocol will be followed. Go back to your quarters or the courtyard or the library, but please do not discuss this with anyone outside the room.'

During the ensuing hubbub, the matriarch turned to escort the soldier out of sight.

Birgitta and Elysia withdrew from the grille.

'What was all that about?' Elysia asked.

'Two days and two nights,' Birgitta muttered. 'The matriarch will lobby each and every one of the sisters during that time and the decision will be inevitable.'

'What does that mean?'

'It means Mardonius will *own* the sisterhood in the long term.'

'Own us?'

'More or less, little sister.' Birgitta gave a sigh and closed her eyes. 'Do you know what he is doing across his lands?'

'I have heard rumours.'

'They are likely true. Now imagine if there were none of our sisters in the way. No, imagine *more* of our sisters were helping him. Can you imagine what that would mean?'

'I suppose it isn't good.'

'No. By the source, it is not good at all.'

'What about this breeding thing that the matriarch said?'

Birgitta's gaze softened. 'For now you should push such thoughts to the back of your mind. It matters not where you come from, but where you go.'

Elysia shrugged. 'I still don't like the sound of any of that.'

'Your instincts are reliable. And the presence of soldiers here is somewhat concerning as well. Violence and intimidation — there is no place for them here. No place for them anywhere.'

'I have never seen anyone like either of them. One of them seemed to be on fire.'

'There are plenty of warriors across this continent, little sister, but I cannot ever recall one crossing the bridge to Jarratox. Messengers, so the matriarch said, but when has a messenger ever needed full armour? No. This is Mardonius's cadre. I've heard tell that those closest to him are possessed by daemons, that they have sold their souls in awful pacts to enhance their skills. One cannot know what lies behind that horned helmet. And the figure that seemed as if it was born of fire . . .'

'Do you think the king was threatening anyone?'

'If Mardonius wanted any of us killed he would have sent an assassin.' Birgitta's posture stiffened. She swayed from foot to foot while she thought. 'No, I would wager these fellows, these *messengers*, were a kindly reminder of the king's power.'

'So what should we do?' Elysia asked.

'Let me think on it, but I fear there is nothing that we can do. I'll take you out for a lesson tomorrow. We'll go beyond the bridge and into the forests. We can be at peace there.'

'Archery?' Elysia was excited at the prospect.

'Perhaps, little sister. Yes. I need to be connected with the earth. It will help my mind.'

Landril's Mask

Three days passed without event. Although, now that the spy-master had stirred up old memories and quiet anger, three days felt like an eternity to Xavir. He felt alive for the first time in years.

To prepare for their escape, Xavir led his men through harder exercise regimes: lifting each other over their shoulders and moving back and forth across the dark cells until they were out of breath and their muscles burned in agony.

On the third day, fifty-two inmates, including those from Xavir and Landril's cells, milled about under the open air, flecks of sleet spiralling around them, with just as many guards watching them from a battlement ten feet above. A few soldiers were in the courtyard itself, keeping an eye out for any signs of trouble. Xavir and Landril sized up the guards, searching for one on his own and of around the spymaster's own height, which was no simple task given that the soldiers mostly patrolled in pairs.

Eventually they found a suitable victim and set about their ploy. The two prisoners began an argument that was loud enough to attract the interest of the soldier.

'I'll kill you if you say that again!' Xavir bellowed.

'Just try me,' Landril screamed theatrically.

As Xavir pushed Landril's shoulder, raising the ire and sword of the guard, a full fight began to break out on the far side of the courtyard.

As the guard's attention was distracted by this new commotion, Xavir moved with lightning speed, smashing his victim's sword hand against the wall, taking the weapon from him and slipping it into his windpipe with surgical precision. There wasn't a sound as the guard dropped and blood pooled at Xavir's feet.

'Well, that made a mess.' Landril winced.

'Just get changed,' Xavir hissed.

This exchange was concealed by a group of Xavir's calm-looking gang members obscuring them from the view of anyone in the courtyard or on the walls. As they removed the armour from the corpse piece by piece, Landril dressed in it – shuddering in distaste at the blood.

Clothes exchanged, bronze helmet in place, Landril assumed the role of the guard whilst the man's heavy form was shunted over the wall. The body tumbled down into the mists. The gang members who had been concealing the act dispersed with the suddenness of a flock of birds.

The violence across the way was broken up and Landril made his way over to the group of guards herding the prisoners back inside. He walked differently now, with the steady, purposeful steps of a soldier.

You had better be good at your job, spymaster . . .

Despite having dwelt for many years in Hell's Keep, these final few hours felt the longest.

Xavir contemplated, for a brief moment, the earlier act of killing. It had been the first time in years Xavir had taken a man's life, and the first time since the event that led to his incarceration in Hell's Keep, but he was surprised at how little the deed affected him. Those mental barriers he had put up long ago still held firm. How many thousands had he killed? If he thought about it for too long, no good would come of it. As for the guard, the poor fool may have had a wife and children somewhere, but Xavir reasoned that no one joined the military if they had not contemplated an early death. It was unfortunate, but that was war for you.

Xavir lay in his cell quietly. As the sun waned and the shadows grew longer, his gang nervously paced, or bickered with one another. They were eager for developments, anxious for news, but Xavir knew as much as they did and told them to relax and save their energy.

Eventually there was the sound of heavy-booted footsteps approaching down the corridor – one pair, slow and with a tired gait. Xavir pushed himself up as a faceless bronze helm looked through the barred view-hole on the door. A heavy *clank*, and the door was unlocked.

Xavir was outside in a heartbeat.

'What news?' he whispered.

Landril responded, his voice muffled by the bronze helmet. 'No one has noticed me, thank the Goddess. They change the watch here often, too often, so that half the men do not know one another. I have unlocked our way back to the inside of the main front entrance, but it's too heavily guarded on the inside for a simple key to suffice.'

'We can handle that when we get to it,' Xavir said. 'Have you freed Valderon and his men?'

'No, not yet.'

'Do that immediately. Do you know where it is?'

'More or less.' Landril replied.

'I will count to three hundred,' Xavir hissed. 'Then we will walk out and wait in the inner quadrangle. We must not leave without Valderon.'

Xavir watched Landril walk towards the quadrangle. Five men were at Xavir's back, itching to get going, but he waved them back.

'We go with Valderon's men,' Xavir cautioned, and began the process of counting in his head.

'Why the fuck should we?' Jedral ran a hand over his bald head in agitation. He had always claimed his hair had been burned off by magic. Probably another tall tale.

'Because it's no longer prisoner against prisoner,' Xavir replied. 'It's prisoner against soldier. Our enemy is different now.'

'Fine, so long as I get to kill someone at the end of this.' Jedral grunted a laugh.

'I can't fight with *them*,' replied Davlor, wiping his nose on his sleeve. 'Call me stuck in my ways if you want, but I can't.'

Xavir looked at the young man harshly. 'You either fight with them, or you die in here – your choice.'

'But they're our *enemies*,' Davlor whined.

'And now I say they are our allies. When have I ever let any of you down?' Xavir snapped. 'When you found flint pressed into your backs in the courtyard, who dealt out your retaliation? When you initiated a fight, who stepped in before you were thrown over the wall? Who demands you exercise so that you do not wilt like a leaf in autumn? Who intimidates the guards to spare you an extra spear in your ribs? Here is your chance to be free men. If we manage to escape, you will find alliances much harder to forge on the outside with a brand on your arm.'

Xavir's attention was drawn to soft footsteps on stone, somewhere in the distance. He was annoyed at himself for having lost count.

'It's time,' he declared.

The prisoners filtered through into the corridor, uniting with more of their own kin as well as those from Valderon's gang.

Xavir held them back at the edge of what was left of daylight and checked that the soldier before them was Landril and not another. When he was certain the way was clear, with a motion of Xavir's hand, the gangs filtered into the quadrangle, concealing themselves in the darkness under walkways. Xavir scanned his surroundings. There was little cover: two large carts up ahead and a handful of wooden water casks down along to the right.

He sought out Valderon, and the two clasped arms openly in front of their own men. Aside from one or two glances of surprise, the others appeared to take this truce with nothing but indifference.

'We have no weapons,' Valderon said quietly, 'save the one sword in the hands of your spymaster.'

Xavir moved across to Landril, took his sword and offered it to Valderon. 'There.'

The broad warrior accepted it with a nod, hefting the blade and testing its weight, the way an old soldier would, getting used to the feel of a sword once again. 'It is cheap and crude but, Goddess willing, it will kill.'

Xavir watched him warily, wondering for a moment if their trust would hold.

Valderon placed the tip of the blade to the stone and stood upright. 'You need no weapon?' His voice was quiet.

'I'll get one soon enough.'

'How will you kill?'

'Easily enough,' Xavir replied. 'Have your men been informed to stay together with mine? That we are no longer fighting?'

'They'll do whatever I do,' Valderon hissed. 'What about your mob?'

'They will show discipline. Now, come. We haven't much time.'

Landril

Amidst the throng of forty or so prisoners Landril followed Xavir and Valderon, warily scanning the surroundings for in-rushing guards. He hoped they'd soon be distracted by an all-out prison riot, as he had thrown a set of stolen keys into the midst of another cell, which meant that it would not be too long until there were dozens more prisoners causing chaos and attacking the guards. He was glad to be finally getting out of here.

Waving for silence, Xavir steered the men down a shallow walkway and into another quadrangle, making sure to keep them in the shadows as they moved. Darkness was almost complete, but Landril appreciated the caution.

Xavir's urgent whisper stopped the men in their tracks. There were footsteps approaching. Xavir and Valderon strode forwards purposefully. Landril could not see the ensuing skirmish, but heard the muted grunts and rattle of armour. Within seconds they had returned to distribute two more swords and pieces of armour back along the lines to the gang. Should all of these prisoners be armed? How much trust could anyone put in a bunch of cut-throats and traitors? Landril was indifferent to whether some of them died on the way to freedom, but Xavir appeared to want to see they were looked after.

The group surged forwards through an archway and stopped suddenly as three soldiers spotted them. Valderon sprinted towards them, Xavir at his side. Valderon smacked back the helmet of one and dragged his blade back across the man's throat. Xavir picked up the fallen man's weapon before it could hit the ground, and within a heartbeat spun it into the throat of the guard behind. By the time the man died, Valderon had already dispatched the other.

Xavir began stripping the armour off the guards again and spread the kit back through the gang members. He whispered for each them to take one item each, be it a sword or a helmet. All would have one item, he instructed. Then all would have two items. They would progress as equals.

As the prisoners trampled over the bodies of the guards and made their way into another small courtyard, a noise erupted from the far end of the tunnel. Though the sound was probably augmented by the walls around him, Landril guessed the rest of the prisoners were now attempting their escape.

Xavir and Valderon's united force burst out into the open and were immediately confronted by guards. Those prisoners with swords, Jedral and Tylos among them, muscled their way into the fight; Jedral slammed guards backwards with force, whilst Tylos deftly opened necks with a flick of the wrist.

Despite the others in combat, Landril was focused on Xavir and Valderon in amazement. The two of them, Xavir especially so, appeared to move at twice the speed of everyone else, as if they inhabited some special dimension of their own. Their swords flashed in blood-spraying arcs as one guard after another fell to their blows. Xavir wielded his blade with one hand, using his other to grapple with his opponent's weapon arm. Every time a soldier made an effort to prevent a blow, he was pounded back against the wall, or sent hurtling back into his fellow guards behind. And with each death, and Xavir's command, weapons and armour filtered back through the throng, another prisoner became armed, and the gangs became more dangerous. Soon even Landril was gripping a blade again, not that it was much good in his hands.

Fifteen guards now lay dead on the flagstones. Xavir and Valderon had killed most of them.

Somewhere in the distance a braying roar went up.

A bell began to toll repeatedly.

Ignoring the cacophony, the veteran warriors moved to a heavy oak door and lifted the beam that barred it. Upon opening it, the gangs piled through into another open space; directly ahead lay one of the main double doors that marked the limits of Hell's Keep.

And standing before that exit were two rows of soldiers, a good forty men in all. Xavir scanned their lines and then ordered his men to spread out into two groups, with himself at the head of one, Valderon the other. Each wing marched cautiously towards the flanks of the soldiers' lines. Still, the guards did not move, and Landril reckoned they had received orders to hold the gate no matter what. The prisoners rushed the final yards in a surging, screaming charge. Xavir was weaponless, but that didn't stop him as he dodged a clumsy stroke, pulled the arm of the wielder forwards and wrenched the blade free. Other gang members surged past Landril, who now found himself at the back of the raucous mob.

The guards separated into two smaller and more manageable forces to face off against their attackers. Xavir was somewhere in their midst, and all Landril could glimpse was the tip of his blade whirring through the air.

He could see where some of the prisoners were taking out years of pent-up frustration on the soldiers, hacking into them beyond the point of death before stripping them of their armour and weapons.

If we get out of here alive and spread our tale, Landril thought, *poets will not want to sing about this.*

He saw one of Xavir's men, Jedral, wrench off one guard's helm and beat his oppressor to death with it. He smiled with a feral grin the whole time. Only the black man from Chambrek, Tylos, seemed to rise above the savagery and killed quickly and dispassionately.

Several inmates were killed in the melee, their lack of armour leaving them exposed to even untrained blows. Landril was glad he had not got to know these faces well enough. As the mob trampled over the ruined corpses of the guards, and the fighting diminished, Xavir gave orders to open the gates. Four men moved with him to lift the heavy beam that lay across the double doors. Meanwhile Valderon moved towards the lever and chains and began to haul open the doors. As the gates drew back with a clamour . . .

'Archers!'

Xavir pointed to the walkway above, where prison guards with bows were hastily assembling. They were also lining up along the walkways above the gate and would have a perfect aim at the fleeing prisoners. One arrow thwacked into the door by Landril's ear, forcing him to duck reactively, as if it would do any good.

'Pick up a body,' Xavir ordered. 'As we rehearsed. Pick up any corpse. Haul it across your back.'

His men stared at each other until Xavir bellowed: 'Just do it!'

'By the Goddess,' Landril sighed, and wincing and struggling, managed to drag one of the dead guards onto his back just in time to feel an arrow thud into the corpse. A man to his right took an arrow to his calf and collapsed with the body on top of him. More arrows began to clatter around them.

'Now link up as best you can,' Xavir ordered. 'Corpse to corpse. Do not leave yourselves exposed.' Xavir and Valderon made the act of carrying bodies look effortless.

Landril stumbled along with the heavy body on his back and joined the remaining prisoners pushing towards the open gate, while arrows slammed into dead flesh, or pinged off armour and stone.

They moved out onto the stony track before Hell's Keep. Landril could not see the mountainside either side of them in this gloom, merely the first few yards of the descending slope. As if to illuminate them, but more likely to send a signal across the Silkspire Mountains, a beacon sparked to life at the top of the highest tower of the keep. The wind assailed them and made the going even harder; Landril's legs already burned with the weight of the body on his back.

'Keep low,' Xavir shouted, gripping the arms of the dead man around his shoulder and wearing him like a shawl. 'Maintain a steady pace and your body will thank you. Do not run ahead if the guards chase us; do not turn back and try to be a hero.'

'The arrows will start up again any moment,' Valderon advised. 'They'll be useless in this wind. We can dump our corpses when we are properly out of range. It's the witches we need to worry about next.'

Landril peered back nervously as the first few arrows of the reassembled soldiers flew from the top of the keep, whistling by in the dozens and clattering into the ground around them in the darkness. There were about a dozen other prisoners surrounding him; grim-faced and covered in blood. Ahead of them was the black void of the mountainside at night, and a single isolated track into nothingness.

Well we're not dead yet, Landril thought.

Witches

They zigzagged down the mountainside, Xavir checking back at the beacon that flared above the prison, but there had been no pursuit and no other prisoners escaping. It seemed that their small group were the only ones to have gained their freedom. Now they just needed to keep it.

Once they were well beyond the range of the arrows, and their corpse-shields had been dumped into the undergrowth, the prisoners stood staring at him and Valderon, waiting breathlessly for guidance.

'Sun will break in a matter of hours.' Valderon gestured towards the east, away from the bright half-moon. It would be a little while until their eyes adjusted fully to the dark. 'We should keep moving so the cold doesn't claim us.'

Xavir twisted back to glance at the others. 'Are there any injuries?'

The remaining prisoners glanced at each other but none confirmed any wounds. Xavir suspected that even if they were injured, they would not admit it. Bravery was all well and good, but they would only be as strong as their weakest man. He counted who made it: Davlor. Landril. Grend. Jedral. Tylos. Barros. Krund. And from Valderon's gang, Harrand and Galo.

Eleven of us. Fewer than he thought had made it out.

'Good,' Xavir said. 'Dump any armour you think you can't carry over a long distance. We run now at a steady pace. Down the mountain track until we get to the bottom. It will take hours until it begins to level off. We will rest, but we must be swift if we are to get well ahead before light.'

'Are we free?' someone asked.

'We still have the . . . *witches* to deal with before we can use that word.' Xavir then turned to Valderon. 'You have the stone?'

Valderon reached into an internal sling he had made for himself out of a rag. Inside this, wrapped in a grubby cloth, was a red witchstone about the size of his thumb.

Davlor gasped. 'There *was* a witchstone! I bloody knew it.'

'How did you get such a thing?' Tylos asked from behind Xavir.

'One of the guards had claimed the prisoners stole it from the witches,' Valderon said. 'It had been traded for an undisclosed favour. That stone made its way into my possession.'

'We have everything we need, then,' Xavir said. 'Let us continue.'

The prisoners ran down the mountain track and through the night. The path was narrow and wound around knuckles of granite and through thickets of spear-tipped gorse. Now and then one of the men fell – tripping those behind – but there were few complaints.

The prisoners rested three times, on each occasion when they were near to fruit bushes to provide quick bursts of nourishment. On one plateau, which the men optimistically thought was the bottom, there was a deep pool, and Xavir encouraged the men to drink water.

Dawn broke over the mountaintops, the presence of light welcomed as a gentle warmth developed and Xavir could fully examine their surroundings. The foothills were far more lush than the sparse, rocky heights they'd been travelling through. Blue-green oak copses dotted the view, but there were no settlements that he could see, no lines of smoke from chimneys. They were on the far side of the continent, on the eastern fringes of Frengleland. It had for centuries been a place where no man had good reason to come. A few merchants might have used the handful of roads through to the old and inhospitable lands, but the more savvy traders used the shipping networks further north.

Xavir paused for a moment. If their journey hadn't been so urgent, he might have enjoyed the sound of birds starting their daily business, or even the sight of dawn breaking, something that he had not experienced in years.

Valderon joined him. 'The run has been punishing. I have been wasting away in that rotten keep.'

'As have I, if I'm honest,' Xavir replied.

'If this is what it is like to be old and out of shape,' Valderon said, half-jokingly, 'it is better to die young and in glory.'

'We're a long way from glory yet,' Xavir replied seriously.

'That may be so.' Valderon's chuckle diminished into an awkward silence. 'You were a warrior and you said you'd tell me more. You fought for Cedius the Wise, I presume.'

'I did.'

'As did I. I am of the Clan Gerentius. I was a sergeant in the King's Legion, First Cohort. I cannot recall your face among the men, though, comrade. What unit did you serve in?'

'I commanded Cedius's private force. The Solar Cohort.'

Valderon's eyes widened. 'The Legion of Six.'

Xavir nodded grimly. While the legion's deeds were legendary, not all of them were deeds to be proud of. Valderon clapped him on the shoulder, with sympathy or comradeship – Xavir didn't care to know. He was faintly aware that the other men had gathered around to watch the conversation.

'How far to the witches?' Valderon asked. There was something different in his tone and posture now. Whereas before Valderon had treated Xavir as equal, Xavir observed a new-found respect — as if, acting on old military instincts, Valderon now viewed him as a more senior commander.

Xavir shrugged. 'I thought we'd be close to the wretched creatures by now.' He peered into the dawn mists below, but an outcrop of rock jutted out to obscure their view. 'Perhaps only a little way to go. I only ever saw down here a few times over the years, on a clear day, but the magic could be seen even in the mist. Have we lost anyone on the way?'

'Fortunately not,' Valderon said, with a smile. 'Nor have we let anyone catch up with us. We can see the track for a good while back up there and no one is in pursuit. Would you say we've done it?'

'Not until we're past the witches,' Xavir replied, focusing on the track ahead.

The land began to level out again. The sky brightened properly and the surrounding hills were filled with lush trees coming to the end of their season. But the escapees were too tired to enjoy such things. They were just glad that their run had now petered out into a plodding march.

Xavir spotted the danger in the clearing ahead: a faint crackle of magic could be seen, almost like a net glowing with purple light. The wall of magic crossed their path and extended along these lower inclines, blocking their route. It disappeared through the trees at the other end and then reappeared further up the slope and around the base of the mountain. It extended in the other direction, too, this vast unnatural barrier.

Xavir called a halt and the men sank to the floor to rest, many of them fell into a deep sleep.

He and Valderon stood looking at the magic that barred their way.

'Have you any experience with witches?' Xavir asked.

'Not much,' Valderon admitted. 'A few of them skilled in elements such as fire were used strategically alongside us on campaign. They had their uses. But apart from that, no, I've had very little interaction. Thank the Goddess.'

'Very well,' Xavir said. 'It's best if I handle this on my own, if that sits well with you. The sight of more than one warrior advancing to their dwelling will be more likely to be considered a threat.'

'You think them near?'

'I do. Though this blasted wall likely extends for miles around the mountain, I would say they are stationed near the path so as to keep an eye on unwanted visitors.'

'You're certain you do not need me?' Valderon asked.

Xavir shook his head. 'One of us needs to remain to keep an eye on the men.'

Valderon nodded and handed over the witchstone.

It felt unusually cold and heavy in Xavir's palm.

Stone held tightly, Xavir handed his sword to the other former soldier and turned to face the bank of grey rock just off the path, where he had spotted a few caves. There were no dwellings here so it was the most probable place of habitation for the witches.

He strode between the wide fir trees, then looked down as his foot twisted on something in the undergrowth. At first he thought it mossed ivory roots, but looking closer he realized they were bones – and not just animal. He had seen enough rotten corpses in his time to know that the bulk of these were human. He took a firmer grip on the stone. Eventually he came to a pathway leading up to the caves.

Sunlight lanced through the trees and onto his face, and he took a brief moment to enjoy the warmth – something he hadn't felt for years in the cold confines of Hell's Keep. If he were to die now, better he die free than in shackles. Protected only by two stolen gauntlets, and still garbed in his grey prisoner tunic and crude strapped sandals, he strode up the stairs and towards the wide cave entrance. He had to duck slightly to enter the darkness and stood there for a moment to let his eyes adjust. There was a faint burning aroma, something charred, then it faded entirely to leave the damp chill of the cave. Around him feathers were dangling on wire from the roof. Etchings were scratched into the rock – esoteric symbols and words in an ancient form of a common language. He thought the spymaster would probably know what they meant.

Xavir stepped further into the gloom, and with every step the remaining traces of daylight began to fade. After a few moments he was far enough inside that he was able to stand tall without striking his head against the rock. Voices suddenly rushed towards him as echoing whispers:

'What does a warrior want with us?'

'Has he come to kill or maim?'

'His hatred of us burns!'

'He has no sword, but he has something else.'

'What does he want?'

'Who are you?'

'What is your name?'

Xavir called out through the caves, making no effort to hide the distaste in his voice. 'My name is Xavir of Clan Argentum.

I was once a warrior in Cedius's Solar Cohort. More recently a prisoner at the keep.'

A moment of silence in return, but then, with startling clarity: 'Cedius died years ago. You have dwelt on the mountaintop for a long time. But you do not fear witches, do you? We can sense that you dislike us. You are . . . *familiar* with our kind.'

'With *one* of our kind,' another added.

'She changed you, did she not?' hissed another.

How could they possibly know? Xavir thought. *It was years ago.* He shook his head and forced the memories away. The witches were playing tricks with his mind.

'What do you want?' one of the witches asked.

'There are about a dozen men outside.' Xavir looked around but could see only darkness. 'We wish safe passage through your barriers.'

'And why should we help you?'

'The magic that is there to stop the likes of you escaping.'

'And to keep others away.'

'I heard tell that the soldiers at the keep may have stolen something from you.' Xavir held out the witchstone and placed it on the floor. He could not bring himself to go nearer. 'I have come to return it. In exchange, I request our safe passage.'

A figure scrambled forwards from the gloom. She stepped into a thin spear of light from above.

Her eyes had been cut out, her eyelids stitched together. She would have been a time mother, a seer, with no reason to look upon the mortal plane. How she managed to pick up the stone without being able to see was beyond Xavir. He had long since stopped trying to fathom how these *things* operated. The witch caressed the stone and scurried back into the darkness. Only then did he notice the two other dark figures alongside her; he turned to address the three of them.

'The soldiers had taken this from you. I came to return it. Will this be enough to let us pass?'

Another silence, and then the whispers again:

'He speaks the truth.'

'The stone is here again.'

'Fire and light.'

'What are the consequences of letting him out?'

'Does it break the pact our sisters made?'

'Why so much anger against our kind?'

Though he could not see it, in the ensuing silence he felt their probing gaze upon him and, worse, inside his mind.

'Why do you want to be free?' one of the witches asked. 'You feel nothing but guilt and shame for your deeds, Xavir of Clan Argentum. Of the Solar Cohort.'

'Famed Legion of Six,' added another.

'You welcomed the punishment. You did not want to escape. We sense this. What has changed?'

'I have business with the world outside,' Xavir replied. 'People have requested my help.'

'The world is changing.'

'Alliances are shifting again.'

'Things have come into this world. Unnatural things.'

'We know much about what is going on.'

'But we cannot say.'

'We know much about the futures that may happen.'

'You may leave,' a witch whispered in his mind.

'She had marked you long ago as to be left alone.'

'Her seal will always be upon you.'

'Our magic will have faded by the time you get back to your soldiers,' a voice said aloud.

'Go now,' came a whisper into his head.

'In haste.'

Xavir strode towards the light angrily, mocking laughter echoing behind him. He scrambled out into the brightness, shading his eyes as he returned down the path and towards the other prisoners, who were still resting.

'Get up,' Xavir ordered them all. 'Get up now. We haven't got long.'

The men groaned and pushed themselves up from the long grass.

Despite his fear that foul hags were toying with him, true to their word, the wall of magic began to stutter and fade, until there was nothing there at all.

'How can we be sure it's gone?' Valderon handed Xavir back his sword.

'There's only one way to find out,' Xavir replied, and strode towards where the barrier had once been.

Strange Noises

'We're in Brekkland now,' Landril said.

A lush forest of oak trees extended before them, smothering the landscape. Ancient ruins, pillars and still-standing arches were tucked away in occasional clearings, but civilization on any significant scale had long since left these parts. A cool wind sent shivers down Landril's spine.

The once-mighty Arjal kingdoms had extended through here in the Seventh Age, with major settlements on the nearby river, but that culture had collapsed a thousand years past. Their crops had failed, and that was that. No wars, no politicking or drama. Just a basic lack of food.

Landril knew how they felt. He hoped that, now the prisoners were out of the mountains, they could seek a village or town in which to feed themselves. Scavenging berries in the forest staved off starvation, but he was in the mood for a haunch of some fat animal in a rich sauce to be mopped up with a loaf of bread.

'Where's Brekkland exactly?' It was Davlor who spoke. 'Never heard of it.'

'That is because you are still young. You have barely left your mother's breast, and now find yourself in a strange land,' drawled Tylos. The man's ebony face was covered in sweat.

Landril had realized only recently that Tylos came from Chambrek, a noble country to the south, which explained the graceful manner in which he spoke. Every word that left his lips possessed a rich timbre, as if he had been an orator in his previous life.

'You can talk, thief, you're only a summer older than me,' Davlor muttered. 'I was only wondering where this place was.'

'Quiet,' Xavir told them. 'The forest conceals eyes and ears with remarkable ease.'

Landril was glad for the silence that followed the order. The last thing he wanted now that he had come so far from Hell's Keep was to listen to the two men bickering.

Xavir and Valderon were in the lead, peering into the gloom of the forest. Landril noticed how the two had found something of a camaraderie, despite their rivalry within Hell's Keep. Landril reasoned that, of any here among the escaped prisoners, those two shared the most similar heritage. Senior military men among Cedius's finest, Goddess bless his soul. There was something reassuring about their manner, too – life on the road, keeping their men safe, looking out for danger – all of this was familiar territory to them.

Whereas Landril felt like a fish out of water: he was used to neither prison life nor countryside route marches. He needed cities and people to thrive and apply his skills. He was grateful for the leaders' presence, especially considering some of the sounds they'd been hearing recently from the surrounding forest. The undergrowth brushed his knees as he moved towards them.

Xavir turned to him. 'You say we're in Brekkland, spymaster. Yet those noises are like nothing I've heard previously in that country.'

'You've been here before?'

70

'Briefly,' Xavir replied. 'And I know enough of any forest to know that some of the sounds around here are not from any animal I've ever encountered. Valderon, have you campaigned out this way?'

'I haven't. Anyway, fighting wars in forests is not my expertise. Open, muddy plains and rows of warriors grinding against another line. That's mostly all I know.'

'You may have to fight in forests yet,' Xavir said, 'if we are to join with the wolf queen.'

'So that's where we're headed?' Valderon asked.

'Apparently,' Xavir told him. 'Landril knows how to find her.'

Both men glanced towards the spymaster, who nodded. 'I do. Her place is only known to me because she wished it to be so. Otherwise she lives very deliberately alone.'

'Where is it?' Valderon asked.

'The Forests of Heggen.'

'What's a queen doing there?' Valderon asked. 'Nothing but trees and farmland for miles around.'

'It is how she prefers to live. I cannot speculate as to her reasons for it. Her home lies a few days away from here, even if we move at a fast pace.'

'This terrain doesn't make for swift travel,' Xavir said, gesturing at the dense undergrowth surrounding them.

'It does not.'

'We have come down on the opposite side of the mountain from the main path. This territory is unfamiliar to us all. But if we can find a road and a town we could find horses,' Xavir continued. 'Sooner or later.'

Landril closed his eyes to recall the maps he had committed to memory before he came to Hell's Keep. They would want to avoid the road that ferried prisoners and soldiers, particularly now that Stravir warriors marched far from their borders on the

71

king's command. There would be toll houses along the way, and each of those would be manned by guards. Landril walked the lanes of his mind. Slowly the lanes became lines, and the map began to take a more coherent shape. Settlements began to spring up, but he could not tell how close their group was to finding these places.

'I think,' Landril eventually declared, 'that I know where the towns are. How far away we are will require triangulation.'

'Do we have time?' Valderon asked. 'Should we not just press on until we find *somewhere*?'

'There is some wisdom in that,' Landril admitted. 'I can use the mountain as one aspect, but if would help if we came across another marker I can use to pinpoint our location. I know there's a river somewhere we will need to cross at some point.'

Xavir nodded. 'We'll head west, then. But tell the men to keep their wits about them. There are unnatural things out here.'

For hours they trudged through dark green woodland, over moss-covered stones and along forgotten pathways that petered out into nothing. Whenever they glimpsed the sky it was filled with grey clouds. The freed prisoners complained endlessly, until they were too tired to say anything at all. None of them had yet attempted to make his own way, though Xavir would not have minded. If one of the men wanted to take his chances on his own out here, Xavir thought, then so be it. But it felt as though there was some unspoken pact to stick together.

As they finally came to a road that ran parallel to the river they had sought, tiredness overcame them and even Xavir flagged. He realized he had been without sleep for almost an entire day and he didn't have the physical fitness of his youth.

They rested by the edge of a clearing a stone's throw from the road, with Valderon taking first watch.

After drinking from the river, Xavir sat on the damp earth and pressed his back against an oak tree. For the first time in years he breathed fresh air as he closed his eyes to the world.

In his dreams Xavir was taken to a distant place, happier times. A younger Xavir. He was eighteen years old and already one of the most able warriors in Clan Argentum. He wore the colours of his family with pride; a tunic the golden brown of the moorland, a golden dragon carved into every silver helm and shield.

A young witch had just been assigned to their clan, as was normal – each clan of import was allocated a member of the sisterhood. She was to study under the witch who had been attached to the family for decades.

When Xavir first met her, he was returning fresh from an assault on the family lands. His face was covered in blood, but he was smiling and full of the vigour of victory. His father had clapped him on the shoulder, welcomed him and his men home on the outskirts of the estate, and rode alongside him through the columned avenue to the stables.

Later, when Xavir dismounted alone and began to wash his bloodied arms with fresh water, he spotted the young witch peering at him from the stone doorway to one of the annexes, the tower in which the magical sisters dwelt. He had no need of the old woman's magic today, as spear and sword had sufficed and he had no injury, but he wondered about this newcomer.

'Why the sour gaze, lady?' he called across the courtyard, wary of her and why she was staring at him. There were few things he felt he did not understand about the world at that age

— in the way that the young consider themselves invincible — but no one could understand the ways of witches.

'You look like a walking animal carcass,' she said. 'There's so much blood on you.'

'Come out of the gloom if you wish to insult me properly.' He chuckled.

She seemed to drift rather than walk, her black cloak flicking to and fro in the evening breeze. Her hood kept her face in shadow, but there were two unnaturally bright blue eyes staring back at him. Witch eyes. She had an elegant, straight nose and a strong chin.

'Are you the new child from the island?' he asked.

'I am no child,' she snapped. 'I am seventeen. But yes, since you ask. I've come from Jarratox.'

Xavir shrugged. 'Welcome to the castle, anyway.'

She paused for a moment and rubbed her arm above the elbow, as if she was cold. 'It is a miserable place, your nation of Stravimon. There is no sun here.'

'I'm surprised they let you out of your tower to notice.' Xavir gestured to the building behind.

She peered over his shoulder at the two swords poking out, and then at his silver shield that bore a golden dragon. 'I have never really seen warriors this close up. Apparently I am to accompany you in war one day. It seems a crude art, what you do. To kill so many people so . . . brutally.'

'Maybe it is.' Xavir shrugged.

'Have you no concerns for what you do?'

'Why should I? Someone has to do the hard work so others can talk of ethics in comfort.'

'Work?' she sneered. 'It is butchery, not work.'

'Even butchery can be an art,' Xavir replied. 'Anyway, I thought witches killed people too.'

'You have an answer for everything,' she declared.

Back then he did. Back then Xavir had fine training not just in the arts of the warrior, but in words passed between poets and scholars, and felt he knew it all. These days, the answers were not so forthcoming, but back then, back then it all seemed so easy . . .

'That may be so, witch,' he said eventually.

'Lysha,' came another voice. The old witch, Valerix, appeared in the doorway.

The young witch standing before him twisted her head to look back to her mentor, and her hood fell back. Xavir was taken aback by her striking looks. She had a very pale complexion and long black hair, tied back and down over her shoulder. Her features seemed even more delicate within the light.

'I didn't think witches looked as nice as you do.' It gave Xavir an illicit thrill to feel attraction to one of their kind. Many of his comrades would have been sickened by the thought.

The young woman gave no response, though the lines around her eyes softened.

'Lysha!' With a crooked finger Valerix beckoned her student back into the old stone tower.

'You do not speak with lay people longer than you have to,' Valerix snapped as Lysha stepped inside. She placed an arm protectively around the young woman, as if Xavir had been trying to harm her. 'I appreciate the world is a curious place, but still . . .'

'Xavir!'

It was Valderon who spoke. The warrior approached Xavir with some urgency and shook his shoulder.

'Soldiers are coming through the forest, a few hundred yards away. Heading west. I think their scout may have spotted us.'

'How many are there?'

'About ten. I'll muster the others.'

'No,' Xavir said. 'We don't want to fight them if we can help it. Soldiers on the road will be reporting to somewhere. If they fail to arrive, there will be more soldiers. There are always more soldiers.'

'But they have horses, we could use them.'

Xavir yawned. 'Fine. Have the men on standby, but tell them to wait in the shadows. Two men on the road will mean nothing, but a dozen of us will raise suspicion.'

As Valderon gave the orders, Xavir pushed himself to his feet. Even though he had been asleep just a few minutes he felt considerably refreshed. The air seemed sharper, as did his senses. After picking up his sword he followed Valderon, passing the watchful gaze of Landril silently.

The two approached the road, towards the sound of horses and idle chatter of travellers. Xavir motioned Valderon and they placed their swords against the nearest tree, at an angle that could not be seen from the road. 'If we are to kill, we should at least get information first.'

Ahead of them came two small columns of riders, men in the crimson garb of regular soldiery of the king's legions. A horse at the rear was drawing a cart, whose cargo was covered up.

The entourage came to a halt before the two men.

The plump man at the front wore the silver stripe of sergeant across his ornate leather breastplate.

'Fine horse you have here,' Xavir announced, his bass voice carrying. He rubbed his hand along the steed's brown neck. 'Looks like Laussland stock.'

'You know your animals, traveller,' said the sergeant in reply. He lifted his chin towards Valderon, who was standing silently with his arms folded. 'What are you men doing on the road?'

Xavir could hear the blades being unsheathed quietly, but clumsily.

'We're just two travellers,' Valderon said.

'You choose to travel in dark times.'

'There have always been dark times,' Xavir replied. Then he indicated the cart at the back. 'I didn't realize soldiers were now tradesmen. What cargo do you carry this far east? I take it you're not on the trade routes back to the west.'

'Bodies,' the sergeant said. 'We bring bodies as evidence.'

'Evidence of what?' Xavir asked.

'That we have done our job.'

'Efficient men, then,' Xavir said nonchalantly, wandering around towards the cart. The other soldiers looked at him. Their faces and uniforms were dirtied and spattered with dried blood. 'And who were your victims?'

'Victims?' the sergeant repeated. 'They were *traitors* to the king. And so we burned them to set an example to the community. The few we carry are evidence of their punishment.'

Xavir tried to repress his anger. 'It must take a great deal of bravery,' he said, 'to slaughter innocent people like that.'

Images of the past came to his mind: the blood of the innocent stained his hands too; he knew it all too well.

'We are soldiers doing a simple job, traveller,' the sergeant continued. 'I might not like this work, but orders are orders. And who are you to question them?'

'True. True.' The skies had by now clouded over and a steady rain began to fall. No one wanted to be there, least of all Xavir. 'Will you let us continue on our way?'

'I'm not so sure about that. You seem mighty interested in business that isn't yours.'

'I don't want any more blood,' Xavir replied, fixing his gaze on Valderon, who was scowling at the soldiers. A bead of water dripped along the man's jaw. 'I've killed enough men for today. And I have killed enough men for a lifetime.'

'Are you serious? Are you threatening *us*?' the sergeant asked, bemused. One of the others chuckled.

'Consider this a warning,' Xavir said. 'I have travelled far today and my patience is thin. You can all put your swords away and just be on your way.'

The sergeant laughed awkwardly. 'I do not think so, traveller.'

Xavir could feel his blood pulsing. Instincts, deeply ingrained, rose within him like a broth coming to the boil.

He saw the glances exchanged between the sergeant and the soldier to the right, who immediately began to slide down off his horse, and knew there would be no stopping conflict now.

Xavir hurled the man's unhooked boot upwards before he could reach for his blade, launching him back up over his horse and onto his comrade, and both of them collapsed to the ground.

Drawing his sword, Valderon quickly dispatched the two soldiers pushing themselves up from the ground while Xavir swept his blade in an upward arc across the face of an assailant, shattering the man's jaw. Three dead now within moments and the sergeant had not even fully drawn his sword. Six soldiers had dismounted and now clustered around Valderon and Xavir.

Then the other prisoners made themselves known on the fringes of the road, each of them armed, and Xavir held his arm out for caution.

'I ask you again, sergeant, to call back your men,' Xavir said.

'These are young soldiers with lives ahead of them. I do not wish to cut them short.'

'You think professional soldiers should listen to scum of the wild like you?' the sergeant asked, sliding his blade upwards. Rain fell heavily on the leaves.

Xavir sighed. *Young men will have to die now. All for one man's pride and stupidity. Nothing has changed since I've been in gaol.*

The prisoners spread out into a line and waited for the attack. Xavir wanted this over quickly, and so launched himself into the soldiers first, with Valderon on his heels.

The sergeant was the first to die. Xavir knocked away his weak strikes and thrust his blade in between the buckles on the side of his leather jerkin. The man's eyes bulged as his life ebbed away, but Xavir did not pause to see him fall. The warrior was already on to the next man, cleaving away the attacker's sword hand and smacking a blade-edge back through his gaping mouth.

By the time the rest of the escaped prisoners had fully reached the melee, Xavir and Valderon alone had reduced the soldiers to just two men.

Xavir called to halt the assault.

'Don't kill me!' said one of the soldiers, a very young man who fell to his knees before the cart.

Xavir looked at his bloodstained, panicked expression.

'Why shouldn't I?' Xavir snapped, rain dripping down his face.

To his right, the other man threw down his sword and held up his hands in a gesture of surrender.

'This is the calibre of the king's men these days?' Xavir spat. 'Cowards.'

'I was wed last month,' the young man spluttered. 'My wife is with child . . . I . . . Please don't kill me.'

It took all Xavir's will not to strike both these worthless soldiers down.

'I suggest you give up soldiery,' Xavir announced. 'Both of you, to your feet. Remove your armour now. Leave your horses. You are both to go through the forest. Separate directions. I will count to one hundred and then these men –' Xavir gestured with his sword tip to the mob of former prisoners – 'will start to hunt you down. This is your final chance. Go!'

The men frantically stripped off their armour and jerkins, then, slipping on the mud, they sprinted into the trees.

There was a murmur of laughter from those watching.

'We don't really have to hunt them, do we, boss?' Davlor asked.

Xavir shook his head. 'Those soldiers think we will. They're frightened and will run for hours just for the chance to see the sun rise tomorrow. By which time we will be long gone.'

'You should have killed them,' Jedral muttered, wiping water off his broad face. He was only about thirty summers old, but looked far older. He had the look of a bird of prey, with bushy eyebrows and eyes that constantly darted this way and that, as if nervous. 'Deserved to die, the frightened little shits. I can still go after them if you want.'

'It's a waste of time,' Xavir replied and turned to assess what the soldiers had left behind.

He stepped over dead bodies to remove the fabric cover that was draped across the cart. Inside there were corpses: old men and women. They had already begun to rot.

'These were civilians, cut down on the king's orders,' Xavir announced. 'Mardonius is insane. This is the world we have rejoined, gentlemen.'

Landril joined him and stared at the remains. 'It has been happening all too much, though I did not realize the purge had reached this far east. Mardonius is operating well away from Stravimon's borders.'

'Is there no one defending these people?' Valderon asked. 'What of other rulers and royals?'

'They are few and far between. A handful of clans have resisted the king's commands and are now his enemies. They fight for their own survival as much as to protect people like these.'

Xavir looked grimly at the bodies in the cart. 'We bury them,' he said. The prisoners muttered a little but quieted at the look in his eyes.

'What about the soldiers?' Valderon asked.

Xavir wiped the rain from his face and spat on the floor. 'Let them rot.'

Rest

They buried the bodies and dragged the soldiers off the road, hiding them in the undergrowth in case anyone should come looking for them. After gathering all food, weapons, clothing and anything of use the men washed the blood off the jerkins in the river before slipping them on.

Landril could feel the anger among the group at the cold-blooded killing of innocent people. Thieves, killers and traitors these men might have been, but they did have a skewed sense of honour. Some muttered of revenge and justice; Jedral in particular seemed to take the deaths hard. Landril wondered what had happened in his past. He talked fondly of his old axe and how he would have taken the soldiers' heads for their sins. Landril thought him disturbed in the mind and did not entirely trust him. Despite that, the man appeared to have a friendship with Krund — one of the very first men Landril had spoken to in Hell's Keep. The wiry old lawyer with a long jaw possessed a laid-back manner that made him easy company. Nothing was too much effort. He didn't complain. He did not interrupt others. He was very accepting of his situation.

But Landril felt more affinity to Tylos than any of the others so far. He was a handsome individual, the man from Chambrek, and he spoke of the arts in a manner that warmed Landril's heart. Everything became poetry to him out here: the sky, the trees. Given enough time, he'd probably write a poem about the soldiers they'd just killed, and it would sound beautiful.

After the exchange of soldiers' clothing they took the horses, and suddenly everyone's spirits were lifted. Especially now they didn't have to walk any more.

The freed prisoners rode through the late afternoon rain. Landril could see how the one-time leader of the Legion of Six enjoyed being once again on a Laussland mare, to be riding at speed through forgotten country, with the wind and rain in his face and hair.

As they continued through the wilderness, the spymaster informed the commander of the history and myths of Brekkland, of monsters that were said to have prowled the dark forests, of the kings and queens who claimed it for their own before the world had forgotten about them. It was now an agricultural kingdom, with petty merchants squabbling over land and power. Few people came to Brekkland these days, save farmers, hunters or those who needed to disappear.

Sunlight drained from the sky. The men made camp around a fire of damp wood that gave more smoke than warmth, but this was the first time that they had properly rested after fleeing Hell's Keep. A couple of them had found iron razors among the soldiers' belongings and had started ridding themselves of their unkempt beards. It seemed that, with clean clothes, a shave and the fresh air of freedom, something of their humanity had been restored and their good humour with it.

Landril listened to the others talk, though he felt little inclination to join in himself. There were wishful thoughts expressed about taverns and whorehouses, jokes and bragging about what they might do there. It was no different from he expected from such coarse men.

Eventually the conversation turned to what everyone was going to do with their freedom.

'My family won't want me back,' said Tylos, who had shared his past. He had been imprisoned not for murder but for thievery on a scale that impressed the others, and this discussion was the first time that Landril had realized he had noble blood.

'Why's that, black man?' Davlor asked.

'As far as they're concerned, the moment I was caught I might as well have been killed.' He shook his head. 'At least death has some honour. People speak more kindly of the dead.'

'After all that time in the cold, you've probably turned as pale as Davlor's arse in comparison to your countrymen,' Jedral muttered.

'Or the back of your bald head,' Davlor replied.

'Quiet, rat-face,' Jedral said. 'At least I wasn't raised in a barn.'

Landril had heard how Davlor had been the illegitimate child of the Duke of Grantax. He had been raised by his mother in a tiny village between the town of Grantax and Golax Hold, got into a life of crime and became involved in a smuggling ring. Davlor had been due to be executed with the others, but the duke, as a gesture to the mother, managed to spare the boy's life – and instead had him whisked away to Hell's Keep.

'Valderon, what'll you do? What did you do to get in put in the keep, anyway?' Davlor asked with open curiosity.

The old, dark-maned warrior remained silent for a while, staring into the fire.

'I was a senior commander in the First Legion,' he began. 'I was disgraced for having an affair with a duchess, whom I was charged to protect on the way back from a campaign. Her husband found out upon his return. He killed her. So I came and killed him as well as several of his men. And that was that. My title was forfeit, my properties taken away and my life spared only because Cedius wished it so for my years of service to him.'

'Typical. You spend your life killing men for your king,' Jedral said, 'and then you kill just one with good connections and your life is forfeit.'

'That is politics for you,' Valderon said. 'I do not ask for sympathy.'

'Won't get it among us poor bastards,' Jedral said. 'This is what's wrong with the world. Different rules, boys, depending on where you were born and whose teat you suckled.'

A murmur of laughter spread across the group. There was truth in such words. It was the way of the world. But Landril knew that many Hell's Keep prisoners were lucky not to have been executed for their crimes. It was only because of some mercy, or some family connection or a favour owed that these men were even alive.

'I can't believe you were in the First Legion,' said Davlor, wide-eyed with awe. 'I thought you were a good fighter back in Hell's Keep. So should we salute you or something?'

Everyone glanced to Xavir, expectantly. The silence was for him to fill, but he was in no rush to fill it.

'Your boss,' Valderon announced, 'is the one who would receive the salutes, if we were to return to our old lives.'

Landril noted that despite their former rivalry, Valderon followed the old military ways still and gave way to rank. Considering the strength of their personalities he was surprised, but glad that there was no obvious tension between the two.

'I thought you were in the king's legions, too, lad,' Grend said quietly to Xavir. 'First Legion?'

'For a while I was,' Xavir said.

Valderon spoke for him. 'He was no ordinary legionary. He

led the Solar Cohort, the best of Cedius's soldiers. They were known as the Legion of Six. He was the king's closest guard and friend, both on the battlefield and in the white-stoned palace in Stravir City. If rumours were true, he could well have *been* the king one day.'

No one said a word. They simply stared in surprise at Xavir.

'What did you do to end up festering with us poor fools?' Tylos said eventually.

'Well said, black man,' Jedral muttered. 'That's quite the fall.'

'We don't even know your real name. Which one of the six were you?'

More laughter eased the awkwardness, though Landril could see the pain flicker behind Xavir's face. 'My name is Xavir Argentum, of the Clan Argentum. I was commander of the Solar Cohort.' Landril saw recognition dawn on the men's faces. He knew what the great warrior had done and – from the expressions of the men surrounding him – so did they.

Xavir continued doggedly, 'You may have heard about what we did. I killed our own countrymen at Baradium Falls. It was not intentional. But there are no excuses for the slaughter of innocents. And I have to live with their deaths every day.'

'I remember hearing something about that,' Davlor said.

'The ale houses talked about little else for a year,' Tylos added. 'Even in Chambrek.'

'The act brought shame to Cedius the Wise,' Xavir continued, 'and to the Solar Cohort. I was taken away to gaol while my five comrades were executed. My incarceration at Hell's Keep was as a public reminder of the shame I brought to Stravimon.'

'You were set up,' Landril called across the flames. 'It was not your fault.'

Xavir made eye contact with Landril and saw anger at the thought burning there. 'So you have said, spymaster.'

'It's true,' Landril repeated.

'Wait,' Tylos said. 'Spymaster?'

Xavir rose to his feet. 'Landril here was a spymaster to Cedius, and then to Mardonius for a short while, but he has long since left royal employment. He came to the gaol specifically to provide me with this intelligence. In a way, you all owe your freedoms to him, so you will respect him. Landril has informed me that the act we committed was deliberately created to cause our downfall. Innocents were slaughtered to get rid of the Solar Cohort. So if anyone was to ask what I intend to do now that I am free,' Xavir announced, 'I am going to find the people who put me there. And I will *kill* them.'

'Who was responsible,' Valderon asked, 'for betraying you?'

'General Havinir and Lord Kollus were two of the perpetrators,' Landril said, 'but much of the planning was done at the estate of Duchess Pryus in Golax Hold. And then of course, the now king.'

He saw the look of surprise on the men's faces.

'I intercepted messages from Kollus,' Landril explained, 'who was, for a while, my former employer. Mardonius was behind it all.'

'Havinir,' Valderon grunted. 'You know, I never liked that man when I was in the army. He was more interested in climbing the ranks at court than in organizing the ranks at war.'

'Agreed,' Xavir said. 'So it is these people who I have business with. They must suffer for their crimes.'

'Sounds good,' Davlor said. 'We don't have anything better to do. Can we come with you?'

Landril wondered if Xavir realized he could not simply abandon these young men to their fates. Most had been in

Hell's Keep for years. The gang life was pretty much the only life they knew now. Even with their freedom, leaving the security of people they could depend upon would be hard.

'I'll certainly go with you,' Davlor added. 'I've bugger all else to do and, well, you're still the boss, right?'

'Why not?' Valderon agreed. 'It is not as if we have important affairs to return to. Our families have disowned us. Our former ranks will not be recognized. We will be hunted, together or apart, as escapees. There is safety in numbers so it makes sense for us to stay together.'

'Someone has summoned me, and alone,' Xavir replied. 'I'm not sure she expected other visitors.'

'Who was that, boss?' Davlor asked.

'The wolf queen,' Xavir announced.

An awed silence fell upon the group. Landril chuckled to himself. Most of these men would only have heard about Xavir of the Solar Cohort or the wolf queen in back-tavern tales. Now they had met one of those famous warriors and were on the way to seeing the other.

'What, the actual wolf queen?' Davlor asked, stifling a belch.

'Of *course* the actual queen,' Landril replied. 'We plan to travel towards Lupara, wolf queen, as soon as the sun rises.'

Xavir glanced towards Landril and narrowed his eyes.

'You are all welcome to accompany me,' Xavir said eventually, 'though I cannot guarantee your safety. I could do with men I trust. I trust that man.' He pointed to Valderon. 'If he walks with me, then the rivalries of Hell's Keep are no more. The world will hate us for our past. It will be us against the world and we are stronger together.'

Xavir swept up a strip of dried meat from the soldiers' rations. 'Sleep on it, whilst I take first watch.'

Away from the fire, the darkness of the forest was complete. Xavir could still hear his men comfortably in the distance.

A twig snapped and Valderon approached him through the shadows.

'It's quiet out here.'

'Apart from the racket the men are making,' Xavir replied. 'Well, who can begrudge them enjoying their freedom?'

'They'll quieten down soon enough. Surprised it hasn't been sooner, given how tired they are.' Valderon leaned on a felled oak alongside Xavir. They both stared into the blackness beyond.

'What was it like, in the Solar Cohort?' Valderon asked quietly. 'I had ambitions of joining their ranks one day myself. To be one of the Legion of Six. Until Hell's Keep, of course.'

'When I joined,' Xavir began, 'there was no greater honour for a clan warrior. The elite went into the King's Legion, or at least they used to. The best rose to the top of that – yourself, included, no doubt. And then for a lucky few, when an opportunity came . . .'

'They say you had to do something special on the field of battle, some selfless act to secure victory, in order to join the cohort.'

'More or less,' Xavir replied. 'You had to prove you were prepared to die for others. Not only that you were good with weapons or shields, but that you did not seek your own personal glory and demonstrably put others before yourself. If Cedius was to thunder into the heart of enemy ranks, then he wanted to do so with the very best and most selfless soldiers around him. We sought no remarkable act on the battlefield. Simply something honest.'

'But what was it *like*?' Valderon asked. 'When the black helms

were taken off and the banners rolled up? When you accompanied Cedius back to his palace . . . ?'

Xavir smiled and told him stories of the camaraderie
between him and his Solar Cohort brothers, the late-night
briefings on the eve of battle, of the wisdom of King Cedius,
of the black banners and how the fate of nations had been in
the hands of a few good soldiers. 'And so we ate in the king's
company. We enjoyed many of the leisures that a man of his
standing enjoyed. We were like brothers. Good wine, and feasting . . . and friendship.'

'And women as well?' Valderon chuckled.

'For those who wanted them,' Xavir admitted.

'Not you?'

'No,' Xavir replied. 'Not me.'

It wasn't for the lack of it, Xavir thought. There had been plenty
of whores, women and men, at Cedius's palace in Stravir City.
Some warriors found it a pleasurable way to unburden themselves after the horrors of war, after seeing so much blood flow
and so many lives fading to meet the Goddess. Perhaps it kept
a great many soldiers sane, but Xavir had never been interested
in whores. Whenever he closed his eyes and brushed his lips
against another woman's skin, he always recalled Lysha's pale
face . . .

Her seal will always be upon you.

'You should get some sleep,' Valderon said. 'You can't take
the burden of the watch all night long.'

Xavir placed his hand on the warrior's shoulder before walking back through the woodland.

Xavir was still awake by the fire, with the embers burning and
the sounds of the horses stirring nearby. A couple of the men

were snoring peacefully. An owl was hooting softly somewhere in the trees.

Whilst he had been in Hell's Keep it had been simple to forget the past. No one knew each other and most wanted to keep hidden whatever lives they'd led previously. There was no point clinging onto past glories, or hopes of a future, in such a place as Hell's Keep. Better to live each day as it came.

But now, Xavir was forced to remember what had gone before. He munched on another of the soldiers' crude biscuits and cast his mind back to one of the more opulent feasts in the Argentum clan castle. It had been an evening of remembrance for the Brigallia Massacre, a dark moment in the Argentum family history. Every year the sons and daughters of those involved read poems under the banner of a golden dragon, while the extended family drank in honour of the fallen. Everyone was invited – even the witches, though they never usually attended.

One feast in particular, many years ago now, was held just a few weeks after Lysha had arrived at the castle. By that point, Xavir and Lysha had met each other on a few occasions, without Valerix's knowledge. Lysha was curious about the ways of the clan, and Xavir was simply curious about her. It was forbidden to approach the witches outside formal channels, which naturally made a warrior of eighteen summers wish to investigate further.

Whether it was down to fate or Lysha's own planning, Xavir could never be sure, but the two often encountered each other in some forgotten corridor of the castle. Their conversations moved from pleasantries to more personal topics. Lysha was frustrated by the progression of her learning, claiming Valerix was too timid, too conservative with her skills and would not allow Lysha to experiment further. The girl was ambitious, young and driven: she wanted to see something of the world and not rehearse boring, unimaginative magics in a forgotten tower. Xavir could empathize. He only truly felt happy with a sword in his hand on the battlefield – the politics involved in being the scion of a powerful family held little interest for him. He was all too happy to encourage Lysha to take more of the freedom she had been craving.

He invited her, boldly, to ride with him beyond the forests, telling her he knew about a stash of witchstones kept by Valerix's predecessor. In truth, he only knew *of* it, not where it was. He simply wanted to speak with her in a place where only the creatures of the forest could listen in.

It was on the night of the remembrance feast that everything changed. Xavir asked her to sit with him at the table, as his guest and, to his astonishment, Lysha agreed.

A thousand candles were melting next to glimmering golden trays and silver goblets, each of which was emblazoned with the clan dragon. Tapestries, old family heirlooms, had been hung to rid the stone walls of their coldness.

The young witch followed him into the hall, her black cloak trailing behind. The five dozen guests fell into whispered conversation upon her arrival. Everyone stared in scorn at the two of them. Even Xavir's father struggled to hide his disgust.

Xavir didn't care. The two of them sat together on the bench, a row behind his father, pretending to listen to the poets, and dining on mussels from the estuary and slivers of venison from the ancient forest. Despite the inherent sadness of the occasion, Xavir – a man who had already trained in the arts of butchery and seen many close friends hacked apart – could feel little grief for the fallen brothers and sisters of the Brigallia Massacre, thinking only of the glory they could have achieved.

Towards the end of the night, Lysha softly gripped Xavir's

hand. He'd known the company of many women in his time, but none had held his attention for quite so long as Lysha. Beautiful was not quite the right word to describe her. There was something *different* about her. Not merely her striking blue witch eyes, but her powerful features, her intense gaze, a smile that could make him storm a citadel if she willed it. For someone who usually felt in control of everything – the precision stroke of a blade, the old Eighth Age postures he had learned from his clan warmasters, the ability to soothe a wild horse – she took all that control away from him. And he did not care in the slightest.

After the final poet had finished his mournful rhyme, Lysha rose to depart and strolled slowly towards the back of the hall. Xavir wondered, vaguely, if she had placed some sort of curse on him to make him think soft thoughts.

Looking back on it all, Xavir wondered how fate had taken him from such innocent pleasures to where he was tonight: an escaped prisoner deep in the old forest.

Although, not entirely alone. Surrounding him were men whom the world had deemed castaways. A clan of men the world had forgotten, who had been hidden away on the orders of those more powerful than themselves.

Xavir did not realize he had crushed the ration biscuit between his fingers. With his thoughts unfocused, he would be a danger to everyone – even himself. Xavir needed to let his rage become something more acute, to whittle it down like a sword-edge; only then could he wield it properly.

The Carcass

Elysia and Birgitta strolled through the forested hills, walking along one of the old hollow ways that led out from Jarratox. Old stones, discreetly marked with symbols and nestled in the nook of tree roots, indicated the hidden pathways used by the sisters.

Sunlight trickled through the canopy of oak, ash and birch. For the first part of the walk, they waded a green lane through bracken until they came upon the region where boars had recently strayed. Here the animals had mowed the bracken for their sustenance; there were now patches of bright flowers carpeting the forest floor, and the journey became not only more pleasant but a great deal easier.

Although Jarratox was only three miles away, Elysia felt as if it was days behind them. She was wearing more comfortable clothing today – brown trousers, grey overshirt and a green cloak, colours of stone and earth. Slung across her shoulder was an ornate bow, with golden details and into which, three years ago, Birgitta had set a chestnut-coloured stone. The two of them had left Jarratox shortly before dawn, passing no one along the hollow way. The green lane turned into a more well-worn muddy track, yet they had still met no other travellers on the route.

The only life they saw were the deer, which made their own paths. And that was precisely why the two women had come to the forest.

'You're getting too quick,' Birgitta said, 'for my old legs to keep up.'

'You're not old,' Elysia said with a smile.

'Compared to you, little sister, I feel it. You are at the prime of your life. You are an active young thing.'

'It's only because of you that I'm active,' Elysia said. 'Otherwise I'd rot like all the others in Jarratox.'

'By the source, you are finally talking like me.' Birgitta chuckled. 'Jarratox is not everything. It has its downsides. The matriarch and her clique could do with spending more time out here. This is where the real magic lies, if you ask me.'

Birgitta was right. They came upon a clearing that still glistened with dew from the night. Milky sunlight filtered down onto two deer grazing on grass. There was a sense of stillness and serenity that Elysia had rarely felt, and she was transfixed by the colours of the light and flowers. The two animals looked up at the newcomers' presence and wandered cautiously behind an old felled oak.

'Two of the grain crops failed last year,' Birgitta whispered, nodding at the deer.

'I know,' Elysia said with a sigh. 'You say that each time. I understand what we have to do.'

'It gets worse, because the villages beyond the hills have not eaten well in months,' Birgitta added. 'People are *dying*. This has added to the unrest that goes on in the world. Remember that fact. People need food, clothing and a peaceful bed to sleep in. Take any of those away and there is unrest. So we will take one of the deer for them today, and people will live a little longer.'

'I still don't understand why hunters never come here themselves.'

'They're too scared.'

'Of what?'

'They're scared of us. Scared of the forest's proximity to Jarratox.'

'Us? Oh. Right.'

Birgitta rolled her eyes. 'Now, let us get the food. Remember, you need to make your shot so that the deer knows nothing about it.'

Elysia nodded. The sisters chose a spot next to a tree and lay down in the long, damp grass. It did not matter that the deer had gone out of sight.

With her throat thick with emotion, Elysia drew the bow over her shoulder, shuffled across to the tree and lifted the weapon firmly. Birgitta passed across a simple arrow – no witchstones, nothing magical.

The rest was about reaching into Elysia's mind.

Birgitta did not need to teach Elysia any more, merely tweaked any bad habits and reminded her not to think too much about what she was doing. Elysia had done this enough times to trust her instincts now. All she had to do was to tap the part of her mind that none of the other sisters bothered to acknowledge existed. It sat aside from where they drew traditional magic; it was something far more primitive, which could not be found in books. Not many sisters could find this place or even bother to look for it, so Birgitta always told her, which was why Elysia was so different.

Elysia nocked the arrow, closed her eyes and recalled the shape of the deer perfectly. She gauged the angle that would be required now it was around a corner. The stone in the bow began to glow fiercely orange.

She released the arrow and watched it fly – then curve to the degree she had willed – until it went out of sight.

A heartbeat later there came a thud, and the sound of an animal collapsing.

Elysia closed her eyes again, this time out of sadness and respect for the animal. It always hurt to do this, even though she knew that so much good would come of it.

'Come on.' Birgitta pushed herself up with a theatrical groan. 'This is only half the job.'

The walk to the carcass was always slow. Elysia recalled the words that Birgitta had spoken to her dozens of times:

First of all you cut it, then you bring it back to the villagers and then you feed the people. There is no other reason to take from the land. The people will be grateful to you, especially in times of need, but you do not ask for money. The carcass is a gift, from people they call witches and usually fear. Other sisters are not so kind, but it will help people think well of the sisterhood. This is how the world works and you will need to know that if you are to live a smooth existence out here. People do not trust the sisterhood. I wonder at times if they have good reason.

'A clean kill,' Birgitta said, peering down at the carcass. 'A good shot. You have almost fully mastered this art. You know, not many sisters have ever bothered with weaponizing magic to this extent. I understand why, and it pains me to say that you and I *really* know how to do it.'

'Why does it pain you?'

'I don't like violence when there can be peaceful resolutions. It is one reason I was never assigned to a clan. I disagreed with all the petty politics they practise which result in innocent lives being lost.'

Birgitta produced a long hunting knife from the scabbard beneath her cloak and handed it to Elysia. With the older woman's help the young sister eased the blade from the felled animal's sternum to the base of its rear legs and commenced the process of removing the guts so that the meat would cool and not spoil. The very first time she had almost fainted at the sight but she was used to the blood now.

'This is the real, earthly business of life and death,' Birgitta said. 'The other sisters will never get their hands dirty like this. We need to understand that, at times, like it or not, blood must be spilled for life to endure.'

Elysia's arms began to ache with the task. Birgitta unfolded a large piece of cloth and a rope from her bag, with which to wrap and bind the carcass. She then tied an end of rope around where the head of the animal was and handed the other end to Elysia.

'You can drag it first, this time,' Birgitta said, and Elysia sighed. 'Don't moan – it will keep you strong and agile.'

For two hours they marched down the hill towards the nearest settlement, taking it in turns to pull the carcass. Thick copses of trees petered out into grassland, and eventually into barren farmland that had once held crops. Cloudless skies had allowed the temperature to rise and, although she had taken off her cloak, Elysia became covered in sweat. Despite Birgitta's original claim about her not being as youthful, the older woman did not appear to suffer at all.

The settlement of Vasille, the largest within the nation of Brintassa, came within sight. At the core of the town were dozens of Eighth Age stone dwellings that had been reworked over the centuries to provide cramped housing. It was said a wealthy man from Stravimon owned these buildings and rented them out to the people in exchange for them working on his land, but now the people survived on his handouts, purchased from other nations.

'It is not out of charity that he does this,' Birgitta explained. 'The villagers are his slaves, more or less. He feeds them to keep his workers alive, nothing more, nothing less. He will not take kindly to our delivery, as it interferes with his unwritten contract.' She smiled to herself at the notion.

There was a merchant's store in the centre of Vasille, which was where the two sisters headed. They strode along the muddied road until they arrived at the merchant's large oak door. Elysia waited outside the stone building with the concealed gift of food, whilst Birgitta went inside to speak with the merchant.

There didn't seem much for people to do around here, and the citizens of the town looked thin and troubled. Men sat silently in the shade of awnings, whilst a few women gathered at a well to draw water. Their clothes were old and dirty. To one side, the temple that had once belonged to the Goddess had been desecrated. There was no reference to the deity. Instead, strange animals had been carved in bright new stone, a stark contrast to the rest of the faded structure. Mardonius's agents had come all the way out here to make their point. They would clearly have had little resistance from people who could barely even feed themselves, let alone fight.

A sharp exchange came from within the store. Whoever was speaking with Birgitta was certainly terse in their response. Eventually the merchant came outside, a short man with long grey hair, and he was squinting in the sunlight. Time had etched deep lines into his face, and Elysia guessed from the permanent scowl that his life had been a miserable one.

He glared at Elysia in a mixture of surprise and disgust, blinking repeatedly, and then looked down to the wrapped carcass. He leaned down and untied the material. Elysia did the same with the rope around her waist. Seemingly pleased with the delivery, he rose and stared at Birgitta.

'As I say, we expect nothing in return. This is gift,' Birgitta said, before adding, 'We are not all the same as those you fear.'

The man had stopped listening to her and began to haul the carcass up into his store. He closed the door behind him.

'He was rude,' Elysia said. 'I can see why last time you had me wait on the other side of the street.'

'Never forget the way he looked at you, little sister,' Birgitta said as they walked back through the settlement. 'Never forget that.'

'Is it because of our eyes? Is it the colour?'

'At first. To them it seems to glow brighter and more blue than normal. It is a sign of who we are and, thus, he knew where we came from.'

'We've done nothing to harm him, though. And neither have the sisters.'

'No, little sister, no. In life, it does not matter what you have or have not done. People will judge you on your differences. On the things they imagine you do. No matter how improbable or unlikely. They discriminate because they know no better and they're afraid.'

The Wolf Queen

Her routine was simple.

Wake up at dawn, get water, start a fire, boil the water, forage, and hunt if she needed meat. Practise the old arts so that her skills were not dulled in the wilderness. Read from the few old texts to keep her mind fresh in many languages.

Her domain was simpler these days, too.

A large wooden cabin in the heart of the forest, a river nearby. A view of the distant hills. A square of land to grow simple food. It seemed so far removed from her old life, where she had needed politics and armies to maintain her hold on her territory. Out here she needed just a sword and her wits.

And the wolves, of course.

She continued to wear her warrior garb, as much to maintain some sense of discipline as it was for protection. There was no need of it really, not unless brigands wandered through her land, which happened occasionally. Down by the river, she followed the water into a still gully and washed her face. Sunlight filtered through oak and elm. Birdsong was vibrant at this hour. The sound of the bubbling water was soothing. If this was to be her queendom now, then so be it. At least she was still alive.

She stared at her own reflection in the water: she had not aged all that much. The familiar features, a strong nose and jawline, stared back at her. Her black hair was tied back with metal bands. Her face was still lean, perhaps more so since she had come out to live in the forests. Stark against her black leather jerkin were the pale and wiry muscles of her arms. That was where she noticed the changes the most: gone were the days of opulent feasting.

Coming out here has done me so much good. Burned away the lethargy that comes with soft living.

Leaves suddenly rustled on the opposite bank. With water dripping down her face she peered up to see one of the grey wolves pushing through the low foliage. He nosed around the riverbank for a moment before sitting down, upright, and watched her impassively.

'I haven't seen you for two days,' she said. 'Have you been hunting?'

The animal gave no reply. He never did, of course, but it never stopped her talking to him. She never gave these common wolves names, since she did not want to become too attached to them. Their numbers rose and fell with the deer. The winters could be harsh in this country.

Another wolf appeared alongside him, this one with black markings around its face, and it, too, sat down to peer back at her across the water. Then came another, this one with more white markings around her legs. She was a little older than the others. The three wolves were lined up, as if waiting for her to make a decision.

She rose from the bank of the river and tried to sense if there was a threat. It wouldn't be the first time that the wolves had warned her of coming danger. On more than four occasions over the years there had been bandits who had strayed far from the road and investigated the woodsmoke coming from her cabin's chimmney.

She marched back along the riverbank and across the blue-green grassland towards her cabin. Three massive wolves thundered over to join her, their paws thumping on the damp earth. Each beast stood as high as her neck, and even from a distance looked far more muscular than any ordinary wolf. A mixture of grey and black furs, she had named them Vukos, Faolo and Rafe. They were not merely her protectors here. They were three of the great wolves that came from her old realm, and one of the few reminders of who she had once been. These were the only royal escorts she needed.

The animals slowed down to maintain a steady pace alongside her, with Vukos, the largest and more dominant of the three wolves, leading the way. She commanded them to follow her to the doors of her cabin. While she sought out her sword they patrolled the fringes of the structure, with Faolo darting in and out of the nearby foliage as if it were some game.

Rafe, she watched the closest. The young, paler wolf had the sharpest senses. The animal lifted its head in the air towards one direction in particular, indicating there was something further out, but he did not seem all that agitated.

Her weapons now in hand, she stepped back outside and looked sharply around the grassland. The edge of the forest, a circular fringe some three hundred yards away from her home, was the object of her scrutiny.

She bid the animals forwards to where the threat – if it was a threat – was coming from, and the creatures slowly padded towards the eastern fringe of the forest. That was strange enough, she thought, given that the major roads were many miles in the other direction. She followed their lead, her sword strapped across her shoulder and a circular shield across her back.

The pack entered the gloom of the trees. Vukos led them

onto one of the paths that were used by wanderers for genera-tions before she had lived there. Rafe paused and glanced towards her with his dark eyes. Soon she could feel the forest floor vibrating gently.

Horses, she realized. *And not just one.*

She slid free her sword silently and focused on the path, her eyes scanning every swaying branch and flitting bird. Eventually, in the relative darkness up ahead, came the form of several riders. King's soldiers, by the looks of the colours of their uniforms.

Vukos began to growl and edge forwards.

'Be still,' she ordered.

The entourage came to a halt some fifty feet away and, after a quick exchange with the others, two figures dismounted from the horses at the front and began to walk towards her. One was much taller and more muscular than the other. She immediately recognized them.

Xavir of Clan Argentum, one-time captain of the famous Solar Cohort, and Landril Devallios, former royal spymaster. They paused several feet in front of her with uncertainty in their expressions, and with the three wolves encircling them.

Both men fell to their knees.

A Royal Meeting

'Get up,' she said. 'Don't be ridiculous. This is not a royal court. It is anything but.'

The two travellers rose to their full height and her three wolves padded away to her side.

'Old habits,' Xavir said, glancing at the animals. 'No, Lupara, this is a long way from Dacianara. Cheaper to run, no doubt. I always thought your palace far too opulent for someone who preferred life out on campaign. So how did the wolf queen end up here?'

'That question can wait,' Lupara replied.

Xavir had less physical presence than when she had known him last. His brown hair was longer, his blue eyes a little more tired. He seemed more handsome now because of that world-weariness; perhaps time in gaol had tempered the exuberance of his past.

But he was alive at least, and that was something she was very grateful for.

'You have company,' said Lupara, indicating the former prisoners in the distance.

'My new clan,' Xavir replied. There was almost a smile on his face. She could never tell when he was being sincere.

Lupara looked to Landril and placed her hand upon his shoulder. 'You told me you could do it.'

'Need you have had doubts, my lady?' Landril replied, brushing one of his wrists, his shoulders hunching as if anxious.

'I am always doubtful of late,' she said.

'It was easier than we thought,' Landril continued. 'The soldiers manning the keep were the dregs of the army. The hardest part was persuading Xavir here away from his comfortable life.'

'The good soldiers are too busy bloodying their blades on the innocent,' Lupara replied.

Xavir gave a nod. 'We came across a military unit that was carrying bodies from a settlement. Innocent men and women had been killed there, too. Far from where Mardonius has any authority.'

'And those soldiers?'

'Dealt with,' Xavir replied grimly.

'Good.'

'You brought your wolves with you,' Xavir said. 'They're bigger than I remember.'

'Just these three,' she replied. 'There are many normal ones scattered throughout the forest. The others, I had to leave behind.'

'Do you have any connections left with Dacianara?' Xavir asked.

'Could we keep all questions for later, my lady?' Landril interrupted. 'Look. I don't mean to be rude, but would you mind if we talked in that cabin of yours? Only, by the Goddess, my buttocks are thoroughly sore from riding on that thing back there, and I'm dying to warm my bones against a fire and I haven't eaten anything properly since I was here the last time.

Wouldn't mind a little of that venison, if you've still got any, that is.'

'You ate all of it,' Lupara said, 'but it can easily be arranged for more to be provided.'

'What about the others?' Xavir asked, pointing back along the path.

Lupara peered through the trees at the entourage. 'How many men are with you?'

'Ten others, including Landril,' Xavir said.

'I have equipment to make camp,' Lupara told him. 'It's what I used when I first came out here. It is no luxury, though.'

Xavir ran a hand through his hair. 'Those men have just spent years sleeping on stone slabs in a freezing hole at one of the world's forgotten corners. Anything you have will be a luxury to them.'

The former prisoners put up four large canvas tents, which were old and musty, but were at least shelter. Meanwhile, Lupara permitted Landril and Xavir to share a room within her quarters. Xavir asked if the stoic, black-haired one called Valderon could join them, but he seemed hesitant to do so.

'I come from a simple background, my lady,' he said. His voice was deep and crisp. He, too, was handsome. His face was broad, as was his nose, and he had piercing eyes. 'I'm not used to sleeping near royalty. I'll stay with the men, if it's all the same. I always did on campaign anyway.'

'You're sure?' Xavir asked. 'You were my equal in Hell's Keep and I wish for that to remain the same. A gesture to the others, as much as anything.'

'These are merely sleeping arrangements,' Valderon replied,

'nothing more. I'll spend the night out here.' He paused. 'Though if it rains I may change my mind.'

While the newcomers washed themselves in the river, Lupara set off with her wolves, bow and arrow to stalk the distant woodlands. She returned in the late afternoon with a deer tied across the back of Vukos and one across Faolo. The food would certainly be enough to feed the men for a day or two. When she arrived back she was initially put out at the fact that her wooded serenity had been disturbed by the presence of the men. It had been years since Lupara had heard so many voices in one place and it stirred old memories within her, of the great hunts of her people as they fought mountainous tribes.

A skinny, wiry man with blond hair, Grend, approached her cautiously.

'I used to be a tracker from Laussland, my lady, and know my way around a haunch of venison. If you'll permit, I'd be, uh, happy to turn them into something tasty.'

With a raised eyebrow she gestured towards the carcasses, and Grend edged tentatively towards the wolves.

Xavir stood alongside Lupara as Grend effortlessly hauled one of the deer onto his shoulder and lowered it to the grass on one side.

'He was imprisoned for poaching from a prince's private estates in Laussland,' Xavir explained. 'But Grend had once helped that same prince's cousin navigate across a vast frozen lake during a harsh winter. A friendly word spared him death.'

'Although some would say death would be preferable to Hell's Keep,' Grend drawled. 'Still, that's all behind us now. When the sun touches that hilltop, we'll be eating, I promise. Guarantee a proper good feast. Might need a couple of lads to search for herbs among the riverbanks for me, though.'

'I'll go,' Davlor said cheerily.

'By the Goddess, I'd not trust you to pick something that won't kill us all,' Landril declared. 'I will go with you, and you shall commence your first lesson in botany.'

'You sure know how to turn fun into dullness, don't you?' Davlor moaned, scratching his arse again.

'You're welcome,' Landril replied.

Later, whilst this activity continued and the other men lay about the long grass in relative tranquillity, basking in the warmth of the sun, Lupara approached Xavir, who was leaning on the wide doorway of her cabin and staring out across the scene.

'This is your army then,' she said sardonically, gazing at the rag-tag bunch before her.

'Apparently so,' Xavir replied. 'It is strange to watch them in this context after having been confined in close quarters for so long. I'm simply glad they're not bickering any more. You have a pleasant dwelling, Lupara. Good food. Plenty of resources. Peace and quiet. You're far away from any politicking in the courts of Dacianara.'

'It is a world away from the past, admittedly,' Lupara replied. 'But I enjoy it here.'

'Really? Despite the lack of power and warfare?'

'Power isn't everything and, as you know, killing to keep it is a necessary deed at times. No, I don't miss it. Here I can meditate and become closer to the spirit-walkers.' Over the past few years she had indeed become closer to them. The lack of distractions, no one to bother her with the business of running a nation, allowed her to concentrate her mind on the spiritual teachings of her elders. The warrior queen was finally at peace.

'So why did you summon me? Why send Landril?' His words were not harsh. In fact he spoke rather softly. Xavir seemed more confused by her actions than anything else.

'You don't sound especially grateful,' Lupara said, 'to be free.'

'I was resigned to my fate,' Xavir replied. 'I felt I deserved it. I had. Life was hard, but I made something of an existence there, commanding a gang.'

'You didn't deserve to be there. You should not have gone to prison.'

'So I hear. But I committed the crime, did I not?' Xavir's voice was perfectly calm, as if he was talking about the weather. 'I killed all those people, I and the Solar Cohort. We did it. You were there with us to watch us. Though they weren't your countrymen you must have felt the shame, too.'

'Why do you think I now dwell out here?' Lupara whispered. 'Because of our nation's role in the slaughter of our neighbours – our allies. Dacianarans spilled Stravir blood, no matter the reason why. There was talk of war because of what I did! In my homeland I was accused of bringing great shame to the elders. To the spirit-walkers. I was forced to leave my position as queen to maintain order. Cedius did not ask me to outright, neither did my people, but some things do not need to be asked. So this mess did not stop when you went to gaol. It was all because of Mardonius's plan, but only now can we see this.'

'I had no idea of the repercussions,' Xavir replied. 'What is your evidence so far of Mardonius's place in all of this?'

'Landril intercepted the communications: coded letters sent all those years ago between the ringleaders. A plot to bring you and the Solar Cohort down. Landril finally decyphered them. We have the names now. We know what they did. Where they dwell.'

Lupara explained at great length what had happened during

the tragedy at Baradium Falls, wanting Xavir to understand the *true* events rather than the shameful act that had hardened within his mind over the years. It was important to her that he regained his pride.

As far as Xavir knew, intelligence had been received by Stravimon's spies that dozens of invading tribes from beyond the Plains of Mica were gathering to make a unified attack on the northern boundaries of Cedius the Wise's hitherto unbreakable kingdom.

Tens of thousands of wild warriors would slaughter innocent Stravir.

Xavir was ordered to lead the Solar Cohort and a contingent of the main army in an unusual series of attacks to intercept these tribes one by one, before the bulk of their armies could coalesce and thunder into the main settlements on the border. Then the orders changed: the legion had been held up, so it was up to the Solar Cohort to engage and delay their enemies.

What Xavir and the Solar Cohort were unaware of was that orders had been given to the people of the border towns, warning that the attack was coming and, to spare as many civilian lives as possible, they were to strip their settlements of any clan markings and instead make themselves look like wild warriors of the northern lands. Crudely armed mobs were ordered out to defend their territory.

But the genuine invaders were days away, if indeed they were coming at all. Oblivious to any of this, the men of the Solar Cohort, and their allies from Dacianara, did not hesitate in butchering clusters of woad-faced mobs in the darkened forests.

All they had been doing was butchering the Stravir.

The attack was halted immediately when the blood-drenched warriors realized their mistake, but it was too late. Hundreds of innocents had been slaughtered like cattle. When reinforcements from Cedius the Wise arrived, led by Mardonius, an ambitious duke, the Solar Cohort were taken into custody and their horrific attack – portrayed as a senseless slaughter – was made known to the rest of the forces immediately. The news flourished and the legendary deeds of the famed warriors were eclipsed by their greatest shame.

Although, Lupara explained, Xavir's sentence of imprisonment rather than the death penalty was probably a gesture from Cedius the Wise, who could not bear to lose his favourite warrior, a man whom he had loved like the son he never had.

Xavir listened without showing emotion.

'How did the knowledge of the trap surface?' he asked eventually.

'One man felt the burden of guilt. He wrote a letter to Landril's previous employer to share what he'd done, and of the plot with Mardonius. The letter was intercepted and never made it to its intended destination.'

'Lord Kollus?' Xavir asked.

'Yes. That letter came into Landril's hands swiftly. Doing what spies do, he looked into getting more information and uncovered many further coded communications between the two. Some minor lords had knowledge of the act, though they were not involved. The main perpetrators were General Havinir, Lord Kollus and Duchess Pryus, but they had all been working for Mardonius, as I believe Landril has told you.'

Xavir glanced out towards his comrades, who were still lounging on the grass. Lupara wondered just what it meant for one of the finest warriors in the land to have been betrayed and manipulated in such a way.

'How did you end up here?' he asked.

'This place is of import to the Dacianarans. One of our elders fell here, two centuries ago, where there now lies a burial stone. To all intents and purposes I came to tend to his spirit. An old mentor of mine, Katollon the Soul-Stealer, stands in command of my kingdom, though he is not a king. I am still legally the ruler and we have exchanged missives over the years, both Katollon and I, and with Jumaha of the Vrigantines. We send them by wolf. They still wish me to be queen, but I do not feel the people are ready yet. The dishonour is still raw.'

'Is this why you want to come out of exile?' Xavir asked. 'To correct the mistakes of the past?'

She paused for a moment. 'Fighting Mardonius would bring honour to me. This is true. But no. I want to fight to correct the mistakes *he has made*, because they are too severe and have consequences that will ruin both our countries.'

'I do not yet understand what is going on in Stravimon, but Cedius would never have let things get so bad,' Xavir replied.

'I could see the look in Cedius's eyes after you were taken away. The old man didn't just lose a friend, he lost his heir. He was broken after that.'

'After Baradium Falls no one would have me as their king.' Xavir straightened his posture, letting any sentiment fall away. 'Mardonius, then. He always was scheming and ambitious; he would have taken advantage of what happened. Ensured my name was sullied. I will never understand how a wretch like him rose through the ranks. He was weak, never a good fighter. Anyway, I am a soldier. I am not a man who sits on a throne.'

'Cedius led from the front once,' Lupara said. 'That would have been you. Instead we have Mardonius, and now look at where our nations stand. Many countries surrounding Stravimon have been beaten into submission and integrated into its borders. There are cairns up and down the kingdom in which your own people have been buried on a breathtaking scale. This is no noble war. This is genocide. Anyone who doesn't think like him or poses a supposed threat is eliminated. The clans have largely sided with him, because those who don't have been stripped of their lands and wealth and driven from the kingdom. Those who are onside do get ample rewards. There is no honour any more.'

'This still does not sit well with me. It does not make *sense* to kill so many innocent people.' Xavir wore a heavy frown and shook his head at the notion. 'Has no one tried to assassinate Mardonius?'

'They have, but those who have tried have been killed by his bodyguard – a man who is said to be possessed by a daemon. The Red Butcher, they call him – for good reason. He is the sword Mardonius wields, whilst he rots in the palace.'

'Mardonius was never a fighter,' Xavir sneered. 'His kind are the worst leaders. They don't know the bloody realities of war. People's deaths do not matter to them.'

Lupara thought she could see fires of vengeance burning within Xavir's gaze, the injustices of what was happening to his country, what had happened to him – all for one man's greed for power.

'You still have not really told me,' Xavir said, 'why you and Landril *wished* me here.'

'I would have you build an army. Protect those Mardonius hunts. Bring back justice to the country.'

Xavir grunted a laugh. 'An army requires money, food and time, Lupara.'

'And magic. We need magic.'

Xavir shook his head and narrowed his eyes. 'There is no need for magic where good fighters stand.'

'Magic is essential in a war of this scale. Landril believes Mardonius will soon move to take ownership of all the sisters – at least to keep them out of his affairs, if nothing else. An army of men cannot fight the witches without aid. But if it is money we need for war, I have access to some wealth still.'

'Not enough to take on Mardonius and Stravimon's forces, I'd wager,' Xavir said. 'It's a fanciful scheme.'

Lupara considered one final way to help change Xavir's mind. 'Will you walk with me?'

The Long Walk

The journey back to Jarratox took several hours, and it was well into the night by the time that the two sisters returned. Witch-stones, sensing their approach, lit up the bridge across the chasm towards the island. In daylight the void below would make Elysia grip the stone sides tightly, but at night there was something almost comforting about the nothingness that surrounded the walk, despite the strange, stirring winds. It was as if they were walking through another realm entirely.

Jarratox loomed ahead of them. Lights lit the arched windows in the numerous spires and towers deeper back within the settlement.

Strange, Elysia thought, that there were not the usual flashes of magic as sisters practised their arts into the evening. It looked like any ordinary city.

'Something does not sit well tonight,' Birgitta said as they stepped onto the solid ground of the island-town. 'The source winds blow ill.'

'How so?' Elysia asked. She was tired, and just two words felt a struggle to say.

'There is a tension in the air. I can feel it.'

They continued under ancient, lichen-laced archways, through courtyard gardens and under trees that had no right to be growing in such awkward places, yet somehow a seed had rooted and managed to endure. Curiously there was no one around on the streets, no sisters on their way to evening readings or to recite ancient litanies. Pale witchstones illuminated only ancient stone.

Eventually a noise could be heard. Following the tendrils of sound, the sisters strode into an ancient quadrangle, where dozens of their kin, cloaked in black, were gathered around a large fire and humming a lament. It was an ancient funeral song from the Sixth Age, written by the legendary poet-sister Alyanda, whose books were still preserved in the libraries, and who was often quoted by the older sisters.

Birgitta tugged the sleeve of the nearest woman. 'What has happened, friend?'

The woman twisted back, her head shaded by her blue hood. 'One of the sisters is with us no longer.'

Elysia gasped.

'Who is it?' Birgitta asked.

'Galleya.'

'I know her,' Birgitta whispered. 'I spoke to her only last night. But . . . how did it happen?'

'She immolated herself with a red witchstone, right beneath the statue of the first matriarch.'

'Immolated?' Birgitta appeared to be confused. 'You mean she killed herself? But, why?'

'A decision was made shortly after daybreak that we are to fully pledge our allegiance with King Mardonius. Not all of the sisters supported the news.'

'Did she explain why she was going to . . . return to the source? Did she leave a letter?'

The woman turned around fully to regard the two of them, and Elysia thought she recognized her as one of the senior tutors. Birgitta appeared to know her, anyway.

'Galleya had spoken of the brutality of Mardonius's regime, and said that she refused to participate with any plans generated by, and I quote, "the royal butcher". Galleya said that she had seen so many evil things done to ordinary people, and that the sisterhood should not join his campaigns. The matriarch had apparently not invited Galleya to an important gathering to inform her of the decision to align with Mardonius. Make of that what you will.'

'The matriarch did not want her to protest during the proceedings.'

'That isn't my place to say.'

Even Elysia could see the fear in the woman's eyes as she turned away.

Birgitta regarded the scene for a moment longer, then turned and steered Elysia back through the throng towards her quarters.

'Should we not remain here?' Elysia asked.

The sound of the lament followed them along the dark passageways, all the more haunting as they stepped into shadows.

Birgitta said nothing.

As they ascended the internal stairs to the young sisters' quarters, Elysia asked: 'Is it true that this is what Mardonius is really doing. Is he killing all these people? We should fight back if that's the case.'

'Fighting is not always the answer. Besides, you should not jump to conclusions if you have not seen such things for yourself. Question everything.'

'I've only heard rumours,' Elysia said. 'But this sounds serious.'

Birgitta sat down on the edge of the bed and looked down into her hands.

'Little sister, I once heard of a warlord who wanted to spread fear,' she spoke softly and very deliberately, her shoulders slumping. 'This was deep in the south. Near the humid swamps, further into thick-leaved forests. His soldiers would mark the houses of those people who worshipped a different god to him, in order to create fear. Nothing would come of it, but people would expect the worst. He could disrupt an entire community without so much as a show of a sword. A simple cross upon their door and that was that. Later he used the trick again, only he was more devious this time. To prevent himself from being deposed, he arranged it so that a rival faction would mark the homes of neighbouring factions with crosses, sowing discontent. Fighting broke out within their ranks, rather than against his own forces. This warlord, he clung on to power for decades. All with a simple cross.'

'I don't understand,' Elysia said.

'Mardonius may not have to be killing all the time to create fear. He is clever. He is a manipulator. He was never a warrior. Take the example of his *messengers* a couple of days ago.'

Birgitta rose and walked to the window, looking down upon the gathering for Galleya. The sisters' eerie song drifted up to them.

Elysia stepped close to her side. 'What do you make of the matriarch's decision?'

The answer came fast and blunt: 'I think it is a terrible thing. I fear corruption has set into the higher echelons of the sisterhood that we should bow to bribery or threats. What is the purpose of the sisterhood?'

'To nurture the source for the future.'

'And?'

'To use it to the benefit of people.'

'Precisely – for the benefit of the *people*. All people. Not just for one man and his greed. We have always stood apart from the power plays of the clans. It used to be that we were allocated to the clans to be healers and advisers but now we are used as weapons,' Birgitta replied. 'Wielded in the wrong hands, our powers can be devastating.'

Elysia felt the urge to say something in response. That surely, at times, there was a need to fight back. But now was not the time to retaliate.

'Sometimes sisters may even end up fighting against each other,' Birgitta said with a shudder. 'It used to be that the sisterhood came first — above all politics. Now I'm not so sure. You can be positive that the brightest and most able young sisters will be sent to Mardonius now, and who knows where their loyalties will lie after a while?'

'That won't be me, then,' Elysia muttered.

'You are very able. The tutors all speak of your potential, but there is a fire inside of you that frightens them.'

Elysia frowned. 'Hardly.'

'It is true — I sense it in you myself. There is a wild abandon, a curiosity about the external world as well as the source of magic. That unnerves them. It is why I teach you, because it was hoped I could channel your passions into hunting and naturecraft. But my personal fear for you, little sister, is that you are now *too* good with weapons and magic. What really frightens the senior sisters is the fact that you are *different*.'

'Why are you not frightened of me?' Elysia asked.

Birgitta regarded her softly. 'I am frightened *for* you. You have skills for combat, never witnessed in recent years. You may end up causing all sorts of trouble once you're out there with a clan.'

'When we saw the meeting,' Elysia said, 'you told me you needed to think. You've been waiting until the matriarch's decision. Well, we've got that. So what do we do now?'

'I haven't merely been waiting,' Birgitta replied. 'I have been asking questions. I have been finding out information. I have been contacting old friends and . . . calling in favours.'

Elysia waited for Birgitta to continue.

'Before dawn. I will come and find you before dawn.'

'And then what?'

'We're setting off from Jarratox,' Birgitta whispered. 'It may be the last time you ever see this place. Pack your things; only bring the most important belongings. Bring clothes for the road. And your bow.'

Elysia's breath caught in her throat. 'Where are we going?'

'It is better that you don't know, because if someone asks, you won't be able to tell them.'

Elysia looked incredulously at her tutor. 'But how can we leave? What about Jarratox?' she asked.

'Jarratox is doomed,' Birgitta replied sadly. 'Take my word for it. Tonight the sisterhood has effectively ceased to be.'

Old Skin

The forgotten warrior and the exiled queen strode through the forest.

A milky light filtered through the canopy, occasionally glancing off the rubble of an ancient ruin. As afternoon slid into evening there was a sharpness to the air. It had been years since Xavir had experienced such surroundings. Every curling leaf, every swaying branch, every darting bird was rendered vividly to his senses. Now and then he would close his eyes so that he could smell the damp earth and the late summer flowers.

The ground rumbled and Xavir watched as Lupara's wolves bounded ahead. Suddenly more wolves, smaller ones, came to the fringes of the path, peering with curiosity at Xavir and Lupara.

'Do these others obey you too?' he asked.

'Mostly not. I do not give them orders like *my* wolves, however. I . . .'

'Go on.'

'I simply talk to them as I would another person. They're good companionship in that sense.'

'Good sentries, no doubt, should you be threatened. Have there been any attacks on you here? Has Mardonius tried to eliminate you?'

'Much as he may wish to, it is unlikely he knows I dwell here. There have only been a few bandits stray this way. My wolves have seen them off. None who enters the forest without my permission leaves it alive.'

'Don't you ever get bored out here?' Xavir asked.

'Says the man who has been in prison for years,' Lupara replied.

'A fair point.'

The path became a little steeper, narrower and darker. Eventually the two of them came to a clearing.

Lupara nodded. 'We're here.'

The three large wolves padded around them and then sat down to regard the distance. A couple of smaller wolves came by to nose the larger beasts, before trotting off into the undergrowth. The wind came and went, leaving them in a tranquil, cool place.

'What are we waiting for?' Xavir asked, noting her gaze scanning the ground.

Lupara knelt down and began brushing back the damp leaves, inching forwards in one direction until she was satisfied she had found what she was looking for.

Eventually she began to uncover an old shield, rectangular in shape, but with no blazon. Lupara gripped the edges and pulled it back like a trap door, revealing a wide hole in the ground. Down inside was a thin wooden chest, a good four feet long.

'Take the other end,' Lupara said, reaching underneath to grip one side of the chest.

Xavir reached down for an iron clasp and together they heaved the chest up onto the forest floor.

Like the shield, the chest had no markings. It had been varnished, once, but the patina had worn over the years.

'Go on,' Lupara urged. 'Open it.'

Xavir felt for the join where the lid met the rest of the trunk, flipped back the clasp and heaved it open.

Inside was a bundle wrapped in black cloth. Xavir pulled it out and laid it on the ground, then carefully began to peel away the material. Within the bundle were two swords in their ornate scabbards. There was a jet-like shimmer to the casing, and an elaborate emblem of his clan sigils in a faint silver leaf, which framed small golden dragon motifs. Upon each of the weapons, set up near the hilt, was a small red gemstone.

It had been years since he had looked upon these marvels. Years since he had drawn blood with them.

Lupara picked one of the swords up and attempted to pull it free from its scabbard, but she could not — both of them knew she would be unable to do so — and she handed it over to Xavir with a smile. The warrior placed his hand upon the hilt, which immediately began to glow — the way it always had. The sword eased free, the hilt returned to normal, and Xavir pulled the blade back. The weapon easily slid from its casing. He held it upright in front of his face, examining the unblemished surface.

'The Keening Blades,' Lupara reminded him. 'Originally cast by the great weapon-smith Allimentrus. Magically imprinted for only your family's use. Your old uniform is in there, as well. Look.'

As the wind rustled through the trees, she pulled back the layer of cloth on which the swords had rested all these years, and revealed the black uniform of the Solar Cohort. Black boots, black leather jerkin with the silver detailing of a shining, crenellated tower with a flaming sun rising above it. Cedius's symbol. A black tunic and breeches lay underneath.

Xavir swallowed. The mere sight of the items brought back raw memories.

'It is one of the few tragedies of Cedius's reign,' Lupara continued, 'that the men who wore such proud uniforms were tricked into shame and dishonour.'

'Did you take anything else?'

'For a man of wealth you had very few things.'

'Every time I left the palace could have been the last,' Xavir replied. 'There seemed no need to be surrounded by trinkets.'

'Ever the soldier,' she replied.

'Priests share a similar outlook; you were barely different, even in that fine castle of yours.'

'*Bahnnash*,' she said. A curse word in her native tongue. 'It was hardly a castle. All my predecessors were warriors too. Luxury does not sway the likes of us, but honour, glory, the feel of a sword in our hand and the heat of battle – that's what truly stirs our blood.'

Xavir smiled grimly. 'What need is there for men of war in peacetime? We are cut from the same cloth, you and I. Trained to kill people. We fought for what was right – what made a better world for our people. Or we believed we did.'

'Does that mean you'll help us?' Lupara asked.

Xavir was still staring at the Keening Blades.

'What good would it do? I'm sure everyone knows of the Solar Cohort's disgrace. If I wore this uniform, people would lynch me as soon as follow me.'

'You don't strike me as someone who would be afraid of what people thought.'

'True, but say I was to lead your *cause* – I am Xavir, the butcher of Baradium Falls. This is hardly a figure who should be at the front of your army.'

'Perhaps.' The optimism began to fade in her eyes.

'Valderon might, though.'

Lupara looked up at Xavir, confused.

'Valderon was a high-ranking officer in the First Legion. Sergeant. A good fighter. He did not go into prison for any barbaric reason as I did.'

'Were you not enemies in gaol?'

Xavir shrugged. 'It matters little now. No, Valderon will not be as infamous as I, and may lead with honour.'

One of the wolves made a grunting noise.

'Even he approves,' Xavir said with a small smile.

The wolf queen grinned savagely. Though it had been many years since Xavir had seen her, she remained both beguiling and fearsome, as she had always been. Age had only given her expressive face more definition.

'I do not know this man well,' she said, 'but I will take your word for it, if you can vouch for him.'

Xavir wasn't yet sure. 'I can,' he lied. *Though I'll need more proof that he's an honest man.*

'And you – will you fight alongside us at least?'

'You speak of *us*, lady, but who exactly do you have?'

'I can summon my own tribe, but we number in the hundreds of good warriors, not the thousands. Besides, it has been many years since I have fought alongside them. We are out of practice.'

'So,' Xavir said, 'we need to build an army. We need training. We will need money to do all of these things.'

'We need to do it quickly, Xavir, as people are dying.'

'People die,' Xavir replied. 'Unfortunately, it is the way of the world. If Mardonius was not doing it then some other tyrant would. There is always someone happy to reave the life from another should it further their own cause. That's humanity for you.'

Lupara nodded. 'Wolves have it better,' she said. 'They think of the good of the pack – not the needs of the one.'

Xavir sheathed his blades and looked longingly at his uniform.

'You might as well put them on,' Lupara said. 'The colours of the king's men do not suit you.'

With reverence, Xavir placed his weapons upon the edge of the wooden chest and leaned in to retrieve his belongings. He paused. 'I should wash, first.'

'The river is just over there. I'll wait here.'

Under Lupara's gaze, and that of the wolves, Xavir removed his belongings and followed her directions down to the river.

The slope was damp, but not too slippery, and he navigated the old boughs and slabs of rock until he reached the bank. He stripped himself naked and waded into the ice-cold water until he was waist high. Shuddering, he waited for his body to acclimatize, then he stared at his shimmering reflection. It was the first time in many years he had really seen himself.

'The time inside has not been kind, old friend,' he muttered to himself.

Slowly he washed away the past.

Xavir submerged himself in the clear waters, feeling its icy pressure around his body, his tightening skin, basking in the chill. Then he rose and stood there, watching the river drift around him. Too long had he been standing still while time and events moved around him. The world had changed so much – and, from the sound of it, not for the better. But no more would he stand by idly. Xavir vowed to himself that he would make up for the deeds of his past – somehow make right what had gone before. This was a second chance. Then could he die happily, for there was very little else in this world left for him.

He waded from the water and, wiping himself down with his old rags, began to don the uniform from his past. Once he was in it, time seemed to fall away. Piece by piece he reconstructed who he had once been. He pulled the buckle on the jerkin and found that it was a little loose, but he would fill it again with proper food and training. Finally he slipped his boots on, and stood tall. Taller.

He felt truly himself again, one of the Solar Cohort. The finest of Cedius's warriors.

Yet without his comrades, without Felyos and Gatrok, and his old friends Brendyos, Jovelian and the great Dimarius, the Solar Cohort, the Legion of Six was just one man. It should never have been this way.

'I will clear your name, brothers,' he vowed aloud. 'I will kill those who caused our dishonour and your deaths. You should have died in glory on the battlefield, swords in hand – not by the hands of some executioner for a crime that was not our fault.'

Xavir marched back up the slope towards Lupara, who was still waiting by the chest. As he returned she handed him the Keening Blades.

'Much better,' she said. 'This is the Xavir I remember.'

Xavir lifted the sheathed swords over his head and down across his back, and Lupara fixed the buckles and straps in place to the rear of his jerkin.

'Better,' he muttered.

'You're welcome,' Lupara said.

'Thank you,' Xavir replied, thinking how he had forgotten simple manners in gaol. 'For keeping these items. For looking after them. For giving me a reason to live again.'

Forest Food

'Well, you should have listened to me,' Landril said, arms folded.

'They all looked the bloody same,' Davlor groaned.

The scrawny man was holding his hand in a huge copper pot, soaking it in a warm herbal infusion. They were standing a few yards from Lupara's cabin with the others, who were busily eating the hearty stew that Grend had made for them. Next to them, Jedral shovelled food down his mouth the fastest, having spent the afternoon chopping wood for the fire. The labour seemed to have done his mood some good, and he even cracked a smile from time to time.

Landril had to admit that Grend knew his way around a cooking pot. Which was more than could be said for Davlor, who currently had his hand within one. Eventually the moaning settled down.

'The only noises I can hear now are Jedral's grunts of admiration for the quality of the food,' Landril observed. 'He was grunting with his axe for most of the afternoon as well. He only seems to communicate in grunts.'

'Aye,' Davlor whispered weakly. 'He has claims to w-wealth, but I reckon he was a f-farmhand like me. Nothing wrong with that . . . Good l-l-living.'

'Oh, by the Goddess,' Landril sighed. 'You sound ridiculous. It isn't *that* bad.'

Valderon approached the two men with a smile upon his face. 'What happened?'

'Picked a dodgy mushroom,' Davlor whimpered.

'*Despite* my advice,' Landril said smugly. 'I said the yellow mushrooms on one half of the path were delicacies, and that the almost identical ones on the other half were poisonous and likely to kill you if ingested. Did he listen?'

'But they all looked the same!' Davlor had been muttering the same thing since walking back from the forest, his hand throbbing as it became engorged with blood.

'We could always cut his hand off,' Valderon suggested. 'Jedral looked quite efficient with that axe.' He winked at Landril.

'You wouldn't?' Davlor asked, wide-eyed.

'This tisane should calm it down,' Landril assured him. 'Leave it in there for a few hours and you'll recover. Then we may revisit the question of removing it.'

'What?' Davlor moaned. 'I've got to stand here with my hand in this pan for hours?'

'You could not, and let the poisons slowly seep around your body,' Landril told him with a grin. He knew that these particular poisons would do no such thing unless taken internally, but he wasn't going to tell the idiot that.

'So how am I going to eat?' Davlor asked.

'You still have one good hand,' Valderon laughed, and slapped Davlor on the shoulder before walking away.

Landril began to turn away as well when Davlor said, 'What, you're not going too are you?'

'My dear Davlor, a conversation with you is no way to sharpen my wits, and I'm guessing the level of entertainment it offers will be sparse also. So I'll leave you be. With any luck, this experience will be a lesson to you.'

'A lesson in what?'

'Listening to what I say,' Landril replied, and followed Valderon towards the rest of the men.

The escaped prisoners had by now moved around a campfire. Venison was still simmering, the smell drifting through the forest and making Landril's stomach grumble. This was good, hearty food and Landril was grateful to dine well again. *Goddess knows what it's like for the others to eat a proper meal after so long.*

'Fine plates,' Tylos said, looking appraisingly at the tableware Lupara had lent them. 'Real silver.'

'You going to steal them, black man?' someone teased, and the others laughed.

'I might have been a thief once,' Tylos began, 'but no. I was merely appreciating the quality. I grew up dining off plates like these.'

'Once a thief, always a thief?' Valderon said, placing a warm hand on the man's shoulder.

'Perhaps.'

A wave of silence washed over the group as Xavir and Lupara entered the clearing. Landril smiled inwardly. This was the Xavir he remembered from the halls of Cedius's palace, and right now he looked as splendid as a warrior king in his old uniform.

It was notable how the others viewed him with an entirely new kind of reverence. These had been his gang members, some had been his rivals, yet in this black attire Xavir commanded an instant respect from them.

Valderon, who was already standing, strolled slowly towards Xavir. 'Are those the Keening Blades?'

'They are,' Xavir answered.

'I'd heard of them, but never set eyes upon them,' he said reverently.

Jedral scratched his chin and said, 'What are they?'

'Blessed weapons,' Valderon replied, 'created by the hands of the great metallurgist and forger, Allimentrus, who died almost seven centuries ago. These blades are what soldiers dream of using. But, it is said, only one bloodline can use them.'

Xavir slid the weapons off his shoulders and unclipped the scabbards. He handed one to Valderon. 'Here, try.'

Valderon placed his hands around the hilt of a sword and tried to pull it free, but he could not. He smiled wryly.

'Would anyone else like to try?' Xavir asked.

One by one, each of the men, save Landril who knew better, and of course Davlor, who still held his hand within a cooking pot, eagerly attempted to pull the sword free from its hilt.

Eventually the sword was returned to Xavir. He placed his hand on the hilt, which began to glow white, and the sword eased free with a whisper.

'Witchcraft,' one of the men muttered.

'Something like that,' Valderon replied. 'I bet not even the witch who worked with Allimentrus could open them up.'

'Nothing so crude as a witch,' Xavir replied, placing the swords back over his shoulders once again. 'Allimentrus worked alone, it was said. Only my bloodline can wield these weapons.'

'Why are they called the Keening Blades?' Tylos asked.

Xavir pulled them free and stood aside. He moved quickly through a series of postures and, with every stroke of the blades through the air, they emitted a quiet scream.

'They keen like a banshee,' Landril observed. 'That will be the magic in them.'

'Indeed they do,' Xavir replied. 'When in war the noise is more intense, but then their work is more intense also.'

Xavir placed the scabbards back over his shoulder, and then attempted to sheath the weapons, but with the blade in his left hand he missed the first time.

'Look at the graceful warrior!' Tylos gave a hearty laugh that echoed across the dark grassland.

'Well, if you're no longer any good with them,' Valderon said, chuckling, 'I'd happily learn.'

'I'm out of practice, sergeant,' Xavir replied with a genuine laugh, the first Landril had heard from him. 'My muscle memory is not what it was.'

'We're all out of practice,' Valderon said, steering Xavir towards the fire. 'But I'm guessing we'll have plenty of time to learn again.'

It was a pleasant night. The men shared stories and laughed, and there was an ease among them that there hadn't been when they'd been confined in Hell's Keep. Only one of them seemed unsettled: Harrand spoke of going to a particular city to settle some scores but none of the others even discussed breaking free from each other just yet.

Landril wondered if following Xavir gave them a momentary sense of purpose. Kept them in a somewhat familiar routine despite their new surroundings. After all, where exactly was there to go in such a remote place?

Things became a little uncomfortable when Lupara retired to her cabin with Xavir. One or two of the others made crude remarks about what they might be doing.

'Boys, the things I'd do to her,' Jedral muttered lustfully. 'I'd make her howl like a wolf all right.'

A couple of the other men laughed awkwardly.

'I know it has been years since you have seen a woman,'

Valderon snapped, 'but have you regressed to being savages this much?'

'Valderon is right,' Tylos added. 'Besides, I suspect that the warrior queen would be the one making *you* howl, and it would not be in pleasure.'

The other men guffawed as Jedral glared at him for a moment.

Landril winced at the tensions that flared and hoped it would not descend into bloodshed.

'This woman has allowed us to share her home with her,' Valderon continued smoothly, 'and has given us food and shelter, the likes of which we haven't seen for years. The very least you could do is speak about her with respect.'

Jedral looked abashed and grunted something apologetic.

'Besides, Tylos is correct,' Valderon added. 'I'd wager that if any of you got close to her she'd cut your cock off before you wondered what to do with it. I have heard of what the wolf queen has done to hardened warriors in battle. I fought alongside her tribe at one point. Fearsome breed, the Dacianarans. There are few who are as skilled as her with a blade. And you think you could better a woman like that?'

Jedral snapped the twig he was holding and looked down.

Landril decided to take a moment away from everyone to make his evening prayers to the Goddess. He would never quite fit in with the other men, and he was fine with that. He would give everyone a chance to settle for the night before going to his own bed in the cabin.

As a spymaster he was used to spending time alone. Whilst others formed bonds on campaigns and shared bread and ale together, Landril's missions for Cedius had been diplomatic affairs, opulent dinners with strangers at the far end of nations, a life of secrets, different names and faces. He was so used to his disguises and alter egos that at times he wondered who the real Landril was.

But the Goddess knows, of course.

Landril found a quiet old tree to settle next to and fell softly to his knees in prayer – yet his mind drifted with his words.

He had studied the ways of the Goddess all his life. His father had been a preacher of her temple in Stravir City, but despite having followed her teachings Landril did not want to become a theologian. He was too curious about the rest of the world; a secular life would never have suited him. He often wondered whether his father had been disappointed in him, but he had never spoken negatively about the paths Landril had chosen.

Any of them. Even when the old man had caught Landril lying with another man, there was no recrimination, no disapproval or disappointment. His father was the epitome of the Goddess's writings: a belief in equality, love, sacrifice, peace and honour. Such an outlook made it all the more unendurable for Landril to see those bodies on the roads outside holy settlements – people slaughtered, villages burned. Mardonius seemed to have a particular hatred for the Goddess's followers, despite their peaceful worship.

All across Stravimon, and well beyond into the eastern and northern duchies, people were being threatened or executed until they left their settlements or joined with Mardonius's crude campaign to eliminate religion.

As soon as the priests and priestesses of the Goddess began publicly to decry Mardonius's crimes, there came sightings of daemons in the largest towns, monstrous horrors that picked off worshippers after evensong and dragged them screaming into the darkness. Terrified men talked of walls that bled, of screams coming from nowhere, cold chills and houses that were deserted after apparitions had scared the inhabitants into leaving. Were they rumours or reality? When Landril tried to warn his father in Stravir City, the spymaster was too late. The preacher had disappeared, along with key members of the temple staff. Splatters of blood across the temple door indicated all too well what had happened.

Lupara had been taking her own steps and had commissioned a network of spies to investigate what was going on in Stravir, disturbed at the rumours of unrest which could threaten the peace of Dacianara. And that was how Landril first came into contact with her. It was clear that desperate measures would be needed to prevent Mardonius from destroying a continent, and together they could think of only one thing. One man.

Xavir Argentum.

During Landril's prayers, a couple of Lupara's smaller wolves headed past him deeper into the forest. One sniffed his leg on the way past and he smiled at the creature, before it followed the rest of the pack. He rose and turned to walk towards the open grassland.

Something cracked in the distance.

Landril paused and looked behind. He could see nothing but darkness and the glimmer of moonlit leaves. He could feel his pulse pounding in his neck when suddenly the canopy rattled — Landril jumped back as a bloodied carcass slammed down at an angle a few feet in front of him. It was the wolf that had just a moment ago nosed him. He barely recognized it, so mutilated was it.

A deeper, fiercer growl came from up ahead.

That was no wolf.

The forest shook.

Without hesitation, without even taking a second glance, Landril sprinted through the darkness, his pulse thumping in his chest.

Night Fight

Xavir and Lupara were sitting under the light of several candles, their fingers gliding across old maps of the continent. It had been a long time since Xavir had seen a map, but cartography was a language with which he was very familiar, and the pleasure of reading the lines of a land came back to him quickly.

Xavir and the prisoners had already come far from the Silkspire Mountains to Brekkland. Beyond lay Brintassa, but their journey ahead would most likely take them through Burgassia, a strange and ancient country. Beyond that lay Stravimon, which to him looked bigger than he remembered. Under Cedius's early rule, before Xavir ascended the ranks, Stravimon had swallowed up surrounding land in the south, nearly all of it negotiated in a peaceful manner. The real fighting always took place in the Plains of Mica and beyond, where the barbarian tribes and more aggressive nations from the north would chance their hands at making inroads into Stravimon territory. They seldom succeeded, as the towns on the border were well defended. Now it seemed that Mardonius had taken the battle to the barbarians, evidently pushing the Stravimon border ever northwards.

Xavir tried to work out Mardonius's military thinking: he had made no real push to the south and west. While Burgassia still had no king and likely never would, Laussland had suffered many attacks, though Mardonius had made no formal invasion on either. Indeed, his military activities had been curious at best: raids on towns by small bands of soldiers, the rough treatment of civilians.

The horses, which had been kept behind the cabin, made a sudden whinny of alarm. Lupara stood up from the table in her cabin. From the look in her eyes Xavir knew something was wrong.

'What is it?' he asked.

'The wolves,' she replied, her senses focused on something beyond what could be seen. 'Something is happening.'

She strode to her door and called her three immense wolves. As they bounded over, casting glances back at the forest, Xavir slung the Keening Blades across his shoulders and stepped outside into the twilight. The other men, still by the light of the fire, showed only casual interest at their activity.

'Give me a hand with this,' Lupara called. Reaching down, she slung leather and metal armour across the backs of the fidgeting wolves. 'Fix the clasps on the other side. Hurry.'

Xavir did as the queen instructed, pulling the straps under the huge belly of the beasts one at a time whilst Lupara moved the armour into place. The leather reached across the spine and under the belly of the animals, whilst the metal segmented plates hung by their ribcages. All the time Xavir had one wary eye on the wolves' gaping jaws as they growled at something only they could sense.

Valderon ran up towards Xavir and Lupara. 'You're expecting trouble?'

'I am,' Lupara replied grimly. 'Tell your men to equip themselves. Something is amiss in the forest.'

'You're sure?'

'The wolves can *feel* it,' she snapped. 'So I can *feel* it.'

'As you command, my lady.' Valderon gestured for the others to get to their feet. 'Pick up your weapons, the lot of you,' he shouted. 'There's no rest tonight.'

'Ugh. We've all been on the road for days,' Davlor said. 'I'm knackered.'

'If you want to see the road again, then get up and arm yourselves,' Valderon demanded. 'There's something coming.'

Xavir, Lupara and her three wolves strode out towards the trees.

Valderon brought the other men in tow, and they quickly formed a second line thirty yards behind. 'What enemy are we expecting?' he called ahead.

Xavir turned back and shrugged. He unsheathed the Keening Blades anyway and waited for Lupara to give her word. It was good to balance the weapons again, to feel their weight in his hands. Only then did he realize how much he wanted to use them on something.

Valderon cautioned for his men to be quiet, and soon all that was heard was the whisper of boots brushing through the long grass and the trees stirring in the wind.

Then came a squeal, a hundred yards up ahead. Moments later, Landril came sprinting out of the forest into the clearing, his arms flailing. He caught sight of Lupara's small force and lurched towards them.

'There are things in there,' he yelled, his voice echoing across the glade. 'Something monstrous. It killed a wolf and threw it through the trees.'

Lupara flinched at the words. Landril joined the other men behind. The spymaster hunched double with his hands over his knees, looking as if he would vomit on the ground, and heaved in his breaths.

A moment later came a sound of snapping branches.

Everyone faced the noise, clutching their weapons tighter. A huge form smashed out of the trees, followed by two more.

'What in the name of the Goddess . . . ?' Valderon gasped.

All three creatures stood a good ten feet tall. Their misshapen forms were covered in a thick-looking hide, with bulbous heads and gaping, dripping jaws. Their eyes burned red with a mindless violence. They had four legs, each one of slightly different proportions, and two thickset arms with hands claw-tipped and the size of meat plates. One of the abominations gave a guttural roar that sent a shudder through the ground.

The cluster of beasts began to charge.

'On my word,' Valderon shouted to the panicked men, 'scatter for twenty paces, then peel back to attack.'

'Which direction?' Jedral muttered, white-faced.

'Any, just make sure they're different.'

Xavir smiled inwardly – it was one of the old techniques of the legions, though Valderon had not called out the formal name of the Broken Shoal.

Xavir glanced to Lupara as the monsters lumbered closer and said, 'Which one will you go for?'

'Whichever of them gets to me first.'

'I'll see to its friends, then,' he replied.

Xavir identified the path being taken by one of the creatures and darted light-footed into the fringes of the forest. He lunged swiftly out of the trees towards the lumbering beast, dragging one of his blades down across the side of the abomination, opening up a fold of skin and forcing the thing to buckle with a ground-shuddering thump. It screamed maniacally, then turned its attention towards Xavir.

The warrior waited patiently for it to make another move. A heavy, clawed limb came forth and Xavir twirled to his left, cleaving through the outstretched hide with a shriek of his blade.

Another roar exploded from the beast.

When it struck again, Xavir surged towards its jutting maw. He deftly sliced through its face, blinding it, and then rolled away through the grass. Now the creature flailed wildly in the same spot, screaming and scattering its own blood in wide arcs.

Behind Xavir came the sounds of the melee, but he kept his focus on the beast's movements. On his feet again, he sliced the Keening Blades clean through the thing's lurching form again and again. Chunk after chunk of thick flesh slopped messily onto the earth, and Xavir ducked under a slow swing to plant both of his blades into the beast's belly, opening up the flesh and spilling its foul innards onto the moonlit ground.

Xavir stepped back as the creature fell forwards. The warrior finished the fight by cleaving the blade through its throat.

Then he ran back towards the others.

Only one beast remained standing. Amidst the mass of human forms that surrounded it were the lunging forms of Lupara's huge wolves.

Xavir arrived in time to witness the final monster collapse forwards, the three wolves each mauling a limb with their teeth. Valderon plunged his blade deep down into the thing's head to silence it once and for all.

In the sudden quiet, everyone looked around at the scene of carnage. They were breathless and caked in ichor. Lupara sent her wolves out to search for any more beasts.

Xavir noticed two men lying in the grass to one side and went to check them. Valderon joined him as he examined their mangled corpses. 'Barros and Galo,' Valderon muttered, scanning their mauled forms. 'One from each of our gangs.'

'A shame,' Xavir replied.

'They fought well, stood their ground,' Valderon continued, 'which is all you can really ask for.'

Tylos and some of the others came to observe the fallen men. 'They knew their way around a fight, but against that . . .' Tylos shook his head. 'Why is it that good men die, while people like Davlor, who can barely hold a sword, manage to survive?'

'Hey!' Davlor said. 'I didn't run away.'

'You did not strike a blow either, farm boy,' Jedral replied.

'So I ain't as fancy as the rest of you. I stood my ground. Anyway, you're just a nutcase that likes killing anything that moves.'

'Must admit I enjoyed that, boys,' Jedral said, rolling his shoulders. 'Good to release some tension. Was prepared to take it out on Davlor with all his moaning.'

'This is not the time for bickering,' Xavir snapped, rising from the bodies. 'Our comrades are dead.'

He looked up for Lupara and saw that she, too, was searching the fringes of the forest with her wolves. Other wolves had also been summoned by her, and a dozen smaller shadows rippled through the grass like wraiths towards the trees.

'Tell you what,' Davlor muttered, standing alongside Xavir. 'Wouldn't like to be on the receiving end of one of her wolves. I've seen normal wolves take down livestock in the blink of an eye, but those . . . Big buggers, I'll say. Her and those three took the first one down in no time.'

Xavir nodded, having seen the wolves fight numerous times. He joined Landril, who was studying the fallen creatures closely, prodding them with the tip of his blade.

'What do you make of them, spymaster?' Xavir called over. 'I have not seen anything like them before. I have not even heard of them.'

'Nor had I until about a year ago,' he replied. 'By the Goddess, they're strange things, aren't they? They are quite extraordinary. Two main eyes, yes, but there are more set further forward — smaller ones, see? And the teeth are in two rows on the top, three on the bottom. There is nothing in our land even similar.'

'What are you saying?' Xavir asked. 'That they come from another land entirely?'

'As fanciful as it seems . . .' Landril nodded. 'I've heard tell of more of these incidents, but this is the furthest south and east that I have known them to be sighted. Admittedly those other incidents feature other strange creatures, not necessarily these. Scholars in a few colleges affiliated with the Goddess were beginning to detail them and categorize them, but that was before Mardonius's rule grew too mad.'

'How many of these incidents have there been?' Xavir asked. The others had begun to group around them now, listening to what Landril had to say.

'Fewer than a dozen,' Landril announced. 'That does not sound many, but they have had a profound impact upon those communities affected. Some creatures have killed livestock. Some have killed people.'

'It's just as well they were simple enough to bring down.'

'*Simple?*' Landril almost choked on the word. 'Simple for you, maybe. I was rooted with fear. I wanted to do something, to land a blow, but I could not get my sword to connect. This is not my skill.'

'You're alive and they are dead,' Xavir muttered. 'This is how victory works.'

'You make it sound so simple.'

'It is. And in the morning I'd like to know more of what you know about them. But everyone here is tired and we have the fallen to see to. Barros followed the Goddess. What about Galo?'

'Him too,' Valderon replied.

'Does anyone here know words of the Goddess?' Xavir asked the group, but looked towards the spymaster.

'My father was a priest,' Landril replied. 'I know of some suitable words.'

'You may not be a warrior, but you have other skills, spy-master.' Xavir told him. 'See to it that their bodies are treated with respect. They may have been prisoners but they died free men with honour. That's all any of us can ask for.'

Leaving Jarratox

Elysia had no inclination to look back.

As the sun breached the hills on a chilly, cloudless morning, chasing shadows back across the grassland and dark forests, there was no urge to see Jarratox one last time.

No sentiment for the only home she'd ever known. No twinge of regret at the back of her mind. She had never felt truly settled there. To her it had been a prison that had restricted her freedom just as much as chains would have. She took nothing from the sisterhood apart from resentment and resilience, of a kind.

With her bow slung over her shoulder alongside a leather satchel of meagre belongings, Elysia turned towards the land ahead glowing in the soft light of dawn. She stared at it with eagerness: she was determined never to look back.

Despite Birgitta having initiated their escape, she appeared more disturbed by the act of their leaving. She had not spoken much since they had left and looked constantly behind her – either aware of possible pursuit or a longing for home. To Elysia's surprise, ten other sisters had accompanied them.

'I am not the only one who has qualms about the sisterhood's path,' Birgitta had explained as Elysia had stared with suspicion at the hooded women.

The escaping sisters planned to part, like seeds scattered in the wind, and establish contact with those who were making a stand against Mardonius. And so twelve sisters had strode in haste across the bridge – blue robes of tutors, grey and red of clan returnees and one other young novice in brown, a year younger than Elysia.

When they finally crossed the bridge, Birgitta and Elysia had made their goodbyes to the others and started north. It wasn't until they reached the farmland communities with their high stone walls and thick copses of trees that they felt they could slow down the fast pace they'd kept up to throw off any pursuit.

An hour or so later and the sun had finally banked high enough in the sky to reveal their new world, the endless horizon, in all its clarity. No more petty squabbles, chores, facing ridicule over not committing certain lines of text to memory; no more bitter scowls from jaded old women whose life had left them. The concept of *fitting in* meant different things out here.

No, Elysia had no inclination to look back.

'So are we *actually* in trouble?' Elysia asked.

'You see danger, little sister?'

'No. I mean are we twelve in trouble with the sisterhood? I noticed you brought the Staff of Shadows with you.' It was a large wooden staff, shaped like a small tree branch with a thick-textured bark. In the top of it was set a black witchstone. Birgitta had crafted it herself and Elysia had seen the staff used only once before. Birgitta had wanted to show her how it cast their immediate surroundings into darkness and how it swallowed up the light from all angles. It was, as Birgitta put it, not a weapon, but more a distraction to get out of a tricky situation. 'If they can't see you, they can't kill you,' Birgitta had said.

The bag of witchstones in the satchel around Birgitta's shoulder suggested that there were weapons if they needed them, though.

'The staff is to aid me walking up the hills,' Birgitta said. 'My legs still ache from yesterday. But now that you mention it, perhaps by now we may be in a little trouble. That's if they care enough about the twelve sisters, which, given the situation . . . well. Our paths are set upon . . . no use regretting it. Now, I haven't slept all night, little sister. We should take a rest now the sun is so high and the land is so hot.'

'Where are we going to sleep?' Elysia asked.

'See how the questions out here are more useful!' Birgitta clapped her hands. 'This is what life is about. Remember this. You are a basic, functioning animal looking to survive. You need food, water and rest. Everything else is a luxury. You are lucky in that you have the source to guide you, but you are still the same as every other creature. Easy to forget in our old home, but not out here. To think like this makes you assess the matters of the world with more clarity.'

'That's all well and good . . . but where *are* we going to sleep?'

'Nature will provide.'

And so it did. They found a bed of soft grass in the shade of a willow tree. It was well beyond any villages and by a large pond that gave off a cool draught of air. The sun had grown intense, so the stillness of the scene and the relative sanctuary made sleep come easily. They took it in turns to rest, with Birgitta declaring that her advanced age gave her the right to go first. Before she did, though, she produced a strange arrow from her belongings. It looked much like any other arrow, but set into the tip was a tiny red witchstone.

'It might create a bit of a commotion, that one, so only use it in an emergency,' Birgitta said. And seconds later she was asleep in the long grass.

Elysia smiled and held the arrow for a little while, wondering what it might do and what need there could be for Birgitta to bring such an item, before adding it to the bundle she had been carrying. What could the older sister be expecting on their journey? Not that Elysia even knew where they were going. There was something rather enjoyable about the fact that there was no strict schedule ahead of her. Was this the freedom she had craved all these years?

Her belongings appeared rather meagre when she laid them out on the grass. A large leather satchel with some clothing in, a book of her neatest work from Jarratox, an attractive plain silver ring that Birgitta had given her a couple of years ago, her bow and a quiver of arrows. Elysia realized that she could now wear the ring – the sisters did not condone 'personal decoration' – and so she slipped it on her middle finger.

While unwrapping a small parcel of food containing strips of salted meat, she noticed one of nearby trees was an apple tree, so she quickly gathered some of the fruits for the journey.

For a while Elysia just sat there, enjoying the birdsong and the sound of the wind whispering through the grass around them.

Then Birgitta began to snore like a hog.

A little while later, after Elysia had taken her rest, the two witches prepared to set off again in the afternoon sun. Just before they moved off, Birgitta said to Elysia, 'There's something I have to do before we go. I need to send a message to someone. Would you mind waiting here?'

Birgitta appeared self-conscious, but Elysia simply shrugged and sat back down on the grass again.

The old sister removed her cloak, picked up the Staff of

Shadows and then strolled through patches of herbs and thick-leaved plants towards the glimmering pond. From a distance Elysia watched Birgitta as she hitched up her dress and then waded into the waters of the pond itself.

Birgitta dipped the witchstone on the tip of her staff into the water, circling it slowly, creating a black whirlpool within the waters. The darkness was a sharp contrast to the surrounding water that reflected sunlight. Elysia could not understand the words Birgitta said, but she grew convinced that the older sister was engaging in a conversation with someone.

Eventually she withdrew the staff from the water and waded gently back onto the grassy bank.

Birgitta composed herself and approached Elysia. 'That's that, then.'

'What was that?'

'A chat with an old friend.'

'Who was it?'

'You'll see. But for now, little sister, we have a destination. We head further north, to an old watchtower many weeks away. We should keep to the main roads.'

'For our safety?'

'There's no guarantee the roads are any safer. No, I would like news of what is going on. Jarratox can be selective in providing information and I want to know what's really happening in the world.'

Two nights on the road and there was barely a change in the land around them. They eventually came upon a stream and followed it until it became a river. The sound of the rushing water grew stronger as it crashed along the rocks of the river-bank. Signs of habitation began to present themselves. First a small, rundown cabin. Then, as the oaks became sparser, Elysia could see twenty or thirty structures made of stone, many of which featured round windows and arched doors. Several of the buildings were whitewashed and well-maintained. Among the dirt-track streets, people in brightly coloured clothing were milling about. Some were walking to and from the river, which cut through one part of the settlement where there were larger buildings and the noise of activity. Several colourful boats were moored to one side. Traders were unloading small boxes from the larger vessels and piling them on the riverbank. Towards the centre of the village was a large timber mill, and half a dozen workers were heading to their homes as the sun dwindled behind the canopy of the forest.

'What is this place?'

'It's a village called Dweldor, if my memory is correct. It's strongly affiliated with the Goddess, which is usually an indicator of a few kind folk to be found here. In fact, many people think the place is blessed by the Goddess directly, due to its relative prosperity.'

'I would have thought its prosperity was down to that timber mill and the river to carry away all the wood.'

Birgitta chuckled and placed a tender hand upon the young woman's arm. 'You are as cynical as me. That may indeed be the case, but no doubt we can find food and rest here. Where there are workers there's usually a tavern close by.'

The two sisters strode through the main street, which wound itself in a gentle spiral towards a stone temple of the Goddess, with steps leading up to a large metal door.

Birgitta paused. Elysia looked up to her and then across to the door of the temple. 'What is it?' Elysia asked.

'The door. Do you notice anything strange about it?'

She shuffled forwards to the bottom of the steps and looked

up. 'There are scratches across it. Looks as if someone was desperately trying to get in.'

'Indeed,' Birgitta replied. 'And to add to this, it is not often the doors of a temple are closed, either. The Goddess is usually more welcoming than that. We may find an answer over here.'

Birgitta gestured to the large two-storey building to the right of the temple. Hanging from a metal frame on its second storey was a sign displaying the words 'The Fat Hog' in faded gold lettering on red.

'A promising name,' Birgitta said, 'and something I can aspire to after our travelling.'

Birgitta showed no hesitation in pushing the heavy doors open and marching inside.

The locals were dressed well, in fine and bright tunics, with a couple of hunters in more rugged attire the colours of the forest. Elysia noticed they also looked healthy, so clearly none of the sufferings of other villages she had seen were being felt here.

Conversation petered out around them. Elysia suddenly became conscious of the two sisters' bright blue eyes, and tried not to gaze at anyone directly. The place smelled of spilled ale and sawdust from the mill. An occasional waft of food came through from the kitchen when a serving boy skittered nimbly around the tables to deliver meals to the tavern's guests. A flaming hearth either side of the establishment filled the room with warmth.

'Don't mind us,' Birgitta announced brightly, her accent noticeable different from usual, as if she was putting on a more down-to-earth tone. With all the eyes fixed on them it felt an eternity until they reached the bar. The chatter returned.

Birgitta grinned at the tall, broad woman behind the bar

who looked as if she could wrestle, and likely defeat, most of the men in here.

'How are you for rooms?' Birgitta asked cheerfully.

'We got some.'

'Are they available?'

'Might be,' the woman said gruffly, eyeing them with disdain.

'But not to *our* type?'

'We don't deal with *types*. Only money.'

'Well, rest assured,' Birgitta produced a pouch from her sleeve with a flourish, 'we deal in that too.'

Birgitta dropped the pouch into the hefty hand of the woman, who inspected the contents with all the scrutiny of a master jeweller examining a strange new stone.

'We have a room,' the woman declared briskly, 'for *your* type.'

'That is good news,' Birgitta said. 'We'll just seat ourselves by the fire, if that's okay with you.'

'That's fine. One of the boys will be along shortly. Mainly fish on the menu.'

'Right you are,' Birgitta said, and the two sisters strode away to claim their table.

Birgitta made a thunderous sigh as she sat on the cushioned wooden chair, taking a view that faced the rest of the room. Elysia could feel her muscles aching as she sat down opposite her, staring into the flames of the hearth.

True to the woman's word, one of the serving boys, dressed in a drab brown tunic that reminded Elysia of those worn at Jarratox, came to take their order. There was only trout or perch on the menu, so they ordered one of each, with a loaf of bread to share and a cup of wine.

Birgitta closed her eyes and the two sat in companionable silence. Elysia was so tired that she just stared at the dancing flames. Only when she glanced at Birgitta a few moments later did she suspect that the older sister was not asleep at all, but rather concentrating.

'What are you doing?' Elysia asked.

'I'm listening,' Birgitta said. 'A place like this is a valuable source of news. I'm trying to find out what the local concerns are.'

'Why?'

'Because such knowledge might come in useful. Besides, we've spent far too much time with other sisters, and the world has been experiencing strange events of late. What people say may influence the road we take.'

'What have you heard so far?'

'Not a great deal, I must admit. The timber mill is doing a good trade, as reliable hardwood is in short supply in more northerly territories, well beyond the borders of Brintassa and along the Forests of Heggen where there have been diseases and fires.' Birgitta closed her eyes again and sat back with a peaceful look upon her face. 'The metal merchants and mine owners are all richer than ever, apparently,' she continued. 'This tells me of very industrious activity somewhere, if wood and metal are required. Someone mentioned fighting in northern Burgassia, where Stravimon's borders now lie after having overcome the nation of Fallobrock. Perhaps it is looking to expand further south.'

Food was brought to the table and their conversation ceased. Huge metal plates of freshwater fish in a thick sauce. And a chunk of local cheese was declared 'compliments of the house', which made Birgitta frown. The two sisters ate heartily. Elysia mopped up the thick sauce with hunks of bread vigorously, as if it had been her first proper meal in weeks.

Eventually, once sated, and leaning back in her chair, Elysia asked, 'What do you suppose the cheese is for?'

'A good question,' Birgitta answered, stifling a belch with her fist. 'That barwoman was a surly-looking lady, and I'm not entirely sure she knows what complimentary means. I'd suspect someone has paid her to give us a little token, something to put us in a good mood. To make us feel welcome. Given the wariness with which most people treat us, I can only imagine that someone is likely to ask for a favour at some point.'

Elysia scanned the faces of the locals to see if any of them was showing an interest in the sisters, but mostly the men were looking at her, not Birgitta; some smiled and winked and muttered something crude to their friends. She glared at them icily and the men soon looked away uncomfortably.

'When someone wants us to feel welcomed,' Birgitta added, 'it suggests ill news of some kind, or that they want something from us. Or both.'

'You don't know that for certain,' Elysia said. 'The people here could be genuinely friendly.'

'They could, little sister, they could.' Birgitta smiled, wiping her knife clean on a chunk of bread, and cutting into the cheese. 'But in my experience, very rarely do people offer anything without wishing for something in return.'

The House of Blood

The two sisters were shown to their room on the first floor. It was a simple wooden affair, with just a table, a chest and two small, comfortable-looking beds smothered in red blankets. The window overlooked the side of the temple to the Goddess and, as she peered out of it, Elysia noticed how empty the streets were.

'Does nothing happen here at night?' Elysia asked the boy who had shown them up. 'There's no one outside.'

The boy, who was no older than fifteen summers, was busy lighting candles around the room. When he finished he looked awkwardly to the floor and shrugged. 'Not for me to say. Goodnight, ladies.'

With that he gave a slight bow and walked out of the door.

'*Ladies*,' Birgitta repeated sardonically. 'They most definitely want something from us. I haven't been called a lady in . . . well, never you mind how long, but something is most definitely amiss.'

A few moments later a young woman could be heard outside singing a sorrowful song. Elysia looked down to see a veiled figure in front of the temple. She was holding a censer and leaving a waft of fragrance in her wake.

'I don't understand what she's saying.' Elysia turned from the window and looked across to the bed where Birgitta was resting.

'It's an archaic language called Ascendella, not commonly spoken. Many of the Goddess's books are read out in that tongue. It's said to have come from the end of the First Age, when the seven founding mothers of our world ascended to the seven heavens – if one believes in such celestial matters.'

'I do. Why else would there be celestial witchstones?'

'That's different.'

'How?' Elysia folded her arms.

'They can return people to the source.'

'It sounds very similar, if you ask me.'

'Well, it isn't. The source is where witchstone energy returns once that stone, or a sister even, is broken down. Like a river flowing to the sea. It is a practical matter, not some ethereal nonsense.'

'Anyway, what's the woman saying?' Elysia asked.

'She's singing a lament for her mother who – if I understand the words correctly – passed away two nights ago.'

Elysia looked back at the mourner as she paced past the temple and through the empty streets. 'I don't even know who my mother was, never mind being able to mourn her. Sometimes, when I think about it, I feel like a story with no beginning.'

'Most sisters are the same,' Birgitta sighed. 'I did not know my own mother. We do not talk about it. That way, the matriarch becomes mother to us all.'

'I don't want to be like the others and just accept this lack of knowledge. And I don't like how the sisters always talk about the subject as if we're bred like farm animals. Our lineage is all *known* though, isn't it? It must be. By someone.'

'By someone,' Birgitta added softly. 'So many questions tonight.'

There came a knock at the door. Birgitta rose with a groan as Elysia marched across to open it.

A man stood there dressed in the black robes of a priest of the Goddess. Upon his chest was one of the symbols of the Goddess – seven silver stars arranged in a circle. He was lanky, and the robes did not seem to fit him well, and his gaunt face led to a pointed chin. A bald man, he looked about forty or fifty summers, but it was hard to be certain in this light.

'I am grievously sorry to have bothered you ladies.' His voice carried well and was full of confidence – even if he did not look entirely sure of himself right now. 'But I wondered if I may speak with you in private for a few minutes.'

'Fine,' Birgitta said. 'Come inside, then.'

The man stepped into the room and Elysia closed the door behind him. He moved cautiously towards the window and glanced out at what Elysia presumed was in fact his temple. He whispered something about the seven heavens – a heaven for each of the founding mothers.

'Well?' Birgitta asked.

The man hesitated before he began. 'Your eyes suggest to me that you are witches.'

'We are of the sisterhood, yes.'

He appeared relieved at the answer. 'My name is Helkor, and I am a priest affiliated with our blessed Goddess. That's my temple, just there.'

'It seems we'll be able to look down on you for a night or two,' Birgitta replied. 'So, Helkor, what business does a priest of the Goddess have with two of the sisterhood?'

'I will be blunt with you,' he began. 'We have experienced trouble in the village and I wondered if you could help.'

Birgitta regarded him silently for a moment. 'What kind of trouble?'

'We have seen . . . events. A couple of deaths, even, which are related to such . . . events.'

'What do you mean by "events", precisely?' Birgitta demanded. 'A drunken party that got out of hand?'

'Occurrences, I should say,' the priest corrected. 'Unnatural things have occurred in the village.'

Birgitta gestured for the priest to continue.

'It is hard to say this without sounding like a madman, but one month ago, in a house at the other end of the village, the walls began to . . . to bleed.'

Elysia opened her mouth in shock, but when she saw Birgitta's calm demeanour she composed herself.

'As in,' Birgitta said, 'blood seeping through the walls? Or blood was merely *seen* on the walls?'

'The former. Walls that were absent of any marking began to bleed. The property was used by one of the senior workers in the timber mill. He invited three other people – myself included – to witness the phenomenon for ourselves. And, by the Goddess, we can confirm it is true.'

'You're certain it was blood, though? Not some kind of strange rain funnelling through an old roof, or . . . ?'

'It was blood, my lady,' Priest Helkor said softly, glancing to the floorboards. 'As sure as I am standing here.'

'You mention occurrences, suggesting there were more than one. What else has happened?'

'Two people have gone missing. Good men, hard workers, with families. There was no reason for either of them to vanish, but they did – a week apart. Just no sign of them.'

'What else?'

'You think these are not enough?' the priest asked.

'I think they represent ill news indeed, but I want to know as much as possible.'

'Livestock has been left half-eaten. We thought it might have been wolves at first, but what creature consumes half a bull?'

Birgitta closed her eyes and nodded.

Eventually she said, 'Show me this house of blood.'

Within minutes they were standing outside the property, with a chill wind at their backs and the priest holding aloft a flickering torch in front of the door. It was an old house, made of whitewashed stone. It was on the edge of the village and facing along the road down into the forest. At this time of night all that lay out there was darkness.

'I haven't been here for two days,' Helkor said. 'The owner is a simple elderly labourer at the mill. He's moved in with relatives since the incident.'

The priest explained that there were two rooms on the ground floor, and one large room above, with a small out-house behind and a garden filled with aromatic herbs. Elysia thought it pleasant, if a little eerie at this hour.

Helkor eased open the door and peered through. The sisters followed him inside. The light of the torch barely touched the shadows, so Birgitta pulled out a white witchstone, muttered the words to activate it and placed the brightening gem in the centre of the room. Light began to pulse towards a dazzling state, until it mellowed, leaving no room at all for patches of darkness to lurk. The priest gasped at the act, but then was astonished at what the witchstone had illuminated.

Elysia turned a full circle to see the rust-red colour of dried blood caked all across the walls and most of the ceiling. And within the dark surface were hundreds of words, in a jagged, harsh script.

'It's almost childlike writing.' Elysia marvelled at how the lines seemed to fill every nook and cranny of the blood-covered walls, winding about each other in strange patterns. 'It must have taken hours to complete.'

'No child did this,' Birgitta said. 'An unsteady hand perhaps, an erratic hand more likely, but this language is old. Oh, by the source, these words are *different*.'

'Do you recognize what any of it says?'

'These words are not from our shores, little sister, and most of this is illegible to me. A few phrases I do understand, from books I thought ridiculous at the time, for they spoke of lands no one of this continent has seen in many a century. Here –' she gestured to a place above a small wooden table – 'it roughly translates as *from the darkness beyond*. Here it speaks of the importance of wisdom and knowledge. And here it says . . . well, not very nice things about the people of our land. Barbarians, it calls us. Simple creatures, or something very similar. This large bit on the ceiling could be translated as *We are coming*. Same here.'

Helkor shifted his gaze from the walls to the sisters. 'This is grave news. I swear that these words were not here previously.'

'No, I suspect it's rather difficult to write in wet blood, which is how it would have been when you saw it. When did you say the workers went missing?'

'About two or three days prior to the event here,' Helkor replied. 'So that would be several days ago now. By the Goddess, you don't think that this is their blood do you?'

'I try not to make assumptions,' Birgitta replied. 'But I wouldn't expect to see those men again any time soon.'

'Who could do something like this?' he asked.

'Do you think it's a wicked trick someone is playing?' Elysia asked. 'To scare the villagers?'

'A good line of thought, little sister,' Birgitta said. 'I know King Mardonius is reaching into villages to purge elements of the Goddess. He is a clever sort, and these mind games wouldn't be too much of a leap for him to scare away folk. But, why bother? Why not just send in some soldiers to knock a statue to the ground and torment the locals as he has done elsewhere?'

'Surely you don't think that would be any better?' Helkor asked incredulously.

'I'm not saying either of these things would be good,' Birgitta said. 'My point is that this is complex. Not only do we have the mystery of the walls bleeding, but we have the added sophistication of someone coming in here, writing on every available space, and in a script that is not from our land.'

'So what are you saying?' Helkor asked.

'That I think your village could be beyond salvation. That this —' she gestured to the walls — 'is likely a warning from something beyond the everyday realm. Yes. Whatever did this has given you a warning. My advice is to get the villagers of Dweldor to move on from here.'

'I cannot do that.'

'Why not?'

'Because Dweldor is their home,' Helkor spluttered. 'These are worrying times and food is scarce, but not here. We prosper. We endure. We are safe.'

'That may well have been the case,' Birgitta said. 'But I'd put a good few gold coins on this village suffering something far worse than a shortage of food before long.'

'But—'

'This is merely my advice,' Birgitta said dismissively. 'You may wish to take counsel with the village elders. But I can only say what I think, based on my experiences of such matters. That is why you asked me, isn't it?'

'Yes, but what exactly do you propose I tell people? That a witch simply told us to leave—'

Birgitta's glare cut him short.

The priest gave a sigh. 'I apologize for the way I spoke, lady. This is most distressing for us.'

'And I understand that,' Birgitta replied.

'I simply don't comprehend what is doing this. The events are not enough to cause us to leave, are they?'

Birgitta paced around the room, scrutinizing more areas of dried blood with scratched script. 'A strange and foreign entity did this. The things that have happened to your village so far are possibly a prelude to something far worse. I believe that the creature – if indeed it has a form and isn't some kind of peculiar manifestation – has targeted your village for some reason.'

The priest opened his mouth without making a noise.

'This room is filled with warnings. Most of the words I can understand are of a threatening nature. *We are coming*, it says. Over and over again. The word wisdom is used quite a bit. Whatever did this has made itself clear enough, and I have advised you the best I can. Now, Elysia and I need to sleep. It has been a long day for us and we must be on the road again early tomorrow.'

Elysia could not rid her mind of the sight of the room. It was not that it worried her – she had seen enough strange things in her time at Jarratox – but that it presented a puzzle that she could not yet figure out. Birgitta had made references to an era and country that was rarely spoken about.

Just what was going on?

They had returned to their room and sipped a little of the local fruit wine. Birgitta had not mentioned much else about the incident, and Elysia had not bothered her with too many questions. They were both tired. Candles burned low. The noise from the tavern had dimmed down to the last few scrapings of chairs, and the two were beginning to fall into slumber.

Another call came: a gentle knock. Birgitta sighed a little. Elysia was the one to rise to the beckoning, urgent words.

'Ladies, are you awake? Ladies?'

She opened the door, casting low light onto the form of the bulky barwoman and the priest.

'We have had an incident,' Helkor uttered, without greeting or apology. His eyes twitched. 'There's something out there now.'

'By the bloody source,' came Birgitta's voice, 'what is it now?'

'A creature at the fringes of the forest . . . it has taken a child,' the woman muttered.

'The boy's mother is in hysterics,' Helkor added. 'Please, can you help?'

Elysia left the door ajar and stepped back into the room. She threw on her leather jerkin, which she had only moments before taken off, followed by her quiver and bow. Then she glanced at Birgitta, who was beaming at her.

'This is the result of my education,' she said, winking. 'The other sisters would have held a council for several hours before deciding to do anything.' Birgitta turned to the two at the door. 'Give us two minutes, priest. I am dressed for sleep not for trekking in a dark forest. We'll see you downstairs.'

The man nodded solemnly, and the two villagers departed.

The sisters joined them quickly, Elysia with her bow; Birgitta with the Staff of Shadows and a bag of witchstones. A group of five villagers and the barwoman greeted the sisters, and everyone moved outside into the dark street next to the temple. The villagers all had weapons – axes or swords. Someone lit a torch, but Elysia looked away to the steps of the temple, where a woman was being consoled by the priest. Helkor placed a hand on her shoulder, whispered something and descended to speak with the sisters.

'Come this way,' he urged, tugging his cloak around him.

Everyone followed him through the main street towards the edges of the village on the side away from the river. He pointed to a tree whose trunk had claw marks in it. 'This is where we last saw the child. The boy was originally taken from his home and was spotted here bleeding and screaming. By the Goddess, we came quickly but there was no sign of him. Only these markings by the tree.'

One of the villagers held the torch towards the markings.

'Would you mind moving the flames away for a moment?' Birgitta asked.

Grim-faced, the man did as she requested. From a pouch the older sister produced a red witchstone. She began to the Calorenda spell, for revealing the unseen, and the stone began to glow as it was burning.

This light would be all a lay person would see, but Birgitta and Elysia were able to recognize patches of colour upon the ground where the boy had once been. The pools of orange and red vanished into the forest.

'At least he was still alive at this point,' Elysia said.

'That may or may not be a blessing, little sister.'

'What can you see?' the priest called across.

'Just tracks,' Birgitta replied. 'They won't be discernible to you, but there are definitely signs of the boy having been here.'

'Thank goodness.'

Birgitta held aloft the stone and pointed it towards the east.

Patches of colour had grown elongated, like long, bright brush-strokes made by a painter, indicating the child had been dragged through the trees. Alongside it were ordinary glowing tracks – of something like a tall man – but there was something distinctly unusual about the gait.

'I do not know if the boy will be in a good state,' Birgitta warned the others. 'I do not want to raise your expectations.'

The villagers silently followed the sisters through the trees. Elysia gripped her bow tightly and was ready to draw an arrow from her quiver. The puddles of heat showed up remarkably clearly, although after a good hour they had begun to be less distinct, as if the signs of life had been drained from the child.

Presently Birgitta handed an arrow to Elysia. 'If we see any-thing, use this first. It will cast a magical net on impact around whatever is doing this. I'd like to get a look at it before we do anything else.'

'You think it's close?' Elysia took the arrow and gripped it in her right hand.

'I do.' Birgitta still examined the patches of yellowing light upon the ground, whilst Elysia turned to the hesitant villagers. She did not think they would put their weapons to good use. Behind them was a trail of bright light, their combined heat fierce in the glow of the witchstone.

'Over there,' Birgitta called. Now she pulled out a white witchstone and hurled it into the distance, casting a bright light all around them. The villagers shaded their eyes.

A figure could be seen ahead. It was no savage-looking mon-ster. Instead it looked like a human, except that it was taller, narrower, and with longer arms. It was so slender that it could almost be mistaken for a tree, and looked so brittle it might snap. The figure wore armour of a kind, a dark copper colour, although it was hard to see in this light. Its skin was ghostly pale.

Birgitta nodded to Elysia, who nocked her arrow and watched the thing to see if it was going to move. She released the arrow and the thing darted to the right – and, acting upon instinct, Elysia willed the projectile to follow. It whipped through the air and clipped the creature's helmet; a magical net exploded across its form, dragging it to the ground.

'You.' Birgitta pointed the priest. 'The child is straight ahead. See to him immediately.'

The villagers hurried towards where the witchstone had landed whilst Birgitta and Elysia rushed through the undergrowth towards their quarry.

A wail came from the group and Elysia's instincts told her that the child had been lost.

The sisters quickly found the figure. It was writhing underneath the net and emitting a sharp hiss as static fizzed across its skin. Clad in an unusual armour, with intricate markings all across it, the figure would have stood much taller than Elysia. Its face was gaunt, its nose slender, and cat-like pupils regarded them fiercely. Birgitta tried speaking to the figure using all manner of words, many of which Elysia had never heard.

Eventually one word appeared to make it look her way and change its manner.

'What did you say?'

'It's not important what I said,' Birgitta mused, 'but rather that the word was one from the same distant language that appeared on the bleeding walls.'

'So this thing did it, then. This is who's responsible for the strange events.'

'I cannot be sure, little sister. It is certainly connected with them. But none of this sits well with me. I'm concerned that it's not alone. I'm guessing it has strayed from its countrymen, if one can call them that, and finds itself lost in an unfamiliar land. Which is why it is hunting around this village. Feeding on whatever meat it comes across . . . That was a very good shot by the way.'

'I barely even realized what I was doing,' Elysia replied.

'Good. Instincts, you see. Can't teach you that in books.'

Suddenly the villagers came running over – one man arced his axe through the air to come striking down upon the trapped being. The others followed suit, trying to bludgeon the figure with cudgels or stab it with blades. The thing screamed horrifically under the torment, but Birgitta was having none of it. She held aloft the Staff of Shadows and called out a short spell. The villagers were cast in darkness and their confusion brought their rain of blows to an end.

'You must wait!' she snapped. 'It is likely this figure killed the child, but we know little else about it. Where it came from. What it is doing here. And, most importantly, whether or not there are others of its ilk lurking in the shadows.'

Elysia could see the villagers, but they could not see anything – not even the sisters. They pressed the air with open palms, seeking the limits of their vision, utterly blind to the world around them. The figure on the ground had stopped its aggressive response to being captured now and lay limp on the forest floor, still enveloped by the magical net.

'This thing you have tried to kill in retaliation is a source of information. Think about that before you try to kill it.' Birgitta reversed the darkness and brought the villagers back to their normal vision. They still stared fiercely at the sprawled being, and two men spat at it.

Priest Helkor stepped towards the sisters. 'I will attempt to restrain our people for now. But what do we do next?'

'This is not our business. It is yours now. I doubt you'll get support from King Mardonius's troops, so look to others for guidance.'

'What do we do with it?' Helkor asked.

'It's up to you.'

'Do we eventually kill it or let it live in a cell?'

'Shall I decide what you should have for breakfast as well?' Birgitta snapped. 'You have a mind, priest. Use it.'

Elysia smiled as the priest bowed and scuttled towards the other villagers, who had by now moved cautiously away from the sisters and were seeing to the remains of the young boy.

'Can these people not think for themselves?' Birgitta sighed. 'This is a lesson for you, little sister. When confronted with things they don't understand, it is a rare commoner that *does not* defer to a sister. We are viewed as otherworldly beings with powers of clairvoyance.'

'I'm sure many of the sisters love that they're viewed that way.'

'That they do, that they do . . .'

Birgitta began to stride back through the trees. Elysia looked back and forth between the felled creature and the older sister, and eventually cut through the undergrowth to catch up with her. 'Are we just going to leave it there?'

'Yes.'

'And so we just go back to bed?'

'With any luck,' Birgitta replied. 'And I know what you're thinking. But we simply cannot meddle too much in the affairs of everyday folk. What we have done tonight is more than enough. We ourselves must show some kind of restraint. Otherwise they would drain all the source from our blood entirely. Worse still, we would begin to see ourselves like goddesses among them. I'm not sure which would be a worse fate.'

Another Night of Dreams

The more comforts Xavir experienced, the more he communed with the ghosts of his past. His vision started with a golden dragon soaring through silver skies, and it arced ever higher until it vanished into the sun.

Xavir was there again, back with Clan Argentum. The golden dragon was now a symbol upon his silver shield. The dream was becoming something stranger: not a tapestry of images, but a single clear event from his past. This felt very real.

Upon a commission from the king, he had returned from a skirmish with coastal invaders, after saving a village from their onslaught. Ten of the tribe had been killed, the rest scattered back to the seas. The other Clan Argentum warriors had little ahead of them now, save feasting and drinking large goblets of wine to celebrate this victory and their name being recorded in the king's favour.

Xavir was not interested in the celebrations, though. The fact they would happen tonight simply gave him an excuse to do what he really wanted.

As dusk began to deepen and the wind brought a pleasant chill to the warm autumn air, Xavir washed away the blood from his arms, changed into fresh clothing and headed out of Castle Argentum.

Lysha was in the normal place waiting for him on horseback, a riderless mare at her side.

The two young lovers thundered through the woodlands, the moonlight illuminating their path through larch, ash and elm. As their horses sped onwards, fallen leaves flashed up around them and descended for a second time to the ground that year.

Less than an hour later they arrived at the old ruins from the Fourth Age, a supposedly haunted site known casually as Castle Rapier for its single remaining, sharp-looking watchtower that pierced the sky like a blade. Inside the broken structure, moss carpeted the stone floor, and where there may once have been coloured glass there was now an open, perfect view across a dark lake.

There was nothing around for miles. No villagers would stray so close to a place they feared.

They lit a fire within the walls, which Lysha had taken the trouble to prepare earlier in the day. She unwrapped some of the sweetmeats she had taken from the castle kitchen. Entwined in each other's arms, the two of them ate their food at a leisurely pace. Once they had consumed it they turned their attention to each other's barely restrained lust.

Lysha lifted Xavir's shirt and kissed around his many healing wounds. She bit his shoulder, wanting to add herself to his list of conquests — although Xavir felt it was Lysha who had been the conqueror all along.

He was drawn to some baser instinct, basking in the wrongness, the pleasure, the heat of the firelight. This was not making love, as the poets might like to suggest, but something born entirely of ancient, almost violent passions.

They lay there afterwards watching the moon sliding past the tip of the ruined tower, with the warmth of the fire on their bodies. They did not talk of the future, but of trivial things from their pasts. For Xavir it was a childhood memory of his father being invited to hunt deer in the estates of King Cedius the Wise, or the first time he bettered his tutor in sword training. For Lysha it was when she could first shatter glass with a witchstone, or when she moved an object with her mental powers that the other sisters could not – a rare technique even for the sisterhood.

Lysha spoke of her wish that Valerix would allow her to use more experimental techniques with the witchstones rather than being so conservative. Xavir encouraged her, saying that when Valerix was out on clan business, Lysha should try doing so behind her back.

Then, before returning home, they talked about the future, making ever wilder promises . . . promises that Xavir had known, even then, they would never be able to keep.

'You're awake, then,' came a voice.

'I thought I was dreaming.' Xavir's eyes scanned the cabin. The light of dawn spilled inside, highlighting dust motes above his head. It was warm. There was no dripping of water onto old stone. No guards mocking him through barred doors.

'Wishful thinking.' It was the wolf queen. 'You were staring at the ceiling.'

Xavir pushed himself upright, the bedsheets falling off his shoulders. Landril was still asleep in the next bed. Lupara, however, was already awake and dressed in her fighting leathers.

'Are we expecting trouble?' Xavir asked.

'Specifically now? No. I have my wolves out along the fringes of the forest on guard. They'll call if there's danger. We can have a leisurely morning.'

'Leisure . . .' Xavir yawned and wondered what exactly people did on leisurely mornings. It was three days now since the attack and he found himself filling the free time with training, exercise and meditation. 'I ache. I'm obviously not used to travel and fighting. I need to improve greatly to be what I was before.'

'It's just as well that's all we have planned for the future,' Lupara. 'Grend is cooking breakfast at the moment.'

'He's a useful man,' Xavir replied. 'I had no idea he was so good with food. I remember him saying how terrible the food was at Hell's Keep, but everyone said that.'

A knock came from the open door. Valderon stood there, waiting for Lupara to bid him enter. She waved him through. 'Good morning, my lady. Xavir.'

'You do not have to show such formalities,' Lupara replied. 'We are all equals now.'

'My breeding, my lady. Hard to shake. You are a queen and I will treat you as one.' Then, addressing Xavir, 'Some of the others were keen on joining you for your training today. They've watched the past two mornings and now they're restless. They feel weak. Old.'

'So, I am to become an instructor.' Xavir smiled. 'This is my life on the outside.'

'They would appreciate learning from someone of the Solar Cohort,' Valderon replied. 'I must confess, so would I.'

'You're good enough to teach them yourself.' Xavir weighed up Valderon's humility. 'To be in the Solar Cohort was an honour, but selection was a matter of being on the right battlefield at the right time. It could have been you on any other day.'

'That may be so,' Valderon admitted. 'But you were in the Solar Cohort. And that means far more. Besides, you would have learned and refined some special techniques. Sharing that with the men can only be a good thing.'

'I'll think of something,' Xavir said. 'I taught my boys a few close-quarter tricks in Hell's Keep, should the guards have tried anything, but I shall see about getting them to use blades more effectively. Tylos is already very skilled – take note of that. Whatever he learned in Chambrek will be useful.'

Landril yawned and presented himself to the group, scratching the back of his head. His sleeping robe, which he had left with Lupara on his first encounter with her, seemed far too loose for his slender frame. 'Teaching others what we know is how we thrive as a people. I am happy to advise on languages or mathematics when the men are ready for it.'

'As hard as it is to believe, there has been little demand for those subjects,' Valderon said. 'I'll pass on your suggestion, though.'

Lupara laughed and placed an arm on Landril's shoulder. He almost buckled under her force. 'I will be happy to test you on some forgotten languages. Though I have kept myself active, I have not had the books and debates that I am used to from my court.'

'That would be my pleasure,' Landril said, struggling to remain upright. 'But we should also start making more formal plans. After your morning training, Xavir, I suggest we convene to discuss our next steps. But first –' he strolled towards the door – 'it is time to eat.' And with that he walked outside.

'Who put the spymaster in charge?' Xavir asked.

'He has been all along,' Lupara replied. 'The reason we're all here is because of him.'

Before breakfast, Xavir dressed in his old warrior garb and stood some distance behind Lupara's cabin ready to practise with the Keening Blades. The morning sun warmed his face, and the grass around him was covered in glistening dew.

Closing his eyes, first he removed the swords from their scabbards then replaced them – a hundred times. He missed their ornate casings on the third and eleventh attempts. Even that was still too rusty for his liking. With his eyes wide open, he moved through some of his old fighting postures – descending eagle, bitter wind, thunderbolt – gracefully arcing the Keening Blades through the air, hearing their gentle wails as he did so.

These morning routines were an exercise he had kept up in Hell's Keep, mostly to stave off boredom, but also so that he remained in some kind of fighting form. Xavir had never really needed most of these postures in gaol – and he had never had a sword with which to practise them – but he had persevered in the darkness. His men had likely thought him strange at first, but if they gave a damn about him they never commented on the acts. It felt good now to have the blades in his hands again, to become attuned to the nuances of these old friends.

Later Lupara came to watch for a short while and offered to spar with him. Xavir knew that Lupara had ascended to rule on the merit of her skills in battle, and that she was no token warrior queen. She threw a slender tree branch his way and brought another for herself from the back of her cabin. Her three wolves came to watch impassively as the sparring began.

The two warriors' moves were slow and deliberate to start with, and their fighting styles very different. Xavir's was more graceful and flowing, whilst Lupara's was more savage. They did this for a while, examining the nuances of each other's technique, sometimes speeding up, sometimes slowing, laughing at their own folly or smiling knowingly at each other's clever series of blows.

By the time they had finished, Xavir spotted several smaller wolves watching from the top of the gentle slope behind the cabin.

'Do those animals always watch you like this?' Xavir asked, wiping the sweat from his face.

'They find us fascinating.' Lupara took the other branch from Xavir and the two of them walked towards the cabin. She placed the wood back on the pile at the rear of the building. The three larger wolves followed at a distance.

'I imagine they think us faintly ridiculous,' Xavir added, 'rather than fascinating. Life for them is admirably simple.'

'But they have the same concerns, fundamentally. Food. Shelter. They find companionship beneficial, though. It's useful to hunt in packs.'

They approached the other men in their makeshift camp. Valderon had them running a neat operation. Four tents were arranged equal distances apart. There was no litter or discarded food items anywhere to be seen. Equipment had been stored inside the tents.

In the distance were the remains of the creatures that had attacked them. The men had attempted to haul the carcasses some distance away and set fire to them two nights ago, but the things had taken a long time to burn and still smouldered even now.

Valderon approached and handed over a bowl of stew to each of them, and the small group sat around the small fire in the centre of the camp. The other men were milling about in the grass or ambling further off, where Lupara's wolves were now prowling. The men stared at the lupine beasts with a mixture of admiration and fear.

Landril was keeping busy reading the parchments that Lupara had brought with her, or that had been sent to her over the years, occasionally glancing up to note the blue-green hills that loomed above the forest.

'Fascinating region,' Landril announced as Xavir approached. 'We're technically in Brekkland still, although the Forests of Heggen remain within that nation's borders. According to this old account these forests were once the site of the Second Massacre of the Donevuls.'

'I've heard of that,' Valderon said. 'The Donevuls were a powerful people. They dominated the Fourth Age. Their lands extended across most of this continent. Some of the First Legion tactics were said to be based on their strategies.'

'And yet they were wiped out within a year,' Landril added. 'No one knows why, for the Fifth Age is largely unwritten about. History was almost all shared over campfires like this and not written down for future generations. Which makes tales like this one –' he rattled the parchment – 'all the more rare.'

'The script halls of Dacianara were few,' Lupara said, 'but some treasures remained within them. I brought a selection of materials with me and from time to time I am sent packages that contain a random assortment of materials to engage my mind.'

'Who sends them?'

'As I remain queen by a technicality—' Lupara began.

'The technicality being?' Landril asked.

'That I remain alive.'

'Forgive my asking,' Valderon said, 'but why did you forfeit your throne?'

Lupara glanced to Xavir.

He shrugged. 'You may as well share it all.'

And she did.

Lupara spoke of her part in the tragedy of Baradium Falls from her perspective, telling the truth behind Xavir's actions on that tragic day, but not shying from their shared shame and what it meant for their people.

'We need an army,' the warrior queen concluded. 'And I need you to lead it.'

'Me?' Valderon's head lifted in surprise.

'You were a senior officer in the First Legion of King Cedius the Wise. Do I understand that correctly?'

'Aye, I was, my lady,' he said gruffly, looking down.

'Then you can be the commanding officer in my army.'

'But what about Xavir? His position previously far, far out-ranks mine.'

Xavir gazed across at the man. 'I am in no position to ask for any soldier's respect now, Valderon. My legend is too tarnished.'

Valderon looked as though he would object but realized Xavir was correct. The shame of the Solar Cohort would not be easy to dispel, no matter what the truth behind it. 'And who am I to command exactly?'

'That is the first challenge,' Lupara said.

'If I may interject,' Landril cleared his throat, 'I have spent some time contemplating this issue. Building an army requires funds and soldiers. If we can't sway men through their own belief in our cause then we'll need to hire them. The people who were responsible for Xavir's interlude at Hell's Keep are, it must be said, not exactly poor individuals. By the Goddess, they have immense wealth, and their dwellings contain a great many treasures they have hoarded over the years. We can take our wealth from them. Our funds for payment of soldiers can be found there. Kill two birds with one stone: revenge and resources.'

'Where can they be found?' Valderon said.

'Two of them dwell at Golax Hold and the other has a manse

on the border of Stravimon. In the meantime, we need to start building a reputation for ourselves. We need a nicely foreboding name and I suggest that we hire poets and minstrels to sing songs, through the taverns of Brekkland, Burgassia, Laussland and even Stravimon, about us being defenders of the people, tales about our heroic stands against tyranny and the despotic leadership of King Mardonius.'

'Propaganda, you mean?' Valderon asked.

'Exactly,' Landril replied with satisfaction.

'So what *is* our grand mission?' Valderon said.

'Defending the weak against the strong, of course. Putting a stop to the genocide of the followers of the Goddess, bless her hallowed soul in the seven heavens. We are here to be saviours, of a kind.'

'Grand description for a collection of former prisoners,' Valderon muttered. 'I'm not sure even the best minstrels will be able to spin that into a crusade people will want to follow.'

'But we have the great leader of the First Legion.' Landril prodded a finger towards Valderon, before turning it towards the others. 'And a member of the legendary Solar Cohort, who were tragically betrayed and deceived by traitors. And a famous warrior queen.'

'And her wolves,' Lupara added.

'And her wolves,' Landril repeated. 'It all adds colour to the minstrels' songs. We'll also need weaponry, of course, but we can easily intercept the smiths that send their wares to Stravimon's ever-burgeoning army.'

'You make it sound so simple,' Valderon said.

'Nothing is ever easy. But people are dying across Stravimon and beyond. We passed soldiers on our way here who had been purging settlements of people purely because they worshipped the Goddess. What kind of world is that?'

Valderon gave a glance to Xavir, and their eyes met in the silent understanding of well-travelled soldiers. That was the world as it had always been: people killing each other over things they did or did not believe.

'So we are creating a rebellion against the crown, then,' Valderon said. 'We kill only those in uniforms.'

'Naturally,' Landril added. 'But there are a lot of them in uniforms. There is talk of stranger things afoot, though I have yet to see them fully.'

'Is Mardonius enlisting foreign troops?'

'That has been one of the gaps in my intelligence – so far as I can tell, no foreign king or queen will lend troops to someone like Mardonius. Diplomacy is not his strong suit. He's no Cedius.'

Xavir leaned forwards. 'How many in Stravir City? How many are protecting the king?'

'I think only ten thousand soldiers wait in the city while the rest are engaged elsewhere.'

'As it has always been,' Valderon said.

'You may as well pull out the heart of this murderous rule directly,' Xavir said, 'and strike Stravir City.'

'I hoped you would say that.' Landril smiled and leaned back.

'So what first?' Valderon asked.

'To start the legend of Xavir's return and strike fear into the heart's of his enemies. We go to those who sent him to Hell's Keep and give them a taste of retribution.'

Lupara stood for some time watching Xavir train with the other men in the hazy, mellow sunlight. He was standing at the front of the group alongside Valderon, and the two men proceeded through the motions of various manoeuvres.

Jedral had requested an axe, not something as fragile as a sword, and one was quickly acquired for him. Harrand, Krund and Grend were of an acceptable quality, managing to defend themselves against some of Xavir's restrained blows. Harrand was angered by his failures, whereas Krund chuckled at his own inability to match Xavir. Tylos occasionally came forward to demonstrate variants in the more elegant techniques he had learned in Chambrek, but he was mocked in good spirits by the other men for his finesse over brute force.

'I would be more impressive if it was not for your Stravir steel,' he declared. 'The quality is poor. In Chambrek, our swords possessed a finer edge and a better balance.'

'Is everything bloody better in Chambrek?' Jedral grunted.

Tylos placed a fist upon his hip and gestured towards Jedral with his sword. 'Everything is an art form, in Chambrek. From the way we make swords to the way we make love, and—'

'To the way you pass wind through your mouth all the time,' Jedral put in.

Only now was Lupara accustomed to having Xavir's presence here. The great warrior, in a remote cabin, teaching former prisoners battle techniques – it felt a world away from the man she had known. But he was *here*.

As she walked to her cabin, she recalled Xavir of five years past. Formerly he had been stronger, more muscular. There had been a vigour in his expression, a self-belief that he could shatter kingdoms if he chose to. Loyal to a fault and morally sound, he had been Cedius's iron fist in the velvet glove, the example of Stravimon's might in one warrior. He and the Solar Cohort were all the same: boisterous, lively, inspiring company. Their mere presence could haul an army up off the knees of defeat and turn the battle around to victory. They were living legends.

Today Xavir was perhaps a more dangerous man because he was so much harder to judge. There was bitterness there and a desire for vengeance – who could blame him? But Lupara worried that, whereas previously he would always place the good of the many before his own desires, his anger now would lead him to seek revenge and nothing else would get in the way. At least he had agreed to fight with them.

Lupara entered her cabin and noticed something glowing in one corner of the room, by her bed. At first she thought it was the reflection of the fire. But the flames had dwindled, and after a second's thought she realized what it was.

From under its cloth wrapping she revealed a large, colourless witchstone. It was perfectly smooth and roughly the shape of a teardrop. The heavy end just about fit into her palm. It was a 'fascinard'. That was that the witches had called it.

The object was a useful tool to the sisterhood, a gift of communication between those who were separated. Sisters used them to keep in contact with the matriarch and with each other. Lupara was no witch and had no use for it ordinarily but had been given it at the insistence of a group of sisters who she had served alongside in various capacities over the years. These witches had travelled through her domain and enjoyed her hospitality.

The fascinard pulsed a gentle white light every few heartbeats. It had never done this in all the time she had possessed it.

Lupara placed it on her mattress and closed the door to the cabin. She moved back to see that the light inside the fascinard had begun to spiral into a vortex and move towards the tip of the object. As she brought it closer to her face, the spiral slowed down.

An image was presented, an upward-looking perspective of a woman's face. It was silhouetted against the sky but before long it became clearer.

The woman's mouth was opening and closing, but no sound came. Suddenly the voice could be heard directly in Lupara's head.

'*Your royal grace, queen of Dacianara.*'

Birgitta? Lupara thought. *It's been a long time.*

'*Too long, my lady.*'

Are you in trouble? Lupara thought.

'*I don't know,*' Birgitta said, still in Lupara's mind. '*I have been forced to leave Jarratox. I do not have the time to go into the complexities of the matter. But you should know that King Mardonius has brought the sisterhood under his control, bribed by the gift of a new vein of witchstones.*'

This troubles you enough to leave?

'*It troubles me greatly. Especially with everything else going on in the world.*'

Lupara nodded grimly. *The sisterhood joining forces with Mardonius is a fell blow indeed. But I'm pursuing my own plans to put a stop to his murderous acts.*

'*This is fortunate indeed!*' Birgitta exclaimed. '*By the source, if it is not too late, may I suggest a union?*'

We only have plans to travel north, but we have no time in mind. We are at a very early stage of our planning. Where is your location?

'*We are currently walking towards Dweldor, a village in Brintassa.*'

Do you know of the ruins in Burgassia, Lupara thought, *the watchtower on the shores of the Silent Lake?*

The image in the fascinard paused for a moment, the sound in Lupara's head slightly out of kilter with the movement of Birgitta's mouth. '*I do.*'

Let us convene there. If you reach it first, set up a camp. No one will be present. We will do likewise. And one more thing, Lupara thought. *You mentioned 'we'. Who else is with you?*

'Myself and a reliable young sister — she has studied under me for the past five years since I returned from your service. May I ask who else is in your party?'

I have some men, a former warrior of the First Legion, a good spymaster and . . . you remember Baradium Falls very well, I take it.

'It is hard to forget such a tragedy.'

I have Xavir Argentum with me.

'He's free?'

He is. In a manner of speaking. We set him free.

'Oh.'

This concerns you? Lupara thought.

'No. But it is most unexpected . . . Most unexpected. I suppose it had to happen sooner or later, though . . . I will explain when we meet, for that will be the best time. Till the watchtower on the Silent Lake, my lady.'

With that, the fascinard relinquished the light and became a colourless witchstone once again. Lupara wrapped it up, stored it away beside her mattress and walked to the door.

Opening it, she called for the spymaster. Landril presently came hurrying through the grass towards her, tiptoeing between her three sleeping wolves who were lying by the entrance to her cabin.

'My lady?' He stood before her, his fingers writhing nervously.

'We have an addition to our plans.'

'In what way?' Landril asked, raising an eyebrow.

'We needed magic, is that correct?'

'It would be a necessary evil, certainly. Needless to say whoever we fight against, they will likely have witches.'

'Then we must leave tomorrow morning, for I believe I have located us two sisters to join our cause.'

'And where are we headed?'

'Burgassia, and the Silent Lake.'

For a moment Landril furrowed his brow in thought, before nodding. 'Close enough. I shall notify the others.'

The Silent Lake

Burgassia was known as the kingless realm. There was no governance here, and yet its pockets of tribespeople and agricultural communes still managed to organize their lives without much fuss.

The region had seen many battles across the eras, and it was littered with ruined settlements that had once promised something much grander. Old palaces lay crumbled. Castles were mostly dismantled, smothered by moss and lichen, and their stone reclaimed for building elsewhere. For some time only the Belgossa lived here, a strange, squat race that had vanished by the end of the Sixth Era, and for centuries afterwards the place was steeped in superstition and visions of their ghosts. It did not help that it was a place of regular sightings of stranger beings, although these days it seemed such sightings were more commonplace elsewhere. After a botched attempt at conquest in the Seventh Era, no king or queen had shown an inclination to lay claim to the region. Birgitta had heard that Mardonius had attempted to push the Second Legion through these inhospitable lands – but the terrain here was . . . problematic, to say the least. Swamps appeared where there had previously been none, drowning an entire cohort. Poisonous animals would swarm among the grasses and bring down half the men in unimaginable pain. Senior commanders issued written statements about ghost warriors slaughtering their scouting units. Burgassia itself seemed to conspire against any military attempts to conquer the place. It was not without good reason that many a king decided that ruling Burgassia was not worth the effort.

Birgitta explained all this to Elysia as they continued on their journey along the green lanes. Many days had passed since they had left the village. They travelled on the back of a tradesman's boat for the first part of their trip, making good speed up the river from the village before they needed to disembark and continue by foot. Four days' travel had been saved by doing so, and Birgitta ensured the owner of the boat was amply rewarded.

'Is this the region where the Akero live?' Elysia asked.

They were walking on a woodland track, passing through towering larch trees as dawn brightened, bringing a yellow sky. Every few steps for the past mile had been over some form of ruined stone, as if the ancient cultures were trying to claw their way from beneath to the present.

'We may well see them soon enough,' Birgitta replied.

'Really?'

'I think they're here most of the year. Rumours are that they fly south like birds, but I don't believe such nonsense. People make all sorts of claims about them: that they are celestial beings; that they have come from the seven heavens; that they watch over people.'

'They're none of those things?'

'It's all ridiculous nonsense,' Birgitta said, banging her staff on old stone. 'By the source, they are simply people who try and scrape by in a world that thinks them strange. And they've been here just as long as the rest of us, let me tell you. They've had their own troubles over the centuries, within their own kind and with everyone else. I've read old accounts of their great battles in the sky. Now they dwindle to just a few communities scattered about the continent. Thankfully they're left to themselves, for the most part.'

The path opened out suddenly and they paused.

'Ah, Burgassia,' Birgitta sighed.

'It's a place of great beauty,' Elysia added.

Perhaps half a mile ahead of them, a river ran along the bottom of a gentle slope. Lush grassland surrounded it, rising up gently for some considerable distance towards angular hills. The skies seemed clearer here, with long streaks of cloud dividing half the sky into shades of blue, and the other into greys. On the ground and scattered about the plains were just a few old dwellings, which looked rundown and uninhabited.

'Oh look! There's one of your Akero now.' Birgitta pointed towards the left. There, in the middle of the grassland, was a conical hill with several cave-like entrances at various levels. There was a winged statue upon the eastern slope that Elysia first mistook for one of the Akero, but when she glanced up above the hill she could see one of them for real.

The figure began to drift towards them.

A male with long, brown hair arced through the sky. His wings stretched out several feet either side of him; great feathered constructs that looked much like those of an eagle. He wore brown breeches, but no overshirt, exposing his tightly muscled torso, and he carried a spear in his right hand.

Elysia had forgotten to breathe at the sight of him. He swooped up towards where the sisters had begun to descend from the forest. Banking above them, he scrutinized these travellers, then retreated swiftly to the conical hill.

'I shall never forget the sight,' Elysia said.

Birgitta chuckled. 'He was a handsome one as well. They're not all like that.'

'You've met them before?' Elysia asked.

'Oh I've seen a fair bit of the world, little sister. I've met all sorts. But we mustn't hang about with our jaws hanging down. We've much ground to cross.'

The sisters continued down into the grassland and away from the strange home of the Akero, down towards a wooden bridge that crossed the river and ahead past lifeless old farm buildings. It took longer than Elysia thought to get across the plains. They ate a late lunch of cheese and salted meats acquired in Dweldor, marvelling at the flashes of orchids among the swaying grass. What clouds there had been in the morning vanished, leaving an ocean of blue above.

'What do you think of it?' Birgitta asked Elysia.

'The food?'

'No, this.' She gestured to everything around them.

'It's a wonderful place.'

'No, I mean life on the road. Travelling out to places like this.'

Elysia gave no deep thought to the matter. 'It's the most natural I've ever felt.'

Birgitta scrutinized the response. 'You are a wild creature at heart.'

Elysia laughed. 'What makes you say that?'

'You are not the only student in the past few years whom I have shown the wider world away from the sisterhood. But they were not at home away from home. Not in the same manner as you.'

'The world fascinates me. I must have made it clear that I've never liked Jarratox that much. I had no friends there, not that it bothered me. The older sisters must have found it frustrating that I wasn't good at what they tried to teach me.'

'It's because they never realized the correct manner of teaching. We all acquire knowledge in different ways, little sister. Listening to old women lecture is not the best method, I must admit. Tell me, how did you feel in the village when we trapped that figure in the forest. Scared?'

Elysia took a bite of the tangy cheese and contemplated what it was she had felt that night. 'If I am honest, I felt very little. I was curious. Then when I saw what it had done to the child . . .'

'Go on . . .'

'I just wanted the thing stopped.'

'Stopped. Do you think it should have been killed?'

'That's not my place to say.'

'When I gave the order you had no hesitation.'

'None at all. Human or animal, it made no difference at the point where I released the arrow.'

'If indeed it was a human,' Birgitta muttered. 'But your answer is of great interest.'

'Everything is of great interest to you.'

Birgitta smiled. 'Of course it is! Now, I wonder if on our journey you had to kill another person. Could you do that so easily?'

Elysia shrugged. 'I won't know until I try.'

'You think you will treat it with the neutrality that you have learned so far.'

'It's habit now, isn't it? Emotions come later. You look worried, though.'

'There is always something to worry about, little sister.'

'Is it my willingness to kill another human?'

'Perhaps. Or the lack of hesitation. Your hunting skills may transfer easily, but I always prefer non-violence to settle a matter. I hope you can remember that.'

'I will.' Elysia wondered what exactly the old sister was thinking of when she mentioned killing other people, but there seemed all the time in the world right now and answers would come soon enough. She found herself thinking at a more sedate pace out here. Even though it had only been a matter of days away from the routines and the formal structures of the sisterhood, she was more relaxed, happier. There were no petty arguments, no posturing and politics, no silly rituals and no one fussing over what so-and-so had said.

Suddenly Birgitta looked about. 'Can you hear that?'

'No, what?'

'A noise. Like someone in pain.' Birgitta rose up and peered through the swaying grass. She closed her eyes briefly in concentration, hitched up her skirt and strode to find something. Elysia followed.

A few moments later they discovered an injured Akero sprawled upon the ground. The figure, a female, was unconscious, but breathing; her brown-feathered wing had been broken and her muscled torso was covered in blood.

'Quick, pass me the red stone,' Birgitta snapped, 'the healing orb.'

Elysia rummaged in Birgitta's bag whilst the woman crouched down to tend to the figure. Once she located the round witchstone she passed it over and watched as Birgitta began to warm it in her hands. The older sister moved it across where the blood was coming from, and the open wound, which was about two inches long, began to close up.

'Can you find me a stick – about as long as an arm, no wider than two fingers?'

'There's nothing around. But two of my arrows might do?'

'Very good. Choose ones without witchstones.'

Elysia did as instructed and, knowing what Birgitta was doing, plucked individual strands of grass from the surrounding field. She began to tie the arrows together until they were firmer. She helped Birgitta bind the broken wing to the arrows, which provided support. Once again Birgitta worked the red orb across the injury.

After a while Birgitta seemed to relax physically; her shoulders softened. She rose up. 'There. That will have to do I suppose. Now . . .' She looked up to the sky, which was empty of Akero.

Birgitta raised her staff and after she chanted the spell of the Four Orders a beam of purple light fired into the sky, and her incantations carried in all directions with great power.

And they waited.

Some time later, a flurry of activity rushed overhead. A moment later, a winged figure skipped to a halt just yards in front of them.

Elysia and Birgitta rose up from the grass, startled. There had been no sign of the Akero's approach, no silhouette in the sky.

He stood before them, spear in hand, strange tattoos spiralling across one side of his wiry torso, his chest heaving with breaths. There was an ornate golden clasp to his belt, and he wore black boots and trousers. His gaze flicking keenly between the two of them, the Akero rubbed his short beard with his free hand and grunted something in a language Elysia did not understand.

Birgitta said, 'Strivova?'

'Ah,' the man replied. 'Two women travelling alone. Brings strange omens to a neglected land like this, yes? What are you doing here?' His voice was bass and rich, as if he was some skilled orator or order-giver. There was a slow and deliberate crispness to his words.

'We're simply passing through,' Birgitta replied and gave their names and told him of their background. 'We found her here.' She gestured to the figure on the ground. 'I have healed what I could, but the wing will need time to mend properly.'

In a lurching movement, the male Akero crouched down, his head twitching as he examined the form.

'Wait,' he declared, then picked the figure up in his arms, pushed down with his wings and vanished into the sky.

True to the order, the two sisters waited once again in the long grass. It was an hour until the Akero returned. He arrived as suddenly as he had appeared.

'The family thank you,' he began. 'An attempt had been made on her life, yes, by one of our own. We believe we know who did it. We will undertake proceedings.'

Birgitta remained silent. Elysia didn't know what to say.

'Our people owe you for what you have done, yes. It is not common for ground-grubbers to be so kind.'

Elysia smiled at his choice of words.

'We're not all the same, you know,' Birgitta replied.

'I can see this. The family and the elders would like to speak with you. In person, yes?' His expression remained unreadable.

Birgitta bowed her head in response. 'It would be an honour.'

Entry to the hilltop home of the Akero was not easy for a so-called ground-grubber. No clear path led the way up the conical hill, therefore the sisters were forced to scramble up the limestone slope.

Elysia's astonishment grew with every step. The structure, perhaps a quarter of the size of Jarratox, was loosely based on a network of interconnected cave dwellings, except that the habitation was far more than that. Everywhere she looked she could see jutting branches, thick clouds of twigs, decayed leaves underfoot. Clumps of grass and moss from the lands around had been gathered and meshed together with feathers. Scraps of brightly coloured cloth hung down like ragged banners, each with a curious symbol she took to be part of the Akero language. The whole place was one enormous apartment dwelling of *nests*. Here and there she witnessed an egg that must have been an arm-span wide, and twice as tall. The place had a pungent, earthy tang about it. Curiously there were nests of smaller birds scattered among the homes, though only of one or two species – eagles near to her and, on the far side, vultures.

The Akero was waiting for Birgitta and Elysia as they reached the first proper level of the bird-people, and he led them up a stone stairway that wove around the many levels of the conical settlement.

Breathlessly, and shading her eyes from the sun, Birgitta said, 'It is not at all easy to get here.'

'For good reason, yes,' the Akero replied. 'And humbling, no doubt, for ground-grubbers.'

Elysia could not tell whether or not there was amusement in his harsh voice. The lower levels of the settlement appeared far dirtier and simpler than those higher up. With every level there seemed to be a more civilized and habitable nest, with more refinement and more artefacts within, and she wondered if a caste system existed here. Akero peered out at them from their dark cave-nests, some guarding their young; others were alone, watching the visitors with a head cocked sideways. All of them wore a similar garb of trousers and boots, with different styles of tattoos, and different coloured wings, from white and brown, to grey and black. One or two came into land with fish they must have caught from the nearby river, which from this distance looked like a glistening green snake that lay across the landscape.

The Akero led them to a level that contained a more elaborate stone dwelling, with a large group of figures sitting in a circle around a brazier. Elysia wondered if the heat would ignite the scattering of dried grass, twigs and branches, but it seemed that mainly a heady smoke rather than heat came from it. A deliberately carved viewing hole stretched like a vast window, offering an almost full-circle view of the landscape around them. From the darkness here, the countryside appeared remarkably harsh and bright, so instead she focused on the several Akero. At first glance they all looked of very similar ages – though they were different sizes and colours. When her eyes grew accustomed to them she could see different tattoo patterns carved across their chests, and two of them were clearly more weathered than others. Elysia spotted, in the far corner of the room, the Akero the sisters had found in the long grass. She was resting peacefully on a heavily feathered bed of twigs.

'I could tell you were witches, yes,' the male Akero announced, beckoning them to sit on the ground to complete the circle. 'But we do not often see your kind, not out this way.'

'No,' Birgitta replied, to them all. 'No, I guess you would not. Here we are, anyway, and we mean no harm by coming through your domain. It is an honour to meet so many of you.'

The Akero questioned them intently in front of the group. He wanted to know just how long they had been in Burgassia, the village that they had come from, their ages, their purpose and why they were carrying weapons. Birgitta handled the questions with a diplomacy and respect that was unusual for her nature. She stressed her admiration for their people and mentioned a community of the Akero that she had once met beyond the borders of Stravimon in the north.

Seemingly satisfied, one of the older, grey-feathered Akero spoke. His voice was harsh, but somehow frail. He first apologized for the questions. 'You must understand,' he continued, 'that figures have passed through these plains, yes, who are not on such honest business. Nor are they necessarily from these lands.'

He twitched towards Birgitta, as if having seen something change in her expression. 'What have you seen?' he demanded.

Birgitta explained the recent figure they had captured in Dweldor, and described the strange language written on the bloody walls of the house.

The older Akero listened without expression to her story, and when she finished he simply gave a slight shake to his wings.

'I have,' he began, 'seen more of these figures. We fly afar and go where others cannot. These foreign figures are there. They are warriors, yes. This much is clear. Always, the warriors come first . . .'

'They are not of Burgassia, no,' one of the others added. It was a female, young and with striking brown and white feathers. 'They are from far away. Our elders know nothing of them. These people concern us.'

'Strange figures do not necessarily mean ill news,' Birgitta added. 'You yourself must know that, given how you must appear to the folk of Burgassia.'

For a moment two of the Akero gave something resembling a smile.

'No, you are correct,' said the elder Akero. 'But when they are warriors who come here we must question things, yes? When they carry weapons and walk the shadows we must question what it is they are up to that requires such delicacy. Also, from what you have just told me, they represent a threat.'

'If indeed they are the same figures we're talking about,' Birgitta added.

'From your descriptions I think it so, yes.' The elder Akero nodded sharply. 'I have only watched them from afar.'

'What do they do?' Elysia asked.

'They come to survey the land, young one, yes.'

'They come in twos or threes, no more, from what I have seen,' the female added. 'They are equipped lightly. Carry swords. Prowl the forests of Burgassia, yes. They look at old buildings and pause as if to question their purpose. These are people who want to know the land better, but for what dark means I cannot tell, no. It is as if they are building their knowledge of our world. To report back to whom, I cannot tell either.' For a moment the Akero tensed and twitched her head in response to some far-off sound, but then relaxed once again, easing her shoulders, and focused on the two sisters. 'I have seen forty-one of these figures to date, yes.'

'Forty-one?' Birgitta leaned on her staff. 'By the source, that is more than I thought. Have they appeared recently or is this over a matter of months?'

'Within the last three seasons,' the elder Akero replied, and ruffled his wing feathers. His gaze lingered at her through the smoke from the brazier. 'Like you they travel the old green lanes, yes, but they do not stick to them for long, no. They bring their own food. And when they run out they will not hesitate to kill. I have watched some closely, for many days at a time, yes. They are tall, and pale like the ghosts in your stories.

Sometimes they follow a figure who wears a cloak, and this one seems the most mysterious of them all, yes, and I cannot get close to it. None of us can. These people have not so far tried to come towards our home. If they do, they will suffer. Perhaps they know this. But more and more are coming, yes. And where they tread, the forest seems a sicker place. The trees under which they have slept are beginning to wilt, I can feel it. These people are a poison to our world.'

For some reason Elysia couldn't help but feel a sense of dread at what the Akero was saying. He looked an impressive warrior and his concerns were infectious.

Eventually Birgitta spoke. 'We are on the road to the Silent Lake. We will be meeting with friends, good people. I hope very much that they will know more of what's going on. If we can help you, we will. You have my word on that.'

The elder Akero gazed intently at Birgitta for a moment before nodding. 'You are genuine, yes. This is welcome news, witch. And with such spirits and after your deed with our kin, you are welcome to pass through our land. Furthermore, yes, we offer our service in return. How will you contact us from afar?'

'Oh, that is most kind. And I know of the old methods,' Birgitta replied.

The Akero shrugged without comment, as if he knew what Birgitta meant. The others twitched their gaze to each other, but now appeared uninterested in the conversation.

'We will not keep you,' the elder declared. And with that, the first male who had met them out on the grassland rose from the floor and bid the two sisters follow him outside, into the bright sunlight and back down, until they were out onto the grass once again.

With a swift downdraught, their Akero guide departed wordlessly.

'Well, that was something,' Birgitta said to break the stillness after the departure.

'What remarkable beings,' Elysia replied, as his figure grew ever smaller in the distance. 'We should probably continue on our way. I was prepared to sleep back on that grass, on a warm day like this. Where should we camp?'

'In those hills.' Birgitta indicated to the north with her staff. 'The Silent Lake lies the other side of them, and will take us many more days yet.'

'You may need to cast us in shadow if the Akero suspect there are more of those strange warriors around,' Elysia said it in a matter-of-fact manner, but she still felt a sense of dread — and primitive excitement — at the prospect of a threat.

'Making ourselves unseen is simple enough,' Birgitta said. 'But that is on the assumption that these other beings are not using any nefarious means to watch us. They might be following our every move, for all we know. It's what they're doing here and what they want that really worries me.'

Entourage

Finally. To be on the road again with a sense of purpose. It was, after all, how Xavir had spent most of his life as a warrior. The road had once given him reassurance that he was doing something useful with his time, that through his battlefield victories, he would make a difference to the kingdom. Such sweet sentiments were the echoes from a younger man's mind, certainly, for today he felt very little.

Food and clothing and weapons. Just the bare minimum. Lupara had ensured essential documentation with which she had travelled out here was carried in leather bags, but as far as a royal entourage went, this was lean indeed.

With Xavir and Valderon's help, Lupara had sealed her cabin at dawn by boarding up the doors. The look on her face had been telling. This had been her home for years, her place of solitude among the wolves and the trees, and it was hard to leave such peaceful surroundings for an uncertain future. Xavir wouldn't have blamed her if she had wished to live out the rest of her days in such peace, yet it was Lupara who was pulling everyone else with her in this crusade. Her passion. Her motivation.

The group rode out in a long line, following a hollow way north-east through oak and elm. Few wayfarers had trudged through here in recent times. The sunken lane was covered with leaves and had begun, in places, to be claimed back by the trees as they made arching roofs of their branches and uneven walkways with their roots. Here and there, tucked away upon the higher ground, the group passed ancient burial mounds, with standing stones smothered by lichen guarding the entrances. Yet the road seemed almost enlivened by the queen and her entourage, as if it thrived at being used again. Even the sun came out, poking through the thick canopy with dappled light, illuminating the route ahead of them.

To reach Burgassia would take a good few days' travelling, even with horses. The sight of the queen of Dacianara riding one of her wolves, with another of the great beasts scouting up ahead and another at the rear, was a novelty to the men at first. After a day of nothing but plodding through the forests the sight became as boring as the rest of the journey.

Xavir purposely rode behind Lupara and Valderon, who spoke in polite but short conversations to each other along the route. He was well aware that Valderon felt unworthy of riding alongside the queen, but if he was to lead whatever army she wished to create, he had to get used to it.

They travelled without event for days. Each member of the group took it in turns to stand watch at night, but, save the noise of distant animals, nothing disturbed them. Not even the wolves twitched in alarm.

Despite the seriousness of their venture, the journey was actually rather relaxed. Xavir supposed anything would be better than the confines of Hell's Keep and it showed in how the men slowly grew at ease with one another. Old rivalries were put aside, the banter became more jocular rather than barbed.

One morning the travellers passed close to a small town built around a forested hill. Instead of making their full presence known, Valderon and Tylos went alone to purchase supplies, including much-needed clothing. Soon enough black overshirts, breeches, tunics, leather breastplates and waxed rain capes were distributed. Immediately gone were the haggard, dishevelled men with mismatched clothing; suddenly they looked like a unit. The men laughed at their new attire but it was obvious they were pleased with it. Xavir had learned more about these men in the last few days than he had in the previous five years.

Tylos, seemingly happier than he had ever been, spoke more about his childhood in Chambrek. Xavir asked him about the lands of the hot south, intrigued as to their cultures and history. Tylos spoke of living in vast white stone houses over-looking turquoise seas, each one filled with objects of art. He told tales of poets who sang late into the night and of walking hand in hand with shrouded women among the forbidden drink houses. Chambrek was a place of high culture, he told Xavir, but it was not like that for everyone. Tylos's descriptions suggested that he had come from an affluent background, more so than Xavir had previously realized.

'In more northerly terms,' Tylos said, 'I think you could call me a duke. Or at least that is what I was destined to become. My family knew the royals well.'

'And you decided to become a thief,' Xavir said, 'despite such wealth?'

'It was more the thrill of adventure, I suppose.' Tylos said. 'My brothers called me a magpie when only they knew about my habits. But I grew more ambitious. What is the point of being average at such things when one can really perfect the art? I had no need of what I took, naturally, so I merely disposed of them at random to poor households. Over a year or so I really developed my arts with a sword and dagger – mainly in self-defence. The end came when I was caught stealing a rare emerald from the house of a powerful lady.'

'You kept this from the others in the gaol,' Xavir said.

'Who did speak truly of their past in that place? It did not seem politic to share my tale back there. Besides, I was not the only one to keep a few secrets.'

'No, you were not.' Xavir gave a half-smile.

'I do not understand your military structures, but the way some of these men speak about you, Xavir, you seemed destined to be a Stravir king one day.'

'Something like that.' Xavir rolled his head and shoulders to work out some of the stiffness from travelling. 'It was not meant to be, and it matters little. The world is a very different place now. We're likely to get into some dark situations on the road, Tylos. Tell me. Had you killed before Hell's Keep?'

'I had, when there was need for it,' Tylos replied nonchalantly. 'I like to think I have more finesse about it than most. Those of us from Chambrek bring poetry to the blade.'

'There may not be much call for finesse so much as being a blunt instrument of war.'

'Such are the ways of the north.' Tylos indicated up ahead with his chin. 'Let us hope that this Valderon will use me wisely. You trust him, despite your once rivalry?'

Xavir shook his head. 'Doesn't matter out here. He has things to prove to the world, and to himself. And he is a man of honour. I can't ask more than that.'

It had taken them a great many days, but soon the travellers crossed the unmarked borders of Burgassia. Landril guided them along the ancient routes, identifying tracking signs and markers left by generations of wayfarers. To the trained eye, symbols and runes had been etched by blades into the base of towering beech trees, informing of dangers ahead and clear roads. In this way their passage remained unobserved.

After days of sunlight, a fine mist developed, which morphed into a steady rain, and their new waxed capes proved invaluable. The hills seemed lost to the blue-grey light that was beginning to fade from the day and they decided to make camp at the mouth of an unused cave. The sandstone cliff face provided ample shelter from a gathering storm.

Lupara and Valderon took their turn to patrol the road up ahead. Peering out at the driving rain outside the cave from the warmth of their fire, Xavir glanced across to Landril, who was busy scrutinizing a map in the half-light.

'We may be seen on this road,' Xavir said. 'I wish to strike at the targets as stealthily as possible, and any strange band of travellers will soon be commented upon.'

'Perhaps,' Landril said. 'But I don't think it'll present too much of a problem, even if we are spotted. Lupara and her wolves are well camouflaged, and we are simply a band of mercenaries on the road. No one knows our identities. We're unlikely to be approached unless by soldiers, and I suspect we would have a few surprises for them if they tried anything. You'll get to spill blood soon enough.'

'How far until we reach the first traitor?'

'Well, first we get to the Silent Lake tomorrow morning. I would say two days beyond and we may arrive at the manse of General Havinir.'

'Will he be there?'

'He retired from the main army shortly after your incarceration, and now he sees to other affairs of state and so forth. But he spends most of his time there.'

'It's almost as if you've planned it this way.'

Landril grinned.

'I've no doubt he'll have protection, though,' Xavir muttered. 'I have no wish to slaughter good men if we can avoid it. Some of them might wish to join us; others may resist. Is there a more direct way through his defences? I'd prefer to kill him quickly, and then see what options the others offer.'

'I will have to assess options at the scene,' Landril said. 'Unfortunately, when I tried to glean more intelligence of his manse in the various records across Stravimon, I had difficulty in finding them. It is often the way with those favoured by Mardonius. Information on key people vanishes from official records.'

Xavir turned his attention back to the flames once again, and Landril returned to his map. Eventually, Valderon returned to the light of the fire and shook his waxed cape free of rainwater. 'Xavir. Landril. Something you should both see.'

Xavir rose and commanded the others to remain by the fire. He and Landril followed Valderon along the muddied path around the face of the cliff, down towards the old road that cut through the forests of Burgassia. Light had mostly faded from the day by now, yet the glistening tops of trees could just about be seen against the indigo sky.

The three joined Lupara, who was standing with her wolves where the road began to bend gently to the right and slope upwards. Water continued to trickle down the road, though the rain had ceased.

She indicated something in the distance. There, over half a mile away, was a cluster of torches glistening like starlight.

'Have you identified them?' Xavir asked.

'Yes,' Lupara said. 'They are refugees. About five hundred of them.'

'Five hundred?' Landril asked. 'From where?'

'From what I could hear from their accents, Stravimon,' Lupara said.

'Unlikely.'

'*Bahnnash!* They were from Stravimon,' she repeated.

'But did they speak aloud of why they were on the road?' Landril asked.

'No,' Lupara said. 'Only of when they were going to get off it. There was a priest among them, attempting to spread cheer, saying that the Goddess was watching over them.'

'I can guess why they're here,' Landril breathed.

'Explain,' Xavir said.

'Mardonius rids the lands of the Goddess's followers. It has been a discreet purging until now, or so I thought. A town here or there would see the subtle incidents that I have already spoken about, but to get hundreds on the road, that must mean incidents of greater violence.'

'Your king. He has visited great acts of horror upon your people,' Lupara said.

'He's no king of mine,' Xavir replied.

'Nor mine,' Valderon agreed.

'I would have thought your people would have been happier if Cedius and the Solar Cohort were still around,' Lupara said. 'This is the result of what has come in their place.'

'We cannot reverse the past. What's done is done.' Xavir turned to Valderon. 'Your thoughts on the matter?'

'I think we should speak with these people,' Valderon declared. For a second he waited as if for a signal to continue, but none came from Xavir. 'And if we are to defend them, or their kin, then we must understand what is going on and get information from them.'

Xavir tilted his head back towards the torchlight. 'We should only have one of us go.' It will be less of a threat.'

Landril was about to speak but hesitated. 'It should be you, Valderon,' he said after a moment. 'If you are to lead whatever army we build, then the people who we are charged with defending should become familiar with you. They should know your name at least.'

'And what do I tell them?' Valderon asked, not quite committing to a full laugh. 'That a non-existent army will save their homeland?'

'Give them hope,' Landril said. 'One man's actions can turn a whole war. Xavir could tell you that.'

'So be it.' Valderon began to march up the slope towards the refugees.

Refugees

They waited in the dark and the cold for Valderon to return. Landril's breath formed wraith-like mists in the air. The scent of the pine forests travelled down on the breeze. In the distance was the sound of crude laughter coming from the other men. Landril was longing, more than ever, for a warm dwelling, for fine wines and for conversation that did not end up in the gutter. Still, at least the rain had ceased.

Instead, in this darkness, he dwelled sadly on what had forced innocent people from the only homes they had ever known. Landril sighed, wishing he had done things differently. Had acted sooner. But even his own father had been resolute that such persecutions would pass, that it was not the first time people had spoken against the Goddess and her followers. He believed that good would prevail and the masses would rise to defend those in need, probably right up until he himself was 'disappeared'.

'I'll never understand humans,' Landril complained. 'Innocents killed, countries overrun, persecution and discrimination, and no one does anything. Why do we wait too long to put right such wrongs? Read any historical text and it's the same throughout the past. We never learn. Why do people simply continue with their lives and not question these incidents?'

'For two differing reasons,' Xavir replied. 'The first is that most people expect decency from others. They expect that any negativity is down to a few dissidents and will be quickly over with. The second reason is that they might simply be afraid of what will happen if they *do* speak out.' Xavir remained expressionless throughout. 'At the end of the day, we are animals still. We have base urges. We fight for territory, for possessions, for beliefs. Rarely do we sit and discuss our way through a situation. People like Mardonius will only ever understand the language of war.'

Landril fidgeted impatiently. 'How long do you think Valderon will be?'

Xavir shrugged. 'As long as he needs to be.'

'Has he experience of this kind of reasoning with people?'

'He was an officer of the First Legion,' Xavir said. 'He would have been out on campaign, where not everything involved slaughter. A good part of it was negotiating – whether with those above, his own men or civilians they needed aid from. People do not get to such stations in life without a certain amount of skill in debate.'

'I can see you're confident of his abilities,' Landril said, 'despite being rivals.' His fingers began to twitch again.

'We *were* rivals. And as rivals, I studied him as an enemy might. He's smart. He looked after his men, as did I. He was a diplomat as much as a dark threat to others. He made wise decisions not to retaliate over simple matters, because he realized we still had to live alongside each other.' Xavir gave a sad smile. 'It seems trivial now to think about it. To be challenging one another over pointless things for so long. Back then these small conflicts were our world and they were everything to us. Now we have much bigger battles to fight.'

❧

The moon eased between the clouds. Up the road the line of refugees had long since paused. Landril remained anxious, but did not see any concern on the faces of Xavir and Lupara. Both of them had found rocks by the side of the road to sit on and remained in silent contemplation, the wolves at Lupara's side.

Landril was eager to press on, keen to start their defence of the people. Although part of him wondered what it would take to stop the killing. Armies. Combat. Politicking. Getting to Mardonius in order to spear the cancerous growth at the centre of the continent.

Standing in the middle of the road, Landril clicked his fingers and stared forwards. The torches still glistened. Somewhere in the distance an animal of some kind cried out and he glanced to the wolves to see if they looked up, but they were not bothered and consequently Landril decided neither was he.

Lupara began to tell a tale of refugees in her own kingdom, just a couple of hundred years ago in the Seventh Age. A crisis had been caused by a shortage of food and lack of support from surrounding kingdoms, and many of her people had fled beyond Laussland to the coast. From there they sailed to find a new home and were never heard of again. Smaller wolves went with them, and Lupara liked to believe that somewhere a new colony of the animals was established. That way the wolves of Dacianara, even if they weren't the great ones, would ensure the blood of her country endured on far-off shores.

'A lack of food is sad enough reason,' Xavir commented, then casually indicated the refugees in the distance. 'If these people are indeed fleeing persecution from their *own king*, then it is a tragedy.'

'It was not quite this bad when I left,' Landril replied. 'There was a will to resist and the purges were certainly not on any great scale. A village here. A farm there. It was more *subtle*. Threats and intimidation, for the most part.'

'We will see what Valderon has to say,' Xavir muttered, glancing along the road to his right. 'He's on his way now.'

Eventually Valderon returned with the ill news that Landril had expected. They walked back to the cave and sat down by the fire.

A few of the other men, who lay on their blankets, came forwards to hear his news.

'Well?' Landril asked.

'They are the people of the town of Marva,' Valderon said, 'on the southern borders of Stravimon.'

'A populous town,' Landril explained. 'Ten thousand people dwell there.'

'I know, spymaster,' Xavir said. 'Many of us are not foreigners to Stravimon.'

Landril tilted his head in apology. 'It was also one of my favourite places. It was a bastion to the Goddess, a town of priests. Other religions were welcome there, too – there were great theological discussions in stone courtyards—'

'Not any longer,' Valderon said. 'The settlement is no more. Priests of all kinds are guiding great numbers of people to flee in different directions from the town for safety. This –' he gestured behind – 'is just one group of refugees.'

'Mardonius?' Xavir asked.

Valderon nodded. 'In the past few months, his armies have ransacked every border town and driven out believers not just of the Goddess, but of any kind. Marva was the last great hope, but even with the militarized faithful they could not withstand the force of . . . well, not exactly the legions.'

'How so?' Xavir asked.

'Some were of the legions, undoubtedly, though their numbers are low and spread widely. A priestess of the Goddess here told me that there were *new* figures among the forces, pale-faced and clad in armour she did not recognize and bearing symbols she had never before seen. These people were using unusual magics to pummel the town's defences. She guessed that Mardonius had hired mercenaries from abroad.'

Landril saw the deep frown on Xavir's face. 'You disbelieve their words?'

'They saw what they saw,' Xavir replied. 'I simply do not understand why a king in charge of a large army has need of others fighting on his behalf. Especially those from a different country.'

'His men have deserted him?' Lupara suggested.

'That's a possibility,' Landril replied. 'I heard tell of soldiers refusing orders. Not forgetting a great many will be followers of religions, too. Mardonius would have need of hired thugs.'

'They also spoke of a warrior in red armour,' Valderon continued, 'some bedevilled being who had been seen leading this purge. He does not seem of the new force. He is described as representing Mardonius – presumably he has some close relationship with the king.'

Landril recalled the glimpses he'd had of this figure. 'Mardonius's bodyguard.'

'They called him the Red Butcher. They said he was responsible for the greater part of the killing,' Valderon continued. 'Him and a few horn-helmed comrades. He came to town on a black steed covered in red armour too. His steps were so heavy, they said, that this Red Butcher could be heard stepping through buildings and along streets by those who tried to hide from him. They said his armour glowed.' Valderon paused. 'They said he was a warrior from hell.'

Landril wanted to know what Xavir made of this, but Cedius's finest remained as impassive and unreadable as ever.

'These refugees have carried the burden of watching their families being killed openly in the streets, their idols torn from temples and their holy books burned by magic. That's a heavy weight to shoulder on a long trip. Now they're taking time to rest up the road. They have travelled for a great many days already, and come far enough for today.'

'Do they have protection?' Lupara asked.

'Not as far as I could see. A few crude swords were piled up on carts, but there were very few among them who looked strong enough to use a weapon well.'

'There will be those among them,' Xavir said, 'who know how to fight. They'll be cloaked and concealed. You'll see the face of an ageing man or woman, but the people of Marva always kept these priestly warriors among their own. What they may lack in apparent strength, they more than make up for in resolute faith — and that helps in a battle line, I can tell you.'

'I remember such tales, though I've not had the honour of fighting with them,' Valderon replied. 'I said to the priestess that I did not travel alone, and that my friends would keep a watchful eye on this side of the road if required. She thanked me for my kindness, but I am certain did not quite believe me. They have little enough reason to trust armed men, having just encountered an army of them who forced them from their homes.'

Xavir nodded grimly. 'Keep a sharp eye out tonight. They are not the only ones who need to watch the road behind them.'

Screams

For a moment he thought he was dreaming of howling winds or banshees, but when Landril awoke he could most definitely hear screaming.

Dawn was breaking and a soft light filtered through the leaves covering the cave mouth. The rain had stopped. The smell of damp vegetation was pungent. The scream was piercing and continuous.

His heart thumping, Landril shoved back his damp blankets and scrambled to his feet.

Xavir was already fixing his weapons into place.

'Get up, all of you!' Xavir shouted to the others. The prisoners scrambled clumsily to their feet. Tylos leaped up with grace. There was grumbling and complaining as they searched for their weapons in the dark, Harrand moaning he was not as nimble as he'd once been and that things didn't work as well as they should.

'Get the fuck up anyway, lest you let innocent women and children die because of your laziness. Arm yourselves and get to the road,' Xavir commanded.

'Why bother?' Harrand said.

'Because I'm telling you to.' With that, Xavir strode through the overgrown path.

Harrand grunted something non-committal after he had left. Landril knew that Harrand had been in Valderon's gang and did not easily bow to Xavir's command.

'You don't have to stay with us if you don't want to,' Jedral replied, waving him on. 'I don't know about the rest of the boys, but I could do without your moaning.'

'And where am I to go?' Harrand said. 'We haven't come close to civilization yet.'

'Just fuck off.'

'Or what?'

'Or I'll—'

Tylos stood between them and pointed his sword to the road. 'We have orders, gentlemen. We should be fighting to save civilians, not trying to kill each other.'

'I can, black man,' Harrand began, still eying Jedral. 'But I'm tired and have had no breakfast.'

Jedral stood fuming, his arms away from his body as if anticipating the fight.

Landril did not hang about to discover the results of the discussion.

He looked across the blade to Davlor, who was wide-eyed and busy scratching his arse. Together they followed after Xavir.

Still the screams came, each one making his heart lurch, wondering what they'd find on the road ahead. Valderon and Lupara had not been at the camp and he guessed that at least they were out here in the pale light of daybreak somewhere. Landril strode through the undergrowth and out to the road itself. He looked into the distance.

Xavir was nowhere to be seen, only civilians rushing towards him, many looking fearfully over their shoulders.

A woman in a shawl, her eyes wide with terror, carrying a child, scurried towards Landril. He shouted to her, asking if she knew what was going on, but she simply shook her head, focused solely on guiding her young to safety, and rushed past him as if he wasn't there.

Then Landril heard another noise, a strange metallic wailing, a rush of magic-blessed swords carving the air, followed by grunts and wails of agony. He ran towards this noise through the parting mass of fleeing bodies, gripping his sword tightly.

As if it would do any good, he thought. *As if you could do anything useful for these people right now.*

The enemy presented itself: strange, pale-faced beings in bronze armour, about a dozen of them with curved blades, spreading their formation out wide with an unnerving unison and grace.

And there was Xavir, grim-faced, black-clad and glorious in combat.

He glided through the throng of newcomers, scattering the warriors. With bursts of startling agility, he severed heads and cleaved through bone, crippling the attackers with the merest flick of his Keening Blades. Bodies collapsed around the former commander of the Solar Cohort like puppets being released from their strings.

Only then did Landril notice the dead civilians on the road, the bodies mauled and disfigured. Family members or friends had gathered around the dead. Upon spotting more of the strange enemy moving in from the trees adjacent to them, Landril shouted for people to leave the dead be, and flee into the trees.

Some would not listen. He physically dragged one wailing woman away from the body of her husband. Most followed Landril's lead as the attackers came towards them, but one tall man remained behind to tend to his child. A pale-skinned warrior strode forwards and cleaved upwards with his blade, severing the grieving man's torso and shoulder. He cried in agony as Landril hopelessly ran towards the attacker, who was now flanked by his comrades.

By the Goddess, where are the others? Landril thought. No sooner had he thought of them than they were there.

Tylos and Jedral spearheaded their way towards the strange warriors. Tylos's swordplay made a quick wound in his opponent's neck and, from behind, Jedral slammed his axe down across its still-open eyes to finish it. The two men nodded to one another and separated to face the remaining warriors.

Landril moved on through the scene, which by now had been reduced to a handful of bodies on the road with all the activity further up. Xavir had chased his fleeing opponents into the fringes of the forest, where the wails of the Keening Blades and the clattering of metal on metal could still be heard.

Eventually Xavir stepped back onto the road, a macabre look of exhilaration upon his blood-caked face, his body heaving with breaths. There was no one left to fight and so he ran with long strides towards the east. The sun rose higher now, breaking the treeline, lighting the scene like an inferno. Landril could only follow Xavir with the other men in tow, conscious that he had not yet raised his own weapon.

Further up the road, where Xavir was heading, stood Valderon and Lupara. The wolf queen's beasts had formed a wall of fur, fang and muscle against a line of the attackers, blocking their charge on the refugees. However, to his right, facing the trees on the other side, Landril noticed two robed and hooded figures defending the refugees. Blades flashed in the morning sunlight as they waded into the armoured foe striding from the darkness of the trees. The fabled warrior priests of Marva were busy protecting their flock.

But even they paused in their defence as Xavir Argentum started towards them. In his black war gear Xavir was like a figure risen from the underworld, and he dealt death just as efficiently.

Lupara's giant wolves parted as he strode through to join Valderon and the warrior queen as they fought more armour-clad figures, at least twelve of them facing the three warriors.

Landril followed cautiously, knowing he'd be little help but wanting at least to even the odds a little. As he did so his professional instincts kicked in and he made a careful study of these strange new warriors. Their movements were fluid and elegant, almost as if dancing, which was surprising given the heavy-looking armour they wore. Their skin was pale, some almost white; their hair, too, was so blond it could have been silver. Among them was a hooded figure in black whose gestures caused the ground to shift where directed. Civilians were tripped up by the strange magics, and a priest of Marva found his ankle trapped in winding roots grown from the earth.

Lupara and Valderon launched into the remaining warriors, whilst Xavir started to advance menacingly towards the magician, who, suddenly, appeared to divide into two and then three, before uniting as one again many yards from where Xavir now stood. Then, with a blue flash: it vanished.

In the absence of this figure, the rest of the enemy fell quickly and by the time Landril reached them, there was no attacker left standing.

Xavir paced, looking down at the warriors he'd just slain, then scanning the road for others. Lupara bid her wolves forwards to scout the forest.

'I killed twenty-three in all,' Xavir called over. 'How did you fare?'

'Fourteen,' Lupara replied.

'Twelve,' Valderon grunted. 'Though to be fair I was dragging civilians from the road and tended a few of the injured.'

'Excuses,' Xavir replied. The two men smiled darkly at each other and then surveyed the scene. 'They had a leader. Whoever it was, it was a magic-user. Did you see how it moved the earth?'

Valderon nodded. A moment later he sighted the warrior priests of Marva, and headed towards them.

Landril stood agog at the carnage, and in particular at what bloodshed Xavir had caused in response. What the spymaster had witnessed in the prison escape was nothing. This morning Xavir had shown a raw and mesmerizing violence, a glimpse into the man's capabilities.

What must the Solar Cohort have been like?

Landril simply looked at the sword in his own shivering hand. Then he surveyed the damage the attackers had caused. The Marvans slowly made their way back to their families and friends, or crouched by the roadside inspecting bloodied faces. The sound of wailing for the dead soon echoed throughout the forest.

'Despite the sad losses, we did well this morning, spymaster. Things could have been far worse.' Xavir reached over his shoulder and placed one sword back in its casing. He examined the other, checking its surface.

'I didn't do much,' Landril said, his hands still shaking. His feet were numb. His spine felt as if it was on fire. 'But you, you knew what to do instinctively. You knew where to go and how to react. I should have done more.'

'We each have our skills,' Xavir said, peering at the blade.

'Do not feel the need to burden yourself with concern about my opinion. It does not suit you.'

'Even so,' Landril said, 'I do not often feel this useless.'

Xavir gestured to a fallen enemy with the tip of the sword. 'Be useful, then, and identify the markings on his armour. I've no idea what it says. You are a man of books. Tell me.'

Landril crouched down with Xavir to inspect the figure. It was slender, with gaunt cheeks and small eyes. The armour was bronze, with serrated panels across the shoulders. Around the edges of each panel was a strange, elongated script that he did not recognize at first. The letters – if indeed they were letters – had been etched in fine detail, a display of remarkable crafts-manship. There were no other obvious symbols or insignia upon the armour.

'Let's look at another one,' Landril said.

They moved to a different body; this one's head had been separated, leaving just the armour. Landril winced as he inspected the blood-drenched metal, but again there was the same script, finely carved within the surface around the edge of each and every panel.

'Would you mind removing one of those plates of armour?' Landril asked Xavir. 'Try not to make too much of a mess now.'

Without comment, Xavir placed a boot on a warrior's neck and levered a shoulder panel free with one of his blades. Underneath was a material that looked like leather. He handed the piece of metal to Landril, who stepped over to the original corpse. He placed the panel alongside the corresponding plate upon the other.

'Ah,' he said. 'Different script on this one. I suspect every panel may be differently worded.'

'But what does it say?' Xavir demanded.

'I do not know,' Landril said. 'Not yet, anyway. I need time to think. This is a strange language indeed.'

Lupara continued consoling many of the mourning civilians, whilst Valderon approached the two of them. Landril half-heartedly listened in on the conversation, whilst attempting to decipher the script.

'There were two warrior priests protecting the people of Marva,' Valderon began. 'It seems they're satisfied there's no one else trying to attack. We can relax, for now.'

'You did well, Valderon,' Xavir said. 'The skills of the First Legion have not left you.'

'I did what I could, mainly by reflex more than thought.'

'Years of training will do that.'

'An old Clan Gerentius trick, too,' Valderon said. 'My father would ensure we had surprises during our youth when we fought alongside the clan. He said it was to keep us on our toes, to think quickly. The old rascal.'

'It must have worked.'

'To some extent. But it was one of the wolves that first noticed there was something amiss before the sun rose, so I cannot take too much credit.'

'What happened?'

'Lupara and I were on watch again. About an hour after you went to rest. The queen sent her animals either way up the road and one into the forest. The creatures returned simultaneously, as if they had communicated with each other over great distances. The big wolf, Vukos, showed signs of anger from up the road and we followed him for some time. The winds were strong this morning, and blowing in the direction of where the attack came from, so Lupara thought the wolves were unable to scent the threat properly.'

'Hmm,' Xavir said. 'They could have concealed the scent and sight of their attack easily with magic.'

'It is possible. But we drew swords and waited. It was too far away from the civilians for me to be able to warn them.'

'Nothing you could do,' Xavir replied. 'Then what?'

'As dawn broke, we saw them, two dozen figures in bronze armour marching up the road. They'd taken the advantage of travelling by night.'

'Wishing to remain unseen, I can only presume,' Xavir said.

'As I thought too,' Valderon continued. 'It was as if they had been hunting these people.'

'More actions that make no sense,' Xavir said. 'To purge a town of people is one thing, but to hunt them down? There seems little strategy to it.'

'As I was saying,' Valderon continued, 'two dozen of the figures came towards us, but I could see others well out of our reach, flanking us. Lupara had the wolves form a defensive line in front of the refugees whilst we intercepted them.'

'How did they strike at first?' Xavir asked.

'Organized. They formed tight cohorts and held their swords behind their shields. It was too efficient, though, because, as you know, while that is a good way to engage with an army, not so effective against two individuals. We did what we could, but with only two of us and the wolves holding the front it was not possible to save everyone.'

'You did what you could, and that kept a good many alive.' Xavir placed a hand on Valderon's shoulder. 'You fought well, friend. And the people of Marva saw you fighting to save them. Just look around.'

At this, Landril also looked up. Men and women were standing behind the two warriors and staring at them in awe. Now that the warriors' conversation had momentarily paused, the civilians took the opportunity to express their gratitude. Xavir stood indifferent to their behaviour, though Valderon seemed almost embarrassed by the attention.

Landril, meanwhile, turned his attention back to the script. Occasionally the shapes of words – or what he thought to be words – seemed familiar. He was conscious that he was starting to read words that were probably not really there in the armour. He was projecting realities that did not exist.

'Why can I not understand this?' he hissed. 'Goddess save me, why?'

'Talking to yourself?' Xavir said, breaking his attention away from the crowd that now surrounded Valderon.

'I have a mastery of codes and many languages,' Landril said, 'and still I cannot fathom what these symbols represent.'

'Give yourself time,' Xavir replied. 'We still have plenty of road ahead of us.'

'I need more armour to examine,' Landril said.

Whilst civilians buried their dead and gathered their meagre possessions, the spymaster drifted from corpse to corpse, scrutinizing armour and levering up small pieces to study.

'Landril, you look like a grave robber,' Tylos called out to him.

'You should know, thief,' Jedral replied, leaning on his axe-head. The other men laughed.

'Pardon me, but I never stole from a corpse,' Tylos protested. 'And if I did steal, it was from the wealthy. Usually quite attractive ladies, for that matter . . .'

Landril ignored their discussion and pressed on with his quest to find a word he could decipher, a key that would unlock the language before him. From body to body he wandered, his fingers tracing the line of scripts. He pressed his fingers into his face, concentrating on the fine detailing, looking for symbols, letters, anything that might give a clue as to where these attackers had come from. Sunlight glimmered off the armour, which appeared to have the reddish hues of copper more than bronze as he had first thought. *A strange alloy, this.* Now and then he'd catch a glimpse of one of the refugees, a confused and pitiful gaze.

He loomed over one corpse which did not seem so badly injured.

Suddenly it opened its eyes, revealing an almost cat-like pupil, and Landril scrambled back with a gasp.

The figure pushed itself upright. It moved its hand along the ground, searching for its blade. No sooner had it attempted to get up than Jedral stepped forwards with his axe and swung it into the thing's face with a firm crunch.

Landril turned to Jedral, his heart thumping.

'You're welcome.' Jedral grinned. His usual maniac look almost seemed appropriate in these surroundings. The bald man strode off to join the others.

Landril regarded the corpse once again. Whatever these things were — they wanted him dead. And everyone else. That was reason enough to find out as much as he could about them.

No Time for Kindness

'We should move on,' Xavir announced.

It was midday and the heat had grown to be unpleasant. Lupara's entourage had removed themselves from the scene, back to their own encampment by the mouth of the cave. They were seated on the ground, around the remnants of the fire, eating meagre rations.

'Can we really abandon the people of Marva now?' Landril asked.

'Yes,' Xavir replied.

'But do they not need our support?'

'Very likely,' Xavir said. 'But I cannot hang about for them, spymaster. If I had to wait about for people to feel safe, I would never have seen any victories in battle. No matter what you do, they will not feel safe. Not now, not for weeks, likely not for years. They have seen their families hacked down before their eyes. Do you think that our presence would relieve them of their sadness?'

'No,' Landril sighed. 'But there might be more attacks.'

'There likely will,' Xavir replied.

'By the Goddess! Do you even care?' Landril snapped. He began cracking his knuckles and twisting his fingers.

Valderon placed his heavy hand on Landril's shoulder. 'You

have a good heart, spymaster. But Xavir is right. With all the will in the world, we cannot help them any further like this. If we are to help the people of Stravimon, and the followers of the Goddess, we must see to it that this cleansing is ended. To do that, we need to move on and find the people directing these armies. Besides, they have those priests among them who know their way around a blade. They are not entirely without protection.'

Landril sighed and stared into the smouldering remnants of the fire. Crows called out nearby, and the tops of the nearby trees stirred in the wind.

'Let us see to the horses,' Xavir pointed to Tylos and Grend, and the three of them walked away.

Meanwhile, Landril examined a plate of armour yet again, watching the sunlight glisten off the surface.

Seated across the expired fire, Valderon began to clean his blade with a cloth. The wolf queen moved to sit alongside the former officer of the First Legion.

'You fought well again today,' Lupara said to Valderon, placing her hand on his arm. 'I am glad we can trust you.'

Landril noticed the way she looked at the warrior, and gave him a dark and disabling stare. There was something other than admiration there. It was still admiration, though of another kind entirely.

If the wolf queen felt any thing other towards Valderon it was not surprising. Landril would confess he was a fine-looking man, broad-shouldered and darkly featured.

Valderon, however, could only roll his lips thinly and glance at the blade without comment at first. Landril saw Lupara's smile. If nothing else, she enjoyed a challenge.

'I heard you were exiled from the legions and put into Hell's Keep because of love,' Lupara began. Landril wondered where she was going with the statement, because she was fully aware of how he had ended up in gaol.

'I would say,' Valderon replied, 'that the whole incident concerned *passion* rather than love. Passion speaks of the intensity involved at all levels. Love needs time – and we never had that.'

'Do you regret your actions?'

'No,' Valderon replied eventually. 'Because, despite all the complications of the incident, I rid the world of an odious man who treated his wife abhorrently. I gave her justice, in the end.'

'And yet you ended up in prison for it . . .'

'I did. I could have been executed. Made an example of. But I was well regarded by many and I had friends in the First Legion who had better friends than I did. Cedius showed mercy, thankfully, and instead I was sent to that rotten place. I lost years from my life there, but at least I am still alive. So no. No regrets. And I would do it again, should the same situation ever arise.'

'Do you feel your reputation ever suffered?' Lupara focused on his face. This brave soldier of Cedius's army could barely look back at her. Landril wondered if it was shame from years in prison, or simply that even a mighty warrior could not meet an intense gaze from the dark-eyed wolf queen.

'The opinions of others can change with the winds. And it is an ill-fated ship that sets sail in such transient conditions. So, though I do not like to think opinions matter to me, I do wish to claim something of the honour I once had. A reason to walk with pride again.'

'That honour of which you speak,' Lupara continued, 'was that being in service to a king?'

'A great man, yes. But the honour came from serving the people of my country. We protected the borders and kept their homes safe. We brought them wealth and glory from other lands. I am simply grateful for the chance to serve them again, with or without their knowledge.'

This seemed to satisfy the wolf queen. The lines around her eyes changed as he spoke and she patted him gently on the arm, then rose and strolled back towards her wolves.

Valderon, meanwhile, continued to check the sword blade, running his thumb along the edge.

Lupara's small force went on the road again. Xavir was eager to reach the Silent Lake before nightfall and no one was in disagreement, save Harrand, who by now had grown into someone who complained at just about every decision that was made. And Davlor, who simply wanted to sleep some more. Landril knew the young farmhand was lucky to be alive. Without any talent for swordplay, the man had survived several skirmishes now and the consensus from the others was that he must have the luck of the Goddess. Then Davlor would yet again say something to reveal his stupidity, and Landril wondered how long that luck would last.

Their horses continued along the main road through Burgassia for a few miles before taking a track that brought them yet again to the ancient, rarely used hollow ways, sunken routes that left the forest high around them.

The day continued to be clear and warm, bringing an almost dream-like tranquillity to the land of Burgassia. Though Landril knew the country had experienced a strange history, today it had blossomed into a quiet garden nation: rolling meadows of bright orchids and softly stirring grasses; untilled earth that had been invaded not by armies, but by vibrant poppies; ancient forests shading strangely shaped fungi. Landril did not know half of the plants around him, and he wished he could spend a little time making notes. There would be treatments and poisons aplenty out here.

Alas, it is not to be.

It was the following day that they actually reached the region around the Silent Lake. The forest died back, and vegetation was sparser here, leaving bare, grass-covered rock undulating for miles. Knuckles of granite protruded from the earth, leading towards steeper mountains in the far distance to the east. The grassland was full of yellow-green and ochre tones, a sharp contrast to the cloudless sky. Now and then the wolves headed up to one of the higher plateaux, nosed the air and scoured the landscape with their fierce gaze.

They continued all morning until, by noon, the landscape dipped to reveal a vast, dark lake surrounded by a lip of pale stone shore. The lake was more than a mile wide and, sheltered by the surrounding land, it remained utterly calm. A few tributaries on the opposite slopes threaded into it. And on the western shore, standing on terrain that jutted out into the lake like an upturned palm, stood a crenellated tower.

'That's the old watchtower in the distance,' Lupara announced. 'That's where we must meet our guests.'

'Are our guests armoured?' Valderon asked, gesturing to the hillside. Four hundred yards to the right was what appeared to be a group of armed figures advancing towards them.

'They should not be,' Lupara replied.

'Then I'm guessing we can expect trouble.'

Earthcraft

Xavir and Valderon marched down the steep grassy slope, careful to not lose their footing. Lupara's wolves bounded ahead of them, with the warrior queen calling for caution as she came behind them. Behind, the prisoners trudged through the long grass.

The sun was bright and falling, meaning the strange figures were almost lost in the hazy shadow of the hillside. But it was clear they were on a direct course to intercept them. *How long have they been here?* Xavir wondered if they had been tracking them all along.

As Xavir examined their adversaries across the steep slope, he reasoned there was more cause for concern. Among this band of five was one who appeared cloaked – like the figure from the previous night, who had wielded magic with alarming skill. The wind around this region was utterly still, and he could hear the harsh and guttural utterances of their language.

Lupara's wolves thundered across the distance and lunged to savage the pack of warriors. But the robed figure held aloft a hand and then shoved the air, as if slamming back a door. The wolves howled and were sent reeling backwards, sliding down the grass towards the lake. With quick readjustments, the animals regained their footing just before they reached the rocky shoreline, but they were a good hundred yards away by now and visibly confused.

The alien warriors withdrew their swords and, whilst protected by the barrier, formed a tighter formation behind their shields. The ground between the forces began to shake and crack. Xavir was forced to leap from one splitting ridge of grass to another. As the magician continued its despicable earthcraft, Xavir found himself isolated, forced to take routes away from his attackers so that he was not swallowed up in the unnaturally swirling rivers of mud between. Valderon stood on the very opposite side of the warriors, and was also unable to find a simple route to fight.

'It's futile!' Xavir bellowed.

'There's no way to them,' Valderon replied.

Lupara, who was close behind, managed to leap across to a bank of grass alongside Valderon. The group of prisoners, Landril alongside them, scurried in her wake, but could not catch up. Between each of them were steaming rivers of earth, which drifted like a mobile swamp.

There appeared to be no way to the foe.

'I can help!' bellowed a new voice. A woman's voice.

Xavir turned, startled. Behind him, at the top of a hill, stood a woman in a fluttering blue robe. She was gripping a staff in one hand.

A witch.

Scowling, Xavir watched her hold her arms aloft like a prophet. In her hand was a witchstone, though he could not discern the precise colour. She began to chant. The air changed, voices began to travel much further. Clouds massed from nowhere and the hillside began to shudder.

Xavir stood with his Keening Blades wide for balance as the rivers of mud began to coalesce into something firmer. The witch touched the head of her staff into the mud and a flash of yellow light skidded along its surface, rippling along the hillside.

A moment later, with the other end of the staff, she tapped the substance firmly, indicating the issue had been solved. Xavir wasted no time. He threw himself across the dried mud, which was like walking on the bark of a flat tree, and made haste towards the enemy.

Ahead of him, the robed and bronze-helmed foreigner made frantic hand movements, which occasionally made the ground shimmer, full of promise, but nothing happened. Xavir jumped across onto their island of earth and slammed the Keening Blades towards them. The invisible barrier that protected the creatures shone, then shattered like glass into nothingness, leaving the warriors fully exposed to Xavir's onslaught.

Two of them held aloft their shields futilely – and died.

Another screamed hideously in Xavir's face as Valderon's blade thumped into its back, whilst Xavir blocked the strike of the fourth with one blade and sliced its throat with another.

Only the robed figure remained, but with a deft twist of its hand it vanished to twenty paces to Xavir's left, further down the slope and towards where the freed prisoners were running to join him. 'Stop the bastard!' Xavir shouted.

One of the men, Krund, raised his own blade to strike the figure. But with a dismissive gesture the robed figure gripped the air and the old man dropped his weapon, clutched his throat and was tossed backwards, screaming, into his comrades.

The figure stared at Xavir as he made his way across the awkward terrain. Whether or not it smiled, Xavir could not tell, but the thing vanished in the blink of an eye and Xavir slipped to a halt.

Breathlessly, the two veteran warriors strode across to the

rest of the group, while Lupara advanced up the slope to greet the witch. The skies cleared. The ground began to heal itself and the mud cracked and split like rotten floorboards. Xavir could see the broken body of Krund, the former lawyer, and realized the worst had happened.

Tylos leaned over the corpse. 'He is dead.'

'You don't say,' Davlor muttered. The young man placed his sword in the ground and began scratching his crotch.

'At least it was quick.' Tylos added.

'That damned thing,' Valderon muttered. 'I don't know if it was the same one who was present last night, but it looked the same.'

'Magic,' Xavir sneered. 'It is a hideous thing.'

'Not all magic.' Valderon gestured with his blade to the woman Lupara was embracing.

'Even that,' Xavir replied morosely. *Especially that.* 'They may well be human. They may look human. But those who handle magic are a different breed entirely. They're not to be trusted.'

Pyre

Funerals were all much the same to Xavir. His view on death was that it was inevitable. Deal with it, or fear it – and if you did the latter you might as well be dead anyway, for all the good it did. Xavir carried Krund's corpse down the shoreline. The men had gathered wood and made a pyre. Their comrade was placed upon it and embraced by the inferno. There were no words – just a solemn silence that spoke of the understanding that any one of them could be next. Jedral's face was hard and emotionless; Xavir knew just how long Jedral and Krund had known each other. The two had spent much time together in Hell's Keep. Xavir, too, had enjoyed Krund's easy company, and knew the old lawyer would be missed.

A smoke trail rose like a thread dangling from a needle, up on the still air of the Silent Lake. Xavir didn't trust this windless place. It was full of ill omen. Blue sky deepened towards nightfall. The flames died down and the men covered Krund's charred remains with rocks from the shoreline.

All the while, Xavir eyed the witch suspiciously. Lupara knew her, that much was obvious, but no formal introductions had yet been made. Xavir was fine with that. He had no time for those belonging to the sisterhood. Not any more.

Eventually, when it was clear they had finished with Krund's pyre, the witch and Lupara approached.

'I was leaving you to mourn your friend,' the witch announced.

Xavir just scowled at her.

Lupara seemed a little taken aback by his response but continued nonetheless. 'Xavir. This is Birgitta. I have known her for many years.'

Xavir regarded the woman's blue eyes and nodded coldly.

'Quiet one, isn't he?' Birgitta said to Lupara.

'I have little to say,' Xavir said abruptly.

'Well, a *thank you* wouldn't go amiss now, would it?' Birgitta replied.

'It was useful.' Xavir had little interest in pandering to the old crone's pride.

'Useful, was it?' Birgitta scoffed. There was a question in her direct gaze that unsettled him. 'Useful indeed.'

Lupara stood alongside Birgitta, her arms folded. 'Xavir has never fought alongside those of the sisterhood.'

'I never had need to. Life is far simpler without magic.' Xavir spat on a rock and gazed across the still waters drenched in shadow, refusing to meet the witch's eyes. Sweat cooled across his back.

'The lad has a point,' Birgitta added cheerfully. 'I have done you no harm, warrior, so why the barbed tongue?'

Xavir ignored her and turned to his men. 'We must set up camp here tonight,' he told them. 'It is too late to travel. I suggest a night watch upon the hill's summit.' He turned to face the blue-eyed woman. 'I am more than happy to take first watch.'

Lupara turned to the witch. 'You will stay with us?'

'No, my dear lady,' she replied softly. 'I ought to return to my companion, on the far shore. I only left her to follow those creatures — wanted to see what they were up to. On the morrow, we will meet around the bend in the lake. By the watchtower.'

The woman smiled to Lupara and turned to walk back along the shoreline. Lupara scowled at Xavir, who simply shrugged.

Davlor slunk alongside his former boss. 'Why d'you hate 'em so much? Thought a man like you'd like a bit of magic on side to weight the odds in your favour.'

'You know nothing about me, Davlor,' Xavir told him with a scowl. 'And you know nothing about witches. If you did, you'd want them as far away from you as I do.'

As if Xavir had disturbed some tomb within his mind again, his night was haunted by the past. Through a fog, faces came and went.

He saw blades through closed eyes, blades slicing at his neck, people screaming his name, a woman's voice calling to him through all of this. Then he saw his brothers-in-arms, again, the Solar Cohort: his comrades hanging from ropes off a tower in Stravimon, their necks broken. Their bodies swaying. And one by one, their eyes opened, their heads tilted unnaturally towards him. And they spoke his name: *traitor*. And suddenly they all had her face. Her.

Xavir bolted upright with a gasp. Sweat dripped from his face and began to cool immediately in the night air. His chest heaved as he glanced across to the campfire nearby. The others slumbered peacefully.

'What ails you?' It was Tylos, sitting cross-legged nearby. Xavir stared at him. 'Forgive my intrusion. I have returned from watch, but before I woke Jedral I saw you thrashing around as if you had daemons behind your eyes.'

'They have been my companions for many years,' Xavir replied, resting his head on his blankets.

'I have heard of such things,' Tylos began. 'The poet Krendansos once said that all events in life are like blades on the bark of a tree. A few gentle strokes allow for effortless growth. Carve too hard and a tree can bleed, maybe never recover. I take it you have memories like that?'

'Not all poets from Chambrek speak shit, then,' Xavir said.

Tylos smiled at that. 'I will take that as a compliment. But your sleep betrays you, Xavir. Who is this Lysha you cry out about in the night?'

Xavir stared hard at him, but the black man's gaze and manner were soft in return. 'A mistake. A long time ago. That's all. Quoting Krendansos's words, I am a gnarled oak ill indeed from wounds.'

'Yet you do not have nightmares from your days of battle? That is what I find most peculiar.'

'If anything, I am wounded from the absence of war, Tylos. Warfare, battle, the killing was all normal for me. I need the danger and the blood-letting to thrive.'

'And Lysha? What part did she play in your wounds?' Tylos asked.

'Enough.' Xavir sighed and rolled away with his back to the Chambrek man. 'That's not something I'm prepared to talk about.'

'I understand,' Tylos said quietly. 'But just remember, such wounds can fester and poison a life if they remain untreated.'

Xavir said nothing and stared into the dark until the sun rose.

Memories

The past few days had remained largely uneventful for Elysia, save the excitement of Birgitta's excursion the afternoon before. Birgitta had only intended to look at the path ahead while Elysia set up camp and prepared food. Elysia had started to worry when the older woman hadn't returned after a couple of hours and was about to set off after her when Birgitta arrived, flushed by her recent adventures. Elysia was astounded by the description of the magical battle and wished she had been there to see it herself.

Birgitta said that her friends would be joining them soon, but obviously felt no need to fill in any details about them. Elysia was used to that, frustrating though she found it: the sisterhood were experts at keeping information close to their chests.

The weather was calm here, with blue skies and warmth, so Elysia occupied her time by practising with the arrows around the shoreline, willing the shafts to follow the line of the water's edge with considerable success. Birgitta meanwhile, made frequent trips to the top of the watchtower in order to study the steep hillside. She seemed jumpy about the arrival of these new companions, and when she did come down to the lakeside and watch Elysia practise gave her a look of such uncertainty and even sadness that Elysia wondered just what these newcomers might be bringing with them.

Eventually, when the shadows were short and the heat too intense for them to do anything practical, Birgitta scrambled down from the watchtower and announced: 'They're here. Come on, let's gather up our belongings.' Birgitta stepped around the fire, gathering a few small books into her bag, and picked up the Staff of Shadows.

Elysia had nothing really to tidy up, so, seated on the ground, she raised her knees to her chest, shaded her eyes and peered up at the surrounding hills. There, to the south, she could see a line of figures zigzagging down the steep hillside.

When they reached the shoreline she stood up next to Birgitta, who started flattening her hair with her fingers.

'You seem nervous,' Elysia said.

'No, little sister,' Birgitta replied. 'Perhaps a little anxious.'

To see the normally unflappable older sister like this was infectious, and now Elysia began to felt unsteady at the newcomers' approach.

It wasn't long until the travellers came close. They were mostly riding on horseback; but three of the animals were clearly wolves not horses, and a woman was riding one of them. There were broad-shouldered men with swords among them, but Elysia remained calmly waiting.

The wolf-riding woman commanded a halt and only three men dismounted alongside her. The four strode along the shoreline towards the two sisters. Two were tall men who looked as if they were professional soldiers, one was thin and nervous-looking, and then there was the black-haired woman who, in warrior garb, looked every bit as formidable as the two tall men.

Birgitta walked forwards to meet them.

'My lady. Queen of Dacianara.' Birgitta paused. 'I am so glad you *all* came.'

The queen placed a hand on Birgitta's shoulder and the two embraced as if old friends.

When Elysia examined the newcomers she noticed the soldier who had two swords sheathed behind him was staring at her with an intense look that was a combination of shock and fear. She scowled back. He was nearly as old as Birgitta, with dark brown hair that reached his shoulders, and a strong, slender face.

The man muttered one, breathless phrase: 'You . . . Lysha?'

Elysia frowned at him.

Birgitta suddenly stepped between the two of them, 'Xavir of Clan Argentum. You may wish to temper your hatred of the sisterhood.'

Xavir replied but his gaze remained fixed on Elysia. 'I had good reason to hate you all. All but one.'

'Well, now perhaps it will be all but two,' Birgitta sighed, shaking her head as she patted Elysia on the shoulder. 'Xavir, allow me to introduce to you to Elysia.' Birgitta bowed her head. 'Your daughter.'

'I'm sorry I never told you,' Birgitta told Elysia, as if struggling to find the right words. 'But he was in Hell's Keep. By the source, I never dreamed you would meet. And you always felt so different from the others. I didn't want to compound that.'

Elysia ignored her, still trying to gather her thoughts. Birgitta had ushered her and her supposed 'father' into the watchtower, whilst the others remained by the sisters' camp. Elysia was hunched up slightly, staring only at the shoreline.

'Xavir, you obviously remember Lysha,' Birgitta continued. 'I am glad of that. She deserved to be remembered.'

The warrior closed his eyes for a moment and let tension fall from his shoulders before opening them again. 'You knew her?' His words were tainted with anger.

'For a while,' Birgitta replied. 'We were friends. Though I was older than her.'

Xavir looked at her fiercely. 'You speak of her as if she was no longer here. Explain.'

'Lysha was allocated to your clan to study under Valerix. And I believe Lysha and yourself engaged in something of a . . . forbidden relationship.'

Xavir scowled at her. His eyes straying to Elysia. 'Forbidden only in the eyes of *some*.'

'Indeed,' Birgitta said with a sigh. 'Some of the sisterhood's rules may seem arbitrary to outsiders. But then sadness came, didn't it?'

Xavir swallowed. 'Lysha was taken from me – dragged away by other sisters, under the cloak of night. Kidnapped. Stolen.'

Elysia looked at Birgitta in surprise. How could she not have told her any of this?

'By the time I even knew what was going on, she and the other witches were miles away. I heard her screams, in my head, through my dreams. It was as if she had projected them there. Even now they come back and blend with all my other madnesses. I searched for her for three days and three nights. I even travelled to your foul isle but no one would let me in. I would have torn down the walls if I could have done.'

'I understand. Lysha was no one's property,' Birgitta replied, 'but you are right. She was taken from you.'

'Then what happened?' Xavir demanded. 'She does not live. I can tell from the look on your face.'

Birgitta's expression was full of sorrow.

'It was a tragedy,' she said sadly, 'and one of the sisterhood's greatest failures. What you could not have known was that, when she was taken from you, she was with child. Your child.' She gestured to Elysia. '*This* child.'

'Tell me what happened to her,' Xavir muttered.

'You have to understand that the sisterhood has its own ways of breeding. Select men are chosen at the right time, when our scryers deem it so, and only then are the sisters permitted to bear their children. It follows the pattern of the source. To have a child outside of these strictures breaks all the laws we abide by and this caused great concern. But Lysha was strong-willed and refused to let the child be aborted. Alas, during the birth, Lysha was lost to the source. But the child! The child lived and breathed. There was talk of ridding the sisterhood of the baby. Having it adopted. But our soothsayers claimed there were portents that could not be ignored and so the matriarch at the time declared the child a gift from the source and she was kept among us. Her lineage was *never* to be discussed.'

Elysia listened in stunned silence as Birgitta's words pierced her like an arrowshaft. A thousand questions ran around her mind.

'For a while I looked after her. I nurtured her. Only a few of us knew of her true parentage, many of the other sisters did not trust her. She is not like the other sisters. Elysia can use magic, but has little interest in it. Her skills lie elsewhere. She has become something of a warrior witch, like in our legends, but the sisterhood was right to be cautious – here is a young woman they cannot control so easily.'

After a silence, Xavir unbuckled the huge swords around his shoulders and freed one of the encased weapons from its leather strap. He handed the sheathed weapon to Elysia. 'Draw this sword,' he said, without emotion.

Elysia looked questioningly to Birgitta, who nodded encouragingly.

She took the resplendent weapon and placed her hand upon the hilt of the blade. It began to glow and, with a noise like a sigh, the blade eased free from its casing.

'It's true then,' Xavir breathed. 'Only those of my bloodline can use this weapon.'

It was all too much: she dropped the sword from nerveless fingers and ran.

Deciphering

'Well, what did you expect?' Landril asked Birgitta.

Landril, Birgitta and Lupara were seated around the remains of the sisters' campfire, where the shoreline met a bank of long grasses. The other men had long since meandered up the shore to take in the tranquil surroundings. Xavir and Valderon had been standing atop the watchtower for hours, surveying the lake, while the wolves were dozing in the shade of the old structure.

Birgitta said nothing in response.

'I'm sure she'll return soon enough,' Landril suggested. 'It's not as though there's anywhere to go around here. We're a long way from anywhere.'

'She needs space,' Birgitta said. 'The little sister is forced to reassess who she is and where she has come from.'

'While I sympathize, we do not have the time for such introspection,' Lupara said. 'Tell me. Is she any good in a fight?'

'Oh yes,' Birgitta assured them. 'Though it concerns me a little, she's got the potential to be better than any sister I've known in combat, if indeed that is a thing to be celebrated. Those of the matriarch's cabal had many words with me about her over the years. They think she harkens back to a time in the past where sisters were wilder and more aggressive. Warrior witches, they were known as in the Seventh and Eighth Ages. I was asked many questions about her development. She was not interested so much in memorizing lines from books, like many of the others; instead I took her out into the forests to learn the old arts. And she adapted quickly. I may have done the wrong thing, but she learned and she enjoyed. Elysia did not know about her background, and about what the sisterhood thought of her. She does not use the witchstones in the traditional manner, and that worried the matriarch.'

'And you can use them well enough still?' Lupara asked with a gentle smile.

Birgitta winked. 'I'm not quite ready for my funeral pyre, thank you very much.'

'You two have much history together,' Landril observed. 'You appear as old friends.'

'We are,' Lupara began. 'Birgitta was one of the sisters who was assigned to my people.'

'Rare for a Dacianaran to take one of us,' Birgitta said, 'though I suspect it was as much the matriarch's doing to keep me out of trouble as it was a way of building bridges between our two peoples. Alas, when Lupara chose exile, I had to return to the sisterhood, where I became a blue robe. A tutor to the younger sisters, as is the way of those who return. From thereon I continued to keep an eye on Elysia. It was wonderful to see how the girl had grown. Now she's a woman, of course. Seventeen summers – can you remember what it's like to be so young and healthy? Quiet, thoughtful, and devastating with weapons.'

'Do you think it was right to bring her to Xavir?' Lupara asked.

Landril had been astonished at the revelation that Xavir had a daughter, and that she was in fact a witch. Xavir had made it plain that he distrusted magic. Hearing his story, it was now obvious why.

Birgitta let out a deep sigh. 'What choice did I have? I need to explain what has happened to the sisterhood, for I believe there is significance to my tale.' She looked thoughtfully into the distance. 'I understand why Xavir hates us. I am no moralist, but he does not seem to be a man who loves often. To have the only woman who touched his heart taken away without a goodbye . . .'

'Well, we cannot know his mind,' Landril said.

'No indeed,' Birgitta replied. 'Now tell me: what are we to do from here and what is the plan? We have none, it should be said. We needed to get away from the sisterhood.' She explained about the movements to deepen the allegiance with Mardonius, and that a dozen sisters had fled in the night in protest.

'We share a common dislike of Mardonius,' Lupara said.

'Dislike?' Landril waved his hand through a clump of grass to one side, beheading a few stems. 'A whole book could be written on reasons to loathe that evil bastard's existence.'

'You and I,' Birgitta announced, 'will get on very well.'

Landril explained about the path from Baradium Falls to the Silent Lake; about how Xavir's incarceration and the fall of the Solar Cohort was to clear the way for Mardonius to take the throne. Mardonius became king, instead of Xavir, and Cedius's honour was tarnished the day the Solar Cohort was shamed. He'd never been the same afterwards. Landril revealed the names of those involved and that they were the next destinations.

'And Xavir is to lead this army?'

'No,' Landril said, leaning back on his elbows. 'Valderon will lead. He was an officer in the First Legion, many years ago. Xavir has no appetite to be at the head of an army again — those days are behind him. He does want to kill Mardonius, for all the man did to the Solar Cohort and all the innocents he has since slaughtered. But our first step is to get the resources we need to build the army.'

'He is still dressed as if he's in the Solar Cohort,' Birgitta said.

'Cedius himself presented me with the items. I am not sure he ever truly believed the Solar Cohort were to blame for the tragedy. And he truly viewed Xavir like a son. He gave me the Keening Blades to look after. I took them with me to Dacianara for a short while, before I too left for the good of my people. Baradium Falls was such a low time.'

'He seems a changed man from the one I heard described in the legends,' Birgitta commented.

'Time changes us all,' Lupara said with a smile. 'And the world has changed with us.'

'That it has, Lupara, that it has,' Birgitta said. 'But certainly not for the better.'

As the light began to fade from the sky, Landril was proved right. Elysia returned to the camp.

The campfire was burning once again on the shoreline, and everyone gathered around it; free men, sisters and queen alike. Elysia said nothing upon her arrival, though the voices around the fire went quiet for moment. Landril watched her take her place alongside her mentor without a word. Birgitta gave her a tentative smile and handed her a strip of dried meat. Xavir glanced at her only once – a lingering, painful look – but then returned his attention to the fire.

With sharp features and raven-black hair, Landril thought she was a pretty girl – if one was into that sort of thing. He noted the stares from the other men and thought it worth advising them to steer clear from any tawdry comments. *Goddess only knows what Xavir would do to them . . .*

Eventually Valderon asked the young sister about her bow and her apparent ability to bend arrows. She replied politely, 'I have trained for about half as long with swords, too, but it is with this bow that I feel most comfortable.'

'Such a skill will come in handy,' he said, indicating the weapon she had placed alongside her. 'Who crafted your bow?'

'A man called Dellius Compol,' she said, glancing to Birgitta for confirmation she had got the name right.

A couple of the men gasped. Even Landril was impressed.

'A Compol bow?' Valderon said with respect in his voice. 'A valuable heirloom. He was a contemporary of Allimentrus, wasn't he Xavir?'

Xavir gave only a nod.

'By the Goddess,' Valderon said, 'now that was a great age of weapon-smiths. You won't get anything like that forged today.'

'I did not know much about it,' Elysia said. 'It appears there's a lot I didn't know.'

Birgitta raised an eyebrow at the comment, but said nothing.

'It shoots well enough, though,' Elysia continued.

'Better than most other weapons, I'd wager,' Valderon said with a grin.

Elysia smiled shyly back.

Landril reached into his satchel and produced the strange piece of armour that he had brought from the attack on the people of Marva. 'Talking of skilled weapon-smiths, is there any chance one of them could have made something like this?'

'Now, what have we here?' Birgitta asked.

Landril tilted the armour in the light of the fire, so that Birgitta could take a better look. 'Took it from our attackers. Been trying to fathom this writing ever since. You know, I can understand at least two dozen languages, but . . .'

'Here, let me have a look,' Birgitta said.

Landril was reluctant to hand over the item, but reached across with it.

'Now then . . .' Birgitta leaned nearer the fire. She appeared confident in her assessment, nodding to herself. 'Yes, I believe I can make out *some* of these words.'

'You can?' Landril knelt up alongside her.

'You see,' she continued, 'I have the advantage of having experienced some similar script to this only recently.'

Birgitta told of the sisters' journey from Jarratox, and of the incident in the village of Dweldor. She explained at great length the horrors and of the strange presence that had made itself known to the locals.

'Elysia here fired the arrow that trapped the creature,' Birgitta concluded, 'but we left it up to the villagers to decide his fate.'

'And you say you saw this script upon the walls?' Lupara asked.

'Scratched in the dried blood of the house. By the source, I think whoever, or whatever, created that mess was far more of a menace than the being we caught in the forest, who seemed like a simple warrior. But this script here —' she handed it back to Landril — 'is of the same kind.'

'What language is it?' Landril demanded.

'He's an impatient sort isn't he?' Birgitta chuckled, nudging Elysia. 'Now, the reason you — and for some time, myself — couldn't understand it was that you were thinking of languages of this continent.'

'I can speak others.'

'How far away, though?'

'The Balanx; the Blood Isles; beyond maybe.'

'Not far enough. Have you heard of the Voldirik people? That's what language I think this is.'

'By the Goddess,' Landril said eventually. 'What is such a

script doing here? Their lands are almost mythical . . . I mean, many scholars even dispute their existence. I have read some very old texts concerning those who have travelled their land, but one never quite knows if it is truth or fiction. It was said by the historian Mavos that during the Second Age, the cult nation of Irik fled its shores and established a new realm elsewhere, and that they became what was later recorded in the Sixth Age as the Voldirik people.'

'It is indeed a most mysterious question,' Birgitta said, leaning back next to Elysia. 'How did their script, on their armour – on their people – end up on our continent?'

Landril inspected it once again. He smiled, slightly, as with Birgitta's information he was able to make out at least one of the words. 'With that in mind then . . . this looks like an archaic spelling of "castle", if one went by the origins of their language from Irik. And this word, the long one, appears to be some kind description of numbers.'

Birgitta furrowed her brow. 'I have read similar texts to you, and I believe in the Irik origin myth. I understand parts of that classical language structure, and I spotted a few things on this armour. Mostly about where the warrior – whoever wore this – came from. I believe the armour itself quite literally tells their story.'

'I wonder if *each one* would be personal to the figure wearing it,' Landril suggested. 'Deeds done in war. Their origins. Either way, this goes to show that whoever wore this armour – whoever came into that village to cause havoc – they are not mere savages. They are people of some considerable culture.'

'Which is even more concerning,' Birgitta added.

Valderon cleared his throat. 'Why is Mardonius siding with these Voldirik creatures to attack his own people, and especially those who follow religions?'

There was a thoughtful silence.

'The thing that bothers me the most,' Xavir declared, 'is this. I knew Mardonius, despite his lowly station in Cedius's court. In the Angelic Court, or even the Celebration of Martyrs, he never even made a speech. He had no real position among those glorious limestone spires of Stravir City. There was no merit to his being there, and Cedius confided in me that he sometimes felt the same. So how can this man – how can this little man with no concern for religion – suddenly be driving the faithful out of settlements?'

The young raven-haired woman with those startling eyes, Elysia, gazed towards Xavir at the mention of his past.

'These things –' Valderon indicated the plate of armour – 'these other warriors. Voldiriks. Do we think they're acting independently in their persecution or on behalf of Stravimon's king?'

'He's no king. And I do not think they are working on their own,' Xavir said, 'going by recent observations, and what Marva's people have witnessed. This new race – whoever they are, wherever they have come from – is walking the lands not merely *unchallenged* by Stravimon's army but with its blessing. This is a bedevilled alliance.'

A bird chittered in the distant trees, stark against the comparative calm of their surroundings. The starlight overhead was mesmerizing.

Xavir rose from the light of the fire and picked up his swords. 'I'll take first watch tonight.'

Elysia's gaze followed him as he marched towards the arched entrance to the watchtower, before she eventually stared back into the fire.

A Second Escape

Nothing disturbed the quiet of the Silent Lake, save the moon's reflection sailing across its gentle surface. The bareness of the landscape appealed to Xavir. The solitude was peaceful. In gaol, and even before that, it had been impossible to be alone, to find time to himself, to relax and not constantly be strategizing and planning.

The wolves were sleeping near Lupara, who had joined the two witches. One of whom was his *daughter*. Xavir walked down the steps, his feet whispering across the stone, his stealth bringing to mind some of the light-footed nightingale postures from his sword training.

Earlier he had moved his few belongings towards his mare and had tied the horse to a tree many paces away from the others. He had needed the distance. He moved there now, the only sounds around him being that of the lake gently lapping on the sand. The air was so calm tonight.

His awareness focused all around him, Xavir made no sound as he untied the mare. He walked the animal along the path, rubbing her neck, and mounted the animal when he was about four hundred yards beyond the others. Even then she moved cautiously at his command, going quietly. The wolves would certainly hear by now if they hadn't already.

Suddenly, as he was ready to move to a faster pace, he heard his name being called.

He turned. There, riding behind in the shadows, was another figure.

How the hell has he seen me?

'I think you must have spotted trouble,' Valderon said. 'That's right, isn't it?'

Xavir didn't turn around now, but called back softly. 'Nothing to concern yourself with, Valderon.'

'Is it not?'

'No. Go back to the others.'

'And tell them that Xavir Argentum, the warrior on whom so many of their hopes depend, is fleeing into the night?' Valderon brought his animal alongside Xavir.

'I am not *fleeing*, Valderon,' Xavir said, 'I'm doing the sensible thing.'

'Sensible for whom? You've just discovered you have a child. That must mean something to you.'

'It is why I am going, Valderon,' Xavir said.

Both men slid from their horses to talk face to face.

'I have no business with her,' Xavir said. 'I have some acts of justice to mete out and a corrupt king to dethrone, which I can do alone. It will help your cause and allow whatever army you amass to walk through the gates of Stravir.'

'Even you cannot storm the city alone.'

'It is possible I will die in the process. But it is easier if this daughter of mine never knows who I am, if only death awaits me.'

'It awaits us all,' Valderon said.

'But she will not grow to form a bond, which would be worse. Trust me. I had formed a bond with her mother and her loss still haunts me to this day. I ache – still – like a spear has entered my flanks. Today has only opened that wound.'

'I know a little of your pain,' Valderon said. 'But I think it is you who is afraid of being hurt again. Elysia will want to know her father. You are all the family she has. From you she can understand a little of where she came from. Who she is. It will give her strength.'

'And what can I bring to her?' Xavir scowled. 'A name tarnished by the blood of innocents? A legend in his own lifetime? My name and my deeds are well known. She will gain nothing from being associated with me.'

Valderon placed his palm above Xavir's chestbone. 'She will want to know *you*, friend. That is why she came back earlier.'

Xavir tilted his chin to one side. 'She was better off running away.'

'She wasn't running *away*, I don't think. Merely . . . running. She came back to discover you.'

'She has barely even looked at me.'

'And you expect it to be easy?' Valderon asked. 'You're a stranger to her.'

Xavir glanced back across the dark lake. The moon had shifted a little in its surface. 'I am a stranger to myself.'

'I know what you mean.'

'It was easier for you,' Xavir said. 'Your whole life *was* the army, a life on the road and few commitments. Being in the Solar Cohort meant . . . additional luxuries and entitlements, and exposure to fine culture. One can get *attached* to such things, even though I tried not to. This –' he thumped his fist to his chest – 'just isn't the same. This is a half-life to what I had before.'

'You may find reward with a daughter. That may bring something more wholesome.'

'I am going to slaughter those who wronged me,' Xavir said, 'and there is nothing wholesome about my future.'

'You mentioned her mother,' Valderon said. 'That she has haunted you. What would you think she'd make of your leaving?'

Xavir closed his eyes and remembered moments of his time with Lysha. He wasn't certain if his memories were real or not.

'She would hate me for it. And tell me so. She would then scold me with magical flame rather than words.'

Valderon smiled at the comment. 'Come back, Xavir. Give that young woman a chance. For her mother's sake.'

'I loathe the sisterhood and what it has done.'

'She is only half witch,' Valderon observed. 'Besides, think what a wound it would be to the sisterhood for you, Xavir Argentum, to have nurtured the warrior in her.'

A smile came and went from Xavir's lips. He ran his hand along the mare's warm neck while he contemplated the suggestion.

'She may prove handy with that bow,' Xavir said.

Valderon rolled his lips thinly and placed a hand on Xavir's shoulder. 'She may indeed. After all, look who her father is.'

The two men turned back along the path with their horses, in companionable silence, the wind still gentle, moon reappearing to cast its light across the calm surface of the lake once again.

Dawn

The former commander of the Solar Cohort went through his morning ritual: stretches, exercising, rehearsing the forms of complex swordplay. The sunlight was warm on his face and a few birds skittered overhead on dawn missions, but other than that and the occasional splash of water, there remained no sounds save those of his exertion.

The sun banked higher. In the distance he could see the little trail of smoke from the campfire as the others readied themselves for breakfast.

'Birgitta told me to say something to you.'

Xavir turned to see Elysia – his daughter – walking towards him from out of the long grass. Placing his blades back over his shoulder, he wondered if she had used some kind of witch trickery to conceal herself.

'Well, you've now said something.' Xavir watched her, curiously. The same raven-black hair as Lysha. Those blue eyes were just as disarming, though for completely different reasons now.

She stood before him, the young witch, just a head shorter than himself. *Tall for a woman*, he thought. Her bow was in her hand and a quiver half-full of arrows slung across her shoulder. She was dressed in browns and greens, with a decorative leather cuirass.

'I don't know what to say to you.' Her voice was absent of emotion.

'That makes two of us,' Xavir replied. 'This is unexpected, to say the least. I had no plans apart from those concerning where my comrades and I were going.'

'Where is that?'

'Dangerous places, is all. I may be killed, and I intend to kill many in the process.'

Elysia shrugged. 'I've only killed deer so far. Birgitta taught me that. We fed villagers with the carcasses, though.'

'It doesn't bother you?'

'Why should it?'

Another silence fell between them, though it was not uncomfortable.

'You shoot them with this bow?' Xavir asked, holding his hand out to take a look at the weapon.

She handed it to him.

Xavir marvelled at the craftsmanship, the way the dark polished wood appeared to shimmer, the balance and tension of it. He noted the witchstone fixed near the grip.

Xavir handed it back, impressed. 'Dellius Compol knew how to make weapons. I used to know a man who lived on the borders of Stravimon who said he had rediscovered Compol's techniques, but they were not even comparable.'

'I'm good with it too.'

'I've never really known of a *warrior* witch in the Ninth Age. Not one that uses weapons other than witchstones directly.'

'The sisterhood doesn't encourage such things,' Elysia replied.

'The sisterhood does not encourage much,' Xavir said.

'You knew my mother,' Elysia said.

'Evidently,' Xavir added, gesturing back to Elysia with his left hand.

His daughter smiled awkwardly. 'What was she like?'

'Proud. Stubborn. Keen to try new magic. Paid little attention to rules, though neither did I at the time. She was sarcastic and had a temper about her. But, we loved each other.'

Elysia sat on the grass and shaded her eyes as she stared out across the water. Xavir, uncertain at first, followed suit and crouched down beside her.

'You look very much like your mother,' Xavir said. 'Yesterday I thought it was her that I saw. I'd only known her when she was perhaps a year older than you, when she first came to my clan.'

'What was that like?' Elysia asked. Again, no emotion in her words. 'What was *she* like?'

Xavir spoke more about his early days at his family estate, about his time as a warrior and when Lysha came to join them. Elysia listened patiently, without comment. This was the most Xavir had spoken at length for some time.

'And you?' Elysia said. 'Who *are* you?'

'I'm sure you will hear from others soon enough. Suffice to say I am a soldier who rose to a particularly high rank alongside Cedius the Wise.'

'I've heard of him. The famous Stravimon king.'

'And a generous, smart one at that. Not like the barbaric fool who now leads. A man may sit on a throne, but that does not make him a king. A man may have the right to rule, but that does not make him a leader.'

'Birgitta told me, late last night, that you might have once been a king. Is that true?'

'People may speculate on that, but here I am – without a crown.'

'Do crowns make kings?'

Xavir said nothing.

'How did you leave Cedius?'

'I was . . . tricked.' Xavir revealed, in short, blunt sentences, how he had ended up in gaol betrayed by others in Cedius's regime. 'So my travels run parallel to those of Lupara and yourselves, it appears. Do not think ill of me for the deeds I will commit.'

'Why would I?'

Xavir gave her an uncertain look. 'It is not my way to kill those who are unarmed, yet I will gladly walk into their homes and butcher them. This is your father now, Elysia. A man who seeks to kill retired generals and politicians, and eventually a man who is not a king, because each of them deserves death. My days of glory are long behind me.'

Elysia did not reply.

'Come,' Xavir declared, rising up. 'I want to see this warrior witch in action.'

The two stepped into a copse of oak trees in a small gully, at the far end of the lake from their camp. The sky remained cloudless, and the vegetation around the shoreline began to smell in the heat. With the tip of one of the Keening Blades, Xavir sliced an 'X' into one trunk. They moved back thirty paces into the gloom.

'Can you hit that, in the centre?' Xavir asked.

'Are you being serious?' Elysia said with a smile. 'That's not much of a challenging target.'

'Then hit it,' Xavir replied.

Elysia reached over her shoulder with one arm and raised her bow with the other. Xavir could see her concentrating, furrowing her brow. She released the arrow and it slammed into the tree. Xavir jogged over to it and could see the arrow had landed perfectly in the centre of his mark.

As Elysia caught up with him, he acknowledged her cocky stance and folded his arms. 'Show me something you consider to be challenging, then.'

Elysia gave him a dark, playful look. 'Stand there. And don't move.'

She walked around Xavir and towards the edge of the copse, skipping over the undergrowth, until she was about the same distance away as before, except from another angle. The major difference now was that Xavir stood right in between his daughter and the target he had carved upon the tree.

'Don't move!' she said again.

Raising an eyebrow, Xavir remained impassive and watched her every move. She was obviously testing him. She took a little longer to nock her arrow this time, but within a few heartbeats he found himself in the centre of her aim. She took her time about it and when she momentarily closed her eyes he wondered if she knew what she was doing.

Elysia released the arrow. It rushed towards him and began to curve when it was three feet from his head. It swerved around him in an arc, just missing him, so close he could feel the rush of air from its passage. And, no sooner had it passed him, than it curved back onto its original trajectory, and once again struck the tree. All within a heartbeat.

Xavir marched over to take a look at the impact. Elysia had missed the centre of the 'X' by about half a finger-width, if that. It if had struck a person, they would have been as good as dead.

'That is impressive.' Xavir glanced back to Elysia, who was striding through the forest towards him with a proud look upon her face.

'Was that you or the bow doing this?' Xavir gestured through the air to mimic the path of the arrow.

'A little of both,' she said. 'It's clearly the source that moves the arrow, but it's the same as any other witchstone in that it's part me, part . . . elements, I guess.' She pointed to the shimmering stone set into the bow. 'This is one of the few witchstones that I am any good with. The bowstone affects the wind around the arrow and curves it to my will. Curving it is the easy part. Knowing what's the other side of an object, a place I cannot see, that's the difficult bit. It relies a lot on memory. And faith, I suppose, though Birgitta never likes to call it that. There are other stones that are set into arrows, which perform different tasks. Some of this is predefined. All of it requires my will, but I have the bowstone to guide me.'

'This is useful,' Xavir said thoughtfully. 'Very useful. Can you use other weapons?'

'I have trained a little with sword, and was reasonably adept – although I have no way of measuring that as there was no one to fight against, other than Birgitta, and she kept saying she wasn't as fast as she used to be.'

'Sword.' Xavir nodded. 'Good. I can help tutor you further if you wish. Anything else?'

'I tried an axe when I was twelve summers, but that was too heavy for me to use. I enjoy the bow the most.'

'What other magics can you perform?'

'That's not really my . . .' She paused. 'Look, as much as I'd like to say I am one of the most talented sisters there ever was, I'm not. Sorry. The sisterhood hated me and I didn't like them.'

'Well that's something we have in common, then.' Xavir said with a sardonic twist to his lips. 'And I also was never that good at studying, but I knew my way around a blade.'

'Birgitta knew I could not be bothered with learning from

books either, so she taught me these ways. She claimed that they were more ancient arts, and that once, many ages ago, this is how the sisters might have been. Warrior covens who moved around the woodlands.'

'Is that true?' He hoped it was. Something stirred within him.

'I don't know. I'm just going by what Birgitta has told me, but I preferred these lessons to sitting at a desk.'

'It is a more practical life, certainly.' Xavir could only assess her in terms of her value to his expedition, and he knew that wasn't the right thing to do. But first and foremost he was a military man – he had no idea how to be a father.

For a while both of them stood there, the conversation having petered out.

Eventually, Elysia said, 'What are we all doing here, in Burgassia? Birgitta has only told me so much, but I don't really think she had a plan other than getting to this place.'

'A good question,' Xavir replied. 'I assume you know about Mardonius and his destruction of his own people?'

'It had touched even the sisterhood,' she said. 'As Birgitta said last night, it's why we left.'

'With my help, Valderon, Lupara and the spymaster, Landril – we shall raise an army to take down the king. I, personally, will kill him for what he's done to me. Though I would have had it otherwise, they will need magic – which is presumably where you and Birgitta will come in.'

'Will we sisters be joining your army?'

'If it's as Birgitta says, then Mardonius will undoubtedly have witches to help his own forces. Birgitta will think it a grave mission, but she will accept, because she is old friends with Lupara.'

'She will,' Elysia said. 'If you were once the commander of the king's forces, why aren't you leading?'

'I don't lead armies any more.' Xavir regarded the distance, his eyes tightening. 'I will help in my own way. The people I am seeking will have resources that will help pay for an army and materials. It will take weeks, months even, to build up enough of a force. In the end Valderon will lead it. He is a man of honour.'

'And you are not?' Elysia questioned.

Xavir shook his head grimly. 'I don't know what I am any more.'

The two walked slowly back to the camp. Elysia went to Birgitta, while Xavir spotted Valderon perched on a large rock a little further up the shore, sharpening his blade with a stone. He walked over and sat down next to him, and for a while continued the silence while he stared out across the tranquil lake, inhaling the fresh air and basking in the sunlight.

'These swords are not pretty,' Valderon said eventually. 'We could do with better weapons.'

'So long as they kill,' Xavir said.

'Speaks a man with fine weapons indeed. Tell me, how did it go?'

'I am not prepared to be a father.' Xavir sighed. 'Whatever that involves. It was awkward.'

'These things do not come overnight,' Valderon said. 'You need to work at them, hone them like I am doing with this blade. It takes time to get the perfect edge.'

'And yet in your case,' Xavir said, 'you'll still not be happy with the weapon.'

'That's family for you.' Valderon grinned. 'So when do we leave?'

'When I spoke to Lupara, she needed to confirm that these two witches would join our party. I have seen what the young one can do, and it will come in useful. Then we will continue on our way. I am just a few days away from our first victim . . .'

'You thirst for blood, friend?' Valderon shook his head, chuckling. 'Unhealthy desires . . .'

'In a manner, but are you not keen to see how this rabble perform?' Xavir tilted his chin towards the other freedmen, who were japing around further up the shore. He could hear their laughter echoing for some distance.

'Some of them will be good fighters. Maybe not Davlor. Tylos knows his way around a sword. Jedral seems to have a lot of skills too. He was a mercenary for a short while, so he tells me.'

'Despite being born into a good clan, he'd fallen on hard times,' Xavir replied. 'He had to make ends meet by putting his skills and connections to use out in the wider world.'

'But that gives a man certain characteristics that will prove useful. The others, despite their upbringing, are barely more than thugs, but we need thugs too.' Valderon finished sharpening his sword, placed his tools down to one side and drew his knees to his chest. 'I'm not concerned about their abilities. They need daily practice, more of being involved in a planned attack and, if you'll permit them to help, your first raid will provide it.'

'I'll not decline their company.' Xavir leaned back on his palms. 'Though we must see what we are up against when we arrive.'

'If I'm concerned at all, it is for what lies ahead in Stravimon,' Valderon said. 'We've seen very few travellers on the road.

That's strange enough, don't you think? I know we've taken the greenways for the most part, but some of these roads used to be filled with travellers, tradesmen and troubadours. Where is everyone?'

The witches had agreed to accompany the travellers on their way, so without much fuss they were back on the road within the hour.

Lupara offered one of her wolves to the two sisters who had ventured so far on foot and declared that she would share a steed with Valderon. Xavir's former gang rival tried his best not to show his uneasiness at the gesture and asked if it would be better if the other wolves acted as mounts so that Lupara would not suffer discomfort. Lupara declined. The other wolves were scouts, she said, and would patrol far ahead.

Xavir could only chuckle, thinking that Valderon had better chances at defeating an army single-handed than escaping Lupara's attentions.

Birgitta was not entirely suited to riding a wolf. Despite there being a fitted leather saddle, it took her a good couple of minutes to mount the beast. Elysia hunched over in laughter at the sight of her mentor going headfirst over the other side.

Eventually the group departed the region around the Silent Lake; they headed through the ancient landscape of Burgassia, into more lush vegetation, undulating hills and eventually thick forests. Xavir felt a keenness and anxiety, a welcome tightness in his chest. It was the same feeling he had experienced on the eve of every battle. He knew that soon he would be facing those who had caused his downfall, betrayed their king, killed his brothers and had him incarcerated in Hell's Keep. It was time for them to pay.

Time to Attack

'He's got scouts patrolling at the moment. About a dozen. No more.'

Tylos had returned from surveying the hilltop on the border of Stravimon, near the fortified estate of General Havinir. His usual insouciant manner indicated there was no threat. Xavir liked the man's calming, even charming, influence out here. Nothing seemed too much trouble for him. He could talk on just about any subject. Whenever the men complained about something, he would have a positive response. And recently, during quiet times around the campfire, Tylos recited poetry from Chambrek, imbuing the drizzle-filled night air with images from a more exotic land. Xavir thought he would have been a good man to have on one of his long campaigns of old.

Tylos sat down, having made his observations. 'Why so glum, Davlor? You don't look that excited. Does the prospect of finally spilling blood make you feel faint?'

Davlor sat a little taller and puffed out his chest. 'Love it. It's just that, uh, well . . . I didn't have to *think* about fighting before. It just sort of happened, didn't it? Things just attacked us and there was none of this sitting around waiting for it to come. I'm not one for thinking too much. Back on the farm we just did what we did and accepted whatever the seasons brought.'

'Thinking can be torture, can it not?' Tylos said. 'Just take heart from the fact that there are not that many men for us to kill.'

'Tylos is right,' Valderon said. 'It will be over before you realize.'

'Then you can go back to sucking your mother's teat,' Jedral replied, nudging him in the ribs with his boot.

'Fuck off,' Davlor muttered. 'I can hold my own.'

'Hold your own what – cock?'

'Least I've got one.'

'Play nice,' Tylos said.

There was no fire tonight, not this close to their target. Everyone threw a blanket around themselves to remain warm. Lupara nestled herself against one of her wolves, whilst the witches did the same with another.

'Some time before dawn,' Xavir announced, 'when the moon touches that hilltop, we will make our move. The wind will be stronger by then, and its noise will work in our favour. Elysia –' he indicated his daughter – 'will accompany me. Birgitta will come with us as well. I anticipate that what is lacking in a military defence around the manse will be made up for in magical wards. The others should wait behind. Here. With Valderon.'

Elysia looked startled at the suggestion. The surprise was shared by others.

'Valderon and Lupara will guide the rest of you, if you are required. But you are merely to come after us if we don't return. The smaller the force, the better in a situation like this. Our mission will be one of investigation, picking off soldiers, and if there is an opportunity then we will go it alone. The rest of you can relax. Even you, Davlor.'

Harrand stood up, his face screwed up, and faced Xavir. 'You'd have these women follow you, but not us? Not after all we've done to help get your noble arse out of prison?'

Someone gave a sharp intake of breath. Xavir's gaze met Harrand's suddenly regretful eyes.

The man turned away with the wave of his hand. 'Ah, forget it. I'm tired and I'm itching to kill someone.'

Davlor muttered, 'You could start with yourself.'

Harrand lurched towards the lad.

Valderon stood up and thumped the top of Harrand's chest with the heel of his palm, sending him reeling backwards into the dark grass. Davlor appeared dumbfounded by the sudden movement.

'We do *not* fight amongst ourselves,' Valderon hissed. 'Especially not on the doorsteps of our enemy. If you want to get yourselves killed, fine, but don't get us killed for your folly!'

Harrand rubbed his wrist lightly, checking for damage from the backward fall. His face was full of rage.

Xavir glanced to Landril, who shook his head and pressed his palms to his face. 'Spymaster,' Xavir continued, 'I will likely need you as well.'

'I am no fighter,' Landril said. 'If you'd prefer a fighter, then surely—'

'I don't expect you to fight.'

'What do you need me for?'

'Answers,' Xavir replied, then added softly, 'my techniques with Havinir are likely to be blunt. Yours are more subtle.'

'As you wish,' Landril replied.

'There is barely any magic here,' Birgitta said, sniffing the chill air. An owl made a noise in the distance as it glided towards some unsuspecting mammal.

The two sisters, Xavir and Landril were standing in the cloak of darkness that Birgitta had cast with her staff.

So far they had seen no threat. The manse was constructed of dull grey stone and could be seen behind thick clumps of trees, with an unkempt lawn stretching out before one side.

'How so?' Xavir whispered.

'Sisters can sense magic from afar. There is none here, save what is coming from my own staff.'

'This is not necessarily odd,' Landril offered. 'He may simply have no witch attached to his clan. He may even feel no need for one.'

'Unlikely,' Xavir said. 'I remember Havinir well. He always deployed magic in battle. The witchstones were crucial to his tactics and he was ever curious as to the ways of the sisterhood. He lobbied Cedius to influence the sisterhood so that he had the powerful witches with powerful witchstones at his side. There ought to be good reason that there is *no* magic around . . .'

Xavir paused, held up his hand, then pointed with his other through the trees. 'A guard up ahead. He wears no helm. Elysia, release an arrow – aim for his head.'

The young woman showed every sign of hesitation and uncertainty, though she did not speak of it. Without looking to her mentor for guidance, she fumbled nervously for an arrow and raised her bow.

We shall see what this daughter of mine is really made of, Xavir thought.

Elysia released it with a quiet gasp. Xavir didn't bother to look at the man, who now fell to the ground in the under-growth. He stared at his daughter, who had just killed her first human. Her breathing had increased and she knelt down on the damp earth.

Xavir crouched beside her and placed a hand on her back, trying to get eye contact with her. 'It was quick and painless for him,' he whispered, lifting her up. 'He was a soldier and he had prepared to die. What you did was difficult and you will remember it. Think of him like a stag in the forest. Soldiers out here are wild game, just like them. You will be fine. But I'll need more of your arrows.'

Elysia nodded and Xavir turned back. Birgitta placed an arm around her young student and steered her forwards.

'He's right,' she whispered, 'and, sadly, it will get easier.'

They continued around the edge of the grounds, taking down five more soldiers in the process, each kill unseen and quick, by arrow or by blade.

Progress is too easy, Xavir thought.

Havinir's residence was a large rectangular building, constructed more for luxury than for withstanding a siege. There were crenellations at the top, and large, arched windows on every side. A moat ran around the immediate building on its eastern flank, and the wooden drawbridge had been withdrawn. At the sentry post by the formal entrance there were two more guards, so the group moved across to the rear of the manse and stood on the edge of the moat's bank. There was at least a twenty-foot gap to the other side.

'Now what?' Landril said.

'She knows earthcraft.' Xavir gestured to Birgitta, whilst taking a step back to see if there were any guards on the battlements. 'She altered the ground previously, so she can do it again.'

'*She* has a name, you ignorant oaf,' grumbled Birgitta. 'Fine, but I'll have to make us appear momentarily, so try not to get yourself shot.' Birgitta set down her staff, pulled out a brown witchstone from her satchel and began chanting.

The ground vibrated. The bank of the moat began to stir and morph, and from out of it sprouted a wide offshoot. Mud and roots twisted outwards, creaking like old floorboards until it punched into the opposite bank and soon there was silence.

'Elysia!' Xavir pointed towards the left and right, where two guards were approaching. 'Hurry.'

She fired twice, in quick succession. One man tried to roll to one side. The arrow curved and followed his lurching movement; he collapsed, sliding dead into the water. The other man's face shattered strangely, and the resulting a plume of blood sprayed back across the wall of the manse.

'Oh, I used one of the witchstone shafts by mistake,' Elysia whispered, cringing at her deed. 'I only needed to will the bow-stone on a normal arrow.'

Everyone watched as the headless form fell to his knees a few moments later.

'The effect was dramatic . . . to say the least,' Landril observed. 'But still, by the Goddess, I've never seen shots like that.'

Swift-footed, Xavir strode first across the earthen bridge, which remained sticky underfoot. Reaching the side of the building, they followed his lead and pressed themselves flat against the wall. The sky had not yet purpled into dawn. Stars still defined the position of the surrounding hills. There was a sharp tang to the air.

Birgitta used her staff to cloak them all in darkness once again, and they advanced, making progress to the front of the building.

Two guards stood in partial slumber by the sentry box porch

at the main entrance, which was a large, arched double door at the top of five stone steps.

In a move known as Akero descends, his arms spread wide, Xavir drew the tip of a Keening Blade across each man's throat; they fell silently down and across the entrance before they could reach for their own weapons.

The door was closed. Xavir thought it likely there was another guard, maybe even more, waiting behind. The group stepped back out of earshot, just a few paces away, no more.

'Can you use black arts?' Xavir whispered to Birgitta, and gestured to the corpses.

'Necromancy?'

'Of course.' Xavir furrowed his brow.

'Certainly not.' Birgitta folded her arms and scowled at him.

'Animate one of these two. Get them to mutter a password to whoever's behind the door.'

'By the source, I'll not listen to such nonsense.' Birgitta shook her head. 'It is forbidden. Not to mention rather tricky in practical terms.'

'How else do we get in *quietly*, then?' Xavir demanded. 'The door is likely barred. We do not know what's behind.'

'Not this one,' Landril observed. 'It's probably just locked. I can see a mechanism.'

'Well, there you go then,' Birgitta said. 'I'll just melt the mechanism. No need for such dark barbarity.'

The old witch rooted around in her bag and drew out a red-hued witchstone. She wedged one end of it in the lock, then began to whisper to it. The lock began to glow to amber, then brighter. Something snapped inside.

'There you go,' Birgitta said, rising proudly.

Xavir eased the door back, then suddenly shoved it back the

final three quarters. Poking his head inside, under the cloak of Birgitta's magic, he glanced either side into the darkness.

'No one here,' Xavir whispered behind. 'There were ten soldiers outside. Tylos counted a dozen, though there may be more. The remainders have probably not come on shift and are inside somewhere. They need eliminating first.'

Xavir led the group around the dreary stone corridors of Havinir's manse. The place had an odd air about it; it seemed as if many parts were disused or neglected, even though there were plenty of people around. Military items decorated the walls: ancient helms and shields, banners from old campaigns emblazoned with iconography, crossed swords and maces. There was a mustiness, though. The aroma of decay. Rats scurried further away, their noise causing Xavir to pause. Eventually he could hear the chatter of men from a chamber up ahead. A warm light glowed underneath a closed door.

With a lightness of foot, Xavir moved towards it and pressed his ear against the wood. On the other side was barrack talk, the idle chatter of men who had nothing to kill but time.

Xavir stepped away and whispered to the others, 'Five men, I think. I will go in, alone, and keep one of them alive for questioning.'

Xavir calmed his mind and breath – then shoved back the door. Four men started to rise from a table, another stood with his arms unfolding to one side, and behind him were several church candles. Xavir cut down two men before they could fully leave their chairs and sent them buckling backwards over the backrest in gouts of blood. The man with his arms folded collapsed as Xavir drew a blade across his thigh. The other two stood facing him and in a flurry of blades they, too, lay dead across the table.

The only one left alive was lying on the floor clutching his injured leg. Xavir sheathed one blade over his shoulder, and with his free hand hauled the soldier onto the table, slamming him on top of his dead comrade. His victim was old and gaunt, with scars written across his left cheek like bad calligraphy.

'Where are Havinir's quarters?' Xavir hissed.

The man shook his head.

Xavir covered the man's mouth with his left hand, and raked a Keening Blade across his other leg. The man screamed into Xavir's palm, his eyes bulging.

'Tell me!' Xavir demanded, removing his hand. 'And I'll spare your life.'

'Up . . . upstairs, on the south s-side of t-the building. Double doors . . .'

Xavir cut his throat, checked everyone else was dead, and left the room quietly. Landril and Elysia looked at him in shock when he rejoined them, Birgitta just glared at him.

'On the level above,' he declared, and moved onwards, ignoring their disbelief at his deeds.

They progressed through the manse, finding the stairwell.

'There are some strange goings-on in this place,' Birgitta whispered. 'I feel it, by the source, though it is *not* magic. It is something else.'

'Do you think there are traps?' Landril asked. 'This place is labyrinthine. If I had to defend it, I'd have traps everywhere.'

'I do not think it is that,' she replied, staring thoughtfully at the ground. 'I'm sorry I can't be more specific. Can you feel it, little sister?'

Elysia closed her eyes for a moment. 'Yes. It feels . . . full of energy. Full of life. Not unlike magic, though.'

'Most peculiar,' Birgitta added.

Thinking it to be no specific warning, Xavir continued leading them upstairs. Again there came a musty smell, a staleness. Everything stank to him of death and decay – a contrast to whatever the witches had perceived.

Along the corridor, under the watchful gaze of ancient portraits that hung at angles, they strode with quiet, considered steps through the house towards Havinir's quarters. There was a double door halfway along the south side that Xavir thought to be his room, and he approached it.

Before Xavir turned the handle he whispered to Birgitta, 'This needs to be me alone at first. Conceal me when I'm in there.'

'Is that an order or a request?' she asked.

Xavir stared at her.

'If the door is ajar, then yes,' she replied.

'I will call for Landril if I need him.' He paused. 'Though not exactly a private matter, it will be better if you do not see it.'

'I understand,' the witch replied.

'Keep me in shadow for a few minutes, and then release me from it. I want him to see me there.'

Xavir eased the door open silently. Birgitta cast a shadow upon him, and he pushed the door back softly behind him.

Nightmares

General Havinir awoke from bitter dreams. They had all been bitter of late.

Was that something outside?

He was surrounded by darkness and found the sense of isolation comforting. The window was open and the curtains shook like banners in the breeze. There was a glimmer of moonlight upon the glass. He sat up on his bed, slid out the ceramic pot beneath it and began to urinate. Once that was over he rearranged himself, kicked back the pot with his heel and lay in bed, staring at the ceiling.

He pondered the great campaigns he had led under Cedius and Mardonius. Long trips north beyond the Plains of Mica and Herrebron, into the tribal territories whose borders ebbed and flowed across the map. Those days had been about tactics and nuance on the battlefield, of great tides of armour clashing across mud and dust. Those *were* the days.

Not now. Not killing idiots who couldn't handle themselves let alone a sword – in his own country, no less. All the best fighters had gone or been transitioned, save the one who stood by Mardonius's side, and even he was not really all *there* any more . . . There were dark glimmers now in his mind. He had done what he had set out to do, for the Voldiriks and for

Stravimon. The alliance was true. His only concern was that this new army was not yet perfect. The transitioning left warriors in a worse state than before, and Havinir preferred campaigns with smaller, more effective forces . . .

I should stop thinking about all of this nonsense now. I need to pay for more girls to occupy my nights.

Havinir suddenly realized that a figure was standing in the room, between the curtains. He sat up and rubbed his eyes.

'This is what you have become then, General,' the figure said. 'An old man with a weak bladder. So much for the great warrior you once were.'

'Xavir Argentum,' he breathed.

Havinir shivered. His stomach curdled. The figure was tall and two swords showed over his shoulders. *Is it really him?* 'The butcher of Baradium Falls. You have tormented my dreams over the years.'

'I've come to relieve you of that suffering.'

'So be it,' Havinir whispered, lying back on his bed. He could hear the gentle wailing of those ancient, powerful swords being unsheathed. It had been many years since he had heard that noise. Those Allimentrus-crafted blades would have been just the thing for his prized collection of artefacts. If only he'd managed to get hold of them before that damned wolf queen had done so all those years ago.

'Why did you do it?' Xavir stepped forwards so that he loomed over the bed. 'Why did you consign me to that place?'

'What was it like in there?' Havinir asked calmly.

'Cold,' Xavir grunted. 'Too much time to think. Why did you send me there?'

'I didn't send you anywhere, certainly not there. We wanted you dead. We wanted you out of the way.' Havinir sighed. How could he even begin explain the complexities of it all?

'Out of the way of *what*?' Xavir demanded.

'Progress, of course. The future. A chance for a better way for our world.'

'You speak in riddles.'

'You don't know the half of it, warrior. This is not about simple politics. Nor the crudeness of war. This is not even about possession of the throne. Oh, such simple desires! This is about much more. This is about surrendering ourselves to a greater force entirely. This is about understanding life and death themselves.'

'Explain,' Xavir growled, still in the shadow.

'Have you explored my home yet?'

'Some of it. I made a mess of some rooms.'

He'd come straight for Havinir, then. No nuance. No reconnoitring. Though older, possibly weaker, he was just as blunt. An instrument of war, nothing more. How he could have been favoured by Cedius was mind-boggling to Havinir. Rule was about more than force and personality. This man had never been fit to be king. 'I cannot be bothered to waste my final breaths explaining it to you. You'll find some of it here, once you've finished me off. Beware of the Voldiriks, is all I will say.'

'You have not explained,' Xavir continued, 'why you wanted me out of the way.'

'You would have prevented so many great things from happening to our world. Cedius should have let you die after Baradium Falls. But he didn't trust what was going on around him. He was a canny old man, I'll give him that, for all his stupidity in favouring you. That's why he kept you alive. Only you. The one he wanted to take the throne.'

'Mardonius is now king. He was part of your schemes, I know this much. He, too, will die. Who else had a role to play in that night?'

'Who do you think?'

Xavir listed the other names Landril had given him.

'You've done your research well.' Havinir chuckled. 'There is a brain in there after all.'

'Why did you set me up?' Xavir demanded, sheathing his swords. 'You haven't given me a good reason yet.'

'You'll find out sooner or later. You were just better off out of the way.'

'Tell me why.' Xavir lunged, grabbed Havinir by his collar and slammed him onto the floor. A surge of pain flashed through Havinir's back. 'Why did you have us slaughter all those innocents? Besmirch our name, have my brothers killed?' Xavir placed a hand on his throat, fingers of iron gripping . . .

'Such simple barbarism.' Havinir squirmed, laughing at the crudeness of it all. 'Whoever . . . has the wisdom . . . has the authority. The Voldiriks will be too much . . . for you.'

Xavir began to slam his fists into Havinir's face repeatedly. Pain came quickly, then thankfully numbness. 'Tell me!' Xavir snarled.

'*Whoever has the wisdom has the authority,*' Havinir spat one final time.

Then he lay there silently smiling, absorbing the agony, staring into this darkened angel of death, until a strange feeling eventually took over.

Xavir hammered his fists again and again into the general until bone gave way and his knuckles sank into something far softer and his hands were covered in blood.

The man's face was unrecognizable. His legs no longer twitched.

Killing General Havinir did not grant Xavir the satisfaction he had thought it would. Revenge had been dealt but the old general had taken the answers they'd needed to the grave. Xavir cursed his lack of control. It was unlike him . . .

Xavir rose from the body in the darkness and called out, 'I'm done.'

The door eased back and he heard the others stepping into the room cautiously.

Landril gawped at the corpse with his mouth open. 'I see you didn't need me in the end, then? It wasn't exactly the most delicate of interrogations, was it?'

'He wasn't going to talk,' Xavir said, walking away.

'He didn't get much of a chance,' Landril said to Xavir's turned back.

Xavir paused by the door. 'Whoever has the wisdom has the authority.'

'What . . . ?'

'That's what he said. Many times over. *Whoever has the wisdom has the authority*. Does it mean anything to you?'

'Not that I can think of,' Landril said.

'We have work to do here,' Xavir said. 'We need to search this place. Summon the others.'

By the time dawn light had broken across the old manse, Lupara, Valderon and the rest of the group had rejoined Xavir. Havinir's corpse had been left forgotten in his bedchamber. Of more importance now was what lay in the building itself.

They investigated one room after another together. In the basement quarters, they found treasures. Once illuminated by witchlight, the stone room revealed glistening items that had been hoarded from Havinir's campaigns: antique weapons and armour, and wooden chests overflowing with coin. Draped here and there, like discarded rags, were banners from extensive military operations: legion colours, great sigils of the Elder Wars and the Desiccation, and of places long forgotten.

'Here is your war fund.' Xavir gestured to Landril, running his hand along the surface of a trunk full to the brim of silver and gold coins. 'You can buy yourself a good army with this.'

'Oh, I should say so,' Landril replied with a grin of avarice.

Lupara looked at the spymaster. 'Get to the nearest settlements quickly. Find clothing, fighters and metal.'

'It will take time, admittedly,' Landril said, scrutinizing a golden cup, 'to acquire such things.'

Xavir nodded towards the weaponry amassed. 'I have counted a hundred swords in this room alone that could be of practical use.'

One item in particular was of interest to Xavir. It looked innocent enough – a flat-topped mahogany trunk of some considerable size – but once the dust had been blown off, the image of a crenellated tower was revealed.

It was the *Citadalia*, the same symbol as was upon his chest armour.

On his request, Birgitta melted the lock. Together Lupara and Xavir inspected the contents.

'Three of these items belonged to the Solar Cohort,' Xavir announced. 'I know them well.' He lifted out a black-bladed two-handed longsword, followed by a double-headed axe and then another longsword in a scabbard. 'The swords were made by Allimentrus, like mine,' Xavir continued. 'They belonged to Felyos and Gatrok. Brendyos used to wield this axe.'

Memories rushed into Xavir's mind: covert operations under the cloak of darkness, spearing into the heart of enemies in distant lands. Fronting campaigns and cleaving through the flanks of powerful foes. The din of war rose again in his mind.

He could smell the stench of mud and blood and horse shit, and recall the camaraderie of the Solar Cohort in their quarters in Cedius's palace.

'I had no idea,' Lupara said softly, 'what happened to these items. I only managed to recover yours, because your life had been spared by trial. The others . . .'

'Were murdered for a crime they did not commit,' Xavir finished. 'These are their weapons and it is a waste that they lie here unused. Valderon — take Felyos's weapon. You wanted a good sword. Now you can have one of the best. It's called the Darkness Blade — a companion of sorts to my own swords. Forged by Allimentrus when he was in his thirty-seventh summer, in the Seventh Age; you can tell by the tiny inscription, "A-37-7", on the base of the hilt. It's inset with a black witch-stone, which makes it a devastating weapon. When it encounters enemy flesh it blackens the skin. You can only imagine what a mess it causes when it strikes a body.'

'Black stones!' Birgitta shook her head in awe. 'By the source, I haven't seen too many of those. Allimentrus must have known some of the old warrior witches . . . They were thought to have vanished by the Seventh Age. Even some of those whom we refer to as Dark Sisters, who are a breed apart, were the sorts to have dabbled in the arts of necromancy too . . . and all manner of forbidden fleshcraft. Allimentrus kept strange company.'

'Allimentrus was a legend,' Xavir said proudly. He had read tome after tome on the great man. 'He was perhaps the only male who could manipulate magic. The Seventh Age was the most glorious time our realms have ever known — a time in which misery was a ghost and all nations prospered. Kings looked upon Allimentrus as a god, but he simply wanted to make better and more interesting weapons. In our Ninth Age we will never know the like.'

'I cannot take such a precious relic,' Valderon breathed. He shook his head, but his eyes were wide and greedy for it.

'It is a weapon, not a relic,' Xavir said. 'It wants to be used, not remain dormant in a trunk.'

Valderon took the blade with both hands and regarded it with awe. A moment later Xavir handed him the separate scabbard. *Havinir didn't even have the decency to look after these weapons properly*, Xavir thought.

'Tylos,' Xavir called.

Someone else called along the corridors for him, and while Valderon stepped away, inspecting the ancient weapon, the black man arrived at Xavir's side.

'There are some remarkable portraits upstairs,' Tylos announced, 'but this Havinir fellow, he has not looked after them.'

'Never mind about that. Take this.' Xavir momentarily withdrew the second sword from its arced casing, and the blade somehow shimmered in the murky light of the room. A red witchstone was set between the hilt and the blade itself, and old Seventh Age script wove itself around the weapon. 'This is the Everflame, one of Allimentrus's experimental items that he forged with a fire witch. Birgitta, you will have heard of those.'

'By the source,' Birgitta murmured from the other side of the trunk. 'This is going back some time. They are forbidden now, but in the Sixth Age – the darkest days of the sisterhood – they were said to have specialized in the arts of fire. The things they could do! Legend has it that they themselves could turn into flame and travel up the sides of buildings . . . but the sisterhood today consider it devilry, and such things have long since been eliminated from our stock.'

'It sounds to me,' Xavir replied, 'that you witches have tried to breed all the fun out of life.'

'That's about right,' Elysia added.

'Don't encourage him,' Birgitta muttered. 'Anyhow, is it not amusing how he can appreciate witchstones when they've been through that weapon-smith's hands?'

'I do not have a problem with the witchstones, lady,' Xavir said. 'I have a problem with those who wield them.'

Xavir narrowed his eyes at the ancient item, contemplating its lack of use over the years, and placed it back in its casing. 'Gatrok once single-handedly held the Stravir flanks against a barbarian horde on the Plains of Mica with this. They had been supported by a cave-dwelling race who venture out in the dark hours, and we had been vastly outnumbered. The bodies this weapon created . . . Tylos, take this sword. It's lighter than it looks and I think you'll have good use of it. When you wield it, the blade leaves a small trail of flames. It gets hotter and hotter in battle, and when it is at its peak it is able to melt through the toughest armour in an instant.'

Tylos bowed his head with grace. 'It would be an honour, Xavir.' He took the weapon in both hands as if it were some holy item.

'Jedral,' Xavir called out. 'Where is he?'

It took longer to find him, as he had been in the kitchens with Grend. Eventually the bald man with the scarred face stepped alongside his former gang leader. Jedral was wiping crumbs from his mouth. 'My apologies, boss. We found some pastries in the kitchen . . .'

'Never mind that,' Xavir replied. 'This double-headed axe was wielded by my old friend Brendyos. You remind me of him, although that's not why I'm giving it to you. No one knows who crafted it, or why it is entirely constructed of a black alloy, only that its blade never needs sharpening. It could slice a hair.'

'Why me, boss?' Jedral, unusually for him, appeared discon-
certed at the gesture.

'I've known you longer than any of the others, and you've
watched my back more than once. You may look like a savage,
you may look like you'll kill any of us given half a chance, but
I know you'd stand alongside us when the time comes. You grew
up using such weapons, so this will be second nature to you.'

'Axes, sure, but this is a fine weapon.'

Xavir used two hands to give Jedral the axe, the weight of
which seemed to surprise even him.

'It ain't light,' Jedral muttered.

'No, it is not,' Xavir said. 'So get used to it.'

Jedral stepped backwards, clutching the weapon. He did not
say his thanks but the look in his eyes was enough for Xavir to
know that this favour would not be forgotten.

Xavir glanced at his daughter, who had a strange look on her
face. Whether or not she believed the tales of her father, he did
not know, but here was evidence of his former life. What did
she think of it all?

He had been impressed by her actions on the way into the
manse. She had not complained, had taken her orders and
actioned them without delay. Her aim had been incredible. Her
skills were one reason they were all in here so quickly. Xavir
would have liked, somehow, to be able to tell her this.

Facing the others, he said, 'Help yourselves to whatever
weapons and armour you see fit from the rest. Some of these
items are decorative trinkets, but there are many useful things
here. The rest we might want to take with us somehow, to trade
or use for building our army.'

'Xavir,' Lupara said, 'we are near the border of Stravimon.
We should use this manse as a headquarters for whatever army
we can build.'

He gave it but a moment's thought. 'Agreed.' Xavir stepped towards the two witches. 'This is just the one room and the others need investigating. We have more work to do before we can rest.'

'We are not merely lockpicks or dogs to sniff out whatever it is you seek,' Birgitta said with some asperity. 'We are people too and we are tired.'

There was a brightness in his daughter's gaze that said she was keen to continue. 'I know,' Xavir said with unusual gentleness. 'A few moments more and we can rest.'

The darkened corridors of the manse contained only dusty paintings, red carpets gnawed by mice, and empty wooden trunks. Floorboards creaked under every step. The old witch brought out a selection of witchstones from her bag and weighed up which of them to use. She chose a blue one and held it up between her finger and thumb. She mumbled an incantation and then both she and Elysia began to scrutinize the walls and doors with more focus, rolling their palms over wooden panels and frames with delicacy. They were perceiving things that he could not.

After a short while Birgitta declared that she had sensed an underground chamber. She marched forwards, got down on her knees and pulled back the rug with a flourish.

A trapdoor.

'There is something strange around this place, though.' Birgitta appeared to sniff the air. 'I have thought that since we arrived. Perhaps it lies beneath our feet.'

Xavir crouched down to find the handle. It had been inset into the wood, hidden discreetly. He levered up the door and lowered it flat the other side, to reveal a large black hole and a ladder that led down into the darkness.

'I'll go first,' Xavir said. 'I could do with some light.'

'You could try saying please, then,' Birgitta snapped, pulling out one of her white stones. Carefully, she dropped it down below. It clattered quickly, indicating a short drop. A light began to emit from it, and Xavir could see a stone floor beneath him.

He lowered himself down into the darkness cautiously, prepared for an attack from beneath. There was definitely something here, something strange. An unusual smell. Using the witchstone for guidance, he began to walk around the chamber, which was so dark that even the witchstone had difficulty piercing its shadows. Birgitta and Elysia followed him down, and the witches soon enough produced more light through other stones.

'By the source!' Birgitta hissed, her eyes narrowing. 'Something feels rotten down here.'

'I know what it is,' Xavir replied grimly.

They were standing before an enormous four-foot-wide container made of thick glass, which was positioned on top of a short wooden frame like a stage. Xavir pressed the witchstone against the container and they saw that within it there was a woman, naked and dead, floating within a translucent fluid.

'Oh, by the source . . .' Birgitta pressed another stone against the glass to illuminate the form even more. 'What devilry is this?'

Xavir perceived another, similar container adjacent to this one. He stepped next to it and again there was another figure, this one male – again, naked and dead, floating in the glass box.

'There must be more light around here somewhere,' Xavir said.

'Ah, a cresset over there,' Birgitta said. For an old woman there was nothing wrong with her vision.

Somehow, without a flame, she managed to light the cresset – and shortly after, another. The stone chamber was illuminated to reveal six large containers, in two rows of three, either side of the room. Each one had been positioned within a wooden frame that acted as support. Warm light shimmered on the glass. Each container was about eight feet high.

Within the glass vats Xavir counted two women and two men; one container stood empty, but the last appeared to contain a human form – albeit one that looked flensed, as if it had no skin at all. He clambered up on a wooden shelf at one side to view the top of one container. It was exposed to the air and the fluids were even more rank close up. An eyeball floated on the surface.

Birgitta spread her palms against the glass and called up to him, 'What can you see?'

'Nothing. It's open. It reeks.'

Xavir jumped back down and began to scour the surrounding shelves. Cupboards contained tin cups and plates, along with barbed tools of a worrying-looking purpose.

'I've found a note!' Elysia said.

Xavir and Birgitta rushed over to her. The piece of parchment was nailed with a knife onto one of the cupboard doors.

'This is the same script as upon the armour,' Birgitta said.

'Can you read it?' Xavir asked, leaning over his daughter's shoulder.

'I can understand *parts* of it . . .' Birgitta replied.

'Do any of the words say the following?' Xavir asked. '*Whoever has the wisdom has the authority.*'

Birgitta's gaze flickered down the page as she scrutinized the language. With a fingernail she tapped on the bottom words. 'These two here, I think, say authority. And this word here just before could mean wisdom or blessing or knowledge. That was what Havinir said, wasn't it?'

'You did hear, then,' Xavir remarked.

'In between his *screams*.' Birgitta's tone was full of judgement.

Xavir shrugged. 'I did what needed to be done. It was a strange phrase. He said it as if it was some religious mantra. Words of faith. And if they're here on this note, it makes it even more curious.'

'Indeed. Most peculiar,' Birgitta said. 'What do you think of it all, little sister?'

'Clearly this place is for experimentation on humans,' Elysia began after a pause. 'I wonder if that has anything to do with the *wisdom* mentioned. Wisdom from seeking knowledge. But what was the general doing here and what was his connection to the people who wrote this script?'

Birgitta's eyes glimmered. 'My thoughts precisely.'

Xavir turned towards the glass containers. The human forms drifted there, almost motionless in the fluid. 'Havinir was mad.'

'A madman's world still appears sane to him. This is not an easy thing to arrange.' Birgitta gestured with her staff to the floating bodies. 'This was logical. Calculated. What was he looking for in these poor souls, we must ask.'

'And what dealings has he had with them? I worry that there are things happening in the country that are bigger than we think.'

'In what manner?' Birgitta said.

Xavir was unnerved by the situation. Havinir had hardly seemed to care about his own death, and now this . . .

'When the refugees were attacked,' Xavir began, 'I suggested that it was likely that Mardonius had a connection with this new enemy. That they were somehow employed on the king's behalf. Now Mardonius's old general has this room, these things, these bodies.' Xavir gestured to the glass containers. 'I may have disliked the man but it was clear even to me that Havinir was not himself, not the man I recalled. Something had terrified him so much that he'd rather die than betray it.'

'Who were the victims?' Elysia asked, pressing her hands against the glass of one containing a woman and taking a closer look. 'They might be mothers and fathers, sons or daughters. Only the source could know what that skinless one over there would have been.'

'That act in itself is not exactly an easy task, little sister.' Birgitta shuddered. 'Someone with exceptional skill has to have done that.'

'It must have been this new foe,' Xavir declared, walking back to the ladder. 'We should bring that note. Landril will want to spend some time with you deciphering it, no doubt.'

Xavir climbed up the ladder and eased himself back upstairs into the main manse.

'Are we finally done, then?' Birgitta asked. 'Can we rest?'

'You can rest now,' Xavir said, as he clambered up the ladder. 'It is mid-morning and I am hungry.'

'How can you be hungry after seeing this!' she shouted back up at him.

Elysia just looked at the containers and felt a slow fire begin to build in her stomach. Someone had tortured these poor people, for who knew what reasons. They should be made to pay for it.

Headquarters

Lupara's small force found Havinir's manse completely unoccupied. There were no servants or administrative staff. No soldiers, apart from those they had killed. Grend had raided the well-stocked pantry and the former woodsman was on the way to creating a feast for all. He had put together a concoction of cured meats, cheese and foraged leaves, with bread that was still reasonably fresh.

To Landril it was a slightly surreal scene: a group of warriors and witches covered in the dust of the road, eating in an opulent if scruffy dining hall.

Lupara and her wolves were surveying the grounds of the estate once more, although Landril suspected that the queen had spent so much of her life alone that she appreciated the solitude. Valderon and Xavir were not present. The two men were inspecting Havinir's quarters to see if there was any information about the strange experiments in the basement.

It had, so far, been an uneventful start to the day. An hour ago, in the calm of the morning, Tylos had caught Davlor handing a flower he had found in the garden to Elysia. She had accepted it politely, but it was obvious that she did not quite know what to do with the gesture. A few moments later, Landril watched the black man caution Davlor, and he overheard him say, 'Even the fool must choose his path with wisdom.'

'What would I want with a witch, eh?' Davlor laughed awkwardly.

'Your affections will go unrewarded at best, punished at worst.'

'What? She's old enough to fend for herself without the boss wanting much to do with her. Besides he doesn't 'xactly show fatherly ways.'

'I did not say it was he who would punish you – she is more than capable of that,' Tylos whispered in his ear, and then turned away, tipping his head politely to Landril as he passed him in the corridor.

Davlor caught the spymaster looking, and simply shrugged. Landril later found the same flower wilting on a sideboard, ready to gather dust with the rest of the house.

Everything about the place felt neglected. Milky morning light flooded in through the tall windows, illuminating thick shafts of dust motes. Outside there was a garden full of weeds, with thick clumps of oak and ash. The wind stirred, brushing a few golden leaves across the scene. Beyond the faded and crumbling statues of long-forgotten warriors, the garden led down to a cliff face. The yellow-green land beyond, where the more remote places of Stravimon spread east until they reached the sea, was covered in mist.

Inside, red and green tapestries depicting battle scenes through the ages decorated the walls, along with old swords and shields fixed above a large, empty fireplace. It was a fine affair, no doubt, and the men made much of the fact. But Landril knew it to be a faded grandeur and couldn't fathom why Havinir had let the place fall into disrepair. He certainly had the money to maintain it, but the general had chosen not to.

'I was born into a life like this,' Tylos said. 'Believe it or not.'

'Were you buggery,' Jedral muttered.

'No, no,' he protested. 'It's true. Albeit my father's estate was a little larger, warmer and . . . well, we had better taste in Chambrek. This military regalia – it's too crude. Weapons should be for war, not for decorating walls.'

'You've got a fine weapon yourself now,' Davlor muttered. 'Both of you. Wish the boss had given me one.'

'Like you could have used it.' Jedral laughed. 'You don't even know what to do with your arms and legs, let alone a pretty blade.'

'Not the point, is it? I've been good to the boss all the while I've known him.'

'You have indeed,' Tylos smiled. To Landril the black man had a broad, beautiful face. 'But I'm sure Xavir gave them to those he felt could use them. These are tools to kill people.'

'Fancy tools, admittedly,' Harrand interrupted. 'Even managed to silence Jedral there.'

'Must admit, boys, I'm not used to gifts like this.' Jedral had placed the axe before him on the table, and he caressed it now and again whilst chewing his food.

'Bet he can't wait to kill with it,' Harrand muttered. 'Take out his rage for being cooped up all these years.'

'And you don't feel that same rage?' Tylos asked.

'Never said I didn't,' Harrand replied. 'Even you, black man, you can't be this mellow all the time. Bet you harbour some desire for payback after being in gaol for so long.'

'I must confess,' Tylos said, 'even I feel a little anger at the time wasted, although I like to think I am wiser for the experience of being there. It makes one appreciate what is important in life and what is not. I remember a Chambrek poet, who—'

'Bloody hell, not another poet,' Davlor interrupted. He

stuffed a soft boiled egg in his mouth, and yolk dribbled down his chin.

'You'd do well to consider the arts,' Tylos said. 'It might make an enlightened man out of you.'

Davlor wiped his mouth on his sleeve. 'Doubt it.'

'It might be all that saves you from letting your anger get the better of you. It might keep you sane.'

'Don't get angry, don't want to be sane,' Davlor replied, lifting his clean chin up high. 'I just want one of them magic swords.'

The others laughed.

'Must admit,' Davlor said, leaning back in his chair, 'I could get used to this place. It's a step up from my old farm. Heard talk that we needed some sort of place to set up our headquarters or something. This would do nicely now that the boss killed the owner.'

'Did you see the mess he made?' Harrand said. 'Wouldn't like to have been the general in his final moments. You talk about rage, black man. Well, Xavir has more than enough. You think we're likely to lose ourselves to anger? Look elsewhere, friend, and don't let a pretty blade distract you from the *real* madman.'

Tylos glanced to Landril, who raised an eyebrow at the comment and said nothing. While part of him agreed, mad or sane, it didn't matter to Landril what condition Xavir was in, so long as he could stop those who wanted to destroy the country.

'Landril,' Davlor said, 'you know the boss's plans better than anyone. Will we end up here for a while?'

'Indeed,' Landril began, then cleared his throat. 'There are a few others on Xavir's list that need dealing with, and they're not too far from here. Two days' riding, at the most. Only

Mardonius will be the most difficult to, uh, visit. So yes, we shall be putting down roots for a while.'

Everyone fell silent for a moment.

'Fine with me. I ain't going nowhere,' Jedral said. 'Got nowhere to go to. I was a mercenary in a previous life, and it feels much the same now. Killing for a job. Except now I've got that.' He nodded to his axe and continued chewing on bread.

'I'll still linger,' Davlor said. 'Doubt I'll be needed on the farm, anyway. If it's still there. I know you lot all come from fancy backgrounds compared to me, but this is as nice as I've had it in life. And you never know, while we're here his daughter might fall for my charms.'

'Or kill you with an arrow and be rid of you,' Jedral quipped. 'Black man, what about you?'

Tylos smiled sadly. 'I cannot return to Chambrek. My family will still refuse to speak to me. If unseating a king is our aim, and to help save those who suffer under his rule, then that, at least, is an honourable quest.'

'You may think you have a point,' Harrand muttered, 'but I'm too old for any ideas of noble causes. Seen too much of that nonsense in my time.'

'You'll leave, then?' Tylos asked.

'I think so. Not right away. A life of going from tavern to tavern and eyeing up the serving girls, that's what I want. Maybe get my hands all over one as well – it's been a while. See, I served my time as a soldier and left the army when I still had my limbs intact. Not an easy life for an ex-soldier out here, I can tell you. No one wants to know the stories of the average warrior, just them like Xavir. The great ones. People like us, we're quickly forgotten about. Before Hell's Keep the most successful job I had was being a bodyguard to a duke, in a place not unlike this one. He spared me death after I got into that barroom brawl. To be honest, I didn't exactly hate life in that place. Keep your head down and things were fine. So, I don't know. What's the point of it all? What's the point in fighting, eh? It's all bollocks.'

'The point . . .' Valderon marched in and everyone turned to look at him '. . . is nothing to do with *glory* and everything about what kind of man you are.'

Valderon placed his master-crafted weapon, the Darkness Blade, in front of him at the head of the table, then turned around a chair and straddled it, with the light of the window cast upon his face. For a moment he stared at them each in turn.

'This cause won't win us renown, there will be no crowds cheering you on. It is *not* so that we can conquer or defend territory for the honour of our king. The complete opposite, in fact. Our king is corrupt: people are being driven from their homes. Homes that you once shared with them.' He pointed at Harrand. 'People who have done nothing to deserve it are being tortured. There are strange beings and creatures walking through our forests. Villages being purged, innocents are being slaughtered. So what we are about to do, Harrand, is nothing to do with winning fame and rewards. It is about keeping the civilized world in order. Because if we do not, there will be no messing about in barrooms. There will be no sly conversations with a serving girl to entertain your dreams of slipping a hand up her skirt. You will not have the luxury in which to be ill-mannered. There will simply be *chaos*.'

Valderon helped himself to some of the food. Harrand glared at him. Landril wondered if something more would come of it.

'Anyone who wants to go can go.' Valderon ripped apart a piece of bread. 'But the world is changing. *Has* changed. You'll have to travel a long way to find a peaceful country, and even then you'll have restless dreams of your old home. It'll be prison all over again. The only walls that exist will be in your head – and they'll be impossible to tear down.'

No one said anything. Heavy footsteps approached from behind.

Breaking the tension, Xavir stepped into the room. He was carrying a small leather-wrapped book in his right hand and tossed it across towards Landril. It landed on the table with a clatter, rattling his breakfast plate and knocking over a goblet of water.

'This is General Havinir's diary.' Xavir folded his arms, leaning against the wall by the window. 'I found it in his room.'

Landril eagerly unwrapped the book and began flicking through the pages.

'Voldirik rangers,' Xavir said aloud. 'That's what he calls our new foe – their soldiers at least. He mentioned the name to me, though it meant nothing. There seems good reason why we don't know much about these Voldiriks. They're not of our land at all.'

Landril began to scan the text until he came across the words Xavir had spoken. He read aloud for all to hear.

They came to my forests today, the Voldirik rangers. They assure me they are here temporarily. They have brought with them one of their wayseers, for which I am truly honoured. Mardonius has blessed me indeed with such favour, though I suspect he is as much interested in their results as I am.

Landril skimmed forwards several pages.

The Voldirik wayseer is a strange woman. She has entirely black eyes, set in an otherwise perfectly elegant human face. In her

*shimmering, many-hued gown she came to the basement to inspect
our specimens. The four townspeople have been dead for five years
now and their decay has not even begun. The flensed victim is
fascinating still, for all the organs and muscles and tendons still
seem healthy. The secrets to life are being unlocked before our very
eyes.*

'That was two years ago.' Landril looked up and shook his head.
'They have been conducting experiments on people.'

'It is disgusting.' Valderon gave a heavy frown, as if he now
bore the burden of their fate. 'And for what?'

Landril continued once again:

*The wayseer does not or will not speak much of our language like
some of the more established rangers, but I understood that she was
impressed. Her obsession for knowledge is typical of the Voldirik
race. They have, under cover, scoured the libraries of Stravimon, the
script halls of the royal palace, and yet she wants to know more
about our land. Their desperation to acquire information and
wisdom knows no bounds. That is how they have grown so much as
a race and come to dominate such a vast territory beyond our shores.
They are wisdom hoarders.*

Landril placed the open book down upon the table and
brought a steeple of his hands to his chin. 'Well . . . some
answers at last.'

'*Whoever has the wisdom has the authority*,' Xavir repeated. 'It is
what Havinir said. It is what we saw written in his underground
chambers. It was as if the mighty general was in thrall to these
people.'

'Vol-di-rik,' Davlor said, stifling a belch. 'Never heard of
them, not that I pay attention to these things.'

'There's not a lot you *have* heard of,' Tylos said, 'so that is not exactly saying much.'

'To be fair to Davlor,' Landril said, 'even I hadn't really heard of them until now.' He tapped the pages of the diary with his finger. 'I would like to spend more time with this. Perhaps Birgitta should be made aware of it too.'

Xavir tilted his head to the window. 'She's outside with Lupara.'

'And your daughter?' Landril asked.

'My daughter,' Xavir repeated, a half-smile upon his face. 'What strange words.'

'I wouldn't worry,' Jedral announced, 'if Tylos's tales are to be believed, he's probably got several of his own offspring scattered about Chambrek that he doesn't know about.'

Tylos gave nothing but a smile. 'I'm certain those words will become natural soon enough, Xavir. Familiarity is a matter of repetition. How did she fare in the mission?'

'Very well. Her skills with a bow are unusual, but I cannot deny how lethal she is. She killed a man for the first time today. Many men, in fact.'

'She takes after her father in that respect,' Jedral said. The others gave a gentle laugh.

'A walk in the garden will do her good,' Tylos said. 'Killing can be quite the burden at first. But these new people, these Voldirik rangers. What are we to make of them?'

'From reading briefly through this diary,' Xavir announced, 'I believe them to be the source of Mardonius's extra military power. Where the Stravimon legions could not be convinced to kill their own people a new race would think nothing of it. Havinir speaks of desertions from the main legions – and rebel groups protecting certain towns. But of "conversions", too, and I do not know yet what this means. There may be hope for our own cause if we can bring these factions together. It is clear that, for the tyrant, all was not as smooth as we thought.'

'Comforting news,' Valderon said. 'But where have these Voldiriks come from?'

Xavir was still facing the sunlit garden. Landril thought him young-looking with the bright light hiding the blemishes of time. 'Stravimon has ownership of islands off the far western shore; there are ports there, for vessels carrying cargo a king wishes to keep quiet. One lies to far the north-west of Stravimon's coast – called Port Phalamys – and that is where the Voldirik ships arrive.'

'This is all getting a bit heady for me.' Davlor rose from the table and sauntered to the door. 'I'm going to find me a decent sword. Who's up for it?'

Harrand said, still staring narrow-eyed at Valderon, 'Why not? Someone needs to make sure you don't cut yourself.'

Harrand, Davlor and Grend piled out of the doorway, leaving Landril with just Tylos, Valderon and Xavir.

'What is your plan, spymaster?' Xavir asked, with a knowing glance. Landril was still too busy watching Harrand leave the room. 'You look as though you have one.'

Landril leaned back in his chair. 'I must investigate the past. To do that I need to visit any of Stravimon's libraries, if anything remains of them.'

'Where is the nearest library?' Xavir asked.

'I believe there is one local to your other targets,' Landril said. 'As it's not in Stravir City and therefore an obvious place, it means that the Voldiriks would not necessarily have gone there to *accumulate wisdom*, or eradicate knowledge of their existence in this world. If I may be permitted to accompany you . . . ?'

'I planned on going alone at first. The witches would be useful, if you could spare them, Valderon?'

'The witches? I see no reason why not,' Valderon said. 'Although I take it by the request that your stance to the sisterhood is softening?'

Xavir shrugged. 'They're useful.'

'You wish to bond with your daughter, at least?' Valderon said, raising an eyebrow.

'I am not completely a monster,' Xavir said.

'Take who you need,' Valderon said. 'It is not as though we have an army yet, ready to march on Mardonius. And our road changes direction with every mile.'

'Here is what I think we must do, then,' Landril said, scraping back his chair. He began to pace the room. 'Xavir and myself — with the help of the witches — we will leave in the morning. We'll head in the direction of Golax Hold, the town where Duchess Pryus has her estate. Lord Kollus oversees the affairs of the settlement. The two have grown close of late.'

'Golax Hold,' Valderon repeated. 'Never liked the place. A granite cesspool. It got far more of the king's coin than any other town, for no good reason.'

'Well, for one reason at least,' Landril said. 'It had powerful residents. Cedius never liked sending money that way, so I've learned, but it was where the influential folk tended to gather, ever since the reign of Queen Stallax sixty years ago.'

'Tyrannical woman,' Valderon added. 'She spilled far more blood than is decent. Might have known Stallax set up a place like that.'

'Cedius spoke of her often,' Xavir added. 'Despite the amount of blood she spilled, much of Stravir's infrastructure is down to her. The trading patterns are down to her. The mines. The lingering tribal hatred . . . King Grendux, Cedius's predecessor, could not erase her trace and Cedius chose not to bother. Which is why a place like Golax still clings onto power. She was a canny woman, Stallax.'

'Well, to this day,' Landril continued, 'that's where coin ended up to buy favours or ease some political point. It won't be easy to get in – the town is, or was, well defended. But it has ample resources and, just as important for me, it has one of Stravimon's many libraries. I need to find out more about who these Voldirik creatures are. If Birgitta is with me to aid with the research, that's all the better.'

'And what of us?' Tylos asked with no agenda as he sat back in his chair. 'We just sit here and wait for you to return?'

'You have work to do as well,' Landril said. 'Valderon and Lupara must build the army that is desired. You have the wealth and a headquarters. You must recruit and train, and gather what men will join you. Your work here will form the backbone of what we do.'

'Administration . . .' Tylos sighed. 'You were my gang leader, Xavir. It seems natural to continue with you.' He leaned forwards to Valderon, and was very frank. 'This is nothing personal, you understand? You are a good man. Merely my loyalties have been with Xavir for so long.'

Valderon waved away the comment. 'Understandable, Tylos, and I respect you for it.'

Xavir, arms folded, still casually regarding the distance as if this conversation was the kind of thing he had been through many times before over the years, said eventually, 'It's important that the men get behind Valderon, Tylos. You have more sense than any of them, and the others look up to you for that, so it will be important that they *see you* supporting Valderon. What I need to do relies upon stealth. I will strike Pryus and Kollus like an assassin, not as a soldier. There is no honour in what I do, but it is a necessity if we want a clear run at Mardonius without his cronies rushing to his aid.'

'So be it,' Tylos said.

'Remember that Valderon was a commander in the First Legion,' Xavir continued, 'not the second, nor third. He knows how armies function. Put your faith in that.'

Valderon appeared faintly embarrassed by the praise.

Tylos offered a hand to Valderon and the two shook. Landril hoped it was the last breaking of the old gang ties and a continuation of the relationships that had been building over their journey. Former foes had become united in a common cause of survival.

Landril closed the book and tucked it under his arm, then made his farewells and walked along the corridor. He stood in the front, pillared entranceway, regarding the overgrown garden. He had tried not to reveal his deep concern earlier. No one else, apart from Xavir, seemed to understand the worrying implications about an entirely new type of people coming into this world. That there had been experiments on people from a nearby town was unnerving. Why were they conducting such research, and what was Havinir's role in it all?

Whoever has the wisdom has the authority.

The phrase had been much repeated, according to Xavir. The general had chosen to utter it as his final words. The note contained it. The diary revealed it. Was this the purpose of the Voldirik people, to deepen their knowledge?

Landril hoped there would be answers forthcoming at Golax Hold.

A Tactical Move

Idle chatter drifted in front of the fire for many hours. Grend had found a good supply of seasoned firewood and managed to build an impressive fire in the hearth of one of the manse's dusty front parlours. Plush furnishings were rearranged and brought forwards to the light. A supply of decent wine had been discovered, too, and Landril thought that such a discovery never worsened an evening.

Upon request from the other men, Valderon told tales of the First Legion, of their huge campaign through the salt flats of the north, into the lands of Kolpor and Roj, and of the enormous Ghosts of the Coast defence where a fleet of Rojan pirates had gathered in their thousands to destroy and raid the settlements in the far reaches of Stravimon. Cedius had given every man who returned from the campaign an extra flagon of ale for his efforts and rewarded the bravest with coin and honours. Not once did Valderon mention his own heroic efforts, but those of the men who had stood around him.

During the entire tale, Landril watched Harrand.

As the fire burned on, the old man continued to stare with rage at the former legionary. Landril didn't like the dark look that glimmered in his eyes or the way he touched his knives while glaring at Valderon's back.

I've seen that look before. Blood will be spilled if we don't take care.

Eventually, one by one, everyone decided to head upstairs to rest for the night. Valderon was first. Harrand stayed sitting by the fire, staring at the flames and sharpening his blades.

Landril returned quickly to his quarters to retrieve the small parcel of mushrooms that he had taken from the forest near Lupara's cabin – the same mushrooms that Davlor had touched by accident. He used a small knife to shave the surface of one of the mushrooms into a tin cup, into which he poured a glug of Chambrek red. He poured a cup for himself and walked back to the parlour.

Harrand was still there, as Tylos, the only other to remain, moved into the corridor, bidding him goodnight.

'Just us two left,' Landril declared, thrusting a cup into Harrand's hands. 'You're a curious fellow, you know.'

'How so?'

'I know so little about you,' Landril said, sipping his own wine.

'Got little to say, spy.'

'*Spymaster*,' Landril corrected. 'Years of training marks the difference between a spy and a spymaster.'

'Such as?'

'A spy merely observes and reports, in order to develop trust. Once trust is established, then the proper education begins.' Landril took another sip of the wine and said, 'These people from Chambrek, they know how to make good wine.'

It was enough of a nudge for Harrand to take a sip, which he did, and placed the cup back down on the side table.

'The guild of spymasters,' Landril continued, 'is an elite institution with its headquarters in Stravir City. For nine hundred years its members have been assigned to royals, businessmen, dukes, courtiers, just about anyone . . .'

Harrand hunched forwards suddenly, clutching his throat. In great heaves he attempted to vomit, but nothing came out. Landril watched him insouciantly as he collapsed, his body shuddering violently as if in a fit. And then, just as suddenly, he became still, eyes fixed to the roof and his face frozen in a rictus of pain.

As Landril checked for signs of life, a voice called out from the doorway: 'I never liked the man, but I had no need to kill him.'

Landril rose, processing the scene in his mind to work out how much Tylos knew or had worked out.

'He doesn't like Chambrek red.'

'Nonsense,' Tylos said, marching into the firelight. His expression was unreadable. 'It is a most agreeable wine.'

Landril placed his hands behind his back so Tylos wouldn't be able to see his twitching fingers. Displaying an utter air of calm, Landril sauntered back to his chair and slumped into it with a sigh.

'Why did you do it?' Tylos asked.

'Do what?'

'Come now.' Tylos sat down next to him, reached for the cup of wine without a thought, and began to bring it to his lips.

'Don't!' Landril hissed, his heart thumping.

Tylos smiled. 'As if I would,' he said, pouring the contents onto the floor. 'Now, I am not stupid. Why did you do it?'

'He was going to kill Valderon.'

Tylos appeared thoughtful. 'Valderon would have killed him, if he had tried.'

'That was possible,' Landril replied, 'but it would have had a bad effect on morale if he had killed one of our own. There would have been mistrust, at the very least, that old politics had been brought into play again. That mistrust would then spread throughout whatever army we bring together. People would talk behind Valderon's back about it. And, besides, I just could not take any risks.'

'You cannot control everything.'

'You are wise, black man,' Landril said. 'But I have spent my entire life controlling things.'

'I am observant, that is all,' he replied. 'Now. What do we do with his body? What is our explanation to the others?'

'His heart gave out,' Landril replied. 'We should arrange him in a chair, by the fire. We should try to make him look serene.'

'His heart gave way,' Tylos repeated. 'I can perhaps vouch for this diagnosis, for I have had *some* training from a physician. That is what I will say in the morning light.'

Landril felt the tension dissolve as the burden was shared. 'We are in this together now,' he said.

'We have been since Hell's Keep, friend,' Tylos replied, staring into the dying fire.

The Road to Golax Hold

Three days had passed since they had burned the old man's body. Elysia found the event sad, largely because no one else did. It was strange how some men – like her father, and Valderon – could kill, brutally, and be looked upon favourably, whereas others like Harrand, despite only being sour in mood and showing little violence, passed from the world with little comment. It was a thought that lingered with her over the days on the journey to Golax Hold.

It was taking longer than Elysia had thought to get there, but she was glad of the uneventful journey. They had taken horses and ridden through peaceful glades under a sunlight that, according to Landril, was uncommonly persistent for Stravimon. She was a little sad to be away from the company of the others. She had enjoyed listening to their pleasant simple banter that was a world away from the politics of the sisterhood, and though Elysia never said much, she enjoyed the snippets of their conversation, even the crude elements that spoke of lives radically different from the one she had known. She wished that her father would talk with Birgitta more than he had done, although at least his bitterness against them seemed to have faded slightly.

Elysia wore a few items that had been gleaned from Havinir's treasury of artefacts: a small adjustable leather breastplate that had a decorative leaf motif across it; brown, calf-high boots to match; and a tough, green undershirt, with gold stitching. It had a strange effect on her: she felt as if she had properly become someone else, that she was no longer one of the sisters. Birgitta, however, still preferred to dress exactly as she had upon leaving the sisterhood, though she made no comment about Elysia's new garb.

The peaceful glades soon became patches of darker, macabre forests. Amidst the thorny thickets, a few old ruins lingered, but old stone had been reused to make farmhouses or surrounding hamlets, leaving only markings on the ground for the most part. This repeated itself for miles into Stravimon.

Stravimon. The vast nation her mother had come to. Lysha – that had been her name. *Lysha*, she repeated in her head over and over. This was the land where Lysha had met the warrior, Xavir. Elysia had always been curious about her origins. Now one of her parents was riding beside her and she had no idea what to think about him, not really. Part of her was unsettled at what he had done to the general back at the manse, when she had seen that rage unleashed, but part of her understood where that anger had come from and even felt that the punishment was justified.

Xavir trusted her and her skills without question since he had witnessed them by the Silent Lake. It was refreshing not to be derided and doubted, as the sisters had done; unnerving but exciting to be relied on for her skills. What worried Elysia more was the thrill she had felt during the act: the rush of emotions, her ability to override them, the fact that each arrow enabled them as a group to achieve their aims. She felt as if she had a purpose, finally, and that she had contributed to something. That she had *meant* something to someone.

Was this normal?

Each night Xavir had handed her one of the Keening Blades and they had sparred calmly under a dark canopy. The blade was light and much to her liking, and though she felt she could somehow activate the witchstone within the hilt, out of respect she opted not to. Her father was being overly gentle with her, and she knew it. Whether or not she was really learning much about swordplay did not seem to matter. It simply felt right.

Xavir had attempted to speak with her about her mother on a couple of occasions. He did not say much. He spoke about the past because he thought that was what she wanted to hear. At first it had been, but soon she just enjoyed talking to him. Xavir had led an interesting life, certainly compared to her cloistered existence, and she enjoyed listening to his tales of campaigns, his friendship with Cedius, his travels with his brothers and encounters with figures out of history.

The one thing he didn't discuss was the battle that had led to his incarceration. She had heard the other men talk about it quietly when Xavir wasn't in the vicinity and understood that those responsible for the slaughter, the execution of his brothers and his fall from grace were what caused his dark moods and the rage that flared in his eyes. She wondered whether, when retribution had been dealt, Xavir would find some form of redemption. From what she had seen of him so far, she doubted this was a man who would ever find peace.

On the second night of travelling from Havinir's manse, heading ever deeper into Stravimon, they reached a settlement of a few wooden buildings bordering the road, which then continued beneath a small forested cliff. This was, Landril said, a place for travellers, yet Elysia observed that the residents, who were sitting on porches, swords or axes at their sides, seemed surprised that anyone at all was coming through.

They stopped at a dingy tavern called the Strong Ox, which looked as if it had seen better times. A large place, with wooden floorboards and candles melting on just about every table, there were a dozen people here at the most, each staring out into the coming evening or into the bottom of their own tankards.

'The only commodity of value here will be news,' Landril whispered to Elysia, 'and I'll be happy to pay for a round of drinks to loosen tongues.'

They approached the bar and waited while the landlord served them.

'Place is a shit-hole now,' one man said, rising from a table by the fire. He gave half his life story in the time it took him to get from the table to the group: his name was Gorak and he used to work for the nearby mining company. He wore a simple, drab brown and black outfit, with old boots, and the travellers obviously broke the tedium for him as he regaled them with the town's history. 'Decade ago when old Cedius ruled, this was a boom town. Even when King Grendux, fool that he was, ruled for so long. Half the place has been torn down and sold on. Few of us stayed. I think I'll take my chances here, given what I've heard's going on in Stravimon.'

'And what exactly have you heard?' Landril asked.

'Beasts stalking the forests, taking more than just cattle,' Gorak declared. 'King's troops turning on his own people. Invaders from another kingdom – can you imagine that? Foreigners here in Stravimon . . .' Gorak shook his head.

'There have always been foreigners,' Landril replied. 'They have bought our wares and put money into our cities.'

'Not this lot, though. They're violent. Bugger knows where they came from. Bugger knows where our own legion is, for that matter. It'd be a brave man who made a prayer to the Goddess about the matter too – not that I'm bothered by such things. Cedius must be turning in his grave. Ain't a world I want to be a part of, no sir. I'm happy here with that miserable landlord and my drink.'

Gorak took a swig of ale from his tankard, leaving foam around his grey beard. Elysia found him vaguely amusing, if crude. He paused and his eyes narrowed at Xavir. 'That's a fancy uniform, lad.' He prodded the motif on Xavir's chest, which was head-height for Gorak.

'It belonged to the Solar Cohort,' Xavir replied.

Gorak made a sharp intake of breath and shook his head. 'Have we ever needed them. Where'd you find it? It looks expensive. You should watch your back – there's a good few thieves round these parts these days.'

'It is mine,' Xavir replied.

'Come again?' Gorak leaned forwards, tilting his head.

'I am Xavir Argentum, former commander of the Solar Cohort. This uniform is mine.'

The man's jaw was agape. Gorak didn't look like a man who was impressed easily. He regained his composure. 'Thought you were dead with the rest of 'em.'

'I'm sure some people wish I were,' Xavir said abruptly, glaring at him disdainfully.

Gorak took a step back.

Landril leaned in. 'Let me replenish your tankard.'

'Aye, that's good of you.' Gorak was still staring at Xavir as he handed over the container and slunk back to his table.

'We're supposed to be making friends here,' Landril hissed quietly at Xavir, who frowned at the spymaster and shrugged. Landril looked at those watching them and gave a huge smile. 'And drinks for anyone else who cares for another.'

Within a few moments the entire place had lightened in mood. They seated themselves at a table out of the way and watched as, with every drink, the patrons became jocular – and more importantly – increasingly garrulous.

It was mostly men here, with a couple of women that Landril explained were probably being paid for their company.

'Which gives me an idea,' Landril said, turning to Elysia with a sly gaze. 'I need a pretty young girl, like you, to keep me company. Along with these free drinks, you'll help loosen tongues – because men can be stupid like that. Tonight you'll be my sister. Yes?'

'I guess,' Elysia replied with a shrug.

'Do you mean to whore her out?' Birgitta snapped.

'Not at all.' Landril said calmly. 'But a pretty face does wonders in making men want to impress. They'll spill all sorts of secrets just in the hope of a kiss.'

'A kiss,' Birgitta scoffed.

'I'll be fine,' Elysia said, 'really.'

'Wait.' Xavir leaned down, withdrew a small blade from his boot and handed it over to her. 'In case anyone tries to be more than just friendly.'

Elysia gave a thin smile and accepted the blade, slipping it down the side of her own boot.

'How fatherly,' Landril said drily. Now –' he turned to Birgitta – 'you and Xavir sit over here and have a drink. Talk about the old days or something – you'll enjoy it. Meanwhile, we're going to glean as much information from this rancid little settlement as possible.'

Elysia looked back over her shoulder at Birgitta's fuming face as Landril took her by the arm, steering her towards a group of men.

'Your name is Brella,' he said, 'and I am Baun.'

They seated themselves at the end of a large table. Landril was no more the cautious, nervous man she had seen privately, but like an actor upon a stage – controlled and composed. 'Gentlemen! I hope your drinks are not as foul as the landlord's face?'

They chuckled at his comment and thanked him again for the free drinks.

'Why're you throwing the coin around?' someone asked.

'Ah well, we have just fled our parental home, having inherited a little money. Given we hated our father so much we decided to give some of his coin away to worthy causes. And what more worthy a cause than drink?'

'Why's she got witch eyes, then, eh?' one man muttered.

'Abandoned. Poor Brella here, her mother was a witch. Our father sowed his seed in just about every field in the country, but we got what was rightly ours, if you follow me.'

'Killed him?'

Landril shook his head theatrically. 'I did not take his life, merely his coin. Now, will you permit us a little of your company? We've been on the road for hours and not spoken to a soul apart from the companions we fell in with – and they are not the most merry of souls.'

They spent the rest of the evening engaged in conversation. On one hand Elysia delighted in the freedom of the locals' speech, which was a world away from the sisterhood's controlled and secretive conversations; yet on the other, she despised the looks she received from two men sitting close to her. She did not want to reveal her discomfort and certainly didn't want to show up Landril. The spymaster was at work and seemed to be enjoying every moment of it.

With the mines closed and people fleeing their homes, times had changed and this settlement had changed with them, recently becoming a smuggler's haven to cater to those who had money to spare and no interest in where the goods were coming from.

Landril learned that out here in the more remote places, things had gone from bad to worse. The clan system, whereby families provided their loyalty and support to the king by keeping the peace in their own realms, had collapsed. Instead a centralized army, the king's legions, filled its place. No more were the soldiers honourable, trained well and fighting for the good of the country. They were mainly paid mercenaries, with no morals and little interest in justice – taking what they wanted and leaving chaos in their wake. For a large amount of 'protection' money they left this place well enough alone, so the town was free to carry out its furtive business.

'I also heard a rumour from a woman on the road about some foreign rangers, not mercenaries, but something else,' Landril said more quietly. 'I heard the word "Voldirik", though it meant nothing to me.' He shrugged and sipped his drink, though Elysia could see he had one eye on the group to judge their reaction.

There was a moment of discomfort, until a younger man with wide eyes said, 'We don't know where they came from, or what they want. But they bring no good to these parts. I heard more than one rumour say they took a man in the forest. Cut his head open. Ate his brains. Wanted to know his thoughts and everything by eating them.'

Whoever has the wisdom has the authority, Elysia thought darkly.

'Stories, Tek, nothing more.'

'Maybe so, but it ain't exactly a good omen, is it?' the local stifled a belch.

'Well, this is a mood killer, no messing, an' I was having such a good time.'

'My apologies, gentlemen,' Landril announced, 'but you can understand the worry of two travellers on the road with such fiends about.'

'She can stay with me,' one of the men said with a leer. 'I'd keep you safe, honey.' The others laughed into their ale.

Elysia gave him a stiff smile and fingered the knife in her boot.

'We have even heard tell of a general named Havinir,' Landril continued, ignoring the comment, 'and were told not to stray too close to his dwelling . . .'

The mood turned dour.

'You'll vanish,' the man called Tek muttered. 'He's hired helpers in the past. Whores and servants. They never return.'

Landril quickly turned the conversation to other matters, asking more about the local soldiery, querying whether any were for hire to protect two travellers on the road. They told him that Golax Hold was the only place that had a standing guard: a handful of its clan's soldiers still protected the place.

'Mind, they won't venture out near here or into the forests,' Tek said, swilling the beer in his tankard. 'Not with all them rebels attacking soldiers.'

Landril looked at the young man with curiosity. 'Rebels?'

'Aye,' Tek said. 'All those that won't kowtow to the army, they've set up camps in the forests. Attack the king's merchants and armies like bandits. Foolish, if you ask me. Best to just accept the way things are and pay for protection. That's if you got the money.'

Elysia thought it sounded hopeful if there were others out there fighting against the king.

'Like the Duchess Pryus over at Golax Hold. Got more money than sense, that woman. Instead of building up an army to protect herself, she has some celebration, they say. Each month. The woman's blind to what's going on in the outside world. Either that or she just don't care.'

'A ball?'

'Something like that. Drinks for rich people, anyhow. Nothing for the likes of us,' Tek said bitterly.

'When is it?' Landril asked casually. Elysia realized this might be the opportunity for them to enter unseen into Golax Hold.

'Next one's in about four or five days' time,' someone replied at the far end of the table. 'She's got more of them planned. Seems to be a gathering for those who once meant something in Stravimon. All different now Mardonius is doing things his own way. Barely holds court himself, and who'd be mad enough to go near that Red Butcher of his?'

Elysia was saddened at the stories of Stravimon. She had been led to believe it a place of grandeur, of nobility, of honour. Little of that was left, going by what these men were saying. There seemed no future or hope, so they just got on with things the best they could.

Landril eventually rose, pulling Elysia with him. The men either side of her looked crestfallen. 'We must bid you good evening, gentlemen. It has been a pleasure, but we are tired travellers and must arrange our rest for the evening.'

Landril bowed and, under the watchful gaze of several men, they stepped back across the tavern.

A Night at the Tavern

'What do you think of her, then?' Birgitta asked Xavir, scowling at Landril's back as he steered her charge towards a group of men across the room.

'What do you mean?'

'Your daughter. What do you think?'

'What am I supposed to think?'

'Something. Anything. Speak!'

Begrudgingly, he had found Birgitta's company on the road tolerable, and that she had fled the sisterhood meant that he did not despise her as much as the rest. But that still did not stop her being irritating from time to time.

He wanted to ask her more about Lysha: if she remembered certain times with her, what she had been like. He wanted to verify his memories, but realized that it would have done little good. Xavir had not touched a drop of ale and was not inclined to do so. Since he had left prison, he found he had no appetite for alcohol, but the witch's commentary was making him reconsider his choice. She would not shut up.

'She's good with a bow,' he sighed eventually.

'This is all you think of your daughter?' Birgitta asked with the sharpness of a blade-edge. 'A girl of seventeen summers, the child of the woman you loved? And "she's good with a bow" is all you've got?'

Xavir shrugged, regarding his daughter from a distance. 'Other men are trying to place their hands on her and I have a simple desire to cut off their heads. Does this make you feel better?'

'Shows you have some feelings, at least,' she muttered.

'They are not fatherly.'

'Oh, but they are,' Birgitta pointed out.

'The word father, the word daughter, they describe a relationship I have no context for. They tell me I should feel protective of her: I translate this as killing those men around her. Is that what fathers do?'

'Some of them . . .' Birgitta had a smug smile on her face as if she had achieved some kind of victory.

'I see her mother in her.'

'Fathers often feel such things. Even those who are commanders of the Solar Cohort.'

'Who *were* commanders,' Xavir corrected.

'Nonsense. So long as you endure, so does the cohort.'

'A pretty thought.' Xavir recalled again the faces of Brendyos, Jovelian, Felyos and Gatrok. And of the great Dimarius, his close friend for so many years. Those men *were* the cohort, and now they were dead. 'There's only me left, Birgitta.'

'You have Valderon too.'

'A good fighter.'

'He looks up to you.'

'He looks up to my name. That is different. He was a good soldier and wanted to be a legendary one. Now he has a chance and that is why he is best to lead whatever can be formed. I am now little more than an assassin.'

'Strange that you two were enemies for so long,' Birgitta said.

'Enemies of a sort. Hell's Keep required some kind of structure, to give us a sense of belonging to something. There was nothing else. The place was hell because we lost our identities and needed other ways to define ourselves. For men of our station in life where honour and our reputation was everything – to becoming nothing and no one in gaol, well, that was torture. We found ways to survive.'

'You feel no need to lead these men?'

Xavir shook his head, giving a wry smile. 'I leave that to better men than me. I have only one thing I care about and that's bringing justice to those who wronged my brothers and me.'

'You care not at all for your daughter?' Birgitta tilted her head towards Elysia. The witch had slugged back a cup of wine and by now was quite voluble. 'Is she not worth fighting for?'

'I am sorry to disappoint you,' Xavir said.

'You crusty old shit,' Birgitta spat. 'You feel *nothing*?'

Xavir laughed at that. 'What do you want me to say, witch? That I will take her under my wing? Well, I'll ask her to fight alongside me as I see great potential in her. That is all I can say.'

'She's nothing more than another weapon to you, is she?'

Xavir sighed. 'I recognize her potential and see her longing to become better at what she does. I can help her do that in a way that the sisterhood never could. Is that wrong?'

'You have a point.'

'Anyway, what does it matter?'

'Because you are a *father*, Xavir. To put it bluntly, you were perfectly willing to stick your cock in a witch without considering the consequences of your actions. Well that's the consequence,' she said, gesturing angrily towards Elysia. 'Now take some damned *responsibility*.' With that, Birgitta rose from the table and began talking to the landlord about rooms for the night.

There was just one room available: a large space at the rear of the tavern. A lantern in the back window and a decent moon illuminated some of their surroundings. These shared quarters overlooked the cliff face, with a few trees here and there and a pile of refuse further along that was likely overrun by rats.

Xavir listened to Landril's updates on Golax Hold, the information that the spymaster had gleaned earlier. That the settlement remained protected was no surprise; that it was only clan soldiers doing the protecting indicated something rotten in the main army, for this was a Legion town through and through. Still, it was nice to know the clans still held some sway and that the old ways were not completely lost.

While the witches and Landril settled in, Xavir headed outside for some cool air. Truth be told, he didn't like being kept in such cramped rooms now that he was free.

He walked the street for a good while, staring across at the ramshackle wooden buildings and trees. In his youth he had passed through this town once, following his father on clan business with the crown, but he could not recall much of it. Memories before Hell's Keep were somewhat unreliable in his mind and he had no desire to scratch at the surface of his past tonight.

It was well past midnight. The tavern had long since emptied, and people – if they had any sense – were resting in their warm beds. He must have walked a good few hundred yards, climbing gently from the foot of the cliff to where the road reached a track carved into the cliff face. Standing at the edge of the settlement, he looked down towards the black expanse of Stravimon. The moon was full, casting light across miles of grassland. A lantern glimmered in a far-off village, and woodsmoke travelled on the gentle breeze.

He was no Dacianaran wolf, but his senses were still sharp enough to detect a shuffling of feet behind a cluster of out-buildings some distance away. He turned to make his way back towards the tavern, ensuring that the blades on his back were loosened in their scabbards.

There were men following him. Two. No, three.

They were hooded and moved in his wake, trying to keep to the line of buildings and out of the moonlight, nestling them-selves behind barrels or crates whenever he paused. Deliberately, he stood in a position where even a fool would think it advan-tageous to attack him, with his back turned to the buildings.

They came at once, three men with long daggers flashing in the moonlight. Xavir knelt and rolled to his right, watching the first man collapse over his outstretched leg; Xavir grabbed the man's flailing wrist and, using the force of his own leap, snapped it. Screaming, the man dropped the dagger. It fell into Xavir's free hand while the other two men slipped in the muddy road to change their line of attack. Xavir slammed the dagger into one man's thigh and he, too, fell to the floor in agony.

Then Xavir eased free the Keening Blades and pointed one of them at the remaining attacker. The man stopped, shaking where he stood, the smell of fresh urine demonstrating just how terrified he was. He moaned pathetically.

Xavir sighed impatiently. 'Take off your hood, Gorak, and drop your weapon. I have no desire to kill you or your friends.'

Sheepishly, Gorak did as he was asked. 'H-how did you know?'

I could smell you downwind, Xavir thought. 'You're the only person I've spoken to in this town; I can tell you're hard up. You see a man in fine clothing and you think that the Solar Cohort have faded into stories, so he must have stolen those items from somewhere. You think it unlikely I am Xavir Argentum. You think he is dead.'

'Times is hard.' Gorak found more interest in the ground than Xavir's face. 'So maybe you *are* him. Why should I give a fuck, though? If the Solar Cohort was here, they wouldn't be letting the king get away with what he's done. Maybe you're just a man who *looks like* he's in the Solar Cohort instead. So yeah. I take a chance. The coin from that pretty armour would feed us for months. That's got to be worth more than chewing wood.'

His accomplices staggered to his side, clutching their wounds. They stood like admonished children before Xavir, but he felt no sympathy for any of them.

'Kill us and be done with it,' one of the others said. 'I'll take my chances in another world.'

Xavir took a single step towards them and they flinched. Two of them winced. Gorak had his eyes closed, expecting the worst.

'Pathetic,' Xavir muttered.

Then he put away his blades and walked back towards the tavern.

Fading Dreams

It wasn't Stravir City as he knew it was now. This was another time entirely.

A decade ago.

A younger man with few burdens. His black war gear was fresh, the leather uncreased, and it felt like a second skin. Xavir was standing in the quarters of the Solar Cohort, which was an annex of the palace of King Cedius. Their station was a crenellated limestone tower, second only in height to the chamber in which Cedius held court. Standing by the short but very wide windows, which to the outside looked as if the building had narrowed eyes, Xavir stared out across Stravir City.

The slate rooftops were glimmering after the rains, miles across the city. Some of the more prestigious white limestone and sandstone buildings shimmered with damp facades. There were numerous bridges in the city, over which hung tendrils of flowering plants. Numerous market plazas – different ones for food, metal, precious stones or leather – could be seen in between the buildings, each one thronging with crowds. The smell of bread drifted up from one of the capital's famous bakeries. A great many soldiers patrolled the distant walls and the river beyond curled like a snake towards blue-green hills, which remained hazy in this soft light. Everything was civilized:

the light, the pale stone, the scents. Here was no shit-and-mud city; this was the seat of Queen Beldrius, the first queen of the Ninth Age, and her three long-lived successors. Whilst other cities had faded from history, Stravir City remained untouched by time, unchangeable.

'It suits us well, my friend,' Dimarius said. 'The craftsmen get better each time.'

Xavir turned to regard him. Dimarius was standing tall in the doorway, having just been outfitted in similar attire to himself. Black leather jerkin. Black tailored breeches. Black boots. A fine cloak. His hair was as golden as the afternoon light that spilled into their chambers, bringing warmth and good feeling. His slender face and strong features defined him as a handsome man. The image of the tower upon each of their chests reflected this light, lending all of the Solar Cohort an almost holy appearance. He gave a wide, genuine smile; here was a happy man indeed.

'The leather is too stiff. They're cutting costs.'

'You complain too much!' Dimarius laughed and stood before his commander. 'We should enjoy this, should we not?'

'We should,' Xavir replied with a smile, 'and I am.'

'Your criticisms come from a need for perfection,' Dimarius said, then turned to the others. 'Gentlemen, you should get used to this. And don't look so serious! This is a grand moment for you all.'

Coming in behind him were Brendyos, Felyos, Gatrok and Jovelian. Together they were the six men whom Cedius would shortly be declaring to the court as his champions. It was the same ceremony each year, on the Day of the Five Deaths – dating back to the Seventh Age where five heirs to the throne were all butchered in their sleep – but now with Brendyos and Felyos having just joined the cohort, it would act as their initiation.

Sitting on the bench with their backs pressed against the white marble wall, the two men looked nervous. In the hour that Xavir had spent in their company, he judged them good men. He had already known them to be smart, athletic, each trained to believe he could do anything, but without any arrogance. No doubt they were comfortable riding out on the plains into battle, or scrambling furtively on some mission of assassination, but they were visibly nervous waiting for the honour of the king to be bestowed upon them.

Remembering what it had been like for him that time, Xavir smiled reassuringly at them. Afterwards things became far more difficult, for he realized he had ascended to the greatest station possible for a soldier, and that came with new burdens. People began to view him differently, with veneration – and expectation. Cedius had encouraged an almost spiritual appreciation of the Solar Cohort, even within his court. He had treated them as his elite force, given them only missions of the greatest importance, which required subtlety, precision and the finest battle skills. It was not always in battle, but in hostage situations or rescuing vital gem-laden cargo when it was rumoured northern war bands would strike at the king's wealth. And, when required, to aid the legions in situations where the Cohort's presence and reputation gave courage to their own forces and brought fear into the hearts of their enemies. As such the Solar Cohort were living legends – they had never been bested so they were idolized by the king's armies, and their mere presence could swing the outcome of a battle. That was a great burden to bear, and new recruits chosen for their fighting skills and bravery knew only the half of the weight of expectation.

Brendyos made a joke to break the tension in the room. Only Dimarius laughed. He held his new axe across his knees and was still staring at it in awe. Eventually the stoutly muscled man rose from his feet, rested the axe on the bench and examined the fineries in the room – the ancient banners hanging from the wall, the plush gold-leaf furnishings, the portraits of great kings and queens to have ruled Stravimon, in whatever form the nation had been known, and the golden statue of the Goddess.

'Worth a pretty penny, all of this,' Brendyos said. 'Not even in our castle did we have this much wealth on show.'

'It's a different life to ordinary soldiers,' Xavir said. 'And I mean no disrespect by that – for there are many, many good men in the ranks of the legions who deserve this life too. But I have been in this brotherhood for two years and only now am I getting used to the fineries enough to ignore them.'

'What's different about the other things?' Brendyos asked. 'I mean, I know about the fighting. But there are always tales about what the Solar Cohort get up to, yet one never knows what to believe.'

'We have wealth,' Dimarius announced, 'greater than many. Our families grow rich and privileged because of our position. There is no greater station in life, save that of the king. Given his only heir died years ago, it is said that Cedius may select an heir from our ranks.'

Dimarius glanced towards Xavir.

Brendyos raised an eyebrow. 'I also heard that the most beautiful women throw themselves at you, and there are fine wines and banquets at the end of a hard fight. I am fully prepared for such challenges, you understand.'

Xavir clapped the man on the shoulder. 'You don't need to try so hard, Brendyos. There may be women if you wish. There may be enough expensive wine to drink until you vomit. But you will grow tired of them.'

'Not all of us,' Dimarius interrupted, smiling.

'Dimarius entertains enough women for all our needs,' Xavir replied. 'But there are great reasons to serve the king. Nobility. Honour. Loyalty. Protection of the innocent and being prepared to give your life for others.'

'I can handle nobility as well as my drink.' Brendyos gave a youthful, handsome grin that could charm a thousand cynics.

'There will be pressure, though,' Xavir continued. 'Expectation will be heaped upon you . . .'

There came a knock at the door. The king's messenger stood there in a regal blue robe with a red sash across his body. 'His esteemed highness, King Cedius, now summons the Solar Cohort to his side.'

The six men picked up their weapons, then followed the messenger through the marbled hallway and up the three flights of stairs that led to the level of the royal quarters. Outside the throne room stood twelve warriors in golden armour, bright swords and white robes – the light of the sun somehow coming through the adjacent window to shine off their armour in a bright ethereal glow. Xavir knew that these guards were largely 'ornamental'. Secretly he thought it indecent that such delicately armed individuals 'protected' the king.

The six men of the Solar Cohort and the messenger advanced upon the double doors, which were drawn open from the inside. The room was drenched in golden light from the setting sun: mirrors were angled by the windows to cast the sun's beams into the space. The floor was polished, almost pure white marble. At the end of the room was a raised platform, on which the king's throne was positioned. The first time Xavir had come here it had taken him a while to realize that Cedius was the only one who could see out of the vast, rectangular windows to the east: they had been constructed eight feet up, meaning ordinary men and women could not see out. Only those on the throne could regard the view, and there was only one man in that position.

The messenger beckoned forward the warriors of the Solar Cohort. Xavir and Dimarius led the way, side by side, their steps in sync, followed by Gatrok and Jovelian, and finally Brendyos and Felyos bringing up the rear of their group. Xavir had walked this route so many times that he knew there were sixty-six paces across the sparsely decorated chamber to the throne. Obscured slightly by the hazy light of the room were the usual courtiers watching the proceedings with quiet respect.

The throne itself was plain. Each king chose his own; Cedius's was forged from the melted armour of fallen soldiers and fashioned into a simple steel seat. It was, he often told people, to remind him that when he made decisions there would be soldiers who died because of it.

On it sat King Cedius the Wise, son of Grendux the Fool.

He wore a cream leather breastplate bearing the symbol of a crenellated tower — not unlike that featured on the black uniforms of the Solar Cohort. His crown was gold and of a plain design; nothing showy or decadent. Cedius was a gaunt, austere-looking man. But his blue eyes were fierce, almost like those of a witch, some said.

The six men of the Solar Cohort fanned out in a line and stood before the king with their hands behind their backs, their heads bowed respectfully. Cedius smiled at Xavir.

'My days of being a warrior king are long behind me,' Cedius began, his deep voice resonating around the chamber, 'but I am not so old to forget the sorrow of comrades dying in battle. The men whose place you take died as heroes and they will be remembered as such.' He looked piercingly at the new recruits: 'Brendyos of the Clan Gallron, and Felyos of the Clan Bryantine, you have been chosen not only for your tenacity and

skill, but also for your aptitude and temperament. You —'
Cedius gestured with a frail hand to the six men of the Solar
Cohort — 'are brothers of war, loyal to the crown and to one
another. Defenders of the people and bringers of justice.'

Cedius rose from his throne slowly and Xavir had to stop
himself from going to his aid. Truly, Cedius was no longer the
warrior king: the aches and injuries of war had come to haunt
him now in old age. He had trouble walking, but was proud and
refused to show weakness in front of his court. Only Xavir
knew how much such a short walk cost him. Cedius descended
four steps until he was level with the Solar Cohort.

'Not only are you brothers, but you are my sons, too. I have
no heirs, they all died in battle. But I have sons made of steel
and light, and that is why I formed the Solar Cohort.' He
turned to the two new recruits and smiled softly. 'Your training
has been demanding. We have shaped you into weapons to be
used only on missions that I decree. You are answerable to no
one but me. In return you have my *trust* and my *love* as I would
hope that I have yours.'

Cedius waved for a high priest of Balax to step forwards.
The elderly hunched man shuffled out of the darkness waving
a censer bearing incense. Chanting a long prayer to the god of
war, he began anointing the new recruits as members of the
Solar Cohort.

Thus began a long day, full of archaic ritual. Having seen a
few of his brothers die and be replaced, this was Xavir's third
such ceremony — including his own. There would be vows, a
repetition of them in his case, readings of ancient script, the
surrendering of clan colours. Then eventually a feast, in Cedius's golden hall, with a thousand candles and breathtaking food
on brightly polished plates.

It was a world away from where he was now. He was a

different man from the proud young commander he had been then.

Xavir closed his eyes, seeing his brothers standing before his king in all their glory. So young, so full of hope, and they had died for following what they believed had been the king's orders. Brought low in disgrace by the ambitions of a corrupt few who had no compunctions about having brave men executed like common thieves. No warrior deserved to die like that and Xavir would ensure that those who had caused their deaths would soon be facing their own.

Even if it cost his very soul.

Back on the Road

'I have purchased a bard and a poet,' Landril declared.

'You've done what?' Xavir replied.

They were sitting in the main tavern in the early afternoon light. Birgitta scooped up mouthfuls of stew which, from the sour look on her face, she was not enjoying, whilst Elysia had returned from scouting the streets with Xavir.

'I have acquired a bard and a poet,' Landril repeated. 'I met them at breakfast this morning. Fine fellows, both with commanding voices and charming grins. One of them toured the theatres of Chambrek for a while.'

'What,' Xavir replied, 'are we to do with these people? Are we to skewer soldiers with stories now?'

'In a manner of speaking . . .' Landril leaned back in his chair, raised his boots to the table and took a sip from a cup of water. 'But they won't be coming with us. They've already left, in fact, for they have much travelling to do.'

'Explain, spymaster.'

'As I have said before. We need to spread news of our cause. Our army.'

'We have no army.'

'We will do in a few weeks. I've heard of rebel groups not far away, and we can offer to ally with them. Meanwhile, to encourage more men to join us . . . we need to spread stories of our noble deeds.'

'What noble deeds?' Birgitta asked. She wiped her mouth with her sleeve and pushed the bowl of stew away from her.

'We have defeated an enemy of the people, defended those who were being victimized in his name and freed the locale from his corruptive influence.'

'When did we do that?' Birgitta asked scathingly.

'We killed Havinir and took his manse.' Landril told her smugly.

'There was no army!' she spluttered. 'Less than half a dozen walked in there.'

'By the Goddess!' Landril exclaimed. 'The truth doesn't win wars. Legends are made by those who talk the loudest and longest. People need to know there is hope so that they'll join our cause, and our enemies need to fear us.'

Xavir tilted his head. 'Fine. What news have you told the bard and the poet to spread?'

'I have said that the Black Clan has gathered in rebellion against Mardonius's army.'

'The Black Clan?'

'That's what we'll call ourselves. This is the resistance, driven by the Goddess herself. Led by a great warrior of the First Legion.'

Xavir mused on the idea. 'It could work, I suppose.'

'I have said also that you have returned. The great Xavir Argentum, favourite of King Cedius. That will mean much.'

'And they'll think nothing of the murderous rampage that Mardonius no doubt has said I engaged upon?'

'The poet didn't think so. He reasoned that history is kinder to those who have served well, even if things ended in tragedy. The people – those who remember you, at least – already speak of the old times, given there's nothing for them to look forward to. Besides, Mardonius has done far worse.'

Xavir was not convinced. He had seen the faces of those around him as they looked at him with fear and horror as the Solar Cohort had massacred their own. He remembered the cold stares of Cedius's courtiers as he was sentenced to be taken to Hell's Keep. Those expressions had haunted him for so long now that it was difficult to imagine that the masses would view him with anything other than hatred.

'Anyway,' Landril continued, 'we are spreading the news that you were betrayed. That there is an evil plot afoot – even if we don't know all the details. There has been enough suffering caused by Mardonius that when we offer them an alternative more people will join our cause. Our numbers will swell more quickly. If the legions still exist in any recognizable manner then many may be tempted to flee to our side.'

'Poets and bards can do this?' Xavir asked.

'It would not be the first time that forces have used such methods to achieve these aims. Wars aren't fought on the battle-field alone. They're fought in the minds and souls of the people as well.'

'Much as I hate to admit it, he has a point,' Birgitta said, waving her spoon towards him.

Xavir rose from the table and stared at the spymaster. 'You've done well. But you do not need me to say that.'

Landril's grin widened. 'Nope.'

They continued on their journey to Golax Hold. Steep-sided cliffs gave way to more agricultural vistas of small, interwoven, untended fields of barley, a picture that lasted the rest of the journey until late afternoon. A cold but gentle breeze brought forth hints of autumn. Xavir noticed the leaves were beginning to redden as they stirred in the wind, and that flower heads drooped down with their petals withered. Summers were always short in Stravimon, but intense.

Xavir felt little comfort at being back here. He had travelled this road many times as it connected with the great road north to the capital. Familiar sites stood around him, but they were noticeably different: a farmhouse or mill had become abandoned; forests were much smaller than he remembered; villages appeared sparse; no one was present to say a greeting on the road. This was a great nation in fear.

The track became a wide well-trodden road surrounded by muddy fields of livestock. A citadel wall loomed ahead of them, and poking up behind that was the spire of a cathedral. Behind the structures was an outcrop of granite rock that formed the rear of the town. It looked larger than it actually was – a trick of the distance, and perhaps intentional by whoever built the place.

Golax Hold, as Landril clearly enjoyed explaining to the witches, was the one-time capital of Stravimon, but as the nation grew in the Seventh Age the capital moved north to Stravir City. Golax first became a garrison for the most part, a military headquarters in the southern region of Stravimon. And with it being a soldier town, it had attracted a reputation for drinking, whoring and gambling on a grand scale.

Kings and queens attempted to challenge this by reducing the numbers of soldiers kept here, hiring more priests, building a cathedral and sending families to settle. But everyone mostly kept drinking through the Eighth Age. It retained its fortified front, protecting merchants and families from any bandits bold or stupid enough to attempt a raid on the settlement.

In the Ninth Age Queen Stallax set her bloody stamp on the

place, though, as she had done elsewhere, and the town became disciplined in its ways. Her statues could still be seen in many a courtyard – partly out of superstition for what would happen if they were removed. It was only during the reign of Grendux the Fool, although Landril said he was far from that, that the place eventually settled down to being a respectable trading post. Banking houses and merchant guilds were established here, outside the capital, and it was in this city that King Grendux managed the nation's finances. No one asked questions, but against all odds Stravimon prospered while the king seemed to do very little apart from drink and dance with ladies of his court.

There were now more people on the road here – hardened types used to weathering storms of all kinds. There didn't seem to be the oppressive air of fear in Golax Hold that they'd encountered in the outlying villages. Perhaps where there was coin there was a will to endure – or perhaps it was something more sinister and the mistress of the hold had made a deal to keep her townsfolk safe while the rest of her countryside suffered.

Wagons and carts were pulled by shabby horses along the different tracks. There was a wider road in the distance, which eventually became the great north road, and Xavir noticed it was quiet too. Strange, for the quickest link to Stravir City.

There were no signs of occupation by the Voldiriks. And no signs of anything unnatural here at all, which was enough of a warning to Xavir, as he knew all too well that this place was full of strange sights and sounds.

Under a rapidly greying sky, the group approached the main gate to the Hold, an enormous wooden double door set into the slab-sided wall, operated by chains. The left side of the door was open, allowing in a goods wagon.

Six soldiers in the legion's colours of red and bronze stood before the doors, inspecting another wagon which they quickly waved on into the city. None of the men was wearing his full face helm.

As the four travellers came closer, Birgitta used her staff to cast Xavir in shadow, 'I think it will attract quite enough attention having a member of the Solar Cohort return from exile in a soldier town, do you not think?' she said to him.

Xavir scowled. 'I will not hide from who I am. Why should I?'

'This is not for your sake, Xavir,' Birgitta replied. 'We want to operate swiftly and without trouble. We can enter this town without blood being spilled.'

'It would be quicker that way, but as you wish.'

The riders approached the two soldiers and Landril dismounted before them.

'Good afternoon, gentlemen,' he announced.

'Huh,' the soldier on the left said. He was a lanky young man whom Xavir could have broken with one hand. Had things really become this pathetic in the army? 'Could've sworn there were four of you a moment ago.'

'A trick of the elements, no doubt.' Landril grinned.

'Sure it isn't a trick of *them*,' the other guard grunted, his face full of cynicism. The stocky man gestured with a lance to Birgitta. 'Them's witch eyes, if ever I saw them.'

'You're quite right, my friend,' Landril replied. 'But they are visitors of his lordship, and old friends of Duchess Pryus.'

'Sure they are.'

'Allow me to present their documentation.' Landril rummaged in a saddlebag and brought out a scroll, which he cheerily unravelled before them. 'It's written in Dacianaran, which I take it all gate soldiers can read? It's on behalf of the Duchess Pryus's

336

summer estates. I'm afraid I cannot tell you their business, for the duchess would have me hanging above this gate with a rope around my neck if I did. You know what she's like.'

'Uh . . .' The tall soldier held the paper limply and looked across to the stocky one. 'What d'you reckon, serge?'

'Let me have that.' The other soldier snatched the scroll and eyed it warily. Xavir, who still hid in Birgitta's shadow, noted how the man's eyes went up and down the parchment unnaturally. He wasn't reading it at all.

'Seems right enough.' He sniffed. 'All fair. Better get on your way quickly.'

'Most kind of you,' Landril said, giving a short bow.

The soldiers waved them through and getting into Golax Hold was as simple as that.

Once they had entered and turned out of sight from the gates, Birgitta released Xavir from shadow.

They dismounted from their horses momentarily. Xavir turned to Landril and asked him, 'What was on the paper you presented?'

'A poem I found in Lupara's cabin,' he replied.

'Does Lupara know you have it?'

'Well, she was going to leave it there and I thought the cadence rather nice. Evidently the guard enjoys poetry too.'

'He did not,' Birgitta replied, 'look as though he enjoyed anything. Do they breed nothing but idiots in Stravimon?'

Xavir looked around to ensure they weren't overheard. 'I want to find my targets and be gone swiftly. How long will your studying last?'

'Who knows?' Landril shrugged and turned to Birgitta and Elysia. 'One can spend hours in libraries, isn't that so?'

'Speak for yourself,' Elysia said. 'I'd rather be anywhere but surrounded by scrolls and books. I've spent most of my life in them.'

'Then you can go with Xavir,' Landril replied.

Xavir raised an eyebrow at the girl who stood straight-limbed before him. 'Are you certain you have no wish for a quiet few hours?'

'No,' Elysia replied.

'So be it,' he said. 'You may as well learn the skills of killing, then.'

'By the source, I will have no such thing!' Birgitta spluttered.

Xavir smiled at that. 'What did you expect me to do here, witch?'

'I expect nothing less from you,' Birgitta replied, 'but I will not have you corrupt a sister so.'

'I'll be fine,' Elysia said. She and Birgitta shared a look.

'That she will,' Landril replied, leading his horse between Birgitta and the rest of the group. 'Now we will go this way, as the largest library in the city lies to the east. We must arrange a rendezvous before nightfall. The Silent Hawk is a fine tavern, if I remember correctly, and lies near the cathedral. At nightfall we will wait for you there.'

'And why, pray tell, did you send her with him like that?' Birgitta was walking with Landril along a cobbled street by the side of the cathedral. It was a cold afternoon, despite the sun breaking through clouds now and then. The seasons were changing and summer would soon be forgotten.

Golax Hold remained cast in shadow – partly because of the tall buildings and partly because of the looming rock face to one side of the city. Dwellings had been built into the gran-ite outcrop, in little nooks and crannies that formed a steep slope. A few large buildings stood on top of the hill, overlooking the settlement, and Landril remembered them as belonging to Duchess Pryus, but wasn't certain they still did.

'Because Xavir and Elysia are family,' Landril replied, 'and it will be good for them to bond.'

'Bond over death?'

'You've seen the girl with those weapons — she has it in her blood,' Landril said, 'so it's only natural that she'd want to hone her craft. Better she be prepared than not, don't you think?'

'I would, in theory,' Birgitta replied. 'But that man has a dark heart.'

'He has no heart, I would say. But that is what years of war — and years of gaol — will do to a man.'

'I hope such an attitude will not spread to his daughter.'

'Do you think a relationship is forming between them?' Landril asked.

'Hard to say,' Birgitta replied. 'For all that Elysia and I have shared over the years, we do not necessarily talk about those things. A woman of her age needs to form her own understanding of the world and doesn't need an old thing like me wittering on. She has always been quiet and reflective, too. Not one for words — always wanted to be out and about, in the hills and fields with her bow.'

'She has certainly had the chance to do that.'

'And she is the happier for it. I think she enjoys her time with Xavir, because he values her skills. Even if he cannot value her as a daughter.' Birgitta sighed. 'I just hope that she does not misunderstand his using her as being something more meaningful.'

'It might be,' Landril replied.

'If Xavir had a heart,' Birgitta concluded.

Landril gave a soft smile. 'Your greater fear, though, is that

Elysia will inherently be a killer like him. I believe instincts are carried in the blood.'

'It does concern me,' Birgitta admitted. Her face looked tired. 'Are these qualities bred in a person from a young age? Are they there already – as you say, carried in the blood?'

'Philosophers have argued for centuries on the matter.'

'With no resolution,' Birgitta said. 'But I do fear it. I can see how easily she has taken to killing at his request. A few days ago she felt guilty at taking the life of a deer . . . now . . .'

'If anything,' Landril replied, 'it is you who have accustomed her to the ways of killing. Hunting in the forests . . .'

'Come now, it's hardly the same, is it?'

'Blood is blood,' Landril replied, 'no matter how it is spilled.'

'Well, in that case perhaps Elysia is destined to be a killer after all. Be it in the blood, or be it part of her education. Maybe it is my fault, but I have always made my views on violence clear to her.'

They continued to the rear of the cathedral, passing traders and locals draped in dreary shawls. A handful of soldiers in bronze armour lingered on certain street corners, and Landril took these to be streets where senior administrators of Mardonius's regime would pass through.

Landril was tempted to go into the cathedral itself and begin prayer, but he knew Birgitta, being a witch, would be uncomfortable. There was always time later. The streets became more illogical and angled, narrow with tall buildings that looked so precariously constructed that they might fall down at any moment – and had probably looked that way for decades. Cloaked figures squeezed by, their faces concealed by hoods.

The library was squirrelled away in a forgotten region of the cathedral quarter. Landril had been here numerous times over the years, for the priests and clerics of the Goddess were known for their sensitive preservation of history. It was located at the end of another narrow street, the buildings made of the same dark stone as the cathedral itself.

Landril knocked on a plain wooden door. It was opened by an old lady in simple brown robes, which gave her the air of a nun. Her green eyes, which scanned between himself and Birgitta, were still bright and keen, even if her broad face had been worn by time. Landril whispered an old blessing of the Goddess, which made her smile.

'Landril Devallios.' Her voice was frail, as if she had been speaking for much of her life.

'Hello, Jamasca,' Landril replied.

'It has been a very long time.' Jamasca looked up at him affectionately and took both his hands in her own. 'Come in, and bring your young friend.'

'Young.' Birgitta chuckled. 'I'll accept that, dear lady, and bless you for it.'

As they walked along the polished wooden floorboards, they skimmed over the past few years since they had been apart, it was light gossip, but Landril was keen to know the current state of affairs in the settlement. From what they heard it seemed that Golax Hold was relatively untouched by events occurring in the wider world. Jamasca had heard of libraries in the capital that had been ransacked by foreign invaders thirsting after knowledge, but she would not accept them as the truth unless there were consistent written accounts of it, or had seen it with her own eyes. Which was unlikely, she added, given she did not travel much these days.

Jamasca had been a great scholar under the rule of Cedius, often venturing out to investigate rumours of bizarre creatures or improbable rituals. But these days her back was playing up. Her bones were frailer than they used to be. Now she dwelt in the cathedral quarter library, dusting down books and rearranging parchments, reading as much as she could – as always. Occasionally she updated some official records upon request, but it was a peaceful life, and one she enjoyed.

'So tell me, Landril, what is it you seek today? I always enjoy it when you spymasters venture here – your requests are far more interesting.'

They were sitting on some cushioned chairs in a small chamber, sipping a fine mint tisane. The mullion window had darkened as day eased into late afternoon, so Jamasca lit several candles to brighten the place up before evening came. A few spots of rain rattled against the glass.

Landril could see her properly now: her face was thinner than he remembered, and he asked if she was eating well.

'When I remember to do so,' she replied cheerily.

Her grey hair was tied back. Jamasca must have been in her sixtieth summer by now, yet her eyes retained the sparkle of her youth.

'We have travelled far and seen many unusual things,' Landril said. 'But I may as well start at the beginning.'

Landril recounted his tale, from before Hell's Keep, to breaking out Xavir, through to their perilous journey back to the wolf queen. Then onwards, towards Stravimon and seeing the plight of the fleeing refugees and their arrival at General Havinir's house.

Birgitta added her own story, from what had happened with the sisterhood pledging its allegiance to Mardonius in exchange for access to witchstones, through to the incidents in the village. Jamasca made no judgement about Birgitta being a witch, though she must clearly have known what she was when she invited her into the library. Such impartiality was one of the qualities Landril greatly admired in the old scholar, and one of the reasons he felt so comfortable in her presence.

'Well, you've had quite the adventure, then,' Jamasca said eventually. 'You mention Havinir's curious diary. I take it you have it with you?'

'Naturally.' Landril reached into his satchel and produced the book. 'He has many things to say, and we —' Landril nodded to Birgitta — 'do not fully understand them. It is why we have come here. For enlightenment. For your advice. We can both independently verify much of what he talks about, notably the people he describes as the Voldiriks, but there are so many more questions.'

There was a flicker of recognition in the old scholar's eyes at the name. She shifted her robes slightly and leaned back in the chair with the book, though it remained unopened on her lap. He knew she was sifting through her mind.

'You wish to learn more about these Voldiriks, eh?' Jamasca asked.

'I do,' Landril replied. 'We have found pieces of their armour with foreign script upon it too. I have that with me if you wish to see it.'

She turned her hands palm upwards, though with her wrists still on her lap. 'I may look at it later. For now — we drink, we talk, and we consider knowledge.'

'I fear that is what the Voldiriks think too. Whoever has the wisdom—'

'Has the authority,' Jamasca concluded, closing her eyes softly.

Landril was agog. His heart thumped with excitement. 'You know of the phrase?'

'Of its translation, at least. The language itself is difficult, with a harsh inflection. It's physically painful to speak; brings out the worst in a human larynx. To be honest, the state of my voice these days, I fear using that language may silence me forever.'

'We need to know about the Voldirik people,' Landril urged. 'If you can help us, if you can enlighten us as to their origins, their history and their actions . . .'

Jamasca opened her eyes. 'I can guide you to the texts, most certainly. I will find out what I can for you.'

'You haven't asked the obvious question,' Landril said.

'Which is?'

'How is it that the Voldirik people are on our continent, are *here*, and that I have armour from them?'

Jamasca sighed sadly. 'My world these days stretches from this seat to the parchment room on the far side of the library. So long as the Voldirik people do not enter this library, I will be fine.'

'And yet, with all this . . . wisdom contained here . . . you may well expect them sooner or later,' Landril added.

'You are a devilish thing.' Jamasca chuckled. Then any laughter faded away and the silence was telling. Her gaze grew distant and reflective. 'I worry, greatly, if they are present in our lands. Stravimon used to feel so secure.' She placed Havinir's book and her cup to one side and rose from her chair. 'Come. Let us find your answers, and I will read this later while you search.'

The library was reasonably organized. If one knew the systems, then it made sense, but to a newcomer it seemed a labyrinth of parchment and old leather. Birgitta lit a witchstone on her staff, much to Jamasca's delight, and the winding, haphazard passageways were illuminated in all their glory.

'There must be thousands of years of civilization recorded here,' Birgitta said.

'And much more.' Landril glanced across some of the titles:

Fescews' Histories of the Fourth Age Battles, Deadly Botanicals of the Southern Shores, Confessions of King Goran, The Child-People of Ancient Herrebron and *Chambrek Poetry, Volume One Hundred and Four* were just a few of the books that caught his eye.

They arrived at a small desk station, a stone alcove in which Jamasca lit several candles to brighten the place up. There was another small mullioned window here, with the last light of the afternoon on the other side.

'Now, that row down there –' Jamasca indicated with an outstretched arm – 'is where you will find the histories of Sixth Age civilizations and of the Second Age, where you will find a good deal of work by Mavos. The shelves to the bottom should have plenty on the Irik civilization.'

'It was they who fled our lands to form a new realm elsewhere,' Birgitta said.

'Indeed,' Jamasca replied. 'In the Sixth Age we hear the first mention of them becoming the Voldirik people. Now, the top two shelves contain scraps of translations of works supposedly written by the Voldirik people. They exist only as parchments and scrolls within other works. I have never truly been able to vouch for their authenticity, but I hope that now you have another piece of the puzzle. The opposite shelf contains a couple of commentaries by scholars during the Sixth and Seventh Ages on those people, as there was believed to be . . . an invasion of some kind, although this was met by a vigorous defence by the savage Queen Demelda. It was claimed she sent them back with their tails between their legs, but only after uniting the entire continent; she vanished shortly after, and some scholars argue she was actually sighted aboard one of the Voldirik ships and sailed with the fleet back to wherever it is they came from. And that's the thing – we know there are lands to the far west, but no one from our shores has ever ventured there. It may well be easier to attempt to sail into the stars themselves. These are the only pieces of information I have for you.'

'Well I'm surprised there is as much as this,' Landril added enthusiastically. 'We have only a few hours before we must meet with our travelling companions.'

'There is a spare bedchamber here. It is musty, and not exactly comfortable, but for late-night scholars it has proven useful over the years.' Jamasca chuckled. 'It is there if you need it. Now, I shall be back at the other end making sense of Havinir's writings. Come and find me when you're done.'

The Art of Assassination

Xavir and Elysia were sitting on a stone bench at the edge of a small courtyard, eating a loaf of bread.

'The bakeries here are awful,' he said idly. 'Not a patch on those in the capital.'

'You haven't been there in years,' Elysia replied.

'Thank you for reminding me,' Xavir said.

'I meant that your memory might be playing tricks.'

'No. The city is famous for it. When we get there, soon, I'll find you one from the master of the Guild of Bakers. You'll never forget it.'

'They have a guild for bread?'

'Good food builds the soul of an army. Never forget that.'

Xavir felt a few drops of rain on his face, and the wind beginning to stir. The traders in front of them were starting to pack up. Very few customers lingered. Darkness wouldn't be far away. Xavir spent time pointing out certain observations to Elysia: the way a man walked indicating an injury likely from falling from a horse; the way another's back was hunched and fingers crooked from spending hours at a scribe's desk; how moss and lichen grew on certain sides of stone, which indicated a northerly perspective; the way everyone avoided a specific route because of its proximity to a certain statue. Xavir said that if she watched people long enough, like when tracking animals, they would show her patterns and predictability. These could then be exploited. Whether or not she cared, he couldn't tell, but she certainly indulged him with her attention. She said she liked to know such things. She said they were practical.

'Anyway, it's a good use of our time as Landril and Birgitta will be hours,' Elysia said.

'Very likely.' Xavir replied.

'You come to a new town to kill people,' Elysia continued. 'You watch them for a while. So what steps do you have to take next?'

'Birgitta would not take kindly to you learning such dark arts, I'm sure.' Xavir chuckled.

Elysia shrugged. 'Death is a part of life.'

Xavir frowned at her. 'These are not usually the utterances of a young woman. An older one, certainly. But you are in your prime. You should have nothing but joy for life.'

'I am not like other young women,' Elysia said. 'Certainly not like those in the sisterhood, which is all I have to measure myself by. It sounds as if my mother may have been a different young woman, too.'

'She was,' Xavir replied, staring into the distance. 'She cared little for the rules of the sisterhood. Perhaps such rebellions at a young age are more common than you think. You may have judged your young peers harshly in their subservience.'

Elysia considered this then shook her head. 'No. They were all too respectful of authority to consider rebelling. They did precisely what they were told – always. They never once thought for themselves.'

'Thinking for oneself does not necessarily come with age. Quite the opposite in some circumstances. You're lucky to think as freely as you do. I cannot believe such an attitude is because of Birgitta — from what I understand, she has taught you *because of* your nature.'

'She's been talking a lot.'

'She thinks that because I am your father,' Xavir continued, 'this information would be important to me.'

'It could just be because I'm part . . . whatever it is you are.' Elysia shrugged and regarded the ground.

Xavir laughed. '*Whatever I am.* Yes, you could well be whatever I am. So, you would like to know more about how someone like me plans on killing two very wealthy people. These are dark thoughts — are you certain you wish to know?'

'I would like to understand what goes through your mind,' Elysia replied.

'It is more complex than you may think. There are rules governing how people may die. Take our situation. I am now, in a way, an ambassador for this Black Clan that Landril is concocting. If I kill two people quietly in their sleep like a common murderer, who would get to know about the Black Clan? Who would fear or respect what we can do? No one.'

'So you create a spectacle,' Elysia replied. 'Something to make other people fear you and pay attention to the Black Clan.'

'Precisely so. But we don't necessarily want *everyone* to fear us. The people of Stravimon may not like what Mardonius is doing to them — in fact, they fear him already — and so this assassination will be a sign. A sign of something changing within the nation for the better. What may be a shock to the victims and their family is actually a great act of kindness towards a nation.'

'Is this acting for our cause, or is this still revenge?' Elysia asked.

'Do not misunderstand me, this is still about revenge as well. They allowed the slaughter of hundreds of innocent men just to destroy my reputation. I lost part of my life – I lost my brothers, my honour, my identity to these people. I cannot take that time back, but I will make them suffer for it.'

'You did not look as if you enjoyed killing General Havinir.'

'There is very rarely pleasure in killing,' Xavir admitted. 'It is a job, one that must be done. A lot of people shy away from it. People are willing to let good men and women die for their country, but want no part in the bloodshed. And afterwards they just want to forget the event ever happened. It disturbs their perfectly formed world too much. So the old soldier who gives up most of his life protecting the borders is ignored by the world. And those people in their comfortable homes with their closeted lives will never know the nightmares he suffers or the guilt he might feel about taking another's life.'

Elysia appeared thoughtful, her keen blue eyes occasionally darting this way and that as people moved through the streets, but Xavir couldn't really read her at all. 'How is it that you struggle to sleep at night? You sometimes awake in a sweat. Is it because of guilt you feel about the killing? Does it haunt you?'

'The killing? No, not now,' Xavir replied. 'The killing is habit now.'

'Then why?'

Xavir considered her words thoughtfully. No one had dared ask him outright in Hell's Keep, so it surprised him that he found himself willing to speak to her. 'It started happening when I went into gaol. That is all I know. I awake in sweat. Sometimes I have flashbacks. But they are not always bad. They just happen. What haunts me in the night? I cannot say. The only thing I mourn is what I was previously, but it only takes me a heartbeat of being awake to get over it.'

'So it won't happen to me because of the people I killed?'

'Has it so far?'

'No,' she replied. 'Not at all. I haven't really thought about it.' There were no clues in her intonation as to how she felt.

Xavir studied her. He wasn't quite sure what to say.

'Is this kind of mission what you always did in the Solar Cohort?' Elysia asked. 'Assassination and the likes? I got the impression you were in battle on horseback.'

'We were not assassins back then.' Xavir straightened his back. 'We represented the king on the battlefield, as age, despite his enthusiasm, kept him bound to his palace. He was a fine king and we were honoured to fight for him. After the battles we would report solely to him in his private quarters. We would be brought fine wines and food, and smoke all kinds of exotic herbs. He wanted to know what we felt, what we saw. He enjoyed the camaraderie, the laughter. It was obvious that he was living the battles through us.'

'You speak of him like a father,' Elysia said. It was an innocent enough phrase, but Xavir couldn't help but try to read things into it, given their relationship. Did he one day want to be spoken of with such affection by Elysia? This was new territory for a soldier like Xavir. It was all uncertain terrain.

'I believe he viewed us like his sons. I could never quite fathom what he looked for when selecting the men of the cohort – there were plenty of good soldiers in the legions, naturally, but why us? I think it was because in each of us he saw something of himself and he enjoyed our company. There were plenty of courtiers, of course, but he was a warrior king. They were not his type of people.' Xavir paused for a moment. 'I'm very likely boring you with the tales of an old man.'

'No,' Elysia was quick to reply. 'Not at all. This may be natural for you, but for someone like me, who's never experienced anything but life within the sisterhood, to hear what a king was like close up . . . it's special. We are always taught how remote and inaccessible royals are. I was told that because of my nature I was unlikely to be assigned to a clan or family who had these connections.'

'The sisterhood sounds like an organization the world could do without. Who are they to tell *you* what to do? The world is yours to claim. Take it. No one will hand it to you. People who cling onto power like those old witches, it's their only way of validating themselves in this world. They will do everything they can to put others down. It is *they* who are weak.'

Elysia smiled. Xavir did too.

They walked for the next hour up the dark roads of Golax Hold. Xavir and Elysia ducked in and out of grimy taverns and stores, gathering information about Lord Kollus and Duchess Pryus. The townspeople were only too happy to gossip about the duchess and gestured uphill, towards the estate that over-looked the settlement. She had banquets every other night to keep morale up – now and then a few of the townsfolk would be invited, but they were typically small gatherings, fifty or so dignitaries from various parts of Stravimon. The thought of these parties did not sit well with Xavir, when people around the nation were living in poverty and being driven from their homes. Some whispered salaciously about celebrations of dark, forgotten idols, though they had no details to offer. Xavir saw that although the cathedral was for Balax, the ancient god of war, both his and the Goddess's presence had long been driven from the town. Only a shrine to the Great Eye lingered. What else was there to worship but hedonism?

They stopped at one tavern, a whitewashed building that looked out across a cobbled market square. At the bar Xavir asked the old landlord, 'I've not seen many men on patrol. Does the town not have a watch?'

The landlord shrugged. 'Used to. All I know's that men keep getting drafted for the main army. Leaves very few here, pal. All go up to the capital for the most part. Some we hear from, others we don't. You look like a fighting man, so I dare say you know how it goes in times of war. Hear the usual tales of barbarian hordes in the north, but we only get that from official mouthpieces of the king. Who knows where the soldiers go? Just there aren't as many around as there used to be, like.'

Lord Kollus had lost his wife two years ago, the man told them. She died of a throat infection, though some said it was strangulation. The two had never been close and Kollus's affairs were well known. The Duchess Pryus had never married, and still hadn't in the time Xavir had been in gaol. She had the wealth of her father and never needed to work. Such a status ensured she held the attention of most ambitious men. They swarmed around her estate as if they were worker bees and she their queen. As such, and as she had been to Cedius, she remained a key ally to the throne. She and Kollus had always been close, but now it seemed as if their power was shared in some other way.

There would be another of her gatherings, held at her estate, tomorrow night.

Xavir told his daughter that then would be the perfect time to strike.

At the Silent Hawk

'Landril was right,' Xavir announced. 'This is a fine tavern.'

They were seated at a table in an alcove of the Silent Hawk. From the window they could see the dark cathedral in the evening light.

The tavern was filled, but not with the usual crowd one might expect in a watering hole. Judging by clothing and accents, the people here were of good stock and weren't short of coin. The wines that were on offer were of vintages and locations that Xavir knew to be greatly desired; the main ale was said to have the blessing of Mardonius himself, which presumably explained its bitter taste and high price. The decor was of good quality, with fine mullioned windows and clean floors. Every polished table had a couple of candles in the centre of it, creating a pleasant atmosphere.

They lingered for a while listening to idle chatter. Golax Hold seemed entirely disconnected from the world. While people suffered elsewhere, the discussion here focused on trade, weather, gambling and society. Their people lived in isolation – these concerns were trivial – and were not at all bothered about the issues that affected the rest of the nation. No mention of the king, no mention of troop movements, or battles, or who had died and where.

Xavir and Elysia ordered some venison stew and bread, and waited for Landril and Birgitta to arrive. About an hour or so after they finished their meal, the spymaster and witch strolled through the door, shrugged off the rain and advanced over to their table. Landril had a spring in his gait, indicating that he had found what he had been looking for.

'Ah, there you are,' Landril announced, as if it had been Xavir who had been away all this time.

'You took your time.' Xavir sipped from a cup of wine, one of the fine Chambrek vintages.

'And it was time well spent.'

Birgitta sat down next to Elysia. 'I take it you two haven't butchered anyone yet, then?' Her tone was judgemental, her expression indifferent.

'The "butchering" will take place tomorrow,' Xavir replied quietly. He went on to describe his discoveries of the afternoon, and that the duchess's clifftop estate would be holding yet another social gathering.

Landril sat down alongside him. 'There will be some influential folk there, no doubt.'

'People to intimidate,' Xavir said.

'Persuade first, if we can, then intimidate later,' Landril replied. 'They might have private troops we can use for our own force. Or indeed they might simply have money, access to good blacksmiths, a supply of ore and horses . . . Try not to kill *everyone*.'

'My business is with two people only, and whoever happens to get in my way.'

'I can't imagine there are many heroes left in Stravimon, so you'll have no problem there.'

'If it makes the job easier,' Xavir added. 'What did you find?'

Landril spoke about his old friend at the library, and waved over the serving boy to enquire about the Chambrek wine that Xavir had been drinking, and if there was any of the vintage from twelve years ago. Indeed there was, and the boy brought goblets to him and Birgitta.

'All very nice, I'm sure,' Xavir said, 'but I assume you didn't spend all your time talking about the old days?'

'No. No indeed.' Landril glanced over to Birgitta.

'By the source, we have discovered *plenty* about the Voldirik people.' Birgitta took a sip of the wine. 'They are, and should be, a far bigger concern to us than Mardonius. A bigger concern to me than the sisterhood pledging a bond between the themselves and the king. Perhaps a greater concern than the purging of religious followers, although I dare say Landril will disagree with me on the matter.'

Landril shrugged insouciantly, swirled the wine in the cup and nosed the aromas. 'It is all connected.'

'Go on,' Xavir said.

Landril leaned forwards with Birgitta, as if conspiring. He encouraged the others to gather closer so that people couldn't eavesdrop.

'What we discovered was not merely in the records of the library,' Birgitta said. 'The journal taken from General Havinir also helped. It has pages written in code and even in ink that could not be discerned by any ordinary methods. Landril's friend, Jamasca, helped us translate the words, source bless her.'

'Turns out that it is true that the Voldiriks are the Irik people who left our shores from the Second Age and sailed into the far west,' Landril continued, 'to realms beyond our knowledge. That much we know. And yes, it is strange that they have returned, in the Ninth Age, is it not? This is not the first time. They have made numerous invasions over the millennia, each one gaining in . . . momentum, if you can call it that. There was even a significant attempt at the beginning of the Ninth Age, when Queen Beldrius defeated them – though the archives are lacking details as to what transpired. Perhaps that was what led the first queen to establish so many libraries about the place. Anyhow. At first, Voldirik incursions were rather primitive affairs – nothing more than the smallest of the barbarian nations casting their ill-equipped ships onto the wind to return here and conquer. Each time, they failed.'

'They're not doing so badly now,' Xavir added.

'Indeed not. They are a very curious race. Over time, in whatever realm they now inhabit, their people changed. Evolved. They developed into almost different breeds of humans. Slender. Pale. Ethereal things. But what they lacked in substance, they made up for in knowledge. In fact, they *hoard* knowledge. They gather information from all quarters and record their findings assiduously, in a manner that we cannot comprehend. Their entire culture was structured upon those who had the most knowledge about the world. Philosophers, astronomers and engineers were regarded as the highest authorities in the land. That is the impression that history has given about them, at least. However, dig deeper into the records and we find that their thirst for information served another purpose.'

Landril took a sip of wine and sighed contentedly at the taste.

'Which was?' Xavir said.

The spymaster placed down his cup. 'They had made a god.'

'They had done what?' Xavir asked. 'Explain.'

'Created a god. Or bred one. That's what we believe the records state. Through magic – via whatever channels of magic the source uses, or perhaps even creating those channels – it is believed they spawned a god, and that their endless quest for knowledge is in order to quench that god's thirst. They made a god of magic. And that god, I suspect, has somehow allowed them to reach out through time itself. Now – as before – they are attempting to expand their empire. This time they have used more nefarious means, and managed to gain an alliance with Mardonius by somehow entering his mind and his beliefs. They corrupted him. I can't imagine it was difficult – he always was weak-willed and greedy. One might suggest that, in this manner, they have already conquered Stravimon without shedding blood. More of them are coming. Oh yes. Many more. They have control of the throne and, therefore, the entire kingdom.'

Xavir leaned back in his chair and narrowed his eyes. He had heard many fanciful things in his lifetime, and this was certainly up there with the best of them. 'The connection with Havinir?'

'My friend Jamasca,' Landril said, 'showed us how Havinir had been . . . researching, shall we say. On the local people. People who had been *disappeared*. They were the subjects of his work with the Voldirik wayseers, who are the most magical and mysterious of all the Voldiriks. Havinir was researching methods of extending life, so that he might one day become immortal. He was using the Voldiriks to help him do this. No doubt, they were just as happy to take the findings for themselves. It is suggested . . .' He paused and glanced to Birgitta. 'In his notes he mentions assistance on some of the materials from some of the sisters, whom he refers to only as "the Dark Sisters". They're referenced here and there throughout the early notes in his journal, long before the Voldiriks get to grips with the locals. The general had forged an unlikely alliance with an ill breed of witch.'

'I believe these could be some sisters who went missing some time ago,' Birgitta added. 'Not even the matriarch knew of their whereabouts. But that they have turned to this darkness is a valid explanation for their disappearance.'

'So Havinir,' Xavir said, 'in his retirement from the business of death, was looking into the secrets of life. If we are to believe that Mardonius and the Voldiriks are in some way aligned, then it would make sense that Mardonius has allowed the Voldiriks to work with Havinir.'

'I had similar hunches. The journal suggests so.' Landril took a sip of wine. 'The Voldiriks are sailing to the far western shores and Port Phalamys. They are coming in to our world and learning – one might reasonably assume – a great deal to please their fabricated god.'

'If it is true,' Xavir said.

'I have no reason to believe it is not.'

'I have no reason to believe it is,' Xavir said, 'not unless it can be seen and proven.'

'Much of history cannot be seen – we have only the records to go on. Is it all a grand lie? No. Of course, one must read between the lines, but there has been plenty written about the Voldiriks and the theory holds true in my eyes.'

'I am a much simpler creature in that respect, then,' Xavir replied. 'I have seen this new race, the descendants of the Irik people, and therefore I believe they exist and that they are likely expanding their empire – with minimal violence. I have not seen this god yet. In that I remain to be convinced.'

Landril shrugged. 'It matters little to us. We know where they are coming from and that they pose more of a threat. I have a much better understanding of them. There is more to learn, so while you pursue your vendetta tomorrow I may well return to Jamasca.'

'I could do with Birgitta this time. The extra magic will be necessary. I have no doubt that there will be some kind of witch working with the duchess.'

Birgitta bowed her head in acceptance. 'If I must. But I'm

only coming to ensure you don't corrupt this one any more with your death-dealing,' she said acerbically, pointing to Elysia.

They spent the night in a room adjacent to the Silent Hawk, in a ramshackle property owned by the landlord. Though he had used it as a storage premises, he quite often rented a few of its spare rooms out to travellers, given his tavern was dedicated solely to drinking and eating. He was grateful for the business. It was a place devoid of style and substance: once they had passed through the flagstoned storage quarters, which were also sparse, they entered a vacant dormitory with beds, tables, chairs, and not much else. A smell of preserved cheeses and cured meats lingered. They lit a few lanterns only to realize there were no windows, but at least it was an improvement on Hell's Keep and so Xavir did not complain.

Once settled, and with the Keening Blades lying on a bed, Xavir began to plan the following evening's attack. Landril described and drew out what he believed to be the approximate layout of the duchess's estate on the clifftop. It was deceptively large, he said, because the cliff's other side was a gentle slope, with a more sedate path down to ground level. It meant a great deal could be built upon it, and her estates sprawled from a central, more fortified building, which was her main residence.

'How good is security?' Xavir asked. 'I haven't seen many soldiers around on patrol in Golax Hold. Mostly off-duty or retired men. I've heard there is a shortage of fighters, but that was just one man's account.'

'It's possible she could have all the decent ex-legion soldiers in Golax Hold lined up on her estate,' Landril said, 'but I doubt it. I have heard similar, though, and the lack of news from the capital does concern me.'

'You know about wars better than us,' Birgitta added. 'Is it natural for soldiers to leave towns undefended across Stravimon like this?'

'To a certain extent,' Xavir replied. 'Some campaigns required a contingent of men from the clans which came from towns like this. Often there would be expeditions to the west, but they were messy affairs with a great loss of life. Usually at the whims of royals – Grendux, Cedius's idiot father, was terrible for launching futile expeditions. Normally the legions are bolstered by the clansmen when there's a threat from the barbarians in the north. The barbarians number in their tens of thousands and are vicious fighters. Now and then they unite – tribes like the Gous and the Joakals – and they make a determined push to gain lands within Stravir's borders.

'It is nothing new. It will probably continue for the next thousand years. Cedius always had the legions patrolling those hills. There was little glory to be found there. It was cold and it was a miserable business just trying to prevent the barbarians from carving their way through to Stravimon. That's what they always wanted – to bring down the glory of Stravimon and one day to be at the capital's walls. If there are troubled times now in the north, then it will draw a lot of men into the legions. I knew there was a shortage of good soldiers at our escape from Hell's Keep. Maybe Mardonius has spread his forces too thinly – a purge of his own whilst still staving off the influx from the north . . . It is unwise to be stretched like that.'

'Then this will work in our favour,' Landril declared.

'Maybe it will, maybe it won't,' Xavir said. 'Depends how many legionaries have so far rebelled against the king. We can take it for granted that there will be some who see sense. All we can hope is that we can get a good two or three thousand before we march on Stravir City itself.'

'As few as that?' Landril asked.

'More would be better. But you are forgetting who we have fighting for us. No doubt Lupara has sent word back to her homeland, which is not that far away, in order to bring reinforcements should we require them. But it needs to be a Stravimon army that marches into the capital. It needs to be made of our own people. It just wouldn't work otherwise. People will see themselves as occupied, and they will fight back harder. If it is us, Stravir, then citizens may join us – especially if they are oppressed.'

'Well, we can only hope, then,' said Landril with a sigh.

A Celebration

'No not over there,' shouted Duchess Pryus.

She gestured angrily at her serving staff who, in their black tunics, were carrying amphorae of wine back and forth for the evening's festivities. Tonight was an important date in the Voldirik calendar and she would see to it that their god was honoured appropriately. It was a shame that none of the foreigners could bless her estate with their presence, but it mattered not: the gesture to the king was reason enough. It would keep him happy – or so she hoped. She hadn't actually spoken to Mardonius in months.

'Put them over here, where the guests will be chanting, so they don't have to walk into another room to get a drink afterwards. No, on second thoughts, take them into the next room. There's nothing worse than a drunken incantation. Go on!'

The duchess stood back, satisfied, hands on hips, watching her staff scurry outside. There would be seventy-odd people coming tonight. Many had travelled from the protected estates of eastern Stravimon. Her hope tonight would be that they, then, would go on to donate some of their resources, land and people to the cause of the Voldiriks. This would please the king, as it would strengthen his bond with this strange and wonderful race. Only backward-looking followers of the damn

Goddess or that oafish god Balax would hinder their progress. The little runts who clung onto their backwater homes making prayers to some false deity were always getting in the way. The sooner Stravimon was rid of them, the better. But that was easier said than done.

She hoped by now that the groundwork laid by Lord Kollus among the guests tonight would have taken effect. For months he had been persuading, on the king's behalf, for these people to be at least open-minded in the new world that lay ahead . . .

'My lady,' one of her serving boys reported. He was standing breathless, in a black tunic like the others, but with a dark red sash. Behind him someone knocked over an exotic plant whilst carrying a statue, and the duchess sighed. 'Still . . . no sign of General Havinir.'

Duchess Pryus rolled her eyes. 'For goodness sake, Celix. He must have received my last message by now.'

'That may well be so, my lady.'

'Is he ignoring me?'

'It's hard to say, my lady. I think not. He was very drunk that last time, and would likely have forgotten what he had done.'

'He was always chancing himself, the dirty old sod . . . Very well. We'll put him down as an absentee. Off you go, Celix.' He was dismissed with a languid flutter of her hand, and he scampered back through the criss-crossing passage of servants.

The duchess turned away to the rest of the room and caught a glimpse of herself in a golden-framed mirror. She was nearly fifty summers old, yet the woman staring back looked no more than twenty-five. All thanks to the wisdom and the skincraft of the Voldiriks. Those people knew the fine arts of life and longevity, a magic that was truly enduring and not as transient as that of the sisterhood. She was lucky that she did not have to commit to being crafted in their likeness, though, as the duch-ess rather liked how she looked.

Her own witch, Marilla, did not trust their ways and had no interest in taking them up on their offer to be skincrafted. As such, she looked like the duchess's mother, despite the fact that they were the same age. *Where is that woman, anyway?*

The great hall was finally taking shape. The grand room was eighty paces by ninety-five. Red and purple drapes hung from the ceiling, which itself was covered in geometric frescoes that had recently been commissioned. The statues around her were also representations of the Voldirik god. Of course, very few people had seen it, and therefore all the artwork was rather abstract. All-seeing knowledge. Wisdom. Power. Strength. These were represented as shapes and colours, by shield and book motifs, and by the complex script that covered many of their items. That same script extended from floor to ceiling, filling in any nooks or crannies that the artwork had left exposed. It was all a bit heady and gaudy for her traditional tastes, but she was happy to do what was required. And that the Voldiriks had donated their own artists for this was a blessing, and she knew it. She was in favour. In fashion, some might say. And she had to make the most of it. No matter what the cost.

Duchess Pryus was soon garbed in a beautiful white and bronze-coloured dress, with a low neckline so she could show most of the enhanced skin created for her by the Voldiriks, and soft white slippers. Her long blonde hair curled thickly down her back. A dab of perfumed oils on her wrists and she was finally ready to welcome her guests.

In the entryway into the great hall she met up with Lord Kollus. He, too, had chosen to benefit from the Voldirik techniques and looked not a day over thirty – despite being twice that. Tall and well-muscled, he strode across to greet her and kissed her hand. He wore a leather jerkin and red tunic, with bronze and gold detailing, with a sword at his side. His oiled black hair and tanned skin gave the merest suggestion of his Chambrekian lineage, even though his family's estate had been in the north for a hundred years or more. His eyes were narrow, his nose elegant and long, his jawline strong. Whenever she saw him it seemed to validate why they had been lovers for many years. Their attraction was inevitable. There was something beyond their altered forms, something deeper.

Hands clasped together, the two of them stood for a while in the short corridor to the hall. Through stone arches she could see the sun setting across the distant hazy hills, and consequently the landscape around Golax Hold was hidden in shadow. Down below her were fifty more of her private guards, the red- and grey-garbed men shifting into their various positions to ensure the safety of her guests. Many of those arriving tonight had written in advance to suggest that they would be bringing their own protection as well, so she guessed there would be as many as two hundred warriors of some description here tonight. No doubt her head of security, Captain Deblan, would see to it that everyone played nicely. Pryus and Kollus advanced into the great hall. Everything was ready. Guests began to arrive, filling the cushions laid out among the statues. She took a sip of wine – just one cup for now, as she had work to do. The others would get drunk. They would be persuaded, subtly, to abandon the conservative, miserable ways of Stravir culture. She spoke at length of Voldirik art, whilst men ogled her and their wives looked on in disgust. Some people found her later in the night – and she knew that others would find her in the morning – to ask how they could understand more about the Voldiriks.

That was the point of victory. A step into the future. A way for the Voldiriks into this world to transform it without violence.

She could see Lord Kollus pressing heady herbs into guests' hands – substances supplied by the foreign race to give them a merry time. People drank and talked. The room, tense and awkward to start with, opened up. This was good. These people would be her people. They would open up their lands and resources to the Voldiriks and she would be rewarded.

Everything was going to plan. It was bliss . . .

When, strangely, she began to hear screaming and shouting in the distance.

Xavir drew both of the Keening Blades and carved through the approaching guards. Under a darkening sky, and in the confines of a high-walled courtyard, he launched into the three – and they fell to the ground in a clatter of armour.

The courtyard was clear. He called for his daughter to follow inside.

She leaped in behind him, bow in one hand and an arrow in another. 'Could you not have tied them up or something?' Birgitta hissed to Xavir. 'Such a waste of lives.'

'We don't have the time,' he replied, and nodded to his daughter. 'Show no mercy.'

Birgitta scowled and bustled inside the alleyway after them. Striding between dark walls that towered either side of cobblestone lanes, Xavir gestured above, and Birgitta cast up her staff and scrutinized the tall buildings with its light. She shook her head. There was no one looking down, no soldiers on patrol.

The three pressed on.

As the spiralling lane began to widen, a rush of guards came down towards them. Elysia unleashed arrows in quick succession. One after another, three men collapsed pathetically. Only four made it through to Xavir – casually he struck aside their blows with one blade and skewered them with the other. He willed his weapons to be quieter, and as if sentient beings, they heeded his thoughts.

Birgitta moaned in disgust.

Bodies lying on the cobbles around them, Xavir smiled at Elysia. 'Good work.' His head at an angle, he closed his eyes and listened hard for any sounds. Some distance up a network of stairways was the great hall, and he estimated, even if he was walking without interference, it would take a while to get there. Xavir signalled to follow a route to the left, which Landril had described to him earlier. The sisters followed him through the passageways, their footfall as light as songbirds. At the exit, he paused when Birgitta tapped him on the shoulder with her staff.

'There is magic here,' she told him quietly.

'Where?'

'Next courtyard,' Birgitta said. 'Inner part of the complex. A sister lives here.'

Marilla was her name, so Landril had informed them earlier, and she was the witch attached to Duchess Pryus. Xavir peered around the corner and could see her standing in the centre of the next courtyard: a woman in a dark cloak, her hands calmly extended out either side as if she was in some kind of trance. Xavir figured it was likely that she already knew of the witches' presence.

Soldiers filed into small units of three at the far end, under an iron-framed beacon that glimmered on the wet cobbles. The different uniforms and armour indicated the various regions and estates that these men had come from. They were private militia, not the king's soldiers.

'You can fight the witch?' Xavir asked Birgitta.

Birgitta frowned at the other woman. 'Oh yes. You continue.' Xavir gestured to his daughter.

She nodded her understanding and the three of them strode out into the courtyard. The witch, Marilla, turned to face the aggressors. Elysia fired an arrow at her but Marilla had a witch-stone in her right hand and with a wave of her left hand she sent the arrow clattering into the wall behind her. Birgitta advanced, as Marilla sent a pulse of light towards her. Birgitta blocked it by holding her staff before her. The pulse of light skimmed around her and struck a building behind, sending debris crumbling across the courtyard.

Xavir and Elysia turned their attention towards the soldiers, who though momentarily stunned by the magical combat, re-focused and moved forwards. As planned, Xavir stood in front of his daughter to shield her from attack so that she would be able to deal quickly with any reinforcements. The Keening Blades wailed in the dusk. Three soldiers collapsed at his feet.

Another group advanced more cautiously – and met death just as easily on his blades.

Elysia launched a magical arrow into a large formation who were equipping themselves at the far end of the courtyard. The arrow's crystal tip shattered, and a green cloud began to fizz and roll outwards. Clutching their throats, the soldiers staggered wide-eyed away from the cloud, but it would do them no good. The poison quickly disappeared upwards, leaving eight men twitching on the ground.

Flashes of magic continued behind them as Birgitta and Marilla traded strange and improbable blows. Xavir steered his daughter through a network of passageways. Guards strode across the exits to block their path, but Elysia fired around Xavir's running form, arrows skimming the brickwork and smashing into the soldiers' faces. Xavir dealt with whoever remained standing and, with swift bladework, sent their blood-ied forms reeling back.

At each exit Xavir cautioned her to press against the walls so that they could remain unseen. He didn't want to kill anyone unnecessarily, not when they might join the Black Clan, depending on if he could reach their masters and have them see sanity.

Three more soldiers in different garb walked by insouciantly, between the dark brickwork, oblivious to the carnage that lay a few corridors away. That there were different private units here tonight was an advantage – they had little in the way of effec-tive communication, and no common leader. Elysia fired three quick arrows, each one striking perfectly between armour gaps – sending gouts of blood from severed arteries. The men crum-bled forwards. No one else remained.

Xavir and Elysia advanced up the stairwells.

The sound of chatter. A lyre playing a soft tune. Heady scents of exotic food and perfume. As Xavir and Elysia ran through the hallways, small arched windows flashed by, revealing the purpling sky and a bright crescent moon beyond. Xavir had commanded that none of the guests – not even those who tried to attack – was to be killed. Wound, if challenged, but do not kill. The soldiers had been kept outside the event – inside were all civilians, servants and wealthy landowners from afar. As a gesture, Xavir sheathed his blades, and Elysia carried her bow across her shoulder.

They entered the great hall to the startled screams of other guests. Xavir scanned the faces through the fug of incense and recognized a few of them. No doubt many here would know him too. His vision locked on Lord Kollus, who hadn't aged a day since he last saw him, and he strode towards the man. A couple of servants attempted to get in his way, but Xavir thumped them aside with the heel of his hand and they tripped over guests seated on cushions impotently. People began to peel away from his advance, scurrying to the sides of the room in a flurry of panicked chatter.

Xavir stopped, staring towards his dark-haired victim. Everyone fell silent. 'I am Xavir Argentum, former leader of King Cedius's Solar Cohort,' he declared.

Lord Kollus, in the far corner of the room, closed his eyes. His shoulders sagged.

'I have evidence,' Xavir continued, his voice booming into all corners of the room, 'that this man was jointly responsible for the slaughter of innocent villagers, the execution of my brothers of the Solar Cohort and my imprisonment in a place known as Hell's Keep. Lord Kollus, General Havinir and Duchess Pryus supported Mardonius's claim to the throne and were respons- ible for the deception of King Cedius and the betrayal of our country in allowing a foreign army to displace and kill our people. I have come to execute Kollus and Pryus tonight, and claim justice in the name of Cedius the Wise.'

Someone fainted to one side. Another gave a cry of anguish. Nearby, Duchess Pryus ran towards Kollus and the two embraced.

'What you're saying is wrong,' Kollus announced, everyone still staring.

Xavir unsheathed the Keening Blades and could see Kollus swallowing hard. 'Explain.'

'Well. Uh . . . what evidence do you have?' Kollus asked.

Pryus buried her head in his shoulder. He shrugged her off momentarily, his mind ticking over for a way out of here. Xavir suspected he'd leave the duchess behind, given half a chance.

'I have written communications, intercepted by a former spymaster of Mardonius's court.'

'Where are our fucking guards?' Kollus shouted, glancing left and right.

'Dead, for the most part.' In the distance Xavir could hear the grumble of magical clashes.

'Oh,' Kollus sighed. 'Shit.'

'You have,' Xavir continued, 'a few moments to tell me if it was all worth it. If your filthy quest to allow a foreign nation to walk right in and claim Stravimon for themselves is all worth it. Tell me, fool. Is it?'

Kollus sighed and peered around again. Vainly, he seemed more embarrassed than anything else. 'Not in front of this lot.' He tilted his head towards the end of the room.

'A trap?' Xavir asked.

'As if I have planned for *this* eventuality.'

Xavir nodded. 'It is wise not to flee.' With his daughter having an arrow nocked at the ready and aimed at Kollus, they followed the two victims through the chamber to a small door at the back. People still stared, some curious, some still in fear. One or two were casually sipping wine and obviously enjoying the spectacle.

One of the older men muttered, 'Welcome home, son,' to Xavir as he passed.

They entered a discreet antechamber illuminated by a few cressets. Kollus waved out the serving staff, who had been using the room as a preparation area. The place reeked of wine, as a few casks had been opened. There were sacks of herbs here that brought about hallucination or relaxation. The walls were panelled in wood, and there was that same old script of the Voldiriks carved across each of them.

'Don't kill us,' the duchess spluttered, her palms low either side. 'I beg of you, please.'

Xavir signalled to his daughter to keep her bow raised.

Kollus whispered something in the duchess's ear and she closed her eyes in anguish. 'At least it will be together,' he added.

'Tell me,' Xavir demanded, 'why you wished for me to be incarcerated. And why you wanted my comrades killed.'

'We didn't,' Kollus began. 'That was not our aim. We wanted the cohort out of action. We weren't to know what would happen. Havinir was in charge of the operation. We didn't expect it to work as well as it did.'

Xavir couldn't decide whether or not Kollus was lying. 'You, Pryus, Havinir and Mardonius – you were all together in this plot.'

'Yes,' Kollus sighed. 'And it was just us four. There was no one else.'

'A noble statement, but if there are any others involved I will find them and kill them too.'

'Trust me. If I could blame others right now, I probably would.'

'Why did you want the Solar Cohort out of action?'

Pryus clasped Kollus's shoulder. She looked to her lover and back at Xavir.

'You and Cedius, you were all too backward looking. You were all so very old fashioned. You had no vision and prevented so many wonderful things from happening in this world.'

'Indeed, it looks like Mardonius is making such a good job of things,' Xavir replied sarcastically.

'He is! And he will,' Pryus added. 'At least he's not reliant on a bunch of savages. Cedius honoured the Solar Cohort too much. You were as his sons, weren't you? He never made major decisions until he had discussed them with you. *You* in particular,' sneered the duchess.

It had never felt that way to Xavir. That was just the relationship they had with the king. 'The cohort had not wronged you personally.'

'At every stage you rejected our plans,' Pryus replied. 'Every single one.'

'I can hardly remember your plans,' Xavir replied. 'We potentially turned down a lot of schemes if the king consulted us on them and we felt they weren't in the interests of the people. And you wanted to remove the king because of this?' Xavir continued. 'Did you plot to kill him?'

'No,' Kollus said. 'Persuade him. The old dog was frail. We knew he wouldn't be around for too much longer. His health was in very poor condition. Why bother? We just needed to line things up for when he finally keeled over, which didn't take long, as it happened. Not after you were disbanded.'

'Explain,' Xavir said. 'Why? Why the trap? Why the need?'

'The Voldiriks, of course.'

'Of course.' Part of him felt ashamed for being so blind to the subterfuge on behalf of this foreign race. 'It has always been about the Voldiriks.'

'They will change our world, Xavir,' Kollus said in earnest, eyes wide. 'You — we could offer you so much. A chance of such power and greatness, the likes of which you have never known. Man of your stature could appreciate that, surely? Hang onto that good physique. Get those years back you spent in gaol.'

'I have known much power and greatness,' Xavir said. 'Such privilege does not necessarily satisfy one's thirsts in life.'

'A miserable Stravir outlook, that,' Kollus replied. 'Anyway, I'm not talking about the simple opportunities of this world. I am talking about *transcending* life and death altogether. The Voldiriks could remake you in a way that you could never imagine. Look at me.' He thumped his chest. 'Look at how young I am. I have never felt better. They have fleshcrafters who can change everything about a person.'

'At what cost?' Xavir snapped. 'Experimenting on our own people? Driving civilians from towns and villages across the nation? You would make yourself look pretty and ruin *everything* Stravimon ever was in the process?'

'A price worth paying,' the duchess replied.

Xavir moved his blades so they were both in his left hand. 'How many of our own people have you killed?' He pointed at her. 'How many people, from *your own* lands, have *you* offered as sacrifice?'

'We do not count such things,' Kollus said softly. 'When you are in our position in life, one must think of the greater good, not the herds of cattle who roam mindlessly in submission to primitive gods.'

Xavir shifted a blade back across to his free hand.

'Look, let's not get carried away here,' Lord Kollus pleaded. 'I can offer you such greatness in exchange for sparing our lives. At least consider it.'

With a simultaneous flick of both blades Xavir severed the heads of Lord Kollus and Duchess Pryus clean from their bodies. Blood sprayed across two walls. Pryus's head rolled into the corner of the room, whilst Kollus's flipped straight into a wine cask. Their corpses slumped to the floor together.

'For those whose lives you snuffed out to make your own better,' Xavir said, staring at the two lovers in disgust. He wiped his sword on the duchess's dress then turned to Elysia. 'You are likely offended by my actions.'

'No,' Elysia replied. 'I didn't like him. He seemed a cruel, self-serving man and she was just as bad. I wonder how many people they've killed because of their pact with the Voldiriks.'

'Countless,' Xavir replied. 'The problem is, as long as their lives were comfortable, they cared not what effect it had on anyone else. At what cost did they gain those new faces? So the Voldirik race can walk into our realm and expand their own empire. So they can take what is ours – our lands, our lives. There has never been, and there will never be, a well-intentioned incursion by other nations or races. Countries will take what belongs to others, or exploit them, to better their own cause. It is the way of the world.'

Xavir sheathed his blades, marched over to retrieve the heads one by one. He shook Kollus's free of wine. With both of them gripped by their hair, he turned to walk into the great hall, Elysia holding the door open for him.

People were still there, clearly in a drug- and alcohol-induced haze. A few had taken the opportunity to leave, but many had waited. Some sat up upon his return and looked in horror at what he was carrying. He placed the heads carefully on the base of a statue and then walked into the centre of the room.

'In case you did not hear me before, my name is Xavir Argentum. I once led the Solar Cohort. I was in command of military strategy for King Cedius. I have –' he gestured to the heads – 'executed these traitors.' He paused to let the deed sink in, and watched the curious gazes of those around him. It always surprised him how people were morbidly curious rather than disgusted. 'Tonight they wanted your lands and the people on them in order to give them to the race of people known as the Voldirik. You may have heard of them and some concocted story of immortal youth. Tonight these two were going to persuade you to join in their madness. They were going to ask you to surrender our great nation of Stravimon to another race. And many of you were likely tempted.'

The room was silent. Faces peered back at him.

'It isn't a great nation any more,' someone shouted.

'Our citizens are being murdered by Mardonius's military,' Xavir replied. 'It is a great dishonour that has led to the collapse of trading routes. It means Stravimon is on its knees. It is no wonder that Kollus and Pryus would persuade you that something greater lies around the corner. I can assure you it does not. What lies around the corner is the eradication of our people.'

An old man who carried a stick, and who appeared not to be drunk in any way, came walking over to Xavir. With a white beard masking a rounded face, he stood a foot shorter than Xavir and wore resplendent purple robes and a blue cloak.

'I know you, son,' he began. 'Name's Councillor Trevik, and I'm in charge of three settlements in the northern borders. You came to my town twice and were very courteous to me.'

Xavir scanned the old man's face and could see the depths of his troubled eyes. 'I remember it, councillor.'

'Thank the *Goddess* you have returned,' the old man rasped. 'I had heard about your incident at Baradium Falls. It's not far from one of my towns. I never believed what they told me.'

'It was true, sadly.' Xavir sighed. 'But it was a trap, so I have learned, orchestrated by General Havinir, Duchess Pryus, Lord Kollus and Mardonius so the Solar Cohort would be disgraced and disbanded and Cedius discredited for having created us.'

'Kill the false king, then!' Trevik replied. 'Kill the butcher that stands by his side and does his bidding. The world has fallen apart in ways you cannot imagine.'

'I intend to kill him,' Xavir replied. Then, addressing the rest of the hall, 'But I cannot bring an end to the madness across Stravimon without your help.'

A murmur rippled across the gathered throng.

'Some of you will be cautious,' Xavir continued. 'I have no doubt Mardonius has spies in this room, watching to see how some of you behave. I have no doubt he was waiting to see who would be quick to join him in his warped crusade with the Voldiriks, and who would put up resistance. What for many years has been a gentle incursion by this strange race has now become something far more serious. They are a cancer upon us.'

'There's no way we can stop it,' said a woman's voice to the right. He couldn't see her face.

'The lady is correct,' said a tall, well-spoken man, who moved a few steps forwards with a gentle gait. 'The legions have been used as bargaining tools by the king's administrators. A clan leader might turn down invitations to events like this, and then finds his lands aren't as well protected by the legions – or what's left of them, anyway. And so we must fend for ourselves. A barbarian tribe suddenly drifts south, or from the distant east, and . . . well. Life isn't easy. He may appear to be a mad king, but he knows what he's doing.'

'And none of us can gain access to Stravir City. The capital has been locked down for months. Mardonius has driven away many civilians. People seem to vanish.'

'What exactly is it you plan to do?' someone shouted.

Xavir turned to face the man to his left and was surprised that he held so many people's attention. Many ought to have fled by now, but perhaps there was a will to be rid of Mardonius at *all* levels of society.

Stepping alongside his daughter, who regarded him expectantly, Xavir contemplated his next move. 'I was in Hell's Keep with a man called Valderon, of the Clan Gerentius. He was a commander in the First Legion. A good man, a good warrior. No one better to lead. The two of us have joined forces with the once-exiled queen of Dacianara.'

'The wolf queen . . .' someone gasped.

'The very same. Valderon and the wolf queen are building an army to march on Stravir City. I am a part of this, though I have no wish to lead the force. My aim is simple: to kill Mardonius. Their aim is simple: to wrestle the crown from his dying grasp.'

During the commotion at his final statement, someone slunk out of the back of the room, no doubt some spy seeking to deliver the threat.

Fine, Xavir thought. *Let that threat reach the king's ears.*

'We have,' he continued, 'occupied the manse of General Havinir near the southern border as our headquarters. As we speak, our force is seeking contact with rebel groups. We need the presence of many thousands of fighters before we can access Stravir City and take on whatever Voldirik and legion-based force stands in our way.'

'The place will be blockaded!'

'If we have to lay siege to it, so be it. I know of weaknesses in the city's structure that Mardonius could not even guess at. We do not plan to kill civilians, but we will kill those in the legion who do not lay down their arms. Anyone who fights against us is a target.'

'What about the Voldiriks?' A short, well-built woman in a blue robe stepped forwards. 'We've heard about these rangers and wayseers, see, who have carried out much of the king's bidding. You plan to fight them as well?'

'I have already fought them, lady, and found that, for a race who is intelligent, they are relatively weak in combat. I have killed many of their rangers already. I welcome the opportunity to kill more. We'll see about the wayseers.'

It was this statement that seemed to ease the mood of the room. Though these people were clearly not front-line warriors by any stretch of the imagination, it was as if they had lived in fear of the Voldirik people. It was a fear of the unknown.

'I am no tyrant,' Xavir said. 'I am a simple warrior. You may leave tonight freely – your private guard may or may not accompany you, and I apologize if this troubles your journeys home, and apologize again if you find your escorts are no longer present. I have met some of you before, in another life, and no doubt you know my ways. But times have changed. A madman rules Stravimon. He wishes to allow another empire to walk in and claim it for their own, in exchange for the promise of immortality. And as you can see –' he gestured to the severed heads – 'all roads lead to death eventually. I will give you some hours to consider the matter. You may find me in the plaza before the main gates, should you wish to join me in this venture.'

And with that, Xavir strode out of the room with his daughter.

Breaking Magic

Both witches were lying unconscious in the cobbled courtyard. A dome of light extended around them, a protective field of magic that none of the dozen onlooking soldiers could penetrate. Elysia did not appear too agitated at her mentor's state, and Xavir took that as a good sign.

'Stand aside,' Xavir shouted.

The soldiers turned and some reached for their swords. Xavir stood firm. 'Duchess Pryus and Lord Kollus are dead. For the rest of you, your masters are still alive. I will not fight any of you until they have reached a decision on their and your future. Some of you may find yourselves fighting alongside me soon enough. Stand aside to let us through.'

Uncertain and not at ease, the men lowered their weapons and moved out of the way.

Elysia strode to the edge of the dome ahead of Xavir, who brushed past the soldiers. None of them could meet his gaze. When he caught up with his daughter, he pressed his hand against the light. A crackle of magic shot back against his hand, and he withdrew it immediately, feeling the heat.

'You won't be able to get in there,' Elysia said.

'What's happened?' he asked.

'Sometimes, when witchstones are used, there's a reaction

where the different . . . forces, in simple terms, bond with each other. They must have attempted to use a similar technique against each other and so the stones bonded. You can see the two stones still clasped in their hands now. It's very draining to a sister when that happens, but they'll still both be alive.'

Xavir rubbed his chin and considered the options.

'With her mistress now dead, I wonder what Marilla will plan on doing,' Xavir said. 'We could likely use another sister.'

'We could persuade her, Birgitta and me.' Elysia said. 'Once she's conscious again.'

He hadn't slept in hours and only now, since the fighting had ceased and he could relax, did his tiredness make itself known. The tavern bed was calling to him.

'How long will they be like this.'

'Until sunrise, potentially. But they could come round at any moment. I'll wait with them. I'll need to speak to them through the magic when they stir, else they won't realize what's going on. You could speak to this lot –' she indicated the soldiers – 'and see if they want to join the Black Clan in the meantime, even if their masters think otherwise.'

Xavir raised his eyebrows; presumably Elysia now felt comfortable enough in his presence to give him orders. Inwardly smiling, he turned to the other soldiers and bid them to follow him to the end of the courtyard, where there were some wooden chests and barrels that could be used as seats.

Once arranged in a circle, Xavir announced who he was. Most of the men knew of his name, and that changed everything in an instant. The fame of the Solar Cohort had carried far, and any bitterness for what he had done to their comrades changed into confusion. One or two did not know how to process the fact that one of their heroes had killed good friends.

He spoke to them of honour, of defending the country, of challenging the invaders and, before long, he felt they'd fight alongside him and he was at home in their company.

A little while later, shortly before dawn, Xavir looked across to see his daughter chanting through the dome of light and walked over to her. She had laid her bow and quiver on the ground, and was leaning over, whispering the strange words of the sisterhood. Birgitta began to stir and her head lilted from side to side as if she was in a trance. Elysia shouted and Birgitta bolted upright. The two talked softly through the light, and eventually Birgitta appeared to realize what had happened. The witch released her witchstone and extended a hand to Elysia, who pulled her off the floor. And the light vanished, just like that.

Hunched double and breathless, Birgitta took a moment to regain her composure. Eventually she rested her hand on Elysia's shoulder. 'That was a complex spell you broke.'

Elysia shrugged. 'I remembered one thing from the sisterhood at least.'

Xavir knelt down by the other witch. Marilla was slightly older than Birgitta, and her slender, strong face bore a scar down her right cheek. Her robe was an unusual dark blue material which seemed to shimmer in the light of the new day's sun.

Birgitta joined him as Marilla began to stir. Her eyes suddenly shot open. Birgitta's tone became more soothing and she held up both her hands in a gesture of peace. The other witch pushed herself upright, clearly dazed. Elysia held out her hand and Marilla eyed it suspiciously. Eventually, after much consideration, she accepted the gesture and Elysia pulled her upright.

'Our source energies bonded,' Birgitta said. 'We've both been out for several hours.'

Xavir announced, 'Lord Kollus and Duchess Pryus are dead. You're no longer bound to them.'

Marilla appeared indifferent to the words and regarded Xavir with her harsh blue witch eyes. She stood taller than Birgitta, but not as much as Elysia. There was a sense of perfect stillness about her, and nobility, like a bird of prey simply scanning its surroundings.

'We want you to join us,' Elysia said.

'We do?' Birgitta frowned, and Xavir nodded for his daughter to continue.

Marilla remained impassive as Elysia described what had happened and why they had come, and also talked about the lands of Mardonius and what was happening to its people. 'We're going to march on Stravir City. A rebel force. We want you to be part of it.'

'And what,' Marilla finally spoke, 'does the sisterhood think of this?'

'I can tell you all about the bloody sisterhood,' Birgitta said, and spoke of the changes, of the slavish subservience to Mardonius.

'So they will likely have sisters,' Marilla replied. 'This united force of Mardonius and the Voldiriks.'

'Which is why we need you,' Elysia said.

'You are a strange sister, one who fights with a bow.'

'She is all the more useful for it,' Xavir replied.

'We shall see. I knew of the sisterhood's full allegiance to Mardonius. I could have predicted that years ago. Tonight, this gathering, it has happened many, many times over the years.' She took a moment to regain her breath. 'As the wealthy deepen their commitment to the king, so do their sisters. These sisters, in turn, will have easily swayed the matriarch. But tell me: what do you know of the Dark Sisters?'

Birgitta looked to Elysia, who simply shrugged.

'As I thought.' Marilla's nobility was something that could easily be mistaken for arrogance. 'You see, this is a greater concern to me. I had thought you one of them originally when you came to challenge me, though you did not wear their usual black robes – their choice, to set themselves apart from the sisterhood.'

'I have heard tell,' Birgitta said, cautious not to give too much away, 'of their resurgence, but little more.'

Marilla gave a cruel smile. 'The Voldiriks,' she said, 'have . . . *corrupted* a few of the sisterhood. Quite a few of them, I believe. We thirst to know more, we sisters – to know how to manipulate the elements. You can imagine what a conversation with a Voldirik wayseer will do to our curiosity. I have not put myself in that position, but some have been seduced. Many have gone back – back with the Voldirik ships.'

'Are they more powerful?' Birgitta asked.

'I am yet to be convinced. They are corrupted in the mind, certainly. They are more passionate about what they do. And their moral code has been utterly altered. It makes them very dangerous, because there is little to guide their magic. But it also makes them wayward. So it is not the rest of the sisterhood that we should concern ourselves with. It is the Dark Sisters. Those will be Mardonius's real weapons.'

Birgitta glanced to Elysia and then to Xavir, an uncertain look about her. 'I struggled with just this one battle tonight. I cannot take on the might of these altered sisters.'

'Join us,' Elysia said to Marilla. 'We are about to build a force. If we can reach out to other sisters, then that will help. There will be all of those affiliated with the people who came here tonight, if they decided to spare their clan forces. We have come this far. And this is Xavir Argentum — he used to serve King Cedius. He's going to slay Mardonius.'

Marilla appeared amused at the comment. 'I know him.' She turned to face Xavir. 'You expect to walk into the king's palace, do you?'

'The battle will offer a significant distraction. I can handle anything else on my way there.'

'Except magic,' Marilla declared.

'Indeed.'

'Will you join us?' Elysia repeated.

'With my masters dead, what little choice do I have in the matter? The world is no longer a safe place for a sister who wishes to dwell alone.'

'Together we have more strength,' Elysia concluded.

'And we will need all of it to have a chance against those who stand against us,' Marilla replied.

Forging

Valderon's horse could not maintain the pace of Lupara's wolf, Vukos. The creature's paws thundered into the damp earth as the queen of Dacianara sped up ahead, back towards the manse.

The day was muggy and overcast. A storm was due to clear the air, but it never materialized. They rode along paths that cut through oak and elm, through thick areas of overgrown landscape. Leaves were changing. Flashes of orange and ochre passed their eyes. There was a heady scent of jasmine here, and a thicket of old white roses had overgrown and sprawled far. Lupara guessed that the estate had not been maintained properly for at least four years, despite it being lived in. Priorities had changed at some point.

The wolf queen commanded her great steed to a halt. Valderon's horse galloped until it was alongside her, and he smiled knowingly at his lack of pace. Together they waited, glancing back along the path. Eventually another sound became more obvious, although she had heard it faintly for some time. The ground shuddered. Minutes later, bursting through the undergrowth came fifty-five soldiers on horseback, men and women, carrying swords and lances. Some wore a mixture of military colours, but most had no specific uniform at all: they were clan exiles who had been gathered from the surrounding villages.

A tall, dark-haired man had been leading them and been their spokesman since Valderon and Lupara had established contact. With a handsome profile and hints of nobility that he seemed to shun in his capacity as an exile, his name was Grauden, and he had fought in the Second Legion as a captain for five years. A dedicated follower of the Goddess, Grauden had abandoned the legion with several others when they had been forced to clear a town of civilians under orders from Mardonius. Grauden refused to enact those orders, but pretended to have accepted them. Carefully selecting warriors who shared his disgust, he marched them to the limits of the town, issued the townsfolk with supplies of food and arms, and then fled with his soldiers into the wilderness of Burgassia.

Once they had rearmed themselves, they re-entered Stravimon and began offering aid and protection to refugees. Valderon, through a network of local villagers, had reached out to contact this famous band of rebels. Valderon and Lupara had met with Grauden in an abandoned farmstead five days ago, where they had offered him a chance to join their own force.

Grauden had known of the both of them and was especially interested in fighting alongside Xavir Argentum. He accepted the offer. He said that he knew of more forces, of Goddess strongholds where ardent followers had begun forming something of a resistance. These bands of rebels would, of course, not stand up to the full onslaught of the legions, and so Grauden had since sent out messengers in order to bring these units together as one greater force. Several hundred men in all would be headed towards the manse. The Black Clan would become a reality sooner than everyone had hoped.

Grauden signalled for his own fifty-strong force to halt, and he nudged his horse alongside Lupara's wolf, peering across her towards Valderon. 'I see not even you can keep up with her animal.'

The big wolf, Vukos, grunted, as if acknowledging the compliment, then turned its head away towards the undergrowth.

Valderon smiled. 'He's a swift beast, but I know this terrain well now. I have less of an excuse. We've been holed up here for ten days.'

'You did well to get it.' Grauden replied, indicating the manse. The roof of the building could be seen above the tops of the trees nearby. 'Were there none of the foreigners here – the Voldirik warriors?'

'Not enough to concern us,' Lupara said. 'We dealt with them on the way.'

'I haven't fought too many of them. They have struck in small numbers, rather than actual brute force. Yet the Stravir army has become eroded with every passing week and replaced by these creatures.'

'I do not believe they are skilled at combat,' Valderon agreed. 'It is their numbers and their magic that concern me.'

'They prey on the weak,' Grauden said. 'Unarmed villagers for the most part. We have heard many sinister tales.'

'There is nothing in them that a blade cannot fix,' Lupara announced, 'and this is a message we need to deliver to many of the communities in Stravimon.'

'What communications have the villages and towns had from the king?'

'Once in a while Mardonius has notices nailed to tavern doors and the likes,' Grauden said. He gave a bitter grin. 'It's been his way of telling the people how wonderful he is.'

'And do the people believe him?' Lupara asked.

'The people are not that stupid. They do not like to be told how wonderful a king is when they can see their nation falling apart. When they can see a fall in trade and know that people disappear, they know not to believe a piece of parchment with a nail through it.'

'What have these messages said?'

'Nothing of note. Mainly that all's well. That their king's well. That he's looking after his people. It's shit, really. And they know it.'

Valderon nodded. 'Nothing like Cedius. In his younger days, Cedius was known to go undercover to taverns up and down Stravimon after campaigns and tell people himself how things went and what he could have done better.'

Grauden lowered his head and shook it. 'Now *there* was a king.'

'Come,' Lupara announced, 'we are close.'

Lupara led the entourage at a more sedate pace through the undergrowth until they came to a clearing before the manse's east wing.

Here the grass had recently been scythed, and the former prisoners were labouring – hammer-blows to metal, sharpening blade edges, hanging up meat that had been caught from the forest. Over the past few days they had transformed the rundown manse into a hive of activity. The place had been cleaned, aired and turned into a suitable headquarters. A sense of military order had been established.

Grauden was agog. 'You've been busy here,' he called across to Valderon. 'By the Goddess, I can remember a year ago, when we surveyed these lands, that the manse was in disrepair. We all thought Havinir mad at the time, but you've rescued the old place.'

'We've rooms inside for your comrades to sleep in. You'll have to use your own bedding.'

'Rooms?' Grauden asked mockingly. He turned to some of

his own soldiers behind him. 'Do you hear that? Rooms. A roof over our heads. This is luxury! I don't want anyone growing soft.'

Valderon remained impassive. 'I have spent many years in a remote mountaintop gaol. In my time here, spending my evenings on feathered mattresses, any signs of softness have not yet revealed themselves to me.'

Grauden altered his manner, and gave a slight bow of respect before straightening his back. Overhead a crow called out across the treetops. 'I'm sure we will not either. My soldiers are now your soldiers.'

'They will trust you more than me,' Valderon said, 'so I'll count your friendship and guidance here as valuable. You know much about life on the roads around here, and much about the terrain. I'll consider us equals.'

Valderon had done almost all of the organizing at Havinir's manse, to the extent that Lupara was beginning to feel like some ruler who did nothing and merely let her staff arrange matters. In Xavir's absence, she began teaching some of the others the ways of the sword – good old-fashioned Dacianaran techniques – but it only went some way to satisfy her. She had begun to thirst and crave the business of war again.

She was also glad to see that Valderon and Grauden had quickly formed a respectful relationship during their short time on the road. Warriors from Stravimon always followed and appreciated structure. That Valderon had yielded without words to Xavir was respectful of their former difference in authority. The same had happened with Grauden and Valderon, and the newcomer was quick to appreciate the chance to fight alongside a former officer of the First Legion.

Lupara led Vukos back towards Rafe, whereupon she dismounted and let the beasts roam free together. Then, amidst a strong wind that rippled the surrounding trees, she strode towards the manse.

Before she and Valderon had left some days ago to establish contact with Grauden, she had sent the swift Faolo to Dacianara with a message. Things had been complicated back in her home nation when she left for exile. Most of all there was the sense of shame that she had brought upon her people – a shame she shared with Xavir, in many respects. Her punishment for it, though not as severe, was not exactly of her own making. Courtiers had circled like carrion seeing a wounded beast, and there were mutterings of challenges. She would happily have fought anyone to defend the Blood Crown, but instead she merely yielded to the nation rather than to a challenger. Exile meant that no one could sit comfortably underneath the Blood Crown if they decided to, but it also left things in a messy state, and she was not entirely aware what power structures there now were in Dacianara.

The message tied to Faolo would now be the key to her future. She had requested *not* for the temporary rulers and administrators to hear her case in light of the evidence. The wolf was heading straight to those she could trust: the warrior cadres who had so often accompanied her into war. Tribal leaders would instinctively ignore any formal legalities and come straight to her aid. She had old friends – Jumaha of the Vrigantines and Katollon the Soul-Stealer, who would not waste any time mustering their tribes to come to her aid. Their families had allegiances going back centuries. Their trust, she could rely upon. Numbering in their hundreds, they would flock to her side.

But the army to march upon Stravimon and reclaim it from the influence of the Voldirik people would be barely a thousand strong. Was that enough? No. Not yet. And she was impatient to get the job done; they all were. Every week they waited would result in more chance for the Voldiriks to entrench themselves. On the road, Grauden had told her of people fleeing the capital to the mountains, forests and coastline. Not merely followers of the Goddess, but people who were said not to have accepted the presence of the Voldirik people within the city.

According to reports, Mardonius had, many months earlier, made a show of them. Sitting upon the balcony of his palace with his red-clad bodyguard to one side, he presented senior Voldirik officials to his people. It was declared as the 'alliance beyond the shores', but the people needed much convincing. When citizens began to jeer at the newcomers, the king took it personally. When the people began to organize protests, he became furious.

In perhaps his greatest show of madness, Mardonius sent squads of his own soldiers in the night to root out the worst dissenters. Soldiers knocked on the doors of those who had organized the protests. Men and women were dragged from their beds into the streets, where they were put to the sword in front of their families. Within days any formal grievances at the presence of an alien race within the walls of the capital were sent underground. No one voiced their concern. No one made eye contact with the city soldiers. No one said a word any more.

That was, according to Grauden, some time ago. What could have happened since then? All they had seen of the Voldirik people were the rangers and wayseers patrolling the woodlands and the old, forgotten paths. The legions seemed to be vanishing.

So who and what would they face when they came to reclaim the city?

The Arrival

Lupara held the scroll tube in her hand once again. It had come via a young man on a fine horse, who had ridden forth in resplendent red clothing, and who only shrugged when questioned, and winced when shouted at. He had ridden back in the morning mist through the trees and quickly vanished. That had been twenty days ago. Standing in the morning rain, Lupara opened the leather tube and emptied the scroll out into her hand. The note was written as if spoken by Xavir — to the point, just the essential details.

> *Have no concern. All are safe. Forces are building. We will return*
> *well before thirty days have passed. XA.*

Twenty days now, and Lupara's concern was beginning to grow. What exactly did he mean by 'Forces are building'?

'Reading it again will do no good.' The voice was Valderon's.

In resplendent black armour recovered from inside the manse's armoury, Valderon looked every bit the glorious leader. Such things were important. Lupara knew that such a visage would inspire others around him every bit as much as his technique in battle, and his skills were not in dispute. It wasn't just his appearance, however. From his training regimen and prowess in practice fights, the others now listened to what he said. And from his ability to listen to the men's daily concerns, no matter how trivial, they respected what he said too. Even Grauden's soldiers, and the other fighters that had since been absorbed into their 'Black Clan' from surrounding settlements, had quickly taken to him. He was a soldier's soldier.

'*Bahnnash!* Time is running out,' Lupara said. 'If Xavir doesn't return soon, even more people will die in Stravir City. News of the brutality there reaches us daily. A priest of Balax tells us of his congregation being slaughtered during prayer. A former guard of the city watch breaks down in the forest to tell Grauden of the sins he had to commit on the king's orders. These are not exactly good times to be living in the city. We cannot wait much longer.'

Valderon crouched down beside her, sitting on the large stone that looked back across the gardens towards the manse. At first she had considered him a simple man, and perhaps he was. She had made advances towards him, which he did not even realize, and when he did he acted like no other man she had known. Others had either feared or enjoyed the honour of her attention, when she had been in Dacianara. But Valderon was already wounded, and to go there again simply made that wound raw again. That is all she could fathom from the matter, and she was done with trying.

They sat in companionable silence for a little while longer when Vukos and Rafe came to her side. One of them grunted and nuzzled her shoulder. Then the third wolf, Faolo, suddenly appeared and she rose to embrace the beast. His fur was damp and he seemed nonchalant at the fact that he had just completed a mission. The other two animals nosed him cautiously, before accepting his return and plodding off.

She examined Faolo for any signs of a message attached to him, but there was none.

'There is no communication,' she said. 'Has my command been received?'

Moments later, her answer came soon enough.

'Lupara!' Tylos came running in great strides across the gardens. 'Lupara, Valderon. You must come and see this.'

Tylos led the two of them to the fringes of the estate, and all three of Lupara's wolves came to sit by her side.

Ahead of them, between the trunks and under the canopy, came the sound of thumping drums. There was her announcement of arrival. Lupara's heart skipped a beat. She could hear the howling of wolves – other Dacianaran wolves – on the winds through the forest. Moments later they appeared, dozens and dozens of her former countrymen, riding slowly and triumphantly before her.

Lupara stared in disbelief. It had been so long since she looked upon so many of her own people. She scrutinized their faces to see if she recognized anyone. Eventually she saw none other than Katollon the Soul-Stealer riding into the wide clearing upon his great black wolf. As Lupara and Valderon moved forwards, smaller wolves hurried up to her, leaping around in joy. The wolves began to circle her, drifting with her across the grass. The line of Dacianarans paused at the fringes of the gardens, as Katollon dismounted and strode towards her. Ever the savage-looking man, he was dressed in leather and furs, with feathers in his hair and black paint around his eyes, giving him the appearance of some cruel bird of prey. Across his shoulder was slung a double-headed axe – it was, he always explained, the real soul-stealer.

'Our forgotten queen,' he called out, using their old language. 'Your wolf is good at finding his way home.'

'Katollon.' Lupara paused for a moment. Then the two embraced, almost with as much verve as grappling wrestlers. She stepped to arm's length, and looked at the lines on his face. She had known him at some forty summers. Now he was closer to fifty. With that came wisdom, she hoped. He had always been a mentor of sorts to her and his presence not only excited her but gave her more confidence about the coming mission. 'Time has been good to you.'

'The Dacianaran plains will do that to a man,' he replied. 'We came as quickly as we could. We know of the trouble you face.'

As they spoke, she glanced across the line of savage warriors and wolves that had travelled all this way. More filed in behind the front row, their faces painted blue in the old ways, and banners bearing icons of blood, fang and claw that set her heart racing. Now, more than ever, she craved the assault on Stravir City.

The wild noise they had made upon arrival was now dying down to such a quietness that they would hardly be heard. Behind her, across the grass, stood Valderon and Tylos, and she beckoned them over.

'You know of the Voldiriks?' she asked her old friend.

Katollon nodded sagely. He had a long face, with a broad nose. His eyes, surrounded by paint, were just as startling as they had always been. 'They have been plaguing our borders for many months now. The Soul-Stealer and his kind did not confront them at first. No. We watched them, silently. They came to the border villages, where Dacianarans and the Stravir dwell together. There was no announcement of their arrival to the villagers. Instead, we watched them pick off those who walked the fields, as a wolf would a stray lamb. It was cowardly. This was no great heroic battle, but soldiers preying on helpless people. Though we could not save the first few, for it was too late, we began to hide ourselves amidst the settlements. The tribal council nominated the leaders take it in turns. Old Nalama, your uncle, has become a wise man in his later years and, in your absence, much respected. He sent the Soul-Stealer and my tribe first.

'So we hid among the people, or in caves that overlooked the fields they worked. When the Voldirik warriors came to attack we were ready for them. They numbered in only the dozens, and came in small groups. They did not understand the nation fully, or where the elements and land can hide a man, so we waited until they grouped together in a valley. Our tribe streamed through trees, down steep hillsides, and our axes slammed into them. It was easy work at first. We left none alive. We burned their bodies so there was nothing left of them. We took their armour and it sits next to the great hall of your castle.'

'How many attacks have there been?' Lupara asked.

'Of late, more than you would think. Jumaha of the Vrigantines has been making good progress with them, though he has lost many warriors to the wayseers. He has learned their weaknesses.'

'Is he coming?'

Katollon shook his head. 'He cannot be spared, but we have many more following us. Nine hundred warriors – it is all we can spare. We know the problem is now with Stravimon. The fool king is bringing these warriors from somewhere. Twenty attacks in the past thirty days, and they look to push into our domain. Each time with more warriors. All the tribes have formed an alliance and marched to the eastern borders – twenty thousand so far patrol the wilderness. This is when the Soul-Stealer got your message. Your wolf has the scent for me!'

Lupara grinned. At that moment Valderon and Tylos arrived

by her side. She changed language to speak to them, recalling that Katollon did not speak Stravir too well.

'This is Katollon,' she announced in Stravir. 'He is known as the Soul-Stealer and he has brought a great many warriors from my homeland.'

'Greetings to you all,' Valderon said, loudly enough for some of the others to hear. Then he added a similar greeting in crude Dacianaran.

Katollon laughed at that, though not in mockery. He seemed to appreciate it. In her native tongue Lupara announced Valderon and Tylos, men who were going to lead the Black Clan. Her old mentor listened to her words with great consideration, nodding here and there.

He reached out his hand and Valderon took it. Then he repeated the gesture with Tylos. He grinned, suddenly, and placed his arm around them both, then steered them through the forest as he continued to talk to them in his native tongue.

'What's he saying?' Valderon asked Lupara.

'He is saying,' Lupara replied, 'that he wants to drink with you.'

'Drink?'

'Drink,' she repeated.

'But it's still morning.'

'That matters not to him,' she said with a grin.

It was an old Dacianaran custom. It speeded up the bonding process, so it was said, although Lupara was never entirely sure about that. Not only had Katollon brought along his Soul-Stealer tribe and two smaller tribes — the Broken Tears and Blood Bringers — but he had brought a case of Dacianaran wine

— famed for its ability to bring a man to his knees as quickly as a Dacianaran blade.

The other men, Grauden's force included, did not appear to object in the slightest to this gesture. Before long, what had been a well-organized encampment before General Havinir's manse had transitioned into a typical Dacianaran celebration. An enormous campfire had been lit, drumbeats echoed throughout the forest, men and women warriors howled alongside wolves.

Only Valderon appeared to be disgruntled at what had happened, but even he began to lighten his spirits alongside the Soul-Stealer. Lupara had ended up being a translator between the two forces and, elsewhere, when words could not be understood, drunken gestures and laughter seemed to get people by.

The Soul-Stealer gave stories of the old days — tales that warmed Lupara every bit as much as the fire, and made her miss her nation more. He spoke of the hunting grounds in the distant mountains, and the old ritual sites hidden within the forests where her father had been buried.

Later she asked him about the fallout of Baradium Falls, where she had helped to slaughter the innocent people of an allied nation. In his usual, clear-headed manner, which was remarkable given how much he had drunk, Katollon neither persuaded her to return to Dacianara nor said otherwise. He said that no one these days remembered the incident at Baradium Falls. That no one really cared. If she came back to take the throne, then no one would say a word. They would welcome her, although traditions were changing. People accepted the council of elders as a way of making decisions rather than that of a single warrior royal leading a council. Any fighting so far had been decided for them — naturally, it was the Voldirik warriors who took up all of their attention these days, and on that the council was unanimously in favour of dedicating all tribal resources to attack them.

It was, he declared with a grin, a matter of moments from receiving her message before the Dacianaran forces were mustered.

Aftermath

His dreams these days were almost always impressions of the past. It was as if he was scouring his own mind for clues as to what was going on in the world. Xavir was, in his waking hours, glad of this, because he no longer woke up in a cold sweat. There were no daemons assaulting his mind, no images twisted in a manner as if to torment him. In the real world, on the road, away from Hell's Keep: his dreams were better.

Tonight his vision was in the Court of Ascendency, the highest legal office in Stravimon. It was a large room, much like a church, but instead of a congregation it was filled with robed clerics and lawyers. Among them, nestled at the back – seated, Xavir now realized, alongside General Havinir – was Mardonius. The two remained impassive during proceedings, their faces cold and aloof.

On the elevated ornate bench at the north end, underneath a enormous arched window that overlooked the city, sat the three elder advocates. Two grey-haired men, and one grey-haired woman, in grey clothes, as far removed from Stravir society as possible, Xavir mused, but ultimately responsible for all civilian life. Behind them, on the golden observation throne, sat a miserable King Cedius the Wise. Cedius seldom took his always-open seat in this room, but he could hardly avoid this day.

Dressed in black silk robes, the six members of the Solar Cohort were seated in a row on an entrenched bench, a position whereby everyone else would look down upon them – particularly the elder advocates. On the streets below and outside the Court of Ascendency, Xavir could hear the braying crowds. At the time he had thought they were clamouring for their execution, but now – in his dreams – he was not so certain. They might have been calling for their release.

Each of the elder advocates gave an oratory performance. The first discussed the past of each of the individuals charged with treason at Baradium Falls. The second discussed the events themselves, calling for witnesses from the site – the watchman Jorund giving the most colourful yet true account of their dark deeds. The third elder advocate, the woman, discussed all the possible outcomes for the individuals, and the significance of each fate. Xavir's only frustration was that what happened was obvious. None of the six members of the Solar Cohort denied this. Why all the rigmarole?

The members of the Solar Cohort were invited to speak last. Gatrok and Jovelian said nothing. Felyos merely apologized. Brendyos, normally the most humorous of the Legion of Six, gave humble, stoic apologies. Dimarius stood up and for some time gave an impassioned defence. He listed the honours, the deeds committed on behalf of the country. 'We are your *sons*, my king,' he concluded. 'We have only ever acted to bring honour.'

'Ah, but instead you have brought *dishonour*, yes?' crowed one of the elder advocates.

'If a hero's deeds be judged ill by crookbacked desk-dwellers who have no experience beyond these cold walls,' Dimarius fumed, 'then so be it.'

'That won't help, Dimarius,' Xavir whispered softly.

'We are dead men,' Dimarius replied, his voice echoing loudly. 'Why not tell the world that these senseless individuals, these people whose only experience of life is to watch ink dry, should have no reason, no moral claim, to tell us how *we* –' he thumped his chest – 'we brothers have behaved?'

There was silence in the court. Dimarius, slowly and deliberately, sat back down.

'And you, Xavir,' Cedius rasped. 'What do you say?' It seemed more of a plea than a question.

'What would you have me say, my king?' Xavir replied, rising to his feet. He clenched his fists. *Say that you do not trust the intelligence given to us. Say that they were your orders. Say what you feel, Cedius.*

There was no dignity in that.

He released his fingers and spoke calmly. 'What's done is done. We are Stravir's finest weapons, no more, no less. It is up to the nation to decide how we should be used.'

The elder advocates conferred among themselves in hushed tones; gods in drab clothing debating the fate of mere mortals. The sun was now setting across the city, and a heavenly light filled the room. The gathered throng in the courtroom remained still and impassive.

The woman elder leaned forwards, and spoke: 'Under the watchful eye of the Goddess, we deem that the gathered members of the Solar Cohort, seated before us, are responsible for the crimes of treason of the highest order, bringing the king's honour into disrepute, bringing the high station of the Solar Cohort into disrepute, four hundred and seventeen counts of murder and eighty-seven counts of grievous injuries to Stravir citizens.'

Collective gasps came from those watching on.

'You are,' she continued, 'hereby sentenced to be hanged from the outer wall of the palace gardens.'

Dimarius rose from the bench and shouted, 'After all we have done for you. After everything we have done in the name of the king.' He pointed right at Cedius, shattering etiquette. 'For you!'

The others in the Solar Cohort stared across at Xavir, but he could only stare at Cedius's face. The man appeared to be shocked by what ought to have been avoidable. Dimarius turned to look behind — *was there a glance at Mardonius?* — then thrust himself back down on the bench, fuming. Xavir lay a hand on his shoulder and whispered, 'Our fate is decided, brother.'

'No,' Cedius shouted. 'No . . .' Everyone fell silent. 'There should be one of the cohort to remain alive — to suffer the burden, to be a warning to all.'

The elder advocates conferred, though they had no authority with the king. They bowed their heads and allowed Cedius to continue. Dimarius cast Xavir a worried glance. This time as the vision replayed, Xavir did not hear the people screaming in the courtroom, the rage shared between those who felt they had been wronged and those conservative clerics who abhorred the deeds. This time Xavir watched the old king's gaze scan across the members of the Solar Cohort. The Legion of Six. His military sons.

'Xavir Argentum, as the commander of the Solar Cohort, shall live with this burden,' the king declared. 'He shall be cast to the furthest gaol within our diplomatic reaches. And there he shall last, permanently, a reminder of the shame . . .'

Now Xavir saw the decision for what it was. *Get away from here*, the king was saying by this deed. *I'm sending you far from this court, for a while, away from the political machinations that I do not understand. Things are happening. You must live. You will return, one day. Only you do I trust . . .*

An hour later and the vision remained vivid, but now as he approached the manse he felt that he was beginning to put right what Cedius knew to be wrong.

Hazy dawn sunlight filtered through the oak leaves and across a scene of carnage. But all the bodies scattered throughout the long grass were still very much breathing. Some were rolling. Others were groaning. Had he limited knowledge of the world, Xavir would have believed the group of Dacianarans sitting up and talking at the far end of the clearing had come to massacre these soldiers, but he knew that was not the case.

Instead, here were two dozen warriors who could not hold their drink.

Xavir spotted Davlor, his former gaol mate, lying on his back, clutching a skin flask of some foul brew, and moaning something about his mother. Xavir dismounted from the white mare he had bought at Golax Hold, knelt down beside the young man's head and bellowed: 'Good morning!' into his hear.

The man leaped up with a start, realized it was Xavir, stared wide-eyed for a moment before leaning to his left and vomiting in the grass.

Grinning, Xavir rose. A few of the others began to stir at his loud arrival. It looked as if Lupara and Valderon had done a half-decent job in adding more numbers to the Black Clan.

A figure came from the direction of the manse. It was Valderon.

'Your men need stronger stomachs,' Xavir announced.

Valderon smiled, holding up his arms. 'Whatever those Dacianarans put in their flasks is lethal.'

'Yet you still stand. What was your trick?'

'I would like to brag about it, but my trick was simply that I did not drink as much as everyone else.'

'That is still something to brag about,' Xavir replied. 'Who has come?'

'A man who calls himself the Soul-Stealer has brought a united force.'

'Katollon.' Xavir nodded. 'I know of him.'

'I'm glad you've returned,' Valderon said, and the two men shook at the wrists. 'How did it go at Golax Hold? You were gone a long time.'

'It was a success.' Xavir briefly recounted his tale from the town, of the assault on the duchess's residence, the slaughter of his two victims. 'There's more, too. Find your mare and ride with me.'

The pair of riders and horses cantered along the forest paths. The morning sunlight was already beginning to fade, in typical style for Stravimon. The vegetation was more pungent. Birds skittered through the stirring treetops. The ground sloped upwards past the ruin of an old tin mine, which was surrounded by different, low-lying vegetation entirely, before entering into oaks again.

Xavir shared, here and there, his observations about Golax Hold and on the state of relations with Stravir City, and he answered Valderon's few questions.

'Does it feel satisfying now?' Valderon said, in reference to Xavir's revenge.

'It never does, does it?' Xavir replied. 'What makes this increasingly frustrating is the matter that my removal – and the removal of the Solar Cohort – was just one move in a political game. I would have liked, at least, there to have been great significance in what those people did. But there was none. They just wanted us out of the way to stop our influence with Cedius.'

'What is the truth behind the matter?'

'Very little,' Xavir replied. 'At some point in the past, Mardonius made a pact with someone from the Voldiriks. Somehow, they met up – this remains unclear. The Voldiriks may have encouraged such a persuadable mind that Mardonius could become king if he permitted them into Stravimon. Given the Voldiriks' previous attempts at expanding their empire, this is much more subtle and insidious a method of conquering a new territory. He then persuaded others to join in, promising them access to the Voldiriks' clever ways with magic.

'There are other concerns, too. We have learned that the witches have their own crisis, larger than what Birgitta had reported. There is talk of Dark Sisters, who also have aligned themselves with the Voldiriks in some way. Many have sailed from Port Phalamys back to the Voldiriks' lands and a few have returned. There is concern that Mardonius has them tucked behind the walls of Stravir City, which could complicate matters.'

'And the bond with your daughter?' Valderon asked.

'You care greatly about the matter.'

'I have no family of my own,' the veteran replied. 'My time is passing. Even my mother and father died when I was in my infancy. A fund ensured a good education, but it meant the army was the only family I knew. The absence of such things makes it all the more noticeable in others.'

'Professional soldiers make for good brethren,' Xavir replied. 'But in answer to your question, I do not know how to measure such matters. She is good in combat, very good. I will likely want her by my side. We have established a good fighting relationship.'

'I think she will value that.'

'Maybe so.'

'It's true. One can see the sisterhood offered her very little. Fighting with you must have given her a sense of purpose.'

'We make these assumptions on her behalf.'

'We do,' Valderon replied, 'but this is the process of measurement. What do you think of her?'

'She is quiet, yet gets on with things without complaint.'

'Mere descriptions.' Valderon laughed. 'What do you *think* of her? Do you have any affection?'

Xavir contemplated the matter for a short while, steering his horse around a few large boulders strewn across the forest path. 'I have long since killed whatever part of me can feel affection,' Xavir replied. 'This is likely not the answer you seek.'

'I seek no answer, friend,' Valderon replied. 'Just a happy comrade.'

They continued in companionable silence, and Xavir enjoyed the eventual peace and the sound of the gentle rain hitting the leaves. Both men retrieved their waxed rain capes from their saddles, and draped them around their shoulders. Somewhere, in the distance, he could hear a hawk calling out.

The two warriors turned off the path and up a steep slope where the vegetation died back. A plateau lay ahead of them, the track now a little slippery because of the weather. Xavir tilted his head down as they rode into the elements.

Pausing at the edge, Xavir gestured with an outstretched palm. 'There.'

Valderon's expression turned from a furrowed brow into surprise, and he dismounted from his horse. 'You were busy, my friend.'

Down in the wide valley below, spread out across the hazy grassland, was a vast encampment of two thousand warriors.

Many were in the process of putting up enormous canvas tents and organizing themselves into neat columns.

'They're made up of the different clans who had come primarily from the north and western provinces of Stravimon,' Xavir declared. 'These were the warriors who likely would have been pledged fully to Mardonius had Duchess Pryus had her way. After the gathering, I received the loyalty of eleven estate owners and wealthy families, and on seeing what the Black Clan might do to the capital, they saw it as an opportunity for regime change. They want to ally with us, no doubt so they can jockey for court positions when Mardonius is dethroned. In fact, I suggested the idea to them in a way that would make them think they *would* receive favours. That, of course, is up to you.'

'It does not matter,' Valderon said. 'We have their soldiers. We change the regime first, and then worry about diplomacy and politics.'

'I should make it clear,' Xavir added, 'that these soldiers are not of the legion. Some of these men are not what you would call professionals. But their numbers are impressive.'

'They will do,' Valderon said, nodding thoughtfully. 'Indeed they will do. We have almost a thousand Dacianarans at our bidding as well, and we have been building up the Black Clan from surrounding rebel groups.'

'When should we march on Stravir City?' Xavir asked, wary as ever that he had declared himself not in charge of the operation. Now that he had killed many of those on his list, a part of him wished it could be him at the helm, spearheading the attack into Mardonius's forces. Old urges in his blood still stirred, but it was not to be. He knew he was going to separate himself from the main force. He would have to advance with a hand-picked band of soldiers to infiltrate the palace and slay the king, for no one else knew the place as well as he.

'We must train first. We must spread communication among the men so they understand what's happening, what our codes are and what our tactics will be, especially if there are many who are not professionals. We cannot simply advance blind, and with our hands tied behind our backs, into the capital.'

'Wise enough words,' Xavir replied.

'But we must not train too long. From what we are hearing, the people of Stravir City may need us very soon.'

Questions

The rain cleared, and sunlight hit the tents from an oblique angle. A hazy orange glow began to cast itself across the encampment and all the people who were milling around underneath the fluttering banners.

Elysia watched Xavir from a distance. Her father and Valderon had ridden up and down the rows of clan symbols and tents for most of the afternoon. It had been impressive to see so many colours and emblems fluttering in the breeze and around the smoke from their fire pits. The soldiers all seemed to look upon Xavir with great respect.

Birgitta took Elysia's hand and the two sisters walked a little way along the fringes of the camp and the nearby woodland. Two crows landed on a nearby branch and overlooked them as the gloom of dusk set in. The air began to chill slightly. Laughter could be heard from the soldiers nearby.

'And what do you make of all this, little sister?' Birgitta asked softly.

'I don't know . . . it's better than being with the sisterhood.'

'You say that now,' Birgitta replied. 'Perhaps not when the fighting begins. Blood will be spilled.'

'I've seen plenty of blood already.'

'You have,' Birgitta replied thoughtfully. 'And I've yet to

question you about the matter sufficiently. You are still my student, after all.'

Elysia gave a small smile. She no longer felt like a student. She no longer felt the person she had been all those months ago. Xavir had been teaching her many new and practical things about life on the road, from simple woodcraft to reading the elements. Landril, too, never missed an opportunity to teach her about history; his passion was infectious – unlike back at Jarratox, where miserable old women gave skewed and embittered accounts of past deeds. Elysia now had many people to learn from, each of them with something different to say and who didn't force their teachings upon her. There was no kind way to say this to Birgitta, so instead she said nothing at all.

'You have developed into someone who reminds me of other types of sisters,' Birgitta continued. They stepped further into the woods, following a dark animal track that cut through the thick foliage. There was a dampness to the land of Stravimon that Elysia couldn't quite get used to, and it was augmented in the country's forests. There was such old history here, such strange mysticism, as if the source ran through its lands rather than rivers. But if it was magic, it was of a stranger, more archaic manner. Despite there being no oceans between this and her old home, it did seem a world away. She was more at home here, in the forests.

'What's that?' Elysia replied.

'They used to be known in the tales as warrior witches,' Birgitta continued. 'There used to be more like you, a few hundred years ago, in the Seventh and Eighth Ages particularly. The sisterhood's breeding programme is designed to produce more malleable witches, because those warrior witches could not be controlled. They learned how to use weapons. Some say that the great Dellius Compol, of whom regular soldiers are so in awe, had a dalliance with many of them, and with their help perfected dangerous tools for violence. These bands of witches – who operated in warrior covens – began to act in defiance of the sisterhood, so I understand. There were wars amidst the ancient places of the world that almost wiped out the sisterhood entirely. Whatever happened to these warrior witches, I do not know. The sisterhood has done its very best to breed more docile sisters, more cooperative and collaborative. But your independent streak is considerable – and I believe quite unlike most other sisters. Perhaps it is down to breeding, after all, but whatever meshed between your father and your mother has become something very . . . special.'

'I could live with a term like warrior witch if others gave it to me,' Elysia replied. 'I never had a problem with the word *witch* anyway, despite the other sisters frowning upon its use.'

Birgitta gave a strange smile. 'You were never much like the others. But would you be happy with such a life, Elysia? You will commit to no clan, you will be subject to no one unless *you* choose to. This is a rare for a sister. The rest of the sisterhood was forced to go out into the world and be a connection with the families that control it. That was our way of influencing the affairs of the world.'

'I'd be able to control things in a different way,' Elysia declared.

'And your father?'

It still sounded strange to hear the word – not so much for its freshness, but because talk in the sisterhood continually referred to mothers and daughters and sisters. To evoke a male relation seemed alien to her. She saw him as Xavir more than whatever it was 'father' actually meant. But she could feel more of his character in herself than any sister's.

'I've a role alongside him. I can't explain yet what that is. I don't understand it myself.'

'You enjoy the combat.' Birgitta's tone was harsher now.

'I wouldn't say *enjoy* is the right word,' Elysia replied, wary of Birgitta's dislike of violence. 'I enjoy helping him, certainly. He's very good at what he does – he's like no other – and it feels an honour to fight alongside him. We seem to work well together. But it all feels so efficient. So easy. So right.'

'You complement each other,' Birgitta said, narrowing her gaze.

'Something like that, I suppose,' Elysia replied. 'Anyway, does it matter?'

'I am thinking of the future when I ask these questions,' Birgitta said, somewhat defensively. 'It is Marilla's talk of the Dark Sisterhood that concerns me. I can only hope those of us who left Jarratox that night will be able to salvage something for the future, for I believe a war of our own could be brewing. It will be the legacy of whatever happens at Stravir City. If the king has such Dark Sisters at his side, possessed by the lore of the Voldiriks, then we will have our work cut out for us when facing them. Not for aeons has sister fought sister.'

'And we'll need people like me to *fight* sisters?' Elysia asked. She shook her head. 'My techniques might not work so well on other witches.'

'We have not had the need to go hunting them yet,' Birgitta declared, 'but that time could be soon. And besides, Marilla is a seasoned old sister, but we can work on ways around defences as robust as that woman's. We may fine-tune our techniques – yours, mine, any of our existing sisters, those who have joined this so-called Black Clan of Landril's design.' She gestured vaguely in the direction of the camp.

'You think it is a bigger threat, then, this Dark Sisterhood?'

'You have heard less than I have. Whilst we have been on the road these past days, and while you spent time with Xavir, I conversed with all seven sisters from the clans who joined us. Their knowledge was limited, but I could put together their pieces to form some kind of opinion. It seems many sisters had difficulty with the power structures of Jarratox. Their resentment towards the matriarch, and those with whom she surrounded herself, meant that they were easy prey for the Voldiriks' seduction.'

'So the matriarch brought this upon herself?'

Birgitta sighed, but gave a gentle smile. Her cloak fluttered in a breeze that swept through the forest, sending leaves skittering around them both. 'I would not say it is as simple as that, little sister, but you may have a point. The politics of the sisterhood is not for everyone. But from what I can gather, it is as if these wayseers could sense the dissatisfaction of the sisters and offered them something else. Something more attractive. I don't know how that happened. I think that there are witchstones from wherever the Voldiriks come. Perhaps it is something more potent as well, I do not know. Whatever the wayseers have done to the sisters remains to be seen. I have yet to observe one of the altered women with my own eyes. Only then can I discern what that difference is. Are they more powerful? We shall see.'

They walked for a while longer, discussing their concern for the sisterhood, until Birgitta turned the conversation once again to Xavir. 'One thing concerns me, little sister. If I may say.'

'Why be so polite about it?' Elysia asked. She stopped by a fallen trunk and the two of them sat down alongside each other. 'What is it?'

'It is the ease with which you kill other people,' Birgitta said eventually.

'Oh. Well, I don't really find it easy.'

'I remember killing for the first time, many years ago. It haunted me so much. For weeks I could not sleep properly. Every sister is different. But you . . . you have done it so easily, and so frequently.'

Elysia contemplated the matter a little further. 'I can't explain why, but it doesn't seem to bother me. What is the difference between the deer in the forest and those whom we fight on the road?'

'Those we fight are people. They have souls.'

Elysia shrugged. 'Blood is blood. Maybe I've just got used to it during the hunts.'

'Soldiers are not deer that need thinning, or to feed other people.'

'No. But as Xavir keeps saying, they *are* soldiers and when they signed up to do the job then they became—'

'Fair game,' Birgitta finished. 'Yes, he says that a lot.'

'It's still true, though. The soldiers can't fight and not be prepared to die. It is the nature of being a soldier.'

'And what,' Birgitta said, 'would you know about being a soldier, little sister?'

'I know enough from Xavir's tales.'

Birgitta glanced to the forest floor. 'The blood bond is strong between you.'

'I don't know,' Elysia said, looking down at the damp, leaf-strewn ground.

'The man has no capacity to talk about such things. Some people prefer words, but others prefer action. He has shown his affection, albeit somewhat perversely, by trusting you to fight alongside him. He will want you to go all the way, little sister. All the way. I hope you know that?'

'How do you mean?'

'He will expect you to fight into the darkest corner of Stravir City. He may well expect you to die alongside him if need be.'

'Then I'll just rejoin the source sooner rather than later.'

'Oh, little sister. The young are too careless when it comes to risk. These attitudes change with age. We become more cautious. When did you become so hardened?'

'A long time ago, maybe,' Elysia replied. In honesty, she could not really tell what the fuss was about. Killing was killing. Death was part of life, and that was that. What difference did any of it make in the grand scheme of things? She would return to the source and there would be peace whatever happened after she died. What was there to fear?

'Come, then.' Birgitta rose to her feet and groaned. 'I am too old for fighting,' she continued, pressing her palm into her back. 'That battle with Marilla, I could have done without.'

They walked back along the forest path, pushing aside the damp foliage, until they emerged once again in the busy camp. Smouldering fires could be seen at regular intervals. Men and women soldiers sat around them, talking cheerily about the job ahead. Black banners had been raised – the stark, featureless sign of Xavir's Black Clan. It was like a town had sprouted in the middle of a peaceful valley.

When they found Xavir, several women were standing alongside him, each one a different age. They all wore cloaks of slightly different hues, and richly patterned grey and red tunics underneath, indicating that they had been assigned to clans. Bright blue eyes regarded her. Marilla was among them, and Birgitta must have known who all the rest were, judging by her insouciance.

Elysia, in her leather jerkin, boots and light practical cloak, and her bow strong across her shoulder always, wondered if she was more like a warrior now than a sister, and as such had no need to stand alongside them.

'These women,' Xavir declared, 'have requested we plan the role of magic in the forthcoming battle. And I agree. Tonight, in the manse, we must group together.'

'When do we fight?' one of the women asked, the oldest, judging by her white hair and withered skin.

'That is not up to me to decide,' Xavir replied. 'Much of what happens now depends upon training.'

'We need no training,' Marilla declared.

'That may be so,' Xavir replied. 'We're grateful for your patience.'

'I wouldn't even be here if it wasn't for my master's whim. One day we're off to visit the king, the next we're fighting him.'

Xavir gave no answer. Elysia could tell by his glare that he was at the limits of his politeness.

'Sunset, at the manse,' Xavir replied, and turned to walk away.

The Wait is Over

Three weeks passed before the Black Clan was ready to march on Stravir City, and Landril enjoyed every minute of the training. There were calculations to make, plans to scrutinize and tactics to theorize. Of course, he didn't actually have to do much physical training – no, his role, he decided, was very much about the *organizing*, and almost everyone else seemed happy to leave him to it.

Landril surveyed the scene around the manse in the morning light, his hands behind his back, his pace a leisurely stroll. The men who had come from the gaol had changed beyond all belief. They had a focus, something to work towards and a cause they believed in. As a result there was now a sense of pride as they went about their business.

He watched Davlor sweating away as he attempted to defend some of Tylos's mock-swordplay. The young fool was no match for the man from Chambrek, though even Landril had to admit he'd improved his technique significantly in the time he'd spent on the road.

Landril tutted as Davlor fell face-first onto the grass, his sword knocked out of his hand. Someone behind laughed.

'Are you actually going to do any work,' Davlor shouted to

Landril indignantly, pushing himself up from the ground, 'or just stand and stare?'

'My mind is a hive of activity,' Landril replied, with a smile, before moving on.

By now, Landril reasoned, the bard and poet should have spread some uncertainty in the settlements around Stravir City as well as inside the capital itself. The news of the Black Clan had already spread surprisingly far, and more joined the cause each day. Those who had come had their own reasons for doing so; some had been displaced by the king's legions or borne witness to their brutality upon the king's orders. Others were soldiers who had disagreed with the king's tyranny. Some asked if the famous Xavir would become king, and Landril did not disabuse them of this notion, although he had no idea what Xavir felt about the situation.

The only thing that unnerved Landril was the lack of news coming back from *within* Stravir City itself. He was a man who worked with information but every attempt he'd made to gain news from inside the walls of the city was met with failure. As he had no idea what they would be up against, he anticipated the very worst.

The rest of the Black Clan had expanded into something of a decent force. They numbered about four thousand, with an extra nine hundred Dacianarans warriors. Training continued day by day. Xavir had coordinated the best of the warriors to educate the lesser soldiers in battle techniques, whilst Valderon and Landril ironed out what tactics to use, considering the geography surrounding the capital. The witches had been the most work but even they were coming together now. Birgitta had convinced them to put aside the usual politics and power-plays involved in the sisterhood. News of the Dark Sisters had clearly unnerved the women enough to forget their egos. The women were rarely to be seen at this hour: instead they convened in the twilight, to manufacture weapons from their witchstones, away from prying eyes.

Things were, Landril conceded, going well. His role was satisfying. But how long would they have to wait?

That answer came soon enough.

A man on horseback arrived that same afternoon. He was one of Grauden's scouts, who had been dispatched to spy on Stravir City. His cloak flying behind him, his mare thundered towards the manse. He dismounted before the horse had properly stopped, landed running, heading straight to Valderon and Landril, who had been talking tactics in General Havinir's old library.

The messenger was breathless and sweaty, hunched double, his face and brown clothing covered in grime.

'The people,' he panted, pressing his hands to his knees, 'are being turned into Voldiriks.'

'Steady yourself,' Valderon cautioned, helping him upright. 'Tell us everything.'

'In Stravir City,' he continued, 'citizens are being . . . they're now being *turned into Voldiriks*. Morphed. The process is in its early stages, but it will begin to happen on a massive scale. Civilians are being herded together. There are things called spawning tanks. People are being lowered and altered. So that they become Voldirik people. Their body changes. Their minds are no more. They are essentially dead – they remember nothing.'

'How do you know this?' Landril said in horror. 'What evidence?'

'Visual. I managed to use one of your passageways – the southern sewer system.'

'The abandoned one.' Landril nodded. 'Go on.'

'I saw it happening. The tanks are within the city. It was a mass execution. Those people who are not successfully transitioned – or who put up a fight – a worse fate awaits them. Their bodies – warped and showing all signs of horrors – are taken to another state, another tank, and they are turned into what I can only describe as monstrosities. Two or three, or more, are bonded together; their skin is discoloured and changes texture; eyes seem to sprout from their flanks. Extra, clawed limbs grow. I saw what I could, and returned as quickly as I could manage. I have not eaten in two days.'

'By the Goddess, the things that attacked us in the forest,' Landril observed to Valderon. 'What this man is describing tells of the provenance of these beasts.'

Valderon thanked and dismissed the messenger. 'Is it simply madness?' Valderon turned to Landril. 'How can a king do this? We must hurry, else thousands will be transitioned. That is worse than death.'

Landril moved to the window, the pale light falling across his face. 'Something does not sit right. I cannot believe that even Mardonius would condone such madness.'

'We can prepare no longer,' Valderon declared. 'No more training, no more acquiring resources. Though we number few, we cannot wait. Are we agreed we march on first light?'

Landril nodded grimly. 'We'd better let Xavir and Lupara know.'

A horn blew repeatedly throughout the valley. Thousands of soldiers fell silent. Birds flickered through the treetops and above the canopy in response. The forest stirred in the waning light of the afternoon.

Soldiers began to disassemble their tents and gather their belongings. Horses were mustered and ration carts made their way through the camp collecting what supplies the men had gathered for the journey. There was an air of discomfort around the scene, Landril observed from the hilltop. Despite all their planning, now the hour was upon them there was a nervousness about what they were to face.

The Dacianarans were first to disappear off into the night. Landril had plans for their barbarian allies to be utilized far ahead of the Stravir fighters, and the savage warriors were up for any challenge. Black paint smeared around their eyes, and draped in all manner of animal skins and feathers, they sped on their mighty wolves away from the manse and through the glade. At the head of the wolf pack was Lupara, with Katollon – perhaps symbolically – situated slightly behind. Their wolf howls could be heard in the distance, but the Dacianarans left the grounds of the manse feeling considerably empty and quiet.

Landril walked in haste back to meet Xavir, who was standing alongside Tylos, in what had been the dining room, but had been changed into a storage facility.

'Spymaster,' he declared, stepping aside, 'I have chosen my men.'

Landril peered behind his bulk and could see only the former men from Hell's Keep seated at the dusty table. 'You're sure you need no more skilled men?' he asked. 'I would rather you get in securely to execute your plans. Your getting to Mardonius quickly is crucial to this operation.' What Landril did not say was how he lacked faith in the abilities of the former prisoners.

Xavir gave a feral grin, obviously knowing what Landril was thinking. 'These men broke out of a mountaintop keep. I think they can break into a walled city without being seen, especially on the route I will be using. Besides, they will be with me. Where there are people in danger, we will do our best to help them — or at least we can hold off whatever atrocities are about to be committed until the Black Clan is through the city's gates. Though we may already be too late.'

Landril frowned. 'And your daughter, will she remain with the witches after all?'

'I will be going with him,' came a voice.

Landril turned around, slightly startled, to see Elysia standing behind him, with her bow across her shoulder and her arms folded. 'I wish you wouldn't creep up on people like that,' he muttered.

'It's a skill that will be of use,' she replied, walking to her father's side.

'Does Birgitta know of this?'

'She does.'

'And what did she think?'

'She thought I could think for myself.'

'Well, there we have it,' Landril replied, addressing them all. 'The battle ultimately rests in your hands if you are going into the heart of the capital for Mardonius.'

'Would you rather it rested in any other hands?' Xavir replied.

He shook his head. 'You must leave before us, then. Get to the king. Cut the head off the snake and, with luck, the rest of the body dies.'

'Our horses are ready, we'll leave now,' Xavir said, patting Landril on the back. There was not even a hint of fear about their plan, which was audacious at the best and hopeless at the worst. Here was a man who had been waiting for a long time to do what he was about to do.

Landril stared at the huge form of Xavir, clad in black and

with the Keening Blades sheathed over his shoulder. It was the vision that Landril had wanted for so long to see challenging Mardonius for supremacy. Now the day had come he wondered if the older warrior was up to the task. 'You are not one for emotional goodbyes, no doubt,' Landril continued, 'but good luck.'

Xavir nodded, striding out of the room, followed by his daughter and the remaining men from Hell's Keep.

Davlor was last to leave, and as he did so he grinned at Landril. 'Don't worry. I'll look after the boss.'

'You can barely look after yourself,' Landril replied, then held Davlor's arm. The two men glanced at one another. 'You do everything you can to stop anything happening to the boss, okay? He is our greatest weapon. Don't get distracted. Don't start going off to save people dreaming of heroics. *Get to the king.*'

'Relax,' Davlor replied, his palms in the air. 'I'm good with a sword now, anyway.' He laughed and walked away.

Landril watched them leave the manse.

Their horses sped away and his nerves grew even further stretched. Landril had been manipulating and planning so much over the past few months – but what was happening now would be outside his control.

There was one more thing on Landril's agitated mind and he strode into the trees to find her. It took several minutes, but Birgitta was there. Weeks ago she had told him to meet her at this hour if he wanted to see a feat with his own eyes, and that hour was now upon them. Indeed, even though he was early, she was there, with the other women standing cloaked, and in a circle, within the darkness of the trees. Birgitta was next to a statue of the old Sixth Age king, Vaprimok, but on the statue itself were perched two large brown falcons. 'You're early,' Birgitta said. 'I knew you couldn't wait.'

'I'm glad I did not disappoint.' Landril eyed the women in the shadows, who were watching him every bit as keenly as the two birds.

'It was not a lie, then,' he continued.

'By the source, did you think it would be?'

'No, no, I merely thought it unlikely. But I like to be proven wrong on occasion.'

'Well, they have come. Marilla –' Birgitta gestured to the woman in black – 'possesses outstanding techniques in communicating with these creatures.'

Landril glanced again at the falcons. Both noble creatures, one had a white head, the other was entirely brown. Their feathers glimmered.

'And you're confident this will work?'

'No,' Birgitta replied, 'but it can't do any harm.'

'Then continue, with whatever it is you need to do,' Landril said.

Birgitta stepped towards one of the other witches, who revealed a net behind her. Inside was what looked like witchstones, but they had been encased within a wooden frame. Birgitta scooped one out with her right hand and showed the object to Landril.

'Two witchstones of opposing forces have been bonded together. It was incredibly difficult to do this, not to mention dangerous, but we managed. And, by the source, they will create a powerful reaction when they are dropped from a great height.'

Landril raised an eyebrow. None of the other witches had responded yet. They, too, were standing like statues. 'And you expect the falcons to do this?'

'No.' Birgitta laughed. 'That would be ridiculous and dangerous.'

One of the birds squawked loudly, its call muted in the confines of the trees.

'I mean no offence, friend,' Birgitta said to them, then turned to Landril. 'No. The falcons are going to transport these five dozen devices to the Akero. It is they who will aid us.'

'The Akero answer only to themselves,' Landril said.

'When was the last time you spoke to one?'

'Admittedly, never,' Landril replied.

'Well, I have recently, and they have vowed to help us rid the country of the Voldiriks. We are not the only ones to suffer from their incursions,' Birgitta replied. Landril spotted a messenger tube inside the net and said, 'This is your message to them?'

'It is.'

'May I see it?'

'No you may not.'

Landril sighed.

'Not everything is within your control,' Birgitta replied.

'More's the pity,' Landril said. 'Does it explain the tactics of battle?'

'You must trust us,' Birgitta repeated more forcefully.

Landril's shoulders sagged. 'Fine.'

'Now then . . .' Birgitta gestured to the other witches, who moved forwards to gather the large net. The one Landril assumed to be Marilla stretched up towards the birds and whispered to them in a piercing tone. Whilst she spoke to the falcons, the other sisters began to strap the net to the legs of the birds.

In unison the sisters stepped back.

The falcons extended their large wings, and with repeated firm downward pushes, as though struggling with the weight, the birds began to rise from the statue and then up through a gap in the canopy.

A moment later, the birds and their cargo vanished out of sight. Landril looked around and the witches were back in their original position, as if this had been some religious ceremony of sorts. It felt as if Landril had missed half of what was actually going on here.

'Well that's that then,' Birgitta said, her mood completely different now, much lighter than before. The oppressive air had vanished. Had there been strange magic lingering all along?

'I suppose we should get a move on,' Birgitta announced.

'How long until the Akero will reach Stravir City?'

Birgitta shrugged. 'They'll come when they come.'

'Hardly words by which I can plan a battle.'

'By the source, you're going to be insufferable now, aren't you?' Birgitta said.

Landril had heard enough and seen enough to warrant heading back to the manse. 'We must gather our things. The Dacianarans are away, as are Xavir and Elysia.'

'She's gone, then,' Birgitta said.

'She went with Xavir.'

Birgitta nodded. 'Let us pray he watches over her.'

'I think,' Landril said, 'that the safest place to be may well be beside that man.'

'Not where he's going,' Birgitta said. Her eyes were welling up, but she composed herself. 'He is marching into the dark heart of this mess, and he is taking the little sister with him.'

Landril began to walk back along the forest track, but turned to ask: 'Why do you call her little sister, when she's taller than you?'

'Because she was not always taller than me.' Birgitta raised her staff, and within a heartbeat Landril could no longer see her.

Scent

Xavir could still smell blood.

Ever since their journey from the manse, for a night and a day, he had smelled it, though there was none around. A memory had trigged the aroma. This was how things always smelled during war. Blood. Horse shit. Mud. Rancid wounds and charred flesh. The air would be full of it. It had been many years since he had prepared for a battle on this scale, and now the memories came back to him. In a curious way, these sensations were calming. They were all he had really known of life.

There was also the damp smell of rain from the night before, and leaves drooped heavy with water. Ahead was a haze of blues and greens. The forest was brightening. He and his men had slept for only a couple of hours, some of the others more so on horseback, and he would permit them another small camp before they reached the city walls.

The other men did not say much. Dressed in armour that had been refined and coloured black at the manse, they looked the part of soldiers, but would they behave like them? Xavir felt responsibility for them – they had followed him to freedom out of Hell's Keep but they'd had no reason to follow him into battle now. This was not their fight. Yet their loyalty to him stood firm – he couldn't have asked for more than that from his own brothers in the Solar Cohort. And so from Tylos to Grend, and even Davlor, these few were *his* men now and he would look after them. He may not have been able to protect his sworn brothers but the least he could do was try to ensure that these men survived the oncoming battle. Tylos approached him now to comment on the conditions ahead. The man from Chambrek rarely showed anything other than a calm and neutral expression, but today it was obvious there was a weight on his shoulders.

'I will look to you to be my second pair of eyes and ears,' Xavir commented.

'It would be an honour, Xavir.'

'Would it?' Xavir asked. 'Would it really be an honour? Of all the things that could be honourable, why walking with me into a city that's far from your homeland?'

'There are people who need liberating,' Tylos suggested.

'But you and I both know that atrocities happen every day somewhere in this world.'

For a moment his eyes relaxed, his gaze became softer. Tylos seemed contemplative. 'Those years in Hell's Keep — we could have wasted them. We could have rotted. I would have been a madman muttering fine poems in the darkness. Don't smile. But you insisted we sorted ourselves out. You made us work in the gloom until our muscles burned. You stopped us killing each other over nothing. You may have used fear at times to achieve it, but those of us who were wise could see that you were doing it to maintain some sense of ourselves.'

The words warmed him to the bones as much as any campfire.

'Now, the wisest of those men—' Tylos continued.

'Naturally you include yourself in that category,' Xavir put in.

Tylos gave a wide smile. 'Naturally. The wisest — those of us who thrive on poetry, say — could see that you looked after us because you missed the brethren. You missed the comradeship, if what we had in there could be called that. Now I can see it was the Solar Cohort that you missed. We will be a poor substitute tomorrow.'

'You all followed me when there was no need to. You had lives of your own you could have returned to after your escape. But here you are. I could ask for no more loyal comrades than that.'

Tylos shrugged and relaxed his posture. 'Why is it that we have not simply vanished into the night? Because we feel we owe you something.'

'You owe me nothing,' Xavir replied.

'There are some debts that transcend material possessions. The poet Tharmantalus once said—'

'You never shut up about the poets, you people from Chambrek.'

'It is how we measure our greatness.' He grinned.

'Enough of this sentimental nonsense,' Xavir said. 'I have a favour to ask.'

'Name it,' Tylos said, puffing out his chest.

'If I fall in the battle before anyone else, I would like you to protect Elysia. Whatever debts you feel you owe me, apply to her.'

Tylos raised his eyebrows. 'Of course, of course. Perhaps not entirely surprising, I must say, but may I ask why such concern for one you have known for so little time?'

'Blood is blood,' Xavir replied.

The man from Chambrek laughed at that. 'As you wish, Xavir. You have the word of an honourable man from the south.'

'That's good enough for me,' Xavir said.

Later that afternoon, when what little sun there had been was obscured by cloud, Xavir felt the heavy gaze of his daughter upon him. She was riding at his side. For some reason he seemed taken aback by how tall and noble she looked when on horseback. She looked composed. Elegant. As if she didn't have a care in the world despite what they were about to face. He suspected it was a mask.

'Do you think we'll die?' she asked casually.

His reply was almost born of instinct. It was always the way before war that people wanted to talk about such things. 'One day. Maybe today. Maybe during the battle. Maybe in a year or ten. Death is the only thing that's certain about life.'

'You don't seem to care much about dying.'

'I've asked myself the same question a hundred times, in a hundred similar situations. One day I became bored of asking it and when I rode to war we stopped talking about it.'

'Well, I am scared.'

'It's fine to be frightened,' Xavir said.

'Really?'

'Really.'

'But everyone else seems to be fine. They're saying how they're looking forward to war. They can't wait to show Mardonius what's what.'

'They're likely lying,' Xavir said. 'They're terrified, for the most part. Relax. It's your first battle. Battles are different from smaller skirmishes, like the one we had at Golax Hold. The latter is more sudden and you have less time to think – and *worry*. Battles loom. There's the weight of politics and tactics surrounding them. There is too much thinking. Such contemplation changes how one views the situation. Everything seems more important. But at the end of it all, it's just swords against flesh, only more of it.'

Xavir's small band continued along the dirt road towards Stravir City. He regarded them once again: black-helmed, black-shielded, and swords at their side, they looked the part, at least. They had received good training, and had decent weapons upon them. Their faces were set grim and attempted to hide all manner of nerves.

These men were only one night's ride away from the capital now, but they would not be heading directly for it. Instead, as the Dacianarans aimed to plan their attack shortly before sunset tomorrow, Xavir would be taking them on another route entirely.

The Tide of War

They poured down into the treeless valley below and headlong into the wind, a thousand savage Dacianarans. Most rode the large wolves of their country, with a hundred archers following on horseback.

This was what life was about. How could Lupara have forgotten?

Thundering down the slopes upon her great wolf Vukos, with Faolo and Rafe riderless at her flanks, she had rediscovered a part of her soul that she had neglected for far too long. Blue and black facepaint was cast around her eyes and cheeks, her hair was decorated with silver ornaments and wolf teeth, a broadsword rested on her back, and an axe was gripped tightly in her hand. Katollon rode only yards behind and had encouraged Lupara to take the position at the tip of the fang formation that was biting into the valley below.

Stone lookout posts on the capital's borders, each manned by five or six Stravir soldiers, were swallowed whole by the Dacianarans. Axes cleaved slack-jawed heads clean from their bodies and wolf-maws savaged those who dared to raise a sword in response. The tribal surge advanced across ruined farmland and abandoned homesteads, vaulting broken fences and clattering into Stravir defences. Up on the hilltop, a beacon was lit, signalling the alarm. *Good.* It was what was needed. If they could lure the full might of the city's defences out of the gates, Xavir's mission would be made that much easier.

Hour by hour, mile after mile, the Dacianarans decimated station posts and watchposts until they caught sight of the Voldirik encampments, their tents tall like a sails, across the muddied fields. Beyond them could be seen the high walls of Stravir City, a stark black against the grey-blue drizzle.

A wild cry went up among her kinsmen.

The shimmering bronze line of forty elegant warriors rose up before them. Instinctively Vukos veered towards the line and Lupara held her axe at the ready. The Voldiriks were slow to respond to this sudden charge; they seemed completely unprepared as Lupara directed her tribe into the mass. There was a sickening crunch as mud, blood and broken shards of wood and armour flew like sparks from a hammered anvil. Bodies fell, almost all of them covered in bronze armour. Lupara broke through the line and surged with her warriors into thirty more of the armoured warriors, who were hastily taking a formation. Ever more Dacianarans filled in behind her to deal with the first line of Voldiriks, easily overwhelming those who were left. Lupara scanned the lines: no wayseer here, no magic.

But from the left there came a ground-shuddering thump and a slobbering roar. A huge beast lurched into view. As tall as a church spire, it clambered out of an old mineshaft, scattering timber frames with its rise. Many-limbed, grey-skinned and with three misshapen maws where only one should have been, it began to lumber towards the battle.

Lupara called for the left flank to attack this new threat, and Katollon broke free from the melee to lead an assault. She focused on the Voldirik massing in front of her. Every one of the strange race had to contend with both rider and wolf.

Consequently, Voldirik warrior after warrior crumbled to the ground before her wolf-mounted kin. A few bronze-helmed warriors showed more tenacity and elegantly whittled some of her men from the flanks, but they were soon overpowered. Drowned by the weight of the wild assault.

The Voldiriks here were finished, and all the riders turned to watch Katollon's savage detachment spiral around the enormous beast. A horn summoned forth the Dacianaran archers. A hundred men and women, their faces covered in red paint and fur draped across their shoulders, rode forwards on horseback. Both hands on their bows, and showing a level of balance and agility that Lupara had almost forgotten, they began to fire repeatedly into the tall beast. The thing groaned with every arrow strike that met its target, but many just bounced away. The archers quickly realized that its skin was too thick to penetrate, so instead aimed for one of its four eyes, or its open maws. Meanwhile Katollon and a clutch of wolf-riders circled the beast, darting in to attack and withdrawing so as to make it take a misstep. Eventually dizziness got the better of it, and the creature slipped on the mud. It tumbled sideways, crunching on top of one rider. The wolf struggled free from the mud but the warrior was unconscious. No sooner had the monstrous figure fallen than Katollon and his kinsmen cleaved their axes repeatedly into its head. Thick gouts of blood drenched the three riders. The monster's arms twitched, but eventually a final axe-stroke connected with a vital nerve at the base of its enormous neck and the thing let out a roar – before falling into silence.

Drizzle turned to rain. Paths turned to bloody mud. The howling cries of the Dacianarans filled the air and the thousand-strong force surged once again along the valley. They vaulted upwards, not wanting to be trapped in the valley bottom and invite a swift defeat from above, and the nimble wolves thought nothing of the ascent.

The Dacianarans swarmed towards the capital.

Xavir rode calmly at the front of his small band of warriors. The din of war rose in the next valley as Lupara's army advanced towards Stravir City. Directly above, on the hilltop, was the fierce blaze of the warning beacon. The brightness up there meant the lookouts would fail to see the clutch of warriors who advanced in stealth down here.

He took a small, lesser-used path from the main road which spiralled down to a muddied track that was covered in overgrown vegetation. Xavir had to briefly dismount and cleave through thicker clumps with the Keening Blades.

Their progress was slow.

'Where the hell are we headin' boss?' Davlor wiped his nose on his sleeve.

'Into the hillside itself.'

'You what?'

'It's the way into the city,' Tylos observed.

'How come you know?'

'We were told,' Tylos declared. 'Were you not listening to everything Landril and Xavir discussed?'

'Well, yeah, but . . .'

'You're an idiot.' Jedral shook his head. 'How you've lived this long is beyond my comprehension.'

'Quiet,' Xavir hissed. 'The watchmen may not be able to see us, but they will hear you.'

'Sorry boss,' Davlor whispered, hunching slightly as if he'd be overheard.

Xavir cleaved one final pine branch out of the way and it

revealed a lichen-covered rock face. He smiled, leaned forwards, paused. It was still here.

There were old markings on the stone — the letters that spelled out Cedius's initials and the tunnel number. This one was the third. Xavir felt for the edge of the rock and eventually found a small crevice. He levered one of the Keening Blades in the crack and gestured for Tylos to do the same with his weapon.

'Will it not ruin the blades?' Tylos asked.

'Ordinary steel, yes, but not our weapons,' Xavir replied.

The two men began to ease back the rock, and a huge slice of the granite began to inch backwards. Inside lay a musty smell and utter darkness.

'What is it?' Davlor asked, his mouth hanging open.

'One of four old mine tunnels that were developed for King Cedius to use as a method of escape, should he need to.'

'How did you know it was here?'

'I had it built. Well, only this one. The other three had been there before my time, but too many people knew of them. This — only Cedius and myself were supposed to know of it.'

A roar went off in the distance, the noise carrying on the wind.

'We should enter,' Xavir declared. 'The Dacianarans are making progress and Valderon's army will likely be marching upon the city very soon.'

'So where's the tunnel going to take us?' Davlor asked.

'Within the second city wall, and under one of the old banking houses. This is a narrow passageway, so take caution. The air will be musty. Don't let it affect you. Elysia, do you have the arrow?'

His daughter stepped forwards without hesitation and withdrew an arrow from her quiver. She whispered something in the witch tongue and the arrowhead began to glow into a white light that illuminated the tunnel.

Xavir placed his hand on her back and steered her into the darkness. Together they entered the old escape tunnel of Cedius the Wise.

Tip of the Spear

It was what Valderon had waited years for – to lead an army, to be at the very front of a line of thousands. He never thought it would be like this: an army of renegades marching upon the city of his birth, to wrench that city free from the grip of a tyrant king. No one had talked about what would happen afterwards. Valderon's future, so far as he could see, ended with this siege.

He rode together with Landril and the witches. They had travelled for a day now, camping by the road overnight with scouts silencing any passers-by who might have spread word back to the capital. With every gathering mile, Valderon felt an increasing tightness in his chest. They travelled in the wake of the Dacianarans, who had trampled wildly across the farmland and empty homesteads as they cut a path through to the capital. Occasionally Valderon observed Voldirik corpses in the mud, sometimes one of the Dacianarans.

'All signs of the battle are fresh,' Landril remarked. 'Lupara and her tribe are perhaps the better part of the day ahead.'

'Should we hasten our pace?' Valderon demanded. 'People may well be dying.'

'We are as expected,' Landril said. 'By the Goddess, we are on course.'

'Then tomorrow morning the fighting commences.'

'If Lupara has played her role,' Landril said. 'One can never fully trust—'

'She will have,' Valderon snapped. 'She can be trusted. It is you that cannot trust anyone.'

'You may have a point,' Landril said.

'If it was up to you to do the fighting then we'd never stand a chance. Her skills are in war, as are mine.'

'No, you can do other things as well,' Landril observed.

'How so?' Valderon had, in a peculiar way, come to see Landril as someone he could confide in. There was a viciously sharp intelligence within the spymaster, and Valderon respected his opinion – even if he did not always agree with it.

'Your ways are with people,' Landril replied. 'That is what makes a leader. Any fool can stand at the front of this rabble and die with a sword in his hand. But you can convince and inspire with all the passion of a Stravir hero.'

Valderon shrugged. 'You have much confidence in a man you barely know.'

'This much I know. You spent time with a great many of these soldiers behind us. Whilst I slept at the manse, you camped out with them. You took to Grauden's men and made them like an extended family to our original band of freed men. Even Xavir – he has been critical of you far less than any of us, and he took your council willingly. These are the qualities that make a leader. I had my doubts, I will admit, in your abilities. I wanted Xavir to lead, but perhaps he is too damaged from what has gone before.'

Valderon remained quiet.

'Lupara, too, is bewitched by you.' Landril left the sentence open but Valderon did not take the bait.

'On that matter,' he replied grimly, 'there is nothing to discuss.'

'An honourable man, I see. Despite the temptations of the wolf queen.'

'Not a concern, spymaster. This is where Xavir and I remain similar: matters of the heart have bruised us more than any weapon can. And while we have mended ourselves, we have also hardened. There are walls in our minds so robust that not even the wolf queen can scale them.'

Landril smiled at that.

The night passed without event. The solders' slumber was disturbed only by each other's noise, jokes and debate, and soon enough they found themselves on the road close to the capital. It was a brighter morning, with sunlight skimming across the damp grassland behind, but as usual, by noon, cloud was gathering.

Valderon, Landril and Birgitta rode far up ahead, away from the main force. Tracking the Dacianarans' trail of carnage, it was not long until they came within sight of the city.

It had been years since Valderon had seen the capital. The hundreds of spires that marked the central quarters were mired in drizzle. A hazy light broke through momentarily, illuminating the mirrored roof tiles of the vast palace – the residence that King Mardonius had made his home. Two large granite walls stretched across the front of the capital. The rock had been carved out of the neighbouring hills hundreds of years ago, and built in a way so it seemed that the two hills either side of the city reached arms around as if embracing the people and their homes. Just beyond, far in the east, was a wide river that met the Sea of Rhaman. The flatlands glimmered in the green-grey light.

Valderon was so distracted by the sight of his home that he almost missed, for a second, what was happening in the plains a mile before the southern, main gates of Stravir City. The Dacianarans were here – and if Landril's calculations were accurate, they had been so since the night before. Opposing them, thousands of bronze-clad figures of the legions and the Voldiriks swarmed across the land. The tribal army had divided itself into five nimble forces. Wolves easily outpaced the horses, drawing and feinting repeatedly to break up the Stravir columns. They had achieved much already on the left flank by the look of it, but the volume of the Stravir forces, largely Voldirik warriors here, was staggering, more than their calculations.

The ground thundered with the vibrations of war.

To Valderon's right, the spymaster unfolded a waxed-paper map of the region. After consulting it for a moment he scrutinized the scene before them like some prophet divining the future. The paper fluttered in the breeze. Cries from the distance came and went on the same gusts.

'We should continue on the valley route in,' Landril declared. 'No need to disappear up into the hills. Lupara's aim was to draw the Voldirik and Stravir forces forth from the city and keep them there.'

'This, they have done,' Valderon replied. 'You looked surprised at it.'

'Relieved.'

'So what are we waiting for?' Valderon asked. 'We must get on with it, for the sake of the people.'

Landril turned to Birgitta. 'When will your avian friends arrive?'

'They were supposed to come this morning.'

'Wonderful – so a no show,' Landril replied, grimacing.

'They will come,' Birgitta assured him. 'But if they do and we are still up here talking, then all will be pointless.'

'You have a thirst for war all of a sudden?' Landril asked, amused.

'I have an urge to get it all over with.' Birgitta rolled her shoulders.

'She's right,' Valderon said. 'We should go. Let's muster the forces.'

They returned to the column of soldiers and the Black Clan continued the final mile to the battlegrounds: the plains before Stravir City. Witches returned to the command of their former clan, spreading themselves out among the throng of soldiers; despite their old allegiances, today they were all one family, all one clan. The witches' first instruction had been to cast each division of the army in shadow as best they could, and to mask its presence for as long as was possible. Staffs were held aloft, and the witches muttering in a tongue that Valderon could not comprehend. A purple light shot from Birgitta's staff back towards one of the other witches; that woman's then connected to another staff, and so on, until all the witches were united by a crackling web. Then that light faded, leaving a strange shadow above them, as if clouds had gathered. He hoped it was more effective than it looked.

Ragged banners fluttering in the breeze, the Black Clan filtered onto the plains from the farmlands of the south. Half a mile or more either side, the land began to rise up into the rocky outcrops that protected two sides of the capital. Right in the centre was this army of shadow, with Valderon riding in the centre of the front column of cavalry. The majority continued on foot, marching at pace. Noises rose up: of metal clashing with metal, of vast numbers of people and horses swarming across the terrain. The main road was covered now in bodies.

Valderon pulled down his helm and prepared to engage in combat. His heart thumped. He rolled his head to loosen the muscles in his neck. Gripped his enchanted blade a little tighter. Birgitta still held her staff, still incanting. His mind began to tick: was it possible that the Voldiriks had not yet seen the advancing enemy? Valderon gave the orders and, in rows of fifteen, the soldiers of the Black Clan began to separate into five separate divisions: cavalry, archers and three blocks of infantry.

Then, flying overhead came a sight Valderon could scarcely believe.

Fifteen figures, each one the size and shape of a man, but with outstretched wings like those of an eagle, entered the grey skies. They formed a triangle of almost perfect proportions.

'Now watch what happens!' Birgitta declared.

A moment later and the Akero fanned out and began to hurl objects towards the ground, right into the heart of the Voldirik army. Upon impact elemental vortexes, spirals of fire, water or wind, shot up from the earth, wrenching hundreds of enemy soldiers with them. The ground shuddered. Screams erupted. Armoured figures caught up in the fire were burned horrifically. Those who were raised into the sky on whirlwinds were scattered hundreds of yards in all directions. Great, strange tides carried others back against the city's outer wall with a sickening crunch. Within moments, a quarter of the Voldirik and Stravir legion had been eliminated.

The Akero continued towards the city walls and in unison they unloaded another cargo of altered witchstones. Red light sparked upwards from the walls, followed shortly by the sound of stone being wrenched apart. Soldiers and rubble were cast away like grains being scattered across a field. Valderon was agape. Only the quick-thinking of a wayseer – who peeled up the land with magic and used it as shelter – saved a hundred of the city's defenders.

The Akero arced skywards, and within moments could no longer be seen.

Valderon gathered himself and gave the order. Slowly, the witches released their shadowy veil and the Black Clan was now revealed.

Valderon nudged his horse forwards, drew his sword – the Darkness Blade – and bellowed as he led the charge of the cavalry.

Underground

The vibrations overhead caused alarm to some of the men. Xavir ignored the tremors. They continued in the gloom, following the light of a single white witchstone.

'By the Goddess's arse, what's that?' Davlor asked.

'They're fighting above us,' Tylos replied.

'For the love of the Goddess,' Jedral said, 'will you shut up, Davlor? I've had to listen to your drivel for weeks and, in these confines, for Goddess knows how long you've been wittering on, it's getting the better of me.'

'What if the others like my questions, eh?'

'Boys, does anyone,' Jedral announced, 'object if I punch Davlor until he shuts up?'

'No.'

'Nah.'

'See?' Jedral asked.

'Fine,' Davlor grunted. 'Your loss.'

Xavir smiled wryly, it was like being back at Hell's Keep once again but he knew that this banter was just to alleviate the strain they were all feeling.

They continued following Elysia, with Xavir at her heels, listening for anything that might indicate their presence had been discovered. Amidst damp smells and chilling breezes, they had come across nothing except the gently arcing pathways that led through the old mines. Xavir had recalled ordering that distracting routes be blocked so as not to cause confusion in an emergency. Should Cedius have needed to flee, on his own if necessary, then he could have done so with the minimum of risk.

They walked for what felt like hours, taking only two opportunities to rest. The others complained of the absence of light, of the passing of time, the damp and cold. 'We're almost there,' he said, at least twice. The second time Xavir believed it himself. The mine petered out into an old sewage network. Darkness revealed glimmers of light as the witchstone picked out pools of water.

'Stinks in 'ere,' Davlor muttered. His voice carried in numerous directions.

Xavir urged for silence with a gesture to his mouth, and guided them along the route deeper into the city.

'How come there's no noise here?' Grend whispered. 'This isn't right.'

Xavir continued onwards once again until they found a time-worn stairwell.

'Is this it?' Elysia asked quietly.

'It is one of the ways in.' Resting his hand on the damp stone, Xavir paused to address the others, their eyes glinting in the light of the witchstone. 'The stairwells here exit into what used to be abandoned buildings. They were part of the palace estate. Of course, Mardonius may have had the wit to make something of these properties since Cedius died, but it is unlikely. You should remain vigilant.'

No one said anything as they nodded their agreement.

Xavir was first to climb the stairwell, with his daughter holding up the light behind him. They spiralled upwards towards a hatch. Xavir nudged it up a fraction, resting the wooden panel on his head, and scanned the room either side: nothing beyond but darkness.

'It smells strange in here,' he whispered. 'Elysia, if you roll the witchstone into the room beyond how long will the light last?'

'Not long. Several heartbeats. Enough to allow you to see. I can run in and pick it up, or I have another.'

'Quickly roll it in,' he said.

She leaned up and across his shoulder, and flicked the stone across the floor.

Dead eyes stared back.

Upside down heads and bloodstained corpses on the far side of the room.

The light petered out.

'There are bodies beyond,' Xavir whispered down. 'A few days old. We will need a second stone.'

Within a few seconds, Elysia retrieved a stone and had the light activated.

'I will go in first,' Xavir said, 'then you follow.'

He didn't look for her confirmation, but pushed up the hatch, jumped up into the darkness and withdrew the Keening Blades with their whispered groan of metal. No sooner had he done this than Elysia brought up the light and stifled a gasp.

Xavir leaned down and cautioned for the others to wait. He then checked their surroundings in the unearthly light of the witchstone, looking at the two dozen heaped corpses.

'Just what is going on?' Xavir said aloud. 'Come closer.' He gestured for his daughter to bring the light towards the side of the room. Dressed shabbily, these men and women had mostly had their throats cut, but something did not sit right about the scene.

The glint of a knife-blade caught his eye. It was gripped in the death-firm grip of a man in the corner. Bald, skinny and elderly, he was dressed like the others, and on the floor by his right knee was a book entitled *Realms of the Goddess*.

'They killed themselves,' Xavir realized aloud. 'This was a death pact. They have all been killed in the same, quick way – severing an artery. This young boy here had his wrists cut too.'

'Why would they do this?' Elysia's voice was full of shock and he could see the horror on her face as she looked at them.

'Because it was the best option for them,' Xavir replied.

'What could be worse?' She stumbled slightly, uneasy on her feet with either the stench of the dead or the shock of the sight.

'We'll discover that soon enough.' He placed a hand on her shoulder. 'Are you holding up with all of this?'

'Of course,' Elysia replied. 'I'm fine with it.'

She probably wasn't, but Xavir had no need to press the point. That she was lying her way through a despicable scene was half the inner battle.

Xavir leaned over the hatch to call down: 'Everyone else can come up now. Be warned, it's not pretty.'

One by one the men from Hell's Keep clambered up and looked in disgust at the sight. Davlor stumbled over to the corner, where he vomited.

'That smell . . .' Jedral moved back two paces, bringing his axe up ready. His eyes narrowed as he took in the scene.

'What in the name of the Goddess happened here?' Grend asked; the former poacher looked less affected than the others.

Xavir explained his theory, before cutting himself short. A squad of soldiers ran by the outside of one wall, turned a corner and then passed the other wall. For a moment no one said a word. Xavir found a blacked-out shutter that had been covered with a mouldy hessian cloth and peered into the street.

He could see nothing but the grubby whitewashed building opposite.

'Let's go,' he announced.

'What about this lot?'

'Nothing we can do for them.' Xavir pulled back the hessian with one hand. He levered open the shutters with his blade and clambered effortlessly out into the street. As the others followed him he inhaled the fresh, damp air of the old city.

He regarded the familiar shapes and styles of the buildings. Memories flashed before his eyes: parading through the streets; drinking with his comrades on his first secondment; escorting Cedius on matters of national importance. He felt a paternal instinct for the rundown bricks, mortar and timber that surrounded him. This could have been his city. Instead a greedy, ambitious, selfish man had run it into the ground and done Goddess knows what to its citizens.

There was a clamour as Davlor caught his foot on a splinter of wood and went reeling into an upturned bucket.

'Be quiet,' Xavir hissed. 'If our enemy discovers us because of you I'll kill you myself and spare them the effort.'

'Sorry, boss.' Davlor winced, rubbing his shin.

Xavir stepped towards the corner of the street. A mist had crept in, but he could see a group of Voldirik rangers stationed to one side, and there were five more figures who looked a lot like the rangers, but they were garbed in more basic undecorated armour. They moved strangely, too, their arms and legs flailing ever so slightly, as if they did not have full control over their bodies.

'We had heard rumours,' Xavir whispered, 'that citizens of Stravir City are being turned into the Voldirik people using some strange craft. Some of these figures ahead do not look natural. It is likely they are the poor products of such a transition. This is what walking death looks like.'

'Who are we really fighting, then?' Tylos asked. 'Presumably they'll be Voldiriks for the most part, but what if they are civilians transitioned?'

'Try not think of it.'

'If so then the city has surely already fallen?' Jedral muttered.

'Then Valderon will take it back. Remember now, we must remain close. Whilst Valderon leads the Black Clan, he will draw attention beyond the city walls. We have a narrow margin to put a stop to whatever barbarity is occurring here and then kill the king.'

Xavir demanded eye contact from every single one of them. Even Elysia, who seemed wide-eyed and eager to get to work.

'We continue through the back streets,' Xavir told them and then fixed them all with a fierce smile. 'Try not to get yourselves killed.'

Din of War

The very tip of the spear, Valderon led the Black Clan's hundred-strong cavalry towards the western flank of the Voldirik army. The many thousands of bronze-clad figures were already in disarray from the Akero bombardment and were surprised to see the sudden appearance of such a large force to the south. With Grauden's men at his back, one of whom held the tattered black banners of their force, and Birgitta following them scanning the air for signs of magic, Valderon thundered towards the infantrymen. The air was thick with guttural screams and bellows of warriors, as the rest of the Black Clan hurled themselves into battle.

True to Landril's earlier predictions, the Voldiriks spent their first moments attempting to realign themselves into formation. With a roar, Valderon heaved the Darkness Blade into the mass of clamouring bodies. Armour and blood spat out with ease. The enemy emitted a horrific hissing scream with every blow, as if their insides boiled over like a kettle. Helms buckled, and every Voldirik he struck crumpled helplessly. The old techniques came back to him, muscle movements ingrained over the years that expressed themselves once again with ease.

Valderon inched his horse forwards, spiralling his enchanted blade left and right. Despite the weapon's capabilities, the thicket of bodies led to a slow, grinding, awful business. Two of his fellow cavalrymen fell along the lines, ripped down into the bronze mass. Everything lost context now, just as it had always done; there were no people in his mind, simply out-stretched arms and spears and swords. He zoned in on the details and ripped them apart with the Darkness Blade. Such was the potency of the weapon that soldiers he thought he had only grazed had their armour cleaved as if he had struck them with all his might. After the first thirty Voldiriks had been rendered useless, he had grown properly accustomed to the weapon's ways.

The gloom above them darkened even further: a hundred yards up the slope, to Valderon's right, the Black Clan's archers unleashed a torrent of arrows into the Voldirik lines beyond. Any reinforcements surging towards this side of the cavalry charge collapsed one by one to the metal-tipped storm.

The Black Clan's witches hurled orbs of magic into the throng. Firelight arced like meteor trails above his head and shuddered into the ground hundreds of yards further back. The stench of burning flesh reached his nose. But, lumbering through the Voldirik tide, came misshapen forms silhouetted by the inferno behind.

Another noise, another charge: the full mass of the Black Clan infantry now drifted into the melee. Landril, presumably still somewhere among them, had held on long enough for the Voldiriks to commit their entire forces before sending the rest of his men in.

The infantry divided into two streams, like an inverse V-formation. They spread themselves either side of where the great beasts were located. Blinding light from the clan sisters shot forwards, only to be intercepted by other flashes. It appeared that the other forces' witches were active, or the wayseers were among them. To Valderon's horror, only yards away the ground suddenly split open like a gaping maw. He steered his horse around it as soldiers surged with him to escape the earthcraft.

What the hell was that?

A red-cloaked wayseer stood nearby, one palm extended in the direction of the destruction. The air seemed to shimmer with spirals of alien symbols.

Valderon called across to Birgitta for cover, then to his right, he commanded, 'Grauden, to the flanks. Eyes ahead.'

Grauden reacted on instinct and the two riders carved their way towards the magical figure. Birgitta, however, could reach only Valderon with protective shadow, and not his companion. The two riders continued on their way, deftly avoiding the clog of infantry, spears jutting this way and that, swords missing their shoulders by inches. Grauden nudged ahead and would reach the wayseer first; suddenly the man was lifted from his horse, his body glowing white like an angel.

Grauden exploded in a red mist. Pieces of his body and armour scattered for yards around him.

As flesh rained down upon the rest of them, Valderon – still in shadow – gritted his teeth, screamed vengeance and cleaved through the wayseer's neck. The thing fell to the ground life-lessly and its head reeled back with a shower of blood. The hole in the ground closed up. Valderon breathlessly looked back to see that half his cavalry had now vanished into the earth.

Choice

The mist deepened. The mystery deepened. The capital's streets were mostly deserted. Only a handful of Voldirik soldiers were seen, their elegant forms occasionally cutting through the whiteness. The majority of their forces had clearly been dispatched to defend the city walls.

But that did not explain the lack of *citizens*.

Buildings stood empty. Taverns, bakeries, meat merchants, lay abandoned. Nothing had been taken, no ransacking had occurred. It was as if the people of the city had simply vanished.

The group hurried street by street, past whitewashed buildings caked in mould, and under crumbling old archways, towards the palace in which Mardonius would be ensconced. Xavir was conscious that the more time they took, the more of their men outside the city could be dying. As they went, there were more Voldiriks, and surprisingly even a few officers who wore the uniforms of the legions. As they continued through the narrow passageways and along the perimeter of forgotten courtyards, another clutch of Voldirik warriors were spotted, blocking the adjacent alleyway. They wore far more elaborate clothing, their armour a glittering silver colour, their robes bright green. To Xavir's knowledge they were barring the path his group needed to take, so he bid his daughter fire an arrow into their midst.

'What do you want to happen?' she asked. 'Take them all out with the one arrow?'

'With minimal fuss,' Xavir replied. 'Otherwise, there could be hundreds summoned to obstruct our progress.'

She pondered the point for a moment and removed an arrow with a bulbous witchstone at the head. 'I only have one of these.'

'What does it do?'

'It removes the air from around them.'

Xavir shrugged and gestured for his daughter to fire.

She nocked her arrow and pointed it almost directly upwards. She released the arrow, which curved in a steep arc, landing directly in the centre of the group with the sound of shattering glass.

The figures took a step back and peered down to regard this intrusion, but within moments they were clutching their throats.

One by one they fell to the cobbles in a heap.

Xavir scanned the surroundings and prepared to leave, but Elysia held his arm. 'Give it a while to make sure the air is clean again.'

'Good work.'

They lingered for a moment in the mist. Xavir listened for sounds of anyone approaching, or for the shuffle of feet on vantage points higher up where the guards might be stationed on walls or bridges.

'Okay, it'll be fine to go now,' Elysia said.

They weaved through the old city streets, hearing the occasional roar drifting from the battlefield about a mile away. Xavir began to piece together what might have been happening in Stravir City. The greater part of the city had been abandoned.

Pockets of taverns and ancient trading plazas remained un-attended. Whenever Xavir saw something especially strange, such as an open door banging in the wind, they ventured, moment-arily, from their path.

And within, they discovered scenes of horror.

People had either killed themselves or been killed in their homes. Blood-strewn bodies lay huddled and stilled in front-room parlours. In other quarters people had been strung up on meat hooks as if they were about to be processed in some way, their naked torsos covered in the strange script of the Voldirik race as if they had been branded. That same script occasionally manifested on the whitewashed walls of buildings themselves, written in the blood of the victims in a manner that suggested certain buildings were being designated for specific purposes.

Most horrific of all was the scene in one courtyard. From a vantage point high up on the brick walls, the group crawled across a grimy path so as not to be seen by those on the ground. But down below, among the dozens of bronze-clad figures, were eight huge vats. People – ordinary citizens – were being hauled up a wooden platform and thrown screaming into one tank. While from other tanks, different figures were being dragged out by rope and hook, caked in ichor and shivering. But their forms were very much different. They were paler, slenderer, and could barely walk. They were quickly clad in basic clothing and armour.

'It is like some breeding programme,' Jedral whispered. 'They are being treated like bloody livestock. Except there is no slaughtering at the end for them, just . . . whatever that is.'

'It's something worse that being slaughtered perhaps,' Tylos replied. 'They're turning people into the Voldiriks.'

'As I thought,' Xavir said, shaking his head. His grip tight-ened upon the Keening Blades.

'I wonder if that's what happened to most of the legions,' Jedral suggested. 'They've been turned into Voldiriks. It'd explain why we've seen mostly just them bloody aliens here.'

Xavir's group continued to look on, aghast at what was now happening below. More people were being brought forwards. Screams came from the plaza beyond, and the sound started off even more people.

'Should we save them?' Elysia asked. 'Sounds as if there are even more through there.'

Davlor shook head. 'Nah. They're too far and Landril said we could not risk the mission for a few people.'

'But aren't we supposed to help the people?' Elysia asked Xavir. She gazed at him with those startling blue witch eyes.

He thought of Baradium Falls once again, where he failed Stravimon's people. He thought of Landril's wise message of haste, that to sever the connection between Mardonius and his troops would see a swift end to the atrocities. Xavir's mind flickered between the two extremes. He had been shamed in the past, and let down his people. That thought, that he had failed, lingered the most.

'A change of plan,' he declared. 'We cannot allow this to happen.'

'Landril said—' Davlor began.

'Landril has not seen what we are seeing with our own eyes,' Xavir said. 'We cannot allow this to happen. These are our people. Mardonius can wait a few moments longer.'

'How do we get down there?' Elysia asked, glancing back to the situation below, her raven-black hair trailing in the wind like banners on the battlefield.

Shouting came from the wall at the end of their platform. More bronze helms came into view.

'We start by killing them,' Xavir announced.

On instinct Elysia turned and released three, four, five stand-ard arrows into their midst, sending the figures reeling over the edge.

With his Keening Blades ready, Xavir jumped into the throng of oncoming Voldirik warriors. Three rushed towards him – and died. Another two scrambled up a stone stairwell and exited onto the platform, only to be greeted by arrowshafts through the face. Xavir cleared the area of remaining soldiers with a whirl of blades, allowing his daughter to recover her arrows from the corpses.

To the right was a network of paths and bridges that weaved like latticework towards the palace. To the left was the route down to the plaza. Looking down through gaps in the architec-ture, Xavir could see dozens of bronze soldiers surging towards them now. Another band of warriors blocked the opposite exit; Xavir rushed into them, knocking their weapons aside and driving one of his wailing blades into necks or severing arms. In the rare event any of the Voldiriks bypassed Xavir and climbed onto the platform behind, Tylos was next in line to the kill – carving a searing blow with Everflame through their bodies. The black man looked as if he was having fun with the weapon.

'Are you actually going to let me use my fancy axe on any of this lot?' Jedral called forward.

'Blame Xavir,' Tylos replied, standing watchful for any more attackers. 'I am merely feeding off his scraps.'

Their chance to fight properly came soon enough.

Redemption Proper

Groans of a thousand hopeless people rose up from the plaza. They had been herded in like cattle, towards where they would be twisted and remade beyond recognition.

Xavir ran down the spiral stairway until he landed on a viewing point that looked down across the site. The group joined him, crouching down low. Xavir peered up over a decorative stone ledge that was attached to an empty apartment.

The plaza was several hundred yards long, and perhaps a hundred wide. It was the largest marketplace in the city, where Cedius had often come to give speeches to the people, and through which the legions toured after victorious campaigns. The road through at the far end had been blocked by rubble. In the centre there had once stood a statue of the Goddess, but it had long since been destroyed. Stone gargoyles lined the tops of the three-storey grey-granite buildings. And, of course, filling all of this were at least two thousand citizens. Men, women and children, they looked grubby, malnourished and miserable. They were sitting on the cobbles, sprawled on blankets and piles of clothing, whilst they awaited their fate. To the left, down on the southern exit of the plaza, just out of sight from ground level, was the route to the enormous tanks.

Voldirik rangers patrolled either end of the plaza, thirty

figures in each unit, and more were stationed by the ruins of the fountain.

'Elysia,' Xavir said, a hand on his daughter's shoulder. 'I need two explosive arrows – one at each end of the courtyard – to eliminate as many Voldiriks as possible. Nothing toxic, the civilians must be protected. The act will cause panic. You are to remain here and cover the rest of us while we head down there. We will start from that end.' He gestured to the right. 'And work our way towards the other. At that point, concentrate as hard as you can on protecting citizens. If a Voldirik moves to strike them, kill it. But be selective, not hasty.'

Wide-eyed and eager to help, she nodded and selected her arrowheads.

'I will meet you back here before we proceed up the city,' Xavir said.

'When shall I release the first arrow?' she asked.

'Count to fifty,' Xavir said, and with that he ran.

By the time Xavir's gang arrived by the bank of rubble blocking the far end of the plaza, the blue fire from Elysia's first explosive arrow had vanished. A dozen charred Voldirik corpses were strewn on the ground, and in the clearing smoke a dozen more stood in confusion. Xavir leaped across the mess and sliced into them with whirls of the Keening Blades. His gang followed, Jedral screaming with rage as he put his axe to good use. Armour crunched. Civilians shifted back, staring in amazement at what was going on. Within moments there were no Voldiriks here. Xavir followed the line of his daughter's arrows from above and moved further into the immense plaza.

As he scanned the faces for signs of the Voldiriks, he heard his name mentioned many times over. He stood tall, allowing the symbol upon his chest to be visible to all. People parted for him as he caught sight of a bronze helm and rushed towards it. Another thicket of Voldiriks turned to face the gang members – and died. Xavir, Tylos and Jedral rendered them useless within heartbeats and, with Elysia's arrows sailing in to pick off those who turned, there was nowhere for them to hide.

Elysia had already thinned the foe from the centre of the plaza, making the group's progress even quicker. Xavir continued across the cobbles until he reached the far end, citizens moving out of the way of their approach, again, some calling out his name.

'He's returned!'

'Goddess bless us, Xavir Argentum is here!'

Xavir ignored their words and focused on the task at hand. The final group of Voldiriks stood before him, already falling to arrows from above. A whirl of blades and metal and the gang moved through the narrow road towards the enormous tanks.

Those Voldiriks on the wooden framework around quickly jumped down from their position and ran towards them. Tylos and Jedral leaped forwards to intercept, leaving Xavir to deal with the figures at the base: a mixture of Voldiriks and Stravir soldiers. Two rushed forwards in the alleyway; Xavir severed their heads. Another three Stravir now marched awkwardly to greet him with more than a look of nervousness about them. They bore colours and insignia of senior officers of the military, and Xavir was beyond rage that, while supposed to protect the people, they had permitted these atrocities to occur. The first man, stocky and short, attempted a blow, but Xavir's defence was so hard it spun the man around; Xavir hauled back his head and cut his throat, allowing him to collapse in front of his comrades. The other two hesitated, and in that moment found their limbs severed and blades forced through their throats. Xavir spun around to check his gang had killed the remaining Voldiriks, which they had. Grend had suffered a cut to his upper arm, yet, typically, it was Davlor who was the one who moaned the most about his twisted ankle.

They approached the enormous containers, which looked like much larger versions of the ones they had seen in General Havinir's manse. There were eight of them in all, arranged in two neat rows with a network of wooden platforms and walkways around them. The stench here was horrendous, a mix of urine and rotten eggs. There were many people in the vessels who were beyond saving: palms brushed along the surface of the glass, hair drifted like pondweed, and now and then a bloated-blue face would manifest.

'This doesn't make sense,' Tylos observed.

'What?' Xavir asked.

'The Voldiriks were merely guards. From what we've heard they are footsoldiers; they would not have the intelligence to process these people into new forms. We should see a wayseer here at the very least, no?'

Xavir turned for a second to see a long-haired figure run past one of the tanks at the far end. 'Halt!' he demanded.

It was a woman, with stark blue eyes and blonde hair, dressed entirely in black. For a moment she stood there, brazenly, in between two tanks, just laughing. Then she pulled her cloak across her form – and vanished.

Jedral ran, clutching his axe, to the very spot where she had been standing, but there was nothing for him to kill. 'A bloody witch,' he shouted back. 'Boys, I swear that was a witch.'

'It was one of the Dark Sisters,' Xavir announced grimly. 'We had heard rumours of this – them having made a pact with the Voldiriks. Now we know they are real.'

'Now what?' Tylos asked. 'There are many people still confused in the plaza and we have a king to kill.'

Xavir made his way back into the open courtyard, through the milling townspeople, heading for the ruins of the statue of the Goddess. He stood upon her tumbled form and looked at the people.

'There is a battle being fought outside these walls,' he shouted, watching their expressionless faces, 'to save this city from the devilry that has claimed it. A force called the Black Clan made up of rebels against Mardonius has come to help you. My name is Xavir Argentum. I am the last man of the Solar Cohort. And you are free.'

A noise rippled across the crowd. People were relaying his message back to the furthest reaches of the plaza.

'You should find shelter,' he continued. 'You are free to go. Return to your homes. Wait in your basements. Block entry. Protect your loved ones.'

There was murmuring as someone began to chant his first name. Others joined in. Soon dozens and then hundreds were saying the same thing over and over again.

'Xavir! Xavir! Xavir!'

And for the first time in a very long time, the last man of the Solar Cohort felt a lump in his throat.

Xavir had returned.

A Task Unfinished

Xavir's men reconvened with Elysia on the balcony and he praised her skills with the bow. He gripped her heartily by the shoulders and declared that she would one day be a hero of the people.

'Now for the next stage,' he said. 'We must tackle the hardest part of our mission.'

The central palace walls were made of a black rock that glimmered with fragments of mica. Immense cressets carried orbs of flame along the front. Numerous spires, each one built for a different Stravir king or queen, layered back up towards the royal residence, which was lost in the cloud. A fine drizzle covered the scene. Along the base of the first wall roamed a dozen Voldirik soldiers, with a few men in the legion colours in their midst. They seemed unworried by, or oblivious to, the war going on outside the city's main walls.

Xavir, Jedral and Tylos clambered down from their position on a higher pathway and ran towards the soldiers. They peeled away sideways from the arched entrance. Many Voldiriks remained as sentries. Xavir glanced back to see Elysia, under the protection of the others, fire the first of her arrows into soldiers; two short explosions later and they lay in a heap. She then turned her attention to the twelve that were charging, weapons raised, towards Xavir. Two at the back fell instantly to her shots. The remaining ten were hewn down like blades of grass in the face of Xavir's onslaught.

Xavir kept only one legionary alive, which was his aim, and dragged him screaming bloodily up against the black wall.

'Name and rank,' Xavir demanded.

'Galwyx. Sergeant.' The man squirmed.

'You know who I am?' Xavir demanded.

'I see . . . the badge of . . . the Solar Cohort.'

'Good.' Xavir snarled. 'What defences are there inside.'

'Three dozen men in the next level. Most are out by the main walls.'

'What else is inside?'

'I don't know . . . sir.'

'What do you mean, you don't know?'

'Haven't been inside for months. No one knows. Just take orders.'

'What have your orders been exactly? To slaughter the people of this city?'

The man gave no answer to that.

'Tell me!' Xavir roared, and raked his blade across the man's thigh.

He gave an awful scream. Blood came from his bruised mouth. 'Don't know! I just took orders. Did as was told.'

'Do the Voldiriks, these aliens – do they run the operation here?'

'No. Orders . . . from the king.'

'Where's Mardonius?' Xavir demanded.

'Top of his palace.'

'Who guards him.'

'Close guards. Red Butcher. We – they – all fear him.'

The man looked desperate.

'Red Butcher indeed,' Xavir sneered, 'I'll give them all something else to fear.' Then he cut the soldier's throat and shoved him to the ground in a gargling heap.

Looking up from the body, Xavir spotted a mass of bronze-clad warriors heading in their direction. Among them were more of the horn-helmed elite soldiers of the legions.

'We've no more time for them,' Xavir declared to his men, and together they progressed inside the palace complex.

Corridor by corridor, marbled room after marbled room, they pushed forwards and kept vigilant and maintained the pattern: Xavir would press himself up against a door and peer inside the next room, before gesturing his cadre inside. They sealed heavy oak doors behind them and blocked them with the palace furniture. They ascended stairwells onto the next floor. Arched windows overlooked courtyards with more of the strange Voldirik figures in them, wearing brightly coloured clothing and working with more of those enormous tanks.

It was as if they had long since made the palace their headquarters.

In the very next room was a hooded wayseer. Its expression was one of utter calm at being presented with Xavir's group. The thing jutted out an upturned palm; paintings were wrenched free from walls and floors and hurled towards them; statues and busts spun in an unlikely manner, caught up in some invisible vortex. Xavir rolled to his left and ordered the group to spread. Elysia attempted to fire arrows at the wayseer, but it brushed them aside with a finger stroke.

Then a statue struck Davlor as he dived towards the corner, smashing his skull against the wall. The man cried out for just a second, looking surprised, and then fell lifelessly to the ground as pieces of statue broke over his still form.

Tylos and Xavir both charged, ducking the objects that

spiralled around, using their swords to cleave a path. Elysia lay flat on the ground and fired an arrow that somehow got through the wayseer's defences, sending the figure to the floor clutching its foot. Immediately Tylos sent his burning blade through the thing's arm. The wayseer hissed horribly, but began to heal in an instant. Xavir swiped his blades through its neck and across one leg, making sure there was no flesh that could rebind. The body still moved, though, and Tylos raised his blade and thrust it down into its chest. Fires rippled across its body until the thing was nothing but a charred mess. Eventually it became still.

'We can ill afford to come up against a few of these,' Tylos said breathlessly, 'if we are to get to Mardonius.'

'It's dead, that's all that matters.' Xavir turned to the others to see them tending to Davlor.

Jedral, who had argued with Davlor on countless occasions, had attempted to see to his head wounds, but even he quickly realized it was pointless.

'He's gone,' Xavir said sadly, a hand on his shoulder. 'He died on a hero's quest, and that is how we shall speak of him. Now, we *must* continue.'

Jedral nodded and rose from the ground.

As they were about to step into the next room Xavir realized there was something peculiar about the walls. Pressing through the paintwork and tapestries were elongated faces. They looked at first like decorative features high up, but they were in fact all around the room.

'Those heads – they're moving,' Tylos announced.

The mouths of the apparitions were opening and closing as if chanting something.

'Who knows what unspeakable things we'll find here,' Tylos repeated, wiping his face clean of sweat.

Xavir elected not to tell the others that he recognized the faces as former members of Cedius's court.

Each successive room was now enveloped in darkness and echoed with thousands of whispers. Strange channels of wind were blowing back and forth along corridors, as if the adjoining rooms were exposed to the elements, yet many of the doors were sealed.

They turned a corner and halted.

A mob of horn-helmed soldiers in the colours of the legions were standing at the far end of the corridor.

The legion soldiers marched in slow unison, twenty in all, towards the infiltrators.

'Fire, Elysia!' Xavir commanded.

Elysia immediately commenced releasing arrows. The shafts steered through the channels of winds, appearing to struggle to stay on one course, but she managed to will them home. After the first three shots she became accustomed to this mid-air struggle, and began to direct the arrows towards weaknesses in their armour. Two of the soldiers fell, clutching underneath their helms. She released more arrows now, these ones charged with the potency of witchstones. Explosions of fire eliminated four more, but even more filed in behind them, filling the corridor ten abreast.

'Keep going,' Xavir shouted. 'Try not to hit any of us. Watch your back as well.'

Elysia nodded whilst she nocked another arrow.

'Jedral, Tylos — follow me. Grend, protect Elysia.'

Xavir waved one blade and led the charge towards the onrushing traitors.

He slammed into the first two, his Keening Blades whirling

their constant wail of death. Heads clattered against the wall and Xavir kicked back their falling corpses into the following rows, sending them reeling. Two more men died.

Jedral and Tylos hurled themselves alongside Xavir. A trail of flame left Tylos's blade as he carved his way into flesh and metal. Men screamed as they fell, but there remained a sea of helms ahead of them. As Xavir hacked down the lines, the scene became a bloody, slippery mess of flesh and shattered armour. Arrows were sailing past the cohort into the masses ahead of them, exploding in the attacking forces and causing havoc within the confined space, but as Xavir inched forwards he had to navigate an ever-growing pile of corpses.

Body by body, Xavir beat down the remaining defences. He grew breathless, and in this tired state his weakness allowed a few strikes to get past his defences. His forearm received a deep cut and his shoulder was struck by something hard. He was drenched in blood, most of it not his own.

Behind him Jedral continued to swing his axe with glee, as if these soldiers provided an outlet for his fury, whereas Tylos nimbly dived this way and that, drawing his glowing blade up only when an opportunity arose.

The three of them inched forwards until there were just a few of the legionaries left standing. Elysia's arrows shattered their armour into tiny, inward-turning splinters, brought them to their knees easily enough for Xavir to rid them of their lives. But he turned to see, to his annoyance, that Voldiriks had entered from the opposite end of the corridor, the direction from which he had come.

Those things just keep on coming.

His former brethren of Hell's Keep had rushed back to deal with them, but by the look of it they had already suffered a loss. Grend was dead, his body shattered against the doorway.

Elysia fired rapidly, an arrow per heartbeat slamming into the enemy. She felled them until they fell over each other as they hurried into the room. Running short of arrows, she dropped a green witchstone from her pocket to her feet and fired its partner arrow: immediately it shot forwards, scattering green light across the fallen bodies. Arrows that had killed targets immediately freed themselves and flew back across the room to clatter by her feet again.

Tylos arrived at the end of the corridor and sent an arc of flame into any more scrambling Voldiriks, smouldering arms and swords ricocheting into the wall to his left.

'Stand back!' Elysia shouted, as Xavir arrived at her side.

Tylos leaped aside, and watched a blue-tipped blur slam into the three Voldiriks that were attempting to push their way through the mass.

In an instant they stiffened like statues, covered in a blue frost. Elysia had to pull Tylos back the final few feet as everything connected with the fleshy quagmire became covered in the same substance.

'It's ice,' Elysia said. 'They'll need a wayseer to get through.'

'Which they will probably have.' Xavir heaved in breaths of the rancid corridor air.

For a moment Tylos knelt on a safe spot alongside Grend's body. 'He was a fine and gifted companion. As the Chambreks are with poetry, so was this man with cuisine.'

'We'll have to mourn later.' Xavir peered back towards the far end of the corridor and gestured with an outstretched blade. 'We must head that way now. The worst of the fighting may be over.'

Very faintly he believed he could see something. A figure in red armour stood in the room beyond.

The Red Butcher, Xavir thought. *The so-called king's protector.*

Without a moment's hesitation he turned and walked towards the figure. Jedral, Tylos and his daughter followed behind.

Melee

One thought kept replaying in Landril's mind: what, in the name of the Goddess, was he doing here?

Thousands of soldiers ebbed and flowed on the bloody tide before him. Metal clamoured into metal and the shouts and screams rose to his ears. There was a stench of blood and mud that rose softly from the melee. How had it come to this? Had this been his plan all along? He was no leader of men. A tactician, perhaps, but he felt out of his depth here. A good thing Valderon knew what he was doing down below. But things were happening that were well beyond his control. When he issued a command for the infantry to maintain its position, some bastard wayseer would move the ground and spread his formations out into a pitiful line. Every man who fell to his death began to weigh heavily on his conscience.

Landril had attempted to initiate shock attacks, where he directed cohorts in short bursts of vicious combat, but the Voldiriks seemed immune to his efforts. The plan that was proving most successful was for the infantry to progress in smaller, circular formations, a protective ring around a cluster of archers. Arrows sailed overhead, thumping into advancing Voldiriks, whilst the infantry stabbed and ground down the enemy with sword and spear.

Consequently, Landril declared that this should be the tactic for the rest of the forces, and where possible men rearranged their positions according to this theory. He found himself continually processing the odds and likelihood of which tactic would work well and when. From the top of the slope, on horseback, he scrutinized the scene for the slightest alteration. He scanned for the standard bearers, the flow of arrows and the direction of the wind . . .

The Dacianarans continued to be the bane of the defensive forces. Having honed their skills against Voldirik forces on the hills of their homeland, they now raced to the left flank of the battle, drawing ever more of the foe to their inevitable fate. At one point they had come to within a few hundred yards of Landril's position, delivering a charge of the Voldirik right into Valderon's cavalry.

And somehow, through all of this, the Voldirik numbers had been halved. This was reason enough for optimism.

The only enduring issue was the two wayseers that were out there, their positions moving with the ebb and flow of battle, and whose magic was causing great difficulties for his forces.

Landril's latest tactic was to manoeuvre the witches in a more unpredictable fashion, and so he bid them walk on foot to join the archers who were ringed by infantry. The witches would then use their abilities to aid the infantry on their progression towards the towering walls of Stravir City. Soldiers buckled under their witchstone trickery: armour crumpled in on the flesh it contained as the women weeded out the more able bronze-clad warriors.

Valderon's men ripped free from the battle itself and returned to Landril's side, the numbers of the cavalry reduced to a little over a dozen now.

'Are you enjoying this, spymaster?' Valderon brought his horse to a halt.

'I can control very little,' Landril shouted back, 'so *no*, in answer to your question.'

'I have never theorized from a distance.' Valderon's expression was surprisingly happy, despite the fact that he was covered in blood and mud. 'I prefer to be in there, where the honest work is done.'

'There is no honest work here. It is a miserable business.'

Valderon gave no reply but gazed across the scene around him. Any remaining tendrils of daylight were starting to retreat. Night would come soon enough, and then what?

'Is it worth fighting through the darkness?' Valderon asked.

'Their infantry is as fragile as predicted. We might grind them down if we continue.'

'A hazardous business, night fighting.'

'I have plans, should we need to. How do the witches fare?'

'The sisters are alive and, so far as I can see, still seeking the wayseers, as you had instructed. I believe they feel they have their own axe to grind with these foreign magic users.'

'We are holding our own,' Landril said, 'but unless Xavir manages his part we may still be lost.'

'No news?'

'No news,' Landril replied. 'Until we get a signal from that young witch of his, then we must continue.'

'So be it,' Valderon said, nudging his horse into a circle around Landril. 'Where are we to be deployed next? You have a much better view of things than I do.'

Landril scanned the scene once again, noting how the attack on the right flank had weakened greatly. The archers and witches were drifting into the centre of the battlefield. The riders who were resupplying arrows to them from the far right were now vulnerable. Should they be cut off, the archers would lose their power, and his small, vicious islands would be rendered useless.

'Head to the right,' Landril pointed. 'It's vital we protect the road we have marked as our supply route if we are to remain much longer.'

Valderon turned in an instant, called for his fellow riders and descended downhill with a bloody cry.

Xavir stepped into the vast chamber, his two men at his heels and his daughter by his side. Every window here had long since been shattered. Wind gusted through the openings, forcing the tapestries to slam repeatedly against the stone walls. Outside, clouds scudded through darkening skies.

This was one of the great octagonal spires of King Cedius – though it was no longer great.

'I know you,' came a hissing voice.

A figure materialized in the centre of the chamber, its armour glowing like embers. Xavir waved for the others to take a few paces back.

There were no eyes within its pale head, merely black orbs, but the shape of the face was familiar enough to Xavir. That long, noble nose and the strong jawline. All that had changed was that his skin possessed an unearthly sheen. The uniform was also familiar. On the breastplate was the crenellated tower and the rising sun above it. Behind the shoulders of the figure were the hilts of two swords.

'Dimarius,' Xavir whispered. And laughed.

'What do you find so funny?' The glow of Dimarius's armour pulsated slowly, as if it was attuned to his mood or heartbeat. The figure paced back and forth in the centre of the room.

'Your presence fills in the void in my knowledge,' Xavir said. 'Baradium Falls – you were in on the plot. This explains much. You worked with Mardonius to see we were finished. You have helped Mardonius claim the throne and this – whatever this is – is your reward.'

'The throne does not *belong* to Mardonius,' the burning figure sneered.

'Explain,' Xavir snapped.

'The throne belongs to another king from another shore. A *god*,' Dimarius hissed, the final word echoing around them. Something in the chamber above – the throne room if Xavir recalled correctly – groaned like some primordial beast.

'And you,' Xavir continued, 'you have done the bidding of this other race? You have killed your own people. Mutated them for Goddess only knows the reason.'

'It is for the people's own good,' Dimarius answered. His eyes glowed like embers, before returning to black. Smoke came from his mouth. 'Greater things in life await them.'

'You have no idea what you're talking about, Dimarius. It was ever the way.'

Agitated, the figure burned vibrantly at the suggestion.

'In the years to come you will go down as a pointless traitor, as someone who should never have been in the Solar Cohort to begin with, and as someone whose skills were not up to scratch.' Xavir goaded him. 'Perhaps it is one reason why Cedius never gave you command. Is that why you felt the need to betray us?'

'There was no guilt in betraying *you*, Xavir. The butcher of Baradium Falls. You were of the old ways. Too unwilling to embrace better things. Forever looking at the past. When one can see greater things in this world, you are but a transient thing. An obstacle, but nothing more. A king's *pet*.'

'This is nothing more than envy of me, then?'

'Not everything is about you, Xavir,' Dimarius said. 'That was always your problem. The world does not revolve around you, but you failed to see it. And Cedius did not help matters. Think on – this world will be so much better without you.'

Dimarius withdrew the two blades from over his shoulders, and Xavir raised the Keening Blades in return.

'I am ready when you are, traitor,' Xavir said.

Elysia raised her bow, but Xavir shook his head. 'Keep to the back of the room, all of you. This is my business.'

His warning was for their own good. None of them would last a heartbeat against this new foe. The next few moments would tell what these strange changes had done to Dimarius's skills.

Xavir strode forwards to meet Dimarius, watching his every move. Each circled to their left. Dimarius had been an aggressive fighter, too keen with his moves at times when they had sparred in the training quarters, and Xavir waited for him to make the first move. The first mistake.

'You look tired,' Dimarius hissed.

'I have had to fix what Mardonius has broken,' Xavir replied. 'But give it a few more hours and I will rest well enough. It is nice of you to care for me still.'

'You must feel anger at what I did,' Dimarius hissed at Xavir.

'Is the first of the sparring to be done with words?'

It was hard to read a reaction on Dimarius's face. He had always been of cool temperament, but the strange sheen upon his skin seemed to fix his face in place. It was difficult to discern precisely what those black orbs were perceiving.

'Anyway, I do not,' Xavir lied, 'feel anger. It is clear that if I am to be angry, it is to be with whatever did this to you, to Mardonius, and whatever you claim sits on the throne. And I pity you for taking leave of your senses. I can see now that there is a greater power at work. You have made a pact with it, certainly, and looking at you I doubt you're satisfied with the outcome.'

'You continue to be an arrogant fool,' Dimarius snapped.

Xavir shrugged. 'I do not dispute my arrogance, but I am no fool, Dimarius. My incarceration left me with a simple mission – to issue justice to those who put me in gaol and killed my brothers. But there is much in the world that is wrong and someone needs to step in and fix what traitors like you and Mardonius have broken.'

'And you think you can be the great saviour?' Dimarius gave a cruel, deep laugh.

'No,' Xavir replied, and Dimarius paused. 'I have seen the ebb and flow of power all my life, and I may not be the man to direct it. If I die, so be it. But before I do, I want to take that damn crown off Mardonius's traitorous head.'

Then one of the Keening Blades sang out as Xavir's right arm whipped through the air. An ordinary man would have been killed in that instant, but Dimarius was no ordinary man. A burning sword met the strike, and a spark shot off into the corner of the room as from a hammer on a smith's anvil.

Dimarius's other sword moved towards Xavir's legs, but Xavir had already seen the gesture and leaped several feet up and to the left; his other weapon did not defend the strike, but rather attempted to cleave into Dimarius's upper arm. The Red Butcher rolled back his torso, stepped apart and the two warriors found themselves facing each other neutrally.

'What exactly,' Xavir asked, laughing, 'did you get out of

your pact with the Voldiriks? You're just as predictable as you always were.'

Dimarius walked towards Xavir and unleashed a series of sword strikes; the heat from each one was like a furnace door being opened in front of Xavir's face. The man's armour burned brightly, as if Xavir was fanning the flames of anger within him. Xavir parried each blow, sidestepping vicious lurches and knocking back any attempts that came close to his body. Dimarius grunted in frustration; there had never been any elegance to his technique.

Xavir turned on his heel and worked through many of the classic series Dimarius had always struggled with – the eagle, the titan, the dancing wolf – each one provoking a slight stumble or potential gap in defences. With his unique armour, Dimarius was light on his feet, certainly, but he was restricted in his movements.

On recognition of the fact, Xavir began to stretch Dimarius, forcing his blades out wide and then making blows towards his body. The Keening Blades sang wildly as Xavir offered no respite. Wide and narrow, high and low, Dimarius was pulled far in his defence and showing signs of struggle.

Xavir saw his moment: he drove one of the Keening Blades through Dimarius's elbow.

But a spurt of flame fired out and burned Xavir's left wrist. Both men dropped their blades.

Dimarius arm was severed now and he staggered to one side of the room. Xavir nursed his hand for a moment, before blocking the pain from his mind.

Angrier than ever, he picked up his fallen blade and kicked Dimarius in the back.

'Pathetic,' Xavir spat. Dimarius turned with one blade but now that he was injured it was nothing for Xavir to sweep it away. The burning weapon fell to the floor feet away from the other.

Dimarius once again regarded Xavir. 'We are one.'

Xavir slammed a sword through Dimarius's neck. This time Xavir rolled to his right to avoid the fire and heat that erupted from Dimarius's body. The corpse collapsed and shuddered into a smouldering, charred heap, leaving nothing but a trail of ash in its wake.

Whatever had been inside the former warrior of the Solar Cohort had not been blood, Xavir realized. Something else had been holding him together.

Xavir knelt down on the floor and gripped his swollen, burning wrist.

Elysia ran to her father's side. 'Your hand . . . What's happening to it?'

It had begun to blacken where it had been burned, but embers began to form there strangely, and grew like a living thing.

'Never mind,' Xavir muttered. The pain began to throb through his entire arm. His shoulder was in agony. 'We must get to Mardonius quickly. He'll be through that door there.' Xavir gestured with his chin.

Xavir led Elysia, Jedral and Tylos through the doorway and up the stone stairwell. There seemed to be some strange substance oozing down the surface of the steps. A foul wind gusted down the passageway from above. Xavir, barely able to hold both blades firmly now, ignored as best as he could the mouths that appeared in the stonework, human faces that moaned and groaned silently, their impossible pleas never to be heard.

'What is this devilry?' Tylos asked.

Xavir just focused on putting one foot in front of the other

– he had one person left to kill, and nothing was going to get in his way.

The royal chamber was before them, a strange and warped room that looked very little like the place he had once known. It was the room in which he had been issued the Keening Blades, in which he and King Cedius had planned and laughed and drunk the finest wines in the kingdom. All of that was a world away. Xavir's body throbbed with pain, a harsh reminder of his realities. He began to see things from the corner of his vision, strange daemonic forms that ought not to have been there. He willed away the pain and saw the room in all its simple clarity.

A strange figure was sitting, slouched upon a plain metal throne, at the far end of the room. The throne, as it had always been, was on the raised platform. From a distance the figure appeared blackened, and there were strange forms as if charred snakes writhed from its crowned head. But they were no snakes. They were wires that looped across to a glass tank that stood to the side of the throne. To the left was the open vista that regarded the city. Instead of a perfectly rectangular viewing window there was a ragged edge of crumbling stonework. Outside, the city's spires were mired in a dense fog.

Feeling time slipping away with every pulse of his burned hand, Xavir cautioned the others to remain at the back of the chamber while he stepped towards the figure.

'Dimarius is dead. There are no more defences. It is time to die, Mardonius.'

'*Xavir Argentum, Xavir Argentum, Xavir Argentum,*' came a voice. Xavir glanced back to the others, who seemed not to have heard a thing.

'The thing is speaking to me.' Xavir tilted his head in the

direction of Mardonius. 'You can't hear it. But it has spoken my name.'

'*So wise, so foolish . . .*'

'Mardonius . . . you're a mess,' Xavir declared.

The thing laughed. '*Mardonius . . . Yes, I remember him.*' Two eyes opened and the figure's head lifted up as if a puppeteer had pulled a string somewhere. Fluids pulsated back and forth towards the glass tank, which contained a murky solution. There was Voldirik inscription along the metal framework that held it all in place.

'Whatever you are,' Xavir sneered, 'you and I have unfinished business.' He felt his left arm burn violently. His hand was beginning to glow red and, realizing he was possessed by whatever it was he had contracted from Dimarius, he knew he had to act quickly. Nonchalantly, he severed one of the wires with a flick of a blade and liquids gushed out across the platform. Mardonius hissed and laughed inside Xavir's head. The platform bubbled violently where the liquid had been spilled. Xavir could smell the stench of strange magics.

'Elysia,' Xavir called out, kneeling down in pain.

'What is it?' she said, rushing to his side and placing a hand to his shoulder.

'I am finished,' Xavir replied, noticing the coolness of her palm on his burning skin. 'Presently I will turn into whatever Dimarius had become. A daemon, or some Voldirik trickery. You must prevent that. On my word, you must kill me. Use an arrow. The most potent arrow that you have. It will be essential that nothing remains of me.'

'What?' She looked astounded at the thought. 'I can't do that. I refuse to—'

Xavir gripped her hand, 'I understand and I'm sorry we did not have more time together.' He paused as mockery came from

Mardonius into his head. He shook himself alert again. His body was in agony. 'But you must do it. I am going to die and I would rather it was while I am still myself rather than whatever this magic will turn me into.'

'You're my father. I can't kill you. I can't.'

Her reaction unearthed in Xavir sensations he never knew he could experience. He barely even recognized them. But this was not the time. There was *no* time. ·

'You will be saving me from something worse than death,' Xavir said with urgency. 'If you have any feelings for me you'll do as I ask. Will you follow my instruction?'

Elysia said nothing, her eyes moist.

'Promise me!' Xavir snapped.

She swallowed hard and nodded.

'You *are* the Argentum family now,' he said, shrugging himself free of his shoulder straps and allowing the scabbards of the Keening Blades to clatter to the floor. 'Whatever I had is rightfully yours, I suppose. Take the blades and keep them in good condition.' He heaved in a breath as a burning pain rippled through his abdomen. 'They'll . . . be proof . . . of the blood bond.'

With his chest half turned towards the others, half facing the ruined king, he gave them a nod, which they returned. Nothing else needed to be said.

'Get back as far as you can. Keep the others away.'

As Elysia took away his weapons and joined the others, Xavir staggered to his feet and used his bare hands to rip away the wires holding Mardonius together. There was nothing for Xavir to feel now: there was no man here, no king, no satisfaction to be found in his defeat.

Simply emptiness.

That was the great sadness which he felt, as each and every

disconnected wire shot out noxious and burning fluids into the room. The realization that there would be no great victory and no triumph of battle, and there would be unfinished business that he would no longer be able to deal with – it was a family matter now. He had passed on the mantle. He lived on through Elysia. And that final thought – that he endured, in blood – gave him just the slightest hope that it had not all been a complete waste.

'Get ready, Elysia!' Xavir's voice echoed in the chamber. Winds gathered momentum, and abstract nonsensical sounds filled his ears. The air was charged with the promise of violence, but he kept on pulling the wires, watching the fluid spill and the figure of Mardonius twitch savagely with every passing moment.

'What the hell *are* you?' Xavir gasped at the thing that had been the king of Stravimon. 'What *are* you?'

A sibilant voice issued from the dead king. '*I am something that you cannot fathom, Xavir Argentum.*'

Mardonius's mouth moved out of sync with the sound.

'*I am the ruler of your nation, and I rule from afar. I will come to these shores once it is mine for the taking. This body gave itself to me. Its soul lives on in me. It wanted power and it got more than it could ever want.*'

'And what *do* you want?' Xavir asked, his legs weak as if under some draining enchantment. 'What is the reason for it all?'

'*Time,*' it replied. '*Eternity.*' It began to laugh and laugh.

'What became of you, Mardonius?' Xavir demanded, stopping to draw in a laboured breath.

'*Mardonius is no more . . .*'

Xavir inched forwards towards the crumbling steps of the platform, feeling his left arm shivering with the ill effects. Then it became utterly numb.

'What you see before you is empty . . . Mardonius was never the king
never king
the never king . . .'

The charred form of Mardonius rocked back and forth. The skull was showing through the blackened skin in places, the desiccated lips drawn back to reveal rows of rotting teeth in a grimace. Every time it moved, a trail of ash was left. The shell was possessed by some form of Voldirik magic. How long had that been the case? How long had Mardonius been alive to enjoy his partnership before the thing possessing him consumed him?

How has all the glory of Stravir, how has the glory of the past, come to this?

Xavir grasped Mardonius's ruined head in both hands. Using all his remaining strength, with a flick of his burning arms that glowed with every moment, Xavir wrenched it clean off. What seeped from its neck began to bubble and burn, its flesh merging with Xavir's own form. Xavir began to laugh wildly, a laugh that wasn't his own. He could see his whole body becoming red and burning with rage.

Xavir managed to find clarity enough to turn and meet his anguished daughter's gaze. He nodded, her name on his lips as a blinding white light filled his vision, and the pain vanished.

Valderon, now on foot, waded into the remnants of the Voldirik front lines, a blur of energy – even now. The skies were darkening and the plains before the city were a quagmire.

Landril found himself, sword in hand, doing what he hated doing the most, and almost certain of the fact that he would die here.

'Defend yourself, man!' Valderon bellowed. 'Tactics are pointless now. The fighting's almost done.'

'Easy . . . for you to say,' Landril replied, dodging a Voldirik spear to his ribs. Valderon slaughtered the offending wielder by cleaving off its arm and then sending it spinning bloodily backwards into a thicket of attackers.

'By the Goddess, I wish it would end now. It'll be pitch black before long.'

'Battles end when they end,' Valderon said, clearing the path before them. 'Even when those . . . half dead on the ground . . .' he sliced through a Voldirik throat, '. . . don't realize the outcome and carry on regardless.'

'Well . . . finally.' Landril looked relieved and a little surprised as a blinding light shot up from heart of the capital, like a star ascending. Elysia's signal.

'Would you look at that?' Valderon gasped.

Across the plains before the city, the Voldiriks began to collapse as if a silent wind swept across the battlefield. Scattered lines of bronze warriors tumbled into the mud. The sudden absence of the sound of fighting was startling. The remnants of the Black Clan were as dumbfounded as any remaining from the opposing legionary forces, who looked in horror at their fallen Voldirik comrades. Most threw their swords down in surrender.

In the distance, the Dacianarans howled.

Into Reality

Night smothered Stravir City, but there was no bustling throng in the streets. Of the tales her father had told her, of bawdy drinking sessions and festivities among the cobbled lanes, there was nothing. Of people starting fires and dancing from balconies, or the smell of roasted meats from around the continent being cooked and enjoyed by all, there was nothing to be sensed.

The streets remained largely empty in the inner quarters. Only down among the crude taverns and rundown buildings was there any activity – and that was where the remnants of the Black Clan were to be found, too morose and tired to celebrate. The Dacianarans refused to enter the city, which they felt was haunted by the evil that had occurred there, and decided to set up camp just to the south.

How do we move on from this? she wondered.

Landril was the one who found her shortly after the battle, after the immense wooden gates to Stravir City were heaved open by both force and magic. The spymaster had ridden inside, raced with Valderon and Birgitta across cobblestone roads and up towards the towering, dark stone palace, only to find Elysia, Tylos and Jedral sitting on various steps up the palace's enormous front stairway.

The Keening Blades lay on the stone next to Elysia, her hand resting on them. He gave her rations and asked, perhaps already knowing the answer, having seen the swords, about her father's whereabouts.

'I killed him.'

Landril was agog.

'It is not exactly true,' Tylos said, and explained what had happened with the Red Butcher and the man who once was Mardonius.

'You poor girl,' Landril said, offering a sympathetic hand.

She shrugged it off. 'I killed him. It was his order. It was his will. That was that.'

Landril narrowed his gaze, but it softened. 'You've taken it rather well, I must say.'

'What do you expect me to do?'

Landril knew better than to press her.

But what exactly did she feel? For a figure she had not really known for most of her life, but who had somehow shaped it, and who had helped her realize her potential and celebrate her differences from the sisterhood and fill the strange void inside. A void that she did not even know she had possessed a year ago.

Birgitta stared at her from her horse, maintaining a distance, waiting for Elysia to approach.

'Are you well, little sister?' Birgitta asked softly.

'I will be,' Elysia sighed. Her stance softened as Birgitta dismounted and came over to embrace her.

'What did you make of this?' Birgitta whispered her ear, stepping apart.

'Of what?'

'The war,' she replied. 'The fighting. The deaths.'

'It's fine.' She stood apart. 'I felt I could have done much better.'

'Better?' Birgitta repeated, shaking her head. 'This is not how I saw you, little sister. Our warrior sisterhood is a thing of the past.'

'It needs to return —' Elysia straightened her back — 'if you ask me.'

Birgitta raised an eyebrow. 'What do you mean by that?'

'This is not a time for softness, not any more. There are sisters out there who committed many sins within this city. We saw how they had been involved with great atrocities. They're the ones responsible for helping the Voldiriks turn so many of the people here into . . . whatever they ended up being. The Dark Sisters must be hunted down.'

'And you base this on what?'

Elysia glanced to one side, her hair fluttering in the gentle breeze. She spoke of the horrors that they had seen, and of the presence of the Dark Sisters.

Birgitta demanded to see for herself. Elysia led Birgitta and Landril to the great vat-like containers that had likely been responsible for generating so much of the evil in Stravir City, just beyond the vast plaza. When the air was still and they hunted the ghost trails of these Dark Sisters, there was no one to be found. No bodies either, save those clad in bronze that had mostly been slain by Xavir. Nothing remained now — not even under the light of Birgitta's witchstone, which she shone in all corners, behind casks and stone pillars, in an attempt to flush out any who might have been hiding. Yet she could sense something old in the air, the tang of magic that had faded away.

Throughout the evening Landril ordered the finest of the Black Clan's fighters to scour the streets and buildings. By dawn they had found nothing except the evidence of wholesale suicides or slaughter in the street.

Of the Dark Sisters, nothing was to be found.

The final thing for Landril to do before he could be satisfied and let Elysia get some rest was to investigate the scenes at the top of the royal palace. She was now numb to the reality of her deeds up there, of the many Voldiriks she had killed and of the way her father left this world.

Landril was slack-jawed in awe as he inspected the debris, the frozen corpses, the bloodstains, the heap of bronze-clad bodies, and finally the ashy remains of the Red Butcher. Then Elysia led him into the throne room. Wind howled through the crumbled wall to the left. The marbled floor had black streaks across it, as if a fire had washed through the room.

In the centre was the charred, broken and headless skeleton of Mardonius slumped upon its throne.

Landril approached the figure.

And as he did so Elysia could hear the intense, deep sound of a beating heart.

'Does anyone else hear that?' she asked.

'Something still lives here,' Landril cautioned, scanning around the room, 'though not through Mardonius. Xavir killed him, you say, right here?'

Elysia shrugged, then nodded, feeling a raw ache at the mention of his name.

The heartbeat intensified and Landril began to step backwards from the skeleton king.

'We should destroy this place,' he declared, 'as swiftly as possible. Bring the other witches.'

Back outside, after the witches had joined forces to purge the place, Birgitta asked the question softly to Elysia: 'What arrow did you use, little sister? At the very end.'

'I used the celestial stone,' she said. 'It's why nothing of him remains.'

'You placed him among the stars . . .' Birgitta said, and gave her a strange look.

'You think I did wrong?'

'No,' Birgitta said. Her eyes were welling up. 'I have just realized there is little else I can offer you now. To make a choice like that in such a situation, and to will that uncontrollable stone home . . .' Birgitta paused. 'Perhaps I have been wrong all along. Perhaps we do need sisters with skills like yours. Oh, the world is a strange place now. It is not for simple creatures like myself any longer. I need to sleep, sleep before I make any more decisions.'

As the rays of the new sun cast themselves across the near-vacant city, Elysia and Birgitta sought somewhere to lay their heads.

They were shown a house that had evidently belonged to someone of great wealth. It had been abandoned with an ample supply of firewood, so Birgitta lit a fire while Elysia lay down, clasping her father's swords.

They slept for an entire day.

Elysia did not realize how exhausted she had been until she awoke refreshed, in the next day's afternoon sunlight. The doorway gave them a view of the damp stone of the city glistening, and the air smelled clean from the morning's rain. The higher towers and spires were in shadow to her right, whilst down below to the left, along the cobbles, a couple of soldiers were throwing pieces of stale bread for a flock of gulls.

'What do people do after a war?' she asked, stretching. Her body ached all over, but it was a pleasant sensation: she had done good work, and contributed to something greater than herself, and the aches were reminders of that fact.

Birgitta sighed and placed her hands on her hips. 'I don't know, if I'm honest. This has been no normal war and I do not really feel as if it has been a victory. We have merely stopped whatever it was for a moment. This is the beginning of things. So I do not think it is, strictly speaking, *afterwards*. Not just yet.'

'We should find food and news,' Elysia announced.

'That sounds as good a plan as any, little sister.'

The two passed a pair of soldiers as they exited, and from them they learned that Landril had ordered them to stand guard outside their house. Tylos was sitting in a wooden chair next to them, half asleep, his sword leaning up against the wall.

'And where is the spymaster?' Birgitta demanded.

'Guild of masons, two streets down. To the left, ma'am,' the taller of the two replied. 'It's a temporary headquarters. Commander Valderon is there with him. As is the queen of Dacianara.'

'And you, Tylos?' Birgitta asked, tapping a leg of his chair with the base of her staff. 'What are you doing here?'

He rose from the chair fluidly, stifling a yawn. Elysia noted how the soldiers eyed him warily.

'Excuse my manners,' he said. 'Xavir asked me that if anything were to happen to him then I was to protect Elysia. And that is what I've been doing, since you retired yesterday. That chair and these gentlemen have been my companions.'

'Have you not eaten?'

He tilted his head towards the other soldiers. 'They found a couple of apples in a storeroom.'

'Let's have none of that nonsense,' Birgitta scoffed. 'Notions of chivalry are well intentioned, but she is more than capable of looking after herself.'

'And speaking for myself,' Elysia interrupted. 'Thank you, Tylos. That's a kind gesture. Your loyalty to my father was strong. But don't feel you have to remain longer than you must. The fighting is done for now. You can go where you wish.'

'I have nowhere to go.' Tylos smiled affably and shrugged, palms upwards.

They started walking down the street together. Elysia noticed a sign for a bakery belonging to the guild of bakers, and smiled sadly at the memory of Xavir talking to her about them.

'I am in no hurry,' Tylos added. 'If you need an escort, I am more than happy.'

'What if I am to go on the road? Must you honour my father's words still?'

'He was an honourable man and gave me my life back. If you have plans to travel and will permit my protection?'

'I don't think we can change your mind,' Elysia said. In a way she was glad of the offer – it was, somehow, a connection to her father; so long as Tylos was still around, it might feel as if her father was too.

'Not at all,' Tylos replied. 'Besides, the nights remain long and you will need entertainment on the road. Perhaps some poems from my homeland?'

'By the source!' Birgitta said. 'If you don't shut up about the poets I'll kill you myself.'

Valderon was sitting with his boots up on the long table, on the top floor of the guild house. Landril, Lupara and two wild-looking, face-painted Dacianarans whom Elysia had never met were seated alongside him. Jedral was standing at the back with his arms folded, a shaft of sunlight falling across his now battle-scarred face. The room was a simple, sparse meeting room with wooden floors and open shutters. Clumps of dried herbs had been nailed to the walls some time ago, but the room otherwise smelled musty. There were cups of wine on the table, along with some slabs of cheese and salted ham. In the centre of the table, Landril had placed a small bust of the Goddess, and positioned her to face himself.

They rose when Elysia and Birgitta entered the room, a level of respect that she was not used to. Tylos came in behind them and moved to the corner.

'You've recovered from the events?' Valderon asked, bringing chairs for them to sit at the table alongside him.

'We're as fresh as spring lambs,' Birgitta replied.

'And you, Elysia?' Landril asked.

'Ready to do it again,' she replied.

Landril smiled. 'Your father endures within your spirit, Goddess rest his soul.'

'What news have you got?' Birgitta asked. 'We have slept for too long in such times as these.'

'You earned your sleep, and the city is secure, so far as we can tell,' Landril replied. 'This much, we know: we have captured fifteen Voldiriks who remained hiding in the aftermath. From what I gather about their appearance and in crude communications with them, these are true, original Voldiriks. Many of those who fought on the field of battle were citizens of this very city who had been transitioned in the tanks that we have seen. Our people were spawned. Changed into things they ought never to have been. Those who resisted, or for whom the transition was not a success, were turned into greater beasts. We have spent the better part of a day killing what is ultimately our own people – although they were already dead. Somehow they were connected to the force that lived through Mardonius, and without that – when Xavir severed that connection – there was no life left within them. The Voldiriks still have access to our nation far to the north-west, at Port Phalamys. There is still work to do. We must cut that connection.'

'By the source,' Birgitta said, 'this is a miserable state of affairs. What's your plan now?'

'We must repopulate the city,' Landril said. Wringing his fingers, he glanced to Valderon and Lupara, both of whom waited for him to continue.

Elysia could tell in their glances that Landril would be defining the future for Stravimon, and that he probably would not mind at all.

'Yes, we must bring those who have left back into the city's embrace. We need to create community, though that will take many months. We could destroy whatever they have set up at Port Phalamys as a first step. We must find out what force still lingers in the shadows of the city and the forests of the east and north, for their foul magics are present yet.' Landril turned to Elysia and Birgitta, his eyes darting between the two of them. 'We will need your help in this.'

'To track down ghosts in the city?' Birgitta asked. 'If it needs to be done.'

'I won't do it,' Elysia said.

Everyone stared at her.

'And what is *your* plan?' Landril asked, eyebrow raised.

'The Dark Sisters,' Elysia stated, 'need finding, and killing.'

'This is true,' Landril said after a moment's pause. He began to tap the table with his fingers. 'Something is afoot with the witches. Their role in this is not entirely clear. That they have been involved in the breeding of Voldirik-like warriors is merely a part of what they have been up to, no doubt about that. But do you think you can find them on your own?'

'I won't be on my own,' she replied and indicated the black man in the shadows. 'Tylos will be coming with me.'

'There are other sisters too,' Birgitta added, 'who left Jarratox when we did. They will need finding, for they will be important assets.'

'So be it.' Landril rose from his chair and walked towards the window. He looked down on the empty streets. 'When I ventured to Hell's Keep, I thought all of this nonsense would end with a few lost lives at most, yet it feels to me as if there is even more fighting to be done.'

Valderon stood by and placed a heavy palm on his shoulder. 'Xavir was right, spymaster. None of this – none of the ebb and flow of power and war – ever ends.'

extracts reading groups
competitions books new
discounts extracts
competitions
books
new books
events extracts
new reading groups
interviews
discounts
new books events
events new
discounts extracts discounts
www.panmacmillan.com
extracts events reading groups
competitions books extracts new

BLEACH
Can't Fear Your Own World — **III**

contents

SHUHEI HISAGI

Assistant captain of Ninth Company. Editor-in-chief of the *Seireitei Bulletin*. His interests include guitars and motorcycles from the world of the living.

Kisuke Urahara

The former captain of the Twelfth Company and founding chief of the Department of Research and Development. He provides Ichigo and the others with transcendental engineering ideas.

Shunsui Kyoraku

He succeeded Genryusai Yamamoto as Captain General of the Thirteen Court Guard Companies. He has been friends with Ukitake since they were at Shinoreijutsuin Academy together.

Nanao Ise

Assistant captain of the First Company. She has constantly been at Kyoraku's side as his second-in-command since her days in the Eighth Company.

Mayuri Kurotsuchi

Captain of the Twelfth Company and chief of the Department of Research and Development. A mad scientist whose internal observations and research continue even in the midst of battle.

Kenpachi Zaraki

Eleventh Company captain. His title, Kenpachi, befits him, as he is the strongest Soul Reaper.

Ikkaku Madarame

A tough guy from the Eleventh Company. Pledges to fight and die under Kenpachi. Can actually do bankai.

Yumichika Ayasegawa

Part of the Eleventh Company. A narcissist who loves beautiful things. Hides his zanpaku-to's power.

MAIN CHARACTERS

Tier Halibel

An Arrancar and the third Espada. She took over governing Hueco Mundo after Aizen left.

Nelliel Tu Odelschwanck

An Arrancar. She lost her memories and powers but regained them after meeting Ichigo Kurosaki.

Grimmjow Jaegerjaquez

An Arrancar. He developed an obsession when he was an Espada after losing a fight to Ichigo Kurosaki and wants to settle things.

Sosuke Aizen

Former captain of Fifth Company. He betrayed the Soul Society and engaged in a war against the Thirteen Court Guard Companies. Currently imprisoned in Mugen.

Kaname Tosen

Former captain of Ninth Company. He sided with Aizen to betray the Soul Society because a close friend of his was killed by a Soul Reaper.

Kugo Ginjo

A Fullbringer and the first deputy Soul Reaper. He led the Xcution group and fought against Ichigo and his team but was defeated and died.

Shukuro Tsukishima

A Fullbringer and member of Xcution. He tormented Ichigo with his powers to alter the past.

Giriko Kutsuzawa

A Fullbringer and member of Xcution. He can manipulate time constraints.

Aura Michibane

A mysterious woman who introduces herself as a representative of the religious group Xcution, which shares the name of the Fullbringer group Ginjo created. She attempts to contact Yukio.

Yukio Hans Vorarlberna

A Fullbringer and member of Xcution. He stole an immense fortune from his father and now runs a large corporation.

Shinji Hirako

Captain of the Fifth Company. He has an aloof personality but a quick mind. He led the Visoreds to battle Aizen.

Kensei Muguruma

Captain of Ninth Company. He was Hollowfied during Aizen's treachery. He was reinstated to his position after fighting against Aizen as a Visored.

Yoruichi Shihoin

Formerly the head of the Shihoin family, she was driven out of her position due to Aizen's scheme. Her nickname is the Flash Master.

Dordoni Alessandro Del Socaccio

An Arrancar. A Privaron Espada. He lost to Ichigo but was resurrected as a zombie by Mayuri for the fight against the Vandenreich.

Cirucci Sanderwicci

An Arrancar. A Privaron Espada. She was defeated by Uryu in the battle in Hueco Mundo but, like Dordoni, was resurrected as a zombie.

Luppi Antenor

An Arrancar. The former sixth Espada. Though he died after Grimmjow attacked him, blowing away the upper part of his body, he is brought back to life as a zombie.

Charlotte Chuhlhourne

An Arrancar. Even after being turned into a zombie by Mayuri, she still has absolute confidence in her own beauty.

Liltotto Lamperd

A Quincy. Her beautiful appearance hides a wicked tongue. She survived Auswählen but was defeated in the battle against Yhwach.

Meninas McAllon

A Quincy. She possesses superhuman strength. It was thought she'd been rendered incapable of battle by Liltotto, however...

Giselle Gewelle

A Quincy, also known as Gigi. Anyone covered by Giselle's blood turns into a zombie. Looks like a girl, but...

Candice Catnip

A Quincy. Uses lightning as a weapon. Her whereabouts are uncertain after the Auswählen.

Bambietta Basterbine

A Quincy. A member of the Stern Ritter who was defeated while battling Komamura. Turned into a zombie by Gigi.

NaNaNa Najahkoop

A Quincy. The power of his Schrift immobilized Aizen, though only temporarily.

Tokinada Tsunayashiro

A member of the Four Great Noble Clans. Part of the Tsunayashiro family.

Hikone

A beautiful child who follows Tokinada.

Ichigo Kurosaki

The main character of the original story.

BLEACH
ブリーチ

Can't
Fear
Your
Own
World

III

Tite Kubo
Ryohgo Narita

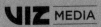

THAT

IS

WHY

PEOPLE

HAVE

A

NAME

FOR

WALKING

THE

PATH

OF

FEAR.

—Sosuke Aizen

INTERLUDE

HIKONE UBUGINU DID NOT REMEMBER the moment that their sense of self germinated.

That didn't quite mean that they had no memories of their time as an infant, in the way that an ordinary Soul Reaper and human would not. The konpaku called Hikone was a warped form created by layering and interleaving the splinters of many different beings. Inside their konpaku were Hollows from millennia ago, freshy dead Quincies, and even miscarriages collected from the world of the living. The konpaku was a compilation of every possible kind of soul with the Fragments of the Reio at its center. Normally, a being such as Hikone would promptly fall apart and lose form. However, because they contained the Fragments of the Reio that the Tsunayashiro family had gathered, Hikone was miraculously able to continue life as a konpaku with a single sense of individuality.

Though Hikone clearly remembered the moment when they had been given the name Hikone and their consciousness had awakened, they were seized by the fantasy that they had a sense of self that reached much further into the past than that.

Or perhaps that was not a fantasy.

After all, the building blocks used to create Hikone were konpaku prior to their decomposition into reishi. It was quite possible that what could be called the dregs of those prior beings influenced Hikone to some extent.

It was the sensation of dozens, hundreds of different selves intermingling within them.

Because they were such an aggregation, there was nothing but chaos that approached nihility.

An accumulation of emotions floated up and disappeared within them.

A certain fragment of soul would forgive slaughter, while another would reject it as absolutely impermissible.

A certain fragment of soul would claim that evil itself was the essence of humanity, while another would extol virtue as the true embodiment of humankind.

Though their individual rationales and memories had vanished, the differences in the *ways of life* etched into those konpaku entangled and, at times, threatened to tear Hikone's soul apart in their rejection of each other.

Because of that, the individual called Hikone found

peace in the instruction that the individual called Tokinada granted them. Tokinada would point out what was definitively "righteous" for the ever lost and perplexed Hikone, which would herd the dregs of konpaku rampaging within the child's head in a single direction.

Hikone's one and only desire, that they themself had come up with, was to become a "good king." For Tokinada's sake—because the Soul Reaper said he would make them king—they would strive to become a leader beloved by the people.

Tokinada had taught Hikone that in order to become king, occasional violence or slaughter was a necessity. And though Hikone had accepted that, a "Hikone-ness" had begun to steadily germinate within them from other pieces of themself.

What it would become would divide Hikone's fate...

However, to Hikone, currently a follower of Tokinada, that was still irrelevant.

And at this moment it still was not.

CHAPTER NINETEEN

"IT'S JUST THAT YOU HAVEN'T SEEN THE STARS YET."

When she learned of Tokinada's true nature, his wife was not shocked or disappointed, but simply replied with the above as though admonishing a small child. The pure love filling her voice did not give him the impression that the words were calculated or had been uttered as flattery toward a high-ranking noble.

And that was something Tokinada could not forgive.

It gave him the sense of someone in a place far higher than himself, looking down upon him as though he were in the position of a supplicant.

His position being in the lowest seat of a branch family, Tokinada Tsunayashiro had taken a woman named Kakyo as his wife at the behest of the head family. Kakyo was a woman the Tsunayashiro family had found by chance, and one who held a secret attainment in the depths of her konpaku.

The Tsunayashiro family's "watchers" had spied her when she arrived to take the entrance exam to become a Soul Reaper.

At the time, the Tsunayashiro family had been searching for those with that attainment. They would deplete such beings through various experiments and then extract fragments of what would become those attainments from the shadows of what the beings once were.

Then the family had begun to ponder.

If one who had the desired attainment bore a child, would that attainment be inherited and fully transferred to the child? Would it weaken, or was it nontransferable, or, possibly, would it multiply in the way that the birth of a child multiplied humanity?

Though they were fixated on their interest in bringing this attainment into the Tsunayashiro family, the woman they noticed was one of the impoverished class of residents of the Rukongai that they scorned. Therefore the Tsunayashiro's leaders decided to use one of the lowest branches of the family for their experiment. Even as part of the same Tsunayashiro clan—or rather, *because* they were the head of the Four Great Noble Clans, which demarcated the world based on social position—there was a clear pecking order within the family.

Tokinada approached the woman, feigning that his bluster had attracted him to her, just as he had been directed to by the main family. Though he was displeased that the main family controlled him to the extent of instructing him to marry her, that displeasure was overtaken by Tokinada's desire to see the face of the powerless woman the moment she fell from the peak of happiness to the pits of hell. What would her face look like in the moment when she could no longer retreat and he thrust the truth before her—when he would say to her, *"I don't love you. You were simply chosen as an experimental subject by the Tsunayashiro family"*?

Fantasizing about that moment, Tokinada was tantalized with sadistic curiosity by the pitiful lamb that was that woman.

Then, using feigned love and his own social position as weapons, he easily captured the woman's heart.

Or so he thought.

The night of the wedding ceremony, Tokinada had laid everything bare.

"If you annul the wedding now, it won't just affect you. Those living in the Rukongai where you come from would likely be blamed and punished. Your best friend Kaname, whom you talk about so often, won't escape unscathed either," he had pressed.

As he turned to look at her, Tokinada's eyes were overflowing with expectation, wondering just what kind of comical expression of despair would show on her face. But his longing was quickly thwarted.

The woman named Kakyo had already seen through it all.

She told him that she had married him despite that. Or perhaps she had guessed that the moment she turned him down, blame would have fallen even upon the friend she had left in her hometown. Yet after all this time, he still could not see into her mind to know which it was— such forms of thought were incomprehensible to Tokinada.

While Tokinada was bewildered and irritated, Kakyo was starting to gain influence as a Soul Reaper. It was rumored she was certain to become a seated officer in the future. Even Tokinada's classmates from his institute years, such as Ukitake and Kyoraku, knew her true abilities at a glance.

At this rate, she would usurp everything.

His very self would erode away.

Though Tokinada felt restless, the main family would not allow him to kill Kakyo or divorce her. To the main family, Kakyo was a valuable experimental subject and Tokinada was nothing more than a tool they had prepared in order to perform their analysis of her.

However, for better or worse for Tokinada, someone discovered the Tsunayashiro's schemes by chance. This person was a Soul Reaper who had risen from the commoners and who, in public, Tokinada associated with as a close friend. This person was also close to Kakyo and might have even harbored feelings for her.

Attempting to save Kakyo from the Tsunayashiro clan,

he had called Tokinada out late one night and questioned the aristocrat's true motives.

Tokinada happily told him the truth, including the fact that he did not love Kakyo in the slightest. He might have been able to follow his family's orders by pretending to love his wife. However, Tokinada's innate character did not allow him to do that.

Ultimately, Tokinada wanted to see it—he wanted to see the man's reaction upon realizing his friend was nothing more than a fiend. As Tokinada had expected, with despair on his face, the man said to Tokinada, "As your friend, I will kill you."

Still smiling, Tokinada had drawn his zanpaku-to.

They matched each other in power, and it wouldn't have been unexpected for either of them to defeat the other. After the clashing blades met countless times, something neither of them had anticipated occurred.

She might have been anxious because Tokinada had left the house in the middle of the night and hadn't returned. Kakyo, who had come in search of her husband, appeared at the scene after hearing the clash of blades.

Coming between their match to the death, Kakyo attempted to stop their swords. In that moment, Tokinada watched for her to turn her back to him and simply *thrust Kakyo's body at his opponent.*

There was no way for the wounded Soul Reaper to

avoid her, and so his friend and wife tangled into each other and staggered.

Then, without hesitation, Tokinada cut through both Kakyo and his enemy Soul Reaper.

Tokinada was thrilled. He was even smiling faintly.

His joy was not a result of having extended his life. He smiled because, though the course of events were unanticipated, he had given his wife, who had devoted herself to a sanctimonious philosophy, despair.

Now—cry, fear, despair. If you are going to burn out the last of your life, then turn the Suzumushi blade you carry against me. You may curse your own naïveté as you strike me with your murderous malice!

Wearing the look of a child stomping on a half-dead bug, he gazed upon Kakyo's face as she passed. However, even on the brink of death, she smiled faintly as she choked out her final words, her expression appearing as though she were admonishing a child.

"I'm sorry... I...wasn't able to clear away the clouds for you..."

Then she simply closed her eyes.

He was in a daze for some time with the two bodies in front of him; then Tokinada's body trembled. He shivered not from regret that he had killed his wife, who had attempted to save him even in her very last moments, but from *unadulterated rage*.

"You...you looked down upon me—pitied me—until your very last moment! You say I have simply not seen the stars? You say that you could not clear my clouds? Don't speak absurdities—don't utter such foolishness, Kakyo! I have been standing on top of the clouds from the very beginning! No, I am the cloud! You were the one who was mistaken! That the stars—that this world—is beautiful...is a gravely mistaken view! Why have you not noticed the unsightliness of the star crud attempting to glisten in the darkness? Your current state is the result of your belief that all would be fine if it was right!"

Tokinada continued to yell as he kicked not the body of his wife, but his already departed best friend. Eventually he steadied his breathing, his shoulders heaving as he did, and the rage disappeared from his face.

"...Too bad, Kakyo. I wanted to more thoroughly show you exactly how absurd the world is. I wanted to teach you that the justice your peace-loving heart treasured was a wish in vain. Had I been able to remake you into evil, at that time I could have truly opened my heart to you... Ah, in that sense, I might have actually loved you."

Another thin smile spread over his face. Had Tokinada's words reached Kakyo's ears?

At this point, now that Kakyo's life was lost, no one could know the answer.

Immediately after that, the Tsunayashiro family members summoned Tokinada to appear before the main family.

Tokinada readily and bluntly replied to his family's interrogation. *"I just could not stand being the husband of a slum dweller from the Rukongai."*

Though the main family branded him as incompetent, they reluctantly accepted his claim. As aristocrats, they were the types who would conclude unquestioningly that it was a disgrace to take one of the poorer classes as a wife.

But Tokinada had lied to his family about one thing.

It was no small lie.

Tokinada did not care whether his partner was from the Rukongai at all. Because, regardless of whether someone was from the Four Great Noble Clans or a commoner—in fact, regardless of whether they were even his own parents—he saw all people equally, as nothing more than playthings for him to toy with.

Although he had been raised in an atmosphere in which it was natural to consider the lower and middle-ranked aristocrats poor and insignificant, it could be said that Tokinada stood out as particularly unscrupulous even within his own family.

"My wife committed adultery with a man who had been my friend, and I caught them in the act. In a rage, the man killed Kakyo, and so I reluctantly struck back."

Having the backing of the Tsunayashiro family, which did not want a criminal among their number, Tokinada shamelessly excused himself in that way. It was very likely that as part of the Four Great Noble Clans, a member of the Tsunayashiro family wouldn't even have to go to trial after making such a claim. However, this time, the circumstances were somewhat different.

A man who had been on the lookout for Tokinada's deceptions appeared, touting a miniscule amount of evidence. Normally, Tokinada would have been able to make such evidence and testimony disappear, but the fact that the man was the second son of a highly influential upper-ranked aristocrat was Tokinada's misfortune.

Shunsui Kyoraku—if only he had not been around, Tokinada Tsunayashiro might have walked a different path.

≡

PALACE FOREFRONT

After arriving beneath the "castle in the air," Kyoraku's first reaction was to once again narrow his eyes at its magnitude.

"You got me. Kyogoku or not, it's preposterous the Four Great Noble Clans could build this thing under everyone's noses."

"I doubt this was built using any hired labor. I wonder if it's floating in the air using the same trick as the Reiokyu."

"The Reiokyu utilizes a hidden technique, if I'm not mistaken..."

Kyoraku shook his head as though he were exasperated in reply to Yoruichi's analysis. Then he turned his eyes to the palace directly under the gigantic castle in the air. Though it was sensible compared to the floating building, when Kyoraku looked at the structure, which was still larger than the Court Guard's First Company barracks, he quietly honed his spiritual pressure. He did so because he felt a familiar spiritual pressure from within that palace.

"So he doesn't even intend to hide? I suppose that means he's already finished preparing to meet our attack."

Kyoraku, still at the forefront, headed to the gate. As he did so, he glanced at Kenpachi and said, "Sorry, Captain Zaraki. I think this will eventually end in a fight, but would you let me do some talking first?"

"Hm? If we're going to fight anyway, jabbering's just a waste of time."

"That is true, but there are protocols to be followed. If we headed right in slashing at him, that act itself would make us traitors. Depending on the situation, we might even end up making an enemy out of the entire Soul Society."

Kenpachi wore a villainous smile as he replied. "Cut the crap. You called me here because you know I couldn't care less about finicky details like that. Having the Soul Society as an enemy? Ain't that great? That's not a problem at all."

"But even so... The reason I had you wear your captain's coat was because that would at least make it reasonable for you to confront the Four Great Noble Clans. Though I wouldn't fuss as much about Yoruichi, since she is also a member of the clans herself."

"I think it'd be an issue for me if you *were* fussing over me, but saying so bluntly that you don't care is odd too," Yoruichi said in a teasing tone and then brought up the name of someone who wasn't present. "It's too bad that kid Byakuya isn't here. If there were a chance we'd be able to legitimately kill Tokinada, I would've liked to let that kid have it."

"Did something happen?"

"Of all things...he insulted Byakuya's wife Hisana to his face. The kid looked calm on the surface, but he may well have been seething in the pit of his stomach."

"I'm grateful for his mettle. Had he drawn his sword then, that itself could have resulted in a civil war."

Imagining the events of that time, Kyoraku let out a small sigh.

Byakuya Kuchiki was presently not in the Seireitei. He had left with Hitsugaya and the others from the Twelfth Company under the guise of an investigation in relation to some trouble Ichigo Kurosaki was having in a certain place within the world of the living.

Though Kyoraku had no intention of calling Ichigo Kurosaki to this place, no matter what route they took, if

that trouble were part of Tokinada's scheme, then their opponent had done an exquisite job of dividing up the Court Guard's firepower.

While Kyoraku was thinking that over, they reached the center of the courtyard.

The man who had appeared high up in the palace, as though he were standing on a balcony, spoke to them directly.

"You're late, Kyoraku."

"...Tokinada."

"Oh, not even a *Lord*? Then should I consider this not a visit from the Captain General of the Thirteen Court Guard Companies but a personal call from an old school friend?"

"I suppose that's right." In response to Tokinada's provocative question, Kyoraku put on a thin, sarcastic smile that didn't reveal his thoughts. "I've come here to stop you—as an old friend."

Before anyone realized it, Kyoraku had already drawn his zanpaku-to. Because he had a second blade that had been created solely to protect the Ise family's Hakkyoken, the Katen Kyokotsu was known as an incredibly rare zan-paku-to making up a set.

While still prepared for a surprise attack, Kyoraku only momentarily glanced at the castle in the air as he inquired, "I suppose I'll at least ask you. What are you intending to do by transporting that thing to the world of the living?"

"Ah, I should have known you'd at least realize that

much. Of course. You've already exposed my lies and subjected me to a trial once."

"I lost that battle the moment you didn't receive an appropriate charge. How regrettable..."

"So you came with that mob in tow to play revolution and exact your revenge? Really, you never change. Just as in the past, you make others think you're deeply prudent, yet you have a penchant for letting your emotions rule. Just as when you turned your back on Central 46 in order to save Rukia Kuchiki, this time you are turning on the Four Great Noble Clans... No, I suppose you're turning on the Soul Society's history itself."

As Tokinada spoke gleefully, Kyoraku shook his head.

"I'm defying history? I give up—how exactly did you come to that conclusion?"

"The Tsunayashiro are the symbol that rules history. The Tsunayashiro family's every move continues to form the foundation of the world. In short, don't you think the moment you defy me as the head of the family, you are committing high treason against history itself?"

"That depends on the history that you're trying to put together. According to Yoruichi, it seems that you're not just trying to govern over the Seireitei, but also the world of the living and Hueco Mundo, aren't you? What is the purpose of doing that now, of all times?"

Tokinada's smile quickly slipped off his face as he replied, "Don't you think the three worlds as they are now... lack respect?"

"Respect?"

"That's right. Just who made it so that those residing in the world of the living could exist through uncountable nights and be showered in the light of daybreak? Whose benevolence enables a ceaseless supply of reishi sand to fall upon Hueco Mundo?" Tokinada feigned vigor by shaking his fist as his oration continued. "This applies to the matter of the earlier war as well. The only ones who know of Ichigo Kurosaki's deeds are the Soul Reapers of the Soul Society. The humans of the world of the living are great only in their number and do not even know that their world was almost in ruin. Do you think it is right to allow such a situation to continue?"

At that point, Nelliel Tu Odelschwanck chimed in. "You can't say that when you don't even know the first thing about Ichigo. He's not the type of person to let such things bother him."

"Oh, Ms. Arrancar, is it fine just because he himself doesn't mind? Are you suggesting it is right for the humans of the world of the living to continue with their carefree lives, letting slip idle complaints when faced with trivial predicaments and living out their depraved days, unaware that they have been blessed with the privilege of being *allowed* to live?"

"You're free to think that. But don't use Ichigo to explain your own selfish reasoning."

Observing this conversation, Liltotto Lamperd asked Grimmjow, who was standing next to her, "Hey, is that Arrancar Ichigo Kurosaki's girl or something?"

"Hunh? No chance in hell. Kurosaki's mate is a human woman who's more happy-go-lucky."

The person that came to Grimmjow's mind was the woman Ichigo had risked his life coming to Hueco Mundo to save.

Disregarding Grimmjow, and recalling the girl who had healed his arm, Liltotto remarked indifferently, "I see, so that prick is a womanizer."

Meanwhile, Tokinada responded to Nelliel with a serious, unsmiling expression. "How rude of me. However, the truth is that I am simply showing my gratitude toward Ichigo Kurosaki. Had he not defeated Yhwach, the boundaries between the three worlds would have disappeared and we would have *returned* to a universe in which there would be no cycling of konpaku, wouldn't we? Such an action would have reduced the Soul Society's history to naught. I would like to make this a universe where he receives commendation befitting his achievement of preventing that occurrence."

Kyoraku, who had been momentarily silent, smiled bitterly as he replied, "Lip service doesn't suit you, Tokinada. Why don't you tell us what you truly want?"

"I am sure I already did, Kyoraku—don't think someone such as the Captain General of the Court Guards can see through me. Do you mean to say you can read my mind?"

"Aye, but not as the Captain General of the Thirteen Court Guard Companies. I see through to your true self as an old friend whose fate is tied to yours whether I like it or not."

Kyoraku readied his two blades as he uttered these words that hit straight at the crux of the matter.

"All you want to do is *see* it, right? You want to see everything that was common sense until now crumble—you want to see the world slowly break."

"…"

"The world of the living is rooted in its own society and religious views. At the current moment they do not even scientifically acknowledge the existence of konpaku." Kyoraku looked at the many-floored building above his head. "You intend to suspend the greatest 'proof' of Soul Reapers, konpaku, and also reveal Hollows over the world of the living to make their existences public. Those who were religious adherents until now would be in chaos, and more troubling, those who did not believe in the existence of that realm will learn of the existence of the world after death."

If the existence of the world after death were proven, even if the world itself remained unbroken, the society and culture that were contained within it would likely be destroyed.

Those who were unhappy in the world of the living might dream of the world after death as a simpler place and more readily kill themselves. Or, more might flock to crime believing that even if they were to receive capital punishment, they would still have the next world anyway. There was even a possibility that countries using religion as the foundation of their social systems would fall into anarchy after being cut off at their very roots.

"Well, in order to prevent that from happening, that castle in the air and Karakura Town might eventually cease to exist. Even if they can't kill Hollows, the world of the living has mountains of frightful weapons to destroy other humans."

In addition, if they were to learn of the existence of hell, it was likely chaos would arise from other vectors.

What were the criteria for ending up in hell? Would that mean that as long as they didn't meet those criteria, they could commit crimes into oblivion within that scope? In that case, how would the significance of the laws of the living change?

Faced with a shared world justice system that forced itself at them from an entirely novel angle, human society could enter a state in which it could not see a tomorrow.

Though that confusion would likely come to an end after a period of time had passed, how much tragedy would result in the world in the meantime?

Or, alternatively, there was a fear that those who had pre-pared themselves beforehand for what came after death might

arrange to meet and create a new religion within the Rukongai that would spread the chaos even within the Soul Society.

After considering those many dangerous variables, Kyoraku purposefully set his sights not on the *result*, but on the *motivation* for it.

"Though they're on thin ice, both the world of the living and Hueco Mundo are in balance right now. When I tried to imagine why you would purposefully set that into chaos and reshape the worlds, I could only think of one answer." At that point, Kyoraku's cynical smile disappeared, and he uttered the outrageous conclusion he had come to with a serious expression. "*It's because you want to see it*. You simply want to laugh and watch as the value systems people believe in collapse and fall into chaos—as they fight and self-destruct you will snack on tea cakes and such. You broke unwritten rules and are trying to push a brand-new value system onto the world of the living simply for that reason. Am I wrong?"

The others who were listening to Kyoraku generally looked bewildered.

They couldn't easily accept his conjecture. Who in the world would believe that a man who had gone to the trouble of committing such dreadful acts would have the ambiguous goal of simply wanting to watch society fall into chaos?

It was likely that only Nanao and Yoruichi, who had had brief encounters with the man's unscrupulousness, had come to the same conclusion as Kyoraku.

Tokinada's eyes quickly narrowed as his face once again broke into a thin smile, and he said, "Oh dear, you really are a difficult man, Kyoraku. It looks like you have a thorough understanding of my propensities... At least, you have a better sense of them than the main family that belittled me."

"Are you saying that you're destroying the ways of the world just to pass the time?"

At Tier Halibel's doubtful words, Tokinada smiled and tilted his head.

"You have the gall to say that, oh, Arrancar queen? You Hollows are beings that are insatiably manipulated by your desires in order to fill the void carved into your konpaku. Some are besmirched by hunger, some are drowning in destruction, some seek companionship to remedy their solitude, some ceaselessly pursue beauty. That is what you are like, is it not?"

Charlotte Chuhlhourne, a member of the Corpse Unit who had been listening, posed and murmured, "Ha ha... you're so naïve. I do pursue beauty, that's for sure...but I've already filled my void. That's because I've already perfected myself! That's right, I exist in beauty...all the way down to my name!"

"..."

Yumichika seemed as though he were about to say something to Chuhlhourne, who was flexing, but he purposefully held his tongue and averted his eyes.

It wasn't clear whether Tokinada had heard Chulhourne's monologue, but his gaze remained averted from the Arrancar as he continued to address Halibel. "Or do you mean to say you have lived a straight and narrow life without having made others into your meals?"

"The world requires sacrifices. However, though I used them for nourishment, I had no reason to turn them into playthings."

"No reason? Do you need anything of the sort? To me, toys and nourishment are equal. A life lived simply eating for survival is nothing better than forever dying, is it not? In that case, if they will die either way, then isn't the *healthy and correct way* to live toying with them as much as possible before killing them?"

As Tokinada declared his intentions without a hint of hesitation, most of those around Kyoraku came to a realization.

It was likely *that thing* had rejected its ties to humanity and was certainly a being with whom they could not see eye to eye.

"*Tsk...* You scum."

Muguruma spat that out while next to him, Kenpachi was searching for their opponents' spiritual pressures as though he couldn't care less about the man's remarks.

Behind him, the assistant captain of the Eleventh Company and the third seat were whispering to each other.

"Hey, Yumichika, you think Captain Kuchiki and Omaeda are actually more like us than the other nobles?"

"That even makes the Shihoin family's impulsiveness look attractive in comparison. Someone who reveals such ugliness just by speaking is not one to scoff at."

As Ikkaku Madarame and Yumichika exchanged these comments, the Quincies and Arrancars were also looking up at Tokinada with expressions of exasperation or disgust.

Giselle Gewelle summed things up in a whisper to Candice Catnip. *"So, that guy's crazy narcissistic, right? Definitely hasn't got any friends."* Grimmjow had also started to hone his murderous impulses at the word *mob*.

"Hm, well, don't you think Luppi's disposition is the most similar to his?"

"You're right. You'd probably be able to get along with him pretty great."

At Dordoni Alessandro Del Socaccio's and Cirucci Sanderwicci's words, Luppi glared at the two with an unimpressed expression.

"Hey, you've got to be joking, right? Don't lump me in with that weirdo. I'm not *opposed* to sadistic stuff, but even I wouldn't indulge in making degeneracy like that into a hobby."

Tokinada looked them over and shrugged, saying, "Oh well, I expected it from Kyoraku, but I can't believe the age has come when Arrancars and Quincies would speak of morality. I suppose this is what you'd say is the end of the world. Well, it was already pretty much over to begin with."

Kyoraku heard those words and stepped forward.

"What's really ending are your schemes. You don't happen to feel like coming in quietly, do you?"

"What crime do you plan to charge me for? Using the Kyogoku as I please is one of the rights of the Tsunayashiro family. If you have suspicions regarding what was in the Visual Department, then I'll kindly ask you to refrain until you have a formal investigation performed by Central 46 and the Gilded Seal Aristocrat Assembly's officials."

"If we did that, we wouldn't make it in time to put a stop to your scheme. I'll kindly ask you to let us press charges that allow us to forcibly take you in."

Hearing Kyoraku's words, Nanao grew dubious as she stood just behind them. When all was said and done, this was an unofficial march, so she wondered if there was any point to questioning whether there had been wrongdoing or not. But Nanao immediately came upon an answer.

Tokinada was the man who was managing the Visual Department.

It was possible this would also be recorded somewhere.

If they let him escape here and Tokinada were to use this record as a basis to gather aristocrats who opposed the Kyoraku family, the situation would be in the Tsunayashiro's favor as it was now.

And in order to make it so that she, Hirako, Muguruma, and the others could consistently demonstrate that they were acting in accordance with "due process," they needed to at least verify there was a crime to charge him with, even if just as a formality.

Then again, since the Arrancars and Quincies had joined them, they could likely expect a ruthless investigation no matter what happened.

"Oh? You think you can sentence me? There are a limited number of charges you could use to arrest one of the Four Great Noble Clans on the spot, so I wonder just what it is you're saying I've done?"

"There *is* one thing you've done. You should know what it is, shouldn't you? It's a crime that resulted even in someone from the main Kuchiki family being arrested without controversy."

"..."

"Hikone Ubuginu. I haven't met this person yet, but don't try to tell me you don't have any recollection."

The smile disappeared from Tokinada's face for a moment.

Then he broke out in another smile, unlike the thin grins he had worn until then—a fiendish, predatory smile—as he muttered, "You mean the 'transfer of a Soul Reaper's powers'?"

To transfer a Soul Reaper's powers to a human was strictly forbidden by the Soul Society's laws.

It was such a taboo that, though it had happened due to Aizen's artifices, Rukia Kuchiki, the adopted daughter of the Four Great Noble Clans, had been arrested with no contest when she had been charged.

"We have retrieved evidence from Shino-Seyakuin. By mixing Soul Reaper konpaku into human konpaku, you were able to compel the Saketsu and Hakusui to function. Regardless of whether it was a corpse or something else, if you have *given Soul Reaper powers to something that was once human*, it could be said that you've stepped firmly into forbidden territory, can't it?"

"Enough with the tomfoolery, Kyoraku. Do you think I am unaware that when Ichigo Kurosaki lost his powers, the Court Guard captains and assistant captains came together to spare him their powers?"

"Well, now. That was authorized by old man Yama, so I'd think of it as a special case. However, I don't remember making such an exception for you. And there's already precedent that it's not allowed even by the Four Great Noble Clans because of Rukia's case."

At that point Kyoraku boldly smiled as he added shame-lessly, *"Though she received the death penalty because of Aizen's tricks."*

As she listened, Nanao felt his argument was such a terrible fallacy she almost wanted to bow her head. Nevertheless, if that problematic provocation could reveal Tokinada's faults, that in itself could be said to be a worth-while plan. Or Kyoraku might have just wanted to bring up this "Hikone Ubuginu" person even a moment sooner.

In any case, if what he had heard were true, the child's existence itself was proof of Tokinada's illegal activities.

However, Tokinada remained unflustered as he replied, "You seem very calm. Aren't you worried about Shinji Hirako after leaving him all alone in a horde of monsters?"

His words indicated that he had realized what one of those who had come to this place might have done.

However, Kyoraku pulled his hat down slightly and shook his head with a cynical smile. "He's an adult, you know. He can handle a child messenger...or rather the 'playmates' of a child messenger, on his own."

The shadow that Tokinada cast from the balcony drew near Kyoraku's feet.

Then, Kyoraku simply sank *right into* that shadow.

In the next moment, his sword glinted at Tokinada's feet.

≡

The valley of the Kyogoku was a desert covered in rocks. At its center, something was enshrined that seemed unbefitting the devastated atmosphere—a gigantic object like a flower. That thing, which was closed like a bud, eventually quivered in its entirety and, in the middle of the white expanse of earth, bloomed into a magnificent flower wreath.

Then the man who had appeared from within it brusquely spat out, "Looks like it's over. Thanks for your efforts, Sakanade."

It was a beautiful, gigantic pedestal formed in a shape that brought to mind a *Dianthus* flower. That was the form of Hirako's zanpaku-to after reaching bankai.

"I really was just beat when it came to the war with the Quincies." Hirako's voice echoed and resounded within the Kyogoku's stretch of rocks. "Since they sprang up in the Seireitei all of a sudden and sent everything into chaos... If they had just created a defined battle formation outside of the walls, I would have been able to clean up most of them by myself."

He muttered as though complaining to himself. "It's not all that useful when I've got allies around. There isn't even much point to using it when facing someone directly. It only really means something when I'm isolated and standing right in the middle of a gigantic crowd of enemies alone. What a pain."

After sighing, he righted his neck, which had been turned upward, and inquired of the sea that surrounded him, "You all agree on that, don't you?"

What was spread out around Hirako was unilateral *death*. A vast white sea composed of a tremendous number of monstrous corpses. Rather than the raging tidal wave they had been just moments ago, they were calm, almost as though in a lull. The several tens of thousands or hundreds of thousands of monsters the swarm had swelled into had all died in a strange way.

They had died by biting each other's stomachs or using their sharp claws to pierce each other—they had expired *killing their own allies.*

It persistently inverted the perception of who was "friend" and who was "foe."

That was the ability of the bankai of Shinji Hirako's Sakanade—Sakashima Yokoshima Happo Fusagari.

"Sorry—Sakanade is a liar. That the hypnosis doesn't work well on bugs was also a lie."

If his normal shikai was thought to be only an illusion of sight and sound, using his bankai, he would prod at the underside of others' perceptions, activating a brutal ability to hypnotize not just their sensory systems, but to confound their very minds.

But as brutal as that ability was, it had immense recompense.

Unlike the shikai, because it could not distinguish between friend and foe, if fellow Soul Reapers were around him, they would also begin to unleash friendly fire on him. Because there wouldn't be an object whose perception of friend and foe he could change in a one-on-one match, the ability wouldn't activate. In a sense, that could also be said to be another form of recompense.

Though if I could do that, I could pretend to be their ally and slash them all I want from behind.

He had thought, just for a moment, that perhaps it would have made sense for him to come to this place alone and

have Tokinada and Hikone attack each other, but he couldn't rely on them conveniently appearing together.

"Well, if somebody on Aizen or Yhwach's level comes by, it might not have any effect in the first place."

Hirako once again sighed and started to slowly walk over the sea of corpses.

He patted Sakanade's handle as though in appreciation, but his grumble revealed the opposite sentiment.

"Seriously, your shikai is for the strong opponents and your bankai is for sweeping foot soldiers... You really are too contrary."

≡

"It seems the horde that Ikomikidomoe created has been destroyed," muttered Aura, who had been probing distant spiritual pressures.

"You've sure underestimated me if you think you've got time to take your eyes off me."

At Ginjo's words, Aura broke into a soft smile.

"No, I'm not underestimating you at all."

Though there was the mood of a conversation before a fight, in actuality, it had already begun.

Before she could start a discussion, Shukuro Tsukishima had turned his sword at Aura in an attempt to insert his bookmark into her. Instead, it had simply passed through her as though cutting through air.

Ginjo had also tried waving his sword as a test several times, but no matter how many times he tried to cut her, her body dispersed like smoke that his sword passed right through, so they had lowered their swords for the time being rather than repeating the process in vain.

"Mere physical attacks will not work on my present self... I will at least inform you of that."

"You got me beat. I can't hold a match to that kido stuff." Ginjo shrugged, then simply went on to question her. "Was that stuff about Karakura Town being sealed off one of your ploys?"

Yukio, standing behind her, answered Ginjo's question. "To be more precise, it was a joint effort. She's been maxing out only her konpaku and Reishi Subjugation stats. That's why when I activate my abilities through her, her performance is next level. It's like she's got a booster or something in her."

"So it's not from the power we stole from Ichigo, then."

Actually, if she can vaporize her own body, her basic Fullbringer abilities must be monster-level.

Ginjo realized that Aura, who was in front of his eyes, was reaching dangerous territory as a Fullbringer. With the utmost caution, he decided to feel out what her intentions were. "I was putting this off, but I at least have to ask what your goal is, founder of a new faith and possessor of divine looks."

"There's no need for flattery. Actually, my goal will change depending on what it is you seek."

"You mentioned that earlier, didn't you? What I seek? What do you expect from me after I died and wandered until I got to the Rukongai?"

As Ginjo questioned her, Aura had a somewhat serious look in her eyes and she responded with a question of her own. "Are you still contemplating revenge on the Soul Reapers?"

"That's none of your business. Did Yukio tell you about that?"

At Ginjo's question, Yukio shook his head slightly.

"It's the opposite, Kugo. She came to me *because* she knew about your past."

"What did you say...?"

Ginjo seemed dubious, and Aura answered, "Michibane is my mother's family name. My father's name was Tensho Agata."

"What?!"

At that point, the look in Ginjo's eyes clearly changed. Tsukishima's eyes faintly narrowed as though he also recalled the name.

"I see...so you're that old Agata guy's little girl... Never would have thought both a parent and their kid would end up Fullbringers."

As Ginjo narrowed his eyes, Aura politely bowed her head.

"I am grateful that you gave my father hope."

"Are you being sarcastic? Your pops ended up dead because I called him over."

It had happened as a result of the Soul Reapers of the Soul Society betraying them. Because they had launched a surprise attack on the Fullbringers who were Ginjo's friends, Aura's father, who was part of their group, had lost his life as well.

A past he did not want to recall came back to life in Ginjo's mind.

However, Aura continued to smile as she shook her head slightly. "No, regardless of the result, you brought light back to my father's eyes, even momentarily, when all he had was fear and despair. Though I am grateful, I have no reason to hold a grudge against you."

"So then why are you here? Based on the conversation, I understand you're working with a Soul Reaper named Tsunayashiro."

"Yes, Tokinada Tsunayashiro is my master. If I can, I would like all of you to gather under Lord Tokinada, and that is why I hastened to join you."

"What did you say? Why the hell would I join forces with a Soul Reaper?"

When Ginjo voiced his justifiable skepticism, Aura said, "The new world Lord Tokinada is building—that place, at least, should allow Fullbringers to join the strong side again."

"…"

"I asked President Yukio about it. And did you not say it yourself earlier? That Xcution is a gathering of those with the ability to change the world?"

Then, still with a gentle smile on her face, she continued, "Will you allow me to describe to you what kind of world Lord Tokinada intends to create?"

"Right..." Ginjo thought deeply and called out to his associate next to him as though in consultation. "Tsukishima."

"What is it?"

Like a surprise attack, the next words he uttered had the effect of reversing the situation.

"*Insert yourself into Yukio.*"

"Huh?!"

In the next moment, the Book of the End's blade was sticking out from Yukio's chest.

"Oh..." a small sound escaped the boy's lips.

It was a perfect surprise. Needless to say, he couldn't evade it, and he wasn't even able to activate his own abilities. However, not a single drop of blood fell from Yukio's body. When the blade was pulled out of him, there was not a scratch left behind. However, the vestiges of Tsukishima's spiritual pressure were certainly there, and it was certain that Tsukishima had inserted his own existence into Yukio's past.

"If you've been brainwashed, this'll cancel that out. First, we'll take our time hearing the truth from Yukio himself."

As a safety measure, Ginjo would first try bringing Yukio back to being unquestionably their ally. If he had been hypnotized or threatened in some way, Tsukishima would be able to preemptively obstruct that from happening. Though it was a stopgap measure, he wanted to eliminate the possibility of Yukio stabbing them in the back.

However, Aura showed no signs of being flustered as she continued to smile.

"It seems you are quite a hasty gentleman." Then, as though she were showing gratitude to Ginjo, she once again gave him a reverent bow. "I must thank you for inserting that *bookmark* into Yukio, just as we had anticipated."

"What?"

In that instant, Ginjo felt something strange in his own abdomen. When he lowered his gaze, he saw the familiar glint of silver.

The Book of the End.

The blade Tsukishima gripped was piercing Ginjo's abdomen from the back.

"Tsuki...shima...?"

As his consciousness grew murky, Ginjo saw Giriko Kutsuzawa being cut as Tsukishima pulled back the blade.

"Wha..."

"Sorry, Ginjo, Kutsuzawa."

Betraying no shame, a pained, somewhat cynical smile crossed Tsukishima's face.

Before they could even ask what the meaning of it was...

Ginjo's past was rewritten instantly through Tsukishima's bookmark.

CHAPTER TWENTY

A CERTAIN KYOGOKU

SHUHEI HISAGI, WHO HAD BEEN DISPATCHED, and Tessai, the person who had done the dispatching, were unaware that when a Tenkaiketchu post was operating on its own, it automatically set coordinates to the center of its effective radius. In this case, the center of its effective range was...

"...This is...a Kyogoku?"

Shuhei Hisagi regained consciousness in a place entirely different from Urahara Shoten. From the moment he was sent flying he had felt a strange sense of drunkenness, like missing his footing in Dangai, but he didn't feel like much time had passed.

"Well...that's because the flow of time in Dangai is weird. So I guess I can't use it as a standard to judge by."

Hisagi, who had been transported through darkness that didn't even exist in Dangai—through the garganta—first dedicated himself to grasping the situation he had been thrust into. Looking around, it seemed he had been transported to an indoor structure that was not much different from any in the Soul Society.

However, there was no source whatsoever for outside light, and the inside of the room wasn't lit by hotaru kazura. Instead, it seemed to be entirely illuminated by the newfangled lighting equipment that was also used by the Department of Research and Development.

"Why, in a building like this..."

He thought that he might not have actually been transported correctly into the Kyogoku and had instead drifted into the Soul Society somewhere, but he sensed that the concentration of reishi adrift in the air around him was indeed different from that of the world of the living or the Soul Society. His knowledge didn't extend to Hueco Mundo, but according to interviews he had done, he didn't think that desert would contain Japanese structures such as this.

"In which case, this definitely has got to be the Kyogoku... Right?"

When he probed the spiritual pressure, he felt something rather large coming from somewhere far below his current position.

Below? Am I on such a high floor?

In addition to the spiritual pressure being distant, because the reishi's concentration around him was irregular, he had difficulty distinguishing between the individual spiritual pressures. However, one among them made a particularly striking impression on his memory.

"Wait, wait...is Captain Zaraki's spiritual pressure mixed in?"

So that means the Soul Society has made a move? I see, since my message to request Gentei Kaijo was cut off...

Because Hisagi had no idea of the separate incidents that had occurred in the Soul Society, he mistakenly came to believe that the Soul Society had independently sensed something was wrong in Karakura Town and started an investigation of their own that brought them to the Kyogoku.

Okay, but are Kyogoku really that easy to find? They might have captured members of the religious group and looked into it themselves...

It'd be a piece of cake for Captain Kurotsuchi if he had a sample of one of the posts... But I guess a lot of time really has passed...

"Well, if Captain Zaraki is here, I guess I don't have to worry about battles... Anyway, I've got to meet up with them and tell someone about Mr. Urahara."

He tried to pull out his Soul Pager, but naturally it was still blocked from communicating with the Seireitei.

Thinking that he needed to first join with the Soul Reapers who were here by following the spiritual pressure, Hisagi once again probed the state of his surroundings.

"Captain Zaraki's spiritual pressure is pretty far off... How many floors has this place got?"

Based on the fact that the other spiritual pressures seemed quite far below, he guessed he was in a tall tower or somewhere near the top of the place.

"Where's the door? ...Huh? The hell is that?"

At that point, Hisagi realized that what he at first had thought was a pillar was in fact something entirely different. The *thing* at the center of the room was a gigantic cylindrical glass case installed on some kind of apparatus. The transparent vessel, which looked like it could easily fit an entire person, was currently empty, and though the device was also connected all over the place with electrodes and what looked like reishi tubing, it didn't seem to be currently in operation.

"When I interviewed the Department of Research and Development, I saw something that looked like that."

Figuring that the device might be related to recent events, Hisagi painstakingly examined it to figure out what it was and whether it had a forwarding system that led outside, but he didn't find any written information or any data at all that indicated what the thing could be.

"Ah, damn it. If I could just get in contact with Akon... Maybe I should just break this thing. But if I break it, it might be one of those things that can't be undone..."

As he was considering that, Hisagi heard a voice from behind him. "Oh, that's supposed to be my *throne*!"

"Huh?!"

"I'd appreciate it if you didn't break it, if possible, since I wouldn't have any other place in this castle to rest if you did. Yes, indeedy!"

It was an innocent voice.

Yet it was also a voice that made him feel mental and physical repulsion. Hisagi had heard that voice before— it was several weeks ago, while he was covering the Shino-Seyakuin.

He turned around to find the child who had been terribly wounded back then.

"You..."

"I'm Hikone Ubuginu! Umm...and you're Shuhei Hisagi, aren't you?! Thank you so much for earlier!"

When Hikone bobbed their head down in a bow in front of him, Hisagi automatically froze.

What is this? This kid's spiritual pressure is making me...

At that moment, Hisagi had a realization.

He realized that his sense of the Kyogoku's concentrated reishi was an illusion. Of course, the reishi in the Kyogoku's atmosphere was already concentrated, but the spiritual pressure that Hisagi stood in was far denser than any regular Kyogoku.

Is the room filled with this kid's spiritual pressure?

Since he had leapt right into the fluctuations of that spiritual pressure, Hisagi hadn't noticed that he was next to the child.

The Soul Reaper, who was neither a girl nor a boy, tilted their head as they asked Hisagi, "But why are you also here, Mr. Hisagi?"

"Oh, I'm..."

"Oh! Did Lord Tokinada call you? If you're Lord Tokinada's guest, then please let me be your host to the best of my abilities!"

"Uh..."

When he heard the name Tokinada, Hisagi's spine straightened. Though he had never met the aristocrat directly, he recognized at this point that it was clearly the name of an enemy.

"Tokinada Tsunayashiro is here?"

"Yes, he's down there right now! Would you like to greet him?"

"Uh! I-Is he?"

Hikone's openness made Hisagi hesitant and vaguely apprehensive. The situation was too strange, and he felt instinctively cautious. However, he couldn't retreat now.

He had no idea whether this had happened by chance or was an inevitability, but it seemed that he had plunged much deeper into the bosom of the enemy than he had

ever imagined himself capable. When Hisagi realized his situation, he immediately steeled himself. At the same time, it once again occurred to him that the spiritual pressure of the child standing before his eyes was indeed very abnormal.

It contained Soul Reaper, human, Quincy, and also Hollow.

That spiritual pressure, which contained the amalgamation of all sorts of konpaku, had transformed into something different from what he had encountered in the past at the Seyakuin. The presence of Hollow had become more pronounced, and as though reacting to that, the other varieties of spiritual pressure had also increased.

This kid was dangerous back then, but this spiritual pressure is on a completely different level now.

It wasn't just instinct, but also his experiences up until that point that brought him to this conclusion.

Seriously, have I ever been so intimidated by a kid?

In Hisagi's mind, the faces of Toshiro Hitsugaya, Yachiru Kusajishi, and Hiyori Sarugaki appeared.

I guess I have been, actually.

Even as cowardice caused him to cringe inwardly, Hisagi corrected his appearance and addressed Hikone with a serious expression. "Hey."

"Yes, what is it?"

"Do you know what this Tokinada guy is trying to do?"

"You mean Lord Tokinada?"

Hikone turned toward Hisagi with their wide eyes,

but didn't leave much time before they broke into a smile and answered, "I don't understand complicated things so much! But if Lord Tokinada is doing it, I think it's the right thing to do!"

"That's not something you should say lightly."

"Huh? Why is that?"

Hikone tilted their head in confusion. Hisagi chose his words carefully. "Just think for yourself for a minute. That Tokinada guy could be wrong about some things, right? Because there isn't a completely perfect person who exists in the world."

What he actually wanted to say was, "That Tokinada guy's a crook, so don't listen to him." But if he said that, Hikone likely wouldn't have even given him a chance to explain and surely wouldn't believe him.

Kaname Tosen, who had edited the *Seireitei Bulletin* in the past, hadn't shied away from concluding that evil was simply evil. On the other hand, he also hadn't written off as fools those who had been tricked by evil. But in many senses, Hisagi still didn't have as much experience as Tosen and so ended up sounding rather crude.

"Wrong? What is it that's wrong with Lord Tokinada?"

"Well, that's..."

"From whose perspective does it seem like he's wrong?"

"Huh?"

Hikone had asked that not out of sarcasm but out of

genuine curiosity. Hisagi hadn't expected such an answer from a child who still seemed full of youthful innocence, so he hesitated.

"Well, you know...I can't say that it's the whole world, but in the Soul Society and the world of the living, well, in each of the societies of those places, it would look that way to them."

"I see... In that case, I don't think he's wrong to me."

"What?"

"For me, my whole world is what Lord Tokinada gave me." Hikone spoke only the truth, matter-of-factly. "I don't know any other worlds. But there's no reason I need to know about them."

"But, that's...!" Hisagi swallowed his words.

Up until then, Hikone's eyes had seemed to convey placid innocence, though they also gave the impression of a profound, cavernous vacancy. However, after the words Hikone had just uttered, Hisagi felt with certainty that they contained within them the light of a strong will.

Looking at those eyes, Hisagi thought for a moment. Hikone wasn't just being swept along by circumstance, but was planting their own roots into the world with their own childlike, yet determined volition.

But...

Hisagi felt that there was something missing. Just looking at Hikone's face, which Hisagi now saw conveyed strong will, he couldn't help but see Hikone also as the bearer of a serious deficiency. As Hisagi's thoughts churned over this conundrum, Hikone continued, "Even if Lord Tokinada was doing something that everyone in the world thought was wrong, it wouldn't be wrong to me."

"Just...stop."

"For example, even if everyone else says Lord Tokinada is a bad person...to me, Lord Tokinada is justice! Yes, indeed!"

"Stop that!"

Justice.

The moment the word entered Hisagi's ears, he unintentionally raised his voice.

Hikone's eyes went wide as though with surprise, then they immediately bowed their head to Hisagi.

"I'm sorry. Did I do something to upset you, Mr. Hisagi?"

Hikone seemed genuinely apologetic, and Hisagi felt guilty and averted his eyes.

"No... Sorry for shouting."

Then he turned his eyes toward Hikone, realizing he couldn't run from this. The face of his blind Soul Reaper teacher flashed into his mind as his hand gripped into a tight fist.

"You should not speak about justice...so lightly."

"Huh? Why not? Lord Tokinada told me that all the Soul Reapers in the Soul Society are principled people who fight for the sake of justice. Oh, but of course, I'm not one of the Court Guard's Soul Reapers. So is that why I'm not allowed to talk about justice?"

"That's not the issue... There isn't just one kind of justice. You can't assume that the justice that Tokinada speaks of is the same one the Soul Reapers mean."

Although Hikone appeared childlike, there were some aspects about their knowledge that were more adult. Hisagi felt troubled, not knowing how to break things down and explain them to Hikone. However, Hikone grasped Hisagi's intentions and even said the words that Hisagi was hoping he would not: "Yes, sir! Lord Tokinada did say that! That's why Lord Tokinada and I might fight against all of the Soul Reapers soon!"

"What did you say?"

"Since it seems like everyone is finally here, I think that Lord Tokinada will be calling me. I'm very sorry I wasn't able to give you a proper reception, Mr. Hisagi."

After saying that, Hikone once again bowed their head and tried to leave. Hisagi was taken aback for a moment, then he tried to stop the child's retreat.

"Wait! Why have you got to fight? The Soul Reapers aren't your enemies! You don't have a reason to fight!"

Hikone turned around when he called out to them and looked at Hisagi with natural curiosity in their eyes.

"If Lord Tokinada says that all the Soul Reapers are enemies, then I have lots of reasons to fight. Isn't it enough of a reason to fight if our justices are different?"

"Killing each other isn't the only answer. To begin with, Kenpachi Zaraki is one of the people you're saying you want to fight—he's a ranking captain. He doesn't care if you're a little kid. He's not the type of guy to hold back against a strong opponent. It's just my impression here, but I think you're probably pretty strong. Still, if you do fight him, you'll end up dead."

"Will I?"

"You will, so..."

He wasn't intending this to sound like a threat, but Hisagi was desperately attempting to stop Hikone. However, Hikone broke into a gentle smile that seemed to indicate acceptance. "Then I will fight until I die for Lord Tokinada. Because no matter what happens, if I can't live up to Lord Tokinada's expectations, then there isn't any value in my being alive."

Hikone wore the expression of a child who was innocently looking forward to picnic plans for the next day.

"You idiot! You don't just say you're going to die, or that your life doesn't have any value, so easily!"

Hisagi raised his voice again, and Hikone bowed their head somewhat sorrowfully.

"I'm very sorry. It seems that I really do just make people angry."

"Don't apologize, damn it... It's not your fault. I know that." After Hisagi's frustrated reply, he started to recite a kido chant: "Bakudo number sixty-three. Sajosabaku."

"Huh!"

Chains of light created from reishi wrapped around Hikone and restrained them.

"Sorry. I think I'm Tokinada Tsunayashiro's enemy, but that doesn't make you my enemy," Hisagi declared. "You wait here. I'm going to have a talk with this Tokinada guy... even if it means I have to get rough with him."

Hikone didn't appear angered or saddened by this and replied almost awkwardly, "I'm sorry...this is hard to say, but I think that's impossible."

"What?"

Pling! The Bakudo chains broke into pieces and were sent flying. But Hisagi had already assumed that might happen. Based on his perception of Hikone's spiritual pressure, he hadn't assumed the child would be restrained so easily.

However, he was still dealing with a child. He thought he might have been able to successfully tie the child up if he exploited the difference in their levels of experience. Needing to get another plan into motion right away, Hisagi started to put together his next kido, but...

In the blink of an eye, Hikone disappeared.

"Wha...?"

Hisagi's eyes opened wide with surprise as he felt something near his solar plexus. It was the palm of Hikone's hand—the child had come right up to his chest before he'd realized it.

Thunk. There was a light press on his solar plexus, and at the same time, an enormous amount of spiritual pressure flowed into him, vehemently shaking Hisagi's Saketsu and Hakusui.

"*Guh!*"

Though he didn't feel any pain or suffering, a deep, chilling darkness began to erode away his consciousness.

"Mr. Shuhei Hisagi. You won't be able to win against me, Lord Tokinada, or Ms. Aura. It's impossible for you to sway anyone with brute force."

As Hisagi's consciousness faded, that voice, which was sincerely apologetic, reverberated in Hisagi's mind.

Wait.

You're not going out there to die. I finally understand. I know what you're lacking.

Hey, wait, just wait…

Though Hisagi tried to shout, he could no longer make a sound. Hikone, who had turned their back to him, was of course smiling as they uttered the next words, which Hisagi heard as his consciousness dropped fully into the darkness.

"So please, please don't push yourself. Please take a rest here! Yes, indeed!"

DIRECTLY BELOW THE CASTLE IN THE AIR, PALACE COURTYARD

The sound of dry metal echoed through the palace courtyard.

The zanpaku-to that had appeared from Tokinada's shadow had been blocked by his own sword, which he had drawn at some point.

"Kageoni, is it? It's far beyond impolite to step on the shadow of a Tsunayashiro, you know?"

As Tokinada cackled, Kyoraku's entire body appeared from the shadow.

"How troublesome. I have to fight someone who knows my abilities from the start."

"That lunkhead! He got a head start!"

Kenpachi was indignant, and a vein popped out on his forehead when Kyoraku launched his surprise attack. From Kenpachi's standpoint, this happened after he had patiently waited through a tedious conversation, and it was clear even to those observing that he was in a bad mood.

Seeing that, Madarame and Yumichika spoke to each other, their faces oozing sweat.

"Captain General Kyoraku might be in hot water later..."

"After all, our captain hates having his prey taken from him more than anyone..."

However, Kenpachi had leapt in order to knock Kyoraku aside so that he could face Tokinada...

"Hikone."

While he continued locking swords with Kyoraku, Tokinada's mouth warped into a grin as he called that name.

In the same moment, an ominous and heavy spiritual pressure broke forth from the castle into the air above their heads.

"Guh...!"

All those who had gathered there were fundamentally powerful, with extensive combat experience. While Nanao, who primarily used kido, was an exception, it could still be said that this was a group that specialized in fighting on the front lines among the most powerful of their kind.

However, even they froze for a moment in reaction to that spiritual pressure.

It was the young Soul Reaper they had just confronted in the Rukongai. Though the child's spiritual pressure was certainly of the same nature, the pressure it exerted had increased many times over in this short period of time.

After Hikone's name was called, just how much time had really passed?

In actuality, it had only been a few seconds, but to those who stood in awe of that spiritual pressure, it felt like it had been several minutes or even several hours.

"The hell is this...?" Candice, who could barely stand it, muttered as her face dripped with a cold sweat...

Then that *thing* fell down to the ground.

The spiritual pressure transformed into a harsh wind and brought up a cloud of dust, making the surrounding air warp just from the impact. Then the child who had disseminated such sinister spiritual pressure raised an innocent voice—too innocent—with delight that seemed to be the polar opposite of the power they exerted.

"Oh, I finally landed nicely! I'm so glad!"

Hikone Ubuginu.

Not much time had passed since they had faced the child in the Rukongai. However, the version of Hikone that Grimmjow and the others saw now gave them the momentary illusion that several years had passed.

It wasn't that Hikone's stature or face had changed. The nature of the child's spiritual pressure hadn't changed either. The child's abnormal growth was in the depth of their spiritual pressure, which now gave the impression that the child had fought in several hundred battles.

"Lord Tokinada! I apologize for the delay! What would you like me to do?"

"Ah yes. Wait a bit, Hikone."

Tokinada crossed swords with Kyoraku and cackled.

"Thanks to you, it's finally complete, Kyoraku." Tokinada just barely warded off the successive attacks from Katen Kyokotsu as he spoke proudly. "That is Hikone Ubuginu... the next Soul King."

The moment those words rang out, some of those present swallowed their breaths and several narrowed their eyes as though that was exactly what they were expecting, while the rest looked as though they had no interest in that conclusion.

In terms of what they had assumed based on previous events, most of those there, including Ginjo, had to completely revise their expectations at this point. Hikone had said they were "being allowed to become the Soul King," but when the actual head of the Four Great Noble Clans, Tokinada, spoke those words from his very own mouth, the gravity of the situation was clearly different.

As though brushing aside the forceful impact of those words, Kyoraku smiled cynically and continued. "Even if you are from one of the Four Great Noble Clans, isn't it unforgiveably disrespectful to say you'll replace the Reio himself?"

"Don't make me laugh. You must know, don't you? *You know what kind of being the Reio is.* If you know that, then don't you think that in fact the most respectful thing to do would be to replace him?"

Tokinada's words as he fought on the ornate balcony were becoming difficult to make out over the bewildering clash of weapons. However, Halibel's ears picked them up clearly. The woman looked at Hikone and, without hiding her repugnance for Tokinada, murmured, "Are you saying you intend to make a little child such as this a sacrifice for the Soul Society?"

"The child isn't even coming to your aid in this situation?"

"Yes. To Hikone, our fight seems like child's play."

Tokinada temporarily moved away from Kyoraku and yelled to Hikone, "Hikone! Hikone! Look at those who are here."

"Yes, sir! I can even see some people I just met!"

"Yes, and do you like them, Hikone?"

"Yes, sir! They all took it very seriously when they fought me! They faced an opponent like me with determination! And they will become my people soon, so I don't have any reason to not like them!"

Not knowing much about them, and though Hikone had previously been antagonizing them, the child readily said they "liked them."

The exchange was more than enough to give the impression of something ominous and wrong, but the conversation that followed made that eerie innocence transform into something repulsive.

"I see. That is more important than anything, Hikone. You must cherish those you love. Do not forget to offer your sincere devotion to them!"

"Yes, sir! Thank you, Lord Tokinada!"

"But also...these are my *enemies*. Could you *kill them for me*, immediately?"

Tokinada gave that cruel order in a booming voice.

Hikone did not so much as twitch an eyebrow as they agreed resolutely, wearing an innocent expression. "Yes, sir, Lord Tokinada!"

Though the child understood the meaning of Tokinada's words, they showed not a single sign of misgiving.

"I will put my whole heart into beating them!"

"Is that…Hikone Ubuginu?"

Just seeing Hikone made a cold sweat break out on Nanao's back.

Outwardly, Hikone appeared to be nothing more than a young child who could not be determined to be a girl or boy. However, that was not in alignment with the concentration of spiritual pressure the being called Hikone contained, which made the child all the eerier.

The young "Soul Reaper-like thing" brightly unsheathed their own zanpaku-to.

"Thank you very much! It finally grew to this level because of the fight you all let me have with you!"

After bobbing their head in a bow, they spoke their zanpaku-to's release.

Of course, the release was entirely different from any of the ones Hikone had used until that point.

"Hatch and perish, Ikomikidomoe."

Then it let out its birthing wail.

Accompanied by a fierce tornado of reishi, the blade of

the zanpaku-to swelled and formed the shape of a single living creature. Compared to the gigantic monstrosity from earlier, it was reduced in size, but despite that, when Ikomikidomoe stood on the ground he was a grotesque object slightly larger than a house.

The impression the creature's form gave off more acutely than before was that it specialized in *indiscriminate killing*.

For how the creature had shrunk, its spiritual pressure had become even more concentrated, as though it had balanced with Hikone's abnormal bearing in strength. This white monstrosity was surrounded by an overwhelming atmosphere that likely would have prevented a powerless Soul Reaper from so much as standing before it. It conjured to mind the image of the beast that would bring about the end of the world.

Hikone, who stood on top of it, looked out at all the surrounding faces with eyes that seemed both pure and empty, as they politely bowed their head.

"I'm so happy I got to meet you all! Even after I kill you, I will never forget our memories! Thank you so much!"

Hikone ran Blut Arterie, characteristic of Quincies, through their hands and did something nearly unbelievable. They created a bow directly from the reishi in the air and used Quincy abilities to condense a Cero arrow, which they fired.

"Seriously. Now you've really done it. Sheesh."

Liltotto's voice was composed, but she clucked her tongue in amazement.

Hollow reishi released using that Quincy technique approached them—and in narrowly avoiding this attack by an element they were incompatible with, the Quincies had a realization. The realization was that the Hollow reishi contained in the arrow was incredibly potent. Had they been hit directly, a normal human or Soul Reaper would sustain a fatal wound, not to mention the Quincies, for whom the Hollow factor was poison.

Meanwhile, Grimmjow and the other Arrancars were turning cautious eyes not to Hikone, but to the monstrosities being created by the zanpaku-to.

"Seems strange. He has the body of an Adjuchas, but his spiritual pressure is on Vasto Lorde level... No, it would be pretty high even among the Arrancars."

With that, Halibel referenced the character of their opponent: "Based on what he's said, it seems he would be an ancient Menos that lived around Barragan's time."

Considering some of what that *thing* had said to them earlier, even if Ikomikidomoe wasn't the oldest Hollow, they could guess he had lived a long life from far before their time. But why would a being like that have become one of the Soul Society's zanpaku-to? Halibel didn't know the reason, but what she *was* certain about was that though he was a Hollow like them, at present, he was not their ally.

The polar opposite of Halibel and Nelliel, who let themselves speculate about what their opponent might be, Grimmjow's mind was set simply and exclusively to pondering how to bring down the opponent before his eyes.

"Cut, Pantera!"

The moment he said his release, a zephyr of spiritual pressure blew around him as well and struck Ikomikidomoe's large body like a whirlwind. In order to release his full strength right from the start, he swung his sword and transformed into his Resurrección form. Then he immediately leapt at Ikomikidomoe.

Taking that as a cue, Halibel and Nelliel also spoke their Resurrección releases.

"Hunt, Tiburon."

"Praise, Gamuza."

The storm of spiritual pressure raged in the palace courtyard like a frothing current.

"Oh!" As he watched the Arrancars transform into their Resurrección states one after another, Kenpachi Zaraki cried out in delight. When the captain saw Grimmjow's form and spiritual pressure as the Hollow immediately accepted the fight, he said with a fiendish grin on his face, "I see. That blue-haired prick isn't all bark."

"Um...Captain. I must at least remind you that right now we're on the same side as that guy."

When Madarame pointed that out, just in case, the corner of Kenpachi's lip lifted and he replied, "He *is*—for now."

Then, while shouldering his zanpaku-to, Kenpachi surveyed the spiritual pressures of Tokinada, Hikone, and Ikomikidomoe and murmured appraisingly, "All right then... which one of them's the strongest?"

However, as though to obstruct his evaluation, there was a change in Ikomikidomoe.

From all sides, the Arrancars—Corpse Unit included—attacked.

Ikomikidomoe remained immobile to the very end while taking the brunt of the attack, but then eventually lowered himself and quietly enlarged his spiritual pressure. Just then a gigantic eye seemed to open in the middle of his body like Fura, and his body started to gleam.

"Hm? What the hell is that?"

"I can't figure out what he's aiming for, but that sure doesn't give you a good feeling, does it?"

Standing in front of Madarame and Yumichika, who were both on guard as they wondered what was happening, Kenpachi narrowed his eyes as he said, "All right, you two, buck up."

"Huh?"

"If you don't, you'll end up dead."

After Kenpachi's breezy warning, he proceeded to unsheathe his zanpaku-to and bring it down in a vertical line. At the same time, an enormous amount of reishi was discharged from Ikomikidomoe's body.

The blinding light swallowed a part of the Kyogoku.

The Cero went in all directions.

It couldn't really be called a Cero so much as a reishi explosion that centered on his body. Just as soon as the ground lifted and the palace's roof tiles were pulled off and sent flying, they vanished.

The Arrancars that had been in Ikomikidomoe's vicinity bore the direct brunt of the attack, but its power was dampened by a water shield that Halibel had instantly put up around them. Though everyone was somewhat scuffed up, they were not gravely wounded.

Considering that concentrating spiritual pressure was usually what made a Cero more powerful, diffusing a Cero in all directions would be pointless. However, because Ikomikidomoe had such a vast amount of spiritual pressure at his disposal, his Cero was even more powerful than a typical one, regardless of the fact that it had been diffused.

Nanao had used Bakudo, and the Quincies had expanded their Blut Vene to its maximum extent in order to mitigate any injuries. As for Kenpachi, he had forcibly dispersed the flash of light by cutting it. As a result, he and Madarame and Yumichika, who had been behind him, were unharmed. Kenpachi cracked his neck as he once again set out to select his prey.

"Well, that sure was close. You've got some nerve," said Kyoraku, who had been hiding in the shadows. He slashed at Tokinada as though nothing had happened.

Though Kyoraku had instantly evaded the flash of Cero by stepping into the shadow that it had created, he had no idea how his opponent had defended against the attack, as Tokinada had not even a speck of dirt on his kimono.

"Oh well, it seems the garden and estate were all for naught. I'll need to have Aura remake them later."

Tokinada smiled sarcastically as he spoke. Kyoraku replied, "You have more friends then?"

"Not a friend. She's simply a pawn."

"I don't know who this person could be, but my condolences. But...I see. Is that zanpaku-to an erosive type?"

"Oh, so you noticed."

Seeing Ikomikidomoe's form directly, Kyoraku was able to guess at the reason Hikone had some Hollow power. For reasons unknown, a pronounced Hollow nature seemed to dwell in Ikomikidomoe, which was already a rarity as a living-creature zanpaku-to. By linking that zanpaku-to with their soul, it seemed that the Hollow reishi assaulting Hikone was being infused into the child's body. Under normal circumstances, Hikone's konpaku boundaries would become unsettled, and the user's body would have burst by now.

However, whether it was due to the influence of the Fragments of the Reio embedded in Hikone's body or

because Ikomikidomoe was regulating it, Hikone was taming that power and had even begun to master it.

What kind of recklessness made that possible?

Considering the nature of Hikone, a newly born Soul Reaper, Kyoraku quietly looked at Tokinada.

"Don't be so deplorable to that child. What are you intending to do with them?"

Tokinada's cruel smile remained on his face as he said, "Now that you've felt their spiritual pressure directly, you know for certain, don't you, Kyoraku?"

Kyoraku did not answer, remaining silent as he swung his sword. Dodging it by a hair's breadth, Tokinada continued to smile.

"They can become the Soul King. Just as Ichigo Kurosaki and Kugo Ginjo are able to."

"So you *were* lying when you said you didn't know much about Ginjo."

"You didn't believe me anyway though, did you, Kyoraku?"

"I have one more question for you..." At that point Kyoraku's smile disappeared. With a serious expression he asked, "Was what you told Nanao also a lie?"

"Hm...? Oh! You mean about her mother!"

"Are you really sure you weren't involved in her judgment?"

"I almost wish I could say I was, but...unfortunately, that was the truth."

Then, though they were in the middle of a sword fight, Kyoraku sighed. "I see... Too bad."

"Hm?"

Not understanding the meaning of Kyoraku's words for a moment, Tokinada was bewildered. However...

When he realized the reason for them, a delighted smile came over his face as he cried out, "So you made a Pinky Promise then! Ha ha ha! That was close!"

"I don't remember telling you about that game."

Kyoraku's Katen Kyokotsu used techniques related to various types of play, such as the games Takaoni and Kageoni. Though it wasn't strictly a game, but just linked to child's play, the Pinky Promise was an ability that channeled the implication of children saying, "Let's play again."

If either of them lied to each other, first, the liar's fingers would stop moving. At the second lie, all the bones in the liar's body would become incapacitated as though a fist had crushed them, and at the third lie, the liar would be assaulted with an intense pain as though their entrails were being pierced by needles from the inside out.

It was a technique to use in battles against opponents who were prone to lying, or for use against people who had been put under his control and whom he needed to retrieve information from. However, since Ohana would become upset when he made pinky promises with other people, Kyoraku did not use the ability often.

And while he had it activated, there was a drawback, in that he also could no longer lie.

"I can tell without needing to see it. Aren't you underestimating me? You really should have used that ability in the First Company barracks! Had you done so, you wouldn't have been so late and you could have settled things!"

"I couldn't have drawn my sword on you, much less used my shikai on you, before you even drew my suspicion, now could I? If that's your way of thinking, I was late from the moment I didn't kill you."

"Ha ha ha! That's certainly true!"

Though Kyoraku was rather pleased that Tokinada's words were not what he had expected, Tokinada continued to provoke Kyoraku while maintaining his smile. "Really now, it's quite irritating to tell only the truth. Oh, right—I wasn't involved in Nanao Ise's mother's execution, but I did make the suggestion that there was a *possibility her daughter carried the divine sword, and that we should torture her!*"

"Guh!"

Kyoraku's face changed color.

Satisfied with Kyoraku's reaction, Tokinada continued to tell the truth with a rapturous look on his face. "To be honest, though, I was confident you had it. But compared to the Tsunayashiro, you are practically a peasant, even as a higher-ranked noble. I thought that you would get ideas in your head if I were to implicate you...don't you think the plot in which I wait to tell you until the girl is persecuted because you hid the sword and it's too late to take anything back would be so much more fun?"

"…"

"Ha ha ha ha ha ha! Don't make that face at me, Kyoraku! Don't worry! Ginrei Kuchiki squashed that proposal. That incorrigible old geezer—he acts hard, but really he's soft!"

"I see... So that's how it was. I need to express my gratitude to Ginrei... Take that!"

Hiding fierce vehemence behind his relief, Kyoraku continued to swing his sword. Tokinada received his successive attacks and, as though to further rile Kyoraku, asked, "What's wrong? What's with your measly fighting? Putting aside the Pinky Promise, you're not using Iro Oni, Takaoni, and Kage Okuri. Are you that frightened of my zanpaku-to's abilities?"

"Yes, I am frightened. It is quite terrifying."

"Hm?"

Kyoraku smiled boldly, and Tokinada was slightly dubious. Then Kyoraku backed off for a moment and asked something strange. "What was the name of your zanpaku-to again?"

"Do you really need me to tell you? You've already looked into it and figured it out, haven't you?"

"Yes, now I'm certain based on your reaction..." A cynical smile came over Kyoraku's face. He looked up at

Tokinada from under his hat with a glare. "...that it's not true that the name of your zanpaku-to is Kuten Kyokoku... Isn't that right?"

"..."

Now Tokinada's expression went blank.

"I'll take your silence as affirmation—since we both cannot tell a lie."

Kyoraku quietly steadied his breath and went on. "I was skeptical. That your Kuten Kyokoku can send your opponent's zanpaku-to's abilities flying is certainly frightening. But, of course, that power seemed slightly underwhelming for the zanpaku-to that the Tsunayashiro family has protected all this time."

"..."

"And as for the name Kuten Kyokoku...it has a similar ring to my own Katen Kyokotsu, doesn't it? So I thought you might have blocked its power with a fake name, partly just to spite me."

There were several examples of zanpaku-to being called fake names in order to limit their abilities. Whether or not Kyoraku knew it, Yumichika Ayasegawa's zanpaku-to, Fuji Kujaku, had a fake name to hide the true ability of Ruriiro Kujaku.

"It's in your nature. Once we came up with a method to defeat that sword and began to implement that, you planned on calling it by its real name to release its true abilities, didn't you? And there was only one reason you wanted to do that—you just want to see our faces in despair. Am I wrong?"

Tokinada sighed at Kyoraku's questioning and then pinned a cold stare on Kyoraku as he said, "You really just cannot read the room, Kyoraku. If you figured out that much, why didn't you at least consider continuing with the ruse for my sake? The term wet blanket was made for you."

"You gave me too many hints. Perhaps you were hoping to pour salt in the wound, taunting me by saying, 'The name Kuten Kyokoku happens to sound awfully similar to your own sword's name, don't you think?' after your game was up. Was that it?"

"You're half right. The other half was a reminder to myself not to forget my suspicion and hatred of you."

Tokinada grinned, raising the corner of his mouth and once again letting out an obnoxious laugh.

"Sip the world and wear the horizon—"

"Huh!"

Realizing that was part of Tokinada's release incantation, Kyoraku used shunpo to close the distance between them and swiped at Tokinada.

He could not allow the man to release his zanpaku-to. Having decided that, Kyoraku had been looking for a chance all along to slay Tokinada when his guard was down. Kyoraku didn't have the time to go through the process of Iro Oni or Takaoni. He simply thrusted, leaving everything up to speed. If the man tried to retreat, Kyoraku was confident he could pursue him and slay him.

However, at that moment something unexpected happened.

Tokinada, who had intentionally stepped forward, seemed to allow himself to be stabbed by Kyoraku's blade, and Kyoraku barely missed the man's vitals. Even Kyoraku hadn't been able to predict that move. He hadn't thought that Tokinada was prepared to let himself be wounded in order to block Kyoraku. That could only mean one thing: instead of interrupting his release incantation, there was enough value in invoking the zanpaku-to's abilities for Tokinada to put his life on the line.

"Duplicate and curtail...all of creation equally, Enra Kyoten!"

Tokinada smiled as he said the name, blood running from his mouth. Then, in front of Kyoraku's cautious eyes, the zanpaku-to blade transformed. The silver blade, stretching from a geometrical hilt of squares and cross-shaped wedges, was bright like a mirror. In the next moment, the sword body began to radiate, and a light brighter than the sun blinded Kyoraku's single eye.

"Huh?!"

A zanpaku-to that controls light?

The extravagant, blinding light momentarily robbed everyone of their judgment. However, naturally it was exactly as the Captain General of the Thirteen Court Guard Companies had predicted. Kyoraku recovered his senses far faster than any normal person and twisted his sword as it stabbed Tokinada. However, one moment prior, Tokinada had moved to kick Kyoraku and pull himself away.

"*Guh!*"

Kyoraku was sent flying, but someone stopped him.

"Are you all right, Captain General?!"

"Thank you, Nanao. That was somewhat clumsy of me, wasn't it?"

Smiling cynically as he stood up, he looked toward Tokinada as his eye began to regain sight. Tokinada stood there, unharmed.

"Huh?"

There was evidence of Tokinada's kimono having been cut. However, though there were traces of blood on the skin revealed by the slashed kimono, Kyoraku did not see the wound itself.

"What's wrong, Kyoraku?"

Tokinada, who had a serious wound until only a moment ago, was delighted. "You wanted to see it, didn't you? This is my...no, it is the *Tsunayashiro's* zanpaku-to that has been passed along from generation to generation, *the oldest one...* it is the one and only Enra Kyoten."

It was not just Tokinada's wound that was missing.

The hilt that Tokinada gripped...and the blade that had been there just moments ago...was gone.

CYBERSPACE

"It seems that Hikone and Ikomikidomoe are using their true power. Lord Tokinada has spoken his zanpaku-to's true name."

"Your spiritual pressure perception is really on cheater level."

"I'm not omnipotent. I have simply 'scattered' pieces of myself here and there throughout the Kyogoku."

"You can turn yourself into a gas and make offshoots of your sensory organs. That's cheating if I ever saw it."

They were in a subspace Yukio had created using his powers. Ginjo and the others had gone elsewhere, leaving only Aura and Yukio in that place.

"So what are you going to do now?" Yukio asked in a cool tone while fiddling with his game.

"If I attempt to assist them at the wrong time, I'll get dragged into it. I think it would be best to wait for a good opportunity."

"What about Kisuke Urahara?"

"Well... I apologize. Let's put that discussion on the back burner."

"What's wrong?"

He'd noticed that Aura's complexion had changed. When Yukio paused from his game to inquire about it, Aura smiled thinly and said, "It seems that our guest who arrived in the 'throne' has awakened. Let us head over there."

She narrowed her eyes at the thought of the invader who was not present as she said with some admiration, "It is surprising he would show up there right from the start... What an interesting individual you are."

≡

PALACE COURTYARD

"Your spiritual pressure has shot up in less than half a day."

Grimmjow stated that as though seeking confirmation, and Hikone smiled and answered while fighting the Quincies high in the air, "Yes, sir! It's because all of you were kind enough to fight Ikomikidomoe! Thank you so much for doing that!"

Hikone's personality itself hadn't changed, but their spiritual pressure had risen in strength by several degrees. Though Grimmjow had voiced his incredulity, he wasn't especially surprised. When they had confronted one another in the Rukongai, he observed that the Soul Reaper Hikone had become strong enough to be mistaken for someone else just weeks after they had fought in Hueco Mundo. In which case, Grimmjow was not surprised that Hikone had progressed further in this short amount of time.

That was because he knew.

He knew a type of Soul Reaper who had made an explosive amount of progress in a short time, in just the same way, and who had continued to show striking progress even while battling.

"So you're the same as Kurosaki," Grimmjow muttered to himself as he dodged Ikomikidomoe's attacks. He asked Hikone, "You said you'd become the king, didn't you?"

"Yes, sir!" Hikone answered with an invigorated smile.

Grimmjow put on a wicked grin.

"I see...and you still believe that?"

Grimmjow was not addressing his question to Hikone, but rather to Ikomikidomoe. The zanpaku-to that had transformed into a beast cackled in a way that reverberated as he answered, **"You may rest easy, young Arrancar."**

The voice, which seemed to resound from deep within the ground, also seemed to have gained power compared to earlier.

"I will eventually consume that brat. I will make Hueco Mundo mine to rule."

"Knew it. That's what it felt like. I don't know why you turned into a zanpaku-to, but you're the same as us."

"You claim I am the same as you? Do not be conceited. Your ilk are a far cry from those such as Barragan and me. You are nothing more than a starved beast that crawls in the desert."

At these words from the monstrosity who clearly disdained him, Grimmjow bared his teeth in a smile.

"Looks like I made the right decision coming here after all."

Grimmjow honed his boiling spiritual pressure and started to walk right toward Ikomikidomoe.

The reason Grimmjow had come all the way out of Hueco Mundo to search for Hikone in the first place was because the boy—or girl—had piped up with words the Arrancar could not ignore.

"I don't care what the hell you are. If you're standing in my way, I'll keep going until I kill you and eat you."

His instincts were driven by a memory from the past.

"Let's walk together. You will become our king."

When he took a step closer, his flesh would rankle. The monster that stood before his eyes and the one who controlled it in the shape of a Soul Reaper child were clearly dangerous beings. The appearance of the Soul Reaper and the childishness he sensed from their tone was nothing more than a papier-mâché façade. The Adjuchas-like appearance of the monstrosity was also nothing more than a front.

He understood that.

The Soul Reaper named Hikone had a spiritual pressure with qualities similar to Ichigo Kurosaki's, but the child wasn't like a living creature so much as a pocket of nothingness that had popped up in the world. If the world itself had a konpaku, it was as though a hole were carved into it the moment that konpaku Hollowified.

The monstrosity called Ikomikidomoe was the opposite of that. The being struck that hole with everything it had, like the incarnation of avarice itself. Ikomikidomoe was perhaps a monster with an equal, if not greater, spiritual pressure than the former king of Hueco Mundo, Barragan.

"We are aware of that now."

"We were destined to be Adjuchas. But you were meant for something greater."

Regardless, he took another step.

Thoughts of losing didn't cross his mind. But these were not easy opponents to defeat. If things went sideways, he understood they could send his head flying with one hit.

However, Grimmjow did not stop walking.

He had no need to fight. After all, this was an internal conflict among the Soul Reapers, and he had no reason to be used by them.

However, Grimmjow had come here. No one had told him to come, and his reason for coming to the Soul Society from Hueco Mundo hadn't changed.

Grimmjow did not smile at Tokinada's words. He didn't doubt them either. Tokinada only destroyed the world because he wanted to see it happen. While Grimmjow had understood that was an abnormal idea and though he had recognized that Tokinada was an enemy to hate, he didn't think the thoughts themselves were entirely foreign.

That was because Grimmjow knew—no matter how trivial a reason it was, if it was one's own path, then that was enough of a reason to make an enemy out of the world.

He had only one reason to fight Hikone.

"...become the king..."

Hikone and the monster that stood before him had each declared that. Had they been normal beings, he could have brushed it aside as foolish nonsense. Had he been the person he was when Aizen controlled him with overwhelming power, he definitely would have ignored them. However, after fighting against Ichigo Kurosaki and remembering the poignant appeals from his friends, those were words he would never turn a deaf ear to.

Because if he did brush it off, in that moment he would be denying his very own flesh and his very own blood.

"Eat us, Grimmjow."

For what this declaration had called to his mind were the voices of his fellow Hollows deciding to give up their paths of their own volition and turning to Grimmjow as their king.

He was not doing this for the sake of his friends.

However, the part of them that had become his own flesh and his own blood stirred Grimmjow's instincts as a beast.

It was because she knew his nature that Halibel, who was the true ruler of Hueco Mundo, did not call herself its king. No matter how those around them viewed it, the moment she took that name, she knew she would begin a fight to the death against Grimmjow.

Grimmjow as he was now, with his instinct back, would likely bare his fangs even knowing he would lose to the likes of Aizen or Barragan.

"I won't let anyone deny me this."

Grimmjow condensed his spiritual pressure into the claws of his hands as he leapt right at the gigantic monster in front of him. He moved like a heroic predator, ready to annihilate even a natural disaster.

"I'm the king."

CHAPTER TWENTY-ONE

A JET-BLACK WIND ROTATED THE GEARS.

A jet-black wind scattered the new leaves.

As though claiming their equivalency, the wind simply circulated life and death.

"Offer."

He felt as though he had heard a voice.

At some point, Hisagi realized that he was standing on top of a gigantic tree.

When he looked around, he felt almost as though he were in a forest, as a vast swath of green leaves surrounded him and thick branches gathered at his feet, through which he could see glimpses of the ground. The view of the ground was far enough down that it looked hazy. The place could fittingly be called the world tree—the existence of a wooden giant like this would be unfathomable in the real world.

"Oh... I ended up here."

Hisagi immediately understood that it wasn't the real world.

"*Tsk*...I guess this hasn't happened since I got done in at the Reiokyu."

Recognizing the sound of rusted iron and a thunderous machine behind him, Hisagi quietly turned around, at which point he saw a gigantic windmill standing on top of a vast plain made up of the gigantic boughs.

Though he thought of it as a windmill, this was a far cry from the pastoral word—an existence clad in rust and the smell of oil contrasted with the embodiment of nature that was the world tree. The rust-covered windmill creaked as its exposed gears, pulley mechanisms, and the chains that connected those parts and synchronized their revolutions moved. Based on the mixture of emotion and corruption in that space, Hisagi knew that it was the spiritual world that interwove his soul with Kazeshini.

Then a black wind raged around him.

The leaves changed color before his eyes as they were buffeted by the wind, drying and falling while the windmill precipitously revolved and started to come alive as it moved.

"*Offer.*"

Once again, the voice resounded.

In reaction to the familiar voice, Hisagi answered as usual, "It's always the same thing. I'm not going to become what you want me to become. I'm not fighting in order to feed you my enemies' blood."

As though ignoring Hisagi's words, the black wind continued to thunderously blow.

The space, which had turned gloomy, was illuminated by a lamp that had been set up in the windmill.

The foliage had made him feel as though life had withered away and turned into death, and the rust-colored windmill that had also reminded him of death now seemed to have a different aspect, as though it were a symbol of life.

"Seriously, I thought we'd reached an understanding."

Then the wind writhed and transformed into a dark humanoid shape behind Hisagi that spoke to him.

*"What you thought you reached an understanding with was this form of **me**, wasn't it?"*

"Huh?"

When he turned around, sure enough, there was the form of Kazeshini that had materialized in the real world in the past.

"Well, it's fine. I am your shadow and I am the shadow of the world you view. Form and words change depending on how the light hits. But, well, if I'm going to talk with you, I'm fine with taking this form."

Hisagi clucked his tongue as though he were irritated by the words of the shadow, which he had the longest memory of conversing with.

"Is that how it is? If you're going to change your nature *and* your form, then doesn't that mean our previous conversations were all meaningless?"

"That's not true. You really did understand an aspect of me, and you learned my name. That's exactly why you can use your shikai and why I...can call you out to this entire Kazeshini world."

In the next moment, the shadow once again turned into a black wind and went through Hisagi's body.

As it did so, it stirred words of intense craving in Hisagi's soul itself.

"Quickly, offer me blood and life that fill my soul."

≡

THRONE ROOM

"Ugh..."

Hisagi, who had regained consciousness, quietly gritted his teeth.

"Damn it...are you telling me to kill the enemy again?"

Since he had first learned its name, Kazeshini had requested blood and life countless times. Though he was

a far cry from the ranks of captains such as Kenpachi, Hisagi had enough combat experience to be called a veteran by the general soldiers. He had killed enough enemies that he could no longer count them, but his zanpaku-to's voice never waned.

"Are you saying I should have killed Hikone?"

Or perhaps it was that the zanpaku-to's voice was pointing out his own vulnerability.

"Like I'd let you use me. The only ones I swing my sword for are the Court Guards."

He didn't intend to say that his own actions constituted an act of justice. He didn't have the qualification to say that. However, the one thing he could not do was renounce his beliefs.

He was a Soul Reaper.

Soul Reapers did not kill Hollows out of hatred. They killed them in order to purify them.

As he considered whether certain actions were appropriate as a Soul Reaper, Hisagi thought that slaying Hikone was not the correct choice for him as a Soul Reaper, or personally as Shuhei Hisagi. Then again, he didn't think that Hikone was an opponent he could kill even if he resolved to do so.

But still, I can't run from this.

Hisagi rose unsteadily and immediately started to search for the exit.

"There aren't any doors. How'd Hikone even get out?"

The walls around him as well as the ceiling were all sealed, and he couldn't even guess how someone would exit or enter from outside.

"Ah well, guess I'll just have to break through."

Hisagi prepared himself to smash through the wall using kido...

"I believe it will be difficult for you to destroy that wall with your abilities."

"Huh?!"

Hearing a woman's voice behind him, Hisagi put himself on guard and turned around, only to find the woman he had just met in the world of the living standing there.

"Aura...Michibane!"

"It is such an honor that a prodigy assistant captain such as yourself would remember my name."

"At this point, that doesn't even qualify as sarcasm."

Hisagi had been extolled as a prodigy in his Shinoreijutsuin days and had cultivated an excellent record. However, when compared to the genius of Hinamori's kido and Hitsugaya's sword techniques, he understood that his natural gifts were next to nothing.

He hadn't been dispirited by that revelation and had reached his current position by continuing to study without pause, but Hisagi himself was saddled with the anxiety of wondering whether he deserved to be an assistant captain. Consequently, he never shirked his training, in order to ensure he was worthy of holding the title.

Even so, there were certainly domains that existed that he would never be able to reach.

Hisagi recalled Hikone's words from earlier.

It's true that someone like me might not be able to win against Hikone or this woman.

However, for Hisagi, that wasn't a reason to stop walking the path he was on.

Once he readied his zanpaku-to, he turned to Aura and asked, "Where is Mr. Urahara?"

"Please don't be worried. We have not harmed him in any way. Our goal isn't to hurt him."

"I see... Then I'll change my question. Where's the exit? And where the heck is this place?"

He wanted to pressure her to release Kisuke Urahara immediately, but Hisagi decided to gather information first instead. Even if he did manage to defeat Aura here, he wouldn't be able to just walk out of the place, which made this plan a nonstarter.

"This is the protective throne. It has been made so only Lord Hikone and Lord Tokinada may enter or leave, to ensure Lord Hikone is not attacked by insurgents. Though I can pass through the walls to enter."

Aura chuckled as she said that, but Hisagi kept up his guard. "So you really do intend to make a Hogyoku to make Hikone the Soul King."

"Because that is what Lord Tokinada wishes."

"So you're planning on using the Hogyoku's power to destroy the current Reio? You're trying to do the same thing as Aizen..."

"Hm?" At that point, Aura seemed puzzled, then after a few seconds, she nodded as though she understood. "Oh...I apologize. It seems that you are not aware, Mr. Hisagi. You seem not to know what kind of being the Reio is."

"Hm? No, I know that. The previous Soul King was killed by Yhwach, but thanks to Mimihagi...the right arm of the Reio that was in Captain Ukitake, I thought things turned out fine in the end."

Though in truth Hisagi had not readily believed the thing that had risen from Ukitake's body into the sky had been the Reio, the fact that the world continued to exist even now meant that he must still have been supporting it even after Yhwach died.

Yet Aura's words troubled him.

"What? Are you saying that's not true?"

"I see... While you are not entirely incorrect...with Lord Hikone becoming the Soul King, the world will become even stronger. What would you do if that were the case?"

When Aura asked that as though changing the subject, Hisagi answered seriously, "That's not something I can decide lightly. But if Hikone said that they wanted to become the king on their own, then first of all, I'd try to stop them."

"And why is that?"

"Because...that kid still doesn't know anything." Hisagi gripped his sword and spoke in a somewhat regretful tone. "Hikone told me that they have only the world that Tokinada gave them. If that's what the kid decided after seeing the whole big world on their own, then I wouldn't say anything. If, after that, they said they were going to become the Soul Reapers' enemy, then I'd be ready to stand in their way as an enemy too."

After stating that clearly, Hisagi continued, "But that kid only knows the world through Tokinada. It's like he's being manipulated. So...I need to teach the kid that there's a lot more world out there."

At that point, for some reason, Hisagi remembered Tosen's face, and after hesitating slightly, he added, "Well... on the other hand, I'd like to know what the world looks like to that kid. Then I'd decide whether I approve or not."

"..."

"So I've got to see this Tokinada guy face to face."

"Are those your words...as a journalist? Or as a Soul Reaper?"

When Aura asked that, her smile gone, Hisagi affirmed, "All together, those were my words as Shuhei Hisagi."

Aura heard him out, then continued after a slight pause. "You can't be sure Hikone would be happy after learning about the great big world."

"Huh?"

"In some cases, happiness is to live and die confined in a tank without knowing anything. There are some who realize they are unhappy only when they find out about other worlds."

Aura's words, which seemed oddly sincere, left Hisagi bewildered for a moment. Then, as though something had just occurred to him, he scowled and said, "You're not... talking about yourself, are you?"

Aura neither confirmed nor denied his suspicions and continued as though testing him. "Don't you think that's the case for Hikone Ubuginu?"

"I thought so too until just earlier, but...that kid has their own will too. It's just...the kid's lacking one thing. I just want to tell them that, is all."

"..."

"If you've come here to kill me, I'll fight with all I've got. In exchange, if I win, I'll make you release Mr. Urahara."

When he turned the point of his zanpaku-to toward Aura, she appeared to be deep in thought. Then she broke into a smile and walked toward Hisagi.

"Huh? Hey, what're you going to do?"

"Please don't get the wrong idea. I simply have one request for you."

"A request?"

He was cautious, but he didn't feel anything like hostility coming from her. Not knowing what her intentions were,

Hisagi was apprehensive as the woman gently brought her face close to his.

"---------------"

She whispered something only Hisagi could hear.

"Huh?"

Not understanding what she meant, Hisagi was perplexed for a moment. However, before he could ask, she disappeared.

"Hey, where did you..."

When Hisagi looked around, he noticed something.

A door that hadn't been there just a moment ago had appeared in the wall of the room and was partially open.

≡

ABOVE THE PALACE COURTYARD

Ikomikidomoe had turned into a monster and was battling the Arrancars while Liltotto and the Quincies faced Hikone Ubuginu overhead. The spiritual pressure Hikone contained was astonishing as the child rapidly fired an endless stream of arrows with enough power to kill a Quincy with one hit. On the other hand, when the Quincies attacked, Hikone used a combination of Hierro and Blut Vene to mitigate almost the entire attack. Liltotto clucked her tongue at their immeasurable opponent.

"This is getting close. This kid isn't as bad as Ichigo Kurosaki, but they're pretty big trouble."

"Since they're trying to actually kill us, *we* might be the ones in more danger. That is scary...." Giselle spoke as though she were talking about someone else while she fired several arrows from her Heilig Bogen. "There we go."

When Hikone swept all of those aside with one arm, Candice tried to strike the child with a thunderbolt.

"Was that lightning?! It's so tingly and fun!"

With those short words, the matter was settled, and Hikone easily dispersed the electricity.

Meninas McAllon took that momentary opening to bring down her fist with full power, however...

Although Hikone dropped toward the ground several dozen meters after taking that hit on the elbow, they fixed the reishi under them in place and held steady while a scraping sound rang out in the sky.

"You're built pretty solid."

Though she had been the one doing the punching, Meninas's fist was warped and crushed with several broken fingers.

Hikone turned their eyes upward toward the Quincies after receiving the blow from the woman whose specialty was brute strength and saw that there were several reishi clumps around them.

"Huh!"

These were reishi bombs made by the zombified Bambietta. When Hikone touched them, the child was caught up in a chain explosion.

The explosive fire brilliantly lit the sky, but not a single one of the Quincies let their guard down. They knew the power of Bambietta's blasts, but based on the sense they had gotten thus far, they didn't believe they had killed Hikone.

In fact, once the smoke cleared Hikone appeared, merely sooty.

Bambietta's power turned the reishi of the parts it touched into bombs. A person on the receiving end would experience their skin itself turning into an explosive, but perhaps because Hikone's recovery abilities were similar to a Hollow's, Hikone's skin seemed to undergo the same superfast regeneration. In addition, it seemed that Hikone had defended against most of the damage from the blast itself, and it didn't appear as though their actions had been impeded.

"That's nice. I'd like to make that kid into a zombie. I think then we'd be invincible too."

"The kid's got Hollow spiritual pressure mixed in them. Nothing good's going to come of that."

Liltotto scolded Giselle for coveting Hikone's power. Though at first glance it appeared as though they were self-assured, in actuality, they were toeing a fine line.

The "Cero arrows" that Hikone sometimes fired as a counterattack were rather strong, and in addition, Hikone could feint using Bara between attacks.

At present, the five of them were able to attack and retreat, but with their fatigue accumulating, that balance would eventually collapse. If even one of them made a mistake, the battlefront would crumble in the blink of an eye. Since Liltotto had made that assessment, she hoped to settle things promptly.

However, Hikone, who had fought and defended in silence until then, smiled and piped up, "I've learned how you attack now."

"What?"

In the next moment, Hikone's movements clearly changed. While earlier Hikone had been fending off Heilig Pfeil directly from the Quincy, they started to intercept those with their own arrows.

In the time that five of the Quincies fired arrows, Hikone fired the same number in the same amount of time. On top of that, Hikone's rapid fire showed no sign of abating, and their deflection shots seemed to anticipate the Quincies' Hiren Kyaku movements, following Liltotto and the others like guided missiles.

"...This is close."

At the same time, Liltotto realized something. Though the Quincies had been dispersed while attacking Hikone, now the child was herding them into one location.

In the next moment, just as she feared, she realized an extraordinary amount of spiritual pressure, different from any before, was gathering in Hikone's right hand.

The timing was such that it would be impossible to evade.

Determining that, Liltotto activated her own ability and, just as she had earlier, attempted to eat the reishi of the Cero.

Oh, this thing might make my stomach explode.

Feeling as though the surrounding space itself was being condensed into Hikone's hand, Liltotto imagined her body scattering in all four directions.

However...

Something that exceeded that spiritual pressure, creating a chill that seemed to freeze them on the spot, ran through the sky of the Kyogoku.

"...Oh!"

Hikone stopped, with the spiritual pressure they were going to release for the Cero still pent up in their hand, and slowly turned around. Death itself in human form stood before them.

"I only got to see a little of it, but...you're the strongest here, aren't you, kid?"

Kenpachi Zaraki looked at Hikone and grinned.

An expansive amount of spiritual pressure overflowed from within the man. The additional spiritual pressure that he pressed together into a foothold was unable to withstand the spiritual pressure coming from Kenpachi himself and would crumble as soon as it solidified.

Since he had never learned proper Hoho, the way he fixed reishi in place was haphazard, but he was able to continue standing in the air regardless, likely due to the many years of battle experience he had cultivated.

"..."

Rather than answering Kenpachi, Hikone turned the Cero stopped in their hand at Kenpachi and shot it. The twisted Cero, which contained black undulations within bluish white light, warped the space around it as it assaulted Kenpachi. However, Kenpachi mowed it down with a single swing of his zanpaku-to that was not even in shikai form, and the pressure from his blade was enough to disperse the Cero's light.

A portion of the scattered light pierced the earth, and the affected area burst as though a meteorite had struck.

Witnessing that, Candice groaned and said to herself, "What is with that guy? He's literally a monster."

"'Course he is. He's the guy even Gremmy couldn't kill." Liltotto, who had been saved by a hair's breadth, spoke impassively while experiencing complex emotions.

Yumichika appeared behind them then and, as though voicing Liltotto's thoughts, said, "That's irony for you. The fact that he couldn't kill the captain ended up being your salvation."

"To be honest, we were ready to assume you might stab us in the back."

Connections ran deep between the Quincies and the Eleventh Company. Half a year ago, during the war, Liltotto and the others had assaulted Kenpachi after he was wounded in the battle against Gremmy and, at that time, had injured and killed a large number of the Eleventh Company.

Though Yumichika hadn't witnessed that scene directly, he had heard about it from the surviving members of the Eleventh Company after the war. He had already seen the zombies of his friends that Giselle had created en masse during the war.

"I wouldn't do something as ugly as that—I'm not like you."

"Is that supposed to be pride? That's sure kind of you."

In the past, when she had partnered with the Soul Reapers to defeat Yhwach, Liltotto had been just as cautious, but in the end, she hadn't been stabbed in the back while working.

Then again, Kenpachi and the others had been in the bathroom when they had gone through the gate and disappeared partway through, so they actually hadn't ended up working together.

"According to the captain, he was most unable to forgive himself for 'not being able to stand after an attack like that.'" In a matter-of-fact tone, Yumichika continued, "I'll just say this, but don't think it extends to us too. Especially when it comes to that zombie tamer, after she toyed with everyone in the company. I don't think anyone's feelings about her will change no matter how many times they cut her down. I don't know how long the agreement is going to be valid for, but you better be thankful the Captain General compromised with you."

Though he spoke in a calm tone, there was a steeliness in his words that indicated he wouldn't take no for an answer. However, it was likely that it went against his personal philosophy to ignore the will of the captain and kill them.

As Yumichika looked at them coldly, Liltotto shrugged with a cold look in her eyes as well.

"You are definitely holding a grudge though, aren't you?"

"Hey, hey, Lil."

"Don't, Gigi."

"*Tsk*. I didn't even say anything though."

Giselle, being Giselle, harbored a strange hostility toward Yumichika for reasons unknown, so Liltotto was at the point of wanting to withdraw temporarily in order to avoid any unnecessary discord.

Madarame, who had just joined them, said with a sour look, "Either way, we haven't got time to squabble with you right now. It's not like I'm completely on board with this either, but you've already got an agreement with the Captain General."

A majority of the Eleventh Company were battle-crazy. In Madarame's case, he had fought under Kenpachi Zaraki and thought that if he were going to die, he wanted it to be in battle.

In the past, he had preached to a Fullbringer boy, "If you're going to risk your life, then do it for someone who would die for you," but if one were to ask Madarame himself who he wagered his life on, in one important aspect it wasn't for others so much as for his own sake.

Many of those who wore the yarrow company insignia wished to meet their end in battle as their ultimate form of self-righteousness, and Madarame also staked his life persistently on his own *dignity*. He wasn't dying for Kenpachi's sake, but instead wished to fight until his last moment under the visage of his revered captain.

It was said that Komamura, who had in the past also claimed that he "left his life with Genryusai Yamamoto," in the end did not risk his life for Genryusai himself, but for the Seireitei, the place the Captain General had been protecting.

Because of that, Madarame thought that to fixate on revenge for his own selfish reasons would only be an insult to his companions who had fought fiercely and were lost in battle. Of course, it depended on what the fight was, but he narrowed his eyes as he stared Giselle down and said, "We've also killed several of your friends, haven't we? I don't like the mouth on that zombie prick, but that's what battles have always been like."

"...Zombie *prick*...?"

"Calm down, slut. This isn't the time for that." Liltotto heard Giselle mutter with a superficial smile but with absolutely no sign of emotion in her eyes and sighed as she soothed her companion. "Well, regardless of the circumstances, it means we're allies right now. But don't expect us to go as far as cooperating with you."

As though he hadn't had any use for cooperation from the start, Madarame put on a bold smile and turned his eyes to Kenpachi.

"Fine, just stay back. Anyone who gets in the way of the captain's *fun*—even us—won't make it out in one piece."

Hikone had released several Cero arrows, but Kenpachi repelled most of them. Though one in five arrows hit him directly, they didn't seem to have much of an effect.

"What's wrong? That can't be all you've got?" Kenpachi said, quickly approaching and swinging his blade.

Hikone met the attack with the top of their shoulder, but it passed through the Blut Vene and Hierro, easily sinking into the child.

"...*Guh!*"

Hikone immediately moved away, but the blade had already torn through their flesh. Fresh blood flitted in the Kyogoku's air. However, the spiritual pressure that circulated the Blut Vene in them immediately stopped the bleeding.

"That Kurosaki also had a strange way of stopping his bleeding. You related to Ichigo or something?"

Remembering the first time he had fought Ichigo Kurosaki, Kenpachi smiled.

"I'm so pleased to be compared to such a famous hero! Mr. Ichigo Kurosaki is supposed to be the same as me, so maybe his Quincy blood did that. Does that mean that you might be Mr. Kenpachi Zaraki?"

"Now that you mention it, I never told you my name. You know about me?"

"Yes, sir! Mr. Shuhei Hisagi informed me about you earlier! He said that if I fight Kenpachi Zaraki, I'll die, so I shouldn't do it!"

Madarame and Yumichika reacted to those words even before Kenpachi.

"Hisagi...? Hey, wait. Hisagi's here?"

At that point, Hikone twisted just their head around to peer at Madarame and smiled, saying, "Yes! He's in the throne room, so I just made him faint and came here! Yes, indeed!"

"What could that man possibly be doing...?" Yumichika seemed shocked as he spoke, then he looked up. "The throne... You don't mean he's in that tall, floating building, do you?"

"What'll we do? Should we go save him?"

Yumichika started to nod at Madarame's words, but...

"I'm very sorry, but you cannot do that." With a hollow smile, Hikone rebuffed Madarame and Yumichika. "Yes, because I was told to kill you all immediately!"

Before Hikone finished speaking, the child disappeared. In the next moment, a tempestuous wind passed between Madarame and Yumichika.

"...*Guh!*"

It was the zanpaku-to pressure from Kenpachi bringing down his sword and cutting Hikone as the child went around to the Soul Reapers' backs.

"You two are in the way. I almost chopped you up with the kid."

Madarame and Yumichika looked at Kenpachi as he clucked his tongue. It was then they realized that they had almost been ambushed by Hikone, who was behind them.

"Sorry."

Breaking into a cold sweat, Madarame and Yumichika immediately backed down.

"That was amazing! I was so close to piercing their hearts though..."

Hikone uttered that disturbing phrase with a smile on their face, and Kenpachi said in irritation, "Quit being greedy. You're in the middle of a fight with me."

"You're right. It looks like I need to kill you first."

Hikone narrowed their eyes and leapt at Kenpachi.

When it came to speed, Hikone was like quicksilver. With Soul Reaper shunpo, Quincy hirenkyaku, Hollow sonido, and Fullbringer konpaku subjugation all combined in their motions, they had reached the pinnacle of movement techniques.

Just as Kenpachi thought Hikone had disappeared, the child was running on a crash course toward him.

The zanpaku-to that Hikone presently carried had transformed into a monster and was taking position on the ground. In other words, though Hikone was empty-handed, by using Hierro and Blut Arterie to enforce their limbs, they were able to create slashing attacks that far outstripped the average zanpaku-to.

In the span of a blink, from beginning to end, Hikone assailed Kenpachi's body with karate chops and kicks. Though Kenpachi swung his sword lightning-quick between the attacks, Hikone just barely avoided the sword and hit with yet more successive attacks.

However, Kenpachi's body was also abnormally steadfast. A Soul Reaper with normal spiritual pressure wouldn't be able to leave a mark on his steel physique even using a zanpaku-to. Though his skin was slightly cut and he was bleeding from Hikone's attacks, they didn't come close to inflicting a fatal wound.

Madarame and Yumichika watched from afar, confident in their captain's supremacy, and actually admired Hikone's skill and spiritual pressure in being able to wound Kenpachi Zaraki even slightly. However...

"I've finally gotten used to how hard you are!"

Once Hikone said this, which almost seemed like something Kenpachi Zaraki himself would say, they saw Hikone cut deep into Kenpachi's flesh, and their admiration was overcome by shock.

A spray of blood spattered through the air, and Kenpachi's captain's jacket was dyed red. However, as Kenpachi was enshrouded in the scarlet mist flowing from his very own body...

As one who carried the Kenpachi name, he laughed.

"Thought so..."

In the middle of the successive attacks, just as the eye patch that had fallen off fluttered through the air, the billowing spiritual pressure that boiled up from under it vigorously agitated the pronounced reishi in the Kyogoku.

Then, the human form that had transformed into a mass of pure violence that might even destroy the concept of death itself, opened its mouth.

"You seem like you'll be the most fun."

REIOKYU HOOHDEN

"Oh, so there you were."

When the Manako Osho high priest, also known as Ichibe Hyosube, called out to him, Oh-Etsu Nimaiya, who had been sitting on a cliff of Hoohden while looking at the empty space, shrugged and stood up.

"Oh my, my, what could possibly be the matter, Osho? It's pretty rare for you to take a stroll all the way over here."

"Well, I thought it was rarer still not to feel your presence in Hoohden or at that bar filled with all your *sword maidens*."

When the Osho stood next to Oh-Etsu, he looked at the empty space that the man had been gazing into earlier in the same way and stroked his deep black beard as he said, "Hm...so Ikomikidomoe is in the Kyogoku?"

"You don't have to ask, do you? You are the Osho, after all. You see everything in this world—you see, all see, see you again, am I right?"

"Mhmm. I have no idea at all what you're saying, but it's exactly as you say."

After that absolutely meaningless exchange, the Osho spoke about what he sensed with his own eyes.

"Karma is a strange thing. A beast that once called itself a Menos among the Menos that did not break its mask fights Vasto Lorde Arrancars that progressed on a different route of evolution from itself."

"You sure we don't need to help? That Tsunayashiro bad boy and the Fullbringer princess seem like they're having free rein."

"Don't mind them. Our role is to strive to make sure the world's bottom continues on as it ever has. For even if the ones who rule the various gardens change, it is not as though the foundation of all creation will change."

"As always, you're quite businesslike when it comes to these things."

"No, no. While I do not intervene in the matters of the world below, I do like the current Court Guards and the world of the living. If we aid anyone, it would be the Kyoraku family's tender lad. Though we have a connection with the Tsunayashiro ancestors who are part of the Four Great Noble Clans, we have no reason to favor their many descendants we have never met."

The Osho crossed his arms at that point and nodded firmly as he surveyed the lower world from high above in Hoohden.

"Whether they have free will or not is one matter, but as long as we have someone who stands atop the heavens to act as a linchpin and continues to center the world as it is now, all is well. All quiet in the world, it might be said."

Then, turning slightly, he fixed his sights on the Reiokyu that floated at the center of the five Squad Zero Riden and the thing that was enshrined at its center. The Osho grinned and murmured, "Don't you think so, Yhwach?"

≡

In the far ancient days...

Before the Seireitei had formed into the shape it is today, and before the Soul Reapers had wielded the weapons that it may be said had given them their roots, a single Menos Grande plagued Hueco Mundo.

It was the dawn of the Hollows as the world formed into the shape it is today, and all evolution was in chaos.

That Hollow was a powerful being above all the rest and evolved into an Adjuchas. The Adjuchas remained an Adjuchas, not wanting to take humanoid form. The old, wicked spirit continued to remain in its monstrous form out of its own tenacious volition.

Barragan Ruizenban and many other powerful beings that had existed even longer than him had evolved to attain forms as Vasto Lordes and Arrancars. When Barragan and the others had their power struggles in Hueco Mundo, the gigantic, sentient beast growing in the sea of reishi sand did not take the side of any group.

A torrent of sinister power, he continued to devour all according to his desires, eventually leaping out from Hueco Mundo to stretch his hands to the konpaku-abundant world of the living and the Soul Society that was crowded with Soul Reapers clad in thick spiritual pressure, continuing to destroy and consume everything like a tempest.

He could not evolve, but the sinister metastasis continued his infinite growth.

Though a Gillian carrying a similar factor later appeared and obtained an ability called Glotoneria, finally becoming known as the Nueva Espada, that is a separate matter.

This Hollow was different—no matter how many he ate, he did not take on their abilities and never acquired further powers than those he was equipped with from the start. In exchange, the spiritual pressure he devoured would accumulate into an inexhaustible supply within his gigantic body. The number of Hollows that Adjuchas devoured finally approached the number of grains of sand on a beach, and eventually, he started to become known even within Hueco Mundo as the "willful calamity."

The gigantic beast that would continue to grow infinitely and Barragan, who had the power of destruction that went by the name of "senescence," had a quandary in that they would end up in a draw due to their affinity. So an implicit understanding was formed between the two that they would not meddle in the business of the other.

In that time, he devoured the multitude of spirits that entered his vision and made them into his own flesh and his own blood.

However, that way of things could not go on forever.

He tried to scale the skies in an attempt to consume the Reio, but as a result of the battle with Soul Reapers such as Shigekuni Yamamoto, who was still a youthful hero at the time, he was defeated at the hands of the Manako Osho and Oh-Etsu Nimaiya.

"已己巳己巳" was his name.

"Since we have the opportunity, how about we give him an elaborate name?"

"You are but a nameless lump of Hollow that only devours those similar to you—己己巳己."

"It is fitting that without reaching any place, you continue to cannibalistically eat yourself indiscriminately."

"That is, until something appears that can tame all those fragments."

Through the Manako Osho's zanpaku-to Ichimonji's ability Shinuchi Shirafude Ichimonji, the empty monster's name was painted over as 已己巳己巳, Ikomikidomoe.

Because of his singularity and his expansive spiritual pressure, he could not be entirely destroyed. After his name and existence had been remade, through Oh-Etsu Nimaiya's hand, he was kneaded into a zanpaku-to and was simply sealed away.

Oh-Etsu had initially planned to hold back the thing by turning him into a full Asauchi, but the Soul Reaper was still in the process of doing that research and was not capable of entirely erasing individuality in those days, so the monstrosity ended up becoming a demonic sword with the ability to devour his own wielder's konpaku.

Since his origins were as a Hollow that had condensed countless konpaku together, he was also not easily purified, and if they destroyed him as a Quincy would, the scales of the world might have tipped.

As a result, they had ended up sealing him away at the bottom of Hoohden's seafloor until a Soul Reaper with the tenacity and spiritual ability to properly use him appeared.

A thousand years had flowed by...

The monstrous sword's seal had been undone, and he had been passed into the hands of a certain child.

A young child, who had been born not long ago.

Into the hands of someone who was created to become the Soul King, the being that the sword had attempted to devour of his own volition in the past.

≡

THE KYOGOKU PALACE COURTYARD

The vast garden had been reduced to a wasteland by Ikomi-kidomoe's violence.

Grimmjow, who stood in front of it, breathed raggedly as a bold smile broke out on his face.

"Hah...that all you've got?"

He spoke as though he were tough, but he was a mess of wounds.

"How insolent, for a mere lowly soldier..."

It wasn't only him that collided with the monster head-on, but Halibel and Nelliel, as well as all the members of the Corpse Unit, on whom deep wounds had been inflicted.

Had Ikomikidomoe simply been a gigantic Hollow, he would have been a small fry to Grimmjow and the other Arrancars. However, this monstrosity called Ikomikidomoe that had been turned into a zanpaku-to was a singularity that contained all the advantages of a Gillian's largeness, the variation of an Adjuchas, and also the density of a Vasto Lorde's spiritual pressure.

The Hollow's large form did not seem to slow him down in the slightest, and the way that he could simply move using sonido was just a nightmare, considering how massive he was. By hurling himself at a speed undetectable to the eye he could break several bones, and even if his target dodged him, his talons were like gigantic trees, raining down on them with the speed of a zanpaku-to.

The scene looked like humans wielding Japanese swords against a Japanese chimera, but it wasn't as though Ikomikidomoe was entirely unwounded. Though he continued to instantly regenerate, the spiritual pressure he consumed to do that surpassed the spiritual pressure that he could take in from his surroundings. Then again, those around him could clearly see that if they eased up on the offensive even slightly, his wounds would immediately heal.

"Oh well, this is so inelegant. I think at this rate all we can do is make you exhaust your energy in vain," Dordoni said, analyzing his enemy's fighting ability.

Next to him Halibel agreed. "I share the sentiment. This isn't the type of opponent we can stop with one effort."

"Yes, there's no reason to be stingy with him."

Looking at Nelliel, who was standing some distance away as she spoke, Dordoni broke into a smile and shrugged.

"Well, well. I would never have believed I'd be fighting alongside the person who stripped me of my number three. I suppose I should think of fate as a way to savor the deep flavors of life, like fruit liqueur in a chocolate latte."

"I don't really understand the metaphor, but that sounds kind of good," Nelliel replied with a deadpan look on her face. "I have many opinions about you, but this isn't the time, I suppose. I'll take my time paying you back what you deserve next time."

Nelliel was staring at him with a strange pressure, and Dordoni was flustered as he called out, "Huh?! Pay me back?! For what?! Did I do something to you, Nelliel?!"

"When I was small, you did plenty of things, didn't you? Like trying to blow me away, trying to kick me to death, and worst of all, trying to use me in order to bring out Ichigo's powers."

"What are you talking...oh, well, wait just one minute! This spiritual pressure and the color of your hair... You couldn't possibly potentially be... Wha?!"

As though a strange thought had just come to him, Dordoni was plainly confused, but before he could respond, Ikomikidomoe's talon rained down and gouged at the surroundings.

"My my, to not allow us even the time for banter is the epitome of inelegance, beastie. However, it has been a while since I have had an invigorating battle. It is unfortunate this is not a duel, but let us dance to our heart's content!" Dordoni yelled, then unleashed his own abilities.

"Whirl, Giralda!"

A tornado wriggling like a two-headed snake surrounded Dordoni, and two giant beaklike bone fragments at the end of each tunnel of wind struck at Ikomikidomoe's gigantic form.

Because of the mods Szayelaporro and Mayuri Kurotsuchi had added to him, his base power was vastly increased from when he fought Ichigo Kurosaki. The speed of his wind was several times faster than before, and their very existence gouged into the ground around him. The earth and sand intermingled into the pair of rampaging wind whips, turning the wind into gales that seemed as though they would smash apart everything within range.

"Fool. You think something as piddling as that could... Hm?"

Though Ikomikidomoe calmly attempted to flick away the attack, the tornado gradually began to transform. As though syncing with Dordoni's tornado, Halibel had drawn turbulent waters close to it. The eddy of water and wind mixed to turn into a waterspout of rampaging hell with cold fangs crossing through it as it surrounded Ikomikidomoe.

"Curse you...you impudent mites..."

After his irritated voice rang out, Ikomikidomoe's gigantic eye once again started to glow. Though Ikomikidomoe animatedly moved to try to release an explosive multi-directional Cero to blow away the whole waterspout, suddenly a section of the waterspout near his eyes exploded and turned into vapor, robbing him of his vision.

"Hm?!"

"Ugh, he reattached stuff I already ditched. That perverted scientist is *so* aggravating," muttered Cirucci, who was in Resurrección form a slight distance away.

The woman, who bore gigantic birdlike wings, had shot her iron Golondrina blade into the waterspout. Her blade, whose rotation had drastically increased in frequency of cycles due to her mods, would instantly scatter any water or earth they touched. She had used that to create a smoke screen from earth, water, and spiritual pressure to blind Ikomikidomoe as she pierced his body.

"...What insolence!"

Ikomikidomoe's enraged bellow resounded.

That smoke screen was able to blind his senses for a mere moment.

However, for the battle-seasoned Arrancars, that was more than enough time.

Nelliel's quiet voice crossed the storming, rampaging space as though permeating through it.

"Lanzador Verde."

The waterspout, vapor, spiritual pressure, and even the space itself was drilled through by the lance that had emerged from her zanpaku-to. It headed toward the enemy in a straight line as it plunged forward. Then, the attack that had once even penetrated through the Hierro of Nnoitora, whose pride was being the hardest of the Espada, deeply pierced Ikomikidomoe's solitary central eye.

"------------"

Ikomikidomoe raised a scream beyond words and bent back dramatically. Chuhlhourne, who had been stationed behind him, struck a pose while speaking in a singsong manner. "My, oh my, oh my! You seemed so high and mighty just earlier. That was such an ugly scream you made there. You had so much to say about Lord Barragan, but too bad for you! Your power and dignity are a far cry from his... And you don't even compare to me as far as beauty is concerned! My condolences!"

Chuhlhourne followed this needlessly long preface by unleashing Reina de Rosas.

"Rosa Blanca."

A black briar expanded and started to wrap around Ikomikidomoe's huge form.

Of course, the briar was unable to cover all of his gigantic mass, but it entangled half of him and rapidly started to draw up the reishi in his body.

"You...all of you...curse yooooooou!"

Regardless, that did not immobilize Ikomikidomoe. Using up all his power, he kicked up off the earth and leapt into the sky in order to tear off the thorns.

However...

"Sorry...this road is closed."

Using a hammer throw with no regard for her broken fingers, Meninas slammed Ikomikidomoe's gigantic body the opposite direction into the ground.

Ikomikidomoe reflexively created offshoots of himself directed toward the sky. However, all of them were disposed of by way of Liltotto's fantastical mouth.

"Gross... Ah, well. Guess we're beating this guy up first."

The Quincies, who had come down in order to avoid getting caught up in Hikone and Kenpachi's battle, shot Heilig Pfeil at the ground all at once from high in the sky.

"Hah, now just get down and grovel!"

Candice shot down a successive Galvano Javelin, and the dazzling flash of lightning harshly lit the surroundings.

"Whoa. That's super festive. Why don't you give him some fireworks too, Bambi?"

Giselle gloated delightedly while she continued to shoot Heilig Pfeil, and in reaction Bambietta smiled, her eyes still blank.

"Okay...I'll try hard. Ha ha... A festival...with everyone... How fun..."

Bambietta's smile was not uncertain so much as filled with childlike innocence as she shot down a massive amount of reishi from her hand. That reishi light turned into a rain as it poured down and turned into explosive fire when it reached Ikomikidomoe's surface, making a dazzling ensemble with the lightning that embellished the waterspout and briar.

"Seriously...I can't believe more of you keep getting in the way of me and my prey," said Grimmjow as he suddenly released the spiritual pressure he had built up in the claws of both his hands and created gigantic reishi claws of five pillars each to his right and left.

Normally he would have fixated on fighting one on one, but just this time, he felt a strange nostalgia and thrill. It might have been his instinct as a beast to occasionally hunt in a pack. Or it might have been that he had remembered others he had walked with in the past who had called him their king.

Then again, Grimmjow himself didn't think about the reason. He simply turned to the enemy at hand and brought down his own attack.

Luppi, who was off on his own and watching from the side of his eyes as Grimmjow used his trump card, smiled.

"That's my line, Grimmjow. I'm going to destroy that goliath."

He started to gather a significant amount of spiritual pressure into the eight tentacles of his Trepadora.

"Not yet... You think this is enough to destroy me?!"

Ikomikidomoe, sensing the abnormal spiritual pressure gathering in front of him, once again created a massive number of offshoots from his body and tried to form a shield of flesh, but...

He stopped abruptly.

When he felt as though everything had gone numb, Ikomikidomoe was bewildered.

It wasn't just that the offshoots he intended to create were not appearing—he couldn't even move a single one of his limbs. One who had been hiding themselves until that moment addressed the monster as he succumbed to the paralysis. "Seriously, you just change your spiritual pressure willy-nilly. I had a heck of a time making the adjustments... But it looks like you got complacent."

"...?!"

"You wrote me off and were planning to get to me later, weren't you? That irritated me, but because of that, I had plenty of opportunity to *observe* you."

The man who had appeared behind the bewildered Ikomikidomoe manipulated his fingers as he continued, "Nakk Le Vaar would probably put it this way, wouldn't he...?"

As he pointed at Ikomikidomoe, whose gigantic body he had immobilized, a delighted smile formed on NaNaNa Najahkoop's face as he spat out what had been the favorite phrase of one of his former associates, "You know what? That was fatal."

"------------"

Somewhere in his immense form his vocal cords were paralyzed, and Ikomikidomoe could not even let out a shriek.

As his body lost all capacity to resist attack due to Najahkoop's ability the Underbelly...Grimmjow Jaegerjaquez's Desgarrón and Luppi Antenor's eight-fold rapid fire Gran Rey Cero kicked in.

Those two acts of violence that were furnished with the "destruction" form of death drove into him simultaneously.

≡

OVERHEAD

"...Ikomikidomoe..."

Hikone murmured that expressionlessly as Kenpachi brought down his sword on the child.

"You think this is the time to worry about someone other than yourself?"

"Oh! I'm so sorry, I didn't mean to!"

Apologizing and dodging by a paper-thin margin, Hikone waited just a moment before saying to Kenpachi, "Will you please give me just a little bit of time?"

"Hunh? What're you getting up to?"

Kenpachi was dubious, but Hikone smiled innocently and answered, "Why, of course, I'm getting ready to kill you! Yes, indeed!"

"...Interesting. Are you going to use a bankai or somethin'?"

A standard strategy would be to kill the opponents before they could use their trump card. However, those kinds of tactics held no interest for Kenpachi. And since only Madarame and Yumichika were beside him, no one was around to scold him for it. Had Kyoraku been there, he would have used that opening to at least try to stab Hikone from behind, but the Soul Reaper was on the ground and fighting Tokinada.

"A bankai... Yes, that might be what it is, but I'm not sure."

"Hunh?"

"Since it's Ikomikidomoe, it might need to be called a Resurrección."

Before even finishing their sentence, Hikone nosedived recklessly to the ground.

≡

THE GROUND

"Impossible... How could I be defeated by urchins such as you?"

"You're still kickin'? You sure are a stubborn dirt bag," Grimmjow said in exasperation as he moved forward to serve the finishing blow.

Ikomikidomoe's gigantic form was at last mostly destroyed and had turned into a statue that could only groan his resentments.

"Curse you! If I just had my name! If I could just get back my true name, what I could do to you...!"

"Hunh? I don't know what you're grumbling about, but you really want those to be your last words?"

Grimmjow used his own fangs to cut his fingertip and started to accumulate spiritual pressure in his hand mixed with his blood to shoot a Gran Rey Cero. However, before he could release the Cero, a voice addressed Ikomikidomoe from above their heads.

"You already have a name, don't you?"

"Huh?"

At Hikone's voice, everyone turned their eyes to the child.

"Ikomikidomoe, you're my zanpaku-to!"

Almost as though he were frightened of that innocent smile, Ikomikidomoe's voice quivered.

"No...not that name...do not call me by that name..."

Ignoring these pleas, Hikone said to those nearby, "Thank

you very much! Thank you for *weakening* Ikomikidomoe to this point!"

"Hunh...?"

Grimmjow knitted his eyebrows, not understanding what that meant.

Hikone simply held their hand out toward Ikomikidomoe and called that last name.

"Ikomikidomoe, Eight Views of the Fall of the Phoenix."

"------~~~~~......"

The monstrosity's gigantic body glimmered, and right as it seemed to crumble away, it turned into a yin and yang wind of black and white that wrapped around Hikone.

In the next moment, Hikone's body transformed into a form like an Arrancar wearing a shihakusho, like a fusion of Hollow and Soul Reaper. The shadow of Hollowlike reishi seemed to crawl and wriggle under the child's skin.

The once-transformed monster Ikomikidomoe had returned to the form of a Japanese sword. Within the pure white of that sword, a blotchy pattern intermixed in the zanpaku-to grasped in Hikone's hand.

It was not only the child's form that had changed.

It was almost as though all the missing pieces had perfectly snapped into place, evolving Hikone's spiritual pressure into something on an entirely different level. Ikomikidomoe's spiritual pressure hadn't simply been set over the top of the child's. As though that ancient Hollow's spiritual pressure had become a key, it seemed to be unlocking limiters that had been in Hikone all along.

Just by being in proximity to the child, a stinging despair seemed to penetrate the skin of everyone around. Those who felt the peculiar spiritual pressure, which was different even from Aizen's, recognized not with words but through instinct... that the child in front of their eyes did undoubtedly have the qualities to become the Soul King.

"Well then...I'll take care of you all afterward!"

Though the child had obtained such expansive powers, their character had not changed a bit from earlier. That consistency made everyone around the child feel an ominous sense of intimidation, and as a result the group hesitated a moment too long.

Using that small opening, Hikone once again leapt high up into the sky.

Hikone reached a height that a normal Soul Reaper could not reach in one breath with nearly the same force as a cannonball. Then, after simply solidifying the midair reishi, they ran through the Kyogoku's sky with the swiftness of a god.

They ran to the man waiting in the sky who was their greatest opponent in that place.

They ran in order to sever the life of the one who bore the title of the strongest Soul Reaper, Kenpachi Zaraki.

INSIDE THE CASTLE IN THE AIR

"What is this spiritual pressure...?"

As Hisagi ran to the exit of the vast, multistory building, he sensed the robust spiritual pressure coming from below and reflexively stopped. His whole body oozing cold sweat, Hisagi realized that a spiritual pressure he had encountered earlier was mixed within that vast spiritual pressure.

"Is that...Hikone?"

≡

PALACE INTERIOR

WE REWIND THE TIME TO JUST SLIGHTLY EARLIER...

While Grimmjow and the others faced Ikomikidomoe, Kyoraku and Nanao were confronting Tokinada, who carried his zanpaku-to in shikai form.

Looking at the zanpaku-to that Tokinada carried, Nanao shivered from a strange chill.

It has no blade?
No, that's not right.
I feel an ominous spiritual pressure...
There really is a zanpaku-to in front of that hilt.

If that were the case, why couldn't she see it? Based on the earlier flash, was it in fact a zanpaku-to that manipulated light? In that case, she could believe the reason why they couldn't see the blade body was because he was using the refraction of light, but that wouldn't explain why the wound on Tokinada's abdomen had disappeared.

As Nanao's doubts piled up, Kyoraku looked at Tokinada with calm eyes as he said, "It seems that isn't any normal zanpaku-to. Do you feel like telling us what its ability is?"

"You really think that I would?"

"I don't suppose you would."

Tokinada of course continued to smile, looking down upon them and simply remarking, "Don't worry, you'll probably know soon enough."

While still holding the hilt of the missing zanpaku-to, Tokinada then said, "In exchange for your life, Shunsui Kyoraku."

"You sure are deranged. I'd like to settle this as peaceably as possible though."

"Did you already release the Pinky Promise? You want peace at a time like this?"

"Of course I do. There's nothing better than settling things through litigation. If you end up dying, the upper-class aristocratic dignitaries will be up in arms about it."

When Tokinada appeared dubious, Kyoraku, who was an upper-class aristocrat himself, smiled cynically. "After all, it would be the trial of the head of the Tsunayashiro family—the head of the Four Great Noble Clans. We cannot allow for the one in a million or even one in a billion chance of being wrong. We *do* have to protect the Soul Society's million-year history."

"..."

"Please have no fear. We will have an aboveboard, proper trial. We will bring the truth to light, even if it takes a million years."

"Kuh!" As Kyoraku spoke these words in a courteous, formal way, Tokinada blurted out in laughter, "Kha ha ha ha! So that's what it's come to! You plan to strip me of my wings with such nonsense, Kyoraku?!"

"The Four Great Noble Clans have their wings stripped the moment they are born. Since in exchange for great power, they themselves become the linchpin that supports the Soul Society of their own volition...or rather they offer their bodies to become the supporting pillar that holds up the three worlds."

Kyoraku's words were mixed with sarcasm.

To Nanao, Kyoraku seemed to be speaking about the responsibility that he took as an aristocrat, but Tokinada seemed to understand what was really meant by the words. Complex emotions crossed his face as he smiled and fixed a stare on Kyoraku.

"Should you really say that, as the descendant of those who only accepted the benefits without sullying their own hands?"

"I can say it. At the very least, there are those who agree with me, even those who are in your position."

"What?"

In that instant, Tokinada felt a chill behind him and reflexively leapt to the side. Because of this motion, the attack on him was somewhat mitigated, but he was still sent flying as a result of the roundhouse kick Yoruichi had landed from behind.

"*Guh...*"

"The conversation's gone on for too long. See, my foot just slipped."

Another Soul Reaper was waiting where Tokinada had been sent flying.

"Bankai...Tekken Tachikaze!"

"Uh!"

From beside Tokinada, who was attempting to stand up, Muguruma's fist and his fist-hilt shaped zanpaku-to stabbed deep into Tokinada's body. Then, a chain of destructive blasts exploded between Muguruma's fist and Tokinada, shredding his organs as he was flung the other way.

"Oh, that was a clean hit. Pretty good teamwork for the short lead-in."

At Yoruichi's aloof words, Muguruma regarded Tokinada guardedly. "Is he dead?"

"Best if we don't get careless. The guy tried to drive his sword into my foot armor more than once even in that state."

"Oh! So it really is an invisible blade then, huh?"

They doubted that was its only ability, but at the very least, it gave merit to their caution if it was invisible.

"Well, I felt like I could see the blade for a moment. Anyway, we can't give him the opportunity to use its ability..."

Though Yoruichi had started to run in order to pursue him, she suddenly stopped.

"What...?"

The foot armor that had been cut by the invisible blade had become abnormally heavy.

In the few moments that she hesitated to observe this, Tokinada chuckled, and he stood up.

"Dear me...didn't I tell you that I am terrible when it comes to fights?"

The only thing about him that was torn apart was his kimono. They could not detect a single scratch on him at all.

"You're...unscathed?"

Muguruma's eyebrows knit together—he was sure he had felt something hit his hand.

The group, who knew they did not have the time to use Kaido, firmed their guard as Tokinada gripped the bladeless zanpaku-to in front of them and broke into a merciless smile.

"So, please do die quickly."

Then, slowly, he readied the zanpaku-to's hilt as he made a contradictory request. "And make sure you suffer as comically as possible."

The statement was contradictory and twisted.

When they heard him say that, Kyoraku and the others shuddered with a sudden chill.

It was not just them.

Ikomikidomoe's fight had ended, and the Quincies and Arrancars that were watching Hikone head toward the skies also felt the sensation. Even Madarame and Yumichika, battle-seasoned as they were, felt the strange chill and turned their eyes to their surroundings. With the exception of Kenpachi, who was focused on Hikone coming toward him, all of the invaders felt the impending danger and tension vibrating in their bodies.

In the next moment, Kyoraku felt the beastlike spiritual pressure that seethed from behind him. He took Nanao's hand and leapt to the side. In that instant, *something* as large as a bear passed through the place the two had just been.

It was a strange sphere, about three meters in diameter that resembled nothing so much as a gigantic mouthful of fangs.

When Kyoraku saw that, his eyes opened wide.

"That's..."

He had a clear memory of that strange object.

There wasn't just one of them.

Looking at the countless objects floating from the courtyard that were nothing more than spheres with mouths, Kyoraku spoke a single name—the name of the

brutal and peerless zanpaku-to that his friend, the seventh Kenpachi, a man named Kuruyashiki, had used in the past.

"Gagaku Kairo..."

"What's wrong, Kyoraku? You look as though you've seen a dead man walking."

Tokinada said that with his arms spread, and Kyoraku smiled cynically as a bead of sweat dripped down his face. "What do you think our job is? I'm used to seeing corpses."

As he spoke, he narrowly dodged one of the gigantic jaws that approached him from behind and sank right into a shadow with Nanao in his arms.

"Oh, so you can even dive into the shadow of a zanpaku-to if it is your enemy. I had no idea."

As Tokinada smiled happily, he started to search for where Kyoraku would emerge.

"Will you let the woman run off to a safe place first? Or will you recognize her as being strong enough to fight with you and come to slay me?"

As Tokinada attempted to provoke them, a blade thrust up near Tokinada's feet as though in response.

Tokinada leapt to dodge it, and Yoruichi approached him from behind.

At some point, she had taken off her foot armor and regained her normal speed, but...

Shiver.

The faintest, slightest amount of spiritual pressure indicated that something was wrong, and all the cells in her
body cried out as she stopped her foot just as it was about
to reach Tokinada.

In the next moment, something like a flurry of cherry
blossoms, which was in fact a group of infinitesimal blades,
passed in front of Yoruichi's foot and grazed it. A section of
them scratched her skin, creating a spray of blood. Luckily the
wound was not deep; however, had she kicked him as intended,
it was clear her foot would have been chopped to bits.

"Was that a trick of my eyes…? I'm sure I just saw the
Byakuya boy's…" Yoruichi was certain she recognized the
storm of blades that had already disappeared.

"It couldn't be…"

It seemed Kyoraku had also seen the blades that had
appeared suddenly, and he broke into a cold sweat as
he guessed at the true power of the Enra Kyoten that
Tokinada carried.

An attack that made that which it cut heavier.

The wound that had healed before they realized it.

The strange creatures from Gagaku Kairo's shikai itself.

And the exact same storm of blades as Senbon Zakura.

Though he wanted to deny the logical path this led him
toward, with the latter two the conclusion had already
made itself clear.

The power to copy another's zanpaku-to's abilities at will.

As though to mock Muguruma next, Tokinada brought out a new power from Enra Kyoten.

Tokinada suddenly knelt and punched at the ground.

Something reminiscent of a chakram, a disk-shaped blade, was gripped in his hand, and the moment he touched the ground with it, the earth around him groaned. The entire courtyard's base warped as it swelled and wriggled like a massive living thing, transforming into lances that assaulted Muguruma.

Muguruma was not the only target. The Arrancars and Quincies that took on Gagaku Kairo's strange creatures were attacked by the ground itself, and they dodged just in time.

"Hey, this guy's zanpaku-to couldn't be..."

Dealing with the earth lances by scattering them with his own zanpaku-to, Muguruma landed next to Kyoraku and Nanao, who had appeared from the shadows.

Then, as though he had timed his reply, Kyoraku addressed Tokinada with a serious expression: "Wabisuke, Hisagomaru, Senbon Zakura...and just now, that couldn't have been Tsuchinamazu."

When Kyoraku said that name—one of the zanpaku-to possessed by Zennosuke Kurumadani who was formerly in charge of Karakura Town—Tokinada smiled faintly as though in admiration and he opened his eyes wider.

"Oh, so you even know about Tsuchinamazu. Does that mean you know about the zanpaku-to of all the company members?"

"To some extent. Despite appearances, I'm the Captain General, so I've at least looked at the data on the generations of those in charge of Karakura Town. Although I didn't think Tsuchinamazu would be capable of this magnitude."

"There are many zanpaku-to powers that will increase in ability according to the spiritual pressure of its user. Hisagomaru is very useful. Though Seinosuke's younger brother can only take in slight wounds, when I use it, I end up like this even after that cut from you went right through my belly."

The zanpaku-to that Hanataro Yamada carried, Hisagomaru, was a nonstandard zanpaku-to that could heal the injured by absorbing the wounds of those it cut. Kyoraku judged that Tokinada had likely used Hisagomaru's powers by cutting himself in order to absorb the wounds that Muguruma had inflicted on Tokinada earlier.

Hanataro's sword shouldn't have been able to absorb wounds when they were serious though. It seems that the abilities are corresponding to Tokinada's spiritual pressure...

Next he had used Izuru Kira's zanpaku-to Wabisuke's power to make Yoruichi's foot armor heavier. The moment Nanao realized that a shiver went down her back.

"It can't be... A zanpaku-to that can use other zanpaku-to's powers."

"Still, we should investigate whether he really can use all the abilities. If its power is that strong, it might have some limitations," Kyoraku said in order to alleviate Nanao's worry as he very carefully examined Tokinada's actions.

However, as though to prevent this observation, Tokinada unleashed his next move. Just as they seemed to see the invisible body of the sword quiver, a dense, gray smoke blew up.

"Oh! Haineko...!" Nanao immediately realized its identity and called out.

In the meantime the strange creatures of Gagaku Kairo approached, and Kyoraku and the others evaded those as they also leapt continuously to avoid the ash that pursued them.

The ash's shadow was too murky and thin for him to sink into. Anticipating that as well, Tokinada set forth to attack them as they fled.

"Hado Number Fifty Eight Tenran!"

A tornado broke out and incorporated Haineko's ashes in the wind, quickly attempting to swallow up Kyoraku and the others. Though he wasn't as fast as Yoruichi, Kyoraku was confident in his shunpo. He was somehow able to escape the ash, but another problem awaited him.

"This is bad..."

He moved away and looked behind him. The wind that Tokinada's kido had stirred up was distributing the ash around a vast area. Those on the ground were being attacked by it one after another.

However...

"Cascada."

The cascade that Halibel had created was like a waterfall that coursed through the sky horizontally and washed away the ash and strange creatures.

"I think I've seen that power before." When she had confronted Hitsugaya in Karakura Town, she had seen the three battling subordinate Soul Reapers use the same abilities from the corner of her eyes. Because of that, Halibel was able to guess Tokinada's zanpaku-to's nature and let slip, "Is it like the ability of Glotoneria in Aaroniero?"

Though the Arrancars could not judge whether he had stolen others' zanpaku-to's abilities or was simply copying them, it made no difference which it was since either way, his power meant trouble.

Quincies included, they all turned cautious eyes toward Tokinada. It seemed that they too had continued to fight the strange creatures of Gagaku Kairo, and they seemed to understand that those creatures were a kind of ability and that their user was Tokinada.

Aside from Hikone, who was high in the sky, further up than the building that floated in midair and slashing as they stepped on reishi footholds to climb higher, and Kenpachi who was taking those slashes while moving higher himself, that meant all the Soul Reapers and Quincies in the place and also the Arrancars were confronting Tokinada.

Additionally, backup had appeared on the scene.

"What is that terrible spiritual pressure up there? Huh? That couldn't be Kenpachi and Hikone, could it?"

After dealing with Ikomikidomoe's offshoots, Hirako had finally come onto the scene.

"Captain Hirako. So you made it out in one piece."

At Kyoraku's words, Hirako grinned and replied, "Of course I did. But that thing I glimpsed earlier wasn't really Rangiku's Haineko, was it?"

"I'll get right to the point. The person over there is Tokinada Tsunayashiro...and his zanpaku-to's ability is to copy other zanpaku-to. He's used at least six different abilities at this point."

"Seriously? He sure brought more trouble."

Hirako's face showed genuine displeasure. Muguruma asked him, "Shinji, if that guy uses Sakanade's power, could you use it on us and reverse it?"

"You ask that like it's easy to do. Well, nobody would be laughing if he copied my bankai, but I'll try something... Though I don't think that anyone other than me could master Sakanade."

As Hirako spoke, he probed the presences of those around him. Because he had spent many years handling Sakanade, he could generally tell almost instantly in what way someone had been reversed. Then again, there was the concern that he would be attacked while he was trying to reverse them back, though it would likely be difficult for Tokinada to make those complex calculations while fighting.

Although if this Tokinada fellow is on Aizen's level, then we'd be at checkmate.

The sense of unease remained in Hirako's mind as he focused himself on Sakanade. He considered that it would clearly be a disadvantage to face so many enemies even while using several zanpaku-to abilities...

"Well, now...it's my first time facing a group of such formidable opponents as this."

Tokinada smiled boldly.

Then, as Halibel's turbulent stream approached him from the front, he projected a different ability using his sword's invisible body. A flame like the sun dispersed and instantly evaporated the water Halibel controlled.

"Ryujin Jakka!"

When Nanao thought back to when Kyoraku and Ukitake had faced Genryusai Yamamoto to attempt to save Rukia, her skin oozed sweat. The arid air dried that sweat instantly, but Kyoraku sounded relieved as he muttered, "Oh good."

"Captain General?"

Nanao was dubious, but Kyoraku replied, "That temperature is a far cry from old man Yama's. It seems that his abilities being based on spiritual pressure can go either way."

Then again, he still could not let his guard down. By Kyoraku's assessment, Tokinada's spiritual pressure was the same in strength as the other Four Great Noble Clans members Byakuya Kuchiki and Yoruichi Shihoin. It could be thought of as a silver lining that although the lineage of the Four Great Noble Clans' spiritual pressure tended to be on a higher level, they did not reach a power that was beyond the bounds of common sense.

"Don't you think it would have been better to have the child Hikone hold that—that zanpaku-to?"

Kyoraku spoke sarcastically, remaining vigilant of his surroundings. Tokinada, while manipulating flames, said, "That *thing* is too meek, and if I did allow them to hold the sword, they would likely devote themself to abilities such as Engetsu and Daiguren Hyorinmaru, and that would be the end of it."

When Tokinada roared with laughter, Kyoraku narrowed his eyes.

So this is the Tsunayashiro family's treasured sword. They certainly can boast about being the governors of history.

Of course, if he used that with old man Yama's or Aizen's spiritual pressure...

...

Aizen...?

Shudder.

As though he had had some sort of premonition, all the cells in Kyoraku's body shivered instinctually. As though Tokinada had sensed that quiver in Kyoraku's spiritual pressure, he snickered and used a move to derail Kyoraku's train of thought.

"Bakudo Number Twenty One Red Smoke Escape."

A red smoke diffused explosively with Tokinada at its center and shrouded the wasteland that had once been the courtyard.

"Huh!"

All those surrounding were vigilant of the next attack that might appear from inside the smoke.

Wait.

It couldn't be!

Kyoraku realized *that* was what Tokinada was attempting to do. To be more accurate, the moment that he realized the ability of Tokinada's zanpaku-to, the possibility of *that* had been in the back of his mind, and he might have been subconsciously afraid of it.

"Don't look! Close your eyes!"

At the same time that subconscious threat connected with his thoughts, Kyoraku attempted to yell, but...

As though calculating that timing, Tokinada's voice made Kyoraku's and Nanao's reishi quiver.

"Bo...

dhi...

dhar...ma..."

"Guh!"

It was one of the games that Kyoraku's Katen Kyokotsu possessed. When an enemy used an attack with spiritual pressure, it was a technique that allowed one to travel along

that spiritual pressure in the shortest distance possible to attack. Since that technique had been activated, if he looked at Tokinada, then it would become his "win" and he would be able to inflict Tokinada with a fatal wound. Further, there was a restriction that Tokinada always should have had to be in a position where they could see him.

Not even a few seconds had filled the void.

When Kyoraku realized that he wasn't being attacked, he looked at Nanao.

As though she were trying to use her own kido in order to clear the Red Smoke Escape that Tokinada had produced, or perhaps trying to set up a defense, she was refining spiritual pressure in her hands.

So he's aiming for her!

Because he had realized it, Kyoraku was not able to not see it. He could not keep from opening his eye.

In order to protect Nanao, Kyoraku opened his remaining right eye and looked at the sword that approached Nanao. It was a zanpaku-to that looked like a swift whip with a spearhead at its end.

—*This is Rose's...*

—*But from the smoke?*

—*Oh no.*   —*That* voice *was a bluff.*

—*He hasn't invoked the game.*

As all these words crossed his mind, he was led to one conclusion...

He couldn't close his eyes to it.

Even if "The Bodhidharma falls down" was a bluff, the blade that was approaching Nanao before her eyes was coming from her blind spot. Tokinada's attacks were not so weak as to allow someone to defend against them while their eyes were closed.

"Don't look! Close your eyes!"

Several moments delayed, the words that he was attempting to say finally came out of his mouth. However, they didn't come in time. Before those around him could understand what the words meant, Tokinada had already finished.

Even though Kyoraku had come upon what Tokinada was aiming for, he ended up already *seeing* it.

It wasn't just him.

Some of them, in order to dodge the approaching Senbon Zakura...

Some in order to intercept the still writhing Gagaku Kairo...

Some before they could escape from the thin smoke of Haineko...

Some, some, some...

They were all carefully watching, trying to determine the infinite number of "zanpaku-to" that Tokinada dispatched.

At around the same time as Kyoraku, Hirako, who had realized Tokinada's aim, looked at the Shinso blade that approached him. His sense of logic was exceeded by his battle experience and the instincts that told him he would

not be able to dodge that attack with his eyes closed, which made him too late to close his eyes.

Because of that, no one was able to evade it.

Crunch. Along with the noise of something being smashed to pieces, all the zanpaku-to in front of their eyes seemed to disperse like water evaporating.

Kyoraku and Hirako had expected that, but for that reason, they were mortified.

The Soul Reapers and Arrancars who understood what it meant opened their eyes in fright.

The Quincies, who had no idea what significance it held, looked on in disbelief.

With the exception of Kenpachi, who only had eyes for his duel high in the sky with Hikone, they had all seen it.

In other words, they had seen the moment that Sosuke Aizen's zanpaku-to, Kyoka Suigetsu, shattered its shikai.

≡

"What is going on here? How big is this tower?"

Even as he complained, he ran through the palace with complete concentration. Although he had been able to leave the throne room, he still hadn't found anything that looked like an exit from the building itself.

He felt that he'd been heading in the direction from which he sensed countless spiritual pressures for quite some time, but the structure was like a complex maze and hadn't allowed Hisagi to escape easily.

He sensed that the spiritual pressure of Hikone had swelled explosively, and Kenpachi Zaraki's had shot up with a staggering force. It seemed they were clashing far up above in the sky.

"Damn it... So I was too late!"

All he could think was that Hikone and Kenpachi's fight to the death had begun.

Though Hisagi continued to move his legs, trying to find a way out even a second sooner, at that point he realized that there was another spiritual pressure he recognized. Though it had been hidden by Kenpachi's spiritual pressure and he hadn't noticed it, there were several other familiar spiritual pressures too.

"Captain General Kyoraku?! And also Ms. Yoruichi...and even Captain Muguruma!"

That so many powerhouses had gathered meant that Karakura Town's isolation had probably become a larger issue, even to them. That was what Hisagi assumed, but...

"Hm? These spiritual pressures...are Arrancars...and Quincies?! What the hell is going on here?!"

Not understanding what was happening, Hisagi suppressed his nerves and his heart thumped as he ran.

After he had run for a while, Hisagi's anxiety grew.

"Their spiritual pressures have started to weaken?"

Accompanying that realization was the beginning of

a fear that was different from the one he'd had until now. Hikone, who had that absurd spiritual pressure, was fighting Kenpachi, he realized. In that case, who was *currently* making the Captain General and the others' spiritual pressure weaken moment by moment?

Is it Aura? No, or is it...?

Since Aura's spiritual pressure was scarce to begin with, he couldn't tell whether she was there from where he was. However, he could make out an ominous spiritual pressure that he had never felt before ensconced where Kyoraku and the others were.

This spiritual pressure...it couldn't be Tokinada's...

Hisagi earnestly held back his unease as he continued to run. Finally he discovered nonartificial light breaking through and used shunpo to run to it at once.

It was likely a window to allow in outdoor light. Jumping onto the window frame, which was big enough for a single Soul Reaper to pass through with room to spare, Hisagi immediately surveyed the situation outside...

That was when he first realized he was not in a multistory tower, but a gigantic building floating in the air.

"Wha...?"

A gale of pronounced spiritual pressure brushed his cheek. The wind that blew up from below cycled around the gigantic building, making the structure that floated in the air seem as though it were in its own cramped world.

"This is practically like the Reiokyu…"

As he uttered this impression, which was the same as Hirako's and the others', Hisagi looked above his head momentarily. From that position, at a height that made their forms hazy, he saw what looked like two stars snapping at each other. If he were to approach them without enough caution, he would likely end up caught and torn to shreds between the two spiritual pressures. In fact, even looking up at them like this, Hisagi was seized by the illusion that his own spiritual pressure was twisting his flesh.

Meanwhile, when he turned his eyes to Kyoraku and the other presences he sensed below, he found a scene that made him doubt his eyes.

"There's no way…"

Seeing it from afar he couldn't be certain, but it looked as though Kyoraku and the others had partnered with the Arrancars and Quincies and that they were being drastically overpowered by a single Soul Reaper.

Hisagi was unable to just stand there. He leapt from the window, falling down toward the battleground spread below his eyes.

He still had no idea what he would learn of the Soul Society's darkness on that battlefield.

CHAPTER TWENTY-TWO

"SO THIS IS THE REIOKYU."

"I understand how you feel, your majesty."

"What are you talking about, Haschwalth? I'm not feeling a shred of emotion from looking at this decaying grave."

≡

UNDER THE CASTLE IN THE AIR,
FORMER PALACE COURTYARD

When he saw Hisagi swoop down directly into the middle of the battlefield, Kyoraku seemed surprised.

"That couldn't be...Shuhei?"

Though Kyoraku did not seem fatally wounded to Hisagi, the Captain General had injuries over his entire body and seemed barely able to stand. Beside him, Nanao was holding

Kyoraku's sleeve, and though she was mostly uninjured, she seemed to have consumed most of her spiritual powers, as though she had used kido to the extent of her ability.

The situation around Hisagi was even more confusing to him. He saw Quincies whom he remembered fighting in the past as well as the Corpse Unit that worked for Mayuri. He even saw the Arrancar woman who had fought against Hitsugaya in Karakura Town's decisive battle. However, none of them appeared to be either the allies or enemies of Kyoraku and the other Soul Reapers; they all seemed to be hesitating over whether to even move, and he didn't see any sign that they would attempt an attack. If he had to guess what they were doing, it seemed as though they were all devoted solely to defense.

When they saw the bewildered Hisagi, the people at the scene responded.

"Is that Shuhei? Why're you here?" Muguruma, who was on his knee, asked in shock. Chiming in, Yumichika and Madarame, who were back to back and vigilant of everything around them, also spoke: "Oh, Assistant Captain Hisagi...so you really were here."

"Hey, wait, Yumichika. We can't assume he's *real*."

Not understanding why Madarame and the others were casting looks of surprise and caution toward him, for the time being Hisagi looked to the person highest in the chain of command for instruction.

"Captain General Kyoraku! What the heck is..."

Though Hisagi tried to run to Kyoraku, he was forced to stop. That was because the point of Katen Kyokotsu that Kyoraku carried was slowly being turned toward him.

"Captain General...?"

"Yeah, I'm sorry, Shuhei—no, Assistant Captain Hisagi."

Even as a trickle of blood dribbled from his forehead, Kyoraku wore his usual gentle smile. Still, he did not put down his sword as he continued, "There are a lot of things I'd like to ask about, like why you're here and what's going on in Karakura Town. But, I'm sorry; it's better if neither of us gets close to each other."

"I don't understand. Just what is going—"

Hisagi was interrupted by an unfamiliar voice from behind him. "You. Where did you come from?"

"Huh...?"

"Well, well... I don't think you were part of the lineup that arrived with Kyoraku. I haven't sensed the barriers or anything beyond them being penetrated, either. How did you break into this place?"

Though he had a Soul Reaper's spiritual pressure, the bearing of the man Hisagi saw then was somehow ghastly and twisted, which made Hisagi feel fairly sure of the answer when he asked, "Are you...Tokinada Tsunayashiro?"

"Well, what an impolite ape you are. Hm...that company insignia..."

Tokinada looked upon the Ninth Company assistant captain insignia on Hisagi's arm with some surprise, then his face twisted with delight and pleasure.

"Ah, I see. I've only seen you on the footage, but I do recognize you. So the Soul Reaper that Aura spoke of in Karakura Town was you. Well then, so you went ahead and used the Tenkaiketchu, you vile thief?" In direct contrast to the tone of his words, he opened his arms wide as though he were actually welcoming Hisagi. "Then how about I answer your earlier question. You're right, I *am* Tokinada Tsunayashiro. What an honor it is to meet a Soul Reaper with such a promising future, Assistant Captain Shuhei Hisagi."

"..."

"Or should I put it like this...I am so pleased that you are penning an article in praise of me, Shuhei Hisagi, editor-in-chief of the *Seireitei Bulletin*."

"You..."

"What do you think? Won't a description of how the fool Shunsui Kyoraku met his unsightly end while mounting an insurrection with Arrancars and Quincies make for an excellent article? If you'd like, you may even watch from a front-row seat. I may even tip you a coin, depending on how the article turns out."

Just hearing these words that were dripping with sarcasm made Hisagi realize something.

The man in front of his eyes was an entirely different type of evil compared to Aizen and Yhwach. Since the incident with Tosen, Hisagi had been reluctant to speak of justice and evil as though they were simple dualisms, but Hisagi's instincts told him this man named Tokinada was quite clearly *evil*.

He would occasionally encounter such people when covering the felons of the Soul Society—those who had not been warped by some pitiable past, but instead were villains from the outset. He keenly sensed a malice even darker than that from the few words Tokinada spoke.

It was clearly a problem that a man like this was the head of the Four Great Noble Clans, a position within the Soul Society that was on equal footing with the Central 46. And the fact that Kyoraku and the others were confronting Tokinada indicated just how terrible a deed the man in front of him was trying to commit.

"I think the readers would enjoy an article about your downfall much more," Hisagi answered, spitting the words out as he reflexively reached for his zanpaku-to.

"Hm. But as an agent of the mass media, don't you think it's inappropriate to involve your personal grudge? As a bearer of news, shouldn't you be consistently impartial?"

"Even from an impartial perspective, from what I know about you I doubt you're a good person."

Though Hisagi had viewed Tokinada as an absolute enemy from the moment the man had attempted to kill

Kyoraku and the others, he didn't attack Tokinada right away. There was something he needed to clear up first. "What are you planning on doing...with that Hikone kid?"

"Hm? You know Hikone?" Though Tokinada was initially dubious, he seemed to recall something and nodded. "Ah, come to think of it, Hikone did say something about that. They met a kind Soul Reaper at the Seyakuin or something of the sort."

"I'm asking you what you're planning on, making that kid into the Soul King."

"Does it matter? In order for Soul Reapers to rule over the three realms, we must have an absolute symbol to reestablish a new set of values in the world of the living and Hueco Mundo. Hikone is able to do that. They were *created* to do it. That is all—it's a simple matter."

At Tokinada's indifferent reply, Hisagi's rage was apparent in his words. "You use people like tools."

"That's a misconception. Hikone is indeed a tool, but I do not think that *people* are tools. I think of people as beings who think with their own free will, shout, scream, and let themselves fall into despair. I consider humans a truly comical show. A tool does not have its own will and instead entrusts itself entirely to my mind—that is a name for something that is *not a person*, such as Hikone."

"You..."

"It is a simple fact. Hikone is no person. Hikone is not a Hollow nor are they a Quincy or a Soul Reaper. They are nothing more than a tool I created—a vessel of power to unobtrusively become king and suppress the three realms. Naturally. But compared to those incompetent, ignorant fools, I do have a preference for Hikone." A sarcastic smile broke on his face as he shrugged lightly and said what he truly thought. "That *thing* is too single-minded when it comes to emotions. If I told them to die, they would simply do it, and if I told them to crush their own lungs and suffer, they would happily pry their chest open using their own fingers. They are somewhat dull to toy with."

Liltotto, who heard that from afar, clucked her tongue, remaining cautious of Complete Hypnosis, since she didn't know when it could assault them. While feeling slightly concerned that the words she was hearing even now might be exercising the power of Complete Hypnosis, she muttered to herself, recalling an exchange from just a few hours earlier.

"So if your pal Tokinada ordered you to die a painful death, would you actually go and die?"

"Yes! And I'd do my best to suffer while I do it!"

"So the kid wasn't speaking metaphorically. That's nauseating."

"Did you...actually order Hikone to do that?"

"What reason do I have to deceive you about something so trifling?"

Hisagi looked at Tokinada smiling down at him and desperately held back the growing rage within him as he said, "...Well, I give up. I'm running out of options other than killing you ASAP."

"You never had that option in the first place, since you're not capable of such a feat." This phrasing seemed designed to make Hisagi feel like a fool. Tokinada then asked the Soul Reaper, with deep curiosity, "But I do not understand—you only just met Hikone once at the Seyakuin, did you not? Why are you so fixated on this?"

In fact, Hisagi had met Hikone earlier, so they had seen each other twice, but he purposefully did not correct Tokinada as he replied, "Even if I'd never met the kid before, how could I stand silently by after finding out what you're up to?"

"What? So then it's nothing more than what you'd call chivalry? Or is it compassion? Regardless, how idiotic." Tokinada responded disinterestedly, then went right on talking about Hikone. "If you're trying to save Hikone, you're misguided. The only way of life that thing knows happens to work out well for me. This is the result of my not teaching Hikone anything else, and also of Hikone never attempting to learn more. I never resorted to reward or punishment; that thing simply believes things are meant to be this way. Don't you think stealing Hikone's happiness would only serve your own sense of righteousness?"

Tokinada was the epitome of composure as he said this, and Hisagi then understood precisely the relationship between the being called Hikone and Tokinada. It wasn't a relationship of control through fear. It wasn't even a relationship of dependence through pleasure. Tokinada had simply used Hikone's innocence and ignorance to his advantage, making the child think that he was their entire world.

He hadn't made himself a god.

He had made Hikone the god and raised himself onto equal footing by becoming all they knew of the world.

How...?

Can that be the only rationale behind all this?

Biting back his anger, Hisagi released his zanpaku-to. "Reap, Kazeshini."

Gripping the zanpaku-to now in its shikai form, Hisagi readied himself, however...

Arriving in Hisagi's blind spot, Kyoraku grabbed the Soul Reaper's collar while still carrying Nanao under his arm. Kyoraku used the hand that was still holding his own zanpaku-to to jerk Hisagi's collar forcefully, then leapt, pulling Hisagi away.

"Huh? Why...?! Wha...?!"

In the next moment, the sensation of solid ground under Hisagi's feet abruptly disappeared. He started to fall immediately, and his vision was seized by darkness.

Tokinada, who watched the whole thing transpire, looked at the flickering flames of the palace behind him. They were flames he himself had created earlier through his Ryujin Jakka. Next, he looked at the shadow it cast under his feet, which stretched out to the point in the distance that Hisagi and the others had disappeared to. A delighted smile broke on his face, and he muttered to himself, "Good grief, could you be more overprotective of your underlings? But are you sure about this, Kyoraku? You truly wish to entrust your last hope to a Soul Reaper such as him?"

三

INSIDE THE SHADOW

"...Kyoka Suigetsu?!"

Hisagi, who had been dragged into the shadow world by Kageoni, the ability Katen Kyokotsu possessed, exclaimed in surprise after hearing what had been happening recently from Kyoraku and Nanao.

"Yes. We suffered an embarrassing blow. Other than Captain Zaraki, all of us saw the moment it was released... I think the Arrancars and Quincies must have also understood the ability immediately. Tokinada has been able to use as many zanpaku-to abilities as he desires while we're immobilized out of fear we'll attack each other."

When Hisagi looked closely, he saw that Kyoraku sported a wide variety of wounds; the Captain General had been burned, frostbitten, slashed, and even seemed to have had holes drilled into him.

Hisagi immediately realized that Tokinada had likely used Complete Hypnosis to make Kyoraku *misapprehend* the type of attacks that assaulted him. If Tokinada's Ryujin Jakka were mistaken for Shinso, even if the target thought they had avoided the blow by a thin margin, they would still end up getting scorched. If it were the opposite, then because the person being attacked would be estimating the speed at which the flames spread, their body would end up cleaved by the lightning-fast strike.

Though Tokinada's other zanpaku-to abilities were not performing as efficiently as before—possibly because he was pouring most of his spiritual powers into Kyoka Suigetsu—still Kyoraku assessed that at this rate they would not be able to escape annihilation.

"Captain Zaraki himself has his hands full facing Hikone. And frankly, considering that the child has been battling him for so long, they must be just as much of a threat as Kyoka Suigetsu."

"Then what should we do? How do we deal with such a depraved zanpaku-to?"

"Tokinada's spiritual pressure is a far cry from Aizen's. That's why I think there must be a limit to his Complete Hypnosis abilities... But even without that power, he's still a formidable opponent."

"Yes, I can't believe he has the ability to copy others' zanpaku-to..." Nanao said, as Hisagi recalled Tokinada's face with irritation. "We can't assume that he can use every ability. He *is* the head of the Visual Department. It's possible he can only use abilities he has witnessed himself."

"Come to think of it, according to Aura, that woman who's in league with him, he was supposedly watching the whole battle in the fake Karakura Town."

"It seems he is well prepared then. The Visual Department was the first to report on Rukia and Ichigo too. Given those circumstances, I wouldn't be surprised if he were secretly connected to Aizen."

Although Kyoraku had suggested that troubling idea, he himself guessed that the possibility was slim. Had Aizen joined forces with Tokinada or the Tsunayashiro family, Aizen would likely have elicited needless backlash from Kaname Tosen. Tosen might have been able to handle all of that, but there was no reason to rattle him on purpose. Either way, given Aizen's personality, had the Tsunayashiro family come into contact with him, it was very likely Aizen would have dealt with them in the same manner he had the previous Central 46.

"Well, regardless, we can't simply assume his powers have restrictions while we're confronting him. Especially since he is obviously the type of man who enjoys pretending he *cannot* do something, then at the last minute revealing to his opponent that he actually *can*, in order to make them despair."

"That's appalling."

"I really did you a terrible disservice asking you to write an article about him. If we survive this, I offer you all my apologies."

Though Kyoraku spoke in his usual tone, even Hisagi could see the man's wounds were not shallow. Kyoraku was likely putting on a show of acting like everything was normal in order to give Nanao peace of mind. But Nanao didn't have holes for eyes. Though she looked uneasy for a moment, she immediately gathered what Kyoraku intended and tried to put on a brave face, the sight of which made Hisagi's hands curl into fists.

"I'll kill him."

"Assistant Captain Hisagi, that's..."

"I know that I'm not strong enough. But I might be able to steal his zanpaku-to, at least."

Kyoraku stared into Hisagi's eyes. Though Hisagi spoke with confidence, it was clear he was frightened. However, when Kyoraku saw that Hisagi was willing to walk toward death while carrying that fear, the Captain General sighed and interjected with a question.

"Tell me...did your Shinoreijutsuin cohort still have compulsory battle drills by night?"

≡

"I know you can hear me, Kyoraku! How about you come out soon?"

In the flames that spread around him, Tokinada was surrounded by his own countless shadows as he raised his voice, looking the epitome of composure. "Do you intend to hide in the shadows until everything is over? If that is the case, I don't mind. That way you can watch as the rebel army you hastily threw together meets its demise."

Tokinada then turned his eyes to Yoruichi, who was close at hand.

"I have an excellent idea. Shihoin princess, how about I use the zanpaku-to of the Fon family maiden who so yearns for you...and slaughter you with Suzumebachi's power? But of course, I won't let you have the second sting immediately. After I engrave the seal of death all over your body, I will take my time administering the Nigeki Kessatsu sting."

"Sheesh, you're even more tasteless than I thought."

Though Yoruichi smiled fearlessly as she stood up, the wounds she had sustained were by no means superficial.

"This is my last bit of mercy. Then how about I make myself look like the user of the blade herself? I wonder what the girl's face will look like when she learns it was Suzumebachi's powers that made you disappear without a trace... Ha ha ha ha ha! I cannot help but anticipate it!"

"It's pretty ironic that someone whose debased character, which would certainly cause his demise if this were a tale from a story scroll, can somehow get his hands on such power in the real world."

"That's how the world works though, isn't it? Hm, or would you like me to take Kisuke Urahara's form to—"

Tokinada paused in the middle of his sentence as he sensed spiritual pressure rising up from the shadow behind him. When he turned around, he saw Kyoraku, Nanao, and...

Hisagi, holding Kazeshini with his eyes closed.

Tokinada was bewildered for a moment, seeing their faces, but eventually his laughter burst out as though a dam had broken.

"Now, now, don't make me laugh so hard, Kyoraku! Surely you don't intend that to be your last hope?"

Seeing Hisagi, who stood in front of Tokinada with his eyes still closed, Tokinada easily understood what they intended. They were trying to ensure that Hisagi, who was not under the control of Complete Hypnosis, did not see Kyoka Suigetsu the moment it was in shikai form.

"Then again, I suppose that cannot be all you are planning."

Looking at their surroundings, Tokinada imperceptibly braced himself.

I see. So you plan on using him as a detector.

The Soul Reaper Hisagi's weapon was a type that could attack from a distance. They likely planned to have Hisagi attack Tokinada with it so Kyoraku and the others could use the position of Tokinada's voice and spiritual pressure to confirm they were attacking not an ally mistaken for an enemy, but Tokinada himself.

How naive. In that case, I can overwrite his voice, form, and the trajectory of his attacks using Complete Hypnosis.

However, in order to fully reproduce those aspects of Hisagi, he needed some time to observe Hisagi's voice and the way the Soul Reaper attacked. If any of it were even slightly off, Kyoraku would realize that and react. Tokinada had an absolute advantage because of Complete Hypnosis, but he did not let his guard down.

Though he would not let his guard down, he also determined he would not kill them immediately, but rather torment them to death. At first glance, his behavior seemed contradictory, but, exactly as expected, Tokinada did not relax his attention as he devoted his entire body and soul to the amusing task of bringing his enemies to the brink of a torturous death.

"Hope does not suit any of you. I will correct that posthaste."

From within Hisagi's self-imposed darkness, Tokinada's voice rang clearly in his ears. The direction Tokinada's voice came from and the place Hisagi's spiritual pressure perception sensed Tokinada were in agreement, as the Soul Reaper steadily honed his awareness.

At Shinoreijutsuin, which was the foundational establishment for a Soul Reaper's education and could also be their gateway to success, they were taught several techniques to battle in the dark of a moonless night. Those techniques included creating light through kido and forging their night vision, but fundamentally, they had to learn to sharpen their spiritual pressure perceptions and reel in their opponent's Reiraku in order to battle.

Naturally, the trajectory of their attacks wasn't as accurate as when they could see, so that method was mainly used to gain distance from the opponent until they could reach a place with light. That was the theory of what they were taught, but at this moment the opponent Hisagi stood before was not some run-of-the-mill Hollow.

This was a formidable enemy whose spiritual pressure rivaled that of the Arrancars and captains, and one who carried Enra Kyoten, a zanpaku-to of endless strategies, as well. The fear of standing up against a powerful enemy who had Senbon Zakura at his disposal, alone and with one's eyes closed, was unfathomable. However, despite the fear he felt, Hisagi was strangely calm.

Did Captain Tosen fight under these conditions? No, right now I can still perceive light through my eyelids, but Captain Tosen probably didn't even have that...

He had heard that the fully blind Tosen had exhibited excellent hearing and spiritual pressure perceptions from a young age. Whether that was true or not, the former captain had trained both senses to perceive the clouds his friend saw in the night sky. When Hisagi recalled how Tosen had been able to sense all kinds of things the seeing could not, he found it plausible that Tosen truly had sensed the movements of the clouds floating overhead, even while he was unable to see them.

Of course, Hisagi was not equipped with the senses of hearing, smell, or spiritual pressure perception to that degree of acuity. Though he could use those senses in a pinch, when it came to overcoming his fear in that darkness, Hisagi reminded himself that this was nothing compared to the "fear" that Tosen had felt. At the same time, Hisagi remembered Tosen's words when the former captain had stabbed Hisagi's abdomen at Aizen's command.

"I do fear something. I've had the same fear for a hundred years. The fear of assimilating and dying as a Soul Reaper."

That was the answer Tosen had given to Hisagi when he had asked why the former captain threw everything away for the sake of power, and what had made him so frightened. Then, after being dropped from a building, Hisagi had almost lost consciousness. But in his empty mind, the words Tosen had spoken to Komamura echoed as well.

"If someone were to join an organization for revenge and lose sight of his true purpose and become complacent in his new life, wouldn't that be depraved? Then tell me what justice is!! To forgive the one who murdered a beloved friend? That certainly could be virtuous! It's beautiful! Blindingly beautiful! But is virtue justice?! No!! To live a drawn-out life in peace without clearing the dead's regrets is...vice!!"

That moment might have been the first time the man named Kaname Tosen had proclaimed his true thoughts. They were filled with endless rage, with fear certainly flitting in and out of view in their depths. The reason Hisagi remained conscious and was able to once again stand was perhaps because he heard that voice.

Tosen had lived on, continuing to carry that rage and fear, for a long while. Unable to abandon his fear or forget it, he had suffered as he continued to walk his path with it. What kind of terrible hell had that been for him? Why did Tosen have to suffer that fate?

The answer to the questions that had risen within Hisagi was right in front of the Soul Reaper's eyes: Tokinada Tsunayashiro...

...the originator of so much rage and fear that those emotions had upended Tosen's life.

With his eyes still closed, Hisagi turned to the place where he felt Tokinada's spiritual pressure and said, "Let me ask you one question."

"Hm? A commoner like you wishes to ask *me* a question? Oh! Is this one of those interviews for the *Seireitei Bulletin*? In that case I don't mind answering, especially for you."

Tokinada shrugged, provoking Hisagi, but the Soul Reaper hid his rage and fear as he asked, "You saw it too, didn't you? The fight between me and Captain Tosen in the world of the living?"

"Did you hear that from Aura or Hikone? Yes, that fight was a useful reference. I rewatched it many times. Although I did have to go to great lengths to sneak the surveillance spirit bugs in so the Department of Research and Development wouldn't catch on."

Tokinada spoke in a casual tone, and Hisagi had to quell his intense rage as he continued to question the man. "Then you should have seen it—Captain Tosen's last moments."

As he took a step forward, Hisagi's roiling heart nearly overflowed. "You heard it, didn't you—what Captain Tosen yelled?"

Then, as though he fully understood, Tokinada agreed and shook his head with a quiet expression. "Yes...that really was deplorable, what happened to him. I regret most of all that I could not be present there myself."

"What?"

"If only I had been there at the point that you pierced through his brain and Aizen *nebulized* him...I could have told him..."

Tokinada then narrowed his eyes, with a smile that was the incarnation of wickedness itself as he continued, "...that his friend's cries as she died were much more exquisite and disgraceful... That's all."

Rage overtook all the other emotions within Hisagi.

"You...!"

He'd been able to keep his eyes closed despite his outrage as a result of Tosen's many lessons, which had permeated his body to the point that they were practically instinctual. Hisagi lightly anchored his sense of reason within the chain of "fear" as he threw one half of Kazeshini toward Tokinada.

Tokinada dodged the attack by a wide margin as he lured Hisagi further with his words. "His yells certainly resonated in my mind! They were so very comical and pitiful that I was almost moved enough to cry! After all the seeds of amusement I cultivated so splendidly, and then he rotted to oblivion without being able to so much as turn his blade on me! Ah, I suppose I should thank you, Shuhei Hisagi. After all, you brought down a traitor who didn't understand his place and came after me!"

"*Hgh!*"

"If I were to say more…I did realize he had an axe to grind. I had no idea he had gone so far as to join forces with Aizen, but when Kisuke Urahara and the others were exiled, I was certain that Tosen was one of the true culprits. Well, it would have been such a chore, so I never did inform Central 46."

When Hirako and Muguruma heard that, they both glared at Tokinada.

"I may not be able to do it now, but that just gives me one more reason to slap you down," snarled Hirako.

Though they could barely move despite the severe wounds that had been inflicted by Senbon Zakura's and Shinso's abilities, it wasn't as though they could act carelessly, due to Complete Hypnosis and the possibility of friendly fire.

Tokinada ignored Hirako's grudging words and continued to taunt Hisagi. "There's something you *should* thank me for. If nothing else, because Tosen was able to keep his rage hidden, he saved the Ninth Company many times— sometimes their lives, sometimes their minds."

Though Hisagi wanted to object, he really had been saved by Tosen, who had continued to hold onto his internal desire for revenge. That said, unable to agree with Tokinada's words, Hisagi answered with another question. "Is that why you won't teach Hikone anything?"

"Is there some problem with that?"

"That kid still knows nothing. All they can do when they come up against a wall is run away to the small world you showed them. Captain Tosen never would've allowed anyone to raise a kid in such a twisted way."

"Don't use another's sense of justice as your own. Why don't you rephrase that with your own thoughts?"

As though his interest had been piqued, Tokinada delighted in provoking Hisagi. The Soul Reaper kept his eyes closed, manipulating Kazeshini's chain and trying to frame the area around Tokinada based on spiritual pressure.

When he confirmed that Tokinada's spiritual pressure was avoiding that, Hisagi manipulated the rotating blade and continued speaking. "Okay, I will. You're a coward. You teach a kid who hasn't got a clue about anything to serve only your motives and raise them in this cramped world for your own convenience."

Tokinada opened his eyes slightly wider, then let slip a snicker.

"To remain ignorant is to run. To refuse to teach is cowardice. Is that what you say as a Soul Reaper?"

At Tokinada's strange phrasing, Hisagi replied in irritation, "What're you talking about? You're a Soul Reaper too."

"I see! I see! You certainly are the editor of the *Seireitei Bulletin*, aren't you?! How arrogant it is to expose someone's personal secrets and believe that spreading them far and wide is justice!"

Tokinada moved far away from Hisagi and stood on the estate's half-destroyed roof as he fired off his invective in a voice meant to reach not only Hisagi, but also all the others who were there.

"None of you have the faintest idea *that we are all living atop the sins of just five individuals.*"

"Huh...?"

Perhaps he was using the power of a zanpaku-to, but while Tokinada did not yell, even speaking in a quiet tone his voice carried far enough to permeate the minds of those on the ground.

As Hisagi was perplexed in the darkness, Kyoraku's voice hit him from behind in response to Tokinada. "Good grief, are you intending to tell that fairy tale? We don't even know if it's true."

"Though it contains some exaggeration, it is a lesson that we, the Tsunayashiro family that rules history, have continued to protect. Someone with as sharp an intuition as you can tell from the scars carved into the foundations of the Soul Society whether it is a fairy tale or not, can't you?"

"You think too much of me, I'm just—"

In the middle of his sentence, Kyoraku disappeared.

According to the indications Kazeshini had given him, Kyoraku traversed the zanpaku-to's chain and closed the distance on Tokinada using shunpo.

"Oh! How impudent!"

Tokinada smiled boldly as he began his defense…

At that moment, Kyoraku was assaulted by an attack he hadn't been expecting at all.

"Is this…?"

It was a collection of patterns floating in the air. Several feelers emerged from them and sprang at Kyoraku. The Captain General narrowly dodged them, but as a result he abandoned his attack on Tokinada. Though the feelers pursued him further, Nanao, who had followed after Kyoraku, used a kido barrier to intercept them. Even as it hit the strong kido wall and part of its form was sent scattering, the patterned whip started to eat away at the reishi itself.

When Kyoraku saw that, he murmured with a groan, "A zanpaku-to...? No, is this...a Fullbring?"

Then, as though in response, a shadow floated up next to Tokinada.

"You realized that it was a Fullbring immediately...you really are the Captain General of the Court Guards."

"That voice... Is that you, Aura?"

Hearing Hisagi's voice as the Soul Reaper kept his eyes shut, Kyoraku kept some distance and said, "Good grief, another challenger after we've gotten this far?"

Kyoraku let out a loud sigh, while Aura bowed her head deeply.

"I extend my sincere apologies for obstructing you." Then she glanced toward Hisagi as she continued. "However... I would like Lord Shuhei Hisagi to hear the entirety of what Lord Tokinada has to say. Please, if you could somehow pardon me."

"And why would that be, miss?"

Though he spoke in a light tone, Kyoraku searched for an opening in his opponent.

In response, Aura quietly smiled and said, "I believe that Lord Hisagi bears the professional duty to know the truth. He can perhaps serve as a good judge to determine whether the world Lord Tokinada seeks to create is right or wrong."

"Me...?"

What is this? What is Aura trying to do?

Though Hisagi couldn't see the woman's smile, he understood that she wanted him to hear everything Tokinada had to say. However, not knowing the reason for that, Hisagi kept his eyes closed and tilted his head.

Is this just obfuscation to confuse me?

Though he was certainly curious about what Tokinada might say, he couldn't slack on his offense. Hisagi manipulated Kazeshini again and tried to attack in the direction of the spiritual pressure, but...

Shinso's blade, which stretched out faster than his spiritual pressure perceptions could detect, pierced Hisagi's shoulder.

"Guh...!"

A sharp pain assaulted Hisagi. The long-distance thrust that surpassed his spiritual pressure perception in speed made the fear eddying under his rage start to swell.

"Hasn't the thought crossed your mind before, Shuhei Hisagi?" Tokinada asked, as though mocking Hisagi's fear. "About whether Kaname Tosen, or rather, Sosuke Aizen, might have actually been right?"

"What are you saying?"

"Even if it was for revenge, can you really comprehend how someone as virtuous as Kaname Tosen would betray the Soul Society itself? Have you ever dedicated any part of that somewhat deficient brain of yours to considering why Sosuke Aizen detested the being called the Reio so much?"

Tokinada gripped the hilt of Kazeshini in order to evade it as it approached and pulled Hisagi along with the chain. "Or maybe I should put it this way..."

Tokinada braced his hand and started to yank Hisagi over. With a supremely sadistic smile, he laid things bare: "Have you considered why Kisuke Urahara would have made the Hogyoku, or what his motives were for doing so?"

He exposed the bowels of what could be perceived as the original sin that shaped the Soul Society's history.

"Huh? What are you talking about? He said that the Hogyoku is for removing the boundaries between Hollows, Soul Reapers, and konpaku to surpass the limits of growth..."

"For what reason would anyone need to do that? In those days, he did not even know about Aizen's rebellious inclinations, and no being could have defeated Genryusai Shigekuni Yamamoto. What would he accomplish by making anyone more powerful?"

"That was...to stop the Quincies' attack..."

"In the end, you were able to survive without the Hogyoku. Although, to be completely accurate, it was likely that he would not have allowed the use of the Hogyoku."

Hisagi recalled the conversation between Aura and Urahara.

"If Ichigo Kurosaki were given a Hogyoku, the world would become very solid for sure. However, that is far from the result you're looking to achieve, isn't it?"

"Yes, I'm sorry. I lied. If I had given Mr. Kurosaki the Hogyoku, it would have been something entirely different, wouldn't it?"

Though he had not understood the meaning of the conversation at all at the time, now things were different. The nature of Hikone's spiritual pressure, which was so similar to Ichigo Kurosaki's... That Aura had said they would use the Hogyoku to make Hikone into the Soul King... All of these assorted elements connected within Hisagi, building to one hypothesis.

Then, as though he were giving the final hint, Tokinada spoke about the man who had been his former classmate. "The Reio's right arm that dwelled in Ukitake's body. Don't you think that was odd?"

"..."

"Why would the Reio's right arm have been lost? Had it dropped to the ground, why would he not have used Squad Zero to retrieve it?"

That was Mimihagi, the thing that had dwelled in Ukitake's body at a young age—in other words, the Reio's right arm. And then there was Pernida Parnkgjas, the one who had claimed that he was "always a Quincy"—in other words, the Reio's left arm.

The Reio's right arm controlled "stillness" and his left arm "advancement." In that case, what did that mean for the Reio who had lost both of those things? He neither stayed still nor advanced, simply existed in the place between stillness and motion.

What did Aizen say back then...?

When Ichigo Kurosaki first appeared in the Soul Society, the words that Aizen had left them with at the end of the rebellion, when Aizen informed them of his true motives... These words resurfaced in Hisagi's mind. The words Aizen said when Ukitake had asked, "Have you fallen?" seemed now to have a different meaning.

"No one ever stood atop the heavens before."

"Not you, or I, or the gods."

Why had he gone out of his way to specify "not you" to Ukitake? Maybe Aizen had known that a part of the Reio dwelled in Ukitake?

If that were the case, Ukitake *was* someone with the right to stand atop the heavens. Until now, Hisagi had thought that the "gods" not standing atop had meant that the Reio was ultimately a king rather than an almighty god. However, Aizen had gone on to speak these words: "But the unbearable vacancy of heaven's throne ends now." In which case...

"The Reio...was dead...from the start?"

When Kyoraku heard Hisagi's whispered murmur, he quietly cast down his eye. Yoruichi did not let her expression change and stared on as Tokinada and Hisagi had their exchange. After a moment of silence, Tokinada smiled cynically and shook his head.

"Close. Very close. The thing they forced the name Soul King on indeed was not living. However, it was not dead either."

"What does that mean?!"

Even in a bewildered state, Hisagi's attacks did not weaken. He pulled on the sword that Tokinada held using his left arm, and he threw the other side of Kazeshini that he gripped in his right hand.

Tokinada sent that flying back using a morning-star-shaped zanpaku-to—Gegetsuburi—and replied to Hisagi's yell. "The Reio was a sacrificial goat. However, he did possess powers that were the equivalent of a god's."

"What...?"

"Before the world took on its current form... In a chaotic place where there was no border between life and death, there was an original protector who stood between the Hollows and humans for the first time. The Quincies, the Soul Reapers, and also the Fullbringers...it could be said that he is the ancestor of them all." Snickering, Tokinada continued. "He was a Quincy and also at the same time a Soul Reaper, and also just a normal person bearing countless abilities like a Fullbringer. He was the symbol of hope who ruled over all in the chaotic world."

Then, as a smile filled with noticeable pleasure warped his face, he told Hisagi of the dark side of the Soul Society. "These three realms were created by sacrificing that man who was both a devil and a savior...

"...by the five people who are the ancestors of our Five Great Noble Clans—the five traitors."

≡

THE REIOKYU

"The founder of the Tsunayashiro clan was a powerful man who was yet more suspicious than any other." The Manako Osho spoke those words in front of the crystal that was sealed away by multiple layers of barriers.

Around him, the silent members of Squad Zero all lent an ear to his tale. The place they were was a throne and also an altar and was not only occupied by them, but also by the imperial guards who were new to protecting the temple. Many of the soldiers had met their end by way of Pernida and Yhwach's other royal guards, so they had needed to supplement the ranks with new ones.

But there was that throne and the godlike enemy Yhwach's remains sealed within it.

The newcomers who had been informed that this was the current Soul King had been considerably baffled by it. After seeing the strife in the Kyogoku, the Osho had likely thought this a fitting opportunity.

He had fetched Oh-Etsu from Hoohden, then he had gathered the soldiers who protected the Reiokyu—in other words, the only people who knew the secret that, at present, a Quincy's remains were being revered as the Soul King— and spoke of the Soul Society's past.

"In that age, in all of creation many things were ambiguous. There was no such thing as life or death, and without progress, there was no retreat. While it swayed to and fro, you see, this was a world where one could only wait for all things to chill over the course of ten thousand or even one hundred million years. Even becoming a Hollow was part of the circulation of reishi." Speaking in a matter-of-fact manner, the Osho recalled the world prior to the birth of Hueco Mundo or the world of the living.

"Eventually, however, the Hollows began to eat humans. At that point the circulation stopped. Had things gone on as they were, all the konpaku would have been reduced to one gigantic Menos and the entire world would have come to a halt. But how curious it was—as though the world were rejecting that outcome, suddenly a life was born. A life that could destroy the Hollows, turning them to reishi sand, and once again allowing the world to circulate."

"Was that...the first Soul King?" a new soldier unintentionally murmured.

As though believing they had been impertinent, the new soldier rushed to cover their own mouth, but the Osho paid it no mind and nodded at those words.

"Indeed. Others such as myself, with special abilities,

had appeared, but the Reio was exceptional. It may even be said he had a power that was close to being almighty, omniscient and omnipotent."

Almost nostalgically, the Osho recalled the form of the past Reio who had long since disappeared from this throne.

"However, it was not as though the stagnation of the world had been averted by the simple act of destroying the Hollows. The Reio continued in that way to protect the world that would have slowly melted into chaos."

Taking a step forward and stroking his beard, the Osho continued. "But there were those who did not believe that was a good world. Although they did not reach the level of the Reio, there were five people who possessed powerful abilities. ...They were the ancestors of the Five Great Noble Clans, the Shiba family included."

The Osho spoke.

Their motives were different.

The Tsunayashiro clan's ancestor feared that the power of destruction might someday be turned against him.

Another clan's ancestor believed a lid was needed to cover the pit that would later become known as "hell."

The Kuchiki clan's ancestor believed a new order was needed to guide the world into stability.

The Shihoin clan's ancestor believed that an even greater cycle of circulation was needed to progress the stagnant world forward.

The Shiba clan's ancestor believed that it was necessary to explore the route of purification rather than destruction for Hollows, as Hollows also had minds.

Curiously, their different motives led them to the same goal: to separate the current world. There would be a reishi world, a kishi world, and also a sand paradise that would be the destination of the Hollows both worlds produced. Or, alternatively, other forms of worlds might come to being, but what was most important was to have worlds with a clear distinction between life and death.

In order to make the separation of the three realms reality, they required the power of the man who had transcended everything.

"It is said that the Shiba clan's ancestor attempted to persuade him, but in that opening, the Tsunayashiro clan's ancestor sealed the Reio into a crystal. I did not view what had happened then firsthand, but everything that followed is the history of the Soul Society itself."

The man who would later be called the Soul King...

Using his almighty power as the linchpin, the five created the foundations of the new world: The Soul Society, the world of the living, and Hueco Mundo.

Souls were given a division between life and death, and through that cycle, the world moved on to a new stage.

At some point, those who were tasked with managing the world came to be known as...

The *Soul Reapers*.

"He may have seen no future where it was avoidable no matter how he struggled, or he may have detected some kind of hope in the new world; it is impossible to fathom his will...but the Reio, it seems, intentionally did not resist."

At that point, the Osho cast his eyes down and returned to his telling. "However, the Tsunayashiro ancestor doubted even the Reio's nonresistance. He was most frightened of the Reio using his powers to escape the seal and destroy them. And so, without letting the Reio live or die, they tossed him into a contradictory spiral of simultaneous, continuous life and death. They even tore away his right and left arms that ruled 'stillness' and 'advancement.'"

The new soldiers held their breath while the members of Squad Zero, not including the Osho, remained silent, each with a unique expression on their face.

Then the Osho himself uttered a cruel fact in the same tone he might use to merely discuss the weather. "Well, that likely was not enough. With the Tsunayashiro leading them, several of the ancestors spent a great deal of time carving out the Reio's heart, whittling away his legs, scraping out all of his internal organs and removing them from his body. They did this in order to carve away his power and to render him simply a convenient figurehead for their benefit."

Taking in the Manako Osho's words, Senjumaru Shutara, who had been silent until that time, smiled as he said, "Unable to have a voice over the governance or the economy, in a body that couldn't so much as exhale, much less incite rebellion, he continued to act as the linchpin for the Soul Reapers. Though they are the ancestors of the Soul Reapers, the deeds they committed to create a puppet 'king' for themselves truly run deep."

At her words, which somehow seemed removed from the situation, the Osho nodded deeply; he then brought up another aspect of the story. "Yes, however, the Reio certainly had his own will. It might be appropriate to call it a 'flow' that essentially guided things over time… It was *because* he had a will that Ichigo Kurosaki and the others were called here. We felt it as well. It can be sensed by those whose bones are turned into Oken who have entrusted a part of their konpaku to the Reiokyu."

In actuality, the Reio's right and left arm each truly had exhibited their own wills and had returned to the Reiokyu in the end. The right arm that had long been worshipped by the Soul Society had done so to protect the world while the left arm had joined Yhwach as a natural-born Quincy seeking to return the world to how it was before. As though to agree with the Osho's words, Tenjiro Kirinji let his long toothpick bob up and down as he spoke animatedly. "Right on! Well, can't comment on his lineage, but the kid raised by the man from the Shiba family coming here under the Reio's will is a pretty entertaining turn of fate! Ain't it?!"

"Indeed. The Soul Reaper who was the ancestor of the Shiba clan opposed the Tsunayashiro clan continuing to forcibly seal the Reio away. 'We must make known far and wide the sin we have committed and entrust our judgment to the world,' the ancestor insisted. In addition, the Shiba ancestor had been searching for a technique to make their own body into a sacrifice in place of the Reio."

"Oh-ho, sure seems like something a Shiba ancestor would do."

"Mhmm. Those who persist in attempting to make themselves a sacrifice are in their own way the most self-indulgent kind. It seemed the Shiba ancestor was determined to become the linchpin of the three realms, had convincing the Reio failed, regardless of whether they had the power to or not... But when you consider that it was because the Tsunayashiro ancestor attacked the Reio that the Shiba family bloodline persisted, it is a very ironic story."

Kirio Hikifune's plump, round shoulders shook as she spoke of the past nostalgically. "The Shiba family, you say... Kaien certainly did have that way about him."

"Well, the Shiba ancestor was obscured from history by the Tsunayashiro family, and as a result, the remaining descendants ended up receiving a cold reception from the Five Great Noble Clans."

At that point, the Osho sighed emotionally and looked up at the ceiling. "However, when a Shiba descendant who bore the right character—Ichigo Kurosaki—showed up and truly did possess the attributes to take the Reio's place, I thought that was also fate. But seeing how that did not come to be, it seems the world might still need him."

Though the Osho attempted to end his tale with a light tone, the newcomers among the holy soldiers looked to each other, and several of their faces seemed pale under their uniform masks. The members of Squad Zero realized this was to be expected, because the truth the Osho spoke of hinted at something...

To wit, the very history of the Soul Reapers...

...had been built upon a crime more cruel than murder, and they continued to commit that sin.

≡

THE KYOGOKU

"If Yhwach is the ancestor of the group called Quincy, then the Reio itself is the source of the Quincies' powers. Whether the Reio left a child behind before he was sealed away or the power shredded away from the Reio took human shape and manifested itself, I do not know."

Tokinada, who had coincidentally finished speaking of the Soul Society's past at the same time as the Osho, happily released Hisagi's Kazeshini. Calculating when the Soul Reaper would lose his balance, Tokinada flung the flames of Ryujin Jakka at Hisagi and tried to burn the Soul Reaper. Had Hisagi not sensed the heat instantly and realized that he needed to retreat, he likely would have been turned into charcoal.

What was dreadful was that, while his opponents were wary of Complete Hypnosis and thus had been passive, Tokinada continued to skillfully evade the attacks on him as he spoke. He wanted to see Hisagi's face in despair. Just for that reason, Tokinada had, in a show of eccentricity, put his life on the line, disclosing the past the Tsunayashiro family had held so tight. Everyone there understood it was specifically his nature that allowed him to employ such a strategy.

"Don't you think it is a humorous story, through and through? The Soul King you so desperately protected is the savior of humanity that my ancestor trapped. That means that Yhwach was trying to save his ancestor, or perhaps someone who should be called father. And the fate he needed saving from was isolation for one million years, unable to live or die!"

Speaking sonorously, Tokinada continued to swing his own shapeless Zanpaku-to.

Liltotto and the others saw an opening and released arrows, but they all missed Tokinada. The Arrancars' Ceros produced the same result.

Tokinada used Kyoka Suigetsu's ability to make them believe that human-shaped clods of dirt created through

Tsuchinamazu were himself. When Hisagi was able to attack properly, they would be able to time their attacks with him to accurately grasp Tokinada's position, but as Hisagi had steadily sustained an increasing number of injuries and the frequency of his attacks had slowed, Tokinada just barely had to move in order to evade those attacks.

"Yhwach wanted to return the world to its original state and release his father through death. I do not know which was secondary to the other. However, as a result, Yhwach consumed the Reio's body and is currently the linchpin of the world in the Reio's place. Don't you think that is so ironic? Eh, Kyoraku?"

When he heard Tokinada, Kyoraku smiled slightly and exhaled slowly as though to show his composure despite being riddled with wounds.

"Well, one does wonder. Though it is slightly difficult for me to ascertain whether what you say is the truth or nonsense at the moment... And in practice, it's irrelevant to our situation."

"Don't utter such transparent lies. You should know, with the position you are in right now, shouldn't you? The information that Sosuke Aizen and Kisuke Urahara knew several hundred years ago—who would believe you that you did not know of it?"

"I don't mind if you don't believe me. The only thing that's certain is that if I don't stop you right now, the world of the living, the Soul Society, and Hueco Mundo will end up in total chaos."

"No, the only thing that is certain is that you will all die here." Tokinada, whose smile was full of joy, continued to provoke. "Hm, right! You Soul Reapers have no such thing as justice! Naturally, I don't either! What we have here is the descendants of villains attempting to steal an encampment, and nothing more. If there were justice in this world, then it likely would have resided in Kaname Tosen himself!"

Tokinada swung his zanpaku-to again and created a large quantity of ice using Daiguren Hyorinmaru, which he broke in pieces using the gigantic blade of Ten Ken, and scattered a barrage of ice chunks across their field of vision.

He made them believe each of those glittering bits of ice were different attacks and, using the difficult-to-evade illusive blades, lambasted the wasteland that had been the courtyard.

In order to protect Kyoraku, Nanao continued to put up barriers that would defend against all kinds of attacks. By developing multiple kinds of barriers all at once, she depleted herself far more harshly than with any normal kido, and her spiritual power was close to bottoming out.

"Don't worry about me, Nanao. Just focus on protecting yourself."

At Kyoraku's words, Nanao scowled and answered, "Prioritizing the Captain General is a given."

"This isn't official business right now. We've come here to

fight under a personal grudge of sorts."

"In that case, I need to protect you all the more."

At Nanao's breezy reply, Kyoraku's expression became complex as he again gripped his zanpaku-to.

"But it's starting to look like a free-for-all. Still, I would think there would be some kind of restriction on it…"

Not wanting to let the barriers Nanao had created go to waste, Kyoraku honed his senses and observed the reishi that flowed between Tokinada and his zanpaku-to.

He felt something off about Tokinada's spiritual pressure.

"Hm? It couldn't be."

Kyoraku's spiritual perception gathered that Tokinada's spiritual pressure itself was changing, or not so much changing as degrading and degenerating, though very slowly.

"This…Tokinada…it can't be that you're shaving away at your own life force?!"

"Oh! You did well noticing that so quickly! Kha ha ha ha! Although, what else should I have expected from you?"

Tokinada spoke matter-of-factly and did not even attempt to keep that fact secret, almost as though he were claiming that such a thing was not a weakness.

"That is the reason why the previous head of the family did not want to carry this zanpaku-to. Enra Kyoten consumes its wielder's life. The more it is used, the more it will continue to consume my konpaku, and that konpaku will never return. It is a curse similar to the Ise family's Hakkyoken."

As though to protect Nanao from Tokinada, who smiled as he fixed a stare on her, Kyoraku took a step forward and queried the man he had once studied alongside. "I really do not understand. Are you really willing to go so far as to wager your life simply for your own gratification?"

"What meaning is there to a life which you do not risk for enjoyment? Even my wife died for her own sacrifice—or something like that. There is only one difference—whether it was virtuous or not. That is the only minute difference there is to society."

The head of the Tsunayashiro family was given the duty of ruling history and keeping the treasured sword, generation after generation. However, most who learned of the treasured sword's peculiarity would relinquish it in that moment, in fear of death. Those who could master it would be proud to wield the venerable Enra Kyoten, which boasted power without peer. But the head of the family could overpower other Soul Reapers simply through political influence, without even needing to use Enra Kyoten. Furthermore, the family was in a position to leave the Hollows and Quincies to the Court Guards, so there had not been many who had willingly pared away their own life in order to use the sword.

Since they also could not allow it to be stolen by the other families, they had continued to seal it away in a secret depository that only the head of family was privy to. However, after that cycle had repeated through the generations, an outlier named Tokinada had appeared. The treasonous agitator who did not fear his own death in the slightest had stolen that zanpaku-to while the previous head of family was still alive. He did not do so for his own dignity, his own morality, or for the sake of another, much less the sake of the world itself; he simply risked his own life for the sake of pleasure.

He was different from Kenpachi, who wagered everything he had in order to whittle away his own life alongside his opponent in battle. Tokinada was an aberration who wouldn't mind sacrificing a year of his own life in order to ridicule the weak for a century.

It was this essential part of Tokinada's nature that made him able to master that cursed zanpaku-to with no scruples, and this was why he was now able to stand in Kyoraku and the others' way using Enra Kyoten as the supreme, unyielding, and indestructible zanpaku-to it truly was.

However...

As those around him were solely focused on defending themselves, a single man was steadily regaining his composure. Kaname Tosen's name had been used, which was one way of incurring his wrath, but regardless of that that man moved calmly as he read the spiritual pressure of Tokinada's attacks and narrowly dodged each one of them.

As though Tokinada himself had noticed that the purposefulness of the man's movements had returned, he asked the man, Shuhei Hisagi, whose eyes were still closed, "You're very quiet... Why don't you speak up, Shuhei Hisagi? I am speaking about the 'truth' that you so love."

"..."

In response to Tokinada's question, the Soul Reaper simply answered with silence.

"What a dull fellow you are. Is your brain not able to comprehend the truth that I thrust before it? I expected at the very least you would cry and shout about Kaname Tosen, as you seem to cling to the man so."

In spite of Tokinada's words, Hisagi remained composed. Had he heard such words under normal circumstances, he might have shouted out, "That's nonsense," and succumbed to his rage. However, the fear that accompanied the darkness of Hisagi's closed eyes kept his mind calm. In this situation of having intentionally shuttered his vision, the tale Tokinada told about his raison d'etre brought something from Hisagi's past back into his present mind.

≡

THE PAST, THE SOUL SOCIETY

The darkness was present.

In that place not a ray of light, no sound, no smell, not even the faintest quiver of spiritual pressure existed—the space was dominated by endless darkness and silence.

Reflexively swallowing his saliva, he only felt his throat move—no sound was produced by the action. He shivered and felt his teeth occasionally grinding together, but of course, he sensed nothing but the tactility of that action.

To Shuhei Hisagi at that moment, the world had contracted to consist only of the pressure under his feet and the feeling of his zanpaku-to gripped in his hand.

Hisagi wondered whether the Muken that he had heard rumors of was a place like this and thought that the criminals who had been trapped in such a place would surely have broken before even a day passed. Hisagi made that abrupt conjecture because he instinctively understood that if he did not think of something, he would end up crushed by his fear.

Just how long would this hell of nothingness go on?

He felt like he could hear something behind him.

However, he only *felt* as though he had heard something.

In actuality the soundlessness had continued, but Hisagi could not help but feel that there was something there.

A monster.

A monster vastly more frightening than any Hollow was immediately behind him, opening its huge maw.

A memory of his old friend's death came into his mind.

In the next moment, the face of his friend's corpse was replaced with his own...

Before he realized it, he had swung his zanpaku-to around toward his back.

However, he wasn't able to complete the swing.

Hisagi started to shout, believing there really was some kind of monster there, but...

The darkness suddenly cleared.

"Huh..."

Abruptly, all his senses returned and Hisagi remembered. This was the Soul Society at midday, and he was in a forest within the Rukongai that few people approached. And he realized what had stopped his blade was the blade of his captain—his superior officer—at which point he quickly lowered his arms.

"...Captain Tosen."

He was soaked with sweat, and slightly delayed, his heart started thumping fast.

The light returned, the sound returned, the smells returned, and Hisagi was surrounded by the feeling of being alive.

"I determined that any longer would be dangerous. First, steady your breathing."

"...I'm sorry. My actions were shameful."

Though Hisagi lowered his head and gasped for breath, Tosen, who stood before him, quietly shook his head.

"There is nothing to apologize for or feel embarrassed about. If your senses are abruptly stolen, it's natural to feel fear. As someone who never had light to begin with, I lost the ability to even move when my hearing was blocked."

"How long was I...in the darkness?"

"Not even a half hour has passed."

Hearing those words, Hisagi, who was convinced that it had been several hours, was once again mortified by his own inexperience. When he looked up reflexively, the black curtain that had been created over the forest before him collapsed and converged into the zanpaku-to blade Tosen held.

"Is this your bankai, Captain?"

"Suzumushi Tsuishiki, Enma Korogi. That is my bankai's name."

What Kaname Tosen first revealed to Hisagi after the Soul Reaper had been appointed assistant captain was his bankai. Normally, one would not share the secret of their bankai so easily with another. No matter how powerful a bankai was, to recklessly allow it to be recognized might eventually become the cause of one's defeat. That Tosen, who was normally so guarded, would purposefully show Hisagi his bankai, was so that Hisagi could be taught the true nature of *fear*, Tosen had told him.

Though he felt ashamed that was the only reason he was being shown the bankai, Hisagi also felt hope that his captain had that degree of trust in him. However, what Tosen said next made Hisagi embarrassed for himself.

"You certainly do have fear within yourself. However, I still do not sense fear from your sword and your words."

With Tosen's straightforward statement, Hisagi hung his head. He understood his own immaturity. He feared only the darkness and had swung his sword blindly. He compulsively brandished his power in order to dispel and shake off his fear. He was far from reaching the level of Tosen, who fought while allowing the fear to lurk within him.

As Hisagi silently wallowed, Tosen said in a steady tone, "Fear takes many forms."

Tosen put his zanpaku-to into its sheath and turned toward the sky. It was almost as though his eyes, though unseeing, were following the clouds flowing by.

"The jet-black world you just experienced would provoke fear in anyone. Whether someone knows no light or sound from the start, when a person is born, and when they realize there is a world they did not know about, they will feel fear just the same. Someone who does not fear that in the slightest wouldn't be human, or Soul Reaper or Hollow; they would be a monster from a place unfamiliar to us."

"A monster?"

"One who does not know fear will eventually become a monster. The more you and I abandon our fear, the more we move away from being warriors, and the more we approach becoming heartless metastases. That is something you should not forget."

"I don't think that would happen to you, Captain Tosen."

To Hisagi, Tosen was perfect as a warrior and as a Soul Reaper. It would have been one thing for this to happen to someone inexperienced like Hisagi, but if Tosen abandoned his fear, it would only have been because he had conquered it. There was no possibility that his actions would ever lead down the incorrect path, Hisagi thought at the time.

But then Tosen spoke as though admonishing Hisagi and even himself. "I do not know the light. Nor do I see the colors that delineate the world."

"Captain...?"

"If a time comes when I learn about those things, and I see only hope and pleasure in the remade world, and I forget my fear—at that time, perhaps, I will stop being a warrior."

Tosen turned his sightless eyes toward Hisagi and expressed simply the words that had been confined within his soul. "We must continue to carry our fear of the path we walk, our pride as Soul Reapers, and we must protect the world itself. Because when we have a path we have yet to know, pride we have yet to learn, and a world we have yet to experience in front of us, we cannot expect that the ground we stand upon will be peaceful forever."

≡

PRESENT DAY, THE KYOGOKU

The world that Kaname Tosen had decided was evil...

Hisagi thought that his mind had accepted it but that his heart had not.

Why did Captain Tosen despise Soul Reapers to such an extent?

It wasn't just Tokinada Tsunayashiro individually, but the existence of Soul Reapers themselves that he hated.

Realizing that answer was in the sin that Tokinada spoke of, Hisagi muttered to himself, "I wasn't afraid of anything... I didn't understand anything."

"Hm? What are you going on about?" Tokinada was deeply curious when the Soul Reaper finally spoke, not understanding the meaning of the words coming from Hisagi's mouth.

However, instead of answering Tokinada's question, Hisagi continued to fire off those words with anger clearly directed at himself. "I was always convinced that I was right. That was why I went into the fight with the resolve to open Captain Tosen's eyes."

Tosen's words were revived in Hisagi's mind, words he spoke when the man had stood in his way as Aizen's retainer.

"You haven't changed at all. Even in those words of yours, there wasn't a hint of fear lurking in them."

They were words that he had recalled earlier when he was speaking with Tessai in Karakura Town as well.

However, they struck Hisagi's heart with a different significance now.

I might be the one who's actually wrong. It might be my sense of justice and the world that I'm standing in that's wrong. I never even thought of that possibility. I thought Captain Tosen had just been tempted by Aizen.

Someone who does not fear the blade they swing has no right to fight.

Tosen always said that. That blade wasn't just a zanpa-ku-to. Tosen likened the justice itself he brandished to a blade. What Tokinada said was likely the truth. There was no reason for him to lie now, and it was consistent with what Aizen had said. Then, most of all, it was more than enough of an answer as to why Tosen had determined the Soul Society itself was evil.

Kaname Tosen had despised Soul Reapers and the Soul Society because the existence of the former and the history of the latter were themselves a betrayal of the wishes of Tosen's own friend.

It wasn't Tokinada individually.

The Soul Society's "justice," which covered the world in clouds that could never be cleared, yet continued to give the false hope that the clouds could be dispersed, might have been Kaname Tosen's true enemy.

I wasn't scared of the Soul Reapers' and Court Guards' justice in the slightest. And the only reason I wasn't was because

I believed in the Soul Reapers' justice! While Captain Tosen went on this whole time carrying his fear...

"If I really feared fighting, then why did I...? Why didn't I try to hear Captain Tosen out? I just kept spewing non-sense about how I was going to 'open his eyes'!"

As Hisagi spoke out loud in frustration and Tokinada listened, Tokinada's expression was permeated with joy, as though he had finally been released from his tedium.

"Ah! I see! So you're regretful then? Because without knowing what Kaname Tosen's true feelings were, you shamelessly insisted that you were an ally of justice! Then what will you do about it? Do you wish to rewind time? Would you return to the middle of the fight, shedding tears as you join Tosen's side under Aizen?" Tokinada continued deliberately, as though tormenting an ant by plucking off its legs.

Ultimately, Hisagi did not turn the brunt of his words at himself, but at Tokinada.

"But I still don't intend to claim that Captain Tosen was right. Even if everything you said was true...regardless of that, I would still probably stand in Tosen's way."

"Hm... Then how about we try to reproduce that?"

Then Tokinada drew a new power from Enra Kyoten.

"What do you think you really accomplished back then? The justice that Tosen adhered to was itself pure. Don't you think that when faced with that, your justice and your textbook truths are flimsy?"

He shot toward Hisagi countless blades that separated into long, needle-like shapes.

"Suzumushi Nishiki, Beni Hiko."

In order to provoke Hisagi, Tokinada had brazenly used Tosen's—and also his own former wife Kakyo's—zanpaku-to power.

However...

The jet-black chain that connected the two blades of Kazeshini swept aside the countless blades with precision.

"What?"

It was almost as though his eyes had seen them all—no, even if he had been able to see them, Hisagi had manipulated the chain in a way that usually would have been impossible for him. Seeing that made Tokinada's grin disappear.

Then, with a transparent hostility that had not been apparent in his words until then, Hisagi said, "Don't talk about justice."

Did he have the right to condemn Tokinada? While accepting that he would walk a path alongside that fear itself, Hisagi wagered his own fate as he challenged Tokinada.

"A bastard like you who hasn't got any fear of death...has no right to talk about Captain Tosen."

CHAPTER TWENTY-THREE

"HA HA HA! I SEE! I SEE! It seems your swipes at me have reached a new level of refinement! How entertaining!"

It was not just the speed that had changed. Faced with Kazeshini's discernibly increasing accuracy with each successive throw, Tokinada was still delighted and smiling as he continued to dodge every attack. Tokinada accurately saw through the angle and force with which Kazeshini flew as well as the shifting contortions of the chain. Reacting to those, he responded to them by calling upon various forms and abilities of zanpaku-to swords.

However, Kazeshini's speed continued to increase until Tokinada was trapped in a cramped space barely the size of a tatami mat. The intervals between swipes contracted until he could hardly step a foot out of that range. The way in which Hisagi manipulated the revolving sickles using the chain and the technique with which he trapped

Tokinada without binding the man's body were like a perfect demonstration of martial arts skills.

Though Tokinada attempted to immobilize the zanpaku-to, cutting it using Wabisuke to multiply its weight, the moment he attempted to manifest that blade, Kazeshini writhed like a living animal with its own will and evaded the attack by a paper-thin margin.

Can he see then?

Tokinada was dubious. In order to test his theory, he created a wall of flames between him and Hisagi using Ryujin Jakka and then tried to cut the blade with Wabisuke, but of course the result was the same.

I suppose that the flames aren't strong enough to melt a zanpaku-to with my spiritual pressure. Even if I dedicated the entirety of my spiritual pressure toward doing that, I wouldn't be able to raise the temperature to that point.

Tokinada looked at Kazeshini's blade as it cut through the wall of flames. As he fully grasped that Hisagi really was perceiving his movements through spiritual pressure perception alone, it also sank in that his spiritual pressure would never reach anywhere near Genryusai Yamamoto's. Had he been able to use Genryusai Yamamoto's actual Ryujin Jakka, he could have burned everything away with a heat strong enough to evaporate even a zanpaku-to; the whole matter would have been resolved using that single ability, without any reliance on Complete Hypnosis.

Still, I need to deal with him before all the riffraff around here recover.

If he dedicated enough spiritual pressure to his attack to burn all of them in an instant, he would have to decrease the spiritual pressure he was putting into Complete Hypnosis by an equal amount, and it was possible that would end up creating an opening he couldn't control.

The scales began to quiver in Tokinada's mind.

He supposed he needed to consider whether to deliberately torture all of them to death, as he had been doing thus far, or first kill 80 percent of his enemies in order to cause Kyoraku despair. As for Kenpachi, if Hikone were to end up at a disadvantage he could simply have Aura, who was not susceptible to physical attacks, deal with him. If Tokinada were the type of man who would choose to kill them all instantly, he likely wouldn't have even thought up this foolish plan to begin with. Because Tokinada's wish wasn't to abandon everything he had to fulfill some great moral cause, but simply to fill the twisted vessel of his own heart with amusement.

However, Tokinada also didn't wish to lower his guard and allow them to launch a counterattack on him. As Hisagi's attacks had become more intense, the offense from those around him had also steadily increased in momentum. The Quincies' arrows and the Arrancars' Ceros followed Kazeshini's attacks. Bringing out the abilities of the zanpaku-to to counter them, Tokinada parried or canceled each one, or occasionally sent them flying back to his opponent.

I see. He's just an assistant captain, so how can he be so...

When Tokinada realized that Kazeshini's throwing maneuvers were faster in speed than they had previously been in the footage Tokinada had seen, he attempted to amend several of his strategies. However, before he could even produce another zanpaku-to ability, the next blow would come down on him.

Hm...? Is he becoming even faster?

As Tokinada determined that his opponent was someone he could not let his guard down around at all, he imagined the moment he would make his powerful opponent submit, letting his mouth soften as he let Senbon Zakura expand around him...

In the next moment, everyone around saw it.

Even as it was scraped by the blizzard of blades, Kazeshini flicked everything away with its abnormally powerful rotations. Then, from a gap that had been wrenched open through Senbon Zakura, the second sickle closed in on Tokinada...

That was the moment that Tokinada's right arm, which held Enra Kyoten, was severed and flung high into the air.

"Guh...?!"

"Lord Tokinada...?"

As Tokinada cried out in pain, Aura's eyes widened.

"Impossible... How could he break through Senbon Zakura's wall?!"

At the same time that his agonized cries rang out, the wall Senbon Zakura had formed around Tokinada and Aura disappeared like smoke, revealing a scene of Tokinada holding the end of his elbow. Those surrounding all began to make their moves at once, as though this were their once-in-a-lifetime chance.

"Hah! You didn't just drop your zanpaku-to—you dropped your entire arm! Pathetic!"

The impetus of Candice promptly driving a Galvano Javelin at Tokinada allowed the Quincies' Heilig Pfeil to pierce through him as well, and Grimmjow enveloped his body in a Cero.

"Once they start to crumble, it's over way too soon."

As Madarame watched Tokinada's broken body collapse on the ground, he shouldered the long shaft of Hozukimaru and looked disappointed.

"Well, even if he could use the same zanpaku-to, he still just wasn't on Aizen's level," Yumichika murmured, though he didn't let his guard down.

Though they had also endured severe wounds, they remained combat-ready through sheer willpower. Tokinada had collapsed, but the mysterious woman who seemed to be a Fullbringer was still going strong.

As the Soul Reapers in front of him surrounded and blocked Aura, Hisagi desperately steadied his breathing in order to calm his thumping heart. Perhaps in reaction to the fact that he had continued to manipulate Kazeshini at a pace that was beyond his limit, Hisagi's spiritual pressure seemed to billow inside of him until he felt as though all the cells in his entire body were going to rip open.

"Did we...do it?"

Feeling that Tokinada's spiritual pressure, which had been present until just a moment ago, had vanished, Hisagi lowered his shoulders in relief.

However, a lingering gloom remained in his heart. He had let himself fall into the maelstrom of revenge in the end, hadn't he? All he had done was kill the man who had caused Tosen despair and who, out of sheer hatred, had stolen the former captain's life.

...I haven't got time to think. I need to do something about Aura and Hikone...

Hisagi forcibly changed his mood, but...

"What you have isn't hate."

Suddenly, these words he had heard in the past repeated in his head.

"All you have is sentimentality for Kaname Tosen and what he left behind after he disappeared."

Whose words were those?

"You would do well to remember this..."

"Regardless of whether you have strong resolve—"

Perhaps those recollections were being revived in his mind by Hisagi's accumulated experiences as a Soul Reaper, in order to serve as a warning.

Back in reality, Muguruma's angry shout reached Hisagi's ears.

"Whoa! Hey! Careful, Shuhei! The woman went that way!"

Oh! Did he mean Aura?!

Aura's spiritual pressure was scarce, so he couldn't sense her using his spiritual pressure perception. In order to grasp her movements, he opened his eyes in a fluster. As he did so, he remembered the last fragment of the words that had just been reverberating in his mind.

"You cannot defeat the strong simply through sentimentality."

Hisagi realized those had been Aizen's words...

...and as he slowly opened his eyes, the blade in front of him shattered almost simultaneously.

≡

"Huh?!"

At the same time that Kyoka Suigetsu's shikai activated in front of Hisagi's eyes, the world that had been shown in Muguruma's and Yoruichi's eyes shattered, exposing the state of reality. Tokinada's body, which had been crumpled until that point, and Aura's body had switched places. Aura, who had been standing in front of Hisagi, had turned into Tokinada.

Looking at Tokinada, who was wearing a strange coat, Yoruichi clucked her tongue.

"A spiritual pressure interception cloak!"

When she saw the cloak that Kisuke Urahara had developed, she immediately realized what had happened. The moment that Tokinada had enveloped them in Senbon Zakura, he had changed places with Aura and invoked Complete Hypnosis. He had made them believe he was Aura and she was him. He made Kazeshini cut through an earthen clump created using Tsuchinamazu and cried out in anguish at the same time but had never actually let go of his sword, not even for a moment.

Then he had made the others believe they saw Aura approaching Hisagi, in order to make them warn him.

While Hisagi continued to stand there in shock, Aura, who had been pretending to be Tokinada crumpled on the ground, slowly stood up.

"That was a terrible thing you did, Lord Tokinada."

Aura, who really had been on the receiving end of all kinds of attacks from those around her, was entirely unharmed down to her clothes.

"You can't be hurt by any cuts or Ceros anyway. Don't complain when all I did was use you as a dummy." Tokinada's words reverberated in Hisagi's ears.

Looking into Hisagi's eyes, Tokinada said happily, "Good grief, what a pity it is that all your friends are such simpletons."

Returning to Aura's side, Tokinada once again swung the flaming blade of Ryujin Jakka and kept those around who had begun to approach him in check.

Snickering, he fired off words deliberately chosen to provoke Hisagi. "Aizen would have easily seen through a trap like this. No, if you just had the prudence of Tosen, he wouldn't have said anything careless enough to cause you to open your eyes."

Then he looked up at Kenpachi and Hikone, who were continuing their fierce clash of swords in the sky, and he said to Aura next to him, "Well then, there's no issue if Hikone can defeat *the Kenpachi* with their own abilities, but...I suppose I'll kill everyone here first. Or perhaps I should leave that reporter as a living witness?" Tokinada shrugged, and then, as though another thought had abruptly come to mind, he asked about something else. "Come to think of it, what happened to the Fullbringers that I left to you? I thought Kugo Ginjo was also here?"

"Oh, but you *are* you. I thought you already knew what happened to them."

"Based on the reports from the surveillance spirit bugs' mock brains, I know they seemed to have fought each other, but...what trick did you use to cause that?"

"It was President Yukio's abilities—after I amplified his powers."

Static noise ran through the air behind Aura, and a boy showed his face.

"It was a piece of cake. I stuck a virus into my 'past,' and when Tsukishima stuck his bookmark in me, I hacked him instead."

"Oh, so your Fullbring is that powerful then, boy?"

"As long as I've got the resources, modding a program is like breathing to me. After that, I just had Tsukishima stick the same virus in the other two."

As though to prove his words, Ginjo and the others appeared from the static one after another. It was almost as though they had lost their emotions. When he saw them stand expressionlessly like dolls, Tokinada smiled happily.

"I see, I see. He had been a close candidate for the Soul King after Ichigo Kurosaki. At minimum, he will likely be of assistance to the linchpin that maintains the three realms."

Tokinada slowly turned his zanpaku-to hilt toward Ginjo and the others. The surrounding Soul Reapers, Arrancars, and Quincies were being restrained once again by the remanifested Gagaku Kairo horde's automatic predatory abilities.

"Just in case, I'm going to show them Kyoka Suigetsu's shikai. You don't mind, do you?"

"Not at all, please go ahead."

Aura bowed elegantly as she spoke, and Tokinada attempted to invoke his Kyoka Suigetsu's shikai, but...

"Hm...?"

It would not invoke.

He scowled, and in the momentary opening when he looked at his own hand...

Ginjo had more than enough opportunity to make a move.

Without a word, he unleashed a blow, seeming to have unsheathed a sword with the most minimal of movements.

The Cross of Scaffold.

The necklace charm that he gripped in his hand instantly transformed into a longsword that he used to dispatch a slashing attack like that of Zangetsu's.

Tokinada attempted to receive that blow using a Zangetsu himself...

...but the newly created Zangetsu blade broke to smithereens when faced with Ginjo's attack, which simply slashed right across Tokinada's torso.

"What is with you? You're way sturdier than I thought you'd be."

Though Ginjo had unleashed a blow with enough force that he thought it should have bisected the Soul Reaper, Tokinada's spiritual pressure might have been greater than he had imagined, since the wound stopped right above the man's ribs.

Tokinada, who had been unable to use Zangetsu, healed his wound using Hisagomaru as he muttered to himself, "Good grief, it seems that Enra Kyoten can only depict Zangetsu's outer form, considering the sword has a special origin."

"Even if you used the real deal, I would've won against a swordsman like you."

With his usual daring smile on his face, Ginjo squeezed his longsword in his hand.

Though Tokinada attempted to invoke Kyoka Suigetsu's shikai again, it was as though it were being blocked, and he could not make it shatter into the form.

"Do you remember the method in which Kyoka Suigetsu can be rendered powerless?" Aura's monotone voice spilled from her smiling face.

Kyoka Suigetsu was a zanpaku-to of absolute superior power once it was invoked. However, it had a weakness as a result of that. If the target were to touch the blade before it was invoked, then Complete Hypnosis could not be implemented.

Had Tokinada been Aizen, he might have been able to fulfill the conditions of having those around him see the shikai the moment it was invoked. However, now that someone other than Aizen was using the blade, another weakness was involved. Tokinada's spiritual pressure was nowhere near Aizen's level, and because of that, it was possible for the shikai transformation itself to be sealed through incredibly strong spiritual pressure.

Then again, there were very few who had spiritual pressure that exceeded Tokinada's and who could also skillfully perform such a feat. Because of that, he took his time creating an opening to show the powerhouses Kyoraku and Yoruichi his shikai.

There were a limited number of people in that place who had spiritual pressure comparable to or exceeding Tokinada's who also were not under the effects of Complete Hypnosis. There was Hikone Ubuginu, Kenpachi Zaraki, Kugo Ginjo...

...and Aura Michibane.

The moment he turned his eyes to her, she had already finished her work. At the same time he felt himself being put under restraints, he also felt something else coming from Enra Kyoten, which he gripped. He realized that, at that moment, every single one of the many different blades that were manifested in that place were being touched by something.

"She's attacking her own people? Why...?"

Nanao saw one of the patterned tentacles that had just blocked Kyoraku's attack twist itself around Tokinada's entire body.

"Don't let your guard down. This might also be an illusion that Complete Hypnosis is creating."

Tokinada and Aura stood between the still quivering flames from earlier, and after looking at Ginjo and the others, Kyoraku narrowed his eyes as he quietly said, "Even if it isn't just an illusion, we probably should not allow ourselves to be seized by optimism."

≡

Aura Michibane was missing something.

If asked what it was she was missing, she could not answer that question. If Hollows acted in order to fill the hole in their chest, Aura herself did not even have a desire to fill anything.

Love.

That was the emotion she was missing.

She had no interest in anything, and since her childhood she spent her days intently carrying out the orders given by those around her. She had no attachment to the world whatsoever; even when she recalled the days she had spent with her father, shut away in the room that was like a glass jar, she still had no deep emotions, even to this day.

Because she had no attachments, she had no hopes; conversely, she did not have the despair to wish to die of her own accord either. In the complex system of the world, she spent her days spinning like a cog. She had thought she was fine with that. She thought she was fine simply adjusting to fit the flow of others and continuing to turn until her body rotted away.

The event that had created a change in that "cog" occurred just half a year earlier.

When she had been ordered by Tokinada to put together all kinds of konpaku and body fragments in order to create a Soul Reaper, no emotion or disgust rose from within her. However, even for her, to take the elements of Soul Reapers and Quincies that normally clashed, as well as peculiar components called Fragments of the Reio, and to put them together to create a life was a nearly impossible endeavor.

The project had sustained her concentration in a way that had never happened before in her life, and finally, at the moment the *thing* created spiritual pressure, which could be said to be a Soul Reaper's pulse of life...

She realized that she was smiling.

It wasn't a smile of relief that she had managed to bring safely to life the work she had been given. Instead, she felt unconditional love for the new life she had created with her very own hands.

The woman who had been only a cog had become someone who could create. That was perhaps the moment she truly took a step out of the glass case. At the same time, that moment was when she learned about fear.

From her own common sense, she knew this life could hardly be said to be a proper being. She knew that it was commonly accepted that lives were equal, but in the Soul Society, where the aristocratic system was celebrated, that way of thinking would not hold up.

Aura realized that because, for some time, she had known...

She knew how Tokinada Tsunayashiro planned to use this life.

All this being would do was reign over the world in the place of the Soul King. When she was faced with the reality that the life she had created was simply meant to execute Tokinada's orders and, as the "next Soul King," act as fuel to make the system that made the three realms, the Soul Society, the world of the living, and Hueco Mundo, continue, Aura's world completely changed.

Or, it may be more appropriate to say the blank sheet her world had been until then started to gain color.

After some time, when the Soul Reaper who had been named Hikone called out to Aura with their own voice, it became even more obvious.

"You're Ms. Aura, aren't you?! Lord Tokinada told me that you're almost like a mother to me! I don't really know what a mother is, but it's nice to meet you!"

Their eyes were innocent and contained not even the slightest hint of ill will. She realized they were the same eyes she saw in her own face when she had stared at the glass wall during the days of her youth. She realized that time had filled her heart, and that, in the past, she had been happy living her days locked away in that place with her father.

But had that really been *right*?

At this point, she couldn't know whether her father had confined her out of parental love, a desire for control, or

possibly for some other reason entirely. Something she hadn't considered even after she had entered the outside world was now being thrust at her. At the same time she learned about love, she realized the missing piece that was somehow warping her all this time was just that. Regardless, Aura thought she didn't mind continuing to be that way herself.

However, for Hikone, this innocently smiling being she herself had created, to be subject to the same fate—no, an even worse fate in which they were to eternally preserve the bedrock of the world—was now something Aura just could not allow.

And this was why she had come to a secret resolve in her mind.

She would rescue Hikone's future from Tokinada's hands.

Hikone might curse at her, telling her that following Tokinada's directions had made them happy. There was a chance that Hikone would shout at her, "Why did you stick your nose where it doesn't belong?" and Hikone's konpaku might rot away from their hatred.

Yet in the same way that her father had shut her away out of his own egoistic desires...

...her own sense of ego compelled her to teach Hikone about the vast world.

Even Aura did not know which would mean happiness and which would mean sorrow for Hikone. It was just that she wanted to give this to Hikone, the being she herself had created. By giving Hikone a vast number of options, she wanted to give them the right to make their own choice, of their own volition.

She wanted to provide the light that would illuminate what Hikone Ubuginu's soul desired.

She believed that even if Hikone chose to follow Tokinada and hated her, that was fine too. She couldn't be certain that what awaited at the end of Hikone's selected path would be happiness.

Even if becoming Tokinada's puppet for eternity might have been far more peaceful than another possible path, one that might result in Hikone caving in partway through, starving and in pain...

She just wanted to show it to Hikone.

She wanted to show them the infinite variety of paths that extended into the future.

That was why she had resolved herself to stop Tokinada.

She would do it even if that meant that her own life would end before she herself had chosen a path of her own will.

≡

"That was unexpected. I had no idea you would attempt something so foolish," Tokinada groaned.

Aura answered matter-of-factly, "Oh, I actually find this even more surprising. You acted as though you didn't trust anyone, with no exceptions, Lord Tokinada."

She hadn't been treated particularly terribly by Tokinada. Because of that, she didn't hold a grudge that caused her to desire his death; Aura was satisfied simply stopping Tokinada. However, the reality was that it would be difficult to stop him without killing him, so Aura had prepared herself to destroy Tokinada for the sake of saving Hikone. Because of that, she had also prepared herself to be cut down and killed by Tokinada as well.

Aura was hoping that in the worst case, things would end in a draw, but...

"What are you talking about? I knew that you would betray me from the start."

"Huh?"

At the moment Tokinada spoke, her konpaku felt something abnormal happening in her physical body.

"What I found unexpected...was the timing. I thought you would betray me a bit before this or a bit after."

"Huh?"

Then, Tokinada, who should have been immobilized, narrowly dodged Ginjo's blow.

"Huh?"

When she saw that her restraints were not working on him, Aura realized the identity of the abnormality she felt in her body. At the same time, she went down on her knee on the spot.

"What's wrong?"

Ginjo was questioning her, but Aura had trouble even breathing, and she couldn't make a sound.

"Ah...uh..."

"Does it feel strange? Do you wonder why you cannot turn to fog and escape? Or why your spiritual pressure is rapidly disappearing?"

Tokinada, who easily cut away the patterned tentacle, looked down upon Aura with a contemptuous smile.

"I see. With your power, you really should be able to touch all of the Enra Kyoten that I have in this place—even the blades that have turned to ash and the ones that have turned into living creatures."

In order to protect himself, he caused more of the strange monsters of Gagaku Kairo to emerge. "I told you, didn't I? The Seireitei is a den of thieves." Tokinada then glanced at one specific Soul Reaper as he said, "Do not forget that a common soldier could be carrying a zanpaku-to that has the exact wrong affinity for them...didn't I say that?"

When Yumichika heard those words, he narrowed his eyes and glared at Tokinada with murderous hostility.

There's no way I'd mistake it for anything else.

The presence he felt from Tokinada's side...

Though normally the spiritual pressures of zanpaku-to could not be distinguished, it was a different matter once one became paired with a blade to the point they could call them by their name. He truly did sense a Reiraku color that was exactly the same as the zanpaku-to in his own hand from Tokinada.

BLEACH Can't Fear Your Own World III

It's likely empty on the inside, but the feeling coming from it is the same.

He had no idea what kind of powers Aura had or what she had been doing. But the one thing he was sure about was...

That Tokinada guy is attacking that woman using Ruriirokujaku's power.

Ruriirokujaku.

The zanpaku-to could absorb all the opponent's spiritual power and debilitate them.

That power had been invoked against Aura. Even if she turned her own body into mist, the spiritual power that controlled that mist was connected.

"When it comes to shunko users and the many kido practitioners, or those who carry zanpaku-to with special abilities, this kido-type of power works right away."

It wasn't the case that Tokinada, the carrier of Enra Kyoten, which could produce most zanpaku-to with a few special exceptions, knew of all the zanpaku-to in the Soul Society. However, he knew enough of the most prominent ones to be able to use them as befitted the situation. For example, the zanpaku-to called Urozakuro, which had been wielded by a prisoner of Muken, could fuse with other materials and had a power similar to Aura's. Tokinada, who knew of that zanpaku-to's power, had dedicated several kido-type zanpaku-to to memory as countermeasures against it.

However, he hadn't done that to battle against that zan-paku-to's master. He had developed that plan in order to serve as a countermeasure when Aura betrayed him, which he had expected from the start...

"Good grief, if you were going to betray me, you might as well have joined Kyoraku's ranks from the start. I thought, after seeing Kyoraku and his riffraff easily taken by Kyoka Suigetsu, you would have waited to betray me until the end, when everything was over and Hikone's power was closer to being perfected."

Aura was on her knees and sweat poured from her forehead. Tokinada spoke to her, seeming both entertained and curious.

When Aura slowly brought up her head, she asked, still expressionless, "How...did you know I would betray you?"

"Hm. That's obvious, isn't it? Ever since you created Hikone with your own hands, it has been like you were the thing's mother. Didn't you experience emotions that you haven't felt before now?"

"..."

"In that case, things are going *just as planned*. I culti-vated those emotions in your insipid mind thinking that it would be entertaining to squash them underfoot, but...you don't look too broken up about it."

He had fostered those emotions so she *would* betray him. Tokinada's endlessly irrational behavior made Ginjo, who had been listening from the side, scowl.

"Well, if you haven't developed any emotions even after raising Hikone, I can't do much about it. But it is so exhilarating to groom someone and for them to turn out the way you intended. I can't say I don't understand Aizen's and Yhwach's feelings as they continued to watch Ichigo Kurosaki—"

Before he could finish, a clash of metal interrupted his words. Tokinada intercepted the flash of Ginjo's blade just as the man stepped in.

"Ha ha! You didn't even hesitate, despite your own companion having collapsed! Well, then again, you only met her today. It's not as though you would develop feeling—"

As he spoke, Tokinada attempted to invoke Kyoka Suigetsu, but...

Of course, the shikai would not activate.

"Huh?"

"What's wrong? You're full of openings."

When faced with the increasing weight and speed of Ginjo's attacks, Tokinada leapt far back.

"Impossible...you're still holding it back then, Aura?"

Though he had absorbed more than half of her spiritual pressure, she was still using a part of herself that she had dispersed in all directions to continue touching all of Tokinada's blades. One of those blades was Ruriirokujaku, but without minding that her spiritual pressure was continually being absorbed, Aura still did not let go.

"Why are you continuing to touch them? At this rate you'll just die meaninglessly."

Aura stood then, even though her breath was faint.

"There is...meaning to this."

"What?"

"There's probably...something wrong with me."

Aura continued to pour her life into sealing Kyoka Suigetsu's invocation as her remaining spiritual pressure was absorbed by Tokinada, who continued to clash with Ginjo.

"Because I'm not doing this for you, the person who looked after me until this point, Lord Tokinada, or for the seven hundred thousand devotees who believed in me despite who I am." While feeling the spiritual pressure of Hikone, who was still clashing with Kenpachi high in the sky, Aura smiled for the first time from the bottom of her heart as she declared, "I'm doing this for a child who doesn't even care about me—I'm wagering everything for their sake."

It was a smile filled with the love of a parent.

In the past, when she had been confined by her father, was such a smile ever directed at her?

Ah, I can't remember any smiles. I wonder if my father did love me. I wonder if my mother, whom I never met, did too.

Though her consciousness began to wane intermittently, still Aura continued to extend her spiritual pressure into the space around her. Exerting enough force that she was practically unraveling, destroying her very own cells and converting them to spiritual pressure, Aura continued to let emotions she had never had before pour out of her.

When Tokinada saw Aura in that state...

"How amusing."

A sadistic smile adorned his face, and he spoke with a voice that was filled with more joy than ever before. He continued to keep Ginjo and the others in check using Gagaku Kairo and the flames of Ryujin Jakka as he said to Aura, "In that case, what do you think of this? What will your face look like as...the very one you are risking your life to protect cuts you down without any emotion at all?"

Tokinada continued speaking to Aura, who was weakened to the point that she could no longer reply. "Oh, oh! How about I give the order immediately? I'll tell Hikone...to kill you!"

Then, as though to increase the turmoil, he tried to call out to Hikone above his head, but...

"Not a chance in hell."

At Ginjo's voice, the Fullbringers went on the move.

Giriko brushed aside the strange creatures of Gagaku Kairo with his swollen muscles while Tsukishima inserted his bookmark into the flames and rewrote their history so that they had "extinguished ten seconds ago," as Ginjo ran along the path that had been cleared of obstacles. He had transformed his appearance just a moment earlier and had white hair as well as clothes that sported a skull motif. He hit Tokinada with spiritual pressure that exceeded the Soul Reaper's.

"So this is how far you've come in mastering the power of a Hollow! I see, you are indeed suitable as a candidate for the Soul King! Then how about you kill me as well as Hikone now and take the throne yourself?"

Tokinada said that as though to test him, but Ginjo snapped back, "Eh? Me as the Soul King? Sure seems like a real bargain for a throne."

"Of course it's not. Do you know how Fullbringers are born?"

"I think I can make a guess... It's through the Fragments of the Reio, isn't it?"

Why was it that Fullbringers were targeted by Hollows from the time they were in the womb?

Ginjo guessed the reason had to do with something that intertwined itself into their konpaku before they were born.

He had no idea what kind of influence the different parts of the Reio could have, but if a Soul Reaper becoming possessed by a part like Mimihagi had ended up like that, then when a fragment fused with a human, he guessed it would have an influence similar to the Hogyoku.

The Hogyoku—a device that would alter the very world as it fulfilled the desires of those around it. If one were to use the Fragments of the Reio in its place, it wouldn't be strange for them to be invoked using Fullbrings that turned attachments into abilities.

So it was possible that defensive instincts would bloom in young souls that had been intermixed with peculiar spiritual pressure, if they were being attacked by highly perceptive Hollows. Or in the opposite case, that people like Orihime Inoue and Chad, who had passed down the Reio's factor generation after generation, would have their defenses bloom alongside Hollow attacks.

Though Ginjo didn't know whether his guess was correct, a bold smile broke out over Tokinada's face at Ginjo's words.

"If you know that much, then what do you think? If someone such as you, who has the power of Soul Reapers, Fullbringers, and Hollows, were to become the Soul King, you could destroy or reshape the world exactly as you wish."

"Got no interest in that. We're going to turn the world upside down the way we want to."

"In that case, why are you lending a hand to Aura? Is it for revenge? Then again, it was the main family, not me, that ordered your friends killed."

Tokinada snickered as he uttered that unverifiable accusation. Ginjo answered at the same time he locked his sword with the man. "I haven't got any interest in that either. Even if I find out who did it, I still became the enemy of the Soul Reapers—that wouldn't change."

At that point, Ginjo narrowed his eyes and drove in his blade as a sinister look crossed his face.

"I've just got one grudge against you." The smile

disappeared from his face, and as he recalled the face of a single Soul Reaper, Ginjo spat out these words: "Ukitake didn't tell me the truth...because of you."

"Gaha...ha ha ha ha! You heard that from Aura? I had a surveillance spirit bug on her, so how did you share the information? Also, don't you think she may have lied to you?"

"I'm not going to tell you our tricks."

In actuality, Ginjo hadn't been informed by Aura. That was why the surveillance spirit bugs' sham brains that Tokinada controlled couldn't have detected Aura's betrayal.

However, Ginjo knew everything.

His fellow Fullbringers Yukio and Tsukishima had ensured that.

Through those two, Aura's will had defied the flow of time and been conveyed to Ginjo.

What Aura had done to Yukio was simple. Using her own ability to rearrange her body even at a molecular level, she had etched a certain pattern into the backside of the business card she had given Yukio. It consisted of multiple QR codes etched not in black, but in a light gray hue nearing white. They were so light that at first glance they only appeared as a background pattern or the grain of the paper itself.

However, with his special power Yukio had immediately been able to read the information etched on the business card, and in exchange for information about the Soul Reaper family that killed Ginjo's friends, he had agreed to ally with her in order to trick Tokinada.

Although that seemed not to be of any benefit to Yukio at first, there was more than enough gain to be had from a business standpoint to get information from Aura's underground believers, who were from various circles of society.

Though it was impossible to know whether Yukio would have acted out of a sense of duty toward Ginjo even without the reward, the result was that Yukio had allied with Aura.

The rest was simple for Yukio, knowing his companions' habits.

First, knowing that if they were to confront each other, Tsukishima would insert himself into Yukio's past, Yukio didn't need to do anything himself. Though he had bragged to Tokinada earlier about sticking a virus into his past, all Tsukishima had really done was find out the situation directly from Yukio in the past. Since the only past that had been changed was Yukio's, they didn't have to worry about the spirit bugs reporting on them no matter what they did.

Then Tsukishima, who had found out the information in the past, immediately inserted his bookmark into Giriko and Ginjo. He did that to transform their pasts so that Ginjo and the others would already have an understanding of the situation that Aura and Yukio were in.

"They say that time is money, but, Mr. Tsukishima, I believe you should offer more gratitude to the god of time for having been given that power."

When Giriko said that, Tsukishima shrugged.

"Sorry, but I'm just not that religious."

"The flavors of black tea as well as fruit wine deepen over a long period of time. Even if your prayers are only superficial to start, eventually time will bring them to ripeness."

At that, Yukio interjected, seemingly fed up. "Giriko, the stuff you're saying is way past old grandpa territory and verging on cultlike."

Even as they had that conversation, the three did not lend a hand in the fight between Ginjo and Tokinada and instead just watched.

That was because they already knew.

This was a fight to settle the past for Ginjo.

While Ginjo once again pushed his blade forward, he answered Tokinada's earlier doubts. "If you asked me whether I was suspicious, it'd be a lie to say that I wasn't. But I've got no trouble accepting you're the kind of person who would do that, based on that earlier conversation."

"Ha ha ha! I see, I see! In that case, your hostility is justified! However, don't you think you've misunderstood something? I didn't have Ukitake in the palm of my hand. It was out of his own unhesitating volition that he snuck a surveillance device into the deputy badge and determined to become your enemy. It is a needless lie to believe the decision was difficult for him."

He said that with a somewhat docile expression, and then the corner of Tokinada's mouth went up again and he started to speak with delight. "After Ukitake was kind enough to make that decision, I simply *did not tell him* about the Tsunayashiro family's cruelty or the truth about the Fullbringers. As a result of his decision, the Tsunayashiro family and I have recently ended up benefitting from that, so I am very grateful to him!"

Even though Tokinada was being held back by spiritual pressure, he was still able to fend off the hatred that was directed at him as though it were a pleasant breeze.

"Oh, and I witnessed Ukitake's face when he made the decision. He was the one most opposed to hiding surveillance devices in the deputy badge at the aristocrats' orders. In the end, when he made the decision himself, he believed in you. He said, 'Ginjo's suspicions are needless and Central 46 will realize that soon'!"

"So then your family used the surveillance device...and killed my friends to gather the Fragments of the Reio. Is that right?"

"Yes. I fiddled with the Visual Department's data to report to Ukitake that 'Ginjo went mad, killing the messenger Soul Reaper and also his own friends.' He didn't believe it, but as a result, you became an enemy of the Soul Reapers and even killed Ukitake's underlings, so I suppose it had the same result. How pitiful that Ukitake believed in someone like you!"

Though he continued to speak to provoke Ginjo, Tokinada's speed was increasing as he did. Even while buying time by talking, he was absorbing spiritual pressure from Aura through Ruriirokujaku.

"I would rather have told him the truth and taken his brothers hostage to keep him silent, but if I made a wrong move, Kyoraku would have sensed it. And if I were to corner Ukitake, I was concerned that I would incite Mimihagi himself to intervene. Really now, what a hardship that was—dealing with the Reio's flesh."

Tokinada said that with genuine regret. Ginjo said, "I don't regret anything I've done, but..."

He unleashed a remarkably strong blow that contained all kinds of emotions.

"I should have made you the first Soul Reaper I killed."

It was a strike that rivaled Ichigo Kurosaki's most powerful Getsuga Tensho. However, through the red flash that Tokinada released, its direction was slightly averted. The strike stabbed into a distant rocky mountain and cut through it, collapsing an expanse of terrain.

"*Tsk*...you still had a trick up your sleeve."

The flash that Tokinada had just unleashed was something from Hisagomaru. He could use the wounds that he had absorbed using its normal power to convert into an attack and release it. The strike, which contained multiple near-fatal wounds, hadn't been enough to cancel out his opponent's attack, but had just barely managed to deflect it.

Well, then what do I do next? Hm...

Responding to Ginjo's powers, Tokinada was deciding which zanpaku-to ability he would pull out next when he realized that Aura's spiritual pressure had started to disappear.

"Oops. It won't be any fun if I kill you by weakening you."

He took his distance from Ginjo temporarily and used Tsuchinamazu and Senbon Zakura to keep the man in check as he turned his attention to the sky.

Hikone! Leave him! Come kill Aura first!

Tokinada attempted to shout that...

"Hiko..."

But at that moment he was assaulted by the sensation of a gust of wind passing through part of his body.

"Huh?"

Before he could comprehend where it came from, Tokinada saw it.

His right arm, which was still holding his zanpaku-to, turned gently as it fluttered in the air.

"What...?"

Then, a moment before the pain was transmitted to his brain, Kazeshini's chain, which had been sent flying, wrapped around that arm and pulled it far, far away from his own body in barely a single breath.

"Impo...ssible...?"

The pain of losing his right arm dominated his whole body. However, the alarm that rose up in him forced that pain back down. The one who was standing in front of him and pinning him with a direct and powerful glare was Shuhei Hisagi.

"You...I'm sure I had used Complete Hypnosis on you..."

Though the shikai had been sealed by Aura, the Complete Hypnosis that he used on Kyoraku and the others had not been undone. Hisagi, who was shown the shikai before it was sealed, should have been put under the power of a very deliberate and strong Complete Hypnosis.

The scene playing out before his eyes, the slight amount of spiritual pressure of inorganic substances, and even the rustle of the wind should have been completely misconceived by him, and he should have been so deep in the dark that he wouldn't be able to move or even think.

However, Hisagi was clearly looking at him.

Since his hearing, smell, and spiritual pressure perceptions were all being misled, it should have been impossible for him to know Tokinada's position accurately through Aura and Ginjo's conversation. Unless he undid the hypnosis by force, using spiritual pressure at Aizen's level, Hisagi shouldn't have even been able to attack him.

In addition, there was something else entirely unforeseen that had been thrust before Tokinada. Something like a cloth that hung between him and Hisagi had been torn to pieces and sent flying. It was the spiritual pressure interception cloak he had been wearing and had just abandoned.

Did he wrap Kazeshini in that and throw it?

Was that why I didn't sense his spiritual pressure? Just before he started letting it rotate...

He sliced through the cloak and my arm...

Tokinada immediately realized what had happened. However, he wasn't able to understand what had led to it. He was sure he had made those around him mistake the cloak itself for sand, just in case. He considered the possibility that Hisagi hadn't seen Kyoka Suigetsu's shikai, but he was sure Hisagi's eyes had been open. It had been clear from Hisagi's surprised expression and his confusion after that.

Confusion?

It was just a second after he held back the pain that was about to assault him that Tokinada arrived upon an idea and turned his eyes to a certain Soul Reaper.

It was Hirako, who had been continually defending against the attacks and had finally gone down on one knee from exhaustion. Regardless of that situation, Shinji Hirako gave Tokinada a smile that was filled with mean-spirited satisfaction.

"I was actually thinking of using that when Aizen tried to show Ichigo his shikai. I really was annoyed when he said he wouldn't use Kyoka Suigetsu on Ichigo."

"Maybe he was already cautious of that happening," Kyoraku said in response to Hirako. At some point, he had come to stand next to Hirako with Nanao and was picking up Enra Kyoten's hilt, which had dropped to the ground. "What a lifesaver that you realized my intention, Captain Hirako. Especially since I didn't tell that to Assistant Captain Hisagi himself."

"Well, had it been Aizen, he probably would have easily seen through that sort of trap."

Hirako's Sakanade in shikai form swung in Hirako's hand. However, Tokinada did not remember feeling as though his vision or senses had been reversed.

In that case, who had he used that power on?

Tokinada arrived at the answer to that, and as his eyes widened, Hirako rotated Sakanade instead of revealing his tricks, and he repeated the word that Tokinada had used for his companions just earlier. "What a help that you're such a simpleton."

Hirako hadn't used Sakanade's activated power on Tokinada, but on Hisagi, the moment that Kyoka Suigetsu was revealed to him. In other words, Shuhei Hisagi, who was seeing front and back in reverse, *hadn't seen Kyoka Suigetsu being invoked.* The reason Hisagi's eyes had been full of shock and confusion was because his vision in front, to the back, to either side, and even up and down had all been reversed.

After realizing this, Tokinada turned his eyes in order to steal back the zanpaku-to that Kyoraku had in hand, but...

At some point, that hilt had disappeared from Kyoraku's hand, and it was nowhere to be found.

"Sorry. Your zanpaku-to's already been hidden by Okyo."

When Kyoraku uttered those curious words, Tokinada tried to raise his voice, but...

"Turning the other way, huh? You've really underestimated me."

He heard that voice from behind him, and it was already too late by the time he remembered the circumstances.

Ginjo's Getsuga Tensho, which had been released to the side and below him, cut upward and once again tore across Tokinada's body.

The fresh bloom of blood scattered high, high into the sky of the Kyogoku.

CHAPTER TWENTY-FOUR

"GAH..."

After suffering a severe laceration that reached his internal organs, Tokinada's clothes were soaked in blood.

He careened backward and was about to turn up to the heavens, but he just barely stopped himself and kept standing. He planted his feet on the ground even more resolutely than before.

Then he laughed. Breaking into a cold sweat, he used kaido he was inexperienced with in order to forcibly stop the bleeding, and he continued to laugh.

"Ha ha...ha ha ha ha ha! I can't believe you would...you would be able to defeat Kyoka Suigetsu with something like that!"

"You stubborn mule, you're still alive?" Ginjo seemed exasperated as he readied his longsword in order to seal the deal.

In the next moment, Tokinada ejected a strange cloth from his left sleeve.

"What is that?"

In caution, Ginjo kept a step back.

The fabric seemed to wriggle like a living creature as it instantly created a swirl around Tokinada like a tornado. It revolved forcefully as it wrapped around his body.

"That's...the thing that was in Abarai's report..."

It was cloth that had been infused with special kido in order to force one to change locations.

Aizen had created the special equipment in an era when teleportation was completely banned. Its existence was confirmed when it was used by Aizen and Ichimaru to escape the scene after having murdered the Central 46 and by Kaname Tosen, when he simultaneously abducted Abarai and Rukia.

"You plan on using this opportunity to run? I think coming in quietly would be best for your sake."

"Don't be so foolish, Kyoraku. If I'm going to spend the rest of my life in tedium until the day I die, I would much rather just die!"

Even as blood dribbled from his mouth, he raised a voice that was so filled with determination that he didn't seem as though he were half dead.

"In that case, let us kill you quietly."

Ginjo swung his sword, but in the moment before, the cloth had closed up any openings. After the fabric was cut up by the longsword, Tokinada had already disappeared.

"Tsk...I let him get away! Where'd he disappear to?"

≡

CASTLE IN THE AIR, ENGINE ROOM

"Ha ha...ka ha ha! I see, I see. This is the first time I've ever been so cornered."

Dragging a trail of blood behind him, Tokinada walked through a room of strange gauges.

"Oh well, I suppose this is how far I will let my fun go this time."

As he started up several of the gauges, Tokinada let his mouth warp into a grin.

"But I will ask that all of you die here."

Tokinada had equipped the multistoried building with secret weapons. He started to activate the fortress equipment he had prepared as a defense against the humans, which included artillery bombardments that were equal in force to the nuclear weapons from the world of the living and reishi cannons that would diffuse toxins that rivaled Konjiki Ashisogi Jizo, but...

"Hm...?"

None of them would activate.

Though he thought Aura could be the culprit, nothing about the weapons had seemed off recently, and most of the equipment was fitted with alarm systems that would notify Tokinada if any of them had been altered by konpaku manipulation.

As his suspicions rose, a jovial voice that was out of place in the castle echoed within the stronghold from all extant communications devices.

"Oh, hello hello! Why, I suppose it's my first time meeting you, Mr. Tsunayashiro?"

"Is that you...Kisuke Urahara?!"

"You know, I would always crush any surveillance bugs I found flying around my shop, so I feel like we've had a long relationship, Mr. Visual Department."

≡

Though Hisagi also had deep wounds and was out of breath, when he heard the voice reverberating from the castle in the air, his eyes unintentionally widened.

"That voice... Is that Mr. Urahara?! I thought he'd been kidnapped."

Yukio interjected from behind. "No way. We invited him as usual. Once we told him everything, he came right with us."

"Wait a sec! You didn't have time to have a conversation like that!"

"Since there were surveillance bacteria inserted into Aura's body, it wasn't like we could just talk out in the open, you know?"

Once Urahara and Yukio had met face to face, they had been conversing in a way that was different from normal talking.

Yukio's use of the compression artifacts that would occasionally run through the screen he caused to float in the air and Urahara's tapping on the floor with the cane in his hand were nothing other than a way for them to communicate with each other.

Since there was a possibility that Tokinada would decipher something like Morse code, Yukio had used computer language codes and converted Japanese into binary, then displayed those as static noise pulses to Urahara.

Urahara, who had noticed the systematic static, responded to that and replied to Yukio. Then, in order to deceive the surveillance spirit bugs, he showed himself actually fighting Aura, and using the explosion of fire he intentionally allowed himself to be captured by Yukio's powers. After explaining that, Yukio shrugged and gritted his teeth as though he were slightly irritated as he glared at the castle in the air where Urahara's voice came from.

"Well, I was obviously a little surprised when he noticed instantly and replied back in my company's proprietary code. Seriously, what's that guy's deal?"

≡

"So you're getting in my way too, Kisuke Urahara."

As Tokinada smiled sarcastically, Urahara's voice replied, *"And from my perspective, why'd you think I wouldn't?"*

"I made Hikone in order to fully release the being called the Soul King. Why is it so bad to sacrifice something that was created for that sole purpose?"

"It makes no difference. Whether it's the revered Reio or Mx. Hikone, it will never be decent to sacrifice a soul with a will in order to maintain the world. I don't think it's perfect or ideal even using Yhwach's remains."

As though he had flipped a switch, Urahara's voice reverberated only in the room Tokinada was in.

Tokinada snickered as he spread the smell of blood and continued, "You hypocrite. Didn't you have the same goal that I had? Didn't you create those dolls you cultivate in your shabby hideout for that purpose? When the time comes, won't you use the Hogyoku and cram all kinds of konpaku into them to use them in place of the Soul—"

Urahara's voice reverberated again, interrupting his provocation.

"If that's what it looked like to you through the surveillance spirit bugs, then let me tell you this..."

Though the voice still sounded cheerful, it was charged with a pressure that could chill the spine.

"You have holes for eyes and terrible communication skills."

"So then you plan on continuing to turn your back to your own desires until the very end?"

"I don't intend to feign I'm a virtuous person. More importantly, how about you finally surrender? Regardless of whether your final trump card Mx. Ubuginu wins or loses against Mr. Zaraki, I don't think they will be able to take on everyone else, and this castle in the sky is now just a floating piece of junk."

Though Urahara matter-of-factly informed Tokinada that he had overridden all the systems, Tokinada did not let his grin disappear as he turned his eyes up to stare at the ceiling.

"I see. So it's just junk floating in the air then."

In the next moment...

He thrust a different-colored Tenkaiketchu that he had produced from his clothes into the floor, and at the same time, he used a special kido to hit the floor of the gauge room.

"That's more than enough to have some fun, Kisuke Urahara."

≡

A dull groan rang out, and the area below the castle in the sky became engulfed in explosive flames.

"Hey, what's going on now?!" Candice's eyes widened.

Then the castle's external bullhorns came online once again.

"Uhh, test test. Everyone down below—can you hear me?"

When they heard Urahara's voice once again from the castle in the air, Yoriuchi asked, "That Kisuke...was he up to something?"

There wasn't any way he could have heard her voice, but Urahara's next words reverberated through the place with perfect timing. *"It wasn't me. Mr. Tsunayashiro has gotten a bit desperate."*

"That's not good. Huh? Is that thing coming down?"

Just as Kyoraku murmured that, they could see that the building in the sky, which was larger than a skyscraper, was slowly starting to fall.

"Well, looks like he's really gone big, but we should be able to escape using shunpo."

"Doesn't seem like it'll be as simple as that."

Ginjo, who had undone his bankai and returned to his normal state, narrowed his eyes as he observed the surrounding reishi. There was pronounced reishi filling the entire Kyogoku. It eddied fiercely with the castle in the air at its center, and the surrounding air slowly began to transform.

"You don't mean...he activated the Tenkaiketchu?!"

Then Tokinada's voice, rather than Urahara's, echoed through the external bullhorns.

"You won this time. Unfortunately, it looks like I couldn't kill you."

"Tokinada!"

Realizing what their opponent was up to, Kyoraku scowled.

"What? I'm just letting some junk fall from the sky. It's not as though the world is ending."

It wasn't clear if he was trying to keep them there, or if this was retaliation for squashing his plans, or if he wasn't thinking at all and simply wanted to see what would happen...

Though they couldn't suss out his motivation, what he was trying to do was obvious.

Tokinada Tsunayashiro had destroyed the system keeping the building afloat and was attempting to transport the structure to Karakura Town.

"Hey, wait. If such a ridiculously large thing falls from that height..."

"Karakura Town will likely be wiped off the map." Liltotto spoke in a chilled tone, finishing the sentence that Yukio had started. "We don't give a crap what happens to Karakura Town. But it's a Jureichi, isn't it? I doubt that the world will be unscathed if it's smashed to bits."

"Well then...what will we do about it?"

Kyoraku refined his own spiritual pressure as he looked into the sky.

I think Captain Zaraki's Nozarashi could cut through it, but he's still in the middle of his battle. Anyway, it's not as though it would stop the teleportation if it were destroyed. As

*for the Arrancars and Quincies, they don't have a reason to
protect Karakura Town...*

Kyoraku fumbled for a solution that involved only the
Soul Reapers, but before he could come up with anything,
the situation deteriorated yet again.

"Wait! The part that got blown away before is coming down!"

They had all realized it when Muguruma shouted. A part
of the bottom of the castle in the air that had separated
from the floating system was falling directly to the ground
of the Kyogoku even before the teleportation went into effect.

Most of those in the area were terribly wounded. Those
who had some degree of stamina despite that started to
move in order to evade it, but...

One figure was a step ahead of them.

At first glance, it looked like someone simply hoisting
their right arm to the sky. However, the spiritual pressure
perceptions of those nearby clearly indicated an abnormality in the figure. Centering on that humanoid shadow,
a whirl of reishi writhed and, just as it seemed to stretch
into the air, entangled itself in the fragment of the castle
as it fell down. The speed of its fall steadily slowed until it
halted in midair as though time had stopped.

The Fullbringers and Shuhei Hisagi understood what
had happened. He looked at that shadow—at the ashen
Aura Michibane—and forgot the pain of his own wounds as
he shouted, "Don't be reckless! If you do that, you'll die!"

At a conservative estimate, Aura almost had no spiritual pressure left in her at all. While in that state, she was releasing even more spiritual pressure and trying to subjugate that gigantic castle in the air.

Based on her complexion, it was surprising that she was still standing. Aura smiled thinly.

"Are you worrying about your enemy? You really are a strange man."

"We're not enemies anymore! I don't know what happened, but I heard that your capturing Mr. Urahara was also a sham. And you're doing this for Hikone, aren't you?"

"No. I'm not doing this for Hikone's sake. I'm simply doing this because I want to."

She turned her eyes to the sky, but it wasn't clear whether what she saw overhead was the falling castle or the small figure that was continuing to fight against power incarnate even higher than that.

Before Hisagi could find out, Tokinada's voice reverberated from the structure.

"Oh, I thought you'd do that. Thank you, Aura. I'm so grateful that you can be the actress in such an enjoyable show even while I am on the verge of death."

His voice filled with twisted delight was enough for them to imagine his unpleasant smile.

"Hikone."

In a syrupy tone, Tokinada spoke his final order.

"This is a matter of utmost importance. Kill Aura."

Those who witnessed that moment felt as though time had stopped around them. Far up in the sky, Hikone, who should have been continuing to fight Kenpachi Zaraki, had come to stand behind Aura.

They had likely used all kinds of hoho to do it. It was not just their speed that was odd. Even coming from such a high point at a speed that was close to instantaneous, they hadn't so much as raised a cloud of dust where they came to stand.

The scene made it seem almost as though they had used spiritual pressure techniques in order to bend the forces of gravity and inertia. Witnessing those movements, which could have been described as beautiful, most of those present weren't able to respond immediately.

There was just one who was up to it.

Only one of them had realized that Hikone would promptly, without any hesitation whatsoever, come to kill Aura, even in the midst of a fight with Kenpachi…

Only Shuhei Hisagi stood guard at Aura's back, getting in Hikone's way in order to protect her.

"Mr. Shuhei Hisagi, would you please move slightly for me?"

Hikone looked different from their earlier form, when they had met Hisagi. Though they had a peculiar appearance, like a Soul Reaper had been mixed with an Arrancar, their essential nature as a young person who still had some youth left—had not changed. However, internally they had transformed to an extent that could not be reflected in their external appearance.

Soul Reaper and Quincy presences that were complexly mixed together, as though Hollow konpaku were forcefully binding them, had formed into a twisted spiritual pressure. Had one looked at their Reiraku, it no longer would have appeared as a long and narrow cloth, but had transformed into a strange globe of all colors collected together.

"Are you planning on killing Aura?"

"Yes, sir! Since that was Lord Tokinada's order!"

"But Aura was trying to protect you. That's why she turned on Tokinada."

"Really?"

When Hikone tilted their head, Aura said, "Please stop them. It's not the child's fault."

Sensing that Aura was smiling bravely behind him, Hisagi couldn't speak but gritted his teeth and resolved to confront Hikone.

With her hand still lifted to the sky, Aura said to Hisagi, "Please don't mind me. You already know that I cannot be slain by any physical attack, don't you?"

"Can you really manage this as you normally do? If you could, wouldn't you already have turned yourself into mist and erased your presence?"

Her silence was his answer.

Hisagi gripped Kazeshini and took a step toward Hikone. No one who witnessed this situation would have thought Hisagi had a chance. Aura understood that well.

"Why are you doing so much?"

"I'm not doing this for you. It's just that I've got to take responsibility for the past in my own way is all."

Aura still seemed as though she could not accept that. Hisagi was at a loss for how to respond for a moment, but then he recalled something Muguruma, who was at the corner of his vision, had said, and smiled derisively at himself.

"Apparently, I'm pretty susceptible to seduction."

Spouting out these words to dodge a proper answer, Hisagi continued on his path.

"I'm helping you out after you risked your life for Hikone because you're a fine woman. That's a good enough reason, don't you think?"

Beside him, the specter of fear he bore accompanied him as always.

"So I suppose you won't move for me then."

Recognizing Hisagi, who stepped toward them, as an obstacle to fulfilling Tokinada's orders, Hikone closed their eyes. At the same moment they opened their eyes again, they slowly turned the blade of Ikomikidomoe at him.

"That's too bad."

Hikone dodged to the side.

It wasn't just Hisagi who was prepared—Yoruichi and Muguruma immediately readied themselves to respond, and the Arrancars and Quincies watched Hikone's actions from afar to probe for an opening or to determine what powers Hikone had. Grimmjow, who usually would have leapt at them right away, was more deeply wounded than the other Arrancar, after having actually done so with Tokinada. He was being restrained by Nelliel.

They were going to move.

All of them felt it in that instant, as the mass of death named Hikone began to shift...

An attack like lightning falling from the sky sent the ground around Hikone flying.

"Guh...!"

Enduring the shock wave, Hisagi swept aside the clods of earth that flew toward him. What appeared in Hisagi's vision was Kenpachi Zaraki, who had the terrifying look of a god on his smiling face, and the sight of him stopping Hikone's blade with his own zanpaku-to.

"We were in the middle of a fight, weren't we?! What're you lookin' away for?!"

"I was planning to finish before you could follow me, but...oh well."

Though Hikone said that, there was a faint joy on their face and an expanse of spiritual pressure started to circulate within their body.

"It's odd, isn't it? I feel like fighting with you has been more fun than other people."

"That's the most important thing!"

It was a fight between two demons.

Just the aftermath of the force from their sword-clashes was enough to make it so that a normal person couldn't stand, and everyone there realized it at the same moment.

Just how long has that Soul Reaper Hikone been clashing with Kenpachi Zaraki?

Though they didn't know how much time had passed, being able to stop Kenpachi's sword even once was abnormal. Those surrounding them were once again reminded what a fiendish being Hikone was as the two of them continued their duel.

"Are you not going to use your shikai, sir?"

Hikone released countless instantaneous attacks as Kenpachi used one brutal swing to drive all of them away.

"Hah! When fighting somebody like you, it's more entertaining to drag the thing out with the most possible moves!"

Seeing the many attacks exchanged up to that point, Candice said in exasperation, "Can you believe this? I can't believe these guys are smiling in the middle of a fight to the death."

"Back when he fought Gremmy, that scary Soul Reaper guy was smiling the entire time, you know."

"Come to think of it, didn't Gremmy seem to be enjoying himself too?"

Liltotto responded, "Who knows? Not like I would notice."

Since she replied in a cool tone, Candice and the others said nothing more.

"Hurry up and finish your observation so you can stop them from moving, you peeping Tom."

At Liltotto's words, Najahkoop gritted his teeth.

"Just wait a little. Their pattern is way too complex. It's different from Aizen's simple and ridiculously strong pattern."

When Najahkoop said he wanted another ten minutes, Liltotto sighed, "I'll just pray you don't get killed in that time."

While the Quincies were having their conversation, Kenpachi and Hikone were also exchanging a few words.

"You're getting slow. You worried about when I'll use my shikai?"

Kenpachi's blow made Hikone fall back dramatically.

"Don't think about crud like that. What's important is fighting here in the moment, right?"

"You're right. Since I'll defeat you with my full power and then kill Ms. Aura and everyone else here like I should."

"Hah! Don't get greedy. If you start thinkin' about the future and get stingy and hold back, I'll slaughter you."

"Yes! I'll fight you with my whole mind and body!"

At the same time Hikone made that declaration, the spiritual pressure contained within them started to circulate in an even higher gear than before, and the balance between Hollow and Soul Reaper started to crumble.

"Their spiritual pressure can increase even more...?"

Just as Kyoraku said that, Hikone's body quivered eerily. They attempted to ready their zanpaku-to again, but...

They stopped for a moment.

Hikone realized that another figure had inserted himself between them and Kenpachi.

"Mr. Hisagi?"

Hikone turned bewildered eyes to Shuhei Hisagi, who stood in front of Kenpachi. They understood why Hisagi had stood in front of them in order to protect Aura. But they could not understand why Hisagi would intrude while they were fighting Kenpachi.

The smile disappeared from Kenpachi's face as though he were also bewildered, and he spoke to Hisagi's back, which was right in front of him. "Hey...what're you trying to do?"

Kenpachi's spiritual pressure, which was crossed with his irritation, scorched and prickled at the surrounding atmosphere. Those around him were bewildered, unable to understand what Hisagi intended. If he had been trying to swoop in to help, it just looked like he was getting in Kenpachi's way. And it wasn't as though Hisagi was unaware what it meant to help Kenpachi Zaraki in a fight without asking.

"Hisagi...?"

"Hisagi...what're you trying to do?"

Madarame was bewildered, and Yumichika forgot to call Hisagi by his assistant captain title, speaking the Soul Reaper's name plainly. The two of them, who knew better than anyone exactly what it meant to get in Captain Zaraki's way when he was brawling, scowled without understanding Hisagi's intent. If Hisagi didn't have a good answer, he would not come out of this unscathed. It wasn't implausible that he might be killed by Kenpachi first, before Hikone had a chance.

Of course, if he *were* just trying to help, he likely wouldn't be killed without argument, but regardless there was a chance he'd end up flying from a punch strong enough to break his neck, with the pithy declaration, "You're in the way." That was why in the past, when Kenpachi had confronted Komamura and Tosen with Madarame and Yumichika, rather than all three of them taking on the captains, they had chosen a path of assistance, and the seated officers took on Iba and Hisagi, who were next to the captains.

However, Hisagi spat out a response that was far more dreadful than "I'm helping" or anything else he could have offered.

"I'll...handle them. *Please don't intervene, Captain Zaraki.*"

The air around them chilled. Those nearby were tense, thinking that Hisagi might not have been in his right mind.

And Kenpachi's spiritual pressure had become so sharp that he seemed to make the air around him freeze.

"What...is he thinking?!"

"Hisagi...you're dead, after saying that..."

Madarame's eyes went wide, and Yumichika seemed to pity Hisagi from his heart as he looked at the Soul Reaper.

Hisagi had just uttered the very words that absolutely no one could say to Kenpachi.

Hisagi had said those words right as Kenpachi was in the midst of enjoying his battle.

He had said, "*Give me your prey*," which was the same as asking for death.

"So I can assume you're picking a fight with me then, huh?"

To Kenpachi, the fate of the Soul Society or the peace of the world of the living were secondary concerns. At that moment, he had an opponent before him whom he could fight against until he ran out of strength. That in itself was everything to him; you could even say it gave his life purpose. In other words, anyone out to steal his prey was a clear enemy who intended to take away his very reason for being.

Kenpachi's zanpaku-to settled on Hisagi's shoulder. He didn't even need to tear through Hisagi. If he were to simply entrust his power into pushing his sword, Kenpachi's exceptional spiritual pressure would have easily crushed the assistant captain.

His life was undoubtedly in far more danger than when he had confronted Tokinada. Sudden, unequivocal death was looming over Hisagi from behind.

However...

Without any regard for the circumstances, Hisagi simply and matter-of-factly said, "That kid...Hikone is *weak*."

"What?"

Weak.

Hisagi had certainly referred to Hikone, the child before his eyes, as such.

He had unfortunately said that.

"You...you're calling that punk *weak* after the kid put up a real fight against me?"

"I am."

"So is that your roundabout way of tellin' me *I'm* weak?"

Hisagi then shook his head quietly as he turned to look at Kenpachi over his shoulder. There was certainly fear in his eyes. He was but a single Soul Reaper who, targeted by Kenpachi's spiritual pressure, desperately held in check his trembling body.

"Hikone. Is. Weak. Weaker than you, Captain Zaraki...no, actually probably weaker than anyone here."

This person who was *only* a Soul Reaper carried fear with him, but still looked at Kenpachi Zaraki as he continued to speak from the depths of his soul.

"For somebody like you, who's inherited the renowned title of Kenpachi... Captain Zaraki, beating on a weak opponent isn't a good look for you... So I'll do it."

Zaraki, who had been listening to him, thought for a few moments, then muttered to himself almost as though he were talking to someone.

"Ah, yeah, you're right, Yachiru. Yeah, that's true, Yachiru."

"Hm?"

Zaraki's usual demeanor returned and he said to Hisagi, who hadn't been able to pick up the earlier words because they had been whispered, "You spoke the word 'Kenpachi.'"

"...I'm sorry."

"If we're talking about the name 'Kenpachi' and not Zaraki, you're right that I shouldn't be picking on the weak."

When they saw Zaraki say such a thing and then withdraw, his subordinates reacted by crying out in shock.

"What?!"

"Huh?!"

It wasn't just Madarame and Yumichika who were surprised. Those who knew Zaraki could not believe that he would back down after finding an ideal opponent. Zaraki shouldered his sword as he turned his back to Hisagi, then immediately stepped between Aura and Hisagi. A memory of the warrior who had previously created the name "Kenpachi" floated in the back of his mind.

"Even just for argument's sake, you brought up the name of Kenpachi."

Then he was quiet—surprisingly so. While turning on Hisagi a spiritual pressure so chilly that it seemed as though it would melt and crumble the moment it was touched, he yelled out at Hisagi, "You put up an unworthy fight...and I'll kill you even before that punk does."

On the receiving end of that spiritual pressure that made the spines of those surrounding them quiver, Hisagi only had a curt reply: "Yes...thank you very much, Captain Zaraki."

Then Hisagi confronted Hikone.

Though several of them considered whether they should lend him a hand, based on the exchange that had just occurred, it seemed Hisagi wanted to make this a one-on-one fight. There weren't many who could take on that *thing* that was in the form of a Soul Reaper.

Ichigo Kurosaki and Kenpachi Zaraki could have, as well as Sosuke Aizen, if he actually wanted to win. Kisuke Urahara and Mayuri Kurotsuchi might have been able to match up to Hikone as well, if it wasn't a match of physical strength, but this was no opponent that an assistant captain–level Soul Reaper could face.

Ginjo might also have been able to put up a decent fight, but he was currently supporting Aura along with Yukio and the others to stop the fall of the castle in the air. No matter how you looked at it, Hisagi was currently out of his depth. However, it seemed that he had met this being named Hikone in the past, and thinking he might have some sort of secret plan, those around him decided to watch what he would do.

Muguruma, who had witnessed it all, ignored his own wounds and stood up, gripping his hand into a fist as he murmured, "Don't be reckless, Shuhei."

Since you still can't use bankai.

≡

Shuhei Hisagi had never acquired bankai.

At the end of his training with Muguruma and Mashiro, Hisagi still hadn't achieved bankai.

"It's too bad…but your power has definitely made leaps and bounds in the last few days. Make sure you show those Quincies the fruits of that."

"Yes, sir."

In the midst of that exchange, Muguruma had noticed that Hisagi's fists were shaking in frustration, but there was nothing they could do about his being unable to reach bankai. However, another thought came into Muguruma's mind.

Mashiro and I were definitely half trying to kill Hisagi. I thought that bankai would be impossible without driving him to desperation, but… We weren't going easy on him. Was Hisagi…really that sturdy?

When he saw Hisagi continue to rise, even after he had collapsed several times, it was like watching some kind of immortal killer from a movie in the world of the living. Muguruma had determined that this tenaciousness was unique to Hisagi and had expected him to awaken himself to his bankai in the middle of the fight with the Quincies.

But not even that had happened, and no matter how many times Hisagi was defeated, in the end, he had been shot by Lille, one of Yhwach's guards, and ended up straddling the line between life and death.

When he heard about that, Muguruma had formed a suspicion. No matter how many times he had suffered defeat, Shuhei Hisagi never died. Was that really due to his pulling through by sheer luck? Or, if it wasn't a coincidence, was that itself the key to Hisagi's bankai?

And now Hisagi faced Hikone.

Most of the wounds Hisagi had received from Tokinada hadn't healed.

When Hisagi stood in their way, in far from perfect condition, Hikone asked curiously, "I don't understand. Why would you not leave me to Mr. Zaraki?"

"I told you, didn't I? Captain Zaraki would kill you."

Hisagi readied Kazeshini and said to Hikone, who tilted their head quizzically, "I didn't come here to kill you. I came to stop you."

"I've already said it, but I think that's impossible for you, Mr. Hisagi."

Smiling wryly at Hikone's words, Hisagi answered, "Earlier I said I thought you were probably strong. I was wrong."

Hisagi gripped Kazeshini and looked straight at Hikone, feeling an emotion that was neither pity nor hostility. "The fact that you're not even agitated that Tokinada isn't here now...means you are definitely weak."

"That's not true! Lord Tokinada told me that I'm strong!"

"No, you're weak. That's why you're not getting anywhere. Not how you are now, at least."

"In that case, I'll defeat you right now, Mr. Hisagi, and prove myself! I'll prove that I've become strong enough to be useful to Lord Tokinada!"

Hikone spoke with self-confidence.

But Hisagi refuted it.

"When I first met you, you were just a kid crying about how you weren't useful to Lord Tokinada and so you'd die..."

"Yes! That's why I became much, much stronger than I was back then! Now I won't lose to anyone!"

"It's the opposite."

Hisagi readied his zanpaku-to, and like an adult admonishing a child, he said in a voice that might have betrayed a hint of affection, "I think...that back then you might have been your strongest."

Hisagi then threw Kazeshini. The vigorously revolving blade approached Hikone, and tearing through the air around them, it traced a complex path. The black chains entangled Hikone and restrained them right away.

However, reality is cruel.

Hikone easily tore off the chains using simple brute force.

In an instant, Hikone's blade flashed as they closed the distance in the space of a breath.

After Hikone passed by him, Hisagi's torso was bisected horizontally.

Hisagi's body, sliced in half, crumpled...

≡

"Yo." The shade spoke to Hisagi.

At the top of a giant tree that made him feel almost as though he were above a forest or a mountain, a rust-colored windmill rotated creakily.

It was the usual scene.

It was a mirror of the world that reflected the cycle of life.

Death and life would repeat, creating something new to perish that would become a new wind continually circulating in the space between the tree and iron.

In that scene, Hisagi saw the form of Kazeshini that called out to him. Just as when Kazeshini had appeared to him earlier, he looked like a jet-black humanoid monster.

"Looks like you pulled something pretty reckless. Did you think you'd win?"

"No idea. I just knew that if I didn't do it, Hikone would've died. It wouldn't have made sense if I had somebody else fight and asked them to hold back in order to avoid killing Hikone."

"Hah! So you're trying to act like a hero? You didn't think you'd be like Muguruma when he saved you as a brat, did you? Did you think you'd be able to emulate Kaname Tosen, when he saved you when you were scared of death?"

"It's not like that. I just...found out about circumstances relating to Hikone, and even then I was only scratching the surface. I couldn't abandon a kid who doesn't even know what it's like to cry." Hisagi's reply was neutral, even though Kazeshini had attempted to rile him up. "And...for some reason, I just felt like talking with you like this."

"You went and got yourself cut in half *for some reason*?"

Kazeshini snickered and leaned onto the windmill in human form as he said, "You've started to get desperate, haven't you? You looked up to the Soul Reapers, but you didn't know what to do. So, recklessly and irresponsibly, you tried to become the ideal Soul Reaper. You kept struggling, trying to follow the manual the Soul Society prepared for you. And the result is this..."

At that point, Kazeshini's expression disappeared for a moment, then a smile different from the one before—as

though he was satisfied by something—appeared on
his face.

"Looks like you've finally gotten me to submit."

"What?" Hisagi inquired, not understanding.

Kazeshini began to speak about his characteristics.
"I'm...not any White or Nozarashi, but I've got a little something that makes me unique. My nature is more shadowy
than the other asauchis."

Though Hisagi wondered whose zanpaku-to White was,
since he hadn't heard the name before, he kept silent and
waited for Kazeshini to continue.

"You looked up to the Soul Reapers and ended up
getting it into your head that you wanted to be as Soul
Reaper-like as possible. So a part of me took on that form.
The form of reaping a life."

"What..."

Hisagi's eyes opened wide with surprise. The shape he
had so loathed had actually been created as a reflection of
his own desires.

"I'm your shadow. When you yourself accepted both
your surface and your underside, and the moment you followed your soul and put your life on the line, you accepted
all of yourself—in other words, you made me yield. So I
needed to ask whether you were finally determined to do
that, and I made things work out so that we could have
a talk."

With a more talkative than normal Kazeshini in front of him, Hisagi put on a pained smile and apologetically replied, "Yeah...I'm sorry I've misunderstood you until now."

Oddly, he felt as though he understood all of what Kazeshini was saying. If Kazeshini were his shadow then that answer would have already been in him from the start. He just hadn't realized it.

Comprehending that, Hisagi declared to his shadow, Kazeshini, "I'll offer it to you. My blood...and also my life."

A conspicuously strong wind swept by, scattering the leaves of the large tree and making the windmill rotate more harshly.

"If you're saying that you're my shadow too...then please lend me your strength."

Kazeshini, who had just been standing in front of him, disappeared before he could blink.

"Life is not just living. By asking you to offer life, I am not asking you to die, and I am not asking you to kill. Life includes dying. And as for blood...that's the oil that has kept your life burning. It could be money, your sense of duty, your pride...or even that thing you call 'fear.' I don't care. Take all of that and add it to my blade."

Hisagi seemed to hear that voice coming from inside of him. He realized that at the same time Kazeshini disappeared, the windmill had stopped and the world became devoid of noise.

"Controlling life, including both living and dying, is exactly what a Soul Reaper—a god of death—is, isn't it?"

Kazeshini's power flowed into Hisagi. He didn't receive a power that increased his spiritual pressure. The power seemed to come in the form of Hisagi comprehending the totality of Kazeshini as a concept. In that moment, Hisagi accepted his own shadow Kazeshini, whose way of being he had hated until that point.

Then the wind died, marking the end of the cycle of life.

≡

"You idiot! You talked a big game to the captain and then got done in right off the bat! Stand up!"

"Um...I think he's a goner..."

Madarame's response to the scene in front of him was to yell, but Yumichika had clearly seen Hisagi's torso cut in half, so he spoke almost as though he had abandoned hope.

Had Orihime Inoue or one of the more powerful members of the Fourth Company been there, Hisagi might have been narrowly saved from death. However, neither were near that place. Those who knew Hisagi sucked in their breaths when they saw Hisagi's body slashed into two separate pieces, while the others just watched with expressions that said, "So he really couldn't do it."

But two people had a different reaction.

"No...he's not done yet."

Kenpachi murmured that, and Kyoraku, as though he had also sensed something, said to the speechless Nanao, *"It's okay."*

Then, in order to make sure that all that occurred next was seared into his vision, he stared at Hikone's back.

"So, I'm looking forward to joining you again!"

Without showing even a fragment of remorse for slashing Hisagi in two, Hisagi whom Hikone themself had judged to be a kind person, the child once again turned to Kenpachi. But Kenpachi remained expressionless as he replied to Hikone, "Don't you think you're getting a little ahead of yourself?"

"Huh?"

Hikone then realized something strange. A black chain that they were sure they had sawn apart was now entangled around their arm. Hikone thought for a moment it might have been a remnant of the broken chains that had wound around them before, but they immediately came to realize that wasn't the case. Hikone was yanked from behind.

"...Huh?"

When they turned around...

Hisagi, the very person who had been *cut in half*, was standing there uninjured.

"What? Huh?"

Hikone marveled while Hisagi stood in front of them, wearing an expression that was no different from earlier. Hisagi looked at them without saying a word. Hikone had no idea what was happening and seemed slightly surprised as they gripped their sword.

"I'm sure that I cut through you, Mr. Hisagi... Was that some sort of kido illusion?"

"That was..."

As Hisagi began to answer, he was cleaved again, diagonally this time.

"I'm sure I felt my sword go through you that time!"

Watching Hisagi, who had simply collapsed, Hikone slashed through the chain wrapped around them and sent it flying. After confirming that it had fallen to the ground, the child turned to Kenpachi and Aura.

"Huh?"

They noticed that the chain was once again wrapped around them. And when they turned around, of course, Hisagi was standing there unharmed. Strangely, even the shihakusho Hisagi wore, which Hikone was sure they had slashed through along with Hisagi's body, had regenerated as though nothing had happened.

Though Hikone thought perhaps they were seeing some illusion, when they looked at those around them, with the exception of Kenpachi and Kyoraku everyone seemed confused to see Hisagi there.

"Hey...you serious..."

NaNaNa Najahkoop, who had been observing Hikone, looked at Hisagi's spiritual pressure pattern and was even more bewildered than those around him as he muttered to himself, "That Soul Reaper...isn't he in rather a precarious situation?"

"Oh...huh? That's strange..."

Hikone, not understanding the situation they were in, simply cut through Hisagi once again in order to be rid of the obstacle in their way, so they could fulfill Tokinada's orders. They cut off both of Hisagi's arms so that he could no longer hold his zanpaku-to. Hisagi attempted to put up some resistance, but unable to respond to Hikone's speed, his arms were severed without his being able to do a thing.

Thinking this was it, Hikone looked to Hisagi in order to give the final blow, but...

When Hikone turned their eyes to him, both of his arms had already returned.

"In that case...!"

Hikone raised their hand and released a Cero at Hisagi. As he was unable to avoid the direct shot, it carved a gigantic hole in Hisagi's chest. When Hikone saw the result of his hit, which should have meant Hisagi had no heart or saketsu anymore, they thought Hisagi must have died this time.

But Hisagi still did not go down.

Though he slumped forward as though crying out, he

slowly raised himself back up, and the hole that should have been carved into him had closed up. Even his shihakusho exhibited not a single tear.

"What...is going on?"

"Try thinking of the answer for yourself. Your Lord Tokinada's not going to explain everything for you anymore."

Tokinada's spiritual pressure had already disappeared from the Kyogoku. They no longer heard his voice coming from the speakers either. Hisagi wasn't sure whether he had died of blood loss, fled the Kyogoku, or if Urahara had done something to him. The only thing that was certain was that the person who defined Hikone's world was no longer around.

In any case, there was no one to describe to Hikone a world that was convenient to Tokinada and pleasant for Hikone to hear about.

"Is this...some kind of trick?"

Hikone was unable to come up with an explanation for what was happening in front of their eyes and so, in order to confirm what kept occurring, decided to *deliberately* kill Hisagi. Hikone purposefully took a shallow step forward and stayed in a position where they could see their opponent, as they once again unleashed a slashing attack.

Though Hisagi attempted to defend against that using Kazeshini, the blade broke cleanly, and he was slashed from his neck down to the side of his torso, cut neatly in half. Hikone approached in an attempt to hastily pursue him and decapitate him.

That was when Hikone saw it.

The bisected halves of Hisagi's body were connected by a jet-black chain—one for each of his wounds.

In the next moment, Hikone thought they heard the chain jangling, and as though a winch were pulling them together, Hisagi's severed sections were reeled together. Instantly, Hisagi was returned to his original state.

"What..."

Unable to understand what they had seen, Hikone reflexively stopped moving.

They didn't even notice that at some point, the chains had once again wrapped around them.

"Hey, Gigi...when did that thing get turned into a zombie?"

In response to Candice's question, Giselle shrugged and shook her head.

"Not a clue. Besides, that abomination's not a zombie."

"That ain't any high-speed regeneration...what is it?"

Grimmjow scowled as he looked at Hisagi while Halibel remarked to Nelliel, "He's not the only thing that's changed."

"What does that mean?"

Halibel directed her attention around her. "The spiritual pressure in this place has been remade into a new form."

Hikone was so bewildered they no longer had the wits to speak. They gathered that this was Hisagi's

zanpaku-to's ability, but they couldn't understand how it functioned.

Hikone had learned about most of the zanpaku-to through Tokinada. All the information about the bankai that Tokinada knew had also been drilled into their head. The aristocrat had told Hikone to be most cautious of Konjiki Ashisogi Jizo, which was a bankai that could adapt based on the opponent, but they understood nothing about the nature of Hisagi's power, which was entirely unheard of. Not knowing how to go about accomplishing their goal, their confusion steadily intensified.

When Hisagi saw Hikone in that state, he said quietly, "I'm going to show it to you—what kind of world you're looking at."

"My world...?"

"Yeah."

What came to Hisagi's mind were the words that Aura had whispered in his ear in the throne room earlier.

"Please don't get the wrong idea. I simply have one request to make of you."

"A request?"

"Please pray, as a Soul Reaper. So that child's world is blessed."

Because she likely knew that Tokinada was surveilling her, she'd had to phrase her request so that he wouldn't recognize her betrayal. In fact, Hisagi had thought that she meant he should ally himself as a Soul Reaper with the world order in which Hikone was Soul King. If Tokinada had heard such words spoken directly, that was likely what he would have surmised as well.

However, Hisagi understood it now, after learning of Aura's true intentions.

She had entrusted him with Hikone's future.

"Seriously. Why me? You could've left this with Mr. Urahara."

He looked at Aura, who continued to extend her power to the sky as she burned away her life. Hisagi let out a troubled sigh. However, he did not disregard her words, and as someone with dominion over death—a Soul Reaper—he confronted Hikone's world directly.

"What I can do...is just show you that."

Then he threw both the right and left sides of Kazeshini.

"All I can do...is forge an understanding between two mutual cowards."

The two sickles he had released spiraled as they rose over Hisagi's head.

As that vortex shrunk, with Hisagi at its center, Kazeshini's two ends continued to fly, and eventually, they came into contact with each other and disappeared into the black maelstrom.

Then Hisagi quietly announced it.

He spoke the powerful words that were a Soul Reaper's culmination.

"Bankai."

The chains condensed in one place in the air, and in the next moment they turned into a jet-black mass that burst open, becoming a wind of spiritual pressure that raged through the expanse.

"Kazeshini Kojyo!"

The wind died down.

Hisagi, whose two blades had returned to his hand at some point, stood in front of Hikone as though nothing had happened. Two jet-black chains extended from his feet and twisted around each of his arms, firmly connecting him to the ground.

Faced with that curious scene, Hikone was even more dubious.

Probing into the nature of that bankai, they extended their spiritual pressure perception all around. However, that only informed Hikone of a strange reality.

They didn't feel any spiritual pressure.

After the raging black wind had died down, the movement of the air itself completely stilled. Simultaneously, even the slightest tremble of spiritual pressure disappeared. The reishi in the Kyogoku, which was more pronounced than either the Soul Society's or Hueco Mundo's, had become entirely stationary as though time itself had stopped.

However, that was only the case on the ground and in the atmosphere.

Aura was still extending her spiritual pressure to the sky, and Kenpachi's ominous vortex could be felt just the same.

Hikone, who had no idea what was happening, decided to attack Hisagi directly instead of waiting to see what their opponent would do. They increased the quickness of their zanpaku-to's attack from earlier. Hikone, who confirmed that there was nothing strange about their own spiritual pressure, was once again confident they had cut Hisagi in half, but...

Hisagi remained unharmed.

To be more accurate, Hikone certainly *had* cut Hisagi, but from the moment they cut him, the wounds closed up as though they had never happened. No matter how many times Hikone attempted to rend into Hisagi with their blade, the moment the back of the blade passed through the Soul Reaper, the wound was already healed. Or rather, it was as though Hikone had never cut Hisagi in the first place.

It seemed that the regeneration power earlier was like a preliminary step toward the bankai. Though Hikone had no idea what had happened within the Soul Reaper Shuhei Hisagi, he had awakened his bankai here, and as part of that process, had invoked regenerative powers through his chains.

Hikone was bewildered as the chains once again wrapped around them.

"Oh..."

Hikone attempted to tear them away as before, but they weren't able to. When they pulled, the chains would extend and continue to wind around them. Where in the world were those chains coming from? In order to find out, Hikone turned their eyes to where the chains led.

Then their entire body froze.

It was high over Hisagi's head.

At about the same height as where the castle in the air had been, Hikone saw it.

It was something of an entirely different nature from anything Hikone had ever known before.

Was it a jet-black moon? Or a sun?

The gigantic black sphere was fixed in place as though to cast a shadow on the ground. Rather than rays of light, it stretched countless black lines down to the ground from the sky.

Hikone's eyes registered the contents of that sun:

Chains.

Chains—the same ones that connected Kazeshini's right and left halves in its shikai form were quickly writhing and gathering to form a gigantic sphere. At about the same time Hikone realized that, Hisagi silently hoisted the blade he'd been gripping.

In the next moment, countless fireworks seemed to launch from the ground as the chains stretched from

the sky like rain in a downpour. The sky and earth were anchored in place by thousands of chains. In addition, a bundle of chains thicker than the others dangled down behind Hisagi like a gigantic black tree stretching to the heavens, connecting the ground to the black orb.

Then, just as Hikone thought the chains connecting to them and holding them in place had come undone, those combined into one chain, the ends twining around Hisagi's and Hikone's necks.

It was as though their necks were being tied together as part of a twisted execution ceremony.

≡

After losing most of its ability to float, the castle in the air had started to gently fall. It had also started to transport itself into Karakura Town.

Within the castle, Urahara was preoccupied with a certain task he was making progress on. But then he saw the gigantic jet-black sphere and the countless chains that extended from it through a window.

He tried probing further into the spiritual pressure around him, muttering with a serious expression on his face but never becoming lax about his work.

"So that's Mr. Hisagi's bankai then. Well now, that's...a pretty nasty one."

≡

"Captain General...what in the world is this?" Nanao was looking up at the black sun that had appeared in the sky.

Kyoraku examined the chains that surrounded Hisagi and Hikone and began to form a hypothesis about the zanpaku-to called Kazeshini. "I did think it was strange..."

"Huh?"

"At first glance, Assistant Captain Hisagi's Kazeshini looks like two swords, doesn't it? But typically there aren't zanpaku-to made of two blades in a set. My wakizashi-style sword Okyo is a zanpaku-to created by Ohana after the fact, and Ukitake said it was likely Mimihagi's influence that created his two swords."

"But Assistant Captain Hisagi's zanpaku-to is..."

Remembering that Hisagi had had command of two sickle-shaped blades, Nanao was confused, but based on what she had just witnessed, an answer came to her.

"Then, Kazeshini's true form is..."

"Yes, I think it's likely."

The shikai form of Hisagi's Kazeshini...

It was a pinwheel or windmill-like blade that would pursue its prey infinitely.

Just how far could the chain that connected those two blades stretch?

"Kazeshini isn't just a sword in the shape of sickles. It's the chain that connects them that is the zanpaku-to's true essence."

≡

Though Hikone had been baffled by the strangeness of Hisagi's bankai, regardless, the child did not waver and continued their attack. Hikone didn't understand what was happening as the chain coiled around them, but it did not attempt to constrict them, and the chains themselves didn't transform into blades or anything of that sort.

There was a chance that Hisagi was preparing for an attack, and in order to defend against that, Hikone used all their power to attack Hisagi before he could invoke something else.

Thinking they could kill Hisagi by blasting away his entire body, they hit him with a full-power Cero, but after the light that encompassed Hisagi's figure faded, he was, of course, still standing there unscathed.

Hikone attempted to extend their Quincy Blut to their exterior and to commandeer Hisagi's nerves, but the Blut went down a chain that extended from Hisagi's finger and was fended away.

In that case, did they need to destroy the gigantic black sphere? They mowed through the thing and burned it through vertically using a sharp and narrow Cero, but...

Chains once again extended from the separated halves of the massive sphere and immediately returned it to wholeness, just as had happened with Hisagi's body earlier.

A bankai that makes the user immortal...?

No, I'm sure that Lord Tokinada told me that was impossible.

There was no past example of a zanpaku-to that could simply make its user immortal. Aizen had obtained his immortal body through the influence of the Hogyoku; that hadn't been a power granted by a zanpaku-to.

Considering the nature of zanpaku-to, it was unlikely. Even a bankai that boasted unparalleled power, as though in equal balance, always had a weakness.

For Zangetsu, it was the relentless spiritual pressure consumption.

For Senbon Zakura, it was the existence of the safe zone.

For Nozarashi, it was the inordinate burden on the user's body.

For Katen Kyokotsu, it was the danger of allies being caught up in its scope and the shared wounds from a double suicide.

And though it was a shikai, even Kyoka Suigetsu had a weakness that prevented it from activating Complete Hypnosis.

So the bankai of Kazeshini that seemed immortal had to have some kind of vulnerability.

In order to uncover that secret, Hikone attacked again and again, but...

No matter what they did, Hisagi would not fall. They weren't even able to tear apart the chains that connected their necks. Though Hikone tried to vacate the area, when they reached a certain distance from Hisagi, multiple new chains would entangle them and force them back under the black sun.

"What is this...? What is this power? With a power like that, why aren't you trying to kill me?"

At some point, the emblem of Hikone's innocence, their childlike smile, had disappeared from their face.

In response to Hikone's sorrowful questioning, Hisagi's reply was matter-of-fact. "Well, I can cut you."

In the next moment, Hisagi unleashed the blades in his hands. The two blades seemed to sink into the shadow on the earth and disappear. Then somehow a new chain entwined itself around Hikone's arm and ran along their skin with incredible force. Each of the links of the chain transformed into narrow blades and cut into Hikone's arm. Though they were nothing like Kenpachi's blows, they ceaselessly abraded the same area of Hikone's arm like a chainsaw, instantly burning through it.

"Ahh... Huh?"

Hikone then noticed something.

Their arm, which they were sure had been cut off, had at some point returned to its original place. They thought perhaps it was some kind of illusion, but the pain of the arm being severed did not seem like any hallucination.

That was when Hikone noticed something else.

It wasn't just Hisagi.

Like their opponent, Hikone had also been given an immortal body.

"You couldn't have..."

"It would've been nice if I had a bankai like Kurosaki's or Captain Hitsugaya's that could defeat my enemies real flashy-like. But apparently I'm just not cut out for that stuff."

Hisagi spoke self-deprecatingly as he explained. "You see...I'm a pretty huge coward. I'm terrified of dying, and ever since I killed Captain Tosen I can't help being terrified of having to kill someone. That might be why I ended up with this pain of a bankai."

A bankai was said to be the reflection of its wielder's soul. Pulling out the power that slumbered within an asau-chi and tempering the zanpaku-to's soul with their mind, they would make that power bloom as a bankai.

In that case, what form had Hisagi's soul taken the shape of once he finally reached bankai?

It was the inverse of the fear he had—another form of dread. If Kazeshini could attain a form that would reap lives in shikai to keep the cycle of the souls in the world moving, then...

The bankai's power was a chain that sealed away the flow of life and brought the world into stagnation. By con-necting everything, it forbade death, forbade life. The black sun even bound the reishi in the atmosphere.

Because of that, it was named Kazeshini—death wind.

The cycle of the world would stop, ending all retrogres-sion and evolution, imprisoning it in chains.

In the circumstance where life was forced into stagnation, there was, ironically, a world with no boundary between life and death.

It may have resembled the form of the world before the Soul Society had been born.

"So then you and I just can't die? What's the point of that?"

"Naturally, this isn't forever. If you keep cutting me, I'll die at some point."

Hikone tilted their head to the side quizzically.

"Why would you tell me something like that? In that case, I'll just keep attacking you until you die."

Hikone did not understand why Hisagi would intentionally tell them how to prevail. The answer was extremely simple.

"Yeah, I'd die from that—and *you* would too."

"Huh...?"

That was when Hikone realized it.

They had killed Hisagi multiple times recently, and with each attempt, their spiritual pressure had faintly decreased.

"But...why?"

Hikone probed with their spiritual pressure perception and, in order to confirm it, cut their own arm. Of course, it immediately regenerated, but they confirmed that a part of their spiritual pressure went through the chain to supply what was needed for the regeneration.

Then Hikone unleashed a Cero on Hisagi.

Of course, he instantly recovered, but in that moment, Hikone felt a vast amount of spiritual pressure being absorbed from them. Their own spiritual pressure went through the chain and was stored in the black sun overhead.

It was as though the ball of chains was accumulating a vast amount of spiritual pressure to use for reverting the injured, or even objects, to their original states.

Their lives were shared, and the spiritual pressure of everyone who was connected to the black sun was being equalized. In other words, the more Hikone cut Hisagi, the more their spiritual pressures would both be consumed, which would end up healing Hisagi's wounds. And the result would be the same if Hisagi cut Hikone.

Hikone then finally realized this bankai's true nature.

This was a system that could be used when people who Hisagi trusted were around. If he were to cancel the bankai chains once they were at their weakest state, both of them would lose their immortal status. However, as long as people like Kenpachi and Kyoraku were there, or those who weren't connected to the chains, Hisagi's enemy could easily be killed by his companions.

In return, he would end up half-dead as well, though as a Soul Reaper, that was perhaps something he was more than willing to abide if it meant that the enemy's defeat was guaranteed.

It was a prerequisite that Hisagi would need friends around, and there were some other conditions that Hikone could guess at. First, though Hisagi's new wounds were healing, the wounds he had sustained before the bankai developed weren't. Therefore that black sun wasn't fully healing his wounds; it was simply an ability that returned things to the state they were in when it was activated. If that were not the case, he would have connected Aura and the other critically wounded people with the chains in order to heal them using Hikone's spiritual pressure.

There was one other thing Hikone could assume—they had come up with a method of overcoming this situation.

"Mr. Hisagi, would you please release this ability?"

"You think I would?"

"Until you release it...I'll torture you."

"Well, I thought it'd come to this."

It wasn't as though pain would disappear.

It wasn't as though he wasn't in agony.

Given that, Hikone could probably drive Hisagi to exhausted pain and force the Soul Reaper to release them.

Once Hikone came upon that idea, they faced Hisagi with a serious expression.

I need to torture him... But how? How can I make Mr. Hisagi feel more pain than when he stood again after I cut him in half and bisected his body diagonally from his shoulder?

Had Tokinada rather than Hikone been in this position, he likely would have come up with many methods for torturing Hisagi, maybe even several dozen, and mirthfully executed all of them. However, Hikone didn't know how to do that. Hikone, whom Tokinada had always instructed to simply eliminate the enemy, could not come up with a way to torture their opponent on their own, no matter how they tried. Because of that, all Hikone could do was lash out and hit Hisagi with all their effort or simply continue killing him.

"I'm...very sorry."

As he spoke, Hikone continued to kill Hisagi.

Unexpectedly, Hisagi put up no resistance.

Had he put his mind to it, he could have at least interfered with Hikone's endeavors by cutting off their arms or legs as he had earlier. Or, had he manipulated the chains connected to his fingers, he could have easily immobilized Hikone.

Of course, Hikone had no plans to allow Hisagi to easily defeat them, but there were methods for Hisagi to significantly delay Hikone's attacks. However, Hisagi didn't attempt to do so.

"I'm...sorry."

Hikone punched with brute strength, gouging through Hisagi's flesh, breaking his rib cage, and easily rupturing his internal organs. Though he immediately recovered, if this continued forever, it would become an agony that surpassed normal injury. Regardless of that, Hisagi stood up again.

Hikone could not understand it. Why was it that Hisagi would get back up no matter how many times he was killed?

"Please...forgive me."

Hikone attempted to swing their sword again, but Hisagi smiled cynically and said, "If you're going to apologize for it, then don't do it. It's not like I'm a masochist."

"But I need to do it for Lord Tokinada..."

"So you're blaming hurting me...on Tokinada?"

"...Oh!"

Hikone's arm halted.

Obvious distress coursed over Hikone's face.

"You understand that hurting somebody who isn't putting up any resistance is a bad thing, don't you?"

"I..."

When Hikone was ordered by Tokinada to hurt someone, they did so without the slightest hesitation. When they were told to kill, they would, and when they were told to let someone live, they would do that as well.

Tokinada would decide the right and wrong of it. If someone were to interfere with Tokinada's orders, Hikone wouldn't hesitate to attack and eliminate that person.

However, what was happening now was different.

They themself needed to determine what was right or wrong.

They were hurting Hisagi because they had to in order to fulfill Tokinada's orders. Though Hikone tried to think about it that way, at the same time, they also began considering whether there was an easier option.

As though Hisagi had seen Hikone's thoughts, he said, "See, you've got a sense of right and wrong in you. Hurting somebody who's not putting up a fight isn't something you really want to do, right?"

"..."

"Or are you gonna put the blame on Lord Tokinada and say it's for his sake?"

"No..." Hikone paled as they replied.

Hikone, who believed that Tokinada could do no wrong and was right about all things in their world though others called him a villain, still couldn't bear to hear their lord being called evil due to their own actions—though they did not know whether what they were doing was right.

"Why...would you say something so terrible? What should I do then?"

"Don't rely on someone else for every little thing. You can't assume everyone in the world will be kind to you."

"But Lord Tokinada...Lord Tokinada would have..."

Hikone pulled from their clothes a tool that seemed to be used for communication, but Tokinada did not answer.

"But..."

Hikone wore an expression like a child about to cry. Hisagi's tone was stern, but his words were gentle as he said, "You're not a villain and you're not a puppet who has to do whatever Tokinada tells you. You're somebody who can walk the path of your own soul."

Hisagi moved one of his fingers to manipulate one of the chains, pulling a zanpaku-to that was the same shape as his shikai from the shadow on the ground.

"If you can't fight somebody who isn't putting up any resistance, then I'll battle you."

"Huh?"

"There's a mountain of things I've got to teach you. I'm saying I'll train you. Don't worry about it."

Hisagi blurted out that offer regardless of the fact that Hikone was by far the more powerful of the two.

Though Hikone was bewildered by what Hisagi was saying, Hisagi thrust out Kazeshini's blade.

"Don't hesitate. If I were an enemy, you would've died because of that opening just now."

"..."

"When you fight an enemy, always keep half a step away from them. You never know what'll happen."

Hisagi gave Hikone the exact advice Tosen had once delivered to him without amendment.

Hikone couldn't understand the meaning of Hisagi's words and, in order to keep from becoming more confused than they already were, rejected Hisagi's advice by sweeping away Kazeshini's blade.

"*Ugh...agh.* Stop...please stop talking!"

They once again promptly killed Hisagi, but of course he regenerated.

Turning the tables, Hisagi's blade stopped right at Hikone's neck.

"Oh..."

"See, you would've been a goner right then. Aren't you supposed to be way stronger than me? You're full of openings."

Hikone might have been a prodigy when it came to combat, but they didn't have nearly enough experience. Taking into account Hisagi's accumulated training, Hikone's agitation, and this peculiar situation in which neither could die from being cut, Hikone's skills could certainly be improved upon.

"No, this is...this is wrong. I became strong so that I could be useful to Lord Tokinada..."

"You need to have more fear. That's what you're missing."

"*Ah...ahhhhhhhhhh!*"

As though to reject Hisagi's words, Hikone emitted a scream that was close to a sob and cut Hisagi down multiple times in a tantrum. Hisagi endured the pain and thrust Kazeshini, always stopping just before reaching Hikone's throat, heart, eyes, and countless other vital spots. The scene resembled an adult Soul Reaper training an admiring child Soul Reaper.

Remembering his younger self, when he wasn't as powerful and cried after being attacked by a Hollow, Hisagi allowed himself to be cut down countless times and continued to stop his blade before hitting Hikone, giving the child pointers all the while.

This scene playing out as the castle in the air threatened to fall from the sky was almost comical, but Aura, who was keeping the structure from falling, endured the agony and seemed to find satisfaction in watching them.

Shuhei Hisagi was neither a prophet nor all-knowing and naturally had no way of foretelling his future.

He was not a hero that would go down in history like Ichigo Kurosaki,

nor was he a manifestation of brute strength like Kenpachi Zaraki,

nor was he wise like Kisuke Urahara,

nor was he skilled like Mayuri Kurotsuchi,

nor did he have the status of Byakuya Kuchiki,

nor did he have the talent of Toshiro Hitsugaya,

nor did he have the experience of Genryusai Yamamoto,

nor the brilliance of Shunsui Kyoraku,

nor the drive of Sajin Komamura,

nor the courage of Kensei Muguruma.

Because of that, specifically because of that...

The only thing supporting him was his pride as a Soul Reaper.

He only had his feet, which walked the path of justice that Kaname Tosen had shown him.

Specifically because of that...

...because he had continued to walk that path with honest integrity...he was capable of withstanding the repeated death, pain, and intermittent nihility that assaulted him.

Though only a small amount of time had passed, in those moments Hisagi revived from over a hundred deaths.

Hikone breathed raggedly as they fell to their knee.

Hikone's spiritual pressure, which was once huge enough to rival Kenpachi's, seemed to have emptied to its lowest point. That meant that Hisagi's spiritual pressure was likewise almost empty. As Hisagi continued to stand in front of the collapsed Hikone through sheer willpower, he spoke to the child with simple self-admonition in his voice. "This world isn't kind. Just being alive is terrifying."

Recalling his past self, then the face of the man who had taught him how to live in this world, he continued in his own words.

"That's exactly why you've got to be kind to everybody around you. And I will try to do that as well."

With Hikone almost unconscious before him, Hisagi glanced toward Kyoraku.

"I'm going to release my bankai...but don't kill Hikone when I do."

"Huh? Do you think I would be such a fiend?"

Kyoraku shrugged it off, but he replied with a serious look on his face. "Well, anyway. If I did that, the young lady over there would probably stop holding the castle."

Hisagi looked over and noticed the clouds surrounding the castle in the air already starting to seem abnormal. The clouds were steadily disappearing, and the edge of this disappearance was approaching the castle itself.

"The teleportation's already gone so far..."

Hisagi understood what Kyoraku was saying and tried to release Kazeshini's bankai.

Now that Hikone had used up almost all their spiritual pressure, they were harmless. He thought that he could just use a simple hakufuku to put them to sleep, but...

It happened the moment he released the bankai with both their spiritual pressures almost fully depleted. Just as he saw Hikone's zanpaku-to light up, a Hollow-like monstrosity—Ikomikidomoe—appeared and assaulted Hikone.

"What...?"

Since it had all happened in the span of a second, those surrounding them were too late to respond.

But there was one who could still protect Hikone.

The one who just barely defended Hikone the moment that Ikomikidomoe's fangs threatened to tear the child's head off was Aura, who instantly came between them. Since she had been directing all of her spiritual pressure toward the castle in the sky, she hadn't been able to fully turn herself into mist, and the side of her torso was gouged deeply as her body was flung into the air.

"Oh..."

"Aura!"

Though Hisagi was almost out of breath, he ran to where Aura had collapsed and held her.

Meanwhile, Ikomikidomoe, now separated from Hikone, was rapidly absorbing the spiritual pressure around him and growing at a terrific pace.

"I was so close to consuming all the Fragments of the Reio."

"That numbskull..."

Grimmjow gritted his teeth as he saw Ikomikidomoe ominously transform his entire form.

"But, right now, a small piece is enough."

When he had separated from Hikone, he must have stolen some of the Fragments of the Reio that were in the child. He was absorbing the reishi in the atmosphere with a force that was incomparable and condensing an incredibly ominous spiritual pressure as he stood in the way of Hisagi and the others.

"So this is a Fragment of the Reio, then! Ha ha, ha ha ha! That was it! I remembered! I remembered it!"

Even a small Fragment of the Reio seemed to have given Ikomikidomoe immense power, to the point that the Manako Osho's zanpaku-to ability had been weakened and he had apparently regained his true name that had been overwritten. At the same time, his spiritual pressure swelled with an explosive force, and he diffused a Hollow presence within the Kyogoku that was far more pronounced than before.

Then, as a first step toward killing everyone in that place and getting his revenge on Squad Zero, he raised his voice to extol his own true name.

"Etch it into your flesh along with your despair. My true name is—"

"Hey."

Ikomikidomoe turned toward the voice behind him, and...

...leaping high from the sky with Nozarashi, a gigantic zanpaku-to larger than he was tall, gripped in his hand, a demonic form filled Ikomikidomoe's sight.

"I'm not lettin' anybody take you from me."

Then a blow like a fierce god's—a blow strong enough to smash a meteor—came down on Ikomikidomoe.

In the end, Ikomikidomoe was unable to say his own true name.

All that was left was Ikomikidomoe in his faded sword form after Nozarashi crushed and dispersed most of the power from the Fragments of the Reio.

"...the hell?"

Kenpachi seemed disappointed as he regarded the broken and battered zanpaku-to blade that may or may not have retained its will, and he spat out...

"Your name might as well've been 'wimp.'"

≡

"Aura! Hang in there!" Hisagi shouted as he laid Aura on the ground.

Though Nanao tried to use kaido on her, Aura shook her head slightly and held her wound with her hand as she stood up.

"Don't...mind me. You should treat Hikone..."

She still held Hikone in her arms from when she had rescued the child. Hikone, who had lost most of their spiritual pressure, slowly opened their eyes, looking dazed.

"...Ms...Aura...?"

"I'm fine. Please, Master Hikone, take your time and rest."

Aura uttered these words as though she were the next Soul King's subordinate, yet when Nanao looked at Aura then, she felt she didn't see a servant, but a mother.

Aura left Hikone with Nanao and once again turned her attention to the sky.

"Hey, what are you planning?"

Aura, still pale, smiled at Hisagi as she always did and told him, "There's something I need to do."

The teleportation had already reached a section of the outer walls, at a point where they couldn't postpone it a moment more. Urahara's voice once again echoed from the external speakers. *"Apologies for the delay!"*

In the next moment, a gigantic garganta opened its maw at the lower end of the castle in the air. Once they saw the jet-black fissure, even bigger than a Menos Grande or the Hollow Fura, all of them realized what Aura and Urahara's aim was.

"I've already discussed what we would do in the event this occurred with President Vorarlberna. I've exhausted all my tricks, and this is as big as I can make it right now."

The Arrancars seemed to have complex feelings about a Soul Reaper like Urahara opening such an unbelievably large garganta. Nelliel sighed.

"A garganta isn't exactly supposed to be a garbage dump...but I suppose with the situation being what it is, we don't have any other options."

"That's more than large enough."

Then Aura subjugated the konpaku in the air and attemp-ted to leap into the sky.

"Hey...are you just leaving?"

When Hisagi saw Aura's injuries, he realized her very survival was precarious. If she were to try to control the fall of the gigantic castle in the air, it would be suicide. At the same time, he understood that he couldn't stop her, no matter what he did.

He thought she would say something to Hikone, but Aura slowly shook her head.

"I was able to hold Hikone in my own arms for the first time. That was enough."

"I see... Well, if that's how you feel, then all right."

"Yes. Please do take care as well, Mr. Hisagi."

Though he felt that the smile on her face at that moment was different from her usual mechanical expression, Hisagi didn't question what it meant.

Hikone slowly reached out their hand from where they had collapsed.

"Wait...please wait."

Aura turned her eyes to Hikone and gave the child a smile filled with more heartfelt affection than the one she had shown Hisagi. "Please, stay in good health."

Though her words were curt, it seemed that they were enough for Aura.

"Oh..."

Before Hikone could say anything else, she had turned herself into mist. She transformed, though they had

thought she was no longer able to just a moment before. Doing so must've been a burden for her, but she likely wanted to demonstrate for Hikone that she was fine.

Then the shape of the castle in the sky changed through Aura's handiwork and slowly disappeared into the fissure of the garganta.

At the same time, as though the teleportation had completed, the clouds floating in the Kyogoku fully cleared.

Hikone's hands were still reaching toward her, but eventually their yearning seemed to fade as they muttered with an unspeakably sorrowful expression, "I wasn't able to fulfill the role Lord Tokinada gave me."

"Yeah, you weren't." Hisagi answered him, though he thought Hikone had probably been speaking to themself.

"I tried to kill...Ms. Aura for Lord Tokinada...I still think that was right, even now...to do it for Lord Tokinada."

"Do you?"

Hisagi noticed a faint doubt in Hikone's eyes. Hikone would soon find the answer. Understanding that, Hisagi didn't immediately condemn Tokinada's behavior.

After Hikone was silent for a while, they turned to Hisagi and asked directly, "Why would Ms. Aura have saved me?"

Though he could think of several reasons, Hisagi felt that at this point it wasn't right for him to give an answer, so he sidestepped the question. "Don't think about it too

much. She did that because she wanted to. That's good enough, don't you think?"

"She did it...because she wanted to? Didn't she have a reason?"

They likely felt the effect of Ikomikidomoe having stolen some of their Fragments of the Reio. Though Hikone should have had leftover spiritual pressure about the same as Hisagi's, Hikone was so emaciated they couldn't move. Still, they continued. "I heard that...Ms. Aura is something like... my mother."

Hisagi's words had given them more confidence about the reason for Aura's actions.

"Was she? Then she really doesn't need to explain."

Hikone was silent for a while... Then, for the first time, they spoke from their own heart, rather than following Tokinada's will.

"Do you think...I'll actually be able to call Ms. Aura 'mother' someday...? No...do I even...have the right to...?"

Hikone's voice trailed off as Hisagi shrugged.

"If you don't know, then I'll tell you."

Despite being wounded all over, he tried not to show his own weakness as he said to Hikone with a bitter smile, "Having a reason or having the right to...these things don't matter when it comes to a mom fawning over her kid."

≡

THE SOUL SOCIETY,
TSUNAYASHIRO FAMILY MAIN RESIDENCE

"Ha...ha ha ha! I suppose when one lives for an extended period of time, things like this occasionally happen."

Tokinada was in the deserted inner parlor of the Tsunayashiro family residence. He had used a small Tenkaiketchu with coordinates set to this room rather than Karakura Town in order to escape from the Kyogoku to the Soul Society.

Still, he had suffered severe wounds, and he left a trail of blood behind him as he slowly headed deeper into the residence.

"Well, that was a good experience. I suppose even a group of cornered rats can kill a tiger. I still have many cards to play, but until I heal these wounds, I should hide for a while..."

As he muttered to himself, Tokinada opened the door to the chamber of the head of family. At that point, he was bothered by the faintest sense of anxiety. The air in the room was slightly different than usual. Though he had been severely wounded, an unrelated chill ran through his body.

"...Huh?"

Someone was in the room. Whether it was a servant or a guest, or a confident assassin, it was not easy to sneak into this place. It was protected by several barriers so that anyone without Tsunayashiro blood would have a difficult time stepping foot in it.

However, it might have been possible for a Soul Reaper with the rank of captain to pass through those barriers.

"Are you the ninth successor of the Fon family...? Or Byakuya Kuchiki...?"

He remembered the face of the Secret Remote Squad head that he had met half a day earlier, as well as that of the other member of the Four Great Noble Clans he had been disdainful toward some time earlier. With his zanpaku-to stolen and his blood loss severe, the likelihood of his surviving a captain was low.

Regardless, Tokinada smiled boldly.

How entertaining. It seems that I cannot survive this much entertainment and won't be making a comeback.

In a test of himself, Tokinada neither ran nor hid, but simply stepped in.

"Who are you? Don't you think it's somewhat impolite for you to step foot into the Tsunayashiro residence?"

From the back of the room, a shadow near the seat of the head of family answered.

"Oh yes, how rude of me."

"You..."

"I couldn't find anyone around, so I thought it was abandoned—my mistake."

"Mayuri...Kurotsuchi."

Tokinada smiled cynically at the man. "You're the one who delivered Kyoraku and the others into the Kyogoku, aren't you? I thought you were thoroughly occupied with that."

"I've left that with a remote-controlled double. The person here with you now may also be a double, but it makes no difference."

"I doubt you came here under Kyoraku's instructions. Did you come to capture me? Or did you perhaps come to see if you could get one of the Four Great Noble Clans in your debt?"

"I don't see much use in making you indebted to me in your current situation. Then again, I wouldn't have much interest in you even if you were in perfect condition." Mayuri's tone was matter-of-fact. "But I was interested that the Tsunayashiro family that heads the Four Great Noble Clans went to some lengths to conduct an experiment to create a Soul King. Though the data from the surveillance bugs I attached to the Corpse Unit is coming back at the same time the barrier around the Kyogoku is breaking..."

Though not much time had passed since Tokinada's flight, Mayuri sighed dramatically and shook his head as though he comprehended everything that had happened.

"Considering all this along with the data you left behind here, it seems that you really are an amateur with only superficial knowledge, Tokinada Tsunayashiro. Had you entrusted the plan to me from the start, I would at least have been able to rapidly perfect the Soul King's vessel."

"Heh heh...but you didn't come here to say you'd help me make my dream into reality."

"The biggest obstacle in the way of increasing the perfection of the Soul King's vessel is the being Tokinada Tsunayashiro himself. Had you entrusted the matter with me, I would have immediately eliminated you, of course. Even if you were to boast about leaving it all to me for the sake of a greater cause, it would be troublesome if you were to meddle according to your whims and indulgences."

Mayuri spoke as though the matter were so obvious he could not possibly understand why Tokinada had even asked the question, and Tokinada let a strained smile form on his face as he endured the pain of his wounds.

"Heh heh...that was very harsh of you. However, there is no way I would have created Hikone for the sake of a greater cause."

Tokinada narrowed his eyes and ridiculed the "greater cause" Mayuri had just mentioned.

"There was no reason behind creating a Soul King other than for my own indulgence. If you've seen the Corpse Unit's data, you understand the depth of the Soul Society's crime that I spoke of, do you not? This world was formed as a result of treachery and spite. There doesn't need to be any great cause in a world where the descendants of criminals fight for their wretched profits! The world should *revolve and rot* around our amusements and desires, should it not?!"

"It seems we do not see eye to eye. To use the crimes of the past as a reason to block change in the world now is just laziness."

"Heh...it's always that way for Kisuke Urahara and the rest of you scientists. You talk extravagantly about making the world turn or creating something new...but no matter how you spin it, you are drowning in your own selfish thirst for knowledge, and you only amount to a servant to the world's profit!"

The moment the name Kisuke Urahara had come out of Tokinada's mouth and he had equated the two of them, Mayuri's eyes narrowed and he shook his head with pity.

"Good grief, it would mean trouble for me if you were to speak so trivially of science. You're almost like a child throwing a fit."

"Yes! I won't deny that! Tearing apart a bug crawling along the ground in front of my eyes and laughing at it is the same as using my influence in the world to achieve my gratification! There is no difference between you and me! We both dance atop the ants and occasionally find one that is powerful—that is all! Aren't you the same, Mayuri Kurotsuchi?"

Regardless of the fact that he himself was half dead, Tokinada grinned and shouted, spewing blood.

"Now what will you do? Will you join me? Shall we kill each other? Or will you take me like the mob of others you dominate, bottling me up in order to make me suffer forever as an experimental subject? No matter which route you take, remember this...the man you see before your eyes is the very karma of the Soul Society!"

Without his position as a noble and without Enra Kyoten, would Tokinada have held sway over Mayuri Kurotsuchi? It was doubtful that the influence of nobility meant anything when it came to Mayuri Kurotsuchi.

Regardless of that, the man prioritized his own amusement.

Instead of answering Tokinada, Mayuri remarked indifferently, "I don't know what you're so angry about, but I only came here to observe your research. Well...regardless, I will apologize for entering this room without permission."

At that point, Mayuri turned his eyes away and continued as though the matter were becoming tedious to him. "And if I were to apologize for other things as well, it would be for not relocking the door."

"Huh?"

Tokinada scowled when he didn't understand Mayuri's words.

In the next moment, Tokinada felt an impact on his back.

"What...?"

He had no time to feel the pain. He realized that something cold was entering his body.

"What...just..."

Tokinada realized that a blade had emerged from his abdomen. After having observed tens of thousands of zanpaku-to, Tokinada immediately recognized it.

It wasn't even a shikai, just a simple asauchi.

Mayuri didn't move a step in front of his eyes. It was as though he no longer had the slightest interest in Tokinada as he looked at the bindings on the room's bookshelves.

"Imposs...ible... Who..."

Tokinada's spine creaked as he turned around and found a girl dressed in black who appeared to be quite young.

"Hm? Who...are you...?"

For a moment he thought that she was Soi Fon, based on her stature, but he realized that wasn't the case. Then Tokinada noticed that the clothing she wore matched that of a family of assassins he himself had framed in the past, pinning the blame for the killing of one of the Tsunayashiro family on them.

"I see. So...the commission has finally been filled, then?"

As Tokinada neared his ironic end, he said something she wasn't expecting.

"C-commission...? What...what are you talking about?"

Her voice quivered, and she gripped her blade as though she did not know any of the fundamentals of swordsmanship. Seeing that, he realized that she was just a trainee who was far from having the skills of a true assassin.

"Everyone's...spite...! Tokinada Tsunayashiro...! You... did that to my whole family...!"

The young girl grew teary-eyed while trying to speak. Tokinada was in a daze for a moment before he spat up a gob of blood and squeezed out some empty words. "Your parents'...enemy...?"

"Th-that's right! You did that to everyone..."

To Tokinada, the emotions in the girl's eyes were nothing like an assassin's. This girl whose name he didn't know was different from the assassins Tokinada had seen. Since she still had feelings for her family, a hindrance an assassin would have immediately abandoned, it was likely she was completely inexperienced.

"You say that you killed me...for something as small as that?"

"As small as...something as *small* as that...?!"

The girl in black opened her eyes wide and raged as she stabbed Tokinada again and again.

Mayuri acted as though he had no interest in the tragedy unfolding before him and skimmed a book that had happened to draw his eye. The sound of the blade hitting flesh and of pages turning filled the room.

How much time had passed?

After stabbing Tokinada countless times with the asauchi in her hand, the assassin sank to the floor, breathing raggedly. However, Tokinada was still standing.

"So...are you...done, then?"

"Uh ugh..."

Seeing his nightmarish behavior, the would-be assassin's fear had overtaken her hatred, and she started to quiver from a different emotion. With such an enemy in front of him, Tokinada slowly straightened his form from its slumped position. The sound of something shredding within Tokinada reverberated, and blood started to flow from his mouth without ceasing.

Death.

It would have been clear to anyone that Tokinada had arrived at that fate.

If he could just squeeze out his remaining strength to fire one kido at her, he would have easily been able to send the inexperienced assassin before him into oblivion. However, Tokinada's eyes had already turned away from the assassin. Tokinada forced out his remaining strength to take his final action.

It wasn't to cry out in fear of death.

It was not even to shake in rage from the fate of being killed by someone he looked down upon.

It wasn't to repent for his wife or Tosen now that he was on the verge of death.

Nor did he slaughter the assassin who had fatally wounded him.

Nor did he leave a message with Mayuri.

"Ha...ha ha ha..."

He simply laughed.

"Ha ha ha ha ha ha! Ha ha ha ha ha ha ha ha ha ha! I get it! So I...I die here! It was not Tosen, who held a grudge for so long, but someone like this...an insignificant nobody seeking revenge has caused me to meet my doom! So this is how I will spend my last moments, after taking everything from the Tsunayashiro family and properly inheriting the karma of the Soul Society! Ha ha ha ha ha ha!"

"Uh...ahh..."

Overwhelmed by Tokinada's laughing even as he spat blood, the assassin was immobilized.

Meanwhile, Mayuri silently lifted his eyes from his book. His expression didn't change as he listened to Tokinada's final words. Tokinada then turned his attention not to the two who were present in the room, but to the man he shared a fate with who was not there.

"See...see what happened, Shunsui Kyoraku?!"

Pouring his disappearing life into it, Tokinada spewed vast amounts of blood as he, the head of the Four Great Noble Clans, simply shouted words of malice and ridicule.

"My life comes to an end here, Kyoraku! That means a girl whose name I don't even know defeated all of you! You couldn't even reach me! Finally! Finally I ruined your plans! How unfortunate! How deplorable! You Soul Reapers! Now you'll never be able to punish me!"

Only the volume of his voice was clear. His face was so pale that it was a wonder he was still alive. Though he shouldn't have been able to speak due to his wounds, Tokinada turned his bloodshot eyes to the void as he continued to yell at those who weren't there, amusement on his face.

"How's that, Tosen?! Do you feel crushed? I will...die without feeling the slightest regret for what I did! How's that, Shuhei Hisagi?! How's that, Ginjo?! How's that, Aura?! Are you being killed by Hikone right now? Even if you survive, you won't...be able...to lay a hand on my soul anymore."

The assassin girl was so alarmed by the unintelligible shouts of her opponent that all she could do was watch. It seemed that Tokinada could no longer see. He was slowly walking toward nothing and no one even as a wicked smile continued to warp his features.

"How's that...Ukitake...the man you tried to believe in...is still going to die...and nothing will change..."

As though a wound-up spring had shot up within him, he spurted yet more blood and collapsed on the spot.

It was unclear what he saw in his last moments...

"How's...that...Kakyo? The stars...you..."

Though his eyes looked peaceful for just one moment, his mouth twisted heinously, as though he were trying to cast away that emotion and his own salvation...

Then he simply came to a halt.

"So it was the sentimentality of an inexperienced assassin that did it, then."

After Mayuri gave the still quivering young assassin a glance, he slowly walked out and left the Tsunayashiro family room behind.

"I see. So it seems that cutting short the Soul Society's karma only required something as small as that."

Mayuri likely would have been able to extend Tokinada's life. It might have been possible for him to resurrect the man like the Corpse Unit or as a living corpse like Izuru Kira.

However, he did not attempt to do so.

Perhaps it was because there was no value in that to Mayuri or for some other reason that could not be guessed. He did not even turn around to look at Tokinada's corpse or try to capture or kill the assassin that had just killed someone from the Four Great Noble Clans. He simply ignored everything as though he had lost all interest whatsoever and wiped all trace of himself from that place.

A while after that, the still-frightened girl in black ran from the room.

Only the miserable corpse was left behind in the bloodied room.

Tokinada Tsunayashiro.

It might have been by design, or because he truly had just forgotten...

In the end, his life was cut short without leaving any words for Hikone in the final moment.

It was a major disgrace for the head of the Four Great Noble Clans.

Yet he continued to remain true to his soul up until his very last moment.

≡

MUKEN

Not a single color was allowed to grace the prison.

Covered by infinite shadows on a jet-black floor, multiple barriers had been set up to prevent even the faintest of light from reaching that underground jail. Those who had been given the death penalty but could not be killed due to various circumstances were sealed away in this prison of darkness. In the prison where silence would normally dominate, a man's emotionless voice resounded through the space.

"So one of the flows...has changed."

Sosuke Aizen.

The prisoner who had spent so much time in that darkness used his incomparable perception to verify that a certain soul had been extinguished in the Soul Society. Aizen, whose body was almost entirely restrained, had guessed that a soul that had a link with a man who was one of his trusted retainers had disappeared, but his face showed no emotion.

Instead, an agreement he had come to with his retainer revived itself in his mind.

≡

THE PAST

"Is there anything you wish for, Kaname? I will give you a token of thanks for following me as my most loyal subject. If there is something that you wish for, you may tell me."

The memory of Aizen asking that of Kaname Tosen, his loyal retainer, revived itself in his mind.

"If you would allow it...I have one wish."

"Oh?"

Curious to know what the man in front of him self-ishly desired, Aizen lent him an ear, but what came from Kaname Tosen's lips was something far from a reward.

"What I wish for is...a warning against a sin."

He urged Tosen to go on with silence.

"If I commit a betrayal and become able to accept the Soul Reapers' world... If this world, that will never achieve evolution gives me peace...at that moment, please wipe my existence from the world and leave no trace."

Though his words seemed strange, Aizen understood what Tosen wanted and asked to confirm it, "It is true that if you stop walking your path...you might forgive the Soul Reapers. However, don't you think that you could accept forgiving them?"

"If absoluteness exists, then you are the only one who would be so, Lord Aizen. Even the one who taught me the way of justice was also a part of the world I despise."

"I see, so the very origin of the justice that stirs you is also the linchpin that may destroy your great cause."

Kakyo.

When Aizen recalled the name of the woman who had been Tosen's best friend, Tosen continued, "If I accept the Soul Reapers' world, that means that I have disavowed my cause. At that moment, the things that I have done wouldn't be justice, they would simply turn into slaughter."

Gripping his hand into a fist, Tosen recalled a past he could not wipe away and spoke with effort. "If I did that... then my friend Kakyo's death and way of being would be sullied. Not only would I be standing here after betraying her wishes, backtracking on my cause would be the same as killing her again."

"But don't you think she would have forgiven you, had she still been alive?"

"Yes. She likely would have. That is why, before I succumb to vice within her innate goodness now that she is no longer here, I would like the mercy of disappearing from this world."

"Mercy, is it?"

"If my cause is a fraud, then I absolutely cannot be forgiven! Before my heart is filled with false salvation, please destroy the entirety of my konpaku. That is my wish."

Tosen asked for something not for the sake of his great cause, but to serve his own emotions. Once Aizen understood the significance of that and Tosen's resolve, he uttered a question that he already anticipated the answer to: "Once I stand atop heaven and create the new world, what do you intend to do?"

"That new world cannot have a prisoner to revenge like me in it. Because of that, after you come to stand atop heaven, I will kill myself to fully purify the world."

"It seems no matter what happens, I will lose one of my trusted retainers."

"I am very sorry. Please forget everything I've just said."

Even he seemed to understand he was a prisoner of his own emotions.

Tosen seemed regretful as he apologized, and Aizen told him, "I don't mind. These are words that originate in your true feelings."

"What doesn't allow me to sever myself from the justice that my friend...Kakyo...extolled, is my own inexperience."

"I don't mind that either. Knowing one's own weakness is the foundation of climbing higher."

Aizen looked at the incomplete Hogyoku he held in his hand as he continued with a daring smile, "Since evolution occasionally requires fear."

Then, Aizen agreed to something that was absolute for the subordinate he trusted.

"Let me promise you that. Before you suffer from the plight of forgiving the Soul Reapers, I will erase you with certainty."

≡

The darkness in Muken quivered faintly.

"Kaname, it seems that those who follow in the footsteps you left behind have walked a path to a rather entertaining place."

After sweeping away the memories of the past, whether Aizen felt something in his chest...

...or whether his heart hadn't been moved in the slightest...

...was unknowable...

The past that had already come to be simply melted into the infinitely spreading darkness.

"Even if they are able to surpass that corpse in the end...

"I will wait with anticipation, looking forward to the time when their journey illuminates my own path."

FINAL CHAPTER

THE KYOGOKU

WHILE THEY WERE LISTENING to Kisuke Urahara tell them the path to escape the Kyogoku, Hisagi stood in front of Kyoraku. Hikone had lost consciousness at that point and was being treated by Nanao using kaido.

"What a surprise. I had no idea you had learned how to use bankai, Shuhei."

As though Kyoraku's words had cut the thread of nerves stringing Hisagi up, he peered away in embarrassment.

"Well...I'm not sure how to say this, but today was the first day I could use it."

"What? Really? Wait a sec! How did you make it manifest and submit?"

"Apparently, that happened before I realized it..."

Though he hadn't been worried about it while using his

bankai, when Hisagi realized he didn't fully understand Kazeshini himself, he apologetically reported the truth to Kyoraku.

"Then, basically, you just had to go straight to using it? Well...I'm glad that Captain Zaraki didn't kill that child and that Karakura Town wasn't slowly wiped off the map."

When Kyoraku considered what he saw of Hisagi's bankai, he questioned something about its ability. "It looked as though that bankai were the culmination of bakudo. Though it seems it'd be difficult to use."

Hirako, who had been standing off to the side, shrugged as he blurted out, "Better than my bankai, at least. It seems that you're able to choose who you connect using the chains, at minimum. At worst, if we end up in a fight, Shuhei will be able to drain the spiritual pressure from the enemy, though he'll sacrifice himself."

"Uh...but if I don't have any allies nearby, all I'd be able to do is hope for a draw..."

"Well, I understand the feeling."

Kyoraku, whose own bankai had an element that required him to share pain, thought over the future suffering that Hisagi would have to endure and silently prayed for him.

Then, as Hisagi worried over Hikone's well-being, Kyoraku told the Soul Reaper something that he felt he needed to say sooner rather than later. "It seems that you've become a

candidate for captain as well, I suppose?"

One of the absolute conditions of becoming a captain in the Thirteen Court Guard Companies was the ability to use bankai. Along with the Thirteenth Company, there were currently several openings for the position of captain in many different companies. Given that situation, there was a possibility that Hisagi could become one of those captains...

"About that...could I just continue being the editor-in-chief of the *Seireitei Bulletin* for a while?"

"Hmm...well, we still have to deal with Tokinada, so I'm not sure what will happen to my position or how the Court Guards will fare from here on. But there are many who can use bankai right now, so I suppose it's all right."

"I see... Thank you very much."

"So you're choosing a path in which you can continue to be a reporter."

Hisagi noticed that those words were filled with complex significance.

He glanced at Hikone.

"I decided that I'd show Hikone all kinds of worlds. And it's not just Hikone. I want to expand the world for the readers in the Rukongai and the Seireitei who can't go to other places on their own two feet."

"I don't mind that, but...there may be some things that are better left in the dark."

"So the things that Tokinada said were actually..."

Kyoraku purposefully refused to confirm Hisagi's suspicion. However, when Hisagi looked at Kyoraku with determination in his eyes, Hisagi told him, "Captain General Kyoraku...if you've decided that keeping the truth hidden forever is best for this world...then kill me and leave me behind before we depart this place."

"We can't assume the truth will save the world. You know that, don't you?"

"Yes, so I won't do anything specific immediately. I will research it for years or even decades if necessary in order to figure out what happened in the shadows. If I just accepted Tokinada's words without questioning them, I'd be a failure as a journalist."

When he heard that, Kyoraku smiled gently and put a hand on Hisagi's shoulder.

"Be careful. If you decide to delve into the Soul Society's past, there are still many, many more enemies out there. Even if the Kuchiki and Shihoin family heads say that it was wrong, there are a mountain of other relatives that won't allow things to be put right."

Then he looked around at the Soul Reapers, Arrancars, Quincies, and Fullbringers as he gave some advice. "If you plan on fighting the world, make more allies. Just as Ichigo did."

"Like...Kurosaki?"

"At the very least, I intend to be your ally. But just as you yourself said, no need to do anything right away."

Kyoraku thought quietly for some time, then pointed out a concrete time frame.

"Right... At least now there is a possibility that the dregs of Yhwach are still wandering about somewhere in the world. I think it won't be too late to wait and see whether those get up to something wicked." Then he considered the history Tokinada spoke of and said thoughtfully, "No... maybe I can't call it 'wicked' anymore."

"If...if the same thing happens again, I'd definitely fight for the Soul Reapers. But if there's something I can do before that happens, I'd like to increase the number of paths we can take."

What was hidden in Hisagi's words wasn't a reference to the war with the Quincies, but to Kaname Tosen. Kyoraku seemed to realize that and intentionally didn't mention it.

They watched Urahara work at removing the barrier for a while.

Once Urahara had released several barriers, Kyoraku received a communication from his Soul Pager. When Kyoraku realized it was a message from Assistant Captain Okikiba, he took it and spoke with a solemn expression for a while.

Kyoraku hung up, and with a complicated look on his face he informed the Soul Reapers, "They found Tokinada."

A shiver ran through the group as they tensed, but Kyoraku went on, seeming baffled. "I have no idea who did it, but...apparently he has already died."

≡

SEVERAL HOURS LATER, THE RUKONGAI SHIBA RESIDENCE

They returned to the Shiba residence from the Kyogoku, and those whose paths had temporarily crossed each headed their own way. Hikone was taken to Shino-Seyakuin in order to be put under the care of Seinosuke Yamada, while the Soul Reapers, Arrancars, and Quincies each went home to their own places.

Ginjo and the others who didn't have a specific place to go back to were enjoying Ganju and his sister's alcohol like freeloaders.

"Seriously, what was with that? If it was such a big deal, I shoulda definitely gone too! I would've taken that Tokinada guy and used my skills to give 'im a little bit of *this* and do a little bit of *that*, like *this*!"

"Lacking in vocab, much?"

"What did you say?!"

"Please calm down. The best medicine for appeasing indignation is abandoning oneself to pleasure occasionally."

"I-is it?"

While Giriko soothed Ganju, who was all worked up about what the boy Yukio had muttered while playing his game, Ginjo said to Yukio, "You're heading back to the world of the living, aren't you?"

"Yeah, along with Kisuke Urahara. It's a pain, but Aura asked me to deal with her religious group. Either way, it seemed like she was going to disappear from the world of the living."

"So you've gotta manage a whole religious group. Seems tough being a young president."

"This is easy mode for me. More importantly, have you got anything you want me to tell Riruka or Jackie?"

As he glanced from his game to Ginjo, the man shrugged.

"I haven't. If they're doing well, anything I could say to them would just be tasteless."

"Would it? Then I'll let them know that."

"You're as charming as ever..."

Ignoring Ginjo's exasperation, Yukio simply called out to Tsukishima, "Right, his name was Moeh Shishigawara, right? Looks like he's been visiting your grave or something. Have you got anything to tell him?"

Tsukishima raised his eyebrows slightly and closed his book. "I'm surprised I have a grave...but I haven't got anything specific to say. I'll pray that he forgets us and comes across a new book."

"Moeh Shishigawara...that's the kid with that irritating power, right?"

"Don't look at me like that, Tsukishima. I'm not about to tell anybody to kill him or something."

Ginjo smiled bitterly and started to ask Yukio about the state of the world of the living, but...

"Hey there, could I cut in for a moment?"

Kyoraku, who should have just gone home, was showing his face.

"What? You're still around?"

"Yeah, I thought I'd tell you some things."

"You've got downtime as Captain General?"

"No, no, I'm busy, of course. Especially since I lost a full day today. I'm about to head around to the government office and Nanao's waiting outside right now, so I don't have much time."

"What're you trying to say?"

Ginjo was skeptical as Kyoraku conveyed the message to him: "First, I already mentioned this to Kukaku and Ganju, but...we will be simplifying the means to move between the Seireitei and the Rukongai from now on. Everyone in the Rukongai will be able to come in more freely."

"Haven't got any interest in that."

At Ginjo's quick response, Kyoraku pulled something from his clothes.

"Since you say that, I've got this for you. I went out to get this just now."

"The hell is that?"

It was a book. It seemed to be part of a series and was numbered with a one next to the title.

"It's the adventure Ukitake was writing. I thought you might be interested."

"...What the hell is '*Warning of the Twin Fish!*' supposed to mean? Looks like some kind of romantic drama."

As Ginjo had no idea how to react, Tsukishima said in an indifferent tone, "Oh, I've already read the whole series."

"Seriously? You'll read anything with pages..."

"It's made for kids, but it's pretty entertaining. In the last volume's scene, where a shrine maiden is being saved, I think the personality of the author really shows through."

He was clearly saying that because he knew about the relationship Ginjo had with the author, Ukitake.

Kyoraku was grateful for the help as he cut in with the main topic. "Are you still having reservations about Ukitake?"

"I told you, didn't I? I don't care about what Tokinada did. I'm the guy who became the enemy of Ukitake and the Soul Reapers. What're you trying to ask me to do now?"

Kyoraku scowled slightly as he said, "Well, Ukitake was constantly asking old man Yama and me to overlook your wrongdoings."

"Huh? What? You want me to be thankful to him or something? Don't make me repeat myself. I haven't got any regrets about making you guys my enemy at..."

"That's not what I mean," Kyoraku interrupted. "I'm not talking about your past crimes. I'm talking about if the time came when you would kill Ukitake."

"...What did you say?"

"It seems that Ukitake was prepared to be killed by you. Of course, he was in a position where he needed to protect his company as captain, so I don't think he would have let it happen without a fight, but...he said if something happened between the two of you, he wanted to shoulder all of the responsibility."

Kyoraku righted his hat and slowly continued. "It might be inappropriate of me to tell you this, but I thought it would be okay to talk about it now. Tokinada also said this, but Ukitake was prepared to pursue you as an enemy when he gave the order to surveil you. It doesn't make that part untrue."

Kyoraku remembered his old friend's face as he spoke that unshakable truth.

"It might be unfair of me to say, as someone who simply saw Ukitake while he was regretful... But even though Ukitake might have been involved with the Tsunayashiro family's motives, he wasn't the type of man to use that as an excuse to make himself feel better. That was all I wanted to tell you."

"..."

"Well, I apologize for forcing you to humor my self-indulgence. With that, I suppose I'll be heading out now."

As Kyoraku started to leave, Ginjo, holding a drink, called out.

"So you were saying it'd be easier to get in and out of the Seireitei, weren't you?"

"Yes, very soon."

"And even I could go into the Seireitei?"

"Depending on what you were intending to do, you could. What are you planning?"

Kyoraku looked somehow relieved as he waited for Ginjo to speak. Ginjo remained silent for a while and then made an honest inquiry. He asked it in order to draw a distinction with his past, so he could walk new paths.

"Could you tell me where...Ukitake's grave is?"

≡

Observing this, Kukaku sipped from her cup and murmured to herself, "Heh... Looks like the time for the Soul Society to change has finally come."

Unnoticed, Kukaku offered up a drink to one who was not there.

"I hope that it'll be a world you like...Kaien."

≡

"I've been able to preserve Hikone's life."

When Hisagi heard Seinosuke Yamada's words, he smiled in relief.

"I see... Thank you very much."

"No need to thank me. More importantly, you're even more severely wounded. Looks like you were reckless when using your zanpaku-to. Your saketsu and hakusui are both worse for the wear."

"I'm sorry."

"Well, I'll heal them. It isn't part of my job to heal anyone except the nobles, but I'll consider this treatment as a pastime during my break."

With that remark, Seinosuke nimbly continued to heal Hisagi using kaido. Hisagi inquired meekly, "Um...so, Tokinada Tsunayashiro is..."

"They brought him here, but a group with documents stamped by the Gilded Seal Aristocratic Assembly immediately came to collect him."

Seinosuke's face clouded slightly as he said, "Even I couldn't resuscitate a corpse. Regardless, his konpaku was already in a sorry state due to the effects of using his zanpaku-to. Even if they treat him by turning him into a zombie, I don't think he would retain his sense of self."

"…I see."

Hisagi gripped his hand into a fist, seeming somewhat frustrated as Seinosuke continued, "Hikone should be waking soon. They might commit suicide if you don't let them know gently."

"Oh!"

"Tokinada, the one who was propping up their mind, died. Hikone might be happier dying. Of course, I don't intend to allow them to die. Even if they said they wanted to, I would make them live, even by force. Giving up is not an option."

Hisagi put on a strained smile and shook his head.

"Hikone is…okay. I think they've developed something new to support them."

Seinosuke looked at Hisagi, who was thinking of Aura as he spoke.

"I see…in that case, I will leave it to you to tell them. I won't ask you to do it immediately though. You may tell them when you feel the time is right."

At first it seemed as though Seinosuke were washing his hands of the responsibility, but when he looked into Seinosuke's eyes, Hisagi understood.

Seinosuke had decided that Hikone should hear it from Hisagi himself, because that was most likely to result in Hikone staying alive.

"It seems that I really don't have a human heart. I'm not suited for such things. Hanataro does have that… It is a talent he has that I am lacking."

Seinosuke let a spiteful smile come over his face.

"If it is a Soul Reaper's work to control life, then isn't giving others the will to live part of your role?"

≡

DEPARTMENT OF RESEARCH AND DEVELOPMENT

"I wonder why it is that you didn't secure this Hikone in the Kyogoku? To think you would allow the subject to be given over to Shino-Seyakuin under your very noses—what a useless bunch you are. If you think you can wander the world doing just what is asked of you, then I have a wake-up call for your future as corpses."

As Mayuri grumbled, Cirucci complained back, "But you electrocute us whenever we do anything on our ow... AGH AGH AGH AGH!"

"Looks like you understand that very well. However, a Corpse Unit that can truly do their work well would take that electrical current, use it to accelerate their neurotransmitters, and finish up their work more efficiently."

"What you're saying is absurd—GAAAAAAH?!"

After Dordoni and the others shrieked for some time, Mayuri cut the electric current and looked over the data collected on Tokinada and Hikone, nodding in satisfaction.

"Well, anyway, you did as you were instructed. As a reward, I will increase your free time by two thousand seven hundred seconds per day. Well then, be sure to show your gratitude."

Behind Mayuri, who went right back to his work, Luppi sighed as though he were exhausted and, with a newly lively expression, said, "Well, all right. Once I'm free, that's when I'll bring Grimmjow to his end."

"You haven't given up yet?"

"All Grimmjow promised to the Captain General here was that he wouldn't let his fight with Ichigo Kurosaki get in the Soul Reapers' way, right? In that case, I'm not a Soul Reaper, so while they're in the middle of their fight I could come in from the side and..."

"Stop right there! What would I do if you killed that orange-haired niño?!"

While Dordoni and Luppi argued, Chuhlhourne smiled as if taking another path.

"Ha ha... Rivalry is a beautiful thing. Yes, though Halibel and Nelliel are both half a step stronger than me, when it comes to beauty, I have a full step lead...and that perfect balance makes me even stronger! And more beautiful! And more radiant!"

Najahkoop watched them from afar and shook his head.

"So, in the end, I'm the only Quincy left here. Luck seriously is not on my side."

When Mayuri heard these complaints, he responded, "I made it seem as though I'd released them. Naturally, I've put a collar on them. Though I'll be using you as a stopgap until the time comes when I call them back."

Once Luppi and the others heard that, they again started to complain to Mayuri.

"Then why us?!"

"What? There's no need to worry. You're already dead, so it's not as though you'd die from overwork."

"That's not the issue!"

≡

A CERTAIN PLACE IN THE WORLD OF THE LIVING

As the Corpse Unit was sighing in the Soul Society, there was a moving corpse crying out in the world of the living as well.

"Seriously! I can't believe two of you got captured because you weren't paying attention! Looks like I've really got to keep levelheaded as your leader!" Bambietta Basterbine, whose skin was the same as always, but whose eyes had a strange liveliness to them, declared sonorously.

"Hey...what's up with that?"

When Candice looked at Giselle with reproach, the zombie-tamer Quincy averted her eyes and spouted out excuses.

"Umm, she ended up getting really beat up by that Tokinada guy, so I healed her, right? And I just accidentally gave her too much blood, I think?"

Candice and Meninas, who had superficially been released from the Corpse Unit but still contained tracking bacteria within them, apparently had some sort of communications equipment installed in their konpaku itself. It was likely that there were other apparatuses that had been inserted into their bodies. Though they had no idea when they would compulsorily be called back, for the time being, they had left with free will, which was a better result than Liltotto was expecting.

"Well, we'll probably have a chance to disable those things at some point. Anyway, let's just be thankful we survived."

They presently weren't in their Quincy clothes, but were instead wearing their personal clothing and were at a cafe in a certain country. Though the zombielike color of Bambietta's complexion garnered an occasional stare, they blended in like normal townspeople otherwise.

Bambietta, who was excited about having temporarily recovered her cognitive functions, was letting her mouth run without reading the mood. "Uhh...so ever since I fought that doggy and then he stopped being a doggy... what happened after that again? Ugh...my head... Well, it doesn't matter! Anyway, if you're saying his majesty is gone, then I've just got to succeed him in his place! I'm the queen for now, so how about we blast one of the countries around here and take over?"

A part of her brain was still zombified, so Bambietta's memories and actions went off the rails occasionally.

"You think we're terrorists or something? Sounds like a pain. If she keeps this up, she's probably going to start offing hot guys again, eh?"

"We'll be in trouble if she causes a commotion..."

"Ah well, guess I'll have to just beat her up to get rid of some of that blood."

"I think she'll go back to normal soon even if you don't."

As they chattered on, just as Giselle had predicted, the spirit in Bambietta's eyes started to wane.

"Huh...? I...what? Uh-huh...cake...is so good."

Seeing Bambietta's childlike smile, the Quincies looked at each other and sighed dramatically. Then, Liltotto half muttered as she ate her cake, "Well, we've got to think about what we're going to do too."

Giselle asked, "You want to go to Hueco Mundo again or something?"

Liltotto shook her head.

"Hollows aside, the Arrancars really are a pain to work with."

"Most importantly, Hueco Mundo hasn't got a ton of grub..."

HUECO MUNDO

Looking at the gigantic building halfway buried in the sand, Aura realized that she had collapsed on top of the soft and cool sands herself.

It was likely somewhere in Hueco Mundo.

Why was she in Hueco Mundo? As she wondered that, Aura confirmed that she was still conscious. She had no memories from after she drove the castle in the sky into the garganta. She had thought she would simply continue to wander within the endless expanse of the garganta and that her reishi itself would simply rot away, but for some reason she was stretched out on this sand.

However, she had done what she needed. She realized that this time, she had lost everything. She might have developed an attachment. But she didn't regret that.

It was more likely that Hikone's world would expand if they were raised by those Soul Reapers, rather than by her. Regardless, she didn't have the strength to stand up. If her blood and reishi continued to flow out of her, she would probably become one with the sand.

Even as Aura thought that, she realized that the pain had disappeared. When she slowly raised her face, she realized her wounds had closed.

Though she was bewildered, a young woman right next to her spoke. "Oh...so you've woken, then?"

An Arrancar woman was standing there with unbelievably kind eyes. There was a thin thread extending from the woman's hand sewing together the wound in Aura's side, all the way down to the delicate blood vessels and nerves.

She heard another voice from a spot slightly further away. "Oh, can you get up already? You're amazing, Roka. I thought she was a goner..."

"You're the one...who was in the Kyogoku..."

"Yes, I'm Nelliel. And she's Halibel, over there."

When Aura looked over, she met eyes with an Arrancar who was leaning on the rubble a slight distance away. Though the woman looked at Aura for a while, as though the Arrancar had lost interest, she turned her eyes to the partially destroyed castle.

"She's just being bashful. Halibel is instinctively kind to children and people who like children."

When Aura looked, the Arrancar called Halibel was looking at a crowd of children—or to be more accurate, Arrancars in the shape of children. The children were playing hide-and-seek in the ruins of the floating castle, jumping around all over the place and releasing Ceros and Baras at each other.

"It seems that the castle you brought here has become the playground for Picaro's child. Though it does not quite match Hueco Mundo, I believe it will become covered in dust and fit in very soon."

"Why am I...here?"

"I brought you here. It wasn't as though I could have left you in the garganta like that, right?"

When Nelliel said that, Aura's eyes widened.

"You...saved me?"

"Ahh...half saved."

"Half?"

"You might not have noticed...but you can't exist as a human in the world of the living anymore..."

When she heard that, Aura understood what it meant.

As a human, she had died in the garganta.

"Since your konpaku was pretty beat up, I called Roka and had her treat you as soon as possible. The air here is concentrated with reishi, so your recovery is going pretty quickly because of her powers, right?"

"Why would you do so much for me?"

"Huh? Well, if we left you, even your konpaku probably would have disappeared."

As though she were an entirely different person from when she had been battling Ikomikidomoe, Nelliel spoke in a mellow tone.

When Aura heard the woman's words, her eyes opened wide again. She was bewildered when faced with the Arrancar's honest goodwill.

Looking at her, Nelliel made a mistaken assumption and asked, "Are you hungry?" and pulled Aura into a building to the side.

"Pesche! Dondochakka! Let's have our meal! And since they're already here, how about we call Halibel and Roka over too?"

When the Arrancars in front of her began to prepare a meal before she had a chance to protest, Aura lost her opportunity to turn them down and was forced to sit.

"Umm, and this is..."

"It's a meal made from Hueco Mundo's lizards and characteristic snow herbs. Don't worry, it's not a person's konpaku or anything."

A meal.

When she saw the unfamiliar ingredients, a memory from Aura's youth revived in her head.

She recalled the rotten foods she had eaten when she first left the glass case and had to steel herself as she brought the food to her mouth. Then, against her expectations, the taste was rich and colorful.

"...It's...very good."

Aura expressed her sensation with wonder, and Nelliel broke into an innocent smile, almost like a child's.

As they continued with their meal, Nelliel asked Aura what she would do now.

"What do you want to do next? If you want to move on properly, I can introduce you to Ichigo."

"No...I have no place to go. I'm not sure if I have the right to go through konso."

"Really? Then do you want to rest here until you figure out what you want to do? Right. I've been interested in learning more about the palate and cuisine of humans in the world of the living! So why don't you help out with our meals here?"

Nelliel spoke as though she had come upon a truly good idea, and Aura felt a swelling sensation.

I thought I wouldn't be able to see Hikone, but...

I wonder what I should do.

Since she had lost her kishi body, there was no point in going back to the world of the living in order to continue serving as the leader of her religious group. She had left the rest to Yukio and would just cause confusion by going back.

As Aura pondered what to do, Nelliel asked her, "Hey, what about you? Do you like cooking? I do. I'd like Ichigo and his friends in the world of the living to eventually try out these meals!"

She would have the humans from the world of the living eat the cuisine of this land. Though it sounded absurd, it made Aura pursue a very specific line of thought.

Someday, after Hisagi and the rest spread out across the world of the Soul Society in front of them...

...eventually, Hikone might once again come to this land.

If that happened, wasn't it likely that Hikone would try the food here as well?

If she were allowed to, she might even develop the courage to visit them in the Soul Society from here.

If she just had a reason—one little reason that would give her a slight push...

I'll see Hikone again.

As she savored the food Nelliel and the others treated her to, Aura realized she had started to cry.

"What's wrong? Were you so hungry that you're crying?"

"No, Lady Nelliel. She must just be grateful for the delicious dessert I made!"

"Or she might've just burst out crying because of how horrible it tasted!"

"No...it's very good." While savoring the meal, Aura answered the earlier question. "I love...food."

There was just one thought that had been conjured in her mind. It was a simple wish to someday feed Hikone this meal herself. In just the same way that her father had fed her when she was young.

"I love eating it... And I'm sure in the future...I'll love making these meals too."

As she cried, she realized she was smiling.

Then, after her modest exchange with Nelliel, she decided in her heart that she would live alone in a corner of Hueco Mundo.

She dreamed of Hikone at some future time breaking out into such a smile.

"What? It wasn't an enemy? Lame."

When Grimmjow saw Aura and Nelliel becoming acquainted with each other, he looked bored and stared out over the desert from on top of the rubble.

Halibel, who had finished her meal with Nelliel and the others, came to stand behind Grimmjow and said, "You're not going to show your face in there?"

"I've got no interest in making friends."

When he answered, somewhere in his lost soul—in his Hollow hole—something burned and seethed.

Though he had finally gotten to fight an opponent that was a true challenge for him, the fact that he had done it with others and that he had been beaten by Tokinada right after was a hard pill to swallow.

"I've got to settle things with the blockhead Luppi too."

In order to make sure he never fell behind a second time, Grimmjow imagined his foe and smiled boldly. He didn't think only of Luppi, but also recalled the face of the orange-haired boy he had appraised as an enemy.

"But he didn't come out even after we made that huge commotion..."

"That Kurosaki better not've gone soft because of the peace."

≡

THE NEXT DAY, THE SOUL SOCIETY

"Peace is...pretty nice."

Hirako made that very out-of-character comment while munching on a rice cracker. Momo Hinamori looked at him and tilted her head, asking, "Umm...so in the end, what happened to the Arrancars in the Rukongai?"

"Right...lots of stuff happened."

"Lots of stuff? So you drove them back without any problems?"

"When I say lots of stuff, I mean there was lots of stuff. Everything's been settled just fine, so don't worry about it."

The series of events from the day before was being treated as classified. Though he had been told he could tell Hinamori some details of how the situation came to be, Hirako found it tedious to figure out how much to tell her, so he decided to handle it however he wanted.

"Ahh..."

Though many questions came to her mind, Hinamori was accepting. Because of that, Hirako decided to listen to some jazz over the Soul Pager that was equipped with music playback features, but...

The moment he put the earphones on, a voice called out to him from behind. "Hey, you baldy, Shinji!"

When he turned around, Hiyori Sarugaki, who should have been in the world of the living, was standing there.

"What? Oh, it's just you, Hiyori. What're you doing here? Come to think of it, I heard you started a part-time job in the world of the living. What kind of goofball situation would lead to tha...OOF?!"

Hirako cried out in agony after taking a kick right between the legs.

"*Gah...guh*...what do you think you're doing?! That's not the kind of greeting you give someone you haven't seen in forever!"

"Shuddup! Apparently you told an assistant captain named Hisagi to *tease* me. And that guy went and did it! So how're you gonna settle this, huh?"

"Th-that guy... He actually went through with it?! Wow, he really takes things seriously!"

Hiyori's hair stood on end out of rage and she half smiled as she said to him, "Huh! So in other words, you actually *did* order that guy to do it, you baldy!"

"Wait a sec...!"

"They're sure noisy."

Kenpachi Zaraki watched from afar as Hinamori desperately tried to stop the fight between Hirako and Hiyori, then he asked Madarame and Yumichika behind him, "Hey, where's Hisagi?"

"Assistant Captain Hisagi is in the world of the living."

"Yeah, he headed over to finish his interview with Urahara."

At Yumichika's and Madarame's responses, Kenpachi clucked his tongue as though he were disappointed. "*Tsk...* ah well. That guy's bankai caught my eye a little, so I wanted to try fighting him...but guess I'll wait until tomorrow."

Kenpachi kept walking, and behind his back Madarame and Yumichika looked at each other.

"Well, guess that's how it is. The captain really would be interested in that."

"Hisagi...I think you're going to be in hot water for a while..."

Imagining Hisagi's future, the two of them each clasped their hands together, offering prayers for Hisagi, who was currently in the world of the living.

☰

THE WORLD OF THE LIVING, URAHARA SHOTEN

"Yes, so that's it for the interview. Once again...thank you for everything."

Completely unaware of the fact that Madarame and Yumichika were pitying him from afar, Hisagi finished the interview and started to make preparations to return to the Soul Society.

In the end, because the plans for an article about Tokinada assuming office had fizzled, he had started to

work toward putting together the reissue. He had also decided to go ahead with plans to interview Urahara and move forward with a special project titled *Be Amazed! The Seven Great Mysteries of Urahara Shop!*

The barrier around Karakura Town had disappeared, and the people Aura had been controlling had a confused recollection of what had happened, but were safely released. The religious organization was likely having a rough time due to Aura's disappearance, but Yukio said he would fix that up, so all they could do was believe him.

"Thanks for your hard work. I'm sure things have been a real hassle with everything that happened yesterday. How are your wounds?"

In response to Urahara, Hisagi gave a fist pump as he answered, "Yes! When I took Hikone over there the director took a look at me, so I think I'm good as new now."

"Well, that's Mr. Seinosuke for you. Is he not getting flak for partnering with Tokinada Tsunayashiro, then?"

"No, the aristocrats made an appeal for him. But even now I really can't tell if he's a good person or a bad person."

Though Hisagi had complex emotions about it, he recalled what Tokinada had said and once again looked Urahara in the face.

Internally, Hisagi reached a conclusion.

It was about why Kisuke Urahara had made a Hogyoku in order to strengthen the limits of a konpaku...

So had he wanted to create a konpaku that was as powerful as the Reio's?

Or had he been trying to make it so any of the Soul Reapers could have the same power as the Reio, so they could all use their powers to gradually support the foundation of this world?

He was likely doing it so that he could release the Reio from his eternal sacrifice.

Hisagi, having made this assumption, said to Urahara respectfully, "This is separate from the interview, but...to me, you're definitely a hero."

"What? That was sudden. You can't use flattery to get me to extend the payment date on your guitar loan."

"I really will pay you back for that! I think..." Hisagi said without much confidence.

Two Soul Reapers who had appeared at Urahara Shoten's entrance, Shino Madarame and Ryunosuke Yuki, called out to him. "Assistant Captain Hisagi! You really did save the town! I knew you would!"

"Oh...no, I didn't really save it..."

"I'm so glad that weird wall is gone! Let's pray that we can ride the trains free from harm from now on!"

"The trains?"

After a brief conversation with the Soul Reapers of Karakura Town who had come to greet him, Hisagi gave the two Soul Reapers a thumbs-up and told them, "It's your

turn to save the town next!" Then he was teased by Urahara for his self-satisfied grin, so much so that his whole body was blushing deep red by the time he disappeared through the Senkaimon.

A little while after Hisagi left, Yoruichi wound around Urahara's feet in her black cat form and spoke to him. "Are you sure about this? Do you really think we can leave Shuhei Hisagi be?"

"Why would we have to do anything to him?"

"He's supposed to be a 'journalist,' isn't he? Don't you think he stepped too far into the Soul Society's...or, actually, into your own internal workings? I thought you'd do something to keep him quiet."

"All this talk about shutting people up really isn't like you, Ms. Yoruichi," Urahara said in exasperation as the black cat leapt gracefully onto the shop's shelves.

"Nonsense. I'm not saying you should kill him, as Tokinada would. You could've used the Kikanshinki Deluxe to wipe his memory or something."

"That's something you're supposed to use on bodies made of kishi, so you know it would only work on humans of the living world."

"I'm just saying, it's not as though you couldn't tamper with a Soul Reaper's memory."

Yoruichi spoke as though she were testing Urahara. The man sighed slightly and then responded with a serious expression, "Mr. Hisagi probably thinks that I created the Hogyoku for the Reio's sake."

"That's not necessarily mistaken, though, right?"

"You're wrong. Entirely wrong. It's the opposite."

There was both regret and self-derision in his words as Urahara looked back at his own past. "All I wanted to do was create something new. The goal for doing so was secondary. I just wanted to open a new door. I used the Reio as an excuse to open the lock to that door. I simply followed my own desires... Fundamentally, I am no different from Mr. Kurotsuchi and how he sacrifices so many in order to fulfill his craving for research."

"Kisuke, you..."

"But Ms. Hiyori did see through me. That's why, to take a neutral position...well to be accurate, it's not neutral, but I decided to entrust some matters to a very *Soul Reaper-like* Soul Reaper." His features softened then as he spoke about Hisagi. "When the time comes that I really do become someone who could be called a villain, it would be best to leave behind someone who can definitively determine that I've sinned, right? I'm sure that Mr. Hisagi, who saw how Mr. Tosen was and saw how he left, well, he would do that. Of course, Mr. Kurosaki or Ms. Kuchiki would work as well."

Yoruichi jumped onto Urahara's shoulder and protested close enough that she could have bitten his ear. "Are you saying I'm not cut out for that job?"

"No, no, but you'd be on my side no matter what anyone says, right? You're not impartial."

Urahara smiled, and Yoruichi acted exasperated, with her tail hanging down.

"I don't even know where to start with that pretentious attitude you've got."

"Also...if you thought I really crossed a line, you'd stop me even if you had to kick me, Ms. Yoruichi."

"I'm telling you to stop being conceited. As if I'd stop at kicking you. I'd snap your neck to stop you."

"You're so severe."

Urahara, who had returned to his usual demeanor, righted his hat as he gripped his cane and said to Yoruichi, "Well, let's head off. Mr. Kurosaki and his friends might really be in hot water."

Ichigo and his friends were in western Japan and had been caught up in some trouble. Though it wasn't particularly urgent at the moment, if this were part of Tokinada's strategy, there was a high possibility that it could turn into a thorny situation. Anticipating that, Urahara closed his store and planned to open an "Urahara Shoten Western Japan Branch" for the next few days.

"Really, you are such a busy man. Don't you think you're coddling Ichigo?"

"A small-town candy shop is supposed to coddle the kids."

As he looked at Tessai, Jintaro, and Ururu, who were

heaping together swim rings, beach parasols, and various other items outside, Urahara started on the path ahead of him in order to open the next door.

"Though I think Mr. Kurosaki is a bit too reliable to call a kid at this point."

He would likely continue on to open another new door that day.

He would head on to worlds through doors yet unseen, carrying both fear and hope.

BONUS CHAPTER

A DECADE LATER, THE SOUL SOCIETY

"THAT'S VERY ADMIRABLE..."

It was the day of Rukia Kuchiki's installation ceremony as the new captain of the Thirteenth Company. Running along the main street that led to the First Company barracks, Tenth Company Captain Toshiro Hitsugaya murmured those words. Hitsugaya, who had just caught sight of Iba going through his captain's training, unintentionally complimented Iba's spirit not to skip out on his training.

"That could be what it takes to be a captain... Wish a certain somebody could hear that."

His assistant captain, Rangiku Matsumoto, averted her eyes and smiled.

"Hmm? Who could that be? Could it be Shuhei?"

Someone from another company who was running just ahead of them heard those words and said, "Yeah. Pay attention, Shuhei."

"I can't let that slide, Rangiku!"

The one who had heard Kensei Muguruma and spoken up was none other than Assistant Captain Shuhei Hisagi.

"For your information, your captain agrees with us."

Finding himself on the receiving end of Rangiku's teasing, Hisagi pointed at himself and objected, full of self-confidence, "I'll have you know... I've already mastered my bankai!"

Stop being so proud of your own bankai.

Muguruma thought that retort internally, but Rangiku and Hitsugaya were already pummeling him with harsher jabs.

"Well, I haven't seen it yet."

"Neither have I."

"This some kind of bankai con?"

The rumor that Hisagi had acquired bankai had certainly spread.

Because Kenpachi had been trying to get Hisagi to have a duel with him by commanding, "Do your bankai," it had spread to the other Soul Reapers.

However, for better or worse, the actual substance of the bankai hadn't spread around, and because the incident at the Kyogoku was classified and they had no idea when he had gotten his bankai, the circumstances remained mysteries to the general soldiers.

Muguruma added, "I haven't seen it either."

"What?! I know you've seen it, Captain!!"

Hisagi was near tears as he desperately appealed to them. "Wh...what am I supposed to do?! I haven't had the chance to use it since that..."

Though Hisagi and Rangiku continued with their quarrel, Hitsugaya was serene as he brought the conversation about Hisagi's bankai to a close. "Well...the fact that he hasn't had to use it for ten years is a good thing."

Thinking of the Quincy war a decade ago and a few incidents since then, he celebrated the world that they had enjoyed since.

"It means for ten years we've maintained peace."

Hitsugaya and Rangiku had been with Abarai and the Kuchiki siblings at the same place Ichigo Kurosaki was during the Kyogoku incident, so they knew nothing about it. However, Hitsugaya might have guessed at something. Though at first glance, Hisagi seemed the same as usual, Hitsugaya had sensed a change in him from a decade ago, which made the captain think that the assistant captain really could use bankai as he claimed.

When Hisagi heard Hitsugaya say "ten years" ago, he remembered a certain Soul Reaper.

≡

The place was a valley settlement that had been part of the Eleventh Company's jurisdiction. However, at the moment the Eleventh Company soldiers, not to mention Rukongai residents, didn't dare approach it. As a result of the great war of ten years ago, when the konpaku balance of the three worlds needed to be adjusted, it was where the Twelfth Company had taken emergency measures and erased the residents of the sector. Though that itself was a secret, no one attempted to approach a village where all the residents had disappeared and no new residents came to attempt to appropriate the place, so the settlement became a ghost town.

However, in a charcoal-maker's hut deep in the mountains of that district, someone was eking out a living for themselves.

Shuhei, who stood in front of the hut, called out to that person. "Yo."

The person in the hut—Hikone Ubuginu—heard Hisagi's voice and replied with the same innocent smile as in the past. "Oh...Mr. Hisagi, you came by!"

After some adjustments had been made at the Shino-Seyakuin, and Hikone was able to live on their own, they left the Seireitei to live in a corner of a desolate part of the Rukongai.

Though Hisagi had thought they could enter Shinorei-jutsuin and take the path to becoming a Soul Reaper, not enough time had passed for them to accept someone who had once been a definitive enemy. Because the incident itself was treated as classified, they had disregarded any wrongdoing, but there was still a high possibility that Hikone wouldn't be accepted by the nobility of the Seireitei. Though the Seireitei's sensibilities were certainly changing, the Court Guards were still on high alert.

And, most importantly, Hikone themself had decided to leave the Seireitei of their own volition.

"I understand now. Until I decided to leave the Seireitei, Mr. Hisagi, Mr. Kyoraku, and Mr. Seinosuke's brother Mr. Hanataro...taught me many things. Now even I can understand what kind of person Lord Tokinada was. But I can't hate Lord Tokinada. I can't scorn him. Lord Tokinada was the one who gave me a reason to live. Because I...was really happy during that time. I think...a Soul Reaper like that couldn't exist within the Court Guards. I want to live alone for a while if I can. Yes...I am very scared. But, Mr. Hisagi, you were the one to teach me that's what it means to live!"

When Hisagi recalled Hikone, whose anxiety and fear were visible within their innocent smile, he once again asked them, "Did you find anything? Something you want to do in the future?"

"Yes, sir! I think...I want to become stronger."

Since Ikomikidomoe had stolen their power, Hikone's spiritual pressure had decreased significantly. Regardless of that, they had spiritual pressure that was much higher than normal Soul Reapers. But they had relinquished Ikomikidomoe to Squad Zero, and their battle power had dropped significantly compared to when they were in their prime.

"Oh, and what are you going to do after you become strong?"

Hisagi asked as though testing them, and Hikone looked straight at him and answered, "I'm going to find Ms. Aura... I'm going to find my mother."

When he heard Hikone say that clearly, of their own volition, Hisagi had complex feelings. Though he didn't know whether Aura was alive, he thought it likely that she wasn't in the Soul Society. He hadn't heard anything about her konpaku reaching the Soul Society, either.

Since Hikone was not formally a Soul Reaper and had lost Ikomikidomoe, who could use gargantas, it wouldn't be easy for Hikone to leave the Soul Society. Despite that, seeing Hikone had found a reason to live as a Soul Reaper, Hisagi believed that Hikone's future would be bright.

"Right...I'll try to help as much as I can when the time comes."

Recalling Tosen and Kanisawa, those who had left him in the past, Hisagi carried the fear of losing them in his heart as he said to Hikone...

"I've also…decided that I'm going to find the 'path of least bloodshed' in my own way."

≡

As he recalled that exchange with Hikone, Hisagi decided anew that he would not let the last ten years of peace go to waste. In order to believe that Hikone and the Soul Reapers' future in turn would be bright, he decided he would do what he needed to as the editor-in-chief of the *Seireitei Bulletin*.

When Rangiku saw Hisagi with a fearless smile on his face, she said, "Come to think of it…Shuhei, you've been going out to the Rukongai more often these past ten years, haven't you?"

"Uh…yeah, well, I started connecting with more people through my interviews."

It wasn't just Hikone. He still went to see Ginjo and the others, and Hisagi was secretly collecting information about the Tsunayashiro family's actions as well. Though many things had become uncertain because of Tokinada's death, he wanted at least to expose their past evil deeds. He'd been battling the influence of a faction of aristocrats while continuing to interview those who were peripheral to the Tsunayashiro family.

"Yeah, because this guy's a 'journalist.' His work is well known among some people. Plus, he's been looking after a kid in the Rukongai."

Muguruma phrased his responses in a way that wasn't lying.

"A child?"

"Yeah, going from a brat who was once reduced to tears after a Hollow attack to someone who helps children is nothing to scoff at. But he's still got a long way to go as far as experience is concerned."

Muguruma shrugged and Rangiku listened to him, tilting her head quizzically.

"Hmm...I can't see any kid becoming attached to a face like Hisagi's..."

"Well I'm sorry for having such a scary face!"

Ignoring Hisagi's complaint, Rangiku thought for a while, but as soon as they got into the First Company barracks, she lifted her head up and pointed at Hisagi as she yelled, "...Is it yours?!"

"No!! Why would you think that?!"

Muguruma responded, seeming exasperated, "Like I said, you seem like you'd be the most likely to be seduced."

"Captain!! You're bringing up something from a decade ago now?!"

It was a lighthearted conversation they were able to have specifically because of the peace they had won, and thus they continued to live their days.

They were Soul Reapers.

They ruled over life and death and were also those who walked the path in the space between life and death.

They feared death, feared life, and clad themselves in all manner of dread.

However, those who live as Soul Reapers can't fear their own world that they bear.

If so, accompanied by the fear of all their days until the last, they would have to sweep away the fears of the next day to reach the world that lay ahead.

And the wind once again circulates through the world.

THE END

AFTERWORD

POSTSCRIPT: TITE KUBO

"ACTUALLY, HISAGI KIND OF SEEMS LIKE main character material..."

That was a discovery we made when Narita told me he wanted me to "write Hisagi as a main character."

Though he's dashing, he's a character you can fiddle with.

Though the people he adores won't pay him any mind, others treat him well.

Though he was a crybaby once, he was saved by a hero and decided to take the same road.

Once he met his teacher, he faced his weakness and became stronger.

Eventually, he has to confront his own teacher who strayed onto the wrong path.

Though I knew that was the kind of character Hisagi was, when I heard Narita's proposal, it was the first time I recognized that he was "main character material."

This work is mapped out to be the final novelization of BLEACH, and it is a grand work that is supported by Narita's usual high attention to detail in his reading and, as ever, by his extreme enthusiasm.

Narita's ability to differentiate between many different characters all in one work and in written form, and his talent for knowing the difference between many different characters' charms in even his own work, all add up to a hardcore intention to serve the readers so they enjoy it.

Hisagi's and Hirako's bankai, which ended up not getting time to shine in the original work, also are now able to play a role thanks to Narita, which has me delighted.

Hisagi!!! Good for you!!! You got to have a big part!!!

TITE KUBO

POSTSCRIPT: NARITA RYOHGO

"I plan on ending BLEACH's serialization in one or two years."

When was it that I first heard that from Tite Kubo's mouth? My reaction upon hearing that was quite blunt.

"Ha ha ha, great joke."

But eventually, one day...

The time for the end of BLEACH arrived.

According to what I heard from the editorial department, when they received a formal intention from Kubo to end the BLEACH serialization in a year's time, apparently the mood felt solemn, as though an era were ending.

However, I am truly grateful that at the same time he reached out to Matsubara and me about his passionate desire and important plans to create a last novelization to add a flourish to his fifteen-year story!

When Matsubara and I met Kubo directly in order to prepare for the novels, we asked him rapid-fire questions about the mysteries remaining in BLEACH's world: "What about that?! What happened in that part?!" "What about that character's past?!" When we heard Kubo's responses, I was blown away by his many charming creations.

"Wh-why didn't you include the past of the Reio and the aristocrats and the underside of the world in the original story?!"

When I asked him that, he gave me a clear answer that I couldn't disagree with: "This is a story about Ichigo and the Soul Reapers' battle, so I didn't want to muddy the story's focus by taking it away from that."

Regardless of the past, Ichigo and the other Soul Reapers were fighting in order to stay true to their souls. If the story's focus were shifted away from that, then it would no longer be a part of BLEACH's original narrative.

However, though he had purposefully not written it as part of the original story, when I heard about the many incredibly fascinating backstories he had, I automatically asked him, "In that case, may I divulge those things you've established as part of my novelization?"

I was sure that would cause him to angrily respond, "Did you even hear what I said?"

However, rather than being angry, Kubo was kind enough to give me even more intricate details about what he had created and gave me a lot of advice about a new character that would need to be created.

Then, as a result of the conversation about which character, who wasn't Ichigo and who would preferably be part of the Soul Reapers themselves, could fight against that malicious head of the Four Great Noble Clans, we chose Shuhei Hisagi as the main character.

When Kubo first looked over my plot, he deliberated carefully about the many BLEACH fans, asking, "But will writing this much of it down take away from the readers the fun of imagining the underside of the story?"

Regardless of that, I unreasonably said, "Yes, that might end up being the case, but even if the ability to imagine it is taken from the readers, I would like to tell the story of the past the Soul Reapers stand upon and how they continue their path going forward. Please let me write it," and he kindly allowed me to write it.

In other words, all of this was my own self-indulgence.

All I can do is convey my gratefulness that Kubo allowed me this indulgence.

If there are any readers who say, "I can't believe you did something so unnecessary! You stole the fun of imagining Hirako's and Hisagi's bankai and also the secrets behind the Reio!" I really do not have any excuses.

As far as that is concerned, all I can do is offer my apologies—I am truly sorry...!

However, I was unable to exhaustively tell the full tale of BLEACH's vast world in these three volumes.

So if, when it comes to the "hearsay" that I wrote from the perspective of the Osho and Tokinada, you were able to spread the wings of your imagination and felt that there was possibly more to the story, or possibly not, and it continued to fit the aesthetics of the BLEACH world, then...

...as a spinoff novelization author and also a fan of the original work, there is nothing that would make me happier.

I am genuinely grateful for those of you who followed this twelve hundred-plus-page story from the first volume to the very end!

By the way, after Matsubara and I heard the story of how Kisuke Urahara and Yoruichi Shihoin met, both of us said the same thing immediately.

"You have to draw that with your own hand as a manga, Kubo!" Or "Really, I'd like to read that as a manga!"

Those fascinating characters as well as a story hidden within the world...

I do not know if the day will come when that will be created in some form, but as a fan, I will pray that the BLEACH story will continue to expand.

To all those who followed along up until this point, and to the editorial department, especially Rokugo, whom I troubled with a several month-long hospitalization as well as several other issues, and to Makoto Matsubara who wrote about an aspect of the story I was not able to as part of the last novelizations...

And also to Tite Kubo, who drew and spread a vast, magnificent world before us, and to the BLEACH opus itself...

Thank you so very much!

October, 2018 while playing *BLEACH: Brave Souls,*
RYOHGO NARITA

A note from the creator
TITE KUBO

BLEACH original creator.
A mangaka who got a dog for the first time at the beginning of spring.
A man who hadn't had any interest in animals whatsoever and had
once thought, "Why do people with pets have phones filled with
pictures of their pets and want to show off those pictures at every
possible opportunity?" until he also got a pet for the first time and
immediately ended up with a phone full of photos of his pet and
spends his days battling the desire to show off those pictures to other
people and has an iron will that stops that desire.
Dogs are great!!

A note from the author
RYOHGO NARITA

BLEACH novelization author number two.
A simple novelist who loves videos of animals and is easily healed by
watching footage of hedgehogs and such.
A snake-loving man who would love wrapping pythons around his
neck at the zoo and always wanted to get a pet snake someday, but
never had the confidence to care for living animals to begin with and
has the will of tofu.
Snakes are great!!

BLEACH: CAN'T FEAR YOUR OWN WORLD III

ORIGINAL STORY BY
TITE KUBO

WRITTEN BY
RYOHGO NARITA

COVER AND INTERIOR DESIGN BY
JIMMY PRESLER

TRANSLATION BY
JAN MITSUKO CASH

PUBLISHED BY
VIZ MEDIA, LLC
P.O. BOX 77010
SAN FRANCISCO, CA 94107

VIZ.COM

Names: Narita, Ryohgo, 1980- author. | Kubo, Tite, author. | Cash, Jan
   Mitsuko, translator.
Title: Bleach : can't fear your own world / written by Ryohgo Narita [and]
   Tite Kubo ; translated by Jan Mitsuko Cash.
Other titles: Can't fear your own world
Description: San Francisco, CA : VIZ Media, 2020- | "First published in
   Japan in 2017 by SHUEISHA Inc., Tokyo." | Translated from the Japanese.
   | Summary: "The Quincies' Thousand Year Blood War is over, but the embers of turmoil
still smolder in the Soul Society...Hikone Ubuginu's mysterious origin story, and the secrets
behind the very existence of the Soul Reapers and all their allies and adversaries, could
be revealed to incite an all-out battle royal. Meanwhile, Urahara and Hisagi face down
formidable enemies in Karakura Town as Tokinada Tsunayashiro's fiendish plan unfolds!"--
Provided by publisher.
Identifiers: LCCN 2020001553 | ISBN 9781974713264 (paperback) | ISBN
   9781974718498 (ebook)
Subjects: CYAC: Supernatural--Fiction.
Classification: LCC PZ7.1.N37 Bl 2020 | DDC [Fic]--dc23
LC record available at https://lccn.loc.gov/2020001553

Printed in the U.S.A.
Frst printing, March 2021